*For Jane,*
*without whose love, encouragement, and sheer hard work*
*this story would never have seen the light of day*

# A Piece of Broken Sky

## SEYMOUR WINTERS

Published in the United Kingdom in 2019

Copyright © Seymour Winters 2019

Typeset in Book Antiqua

ISBN 9781787233249

# AND SO IT BEGINS ...

A pair of yellow eyes, crazed with fine red veins, watched the scene in the valley below with confused fascination. In the fields below him, man, both predator and prey, acted out a role the boar struggled to understand. He had heard the sound of gunfire before. Then, men had hunted the forest around him, using weapons to kill his kind and others. Normally, the very sound would compel the boar to flee, searching out favourite lairs where he could remain hidden until the hunters and their dogs had passed. But this hunt was different; instead of seeking animals of the forest for prey, the men turned their weapons upon one another, littering the fields with the carcasses of the fallen.

The boar flexed his stiff muscles. Concealed in a thicket of dense briar and bracken, he was hypnotised by the prospect of the generous meal below. He had witnessed this before when, to his delight and puzzlement, men had discarded their prizes, leaving bodies to the scavengers of the forest. Why did they kill each other if they didn't consume their prey? The act was beyond the understanding of the boar. The last time men such as these had passed this way, leaving carnage in their wake, he had developed his taste for their flesh. Now, once again, a carpet of green and grey uniform-clad bodies stained the snow covered fields below.

The smell of blood, carried on clouds of smoke, twisted the hunger in his belly. With the ground hard frozen for several weeks, the boar hadn't eaten for many days, and the temptation to expose himself and gorge on the opportunity below was almost overwhelming. Yet, the instinct for self-preservation stopped him; darkness would soon arrive and there would be time enough to fill his belly from the discarded carcasses.

Unknown to the boar, another dormant force stirred within him. Incubating in his blood stream were strings of cells, constantly growing, mutating, adapting. He, like so many of his kind, was the unwitting host to a virus that left the boar largely untouched and from which he had soon recovered. Latent though it might appear, the virus would eventually strike mankind with unimaginable contagion and virulence. The boar had no knowledge of the immensity of his potential power, a power that would guarantee his lineage for aeons to come. Yet that didn't prevent a primeval feeling of his ultimate superiority over the men, now slaughtering one another, in the fields and buildings below him.

And the name of this potential human killer?

It would be known as Swine Flu.

# 1959

It had been a night of the best sex Sam could remember. The following morning, he felt invigorated as he stood in the lime-rimmed shower of the shared bathroom on the landing of the cheap hotel. Tired after the long journey from Rangoon, Sam and his travel companion, Mona, had agreed to share the only low-budget room they could find in London in the middle of the night. They had met as seat companions on a BOAC flight that had started twenty-four hours earlier, and passed the long hours of the flight with animated conversations about their separate times in Burma. Sam had amused Mona with hilarious stories of his experiences in the six months he had spent in Burma, but didn't talk about when he had been seriously ill with influenza. Making light of his time in her country, he glossed over the part where his life had been saved by the intervention of a young Buddhist monk who had spent long hours serving him herbal remedies during frequent visits to his bedside.

Oval-faced, with traits of her European ancestry, and long blue-black hair, Sam had been smitten by Mona from the very start, and their free and easy conversation had passed the journey quickly. Both had limited money, so sharing a hotel room on their arrival in London had seemed a sensible solution. Mona had occasionally flirted discreetly through the long hours of their flight until, arriving in the hotel room, Sam found that her demure Asian personality hid a voracious sexual appetite that had taken him totally by surprise.

Refreshed, Sam returned to their room to find Mona still sleeping, and dressed quietly to avoid disturbing her. He would leave her to rest while he attended the meeting with the company who had sent him to Burma to investigate their expansion into large scale boar farming. He needed to collect his back-pay, and with some money in his pocket perhaps he could afford a few more nights of fun in the hotel room.

Sam checked Mona's sleeping form in the bed. Her dark hair, still damp from the energy of their love-making, lay spread out in a

fan across the pillows. For when she woke, he filled a glass with water and set it on a bedside table with a scribbled note;
*I'll be back in a few hours. Bathroom is just down the landing xxx*
Planting a kiss on her forehead, her skin felt burning hot to his lips. For a moment Sam hesitated, then found some aspirin in his backpack and left it next to the glass of water. Mona was probably just exhausted by their long flight. He would only be gone for a few hours and it was probably best to let her sleep.

Sam had forgotten how long it would take to get across London and he had to wait in a long queue for his appointment. Before he had left Rangoon, he had posted a long and detailed report on his findings on the Burmese intensive boar farming programme. Disturbed by his reports of the increased aggression of the captive boar towards the farmers in Burma, his employers now spent several hours questioning Sam and challenging his observations. They were already committed to intensive boar farming in Britain and his findings drew unpleasant conclusions for their investments.

As a result it was early evening when he finally returned to the hotel, to their 'love-nest', looking forward to continuing with Mona where they had left off, exhausted, in the early hours. At the hotel entrance, Sam found an ambulance. An alarm bell rang in his mind. He avoided the decrepit lift and, with growing apprehension, scaled the stairs, two at a time. The door to their room was open; inside, two ambulance men and a doctor, all wearing gauze masks, filled the small space. The bed was empty; a shroud covering the profile of a body was lying on a stretcher on the floor. Without waiting to ask, Sam knelt down and folded back the covering sheet to reveal Mona, her body now ice cold, eyes closed, skin as white as powder. She was dead.
The pandemic had arrived.

# 1964

## ONE

Profiled by reflected candlelight through the window, Gilmore stood in the darkness, aware that something was out of place in the night air; a biting tang that didn't quite belong amongst the smells of the farmyard.

His subconscious mind sought a memory from the past but, camouflaged by the other smells of the farmyard, he couldn't place it. He bent his head, listening for a sound that might act as a trigger. Nothing stood out. Beside him, Tess whined softly, the sheepdog tuned to his concerns, scenting the same air that was causing the anxiety in the man standing beside her.

Gilmore hefted the scythe in his hand. He and his family were Quakers who ran a braille school, usually for a dozen blind women at any one time. With his pacifist beliefs he kept no firearms in the house, though he had to admit that at a moment such as this, a shotgun would have brought comfort beyond his moral principles. Behind him, the door opened and his son appeared in the threshold, armed with a broomstick. Gilmore stroked Tess's head for mutual comfort, and sharing unspoken words both men stared into the darkness. Something was wrong, they were both certain of that. The question was; what was it?

Pairs of yellow eyes, distanced from their forefathers by unnumbered generations, watched the figures at the house. The scent had brought the boar here. Now, only these men separated them from the prize for their hungry bellies. Eyes followed the men's movements, the roles of hunter and hunted were now reversed by timeless patience. With a barely audible growl from deep in the throat, the alpha male communicated his intentions. Around him, dozens of eyes semaphored agreement. The men moved nervously away from the front of the house, alert to something, unaware of their peril. In silent shadows, eyes blinked and dark bodies fanned out to form an enclosing crescent. Inevitably, fate had rolled her dice, destiny was sealed.

Sam Morten had spent much of the previous day hefting straw bales. As a consequence, when the alarm call arrived he was still deeply asleep. His beard was now flecked with grey, and the crows-feet around his eyes seemed more pronounced, but Rachel had got used to his changing looks since they met five years before. At the sound of the alarm, Rachel jumped out of bed and had to shake Sam vigorously to wake him; he would have happily slept on despite the demanding tones of the bell.

With the bell ringing in his ears, Sam fumbled with the keys to the Landrover, barely aware that Rachel had thrown his rucksack and rifle onto the spare front seat. The engine barked noisily into life, quickly filling the garage with grey exhaust smoke as she jumped onto the side step and hugged him.

"Keep safe," Rachel shouted above the deafening echo of the engine.

"Probably no more than a haystack fire like the last call-out," he grumbled, lingering for a few more seconds with his face covered by strands of her long blonde hair. Reluctantly, he let her go. "I'll be back before you know it," he said, managing a false smile as he grated the gears in the battered Landrover.

Sam nodded and Rachel hastily wound up the garage doors against the tension of weights which would slam the doors closed the moment he was clear. Headlights blazing, he sped down the drive, spraying gravel from overworn tyres. He swerved onto what remained of the tarmac road and turned south towards Newport. Ignoring cracks and potholes in the road, Sam floored the accelerator; normally he drove to conserve fuel, already in short supply, but a 'call-out' was different. For the moment, speed was everything .

All the farm hamlets held a majority of blind women, supported in each case by a handful of sighted survivors. When a crisis occurred, immediate help would be an absolute priority. Their plans had anticipated that in the event of an alert, every hamlet would provide someone sighted as an immediate responder. If the plan worked, at that very moment some thirty men or women should be speeding towards Newport. Perhaps more for comfort, Sam looked around as he drove, with fleeting glances, for other moving beams of light.

Within minutes, he was passing the skeletal remains of buildings in Newport, nearly all of which were unused and abandoned. With a population of barely a thousand, all efforts on the island had to be focused on farming. For administration, and as a centre for their island's governing 'forum', they kept open the Jubilee store building beside the Medina River. Sam was an elected member of the forum and the night's alert was to be organised by another member, Connor Rigby, renowned for his hot temper and inclined to be impulsive. Despite those traits he was the ideal man for a difficult situation, though Sam hoped, as he braked to a halt, that tonight was no more than the usual haystack fire or a false alarm.

The Jubilee store building blazed with lights, another sign of exceptional circumstances. Sam entered in the company of several others, including a woman he only vaguely recognised.

"Another haystack fire, do you suppose?"

"I didn't see anything burning south of here as I drove over," she said, yawning through the words.

"With luck we'll all be back in bed within the hour," someone else ventured optimistically.

Inside the building, Connor Rigby was counting heads in the assembly room. Thirty people had been summoned; so far, including the group Sam had walked in with, only eighteen had arrived.

"Listen everyone," Rigby bellowed. "Time is critical and we need to be going. We've received an emergency message from the Gilmores' farm."

He held a thin red slip in his hand, brought by carrier pigeon. "It reads, 'Boar in the house. Come quickly'." Rigby waited for the sounds of shock and surprise to die away. "Also, the neighbouring Stanhope farm have sent a message saying they've seen a red distress flare from the direction of the Gilmores. That was timed twenty minutes ago. I've already sent four men on motorbikes to the Gilmores; the rest of you will follow immediately in the Landrovers. Remember, the Gilmores are Quakers; they don't support violence and they won't have any guns in the place."

Within a few minutes, the building reverberated to the sound of engines as the lead group set off, quickly followed by the support lorry. Sam joined one of the Landrover teams as they raced at speed in the wake of the motorbikes. He stared ahead into the headlight beams; he had a disconcerting feeling the night held far more drama than a haystack fire. The distress message said there were boar in the farmhouse. If that was true, the few sighted occupants would have little to protect themselves with. Their only hope would be to barricade themselves in on the upper floor.

A man wearing a motorbike helmet stopped them at the farm gate. Beyond him, another man clad in leathers was bent double. Sam could tell from his posture that he was vomiting. Rigby left the lead Landrover, spoke briefly to the man at the gate and then beckoned the following vehicles to park either side of the darkened shape of the farmhouse. As they climbed from the Landrover, the driver illuminated the grounds with the spotlights positioned on the roof. They were just fanning out to form a protective screen when Rigby arrived.

"It's as bad as we feared in the house. I'm about to go inside with my team. Send a message for medical help as soon as possible. There are no boar left inside, but they could be hiding in the woods that run up to the boundary. Be ready, just in case they pay a return visit."

Rigby left without waiting for a reply and disappeared into the house with his team, leaving Sam to search for the box containing their carrier pigeon. Sam scribbled a message on a red slip and in seconds the bird had disappeared into the darkness, his request for assistance rolled in a tiny tube fixed to its leg. Inside the Landrover, the driver was swivelling the spotlights to cover as large an area as possible. Just beyond the range of their beams, the cleared ground gave way to tall lank grass backed by a stand of dark conifers, casting ink black shadows.

"You could hide a herd of elephant in there and we wouldn't see them." The woman he had spoken to earlier arrived at his side, nervously gripping her rifle as she nodded in the direction of the trees.

Sam nodded. "Best we fan out and stay alert."

The woman shuffled uncertainly away; there were only six of them and it left big lonely gaps between them. Once the arc had been created, they stood still, unconsciously fingering their rifle bolts and safety catches, as if the act of repetition would make them safer. Sam had a disconcerting feeling that their aged rifles would be of little use if an angry boar pack appeared and made a determined charge.

In the house behind them, flashlights flickered, accompanied by shouts and curses. Sam tried not to think about what might have been found. They had heard stories from the few survivors still arriving on the island that packs of marauding boar had become far more aggressive. Until now, without any boar on the island, they had no way of telling to what extent that had become a problem.

Beside Sam, someone lit a cigarette, its glowing tip a surprising comfort against the loneliness of waiting. Their eyes strained into the darkness, convinced that shadows were moving. Someone called out a hopeless joke.

"What do you call standing cold and shivering in the dark?" to which they all chorused, "boar-ing."

It wasn't funny, but they laughed nevertheless, and it eased the tension.

Endless minutes ticked by. How long had elapsed between the distress message and the first squad arriving? How much carnage could a pack of boar create in half an hour? So far, no casualties or survivors had been brought out of the house. Sam was trying to decide if that was a good or bad sign, when a shape moved, just on the limit of the arc of their lights. His mouth felt dry, nerves evaporating saliva. For the umpteenth time he checked the catch on his rifle. The shape moved, unmistakeable silver tusks glinting in the thin light.

"My god, there's dozens of the bastards."

The shout spoke for them all. Sam looked from left to right, seeing a long curving arc slowly surrounding them. Directly in front of him, a large boar male, perhaps the alpha male, stepped more clearly into the light, as if determined to declare his presence, emitting a deep throated growl as he did so. Sam eased the pressure on the rifle trigger; he was a poor shot at best. If the boar charged, it would be no better than an evens chance that he would hit the animal. If he missed, dodging the tusks with a hundred kilos of charging boar would require the skills of a matador. Plus there were at least two boar for every human. Instinct screamed to run for the Landrover, but that could provoke the boar to charge, and Sam doubted they could all get to safety in time. He braced his rear foot against the turf, trying to stiffen his resistance to flee as more shouts from the house were heard.

Almost unnoticed, the sound of approaching engines driven at high speed broke through the tension. Within seconds, headlight beams and clouds of dust swept into the farm. Unable to resist turning in relief, Sam saw half a dozen Landrovers disgorging more teams of armed men and women. Help had arrived. Sam quickly turned back to face the boar, only to find, as if by an illusion, they had all disappeared.

"Praise be for pigeons," Sam muttered to himself in relief. Simon Grey, the team leader from the opposite side of the farmhouse, jogged over. Grey had faced a similar situation until the arrival of reinforcements and was as puzzled as Sam by the abrupt disappearing act of the boar, seemingly into thin air.

"If I didn't know better," he said as he offered Sam his hip flask, "I'd say they were working as a team. Uncanny coordination wouldn't you say?"

Sam pulled a face; the brandy in the flask had a powerful bite. "It's been five years since we last confronted them. I guess you forget."

He stared at the dark woods. They were safe for the moment; the boar had chosen to retreat from confrontation. Sam and his team would wait until daylight before venturing amongst the trees. Even in daylight, the task of hunting the boar would be dangerous enough.

Behind them, a steady stream of vehicles arrived. A generator had been started and lights shone from many of the windows of the house. Sam saw that a medical team led by Henry Morgan, one of their only two doctors, had arrived and entered the house. A women's team also arrived, led by a small dark haired girl called Ruth who Sam vaguely knew. They joined Sam's team, reinforcing his perimeter guard. One of the women, Gloria, carried a machine gun, and being quite a large lady her presence went a considerable way to reassure everyone.

The promise of daylight arrived with brooding storm clouds. The eastern sky had begun to show the first faint veins of dawn when Rigby appeared from the house and came to find Sam. His hands were brown with dried blood, and black soot filled the lines on his face. Even the indomitable character of Rigby looked spent with what he had found in the house. Someone handed him the drink of crisis, a mug of strong tea with plenty of sugar, as they gathered in a loose circle around him. Beyond, in front of the house, they could see the first stretchers being laid out in a line. All were covered by blankets.

"Okay, this is what we've found," Rigby paused to take a swig of tea to ease his smoke dried throat. "We found Gilmore and his son dead at the front door where they had been gored to death, leaving the front door open. Inside, a woman and daughter had tried to protect the dozen or so blind women who were trapped on the ground floor. They were both killed by the boar, but not before they had locked the blind women into the study for safety." Rigby paused, staring for a long moment at the increasing line of shrouded bodies. "Unfortunately, someone in the study knocked over an oil lamp; ironic when you think that the women in there were all blind," he mused grimly.

"The fire didn't take hold, but burnt enough to fill the room with smoke. In their panic, the blind women must have tried to escape from the smoke using the French doors into the gardens. Sadly, enough of the boar were outside waiting for them and turned it into an unimaginable carnage. Defenceless, the women wouldn't have had a chance." Rigby stopped, allowing the horror of the scene to sink in.

"But it's not all bad news; there were four young children in an upstairs bedroom. Seems the boar ransacked the house, but the elder child had the presence of mind to lock themselves into a cupboard and they've all survived; orphaned, but alive."

For almost a minute, everyone was silent, as much in shock as respect. It was Simon Grey who asked the question at the forefront of their minds.

"So where did they come from? In five years we've never seen or found a boar on the island, yet tonight, out of the blue, we find at least a score here around the farm. And those we saw were all large males, which implies the main group could number fifty or more. A group that size couldn't remain invisible for long, so where have they been hiding or, more to the point, where did they come from?"

The question had no immediate answer. Rigby departed to supervise loading of the bodies into a large van which had just arrived, leaving Sam and the teams to await daylight before scouring the woods for the culprits of the massacre. A steady flow of people arrived and departed and he noticed a car take away four children, wrapped in blankets so they wouldn't see the covered bodies outside. As they gathered in a group to discuss the strategy for flushing the surrounding woodland, a van arrived with a team of dogs and their handlers to help with the search, which made the thought of entering the dense thickets of trees marginally more appealing.

By the time the last of the casualties had been removed from the house, they were ready to begin their hunt. The scent of the boar must have been powerful, judging by the strain the dogs placed on the handlers, and the search began at an energetic pace, accompanied by the baying of excited hounds.

Whether it was the dogs, or the boar' instinct for survival, their hunt proved disappointing. The dogs excitedly followed the scent trails through the woods and eventually into the open fields beyond without finding a single boar. Thereafter, the trails parted, with the dogs identifying at least ten separate tracks all leading off in divergent directions.

Breathless, Simon Grey caught Sam by the elbow.

"Too damn clever for words if you ask me; even the dogs can't work out which trail has the strongest scent. If we follow them all, we'll end up chasing them in circles around the countryside until they see fit to ambush us again," Grey said, shaking his head.

Sam nodded wearily. He had checked some paths the dogs had found, but the ground was dry and animal prints were scarce. The boar had simply vanished into thin air, almost as mysteriously as they had arrived.

"They'll be back, you can bet on that," Sam said, gazing into the distance. "This has the markings of a first-round all over it. We need to be better prepared for the next time."

By mid-morning, most of the teams had returned to Newport. Sam found Albert Jamieson, the forum chairman, waiting in the Jubilee store building to greet everyone on their return. It had been a harrowing night and the lines of strain were etched into

Albert's face. A side room had been set aside for the bodies, finally amounting to sixteen in number.

Before the flu pandemic, Albert Jamieson had served in local government for most of his career, stretching right back to the dark days of World War Two in the London blitz. To Albert Jamieson, death wasn't a stranger, but the shock of the night's events had taken their toll. Sam watched him greet everyone in turn, offering a word of encouragement or supporting hand on the shoulder, raising morale, often at the cost of his own. Albert nodded to Sam across a sea of heads and gently eased his way through the throng towards him.

"A tough night," he said, gripping Sam's hand. "We have always expected this could happen, but not with such tragic loss."

Sam stretched his tired back muscles. "It's fair to say more went wrong than right. We need to learn lessons fast. This has the hallmarks of unfinished business. We lost the trails of the boar beyond the tree line; they could have made off in any number of directions. We need to be quicker and smarter and better prepared," he added wearily.

For a short time, Albert appeared lost in thought as he gazed around the room.

"I need to show you something," he said with a frown, "in the room we've set aside as a temporary mortuary, before it becomes common knowledge."

Without waiting, he moved away across the room and held open a side door for Sam to enter. The room was brightly lit, with rows of trestles set up to support the lines of bodies covered with white shrouds. There was a strong smell of antiseptic, another of their limited supplies. Linda Hue and Karen, both clad in blood spattered gowns and masks, moved methodically amongst the rows of bodies.

Linda Hue was their only qualified medical scientist and performed every role from pathologist to coroner. Linda was in her early thirties and like most of them, the heavy demands already showed on her face. Linda's once jet black hair already showed veins of grey, and the corners of her eyes bore deeply creased crows-feet.

Karen was one of the small team of nurses; an indomitable spirit who carried a conspicuous scar on the side of her face as a consequence of the pandemic. Seeing them enter, Karen washed her hands and made tea for Albert and Sam from a recently boiled kettle.

"You look as though you could use something stronger," she said with a concerned smile as she handed out the mugs.

"It's been a long night," Sam said exhaling, mentally counting the shrouds around them.

The door swung open as Rigby arrived, striding purposefully across the room to join them, the bright lights from the ceiling throwing the deep scars in his bald head into stark relief. Sam guessed they too were a legacy from the post pandemic crisis from which most of the island inhabitants had fled when they sought sanctuary on the Isle of Wight.

"I need to show you both something," Linda interrupted, wiping her hands on a disinfected swab.

She joined them, carrying a steel sample dish containing an antiseptic solution in which floated a torn rectangle of plastic. The torn end still held a large pin, attached to which was a tuft of coarse hair with roots of bloody flesh. Sam could just read a number, written in black pen, on the rectangle.

"Anyone recognise this?" Linda asked.

"It looks like an ear tag," Rigby offered. "Some of our older cows from before the crisis still have them." He looked at Linda, puzzled.

"Quite right, I suspect. We found it still gripped in the hand of one of the dead girls. She must have torn it from the ear of the boar as she tried to defend herself." She swirled the solution in the dish for a moment as they thought of the implications. "I think you'll find it answers at least one question about tonight's attack."

It was Rigby who provided the answer. "That these boar aren't a wild feral pack. They've been bred by someone and raised to attack humans?"

"It could be a one-off I suppose," ventured Albert Jamieson. "You said the boar were mature," he glanced at Sam, "so it could have come from one of the boar farms from before the pandemic and then it joined a wild pack?"

"Possibly." Linda slid the dish back on to the specimen table. "But we know for certain that there weren't any boar on the island in the years preceding the pandemic. To get a clearer answer we need to catch a few of these aggressive boar, preferably alive."

"Alive?" Rigby responded with a note of horror in his voice, backed by the memory of a night of carnage.

Linda nodded. "We need to find out why they attack with such ferocity." She paused to cast a glance at the shrouded bodies around them before adding, "and how they've obtained an almost rabid desire for human flesh."

# TWO

For most of the journey home to the farm, Sam imagined voracious eyes watching him from every wooded vantage point. The blustery storm that followed the boar attack had passed, swept away by a fresh south-westerly breeze. In its wake, the day sparkled with light as clear as a jewel, veined with the fine lines of cirrus clouds racing in the high jet stream. During the course of the night's drama, someone had taken his Landrover for emergency duties. By mid-morning it hadn't been returned, and anxious to forewarn the farm that boar were loose on the island, Sam borrowed a horse from the stables and rode home.

The grey mare had two speeds; slow and very slow and so a journey normally completed in a matter of minutes took several hours when including the time took by the horse to browse the spring grass and clover on the overgrown verges. Normally, such conditions would lift the spirit of even the most determined pessimist, but Sam found he couldn't throw off a pervading feeling of foreboding. He suspected it wasn't just caused by the sudden appearance of boar on the island. They had always prepared for it to happen. Human occupation was thinly spread and it was always possible that a breeding group of boar might just live unseen, hidden amongst the island's dense tracks of woodland. But the numbers didn't add up; the large group of fully grown male boar they had encountered pointed to a population group many times that number.

Sam nudged the mare slowly up the track towards Sky Farm. In the distance he could see the main farmhouse where they had built a platform at chimney level to help communication between neighbours. With binoculars, you could see a large portion of their farm and several adjacent farmhouses. At a masthead above the platform, a red and white halved pennant snapped taut in the breeze. That would be swapped for a full red pennant the moment an emergency arose.

Lorna, their adopted teenage daughter, was on the platform keeping watch and waved energetically as soon as she saw Sam approaching. With eel-like agility, she slid down the ladders. At eighteen she was already one of their most capable and energetic members of the farm. Sam and Rachel had found her in the terrible aftermath of the pandemic, trying to bury the bodies of her dead parents. They had dug the graves together and it came as no surprise that she adopted them without hesitation, following in their wake as they all sought to survive in the chaos. Lorna greeted Sam with a hug that mixed relief with delight.

"I'm so glad to see you back safely. We heard there had been a nasty incident at the Gilmores' farm. Isn't that the Quaker place where they teach braille?"

Sam nodded. "There's been an attack that led to a tragic accident," he said, emphasising the word 'accident' to avoid frightening Lorna until everything became clearer. "Where is everyone?" The farm seemed unnaturally quiet.

"Rachel has gone to the top pasture with Jake. When Marcus and Peter went out to check the ewes and lambs this morning they discovered that many had been killed." For a moment her usually sunny disposition was replaced by a worried frown. "They've never seen anything like it before. It must have been a pack of dogs. Something has literally torn them to pieces," she said with a shudder.

"How long have they been gone?" Sam asked, trying to keep a note of anxiety from his voice.

"What?" Lorna asked, suddenly alarmed. "About an hour, no more. Why?"

"And everyone else is here, in the farmhouse?"

"Yes, but Peter has gone with Marcus to bring the remains of the flock back closer to the farm."

"Okay. Look, I need you to do exactly as I tell you. Lock all of the farmhouse doors. Don't make it appear unusual, try to make it seem like a game. We don't want to start a panic. Tell everyone I've asked for a practice, a rehearsal. They must all stay inside until I say otherwise and keep all the doors locked and bolted. Then get back to the roof platform. Take your rifle and if anything turns up, fire two shots into the air."

Lorna wouldn't panic easily, but a worried expression crossed her face. "What am I looking out for?" she asked.

Sam was already hastily placing his leg on a stirrup. "You'll know soon enough if they appear." He nudged the mare hard with his heels and she shook her head angrily with offence. "Just stay inside until I get back," he shouted, and left the farmyard with surprising speed.

He covered the two miles to the top pasture at a gallop, or at least as close to one as the affronted mare was prepared to give him. On the west boundary, the farm ran against a dense coppice. Some sections of the dry stone wall had fallen in and logs had been drawn across the openings until there was time to repair the wall. It was sufficient to keep sheep in the field but totally inadequate to keep out foxes, or boar.

Sam found Rachel and Jake backfilling a recently dug hole. No doubt they had buried the remains of their dead animals while two horses grazed a short distance away. With a pang of concern, Sam noticed their rifles were still in the scabbards on their saddles. From his experience, horses were terrified of the smell of boar. If they were the cause of this attack on their sheep and decided to pay a return visit, the horses wouldn't stop running until they got back to the stables, leaving Rachel and Jake with only spades to defend themselves.

"Stop what you're doing and get your rifles immediately," he said more abruptly than he intended. "And tie your horses securely."

Rachel looked startled at Sam. "And hello to you too," she said with more than a note of sarcasm.

He moved past them, gathered the reigns and led the horses back. "Seriously; the attack last night on the Gilmores was made by a mob of very aggressive boar. Virtually everyone at their farm has been killed. The boar pack responsible gave us the slip and got clean away so I don't think this attack on our sheep is the work of dogs; it's too much of a coincidence." Sam reached to their saddles and threw rifles to them both. "Don't go anywhere without these. If the boar reappear it won't be to pass the time of day."

For a moment, they were silent, trying to reconcile the dead animals they had just buried with what Sam had just told them. It was Sam who spoke first.

"Any idea what time this happened?"

"Marcus' son Peter heard a commotion sometime around six-thirty."

Sam frowned. "Two miles is a good distance for sound to carry?"

Rachel shook her head. "Peter said it was birds he could hear, a large flock of starlings. It's the wrong time of the year for them to gather in large numbers so he was suspicious that something had spooked them. We decided to risk breaking the alert curfew and come and find out. This is what we found." She paused to look around the field. "It was carnage. At least ten lambs have been torn to shreds; some of their mothers must have tried to intervene. The remains of four of them are buried in this hole," Rachel said with a grim note of finality.

"We supposed it was dogs," continued Jake, "or wolves. There are rumours of sightings, animals that escaped from the island zoo. But boar? Surely they wouldn't do something like this?"

"The ones I saw last night are more than capable of killing a few sheep." It was Sam's turn to bear a worried frown.

"What? Rachel asked abruptly.

"The Gilmores' farm must be a good eight miles from here." He felt his stomach tighten at the next thought. "If this is the work of boar, it can't be the same pack. They didn't clear off until sometime around five o'clock so …"

"Then we were right," Jake interjected. "It must have been dogs."

"Or another boar pack," Rachel said, anticipating Sam's thoughts.

"Which, if correct, means we're in big trouble," he added grimly, bending down to pick up their spades. "Come on. We'd better find Marcus and Peter and get back to the farmhouse before we have a crisis on our own doorstep."

They caught up with Marcus and Peter and helped shepherd the flock back to a pasture closer to the farmhouse. Rachel noticed that Sam was constantly looking over his shoulder, fretting that the boar might appear at any moment. As he had instructed, the house was in lock-down when they arrived and found everyone assembled in the kitchen preparing a late breakfast. Sam described the events of the night, putting emphasis on the consequence of the fire in the presence of the children rather than the aggressive tactics of the boar. His main concern was their immediate security until the forum had devised a plan to deal with the threat.

"I can't see fencing working, unless we build a timber palisade around the house," Marcus said, his thoughts still distracted by the savage attack on his flock. "If it's boar we're talking about they'll bring down anything we can erect unless it's buried deep

into the ground, solid and tall. It'll be like living in a stockade."
Everyone murmured their agreement.

"For the sake of the children, we need to avoid another repeat of the Gilmores' tragedy. Surely a thorough hunt to eradicate the boar is the simplest answer," offered Monica, Jake's wife.
Sam nodded. "The problem is how to be certain you've got them all. Meanwhile, we need a simple effective solution until we resolve things. Anyone have ideas, apart from a wall?"
A ripple of laughter lightened the mood of room.

"What about a ditch, encircling the houses and stables," Lorna offered enthusiastically. "We could dig a vertical face on the inner side and grade away the outer. We would need extra fuel to do it, but we've got several machines that could do the job. Working together, we could complete the task in a matter of days."

The challenge obviously excited Lorna; she had only fading memories of life before the pandemic that had killed her family, and each day now held another surprise adventure. Sam found this was a common tendency amongst the teenagers on the island. Forgetting the past and treating each day, despite the challenges, in a positive light, was one of the brighter rays of hope for their future.

"If we put the spoil on the inside we can easily raise it to a height they couldn't scale," Jake added. "In the short term we can use the fuel from our harvest allocation. Then, by September, the problems should be history."

Sam stood aside, watching the enthusiasm spread for an idea that offered an easy solution. There were a number of things he had left unsaid and it was best left at that. At least for the moment they were working as a team and had found an answer. Somewhere at the back of his mind lurked a feeling that things wouldn't stay that way.

The emergency forum meeting called for that evening posed a problem. All on the island were invited and most wanted to go, but the consequences of the boar attack weighed heavily on the minds and many were afraid to travel at night or leave their homes undefended. As a forum council member, Sam left early, taking Lorna and two blind women from the farm. It was agreed that Marcus and Jake would follow later when they were satisfied the farm and cottages were better secured. On the roof the crows-nest, as the platform had been named by Lorna, had been equipped with a spotlight, and access from the roof dormer window improved to avoid the need to use an outside ladder. In the event of another attack, Sam felt reassured by a pair of carrier pigeons who were now warming themselves in the kitchen instead of the stables. If an emergency arose, the call for help would be in Newport in a few short minutes.

Despite the short notice, every available seat in the public area was taken, with more people standing in the side aisles and at the back of the hall. From where Sam sat to the right of Chairman Albert Jamieson, it looked as though all of the island's community of hamlets were represented. With everyone gathered, Albert struck his gavel to commence proceedings. Although slight in stature, Albert had a surprisingly deep and assured voice which he used to project calm in difficult situations. Tonight was no exception. He faced the islanders with the forum gathered around him. In recognition of the serious matter at hand, he wore his sign of office, a midnight blue velvet sash embroidered in silver with the names of all the hamlets on the island. Thirty names, the first of many to come it was hoped; the embodiment of their determined efforts to establish a decent community amidst the crisis.

"Thank you all for attending this special meeting of the forum. I know it has been difficult for many of you to be here. I think we need to start with a two minute silence for our friends who died last night. Following that, I'll keep the agenda as tight as possible so that you can get home to your families."

Without bidding, everyone was silent, lost in thought of friends they would never see or speak to again.

"There are two items on our agenda. We'll begin with the consequence of last night's boar attack at the Gilmores. Most of you will have heard about this tragic event already. It's the first since we established our community here five years ago, no less shocking despite the security of the intervening years."

He paused to allow the secretary, Mary, to keep up with her shorthand note taking. During the pause, Sam scanned the faces of his adjacent councillors. He had expected only a single item on the agenda; the look on many faces confirmed they shared the same thought.

Albert Jamieson continued. "To keep proceedings on schedule, the agenda will be presented in a series of detailed reports. On completion, I'll throw open the forum for debate. Please keep your questions short and on the topic under discussion. Everything will be recorded and answers provided wherever possible. Then, after a break, we'll discuss recommendations for improved safety."

He could well have given the same opening address some twenty-five years before at the height of the London blitz; Albert Jamieson was a stickler for procedure, whatever the circumstances, which made him so successful as their chairman. But the strain of the job was etched in the deep lines that furrowed his face, along with thinning hair now prematurely grey.

To explain the details of the attack, Albert Jamieson handed the meeting to Connor Rigby. Rigby lacked Albert's calming skills; a blunt, no-frills speaker who spared no detail in describing a grim picture of events and didn't avoid criticising the failure of their plans or individual performances. He reserved particular criticism for their collective complacency. None of it was pleasant to listen to.

Rigby was followed by Linda Hue who was more diplomatic with her language, presenting the facts only borne out by evidence. She made the important distinction that the tragedy of the night's events had been created by a series of unique circumstances and an unfortunate accident. If the Gilmores had been armed and an oil lamp left unlit, the outcome could well have been very different. That much was speculation, but at least it served to counterbalance Rigby's negative appraisal of their situation.

As the reports wore on, Sam noticed the audience becoming restless and talking to each other, hanging sharp anxious questions over the words of the forum. Albert Jamieson chose to ignore the undercurrent, moving presenters briskly on to prevent spaces forming for counter arguments.

Naomi Taylor nervously stood to give her report. Sam had seen her arrive at the Gilmores just as he was leaving. Naomi was a biologist, normally occupied with collecting samples from diseased crops or sick animals. At the Gilmores, her role was more forensic and she had been sent to search for evidence to confirm the timeline for the attack which would be crucial if more tragedies were to be avoided. From where he sat, Sam could see Naomi nervously massaging her left hand, from which two fingers were missing. The wound wasn't recent and was normally hidden by gloves. Tonight it stood out raw and visible, a reminder of the price they all paid one way or another.

Naomi read out the facts, giving the predicted sequence of events and the timescale likely to be involved. It shocked most of those assembled that, from start to finish, it all occurred very quickly. Sam was relieved that she avoided making reference to the aftermath, when the boar had enjoyed their dinner. She appeared to have reached the end of her report when she stopped to take a drink, but continued again before Albert Jamieson could intervene.

"I have discovered one factor for which there is a clear evidence trail," Naomi said, clearing her throat nervously. "It seems logical that boar must have arrived at the farmhouse in a pack. We know there is woodland to the north, but there is a field of spring barley to the north-west and across this field is a path, quite wide and newly tramped. I followed the path and collected samples of dung; I'm certain they belong to boar. The trampled path leads directly to a shingle beach about a mile away; not a large distance for a hungry boar to travel I'm sure you will all agree.

"Unfortunately, here the trail ended. By the time I got to the beach, high tide had arrived, washing away any evidence, although on the very limit of the tide on the beach a pair of grooves about twelve feet apart were just visible." Naomi paused to take another sip of water. "And the beach faces north-west across the Solent," she said, not advancing conclusions, but leaving her thorough work of evidence to speak for itself.

Her presentation completed Naomi sat down, leaving conversation to bubble to the surface amongst the public. Albert Jamieson sensed problems were building, driven by the stark reality of grief and shock for lost friends. In the interests of transparency he generally tried to avoid hidden agendas, but now he realised that so much undiluted information might have caused anger to swell in certain quarters. It was unusual for so many of the island's population to be gathered together, an event in itself which appeared to create a unique atmosphere in the hall. Ever the consummate professional, he chose to announce a short break in an attempt to diffuse the agenda of certain well known troublemakers.

Water urns were already hissing steam when Sam left the platform. Amidst the sea of faces he saw John Evans. John stood out in a crowd; a tall, gangly Welshman, with curly red hair that exaggerated his pale skin and emphasised the freckles on his cheeks. Sam hadn't seen him before at a forum meeting and was struck by the rapt attention with which he studied a manila folder throughout the proceedings. John's speciality was with radio and for some time he had being trying to establish a radio station to broadcast across the entire island, but the lack of a suitable transmitter and regular supply of electricity had continually thwarted his efforts. As Sam moved through the throng of islanders, he exchanged greetings with many he seldom had chance to meet and was working his way towards John Evans when a hand grasped his arm.

"Can I have a word?" Naomi Taylor asked. Without waiting for an answer she headed towards a quieter area of the hall, away from listening ears where she paused to wait for Sam. "When the next boar attack happens can you help me with some ideas I have?"

"Don't you mean if there's another attack," Sam tried a light touch.

Naomi frowned. "I don't think either of us believes that last night was an isolated event. The rain washed away much of the evidence, but a clear trampled path led to the shingle beach about a mile away. Okay, high tide occurred before I got there and everything was washed away. There are no clues as to how the boar might have got there or what led them in such a direct path from the beach to the house. I've got one or two suspicions, but no evidence," she paused with a shrug. "If I'm on the right track, I need a member of the forum to validate my findings, so will you make yourself available to help me immediately there's another attack? We can't make progress until we find out where the boar are being sent from. I don't for a minute believe they originate from the island, do you?"

Although he didn't know her well, Sam warmed to Naomi's direct style, despite her intensity and occasional lack of humour. She had a petite elfin face with fine brown hair cut to jaw level.

With a wry grin he nodded agreement and she departed with a rare smile of satisfaction.

Sam lingered for a few precious moments, listening to the mood of the hall and how it had changed, which was probably exactly as Albert Jamieson had intended. Gone was the rising electricity of anger and fear, diluted by the balm of socialisation, and just as laughter erupted simultaneously amongst several groups of islanders, Sam smiled to himself with amused thoughts of the skills of his chairman.

Albert, now satisfied that balance had been restored, called for everyone's attention once again and gently chided them to take their seats. Magic had been at work; important matters required objective debate, free from the distortion of bias, either one way or the other.

Over the next few hours everyone had their say. Most people were more anxious at the thought of virus-bearing boar loose in their midst than the aggression that the current generation of boar displayed at the very smell of their prey, serious though the latter was.

Linda Hue tried her best to reassure them that the pandemic virus, carried by boar and their cousins the pigs, had long burnt itself out. If they had survived the ravages of the pandemic, their immunity was virtually guaranteed. But that was what scientists had said the last time and it had not protected them from a virus intent on the extinction of its target of mankind.

Questions were many, answers few. An air of restlessness began to roam the hall as the list mounted up. The promise of a sub-committee would not ease anxieties when the need was for answers. Sam felt a gentle nudge on his elbow and Mary passed him a paper slip from Albert Jamieson.

*'I need you to speak on protection measures. Sound upbeat!'*

Surprised, Sam glanced at Albert but found him staring blankly beyond the gathering, a thin smile on his lips but with eyes clouded by unseen images approaching from over the horizon.

Albert interrupted the flow of discussion, announcing Sam as a specialist on boar behaviour, making it sound the opposite of an ad hoc improvisation. With barely seconds to prepare, Sam rose, hands shaking, a fixed smile hiding the apprehension he felt. He paused as he placed his hands on the desk top with authority, disguising how he really felt. 'If only it were that simple,' was what he wanted to say and narrowly managed to swallow the words before he started.

Absorbed by events in the hall, no one saw the red flare arc through the night sky to the north, or see a frightened feathered messenger flying like an arrow from its loft. While the islanders argued over their fate and what steps should be taken to protect them, an invisible foe had once again shuffled the cards of fate.

# THREE

Nearly four hundred faces stared at Sam in eager anticipation. Announced as an expert on boar behaviour, they anticipated answers on the matter of their greatest concern; the immediate safety of their families and farms. Caught on the spot, he was dry-mouthed, his memory searching back across the years to a college holiday spent working on a boar farm. What could he tell them that they didn't know already? Boar had always been aggressive and had become even more so in recent years while at the same time developing a disconcerting appetite for human flesh. But telling them the bad news wasn't what Albert Jamieson expected from him. He knew he must sound reassuring, even upbeat if possible. His own experiences were sketchy at best and mainly involved fighting off boar to protect his family. For a moment nothing sprang to mind, until Lorna caught his eye and smiled, reminding Sam of her earlier idea for a continuous trench around the farm. Sam cleared his throat.

"I know how anxious you must all be," he began. "There are a number of things we can all do while our teams hunt down this marauding pack and deal with them. It seems to me that speed is essential. Some things will take longer to action than others, but there is one thing we can all do which will be much quicker to implement than the others."

Sam paused to take a sip of water. When he looked up, a commotion had started at the back of the hall. A woman he vaguely recognised was pushing her way through towards the forum, a red slip of paper gripped firmly in her hand.

With a feeling of stark apprehension, the meeting hastily broke up and set about putting a rescue plan into action for the second time in twenty-four hours. There had barely been time to digest the lessons from the previous night before things repeated again. Albert Jamieson had read the red slip, handing it to Rigby as he called the forum to a close. For a moment a flurry of confusion arose; Rigby called for all squad members to assemble in the car park while Albert shouted at full volume above the commotion.

"Will all forum members stay behind."

Mary caught Bill's arm as he passed by, saying, "All forum members in the chairman's office," and was gone in a second.

Puzzled, Sam found Lorna.

"I'm still needed here. Take the Landrover and get home as soon as you can. Don't stop for anything, most of all boar. I'll borrow a horse and ride back in the morning when it's light. Did you get the extra batteries up onto the roof platform?" he asked, distracted by the shouts from around the room.

Lorna rolled her eyes and smiled indulgently. "Yes, would I forget?"

"Good, good," Sam continued, watching other forum members moving hastily towards Albert Jamieson's office. He couldn't think why they should be needed when another attack was just beginning. He began to move to follow them, still talking to Lorna over his shoulder.

"And don't forget, if you are attacked, no one goes outside; fight them from inside the house and release a pigeon immediately; help won't be long in coming."

His words couldn't hide the frustration of his feelings; this was not the time to prioritise meetings. Reading his concern, Lorna gripped his arm to reassure him.

"Go. Don't worry, the farm will be fine," she said with a confident smile, and left him.

Sam watched her back as she blended into the crowd hurrying home to their farms. He never ceased to be surprised by the maturity and self-confidence in one so young; the consequence of survival in their new world.

Albert Jamieson's office, usually airy and spacious, was full when Sam arrived. Though some members were absent, mainly men who had missed the call to stay behind, most had made it to the chairman's room. Usually, the forum comprised an equal gender balance but now, more women had gathered than men. Over the excited babble of voices, Albert called for attention.

"I'm sorry to delay you at this time, but we have a matter of urgency still to discuss. I'm afraid this won't keep until later," Albert had to shout to make himself heard. "Mary, we're missing forum members. Remind me how many we need to make up a quorum?"

"Twenty percent Mr Chairman. As long as we have more than six present you can hold a meeting. I count twenty-four members present."

Albert Jamieson nodded. "We'll append the minutes of this meeting onto the previous one. I'll keep things brief, but I must hold a vote before we convene. A matter has arisen which we must address, so I'll hand you over to John Evans."

John looked awkward as he moved through the room to face everyone. He was nervous in the glare of the lights, his skin resembling the tone of a salamander. He paused to clear his throat.

"Thank you Mr Chairman. Those amongst you may know I'm trying to set up a radio network on the island. We have some equipment, but it's proving hard to get my hands on certain crucial pieces. Recently I've been experimenting with aerials on balloons to increase my range; some of you would have seen my attempts bobbing around in the wind."

Laughter bubbled around the room as the memory of some of John's escapees lightened the atmosphere.

"I've had mixed success; progress has been slow. Then one night three weeks ago, I made a surprising break through." John paused, checking his notes.

"Now, you know we've not heard a whisper from the mainland for almost three years. What helicopter reconnaissance we've been able to do has shown the only thing we've seen alive on the other side of the Solent are roaming packs of feral boar. We've searched about ten miles inland but there's been no sign of any human existence.

"From time to time I search radio frequencies; my receiver is stronger than my transmitter, and three weeks ago I was testing a balloon assisted aerial to see if it improved the range for broadcasting to the island. To my astonishment, I picked up a signal on the old emergency frequency. It was faint at first, but I wound the balloon cable to a greater height and it improved the signal strength."

In an instant, John had the attention of everyone in the room. Sam noted with amusement how everyone leant forward when their interest was aroused, as though a few extra inches would improve their hearing. John sipped water from a glass and continued.

"The signal was coming from the direction of Dartmoor, I estimated somewhere north of Buckfastleigh. It appears they had been hearing my test signals on and off for several weeks but couldn't get the signal strength to make contact. In the end it was pure chance I heard them. I reported my contact to Chairman Jamieson and he gave permission for me to increase the strength of my signal; it meant using more generator power but we felt it was essential given they were using the distress frequency and sounded pretty desperate.

"So last week I made contact again. They're a group of twenty; nine sighted including young children, and eleven blind. Hidden away on a farm on the moors, they seem to have survived the post pandemic crisis reasonably well. They were always reasonably self-sufficient, and boar seem to be thinly spread on Dartmoor. But during the past two years things have been tough. They've run into crop disease and their animal stocks are dwindling along with all other resources. They're now low on fuel and have seen the first signs of malnutrition in the younger children and don't have any medical supplies left.

"As if that wasn't bad enough, there are rumours of a vigilante group raiding what few farms remain to the north of them. Then a week ago, the rumours became reality when they saw smoke rising in the sky in the direction of their only neighbours. One of the sighted men made a search and confirmed their worst fears; farm burnt down, everything plundered, all the men murdered and the women …"

"We can guess John, we don't need details." Albert Jamieson quietly intervened.

John swallowed and continued. "It's only a matter of time before these men also find the group I'm in contact with. Their call to us is a plea; a plea for help. They're asking us to rescue them as soon as possible."

At the conclusion of John's words, people in the room began to murmur, though as to opinions, Sam could only guess. Phrases such as "help immediately" and "enough on our hands" rolled by in the low grumble of conversation. Albert Jamieson allowed things to run their course, while John pinned a battered road atlas map to the wall showing the area he thought the distress call was being made from. Pins were placed on the Isle of Wight and the estimated spot on Dartmoor and connected by a red line. Given their resources and the conditions existing on the mainland, the distance looked intimidating.

Albert beckoned over Chris Woods, a forum member who was also one of their few qualified pilots. Chris stood in front of the map and scaled the distance with the span of her hand. She flicked a glance at Albert.

"Even if we carry extra fuel it's too far for our helicopters."

Albert Jamieson nodded. "But if one only carries fuel for itself and another …? Like a re-fuel tanker."

Chris frowned. "We'd still need two stops each way and face the slow process of re-fuelling by hand in unknown conditions? Our helicopters are small; we'd need to make five or six trips to get them all out. If there is a vigilante gang anywhere within miles, they'd hear the helicopters and zero-in before we even began the second pick-up." The situation answered itself.

Sam noticed Helen Millar standing apart from the main group. Helen was their most experienced sailor and though not a member of the forum, had been invited to join them by Albert. It made Sam smile; Albert had an art of reading a situation in advance and making sure the right people were on hand to resolve the problems along the way. Helen was one of the few sighted survivors to have made it from the north, having arrived on the island with a deep sea fishing trawler, *Lupin*, and a crew of blind trawler men. Now *Lupin* was the main stay of their fishing fleet, the only usable deep sea vessel they had on the island.

"Helen." Albert beckoned her to join the discussion along with Dave Bartlett, Rigby's deputy. "Could we use *Lupin* to get to a port close to this group? Somewhere on the south Devon coast perhaps?"

The smile on Sam's face broadened as Albert's intentions became clearer. For a moment, Helen studied the map.

"Distance won't be a problem, if we can make the fuel available. Getting into a port we can use might be a different matter. I'd favour Dartmouth, mainly because it's somewhere I know and the river channel is deep. Do you think these people could make it to there?" she asked, looking at John as she traced the maze of road networks inland from the town. "They'll need to cover at least twenty-five miles with children and their blind people. Do they have fuel for tractors, or horses and wagons?"

"I'm sure they'll have something they could use. Given their level of fear now that the vigilante group have come so close, I'd say they would walk if they knew for certain we were coming for them."

"Why can't they negotiate with these supposed vigilantes?" a voice from the back of the room asked. "Perhaps the other farms resisted with force; doesn't it really come down to who fired the first shots? Things very soon get out of hand when tempers flare and people start getting hurt on either side, especially when aggravated by the prospect of starvation if the ones who have food won't share it."

Bartlett raised a nicotine stained hand to gain attention.

"Mr Chairman, over the years we've heard rumours about a vigilante group, generally raiding and plundering in the Midlands and East Anglia. From what we've heard, this group is comprised of hard-core criminals, some of the worst elements of the prison system, men with a grudge against society. Don't forget, the prisons were in lock-down when the pandemic took hold, so most prisoners were isolated from the virus. Days of lock-up followed when the staff became too sick to report for duty. By the time the prisoners released themselves, the worst of the virus had burnt itself out.

"It's not hard to believe that once free, they then formed gangs, and I heard that inter-gang warfare raged for several years with no police, army or government to control them. It was thought these gangs would eventually exterminate each other and solve the problem, but the latest rumours suggest that a large gang has evolved out of the anarchy. Hearing of John's conversation with his people on Dartmoor, I think it's imperative we treat their information seriously."

Bartlett's words had a cold ring to them. He was a shadowy figure; no one seemed to know much about his past but his knowledge of military matters was second to none, and a hushed silence followed as members digested his opinions. Eventually Albert Jamieson intervened.

"I need to call the forum to order; time is not on our side and we need to make a decision." He nodded to Mary. "It seems the evidence is pressing in favour of a rescue mission. The first clause in our constitution calls upon us to protect and nurture human life wherever we find it. But before I call for a formal vote, I ask for any counter arguments."

Several hands rose quickly and Albert dealt with them patiently. A member Sam knew vaguely offered an impassioned perspective.

"Mr Chairman, I would challenge your personal interpretation of the constitution. Can I point out that the primary responsibility of this forum is the protection of our community on the Isle of Wight. I would argue that any rescue operation at this time can only put at risk our security and would be flagrantly irresponsible. We simply don't have the resources to tackle more than one problem at a time and this rescue mission, for those who have chosen to ignore us until circumstances suited them, contravenes the most important fundamental obligation of the forum. We would welcome them with open arms if they can make their way here, but we mustn't put ourselves at risk to rescue them. To do so, I contend, would place us at even greater danger than we are already, and that contravenes the first principle of our obligations as a forum."

It was an impassioned plea and for a moment, Sam was almost persuaded by the conviction of the argument, though in part he recognised it was aimed at the opinions of the chairman. Everyone fell silent, waiting to see if anyone would rise to second the contrary point.

Before that happened, Chris Woods interjected with an impassioned plea.

"Mr Chairman, we can sit and argue points of protocol and constitutions all day long but it won't change the fact that the people we're talking about, who have pleaded for our help, may well die if we don't help them. If our decision not to assist them is based on our fear of the vigilantes," Chris paused and shrugged, "then our very humanity is called into question. Likewise, if we don't act because we're afraid of the boar, then we're clearly losing our fight to survive as a species. I believe that the way to protect ourselves and our future can only be sustained if we retain the one thing neither of them have; our desire and instinct to help each other, whatever the cost. Without it," she hesitated to allow forum members to digest her words, "is to admit we're finished as a civilised species. Either way, the bad guys, or evolution, have won and we will eventually reap the defeat and extinction that will bring about."

For a moment Albert Jamieson busied himself with his notes, allowing space for members of the forum he would call upon to vote to consider a course of action, each balanced against the risks.

"Okay, we've heard some passionate points of view," Albert said, finally interrupting their thoughts. "In a few moments I will call for a formal vote on the matter, but first, can I have a show of hands to see how your opinions lie." Albert paused, allowing Mary to open a fresh page in the minutes book. "All those who say 'yes' to the proposed rescue using *Lupin*, please show."

Immediately, twenty hands rose.

"The no's?" Three isolated hands appeared.

"Abstentions?" One hand was raised.

There was no question they had their majority, but Albert hesitated before continuing. He spoke without looking up from his desk.

"Before I call the formal vote, I would ask all respected councillors to reflect. In years to come our successors will honour this book," he held up the leather-bound minutes book, "in which all our decisions are recorded, often in the most extreme circumstances. For perpetuity it would be a statement of our humanity if the vote was recorded as unanimous," he said, looking at some distant point beyond those gathered around him. The gavel struck once again.

"All those who vote 'yes', please show."

Twenty-two hands were raised. The chairman waited; time stood still. Slowly, reluctantly, two more were raised to join the others and the gavel struck for the last time, recording the decision Albert Jamieson had so hoped for. The motion had been passed.

"John, go and tell the survivors that we are coming to rescue them."

As he savoured his words, Albert couldn't resist a smile that symbolised his success, only marred by the ominous feeling that in the future there would be very few such moments.

# FOUR

With a feeling of optimism the forum dispersed to get their rescue plan underway. Sam closed his files and left to find Naomi, but his search of the building came to nothing. She had left already with the first squads to investigate at the Collins' farm. All efforts were being made to organise back-up squads and there was no space for Sam in any of the Landrovers. With the prospect of a long night of waiting ahead, he poured himself a mug of stewed tea and inspected the detailed map pinned to the wall of the entire island. The Collins' farm was on the north-east coast, some twelve miles from the previous attack. This surprised Sam, as it was a considerable distance for a boar pack to have covered in twenty-four hours, especially if the same group had been responsible for the attack on his sheep. The Gilmores' land ran down to the sea on the north-west coast where the island was closest to the mainland, but the Collins' farm was farther away. If Sam expected to see a pattern, this attack didn't seem to fit.

It was a dry night and high tide was still some time off, so Naomi might find more clues; anything would help to give them an idea of what was going on. Sam felt a twinge of unease and hoped she would resist her impulsive instincts and wait until Connor Rigby and his teams had thoroughly cleared the area first. He knew only too well that boar, despite their substantial bulk, had an unnerving instinct for concealment and ambush.

Voices entered the hall behind him and Sam turned to find Albert Jamieson, in company with Helen Millar and Dave Bartlett, walking towards him.

"Just the man we're looking for. Sam, I think you know Helen and Dave."

Sam nodded, surprised.

"Good. We've discussed the outline plan for the mission. As it is an operation proposed by the forum it seems only right that one of our members should be on hand to take an overview. I would like you to undertake this role on our behalf and Helen and Dave have agreed to that."

The proposal left Sam reeling. "Wouldn't Rigby be better qualified for a task like this?" he exclaimed. He didn't want to say no; he had too much regard for Albert to do that, but Rigby was their defence leader and, more importantly, Sam was a poor seaman. The thought of pitching around in *Lupin* on rough channel seas offered little appeal.

"No, we need Connor to remain here to deal with any more boar attacks. On this mission, Helen will captain *Lupin* and Dave will be in charge of two of our best defence groups who will accompany you, just in case."

Albert Jamieson omitted to expand the 'just in case' scenario but Sam suspected that Albert was taking the stories about the vigilante group more seriously than he liked to admit.

"I need you there to make the final decisions on the rescue of these poor people. At the same time, you must avoid any unnecessary risk to the lives of the islanders involved, or *Lupin* for that matter. She's the only deep sea vessel we have and we need her back in one piece."

Though it remained unsaid, Albert probably thought that Rigby was best suited for a situation that would involve a fight. He wanted someone on *Lupin* who would prioritise avoiding one.

Sam felt his stomach tighten. He never sought out leadership roles; life made enough demands in just surviving. With Albert asking him in front of the others, it placed him in a position of credibility. If he refused, it might well create doubts on the chairman's judgement and so, with concealed reluctance, Sam accepted.

"Of course Mr Chairman, I'll need some form of guidance on the limits we should set."

In reply, Albert smiled briefly and turned to Helen. "How long do you need to get *Lupin* ready to sale?"

A frown creased her forehead as she thought for a minute. Helen had spent more time at sea than any of them, evidenced by her weather-beaten complexion. She was the same height as Sam and was probably tougher than most men he knew.

"If we can have immediate access to everything we need, two or three days should be plenty. I'll need extra crew with some knowledge of operating boats and the mechanical skills to fix things if they go wrong. Dave, Sam?" She paused, looking expectantly at both men.

Bartlett paused, drawing heavily on his roll-up. He was a chain-smoker, with fingers stained yellow from his unfiltered cigarettes.

"Assuming no casualties tonight, my squads can be ready in that timescale. I'll need access to the armoury; rifles won't be any good for the close confines of a town."

"We'll open the stores first thing," Albert Jamieson confirmed. "I suggest you take one nurse and a trainee. I can't risk either of our doctors I'm afraid, so hopefully, you won't run into anything serious."

Through the blue haze of his cigarette smoke, Sam saw Dave raise a sceptical eyebrow but decided to ask him later for his private thoughts on the operation ahead of them. This was the first time they would be venturing away from the precious security of the island in almost five years, and now he had been placed in overall charge of an enterprise in which he had strong reservations. Sam was not sure the churning in his stomach was excitement, fear, or his dread of the sea. He hoped it was only the latter.

With so much to prepare, the building emptied quickly and the next hour saw three more squads set out for the scene of the latest attack at the Collins' farm. There was still no room for Sam. He was tempted to leave for home, and in normal circumstances he wouldn't have hesitated. But, by a conservative estimate, there were at least thirty boar loose in the darkness; not the odds a man alone on a horse would risk confronting.

At some point in the early hours, the building fell silent. Just a handful of people remained at tables lit by isolated pools of light, so Sam hunted for a spare bedroll and a quiet dark corner. There was nothing more he could do except wait for someone to return or daylight to arrive, and then make his way homewards. Besides, he had a premonition that time for sleeping could be in short supply in the days to come. It would be best to take full advantage of the moment.

Even allowing for a hard wooden floor, sleep came surprisingly quickly, accompanied by the usual tapestry of dreams which he could recall only in fragments. Dreams without images, often just darkness and a lonely voice, calling, pleading for help. Sam never recognised the voice; perhaps it belonged to his sister, alone, lost and blinded like countless millions of others, still wandering somewhere without family or friends to help them. In his sleep, Sam extended a hand into an unknown void, unspoken words spiralling around his head until everything exploded into shards of silver light. He woke suddenly, disorientated by the dreams, to the crash of a door being thrown violently open.

"For god's sake, when will people start to listen to instructions."

In the dim light of early morning that stole around the cracks of the window blinds, Sam saw that Rigby had returned, ablaze with anger. He must have slept for longer than expected and struggled to his feet as someone flung open the blinds. Albert Jamieson reappeared, almost as a ghostly apparition. Sam suspected he had a camp bed stored away in his office for nights such as this.

"Connor. What's happened?" Albert knew Rigby and despite the obvious provocation of his anger, managed a calming tone to his words.

"I explain time and time again, obeying instructions is critical, life and death, and what do they do …?" Sweat gleamed, wet and shiny on his soot-blackened skin and someone produced a hip flask to pass around as more men arrived and spilled into the room.

"We were doing fine; we found the Collins had barricaded themselves in and were holding off the boar from the upstairs windows. There seemed about the same number as the previous night." Rigby glared at Sam for a moment, seeking a target for his anger. "Since when did the bastards learn to count?"

Albert pressed Rigby's arm and handed him the flask in an attempt to cool his anger. Rigby took a deep swig and carried on.

"As they hadn't broken into the house, we fought them from the Landrovers. No need to expose the men until we were on top of the situation. Just as well really as most of our people are poor shots with a rifle. The boar are cunning devils though, they manage to keep just on the cusp between light and darkness, so you can never quite see them. As happened last night they seem to be able to judge the numbers against them and just evaporate into thin air when the odds are in our favour."

For a moment, anger was replaced by a bemused expression until the real cause for his rage returned to Rigby.

"Everything went to plan until the final stages, when suddenly your friend, Naomi Taylor, turned up. I told her, 'Go nowhere until we've mopped up the last of the situation.' I couldn't be clearer; the boar had disappeared again, but they had to still be around somewhere. I even allocated the young Calder boy to keep an eye on her; stupid pup, instead of paying attention to what I told him, he went mooning off after her and before we know it, they both disappeared on some wild goose-chase."

Sam felt an ominous premonition rising inside him; Naomi's request of only a few brief hours before was chiming loud and clear in his ears.

"It must have been an hour before we realised they'd gone," Rigby continued. "We were searching a small coppice not far from the farmhouse and had found a group of boar lying in wait for us. Aggressive bastards; I'm sure they're moving faster than ever before. We had to use a lot of ammunition to frighten them off but at least none of the team was hurt. It was shortly afterwards that we found the Taylor girl and young Calder in a nearby clearing; the same boar pack must have ambushed them. Calder hadn't even had time to fire a shot." Rigby paused, re-living the moment in his mind's eye. "They're both dead, they wouldn't have had a chance if they were surrounded. And it's all totally unnecessary. This will happen again and again if people don't start following instructions."

Rigby talked with a show of grim indifference which Sam suspected was to hide his emotions.

"It won't have been for nothing." The words tasted like ash in Sam's mouth as he tried to balance some value against the shock of their loss. "Naomi knew how desperately important it was to try and trace where the boar are coming from. She said the last time their tracks seemed to disappear very quickly, almost into thin air. This sense of urgency would have driven her to take a risk, which she wouldn't have taken unless she was onto something."

Albert Jamieson nodded in agreement, his face looked grey and haggard; every member of their small community was precious to him. Rigby just scowled and shook his head. Leadership came in many guises.

Slowly, the group dissolved; there were more tasks to complete and time didn't allow the space for grieving. As Albert moved towards his office, he spoke quietly to Mary, who shadowed him everywhere he went.

"We'll have to arrange for their bodies to be brought here as soon as possible. Contact Doctor Morgan to examine them; we can't ask Linda." He hesitated with a heavy sigh. "She was very close to Naomi." Albert Jamieson's discretion with island secrets prevented him saying more.

For a while Sam contemplated going to the Collins' farm to continue Naomi's search for clues. He felt it would be respectful to do so, though more likely he was driven by the need to assuage his own conscience; if he had gone with Naomi as she had asked, she would probably still be alive. Or, more likely, he could have been killed as well. Either way, nothing would change the fact that Naomi was dead.

He checked his watch; it was now daylight and he had probably little more than twenty-four hours to complete his preparations for their Dartmouth operation. He would borrow a horse to get home to the farm to tell Rachel and the others and get his farm tasks re-scheduled. Sam had the distinct feeling that their peaceful years on the island had in many ways left them unprepared for the pace at which events could arise and sweep them along in their wake. They were starting to behave in a reactive way rather than control what was happening proactively. It all left Sam with an ominous feeling about Rachel's opinion on decisions he had already made.

Sam walked to the stables and saddled another of the 'taxi' horses to ride home, aware that his hasty one way trips were filling the stable at the farm. The rules required the horse to be returned on the next visit, and he already had a string of borrowed horses to return to Newport. The only available horse was an ageing chestnut mare with large docile eyes. Sam suspected she would be little faster than the horse he had used the previous morning. On the positive side, he would benefit from the time and space to come to terms with his own feelings over the tragic news about Naomi.

He was tightening the leather girth strap when Dave Bartlett appeared at his side, for once without a lit roll-up on his lip, the fire hazard in the stable being greater than his need for a cigarette.

"That your rifle?" Dave looked at the wooden stock protruding from the saddle holster.

Sam nodded.

"Then I suggest you leave it at home and take this instead." He handed Sam a sub-machine gun of some vintage, gleaming with fresh oil and complete with a spare magazine. "If you're not a crack-shot I doubt you can hit anything with a rifle at much more than fifty yards. The Sten isn't very accurate beyond that range either, but at ten rounds a second, you've a much better chance of hitting something than with a rifle. I've loaded the magazines with some tracer rounds, so use the trigger sparingly. That way it will even the odds if you get ambushed by boar. With only a rifle, the Calder boy sent to protect Naomi Taylor wouldn't have stood much chance in the woods, even if he had a warning," he said with a note of caution.

"Thanks." Sam measured the weight of the gun and slid the strap across his chest. Bartlett nodded. "Take it everywhere you go and get to know it better than your wives. Especially in the dark." He noticed the use of the plural; how necessity changed morality. "That way, you might stay alive."

"How are we managing for ammunition?"

"Getting through it. Always collect spent cartridge cases whenever you can so we can make replacements, though we'll have to find something better than bullets if these attacks continue or increase."

"Can we use phosphorus?"

Bartlett shrugged. "I've heard we can, but I'll leave that to the brains amongst us. I just hope they don't take too long to come up with something." Both men managed a somewhat grim laugh. "Did you know the Taylor girl well?"

"Not particularly. She was a nice girl, very good at her job. We'll miss her," Sam replied, the past tense catching in his words. "Some said she was too intense about her work, but she knew the threat the boar would represent if they ever arrived here. I think she must have been onto something to make her act so carelessly. Now we won't know what it was."

Without offering a response, Bartlett walked away, intent on finding somewhere safer to smoke. Sam didn't know him well, but found his matter of fact approach reassuring. The fact that they'd be able to work well together helped to assuage some of his misgivings over the forthcoming trip to Dartmouth.

The day was clear with isolated clumps of cloud pushing through on a south-westerly breeze. The mare seemed to know her way to the farm. Like most horses of a similar age there was no point in rushing, so she wound slowly along the empty roads and lanes from Newport towards the farm. It was warm for April, and after a mild winter, crop sowing was already well advanced in what fields could be cultivated. He guessed they were early by as much as two weeks. It promised to be a good harvest, much needed after the two previous disappointing years.

His journey took about a couple of hours as the mare sauntered north, insisting on stopping at every opportunity to crop the young grass shoots which had appeared in the overgrown verges. Approaching the farm he saw Lorna and Marcus digging the ditch to surround their cluster of farm buildings. Even at eighteen, Lorna was a capable machine operator and Sam watched as fresh black soil was sliced out of the ground and levelled on to the inner side of a slowly forming circle. It was essential work but ate dangerously into their fuel reserves for the harvest, leaving Sam to wonder how they would manage if it was as good as was promised.

Sam skirted the farmhouses, directing the mare to the stable, the promise of fresh oats nudging her finally to a brisker pace. As luck would have it, Rachel was already there, attending to one of their mares who had recently foaled. At least he would have a chance to explain things to her before everyone else pushed in for an update.

"Hello stranger. You still live here then," Rachel teased.

"Well, I considered another offer, but decided your blueberry pancakes win the day."

Sam just managed to duck below a playful slap, bear-hugging her before she could try again. For a moment, they remained locked together, each enjoying the familiarity of the others' warmth and body scent. It was not going to be easy to tell Rachel he was going away from her for the longest time since fate had drawn them together. They sat together on a bale of last year's straw, Rachel sharing her tea flask with Sam while he added to what she had already heard from Lorna and the others. She couldn't hide her surprise at the rescue mission to Dartmouth and his prominent role. He tried hard to be downbeat about his position, but knew he didn't sound convincing.

"I can't see why Albert Jamieson should ask you to go. It's not the sort of thing you have any experience with and surely you'd be more suited to deal with the boar attack, while Rigby goes to rescue these people. You had plenty of experience with dealing with boar before we escaped here to the island and don't forget you're a lousy sea-man; you'd be seasick on a duck pond."

There was genuine concern in her voice, far greater than he had expected, but then Rachel caught sight of the Sten gun Bartlett had given him. Silently, he cursed himself for not hiding it until she had got used to the idea of him being sent to Dartmouth.

"Why have you been given that?"

There was alarm in her voice. Sam tried again to shrug it off. "Just better protection against boar. I think we'll all have to have them if the menace continues."

He knew it was only part of the reason he'd been given it. Dave Bartlett had made no direct reference to the vigilante group when he gave him the gun, but Sam was well aware of the implications and he was trying hard to avoid sharing those concerns with Rachel. She stared long into his eyes, searching for what she knew he was trying to conceal from her.

"I can understand your feelings of responsibility to protect us and the island, but I'm not happy with Albert Jamieson putting you at risk. Can't this group you're being sent to rescue get here by themselves? Or at least find a port closer than Dartmouth?" she said, folding her arms, her usual sign of taking up an unmoveable stance on a matter she had strong feelings about.

Sam took a moment to reply and tried to decide if her unhappiness was the result of her intuition of something seriously wrong with the proposed attempted rescue or simply because he had taken on the decision without discussing it with her first.

"Look, I suspect Albert has asked me for a number of reasons. Rigby is good at what he does, but he can be very hot-headed sometimes. Everything we do involves risk, some more than others, but we can't protect the present without regard to the future. Albert seems to think I'll be a safer pair of hands. Helen Millar will captain *Lupin* and she's very capable and cautious. I can't see Helen putting her ship at risk on a foolhardy plan. Dave Bartlett will bring his best squads, so I'll have nothing to do but make sure things run smoothly and no one argues."

Rachel looked at him, her blank expression hard to read. "So don't go then. Do it for me; I'm asking you not to go."

Sam noticed a look of vulnerability in her eyes. Despite his efforts, he knew she had read the risks, even without knowing the details. Covering up wasn't working, but neither could he go back on his word. Someone had got to get the job done; he hadn't sought it, but now it was his, like it or not. Sam stepped forward to embrace her again, trying to recapture the magic of a few minutes earlier, only to find her back away from him, palms now raised like buffers.

"Don't go."

Defeat settled on his shoulders in a way he couldn't understand and now he felt wretched.

"I can't change my mind, not now, you know I can't."

It only took a second; that moment you remember for a lifetime. Her pale blue eyes held his for no more than a heartbeat, and then she was gone before he realised she had left.

# FIVE

*Lupin* sailed on the morning ebb tide. The sunny weather continued and the Solent was whipped by a stiff south-westerly breeze, combing the crests of the swell into a translucent blue fringed with white foam. As they passed through the narrow neck of water to the south of Hurst Castle, *Lupin* dug into the rolling open sea which broke over the bow, washing across the foredeck.

Including Sam, the ship's company now totalled seventeen, with Helen as captain, three engineers, two nurses, Dave Bartlett, and eight men and women in two squads who doubled up as crewmen and landing crew. John Evans had also joined them with his radio equipment. For a while, Sam wandered the decks of the ship introducing himself and trying to memorise names and faces. Despite being the largest boat they had, and displacing some five hundred tons or more, *Lupin* was soon pitching, bow to stern, in a rhythmic manner that had an unpleasant effect on Sam. By the time he reached the wheelhouse, manned by Helen and an engineer called Tony, his face had taken on a white pasty complexion, sheened with sweat.

"How long to Dartmouth?"

They were barely two hours out of Newport; Sam knew the journey would take them at least twelve hours but hoped it might have miraculously shortened. Helen didn't answer his question, instead she took a folded paper rectangle from a small box in her pocket.

"Go to my cabin, drink this in a glass of water and lie down on my bed. It should do the trick."

If anything, conditions below deck were even worse; the rhythmic throb and fumes of diesel engines were woven into a noxious cocktail with the lingering smell of an earlier fish catch. It was all accentuated by the nauseating sensation of bow to stern pitching. With difficulty, Sam found the 'cupboard' that was Helen's cabin. He filled a glass with water and added the white powder from the paper spill she had given him. He almost gagged swallowing the contents as *Lupin* chose that moment to hit a particularly large swell, throwing him off balance and into a heap on the bunk. Groaning, Sam faced the miserable thought of many grim hours ahead. For the first time since they had met, he and Rachel had parted with disagreement hanging between them. This, added to the boat's motion, left him feeling utterly wretched; he had to admit Rachel had been right about one thing; he was a lousy sea-man. Sam felt the bed drop alarmingly beneath him, leaving a moment of weightlessness until the hard mattress sprang upward under the force of the next rolling swell. At this particular moment, he would give his right arm to be anywhere else than curled on the bunk in a foetal position, head spinning, stomach churning.

During the previous twenty-four hours Sam had been trying to understand Rachel's opposition to this expedition. Normally, she was adventurous and pragmatic, with a logical position to deal with most things that arose in their lives, especially now things were so dramatically altered by their circumstances. It was Rachel who had supported the rational new morality that fertile men must father children by multiple women; in her view it was simple mathematics; there just weren't enough men alive to sustain a human population in just single partner relationships.

It appeared that Rachel's argument against him going to Dartmouth was entirely based on female intuition, a position that defied explanation beyond the feeling that something was fundamentally wrong with the principle of the entire plan. Coinciding with the sudden murderous appearance of large numbers of boar, it only served to exaggerate her feelings. Haunted by tiredness, Sam felt irritated by the obstinacy of her point of view. He knew he couldn't win an argument with a woman on matters of her intuition and he wished more than anything he could have found another way to avoid the rift that had forced the distance between them. As sleep drew him mercifully into its grasp, he could only hope for a successful outcome to the operation to heal their rift.

Sam awoke with a start to the sound of the hard metallic rumble of the anchor, resembling the chains of a dozen ghosts. It was still dark beyond the small porthole. The engines had stopped and the boat was silent, rolling gently. With cramped limbs, Sam eased himself from the bed; whatever Helen had given him in the paper sachet, it had knocked him out for most of the journey. He looked at his watch; it was one o'clock in the morning. Standing up he was relieved to find the nausea had gone, leaving him with a dull headache and a sour taste in his mouth in its place. Collecting his things he left the cabin and followed the gangway towards the lights of the wheelhouse and a low murmur of voices.

He found Helen clad in a duffle coat, sharing a celebratory mug of hot chocolate with one of the engineers. Sam was surprised, chocolate was a luxury, saved for rare occasions. Once their meagre stock was exhausted, it would be many long years before any of them tasted the like again.

"So, did you enjoy your slumbers?" Helen grinned with mischief as she poured half of her chocolate into a separate mug for Sam. "I looked in on you several times; you were sleeping like a baby."

"What was in that witch's potion you gave me?" he smiled, gratefully accepting the offered treat. He swirled the contents to release the precious aroma before taking a sip, smacking his lips in delight. It had been a while since he tasted anything as good.

"Witch's potion?" Helen pretended outrage. "Just a simple herbal remedy I always carry for the land-lovers amongst us. Though by the way it knocked you out, I may have gone a trifle heavy on the ingredients." She paused to give their mugs a celebratory tap.

"And just in case you hadn't noticed, we've arrived on schedule, just off the river entrance to Dartmouth. The last five hours of our journey were in darkness and judging by the absence of lights, there's no one along this coast."

The only light in the wheelhouse came from the pale green glow of *Lupin*'s few instruments. Beyond the glass screens, Sam could see a clear starlit night descending onto black velvet shadows of the mouth of the estuary about half a mile away. Around them, the ship was cloaked in darkness, their crew sleeping in hammocks and bedrolls wherever space allowed.

"When will you take us up river?" Sam asked.

"Not before it's light." Helen looked landward. "Although there's no signs of life on this part of the coast, we can't see any of the town from here, so we've no way of knowing if anyone's about. Also, I suspect the river will be strewn with wrecked and sunken vessels; the main channel is deep but I'd hate to take a chance and risk running into something. We'll take time to plot our route up river when we can see what's in front of us."

"Any word from the survivors?" Sam asked.

Helen shook her head. "John Evans has kept radio watch all night, but he's receiving only static."

Only a few years ago, Sam thought, the night world around them would be full of light; streetlights, car headlights on the coast road, a warm glow from houses and offices, all sending a yellow aurora into the night sky, and the air would have been filled with radio and television signals. Now all was darkness and silence, haunted by the dark shapes of hunting boar.

Dave Bartlett always considered the middle watch on board ship was the hardest. It lasted from midnight until four o'clock in the morning and for most watch-keepers it was the most difficult period on which to stay alert. For that reason alone, he had split the watch in half; he and Sam would cover the toughest period from two until four.

For two hours they walked, separated by a ship's length, on the upper deck. Occasionally, Sam saw the red glowing tip of Bartlett's cigarette behind him. Around them, the night was silent, empty, holding nothing more than the gentle wash of wind and sea. For Sam, this silence, with human numbers depleted to a level approaching extinction, underlined that their grip on the world hung precariously in the balance. As he wandered the decks, he tried to work out where the tipping point came; when would a moment of collapse be reached from which human recovery became impossible? Perhaps that line had already been crossed and their decline into yet another forgotten epoch of history was now inevitable. Would that final act take five, fifty, or a hundred years? And boar? Would they now step forward in the evolutionary chain as the dominant species and rule the earth? Somehow he couldn't imagine that; after all, mankind had grown from a tiny tribal sub-group, somewhere in distant pre-history. It was just possible to believe they could hang on, no matter how precariously, until the moment was right for their renaissance. Sam stared at the dark outline of a hostile coast. The question had to be where, if not here, this could be achieved.

*Lupin* was moving shortly before sunrise when the light was still soft and hid the harshness of the day. Ahead, the river estuary sparkled with tiny sunlit jewels; astern their propeller turned at 'slow ahead', barely troubling the surface. Helen had chosen to enter the river one hour after low tide, conscious of the need to test the depth carefully as she proceeded. A river she knew so well was as likely to have changed dramatically over the past five years. Out in front of *Lupin* two men led the way in a skiff, one guiding a route in the central channel while the other tested the depth with a measured pole four metres in length, more than sufficient depth for the draught of the trawler. At intervals, they dropped marker buoys into the river; red-painted plastic drums attached to building blocks by lengths of rope; Helen needed to be certain of her escape route in the event she had to leave Dartmouth in a hurry.

It was still early morning when they eventually anchored between Dartmouth and Kingswear, both located on opposite sides of the broad river. Helen spun *Lupin*, finally dropping anchor with her bow pointing seawards. On either side of them, the landing ramps once used for the car ferry were littered with debris and wreckage. On the Kingswear side, the flat-bottomed ferry had partially sunk, leaving only the blackened bow end pointing skywards above the surface like an accusing finger.

For an hour, Dave Bartlett and Aiden Cooper, his senior squad leader, scoured the riversides with binoculars and telescope, searching for any signs of life, human or otherwise. Sunlight illuminated a picture of empty desolation; a few roofs had already collapsed and windows swung broken on yawning casements. Around them, in the river, mastheads nodded mockingly, marking the graves of sunken vessels. Perhaps most striking of all was the eerie silence, punctured only by the occasional sound of doors and shutters banging in the gentle morning breeze.

"Not even any dogs barking," Bartlett muttered to Sam, standing thoughtfully at his side. "Nothing. You would have at least expected a few feral packs roaming around. I haven't even seen a rat yet." He blew surprise through pursed lips. "Boar have picked the place clean."

"Have you seen any?"

Bartlett shook his head. "Even boar don't stand around to starve. But it will make things easier for us if the bastards have moved on; one less problem to have to deal with," he added with a note of irony.

Within minutes of completing his visual search, Bartlett loaded four armed men into the skiff and set off towards the ferry landing ramp on the Dartmouth shore. They towed a line attached to *Lupin* in their wake. Arriving ashore, two men secured the line while the other pair scoured the buildings in the immediate vicinity. They found nothing; even skeletal remains had been scattered, most probably by hungry dogs before the boar caught them too. A pulley block was secured to a steel hitching post and the line fed through while two men returned in the skiff to *Lupin* and connected it to a winch before it was secured to the large raft which carried their trailer and an assortment of jerry cans and crates to store whatever they could scavenge.

Their expedition was ready to begin. With a feeling of trepidation, Sam joined the men in the skiff as they returned to the Dartmouth shoreline. The aged outboard motor left a trail of blue exhaust as the sound of its asthmatic engine echoed back from the surrounding buildings. To Sam, the town appeared haunted. For most of them, it would provide their biggest challenge in the days ahead.

It was mid-day before they were ready to set out and explore the town. John Evans had spent the morning scanning radio frequencies, but heard nothing; no word from the survivors. Having searched most of the surrounding area and drawn a blank, Sam suggested to Bartlett that he begin a scavenging hunt to use the time effectively. He drew up his squad into their usual star formation, hauling the empty trailer along the centre of the road, while Sam volunteered to take the lonely position behind the tail end of the group. He was only twenty yards behind, but felt surprisingly isolated from the others, despite the comfort of the Sten gun strapped across his shoulders.

Clear of the foreshore, Bartlett made for what had once been streets full of busy shops and traders. After five years of sanctuary on the Isle of Wight, it shocked most of them to see at first-hand how quickly things had deteriorated on the mainland. Abandoned cars littered the roads and pavements, often sitting lopsided on perished or punctured tyres, doors hung open, windscreens smashed, bodywork rusted, flaking red oxide stains into the gutters. One car they passed contained two human skeletons, clad in tattered clothing, sitting upright still holding hands in the front seats. No matter how many times you saw such scenes, Sam still felt a pang of despair that was almost overwhelming.

"There but for the grace of god goes all of us," he muttered as he passed them.

Without speaking, they walked down what appeared to be a main street, now with smashed glass shop fronts with dagger-shaped shards littered over the pavements. Doors and security grilles were broken, forced open in desperation by axes and sledgehammers, and debris lay everywhere. A headless mannequin sat in a chair at a deserted road junction, arms arranged for traffic duty, in a macabre attempt at black humour. Amidst the silence of desolation, everywhere was lifeless; not even a seagull cawed or a wild dog barked, and Barrett was correct; there weren't even any rats to be seen.

Bartlett called a halt outside a pharmacy, its entrance door hanging drunkenly on broken hinges; although it was unlikely, any surviving medical supplies would be a priceless gift. Four of them, including Sam, entered the darkened interior. The shelves had been swept clean; in one area, a mosaic of dark blood stains patterned the walls. They moved wordlessly through the shop, each man alone with his thoughts. Nothing remained, it had probably been stripped bare years earlier. Kicking through the debris, Bartlett stopped in front of a broken cabinet which partially hid a door: the door was locked. Within a few minutes the cabinet was moved and the door broken open with a sledgehammer. They entered an Aladdin's cave; Sam thought it was like opening a pharaoh's tomb for the first time. The shelves were stacked high; somehow the storeroom had been missed and left completely untouched.

"Bingo," Bartlett announced with a note of triumph.

"I wonder how it was missed?" Sam mused.

Bartlett shrugged. "I guess most of the looters were blind; they'd strip the shelves in desperation and wreck the place in the process. Whatever, it's our lucky day, even the rats and mice have not been able to get in, so let's get busy."

It took half an hour to transfer the contents out to the trailer, loading everything; most of the medicines would be out of date and useless, but that was for others to decide and Sam noted the bandages and dressings still looked useable. There was an ample supply of bottled antiseptics and disinfectants; even the boxes containing painkiller tablets appeared intact. By the time they had finished, the windfall had lifted their spirits.

Farther along the street, the remnants of a grocer's shop revealed a stock of tins with no labels, mostly buried under a collapsed ceiling. As they added these to the contents of the trailer, one of the group noticed teeth marks imprinted into some of the tins. Sam saw the look of horror on the young man's face as he took the tins away from him.

"I shouldn't worry too much; it's only rats," he lied.

They moved on through the town and eventually stopped for a break on a wide road with a fallen nameplate. College Way climbed steeply towards the imposing buildings of the Naval College. From a distance it appeared to be intact, even the windows still held their unbroken glass. A sun bleached and tattered ensign still hung limply from the flag mast as a salute to the lifeless campus.

"We need to find a petrol station or garage, but there's no point hauling the heavy trailer up the hill until we find one," Bartlett paused to light a roll-up with a pink-headed match. "I'll leave you here with two of the squad. Stay alert; just because the place appears deserted doesn't mean there's no one about who wouldn't help themselves to our treasure trove given the chance."

They backed the trailer onto a walled forecourt beside the road before Bartlett set off at a brisk pace with two men up the hill, leaving Sam with the two youngest members of their squad to await their return. Away from the river, the breeze had dropped and the sunshine felt unseasonably warm which created the rare sensation of a calm relaxed feeling. Following Bartlett's instruction, they took up positions a short distance apart in an effort to avoid being surprised, though it made conversation difficult and isolated them from one another, leaving each alone with their thoughts in a dead town.

Sam sat in the sun on a brick wall, his back propped against a timber post. As the silent minutes ticked by, a feeling of drowsiness enveloped him like a summer mist. He tried to focus his thoughts on Rachel; their misunderstanding still hurt and made him miss her all the more. Deflecting negative thoughts he tried to imagine the perfect homecoming, hoping that the anguish of his departure would be salved by absence. He tried to think of something he could take her; a small gift to bring a smile to her face would be good. But even half asleep, he was not too drowsy to miss the sound, no matter how faint, one he could never mistake.

"Boar."

Sam's shout shattered the still silence. Surprised, one of the squad dropped his gun with a metallic clatter while the other, the only girl amongst them, was on her feet in a second, alert, helmet and visor lowered as she back-stepped anxiously towards Sam.

"Where?"

Sam squatted to his haunches, pressing his finger to his lips as he strained for the sound again. Gathering their composure, they formed a loose outward facing triangle. Was he mistaken? Once heard, you would never forget the hungry growl of a stalking boar. He knew from bitter experience of their cunning skills when it came to ambush. The gardens and alleyways of a town held perfect cover, providing camouflage amongst the buildings and pathways. To the accompaniment of their heartbeats they squatted, straining for the slightest sounds. Nothing.

"Are you sure you heard one?" The girl was nervous, but tried to hide it.

"Yes, probably close by, watching us."

"Shouldn't we start searching?"

"No. We're safe enough here. If it's not attacked us than you can bet it's waiting for us to make the first move to try and find it."

Sam wiped the sweat from his palms; he was gripping the Sten gun too tightly. He tried to take a fix on the direction the sound could have come from; not in front of them, the road was too wide, so it had to be from behind. Slowly, he eased them forward into the road; the more open space around them the better. Only three in number, their triangle left blind spots, but in the middle of the road he felt safer if a boar charged them. It was hot under his helmet and more sweat trickled down his face from the brim, stinging his eyes.

"There." The boy shouted, pointing, but it was only long discarded litter billowing into the air on a shoulder of breeze. For what felt like an age, their nerves sat on a razor edge. What happened if they were suddenly rushed by a large group of boar?

Sam had only heard one, but that could be the alpha male directing his silent pack. Endless seconds slowly ticked into waiting minutes and still nothing moved. The world seemed to stand still, waiting for one side to make the first move.

With a clatter of boots, Bartlett and the others returned, breathless, having heard the distant echo of Sam's shout of alarm.

"Anything?"

Sam shook his head. "No. But the bastard's out there somewhere."

Without speaking, they merged into a larger group, assuming a broader radius to improve their protection.

"Aye," Bartlett agreed, now standing up. "And you know what they say."

Sam stood up to join him. "Where there's one there'll soon be a dozen."

Bartlett nodded. "Come on; time to move. We're sitting ducks sitting here waiting for them."

With that he moved in the direction of the trailer, still stacked with empty jerry cans. When they had heard Sam's alarm call they had just discovered a petrol station, surprisingly with fuel still in its storage tanks.

"Let's go and fill some cans and leave the boar to wonder where we have disappeared to."

Hauling the trailer, Bartlett set off up the hill and as he took the strain, Sam saw that he still held a smouldering roll-up clenched tightly between his lips.

Late afternoon was moving towards dusk as they hauled the heavily laden trailer through the narrow streets. Now it took three of them to pull it along, heavy tyres crunching over broken glass and masonry. They had already had a puncture and without a spare tyre they now had to move with caution. Sam had taken his turn on the tow bar and was again following the group as the rear guard. The boar had not materialised, but Sam was not reassured, sensing they were being watched or followed, the boar waiting for them to make a mistake or lapse their attention. Despite the booty in their trailer, he felt decidedly on edge.

It had taken two hours to pump fuel into the jerry cans. The underground fuel tanks that Bartlett had found were still a quarter full and they had used a hand pump to draw the petrol from the deep tanks and into the cans. Two hours of back-breaking work and blisters for a meagre reward. If the survivors they were waiting for didn't arrive by the following morning, they would return to the tanks and repeat the process again; blisters and all.

The streets were now filling with shadows, changing the appearance of the desolate abandoned buildings as they passed. At the rear of the group, Sam missed the teasing banter which helped to bind them together. He wondered if this was inflaming his unease. He walked alone, continually turning in circles, leaving nowhere unseen, checking, searching for someone or something that might be following them.

It could explain how he saw, or thought he saw, a pale oval face at a window. It disappeared in the blink of an eye, but Sam was certain he had seen someone, as convinced as he had been that he had heard the hungry growl of a boar earlier that afternoon. He hesitated. As he lingered, the others were already fifty metres ahead of him and about to turn the trailer onto the landing ramp and begin transferring the contents onto the raft.

"Hello." His voice stirred the shadows. "Is there anyone there? We're from the boat in the river and we're here to help you."

Only silence answered him as he waited, finger instinctively curled around the trigger of his gun. With a nervous step, Sam moved back a few paces to get a better view of the window where he thought he had seen the face. It had been small; no bigger than that of a child or young teenager. He crossed the street to the opposite side; the window was at first floor level and, although the glass was broken and the casement shattered, he still couldn't see inside.

"Is anyone there?"

He called again and dismissed the thought of entering the building alone. The rest of the group were now out of sight and preoccupied with transferring their scavenging to the raft. They might not notice he was missing for some while yet. For a minute, Sam remained, looking up to the window, willing the face to appear again. A noise made him start; the sound of something dry and loose, like broken masonry, sliding and falling. It came from behind him.

Sam moved briskly into the middle of the street. Was there more than one? If there were, they had probably worked out that he was now alone. He moved a short distance farther along the narrow street, alarmed that he had left himself open to being surrounded. Shadows were deepening quickly, turning grey light into deep purple, recesses already ink black. Danger was palpable but he felt reluctant to leave without some proof, one way or another.

Slowly, Sam removed his rucksack. He still had some of his day's rations and, finding a piece of card, he removed the remains of a sandwich, an apple and a small pack of biscuits, and placed them on the ground, using the card as an improvised plate. If anyone had lived in this desolate place, hunger would be a constant friend he decided, so the gesture might just work. With a nervous shiver, Sam checked behind him and slowly walked backwards in the direction of the others, dropping to his haunches to wait, hoping his withdrawal might encourage results.

He guessed his absence would very soon be the cause of concern and the others would return and break the spell of the moment. Was someone hiding in this desolate place or was it merely his imagination playing tricks? Some way off someone was shouting his name. Time to call it a day he decided, reluctantly accepting that he was probably mistaken and there had been no one there all along. The shouts were increasing, so Sam set off down the street at a slow jog, feeling the hairs on the back of his neck stand on end in an odd sensation and was relieved to see Bartlett when he turned the corner.

"For a moment you had me worried."

"Sorry, I just stopped to check something. Can I borrow your binoculars?"

Puzzled, Bartlett lifted them over his head and handed them over. Sam could just see the spot where he had left his token gesture. It took a second to clear the focus and magnify what he was looking at. Only the square of card remained.

Bartlett frowned in question as Sam returned the glasses, unable to resist a broad grin in reply, before nonchalantly adding.

"I think you'll find we're not alone here."

# SIX

By the early light of morning, *Lupin* retraced the line of buoys in the river. On his return the previous evening, Sam had been confronted with a disagreement. It had brewed all day while he was ashore, eventually flaring into an argument between Helen and John. No sooner had he arrived back on board, than it burst upon him.

"Did you know it was always Helen's plan to up-anchor at the first opportunity and sit out the night in the estuary?" John asked, his Welsh accent intensified by emotion. "It's irrational and unreasonable. These poor people could arrive at any moment and what will they find; no one here. You must do something. It goes against everything that Albert Jamieson intended."

John was seething, beyond listening to reason. It was obvious that *Lupin* was being prepared for casting off with the rumble of her engines already vibrating the decks, so Sam made his way quickly to the wheelhouse. He found Helen preparing to depart as John had predicted and, with cargo and crew loaded, she was making haste to move out of the river before darkness fell.

"Hi, Helen. Hold casting off for a moment, please."

In mid-command, she turned towards Sam. "Why? I'm only fulfilling my instructions; putting the safety of *Lupin* and her crew before anything else." She folded her arms intransigently and cast a dismissive glance in John's direction. "Are you questioning my judgement, Sam?" she challenged.

"No, I just want clarification on the options here." With the engines running, Helen's hand rested only inches from engaging the propeller. "John, have you heard anything at all from the survivors that might make us change our plans?"

John shook his head. "Nothing yet, but that could change at any moment and if we're stuck out somewhere in the estuary it could be hours before we can help them. Who knows what problems they are having, especially if this vigilante group are still tracking them ..."

Helen cut across him. "Which serves to make my point; if they arrive here and things are that desperate, we need to have a plan that doesn't make us sitting ducks and put all of the crew and this ship at risk."

Her hand moved back to the lever on the engine control console. "Dave." Sam spoke more sharply than he intended. Bartlett had arrived in the wheelhouse and was watching the interplay with an amused expression. "If we remain here overnight, how well can you protect us?"

For a moment Bartlett looked thoughtful, evaluating Sam's question.

"Protection against boar? That's easy, a hundred percent; they can't swim. Other humans who might be about? That's a different matter. Overnight, in the narrow confines of the river? I'd need to double the watch, keep the generators running for searchlights and, as there's no moon, fire flares every half-hour to illuminate the banks as well as the river. So no one gets any sleep, we'd use twice the amount of fuel and we've probably only got enough flares for one, possibly two, nights. But it should keep us safe, though from how serious a threat, your guess is as good as mine."

Sam pursed his lips; he had just caught sight of a large white panel leaning upright on the upper deck. "Have we got any red paint?"

Helen looked surprised. "We've got cans of red oxide for rust treatment."

"Bring a can, some brushes and a stout post; we're going to make a sign."

It took thirty minutes to carry the improvised sign back to the shore. Sam kept the message brief.

*'We're here for you. Back in the morning. Fire flare in emergency.'*

Against a white background, the message would be seen clearly, even in the darkness. They nailed the board to a post and stood it in an upturned drum together with a flare gun wrapped in plastic, and positioned it at the bottom of College Way, the most likely approach route the group might take. Friend or foe, as Bartlett cryptically reminded Sam.

Back on *Lupin*, Sam took John aside, hoping to placate him.

"The sign should be sufficient if they arrive overnight. Dave can't adequately protect us if we stay in the confines of the river and that has to be our first priority. I'm sorry for the decision, but we can't afford to risk the ship. The success of the entire operation depends on her."

Before John could reply, the first of the red marker buoys passed on their starboard side. Almost without thinking, Sam had made his first major decision and hopefully healed their mood of disagreement with an even hand. At least their second night could be spent out in the security of the estuary, waiting for things to unfold, leaving Sam to ponder the fate of the oval face he had fleetingly seen at the window in town.

It took until mid-morning to reconnect the winch lines, raft, and the day's paraphernalia. The price of their security was time consuming, which was tiresome but essential. At least it had guaranteed the crew a decent night's sleep. Repeating the steps of the previous day, Bartlett was soon standing on the landing ramp with a fresh squad, intent on filling a trailer of empty jerry cans with a scarce commodity; petrol. When it was Sam's turn to go ashore, he found the raft wallowed alarmingly in waves now whipped along on a strengthening breeze. Perhaps weighed down with cargo on the return journey it would feel more stable.

In the town they formed up as for the previous day with Bartlett out in front and Sam again at the rear. Bartlett started with the same route as before, aware that the streets provided the clearest access for the trailer. Soon after setting out they passed the building in which Sam had seen the face, but as they were anxious to get to the filling station for petrol he passed it by with little more than a sideways glance. Intuition told him there was no one about, but he thought he would try again on their return later in the day.

They made quick progress and Sam took comfort from the light-hearted mood of their young squad members, creating an illusion of normality in a place where very much the opposite was true. As they walked he allowed himself to daydream and imagine the world as it once had been; a daydream that came to an abrupt end when Bartlett stopped suddenly, mid-stride. Paying scant attention, the leading squad member almost walked into his back as they all stumbled to a halt. Bartlett sunk to his haunches, arms outstretched, palms downwards. After a few seconds he turned and called Sam forward to join him while the youngsters maintained their positions. As he arrived, Bartlett handed binoculars to him.

"So, what have we got here," he pointed forward, along the road.

At first, Sam struggled to focus, debris littered the side paths, but the roadway was largely clear. But there was no mistaking what Bartlett had seen. A human skeleton lay, spread-eagled in the middle of the road, blocking the route ahead of them.

"Unless I'm mistaken, it wasn't there yesterday." Bartlett added with a note of black humour.

Sam handed the binoculars back. From the previous day, he remembered the barber's red and white striped pole on a building to the right and the shattered remains of a café opposite as they had walked down the same street. Then, there had been no skeleton to avoid.

"How ..." Sam muttered.

"More importantly, who?" Bartlett said. "Can't be boar; there are no dogs about and anyway, they would have dismembered the skeleton for the marrow in the bones. So ..."

"As I said yesterday, we're not alone."

"It would look that way," Bartlett said. "What did you mean last night? I thought you were joking."

Sam shrugged. "I saw someone; a face at a window."

Bartlett laughed. "We think we see those all the time. Any evidence?"

Sam shook his head. "Not that I actually saw, but I tried the hunger trick and left the remains of my lunch in the middle of the road just before you called me. I waited a little while but decided I was imagining things, but when I looked back from the corner, the food had gone."

For a moment, both men looked at the figure in the road ahead.

"Maybe you weren't imagining things after all," Bartlett added, softly, so the rest of the squad wouldn't hear him. Keen to move on before the youngsters behind them became spooked, Sam started to walk forward to examine the skeleton, but Bartlett grabbed him by the arm.

"The last man I knew who did that had his leg blown off. It was booby-trapped. You stay here, I'll go and check it."

With an experienced ease he slipped past Sam, adding, "If anything goes wrong, get the squad back to the ship in quick order. It will be a clear sign the natives aren't friendly."

He was gone before Sam could reply.

Sam moved back through the squad members behind him. They were young and curious; two boys in their late teens and two slightly older girls. Bartlett had trained them well and despite the air of nervous curiosity, they hadn't moved from their positions.

"Why have we stopped?" Ruth, who was towing their trailer, asked what they were all thinking. She was a slight, dark-haired girl, who walked with a limp from a leg injury that had healed badly.

'We're all maimed, one way or another, in this new world in which we live,' Sam thought silently to himself.

"Nothing serious; Dave just needs to check the way ahead before we go any farther."

Squatting at road level they couldn't see the skeleton; Sam decided to keep it that way until Bartlett called them forward, and he turned to watch Dave as he quartered the area around the skeleton on soft feet, prodding and searching with an extended cane, gently lifting and scanning beneath the street litter. It took a few minutes before Bartlett was satisfied and beckoned them forward. There was room beside the skeleton to pass the trailer through; he had decided not to move the body, thinking it might be a test or hold some ritualistic significance. Bartlett positioned himself in front of it, giving instructions to keep eyes forward, dead-ahead, and in seconds they were clear, though the event created a few questions in many young minds.

Aware that a change of mood was needed, Bartlett stopped after a short distance, calling a halt outside what had been a tailor's shop. Without a word he disappeared inside the ransacked building, returning a few minutes later with a small velvet box. He beckoned the group to gather round as he tempted them with the act of slowly opening the lid, only to eventually reveal a pair of gold cufflinks.

"Cufflinks?" an incredulous voice asked, deliberately turning to gaze at the chaos around them. "Why on earth would anyone want cufflinks?"

Bartlett looked pained. "To wear with my dinner jacket, of course. I'll have you know I'm frequently invited to black-tie dinners. One must dress the part."

For a moment everyone was silent, absorbed by Bartlett's serious expression, until Sam exploded into peals of laughter at the image of anybody in a dinner suit in their now bizarre world.

Laughter soon applied its healing balm as the banter and teasing returned. Bartlett might well be a tough disciplinarian, but he was not adverse to a trick to bolster morale.

With renewed vigour, they pushed on to the petrol station that had proven so profitable the previous day. On this trip they carried an extra pump to speed the filling of the jerry cans. The late morning cloud had cleared; it was going to be another hot day, but as petrol was worth more than gold to them Sam decided they could get back to the raft and still make a return trip. When they arrived back at the service station the hottest part of the day had passed, and to speed up their back-breaking task, they raced each other to fill the jerry cans. Ruth won; she might be slight but she lacked nothing in fitness. For a few moments the brutal surreal world around them was forgotten.

But fate played her hand. Sam should have known better; they all should have. Their world wasn't a place in which the rules of normality existed. He saw them approach from the corner of his eye, first feeling bewilderment, then surprise and total alarm. There was no approaching growl to warn them; they came in silence; six large muscular male boar, tusks yellowed and stained, razor sharp. In a crescent, they positioned themselves between the team and their guns in an uncanny resemblance to their tactics at the Gilmores.

Sam heard Bartlett make a sharp intake of breath. "Well, what have we here." A bayonet rasped on its scabbard and Bartlett rammed the handle onto the stave he carried. "Form a star."

"We can't fight them with just knives," muttered one of the boys nervously.

"Do as you're told and don't run. It's what they want you to do. Face them and watch. You know the drill."

Stumbling and unsure, they formed their star, trying hard to avoid bunching. Bartlett took the nearest point to the advancing boar. Six humans with short knives, facing six boar, each armed with tusks and sharp stabbing teeth, weighing twice that of a man, with muscle to match. In a previous time it shouldn't have been a contest, but Sam knew the odds had changed and the six of them represented a tempting meal the hungry boar were keen to have.

The warm benign afternoon mocked them as boar and humans slowly circled, each waiting for the other to make the first move. A trembling voice in the group suggested, "Why don't we split up, try to run in different directions; at least some of us might make it to safety."

Bartlett barked for silence, nerves rasping as the dance rotated. To everyone's surprise it was Ruth who made the first move, balancing slowly from one foot to the other, goading one boar as it started to lean forward, head slowly lowered, contemplating a charge. With almost invisible grace, Ruth was closing the gap, knife extended, blade held horizontally. She had no intention of waiting for the boar to charge. Instead, she swayed slowly, like a pendulum, each gesture progressively accentuating her movements, as she puzzled and mesmerised the boar. With the speed of a dervish, she spun on the spot and threw herself to the ground as the disorientated boar lost its focus and charged. As it lunged and missed, she whipped her knife under its chin, thrusting hard in a slashing motion, severing its jugular and windpipe with the razor sharp blade. The boar's falling body knocked the knife from Ruth's hand; she was now defenceless.

Another boar began to turn towards Ruth, an angry growl rumbling from deep inside its body, its head descending, anticipating an attack. Ruth was unlikely to be able to pull off the same gymnastic feat again. Sam shouted and skimmed his knife to Ruth across the space between them; at least she would have a chance if she was attacked. He was nowhere near as nimble as Ruth, but with the boar distracted he scrambled to grasp a discarded length of rubber filler hose with its metal nozzle attached. The boar was backing Ruth towards the blank wall of a building so with the hose in his hand, Sam began to swing the heavy length around his head, like a ball and chain. He would only get one chance; he swung it toward the boar's head at the moment it charged at Ruth. Hose and nozzle struck the boar with a force that tore at Sam's shoulder joint, wrenching the hose from his hands and flattening the boar. In an instant, Ruth grasped the knife Sam had thrown to her and slit the boar's throat, her second of the day. Breathless, they grabbed Sten guns and scurried past the dying boar. Bartlett was locked in a one-sided fight to hold off two more animals. It was close-quarter fighting and difficult to use guns, but suddenly the remaining boar turned and retreated into the maze of overgrown pathways and gardens behind the filling station.

"Leave them," Bartlett barked. "Following will only risk another ambush."

He was furious, mostly with himself for allowing them to get caught in such a situation. A blood stain soaked his trousers, ripped through on the side of his leg. "Bastard glanced me," he said with a painful grimace.

Sam hastily found their medical pack, tearing out a tourniquet as he ran over to Bartlett. He tore open the side of his trouser leg, half expecting the worst. A deep cut ran at an angle from shin bone to the back of the calf muscle, gouging deep into the flesh, mercifully avoiding the artery.

"You're one lucky guy, Dave Bartlett," he said, exhaling through tight clenched teeth.

Thoughtfully, Bartlett looked at the wound.

"Now that's what I call luck. You'd almost think they know where we're most vulnerable the way they twist their heads to try and slash the artery with their tusks."

No one sought to contradict him.


It was late afternoon when, towing the trailer, they approached the landing ramp by the river. It wasn't a difficult choice to leave the petrol station, even though some of their cans were still empty. The possibility of more boar returning, and with two squad members badly shaken by the ambush, was enough for Sam to make the decision to return to *Lupin*. Despite his calm exterior, Bartlett was distracted with anger at himself for allowing such a situation to arise.

"Next time, we won't be so lucky," he muttered with self-recrimination.

The trailer was heavier than the previous day and manhandling it down the steep hill required all their strength. Without thinking, they took the same route passing the windows where Sam thought he had seen the human face. Bartlett didn't question when Sam said he would stay back while they loaded the fuel cans onto the raft. It was only a short distance to the landing ramp.

"Fire a shot into the air if you need help," Bartlett called out as they disappeared around the street corner.

With the group out of sight, Sam felt uneasy, the hard hand of desolation resting on his shoulders. For a while he stood in the shadows, watching, listening. Then he spoke. "Hello. Is anyone there?" His words echoed back unanswered. "Look, I'm a friend from the boat in the river; I'm here to help you. We've got food and medicine to share with you."

Minutes ticked away; dusk was already beginning to colour the sky and Helen wouldn't want to delay departure for too long. Sam made a pile of bread, cheese and biscuits on a sheet of card in the same spot as the previous evening and once again he imagined eyes watching him. He paused to look around at the empty windows that stared back like vacant black eyes. Instinctively, he backed away, turning occasionally to check behind him, then stopped and squatted down, arms outstretched, palms raised. In the silence, he noted that even the seagulls had abandoned the town, presumably due to a lack of food. Or were they also aware of the same malevolent presence that taunted Sam's imagination?

Then came the noise of falling masonry, slipping, sliding, crumbling. Someone, or something was moving amongst the ruins. Instinct made him turn forward again. In the gloom a deep shadow moved, like a black velvet curtain falling to the ground. With the action of a spider, long stick-like limbs slowly extended through a half-open doorway, stretching towards the road. Sam held his breath, convinced it must be some malformed creature sliding along the ground, arms following legs in a flowing motion, like silk drifting in a breeze. He blinked and saw the white oval face gently bobbing with the movement of the limbs, its dark sunken eyes fixed on him. A hand extended toward the tempting food, while the eyes held Sam in hypnotic fascination. With lightning speed, the hand snatched the biscuits, pressing them into its mouth with bruised swollen lips and blackened teeth. Sam could only think of the creature as 'it'. Stick thin, with matted fair hair and wearing rags made gender and age impossible to guess.

"Hello. I'm Sam. What's your name?" he struggled to speak, made breathless by what he was seeing.

For a moment the creature froze, jaw suddenly locked, head tilting to one side, eyes immobile, staring.

"I'm Sam," he repeated, "from the boat in the river. We're here to help you." He could feel cramp setting into his legs and urgently needed to stand. "Don't be alarmed, I'm just going to stand up." Sam had no idea if he was understood, but rose anyway, rubbing and easing his cramped leg muscles.

The figure started to eat again, at the same time hastily pushing the remaining food into hidden pockets. Sam tried a small step forward; immediately the figure began to move in response, with the same flowing action, backwards across the street towards its lair. Sam paused and the figure stopped, shimmering with a cat-like tension, a coil spring waiting for release.

Sam called quickly. "Please, don't go. I need to talk to you, find out what you need, what we can do to help. Are there others? Do you have family? We can help you all if you'll let us."

Sam's voice appealed, but there was no response, just a continued hard unblinking stare. It occurred to him that it was possibly a child who couldn't speak or hear him. Sam's motives were being driven by compassion and he knew for certain he couldn't leave another human being in this state. Without thinking, he took another step forward, hands outstretched. A step too far. The figure vanished like a dawn mist at the same moment that Bartlett called his name from the end of the street.

"Sam," he bellowed. "You'd better come now. It's John. He's had a radio message. It's not good news."

Aiden Cooper intercepted Sam as soon as he climbed the short ladder onto *Lupin*. Hastily leading aft, Aiden gazed apprehensively over his shoulder.

"You need to know that John has got himself worked up again. The people we are waiting for have walked into an ambush, somewhere just north of Totnes. It seems the same group that were raiding the few remaining farms on Dartmoor have caught up with them. John knows more detail. He wants us to go to their aid and mount an immediate rescue mission. I've already said that would need virtually everyone we've got and would end up putting *Lupin* at risk if anything goes wrong or the unexpected crops up. But you know our John, once he starts to get emotionally involved, logic and reason fly out the window."

Sam nodded without commenting. He was bone tired after the events of the day and needed a shower before addressing the next problem. On his way to his cabin, he felt *Lupin* tremble as Helen got underway for a second night outside the river estuary where they might find a solution to the latest problem in peace and quiet.

Revived by a shower, Sam made his way to the radio room. He had already sent out a message for Bartlett and Helen to join him and timed it to get a few minutes alone with John before they arrived. Darkness was settling around the ship as he walked the deck and opened the door to find John, wearing headphones and tuning frequency dials that cast a luminous green glow in the cupboard that served as their radio room. John turned as he entered, red eyes ringed in tired grey shadows.

"Hi, John. Care to fill me in on the latest." Sam perched on the edge of the desk beside him.

"I've found the frequency they're using. 'The men from the north' they call themselves. Signal is weak and intermittent so I'm only hearing fragments, but it tells enough; they've murdered the men in part of the group they've captured, but not before they told them of the other family. And about us."

John's face was ashen, a mixture of anxiety and overwork. Sam stiffened at the implications of his news. It was a nasty shock but he wasn't completely surprised. "Okay. I don't think that changes anything. How are the surviving group?"

"Terrified, as you could well imagine. They've abandoned their tractors and all their possessions, and left the roads to hide in the woods, moving only on foot and following the river Dart towards us, sensibly hiding during the day and walking at night for safety."

Sam nodded. "That sounds the best way. When will they get here?"

"Tomorrow, they hope, but quicker if we send a group to help them. They're really frightened, Sam; they need our help," John said, on the cusp of losing control of his emotions.

The door swung open and Bartlett entered in time to catch John's last words.

"How many people would you need to send to help the survivors, Dave?" Sam asked, not taking his eyes from John, who was now shaking with emotion.

It was pretty obvious that Bartlett had already been considering the question, but at least he made a pretext of giving it serious thought.

"We don't know how big this vigilante group is, so we would have to send both squads at least. That would leave the ship vulnerable, which given they now know about our presence here, might not be the best of situations."

He allowed a note of scepticism to hang in his final phrase. The master of understatement, Bartlett arched a questioning eyebrow as the door opened and Helen arrived. Things were becoming tight in the tiny room. Sam didn't need to ask for her opinion as ship security was always her first priority, even before that of the crew, he suspected.

"John, when will you next be in contact with the group?"

"They said they would try to put in a radio call just before they start walking again tonight. They've stayed hidden during daylight," he repeated, wringing his hands anxiously, "and will start to move as soon as it's dark. They're all exhausted but I'm sure it would energise them if they know we're coming to rescue them."

John glanced at them hopefully. Sam sat in thought for a minute, weighing the options.

"Using the cover of darkness sounds their best chance. Tell them we'll have help in the town as soon as they arrive, but they must get here on their own resources. We've no detailed maps and no way of being certain of their exact location, so it would be pointless to set off on a wishful search. It's asking for trouble and has the hallmarks of disaster written all over it," he said firmly.

"But that leaves them on their own against this gang of killers," John cut across Sam, raising his voice.

Sam shook his head sadly. "As I said, they'll have to use their own resources. Once they're in Dartmouth we won't leave without them, but we're not chasing around on the vague chance that we might find them." He looked directly at Bartlett. "Any ideas how big this vigilante group might be?"

"At a guess, more than twenty, less than thirty. Too big for us to handle even if our people were trained for that role. Remember, a lot of this group could be ex-military. We're just a bunch of amateurs."

John looked appalled for the second time in twenty-four hours.

"So I tell them we're just abandoning them."

"No, we're not. Their best chance is to get here as fast as possible, but they must use caution. Tonight would be good. They're a small group; tell them to leave everything behind in the interest of speed. If they can make it before first light, all the better, and we can be gone before daylight, just in case the vigilante group arrive and want to pick a fight with us."

John stared in reproach at Bartlett and Helen in turn, silently accusing them of influencing Sam against him. Abruptly, he jumped to his feet.

"Stop the ship now; give me a gun and a rucksack; I'll go alone; it can't be that difficult and you two can't stop me," he said, glaring angrily at all of them.

"True, they can't stop you," Sam intervened. "But I can, and you're not going anywhere, John, noble though your intentions might be. If we lose you, we lose what little communications we have and that could be disastrous. Plus, if you're caught by these 'men from the north', you know too much about *Lupin* and the island. So, sorry John, you're staying put, right here."

Enough had been said; too much perhaps. With nothing more to add, Bartlett and Helen left. Sam placed a hand on John's arm as he moved to follow them, trying to reassure him. But John only stared grimly at the dials in front of him, resigned to the fate of those he so wanted to help. Sam left the radio room aware that the responsibility of his decision had cost him a friendship he most valued.

# SEVEN

When problems are unsought, they still hunt you out nevertheless. Despite his fatigue, Sam had slept badly, anguished by a problem he couldn't have expected. Following dinner, with *Lupin* securely anchored in the estuary, he had volunteered for the midnight watch. Bartlett allocated him his favoured patrol on the top deck, an area small enough to cover alone. Slowly rotating his beat, fifteen minutes at each quarter, Sam had his father's pocket watch for company. It was the only family possession that remained; already faces were beginning to fade; from colour to sepia, black and white to ... nothing. Despite the passing of the years, it was the thought of never knowing their fate that caused him the greatest pain. Separated by chaos, overwhelmed by the magnitude of trauma, the pandemic had spread panic as control and governance collapsed. In a final radio message before she died, all the Prime Minister could offer was 'every man for his, or her, self.'

Brutal, but the truth.

It was in the middle of his watch when Sam came across them, coupling naked in the partially covered lifeboat, on davits just below him. If they had kept silent, they would have been invisible, even to the lower deck. They obviously hadn't anticipated someone patrolling on the deck above them. Sam's instinct was to look away. Privacy, for the few youngsters on board, was hard to find, even in the dark hours, but in that instant he fleetingly recognised them. Teri, the teenage nurse who worked with Karen, with a boy holding her in a passionate embrace who shouldn't have turned his head at that precise moment. Then the problem would have never arisen, a problem not of act, but relationship. Sam recognised the boy immediately; Ryan was one of Bartlett's younger squad members. But that wasn't the problem. The island had strict laws preventing relationships between family members. With their small population, inbreeding was something they couldn't possibly allow. It was a trap so easy to fall into and they decided at the very outset that protection of their genetic blood line had to be paramount. The problem was that Ryan was Teri's first cousin.

It was still dark when breakfast was served the following morning. The mess room, which doubled up as meeting place, dormitory and emergency clinic, was rich with the smell of hot porridge and baking bread. Teri, who doubled as one of the cooks, ladled thick steaming oats into Sam's bowl. She showed no sign of having seen him the previous night and was her usual bubbly self. Sam liked both her and Ryan, which only made his dilemma feel worse. They had both lost their entire families in the pandemic and Ryan had protected Teri in many dangerous situations before they had reached the sanctuary of their island. It was no wonder that their affections had grown in the way that they had. Island rules tried to be as liberal as possible, but if Teri became pregnant and their relationship disclosed, she would be compelled to have an abortion. If they persisted with their relationship, Ryan would be sterilised. The forum made and enforced the rules, and Sam had little doubt of the trouble they would be in the moment he reported what he had seen.

At breakfast, John seemed more like his usual self when he and Sam shared the same table.

"Have you heard anything from the survivors?"

John shook his head. "Only from the thugs that are chasing them. I caught fragments of their radio messages. Sounds as if they found an intact pub cellar on the outskirts of Totnes last night and drank themselves senseless. They know their prey have resorted to travelling on foot so they'll catch up on their motorbikes when daylight comes."

Sam nodded his head. "Let's hope they have mammoth hangovers and sleep late."

Ruth joined them at that moment and a passing idea came to Sam. For a few minutes he ate in silence, listening to conversation bubbling around him. Ignoring Sam, John was keen to hear first-hand about the confrontation with the boar at the petrol station and Sam was surprised by the way Ruth played down the drama of the event, making no mention of her own role or the panic of some squad members.

"That was modest of you," Sam said when John had finally left the table. "There might have been a different outcome for all of us if you hadn't acted as quickly as you did."

Ruth shrugged, her dark eyes, almost as black as her hair, flashed for an instant. "I hate boar. They killed my mother and sister so I have a score to settle." Her words were calm, matter of fact, but laced with venom.

"All the same, be careful. There's a lot of them about and they seem to be ever more cunning by the day. A majority of the group that have attacked us on the island are males and they're bigger and faster than I remember."

Sam paused, leaving Ruth to finish her breakfast. He had an idea but needed to find a quiet space to talk; he waited for her to finish while filling tea mugs for them both.

"Thanks."

"Care for a stroll on deck for a bit before the day hots up again."

His tone implied more than just a casual request, so Ruth followed him out onto the deck, her limp more pronounced following the exertions of the previous day.

"Your leg okay?"

Ruth nodded. "It aches. I broke it when a boar I had to fight fell on top of me."

"Ouch."

Again Ruth shrugged. "It had killed my sister some days before. Bastard was hanging around for another meal."

Sam winced at the thought. Boar had developed an appetite for flesh; especially of the human variety.

"Ruth, I need to discuss a confidential matter with you." He tried not to sound too formal, but she suddenly looked alarmed. He pressed on regardless.

"How well do you know Teri Macklin?" Sam lent on the rail, trying to fix his gaze on the shore in the gathering light. The subject was awkward and made him feel self-conscious.

"Quite well. She's a couple of years younger than me. She seems to spend a lot of time with Ryan. I think they're cousins, and only just survived together."

"So that makes them close would you say?"

"Virtually no one has any family members who made it to the island with them, so that's only to be expected."

"How close, would you say?"

"Why?" Ruth sounded suspicious.

Sam drew a breath. This wouldn't be easy. "While on watch last night, I came across them. They were careless," he paused. "Let's just say they're far closer than they ought to be."

For a moment Ruth was silent. "Are you sure? If it was dark …"

Sam sighed. "They were both undressed. I wasn't mistaken, I wish I was."

Ruth glanced at him, well aware of Sam's status as a forum member. "So you'll report them."

"I don't want to, but that's my dilemma. If she's not already pregnant, and if they could be told to find other partners ..."

For a time they both stood in thoughtful silence.

"Silly girl," Ruth muttered under her breath, well aware of the consequences for both Teri and Ryan. "Why are you telling me?"

"I hoped you would be able try and talk to Teri. It might come better from another woman."

"Does she know you've seen them?"

Sam shook his head. "No, I'm pretty certain they didn't see me; they were rather preoccupied," he said, adding a lighter note. "Even if you tell her they've been seen, she'll probably still try to deny it, so you'll need to emphasise what could happen to them if they are caught. Don't mention my name unless you absolutely have to. I'm using my personal judgement on this matter, but the next person who sees them, and someone will if they continue, might not be so fair-minded."

Ruth took a few moments thinking it through. There were serious implications for her also if she stayed silent and Teri became pregnant. Sam read her thoughts.

"In case you're worried, you've fulfilled your obligations by discussing the matter with a forum member. I'll answer for it if this comes out, not you. Hopefully, our silence will reassure Teri and Ryan enough to change course before it's too late." Sam paused before adding, "You can have that in writing if you want."

"No, I'll take your word for it. I'm not sure if I can make any difference, but I'll try. If she's in love with Ryan it won't be easy to persuade her."

"Well, try is all you can do. Let me know what she says. Meanwhile I'll plan for the best and prepare for the worst." Sam tried to finish with an encouraging smile.

It was now light; there were others on deck, so without another word they parted and Sam turned and made to walk away. As he did so he just heard Ruth's words.

"Thank you. I just hope they appreciate the risk you're taking."

The day started with a delay when *Lupin* snagged a hidden underwater obstacle as Helen tried to moor in the river. A metal line or cable from a sunken vessel had wound itself around the screw and it took forever to untangle it. Impatiently, Helen, huddled in an old duffle coat, watched from the aft deck with Sam.

"It's a good job that didn't happen when an emergency arose. Strange though, we've come about in the same spot every time and not caught it before."

Sam shivered. The day was heavy and overcast, the breeze was now from the north, a reminder that winter hadn't completely released her grip.

"We'll sail tonight regardless?" Helen questioned. "Three days is long enough to sit around in this river." She gazed anxiously at the desolate townscapes either side of them.

"Unless the situation develops to keep us here. Last night John thought the survivors were within ten miles, so if they don't make it today, things won't look too good for them."

"Or for us. If this vigilante group we hear so much about arrives looking for a fight we could be in real trouble."

Helen's tone was matter of fact but she hadn't failed to notice Bartlett and his squads on the upper deck now donning helmets and webbing for the first time. Sam followed her gaze.

"It's just Dave planning for the worst. Don't worry about it, Helen."

Beside them the grey day made Dartmouth look even more dilapidated and ruined. Would things ever recover? Not if the handful of survivors started fighting one another. Everywhere looked empty and deserted, but Sam guessed there must be some humans hiding amongst the ruins, in a landscape in which boar also stalked and hid, waiting in ambush for the unwary.

Eventually, the engineers disentangled the cable and the raft was winched ashore. Bartlett assembled a larger six-man team for this trip ashore, including Ruth to assist him with her steady nerve and the skill she had shown the previous day.

"Extra lunch, I see." Bartlett noticed Sam was carrying a second rucksack.

"I'd like to entice out of hiding whoever I saw yesterday. I'm hoping a full rucksack of good things might do the trick."

"Well, good luck with that. I wouldn't hold your breath if I were you."

Sam felt Bartlett's pessimism was misplaced and the thought of leaving someone behind in this desolate place created a hollow feeling inside him.

Once ashore, they left the landing ramp by the usual route, turning right to follow the road through the town. Despite his personal feelings, John had repaired a small mobile radio set. It had limited range but worked well enough and for the first time they would have a direct link with the ship. They soon passed the spot where they had been held up the previous morning. The mysterious spread-eagled skeleton had disappeared. Once well clear, Bartlett stopped the squad and dropped back to the rear where Sam was once again the lonely rear guard.

"Seems like your new friend could be playing games with us."

Sam shrugged. "Maybe. I suppose there could be others about."

But around them were only shattered windows and broken doors, which seemed to gape and mock their passing. A short distance farther, Sam peeled off from the group. He had arranged with Bartlett to stay behind for a while and spend some time alone trying to tease out the mysterious spider-like figure he had seen the day before. Bartlett was clearly uneasy about Sam staying alone, but eventually agreed, handing Sam a flare gun to use if an emergency arose.

With a feeling of misgiving, Sam watched the others disappear down the street. Their priority was the group approaching from Totnes, yet he couldn't leave without one more attempt to rescue the solitary figure. Another half-hour spent alone might just make the difference. Nothing remained of the previous evening. Not a crumb or cardboard plate remained. More in hope than expectation, Sam surveyed the streetscape around him.

"Anyone here?"

Only a hollow echo of his voice replied so Sam dropped the spare rucksack in the same spot in the middle of the street. He repeated everything as before, backing away twenty paces and squatting on his haunches. At least he was fresh this morning, so cramp wouldn't be a problem. Sam shivered again as the cold wind funnelled between buildings, lifting dust and debris in spirals that resembled tiny whirlwinds. Despite his parka, he felt cold and pushed his hands deeper into his pockets to hug the jacket closer.

"C'mon kid, don't keep me hanging around," Sam muttered to himself.

A weak sun broke through the cloudy cover, immediately creating shadows cast by dying buildings. He wondered how much of this would still exist in a hundred years, as mankind's presence became erased by time and weather, and now it seemed, boar? He cast the thought aside; it only made him feel gloomy, a luxury he couldn't afford.

From the recesses of the shadows, came a spider-like movement as limbs began to unwrap themselves from amongst the debris and wreckage, moving towards the rucksack. No normal human gait; more insect than man. So this was what the bare basics of survival was reduced to, no less shocking despite being a repeat of the previous evening.

"Hi, I'm Sam. I was here yesterday," he called, his voice interrupting the flow of motion, as hands reached for the rucksack, eyes locked unblinking on Sam as before. It drew the rucksack closer, sniffing pockets and cover flap, more animal than human.

"I need to talk to you," Sam continued. "I'm going to stand up. Don't be afraid."

He stood slowly, hands outstretched. The child moved; from its size and shape it was clearly not adult, and opened the rucksack, gaze fixed on him, head tilted unnaturally to one side.

"I'm going to walk towards you," Sam called. "I mean you no harm; I'm here to help if you'll let me."

He took a step forward; there was no reaction, so he took another, and another, balancing on velvet toes. Slowly the limbs unfolded. As Sam stepped closer, the child began to stand, rucksack now locked in the grip of one hand, a stiletto-pointed knife just visible in the other. Alarmed, Sam stopped abruptly. Had he not anticipated a knife or weapon? They were closer now and as the child stood, its human form became more apparent. Sam guessed it was a boy, though age was harder, perhaps somewhere between ten and fifteen years old.

"My name is Sam," he pointed to his chest as he announced his name. "Sam. What's your name?"

The boy, if that's what it was, slid the rucksack over his arm, index finger pointing at Sam.

"Sam?" The voice sounded unused; more a grunt than a word.

Sam nodded encouragingly. "You?" He pointed his finger in the child's direction. "You," he repeated.

For the first time, the eyes blinked, brain digging in dark recesses for something invisible, hidden in a recess of distant memory. For a while, as the silence of uncertainty sat between them, Sam waited patiently. A finger turned and tapped a bony chest several times, the eyes rolled.

"Stupid bastard."

He said with a triumphant punch to the chest, as though memory had returned through a dark fog.

"Stupid bastard," he repeated again, louder and again, louder, gathering to a crescendo, as if for the first time announcing his presence to the buildings around them.

Sam experienced a feeling of euphoria at the same moment. Though the words were more a pronouncement of savagery than identity, compassion then jolted his emotions with the realisation that this was what others had called him in past times. Despite himself, Sam took an involuntary step backwards, as much from the eye-watering smell that emanated from the boy as the triumphant shout of his name.

"Are there other people here with you?" Sam was somewhat at a loss but it seemed the next logical question to ask.

"Alone?" The word required thought.

"Family, friends, a group of you who need our help?"

"Alone?" the boy repeated.

"Yes." Sam said. "Alone." He pointed again to himself and then in the direction of the boy. "Not alone?"

Another silence followed, it was progress that the boy appeared to be thinking. Sam waited, holding his breath in anticipation. He barely caught the word when it came.

"Alone," uttered as a hoarse whisper, the moment shattered by the shrill of a whistle from the far end of the street.

Sam felt the pain of despair. In the split second it took to turn and see Ruth calling him, the boy had vanished into thin air. The only evidence that he was not a figment of imagination was that the rucksack had disappeared with him.

"Don't go. Come back. We're all here together. Come back, we can help you," he called forlornly after the boy.

There was only silence in answer to his plea from the empty buildings around him and he knew he would have to abandon the boy to his fate. Sam only had seconds. He knew an emergency must have arisen; it wasn't hard to guess why Ruth had interrupted him. She ran up to him, breathless from the weight of the full equipment on her back.

"John has heard from the survivors; they've just entered Dartmouth, with the 'men from the north' hard on their heels. Dave says you're to come immediately."

Despite the urgency of the moment, Ruth delivered her instructions clearly, between gasps, without emotion, though apprehension clearly lined her face. Sam hesitated briefly, taking one final look at the buildings around them with a feeling of certainty he wouldn't pass this way again any time soon.

'Close, but not quite close enough'.

It paraphrased an experience that shadowed the life of every survivor.

# EIGHT

Javed slid down the pole of a streetlight as Sam and Ruth caught up with Bartlett and the rest of the squad. Javed was from an ethnic Pakistani family who had emigrated to Britain during the partition of India years earlier. His instinctive climbing skill allowed him to tackle almost anything, with or without safety ropes, a talent Bartlett was keen to put to good use.

"There's a group at the top of the hill, moving this way. I can see a handcart being drawn by two men, and what looks like seven women and children tagging along behind. And there was a distant sound, like a chainsaw being used intermittently, but I couldn't see anyone else."

Javed's report was tight and concise, without any guesswork, which Bartlett preferred.

"Any luck?" Bartlett asked as Sam arrived.

He shook his head. "No. I needed more time. Another half-hour would have done it."

Bartlett shrugged in resignation; he had more pressing matters on his mind.

"The survivors are coming and I think we can presume the noise Javed heard is motorbikes, so we'll need to get a move on."

Sam and Ruth quickly returned to their squad positions. Sam felt a surge of nervous excitement replace his disappointment over losing the boy, and eased his webbing and straps and checked the safety catch on his gun for reassurance. For a moment, Bartlett ran backwards, still facing them, shouting final instructions.

"Okay, listen. Remember your training, everyone, and don't forget to keep a look out for boar, we know they're about. No one leaves their positions or opens fire without my permission; that's how misunderstandings arise and lead to problems. We're a team, we work as a team and that way everything will be fine."

With that confident note, Bartlett led them uphill towards the approaching group, leaving Sam to marvel at his fitness despite constantly chain-smoking roll-ups. Yet he felt the pressure to move faster still in an attempt to get the approaching group to safety before their pursuers caught up with them. No doubt Bartlett had his reasons to keep things measured and it wasn't Sam's role to contradict him.

As they crested the top of the hill, a small group approached, suddenly running directly towards them urgently. One member stumbled and fell, exhausted, onto the road. The small cart they were pushing ran out of control and skewed sideways, only stopped by a low brick wall. Bartlett broke into a run with the squad following him, their equipment jingling like discordant sleigh bells. Despite the cool day, they were all panting and sweating; Sam began to understand why Bartlett started slowly. Running uphill in full kit was hard work, regardless of their fitness.

As they arrived, some of the approaching group showed signs of considerable distress. Sam could make out an older man struggling to manage the cart with the help of a teenage boy. An older woman was stretched out on top of bags and possessions heaped in the cart. To one side, another teenage boy was helping a pregnant girl who had fallen and was now lying on the ground. Two more teenage girls, each carrying an infant, were trying to help. Sam quickly counted how many they were; nine, but from his radio conversation with John earlier that morning, Sam expected to find ten.

"Thank god you've found us," the older man gasped out the words. "They're right behind us, closing fast. You can't imagine what they'll do to us if they caught up," he said, the fear of the moment clearly etched on his face as the words tumbled out.

Exhausted, they all looked close to the end of their tether.

"Where are the rest of you?" The old man stared at the small squad in front of him, eyes wide in confusion.

"This is all we are; it's enough," Bartlett answered, ignoring the man's panic and directing two of the squad to help the girl on the ground.

"What? Don't you understand, there's at least thirty of these evil bastards chasing us. They'll overwhelm you when they get here, you must call for extra people immediately. They do terrible things. When they caught our friends they were savages, absolute fiends, butchering the ..."

"That's enough," Bartlett barked. Fear spread like a wildfire and needed to be stamped on before it infected his young squad members.

Within moments they had made space on the handcart for the pregnant girl who had collapsed and seemed beyond exhaustion. Water canteens were passed around and extra ropes hastily attached to the cart to slow its downhill journey. They were ready to move off but even in that short space of time, the buzz noise of approaching motorbikes had become distinctly louder.

"I thought there were ten of you?" Sam asked again, more abruptly than he intended.

Eyes flickered, unspoken messages signalled between the group.

Puzzled, Sam asked, "What?"

Collectively they hesitated, speechless to the question until the younger boy broke the silence. "She couldn't keep up, we had to leave her behind. There was no alternative." He looked as wretched as he sounded.

Sam frowned. More questions sprang to mind, but Bartlett was leaving without any more delay. It was the hawk-eyed Javed who spotted the lonely figure. "There's someone else, much farther back, along the road."

Sam followed his outstretched arm, unable to see anyone until Javed handed him binoculars. As the focus cleared, he could just see a slight figure in a dirty blue dress, frantically searching her pathway with side sweeps of her white cane. A silent thought sprang to mind; blind, abandoned. Why?

"Sam, we're not waiting," Bartlett said sharply, already in the act of leaving.

"I'll go." Ruth read Sam's mind and had already removed her helmet.

She'd have to run the distance between them to have any hope of saving the girl. Capable as she might be, Sam knew he couldn't let Ruth go. Hastily, the group members were already moving past them.

"No, Dave needs you. Take my rucksack. Tell Dave to get everyone to *Lupin* as fast as possible. Take the raft and leave me the skiff."

Sam paused, tearing off his webbing, trying to ignore the nagging thought that this wasn't going to be easy. So why do it? The girl wasn't his responsibility; he hadn't made the decision to leave her behind.

"Radio Helen. Tell her to start the engines immediately and prepare to leave." He was already starting to run, shouting back.

"Hang on as long as possible, but save the ship at all costs. If I don't make it, tell Helen to check the beach at Blackpool Sands tonight."

It would be a long shot, the best he could think of at short notice.

Though he ran with only his Sten gun strapped across his chest, the incline of the hill became steeper and he was soon panting from exertion. The girl was closer now, a forlorn lonely figure as she struggled, half running, half stumbling, with only her white stick to guide her way. He tried to do the numbers as he ran; three minutes to cover the distance between them, the same for them to return. Ahead, the road was littered with wreckage, which would slow the men on motorbikes more than on foot. Farther on, College Way was much clearer. He calculated it would take at least twelve minutes to get to the bottom of the hill, perhaps twenty minutes in total. Above his gasping breath he strained to measure the drone of bike engines, certain that there wouldn't be enough time.

The girl heard Sam. She hesitated, moving sideways, her cane raised like a sword in front of her.

"Who's there? What do you want?" Blind terror was literal.

"I'm Sam, from the rescue boat in the harbour. I've come to help you," he gasped between gulps for air.

He stepped forward, hand extended. The cane sang past, narrowly missing his head as she swiped out in self-defence, deaf to anything other than her imagined fears riding the braying engines of the motorbikes stalking her.

"Hey," Sam shouted. "I'm here to help."

He just ducked under the next swipe of the cane, aimed at the sound of his voice, and side-stepped the return thrust on the backward stroke. He was desperate to move inside the arc of her stick, aware that the girl was fighting for her life.

"Stop that," Sam shouted angrily, lunging for her hand, ducking as he did so, and took the blow across his back. Howling with pain he grabbed her wrist, sending the cane spinning from her hand and twisting her body sideways as she kicked out painfully for his shins. Fortunately, the kick overbalanced her and she fell backwards against him. Opening both arms he caught her, stumbling backwards with the force of the impact despite embracing a body that was little more than skin and bones.

Though disorientated, she still managed a final kick backwards hard against his shin.

"Stop it. You're safe," he shouted, her ear only inches from his mouth.

He now had her locked in a bear-hug, trying to squeeze reason into her. He felt her kick out again, aiming for his groin, but managed to parry the blow with his thigh. In other circumstances he might have admired the fight of this little spitfire.

"For god's sake, stop, or I'll leave you to the mercies of the bastards chasing you."

If she kicked out once more, he'd push her away, abandon her and save himself, but as seconds ticked by, Sam felt the fight slowly drain out of her, her voice half sobbing, panting in his ear. He was still wary as he released her, expecting a renewed attack at any moment. He watched, her expression suddenly became one of bewildered hope; a pale face, with lightly freckled skin framed by long titian hair that hadn't seen a brush in days. A canvas bag and blanket were tied across a flat chest, her once blue dress was filthy, the hem shredded and torn. Worse was her feet, clad in thin soled shoes that had worn through, leaving her feet blistered and bloody.

"Okay. Let's start again," he managed with a gasp. "I'm Sam and you are …?"

"Claire."

"Right, Claire. We have one option; run. Forget your stick, grip my hand and whatever happens, don't let go. Just run for your life. I'll find the route; there'll be nothing in front of you, so just pick your feet up and run like the wind. If you fall, don't let go. We'll patch you up later."

Sam grabbed Claire by the wrist and she followed his lead, holding on with iron-locked fingers for what she now recognised as her only hope of survival. The motorbikes' noise was ever closer, the engines now reverberating through the empty streets. If he and Claire tried the road down the hill he had just climbed they'd be run down long before they reached safety. But there was just a chance they could disappear into the maze of side streets before their pursuers saw them; a slim chance at best, but better than nothing. The side roads posed a greater risk of encountering boar in the overgrown paths and alleyways but it offered the best worst option. Taking the decision, Sam pulled

Claire into the nearest side road. She took her first tumble as they changed direction, falling heavily onto her already bleeding knees.

"Tell me when you're going to change direction," she said, wincing with pain.

"Sorry."

Sam couldn't imagine what running into complete blackness must be like. There was much more wreckage and debris amongst the narrower side roads, which slowed them down while at the same time providing more immediate cover. They were now off his mental road map of the area; all he could do was keep running downhill and hope he didn't get them totally lost. Running hard, they passed what had once been immaculate gardens now reduced to a wilderness, and expensive cars abandoned on flat tyres, discarded like so many unwanted children's toys. From a lamp-post hung a skeletonised body, held together by the ragged clothes that still bound it. Even urban middle class Britain had not been spared the tsunami of terror and desolation. At least her blindness spared Claire the visual trauma of degeneration around them. She stumbled twice more as they threaded their way through the maze of streets, the sounds of motorbikes still echoing around them, now distilled by surrounding houses. Several times they had to backtrack when their path came to a dead-end. Losing track of time, the minutes felt like hours. But at last the streets led onto a broader tree-lined road that dropped to their left towards the river. Sam could still hear the bikes, but the noise was definitely farther away. If they moved quickly to the river, they might just get to the landing jetty before they were discovered. He hoped that Ruth had given Bartlett his message and left the skiff for them. Without it they would have to swim for *Lupin* and Sam knew that Claire was close to exhaustion after days on the run.

"We're going right," Sam remembered to warn Claire as he turned.

The road was clearer and they made quicker progress but were more exposed. He tugged her wrist with the irresistible urge to move faster and a short distance later she fell again. This time she hadn't tripped. He tried to pull her up.

"Come on. We're almost there. Just one more effort."

Claire lay where she fell, chest heaving, gasping for air that would not fill her desperate lungs, leaving her speechless and barely conscious. Worryingly, there was blood on her lips, diluted with saliva, running in a thin stream from the corner of her mouth. Sam managed to pull her upright but she could only stand if he held her. Her legs had given out; she looked too far gone to even care about the consequences. Sam looked at her anxiously. The time for their escape window would be closing fast but she needed more time to recover than fate could grant them.

"Hold on. It won't be comfortable but I'll have to carry you."
Without waiting for an answer he lifted her slender body over his shoulder.
"Grab on to my collar, it will stop you sliding off."

And so it was with Claire over one shoulder and his gun on the other that Sam Morten began the hardest run of his life. For both their lives to be precise. 'All I need now is a group of boar to show up,' he thought with grim humour. Five years of farming, hefting lambs, and lifting bales had toughened Sam, but running several hundred yards with Claire over his shoulder left him breathing hard, lungs burning.

An alleyway appeared, offering a short-cut to the lower road and the landing slipway. Gasping to regain his breath, he had to weigh his options. The alleyway could offer the perfect ambush for a boar. But on the other hand, it promised the opportunity to get ahead of their pursuers and be first to the skiff, if Bartlett had remembered to leave it for them. He strained his ears, his rasping breath drowning out other sounds. The sounds of motorbikes were moving in his direction again; hesitation was not an option so the alleyway it had to be. The narrow path dropped downwards in a series of ramps and steps which were harder to negotiate than the roadway; overhanging vegetation cast black recesses where almost anything could hide. Struggling to keep his nerve Sam plunged through, scored by brambles with barbed spikes and stung by head high nettles. At least there weren't any boar. To his surprise, after a short distance the alleyway led onto a street containing the derelict remains of shops and instinct told him he was closer to the river. He stepped back from the roadway into the protective lee of the buildings and kicked open the door of the first house he came to. Once inside, he lowered Claire onto the carpeted floor of what had once been someone's living room. He eased her into a sitting position and fumbled for his canteen.

"Drink that. I need to go upstairs to check where we are. I'll only be gone a minute or two."

Her face looked brighter, having regained some colour, but her eyes gave away her fears, darting erratically from side to side as he made to leave.

"You will come back won't you?"

Sam nodded, only to realise it was pointless; she couldn't see him.

"I'll be gone two minutes, no more. Here," he fumbled in his jacket pocket for the flare pistol Bartlett had given him earlier. It won't do much damage but you're sure to scare the pants off anyone who might be following us. I'm only upstairs; I'll be back before you know it."

Sam hooked her finger round the trigger and headed for a door that led to the staircase. The building had three stories, so he reasoned the attic would give him a decent view. On the first floor he saw an open door; on a bed lay two skeletons, locked in the embrace of lovers. Sam numbed his emotions and moved on quickly. It was hard enough to stay alive without continually mourning the dead. From the attic Sam could see the river beyond a landscape of roofs. To his left, he could just see *Lupin*'s funnel streaming grey smoke. He moved to an adjacent dormer window and could clearly see the raft alongside the ship, empty and unloaded. At least the others had made it safely back to *Lupin*. From the quantity of smoke rising from her funnel it was obvious that Helen was making plans to sail. The question was, how long could they wait for him and the girl.

A sudden noise from behind gave Sam a start. He turned to see luminous yellow eyes staring at him from a dark corner of the attic. An enormous black rat materialised, carrying a bone in its jaws that looked suspiciously like a human femur. Sam shuddered; no matter how many times you saw such things the sight still appalled him. For a moment, man and rat eyed each other. He slid his knife from its scabbard, while the rat stared back contemptuously. On the farm, Sam would have shot the rat on sight but here that wasn't an option without attracting attention to where they were hiding. Bored, the rat withdrew. It had no need to attack; it knew instinctively that it could leave that task to a boar and scavenge the remains at a later time.

As Sam was about to leave the attic, the hard metallic sound of gunfire reverberated around the town. From the window he saw *Lupin* in the grey waters of the river, now framed in continuous fountains of water from the firing. Sam was certain the landing ramp was a short distance off to their left. If he and Claire followed the road in front towards the direction of the shooting, and then dropped right towards the river, they should end up opposite the ramp and the waiting skiff. He could only hope it hadn't been already discovered.

"It's me, Sam," he called out as he entered the living room.

Water and a brief rest had worked wonders in reviving Claire, enough at least for her to stand and make some attempt at walking. Sam took hold of her left wrist once more.

"We're going to have to go towards the sound of shooting. Only for a short time, so don't be afraid. We'll skirt round the buildings, so keep close to the wall. Farther on we'll need to cross the road to more buildings on the right side before we turn down to the landing ramp where there should be a boat waiting for us," he explained with as much assurance as he could.

Claire nodded, memorising his instructions.

"It's not far; just don't let go of me, whatever happens." With her returned grip on his wrist there wasn't much chance of that happening.

The street was empty, the sound of gunfire intermittent. For fifty yards, they walked Indian file; Sam could feel Claire's nails digging into the flesh of his wrist. He stopped and they bumped together like train carriages. Beside them, two abandoned cars were partially blocking the road. He turned, pressing his mouth to her ear, conscious of her hair against his lips.

"We need to crouch down to cross the road just in case there's anyone about farther along. There are two cars we can use for cover but we must keep as low as possible. It's not far."

Claire nodded her acknowledgement. They scurried across in two stages, pausing briefly behind each car before making the final short dash to the buildings on the opposite side. Tightly pressed into a doorway, Sam could see only a short way ahead.

"Well done," he whispered encouragingly. "Just the same on this side until we reach the next right turn which leads to the boat."

A sudden burst of firing made Claire stiffen. It sounded much closer. Sam tugged her hand; there was no time to delay. The turn to the landing ramp seemed farther than he thought. For a moment, he feared he had made a mistake, until a curve in the fading road lines swung to the right just ahead. Keen to get to the skiff, he pulled Claire's hand with renewed urgency, only to find her frozen on the spot.

"What?" For a moment he thought he would have to carry her again.

"I can hear voices," she whispered back.

"Are you sure?" Sam asked. All he could hear were reverberations of the gunfire in his ears.

Claire nodded. "I can hear two men's voices. They're in the next building ahead of us."

Sam felt a chill down his spine. If she was correct, they would have walked straight into them in a matter of seconds. The door against their backs was locked and the recess just deep enough to hide them both from view on the same side of the street. If the men stayed put, their only option would be to backtrack and find another route to the river front, using up precious time they didn't have and involving a swim in the river where the path ran out. Seconds ticked on as they waited. The firing had stopped. Were the men changing position? Sam strained his ears but still couldn't hear anything. He had just thought Claire might be mistaken, when two men, clad in black leathers, came out of the next door along. He could see their reflections in the window on the opposite side of the road. Both were armed. He held his breath. If they looked at the same window, they would clearly see them hiding. For a moment, the men jostled playfully over something they had found in the building they had just left.

Salvation came from a distance when a sudden shout echoed down the street. The fooling around ceased and the two men walked off, complaining, and without a backward glance. Sam let out a gasp.

"Could you hear what they were talking about?" he asked.

"Just a little. Something about avoiding the others until they had boarded the ship."

They waited an impatient minute before daring a glance into the street. The two men had disappeared. It was only a short distance to the turn to the ramp, but the feeling of exposure as they ran made the gap feel ten times greater.

At the ramp the tide had begun to ebb. With a wave of relief, Sam found the skiff still there, tied by its stern to a mooring ring, bow pointed into the river. Without pausing he lifted Claire into the rear of the boat. Cradled in his arms, she felt little more than skin and bones, returning him to the disturbing thoughts of what had happened in her family group. The others showed little outward signs of under-nourishment. Once she was positioned on the stern seat, he tucked the rudder bar under her arm.

"It's essential to keep this pointing dead ahead, like this. Don't move it until I tell you to."

Sam turned to untie the painter; in just a few seconds he could push them into the river, rowing towards safety. One word altered all of that.

"Voices," Claire called in alarm.

Without hesitating to question her, Sam cut the painter with his knife and threw his full weight against the skiff, pushing hard until he was waist deep. The boat rolled heavily as he hauled himself on board, throwing away precious seconds when he snagged on the gunwale, before tumbling headfirst into the bottom of the boat. Their one saving grace was that Bartlett had thought to secure the oars into the rowlocks.

"Getting closer," Claire called urgently.

Sam couldn't hear anything above the continuous clamour of gunfire, directed at *Lupin*. He hauled on the oars, desperate to gain distance from the shore. Each stroke carried them a yard; the wind was to their stern and a line to a winch on *Lupin* was tied around the bow post. What they most needed now was someone to start the winch. As he strained on the oars, three men walked into view at the end of the landing ramp. They were talking animatedly but didn't look in their direction. In a few seconds they were gone from sight. Sam closed his mind, concentrating all his efforts on rowing as he hauled frantically on the oars. From behind him on *Lupin*, came the rumble of the starting winch, immediately drawing in the slack cable. Sam glanced at the ship; John Evans stood on the stern, waving encouragement, only for a burst of gunfire to send him scurrying for cover. A shout echoed from the landing ramp. The three figures were back, now running towards the water edge. Before Sam could even shout a warning, shots rang out, the sound of supersonic bees whipping past them. With no time to think, he reached for Claire and pulled her into the bottom of the boat and swung the gun from his back. Sam aimed in the general direction of the jetty and pulled the trigger. The Sten wasn't an elegant weapon but at short range it could be highly effective. Without looking, he fired the entire magazine in the direction of the landing ramp they had just left, filling the narrow space with flying mortar fragments and dust and sending the three figures sprawling for cover.

With a sharp jerk, the winch line went taut. The bow reared up and their speed suddenly accelerated. There was no point in trying to row anymore and sitting up in the skiff offered them as an easy target. Amid the clamour, he could hear a constant 'zip-whoosh' sound as shots made fountains in the river around them. The crew on *Lupin* were making a valiant effort to suppress the gunfire from the shore, shooting at the flashes on the shore whenever they appeared, but shots were arriving in increasing numbers around the skiff. Afraid for their prospects, Sam took a huge gulp of air, shipped the oars and threw himself on top of Claire in the bottom of the boat, just as a bullet struck the gunwale, covering them both in needle splinters of wood. As he landed on top of her, he felt Claire wince. They were ducks in a shooting gallery; he could only hope the winch could haul them quickly to *Lupin*. All they could do was lie there, soaked by river water as it spurted through increasing numbers of holes in the side of the hull. The anchor chain started to groan on *Lupin* as it slowly rose, adding a rusty cloud to the grey cloud of gun smoke now enveloping everything, her screw threshing the river surface as she began to make way, towing the skiff with increasing speed behind her. The lunacy of their position wasn't lost on Sam; he could well imagine any watching boar regard the unfolding situation with deep satisfaction as they watched their enemies begin to murder one another.

"We're doing their damn job for them," he shouted in frustration as more bullets riddled the skiff, racing like a motorboat in the wake of *Lupin*.

Rapidly, the line shortened. Ahead, John and Ruth had found a sheltered position and were extending boat hooks to drag the skiff clear of the stern and its wildly threshing screw which would suck them in if they came too close. Sam looked at *Lupin* as they approached and was appalled to see the wheelhouse riddled by bullets, its door and windows broken and shattered. It was the obvious focus of most of the gunfire and he dreaded to think what may have become of Helen and her crew. John and Ruth managed to drag the line around the stern, bringing the skiff into the protection of the port side. It was far better that the hull took the hammering when the time came to climb up onto the ship. Helen's coloured buoys were now flying past as the ship accelerated to full speed, throwing up a white foaming wake that raced from the bow and down her flanks. Trying to stand in the skiff was close to trying to walk a tightrope as they pitched and bucked along the side of the rusty hull. Sam raised Claire to a sitting position. She would have to go first, a terrifying prospect for someone with no sight. As the skiff struck the steel side plates, several of the crew had gathered, arms outstretched, shouting encouragement. Claire stretched up towards *Lupin*. As she did so, Sam noticed with alarm a large blood stain on the side of her tattered dress, a long wooden splinter the size of a large nail protruded through the fabric in the centre of the stain. He braced himself and wrapped his arms around Claire's waist. Despite the drama of the moment, he felt a sharp jolt of static electricity that seemed to pass from her body into him. In a single motion, he thrust her upwards into waiting hands that caught her outstretched arms and pulled her over the side, winching with pain, with all the grace of a landed fish.

Alone in the skiff Sam felt *Lupin* give a shudder and then surge forward. A foot of water now washed violently around inside the skiff; it was long past time to leave before it sank beneath him. Without looking, he threw his gun upwards over the side rail and grabbed the edge above him hauling himself upwards by his fingertips. Waiting hands grabbed his shirt and literally flung him onto the deck of *Lupin* just as the skiff bucked violently, reared, and ploughed into a combing green bow wave before disappearing into the river.

# NINE

Escaping from Dartmouth pushed the crew ever harder, and for a while no one had time for yet another blind girl. *Lupin* was on fire at the stern, and gunfire was pounding her hull from all angles. Blind and disorientated in her new surroundings, Claire found the edge of a bulkhead door and was trying to pull herself up to stand when Sam caught up with her and offered a hand to help. The blood stain on her dress was growing.

"Come on, let's get you somewhere safer," he shouted as bullets ricocheted around them.

She was soaked to the skin, which made the wound in her side look more serious. He guided Claire to the mess room, now converted to a casualty station, and found Karen and Teri working at full stretch. Mattresses were laid out in lines on the floor, some already occupied. Amongst the serious cases were the elderly woman they had brought in on the cart, and the pregnant girl, who had started in labour.

"Am I pleased to see you," Karen appeared beside Sam, smiling with relief, her white coat already stained with blood. "I can't spare long. We've got our hands full at the moment. Can I have a look?"

Sam stepped back for her to examine Claire and took the opportunity to look around the room. The group they had rescued were gathered at one end and three crew members were there too, but thankfully no one appeared seriously hurt.

"It's only a splinter wound," Karen was wiping her hands in antiseptic. "Nasty though. It needs to come out."

A loud moan came from the direction of the pregnant girl. "Can you manage?" Karen said to Sam, and was gone before he could reply.

He found Claire a space at the far end of the room on a white plastic garden chair, a reflection of their limited resources, but better than nothing. From one of the equipment trays, Sam grabbed a scalpel, tweezers and dressings. The past five years had taught him many skills, first aid not the least of them, but this wound still looked nastier than he was used to. He was part way back to Claire when the shouting started. Thick black smoke was seeping underneath the door to the rear passageway. The fire was in the stern of the ship and the crew were already dealing with it, but nevertheless, the dense smoke was a worrying development. He hurried back to Claire, and soaked a dressing in antiseptic. He slit the dress fabric around the wound and applied the dressing.

"Hold this while I go and investigate the smoke. Five minutes, I'll be back."

As he left, Sam grabbed some spare towels and soaked them in the sink, rolling and pressing them hard against the bottom of the door. It would have to suffice until he could work his way to the other side of the deck. Moving quickly, he took the route to the wheelhouse and upper deck, running and climbing the stairs two at a time. He found the wheelhouse in pieces; the windows were shattered and the walls traced with bullet holes. Inside, even the compass and wheel had been mauled. One of the engineers was steering *Lupin* with improvised levers. Spare decking plate had been propped against the bullet riddled walls, an almost too late afterthought. To his relief, Helen stood at the rear behind the protection of the plating, one arm in a sling and her head bound with a blood-stained bandage.

"Thank god you're okay," he managed to shout above the din.

Helen grinned. "More by luck than good judgement. Next time you bring me on one of your trips please be kind enough to provide the proper protection. When you need this ship to go anywhere in a hurry, the least you need is a functioning wheelhouse."

Helen's words made it sound as though he was personally responsible for the wreckage around her. Sam took it as a good sign; Helen was well enough to moan.

Two more shots struck the decking plates, ringing their ears with the hard metallic impacts. The men flinched; Helen stared stoically ahead.

"Well, I'm glad you're in one piece," Sam said, with a look of concern at her sling and bandages. "There's smoke in the mess deck so I'd better get aft and see if they need help."

Sam found Aiden Cooper and three others hacking at burning equipment and stores with axes. The smoke was black and acrid and they were donned in goggles with wet towels covering their mouths. Nothing seemed to be seriously ablaze but the fire was generating huge quantities of smoke. Aiden moved to one side, removing his towel.

"We've too much equipment stored externally and they've used tracer to set it alight." His voice sounded dry and his eyes streamed from the smoke. "It's under control; more a heavy smoulder than a fire. We need to cut it clear and dump it over the side."

"Can you manage that as quickly as possible? There's smoke filling the mess deck," Sam said as he sped away.

Above, the exposed top deck had the look of a war zone. Bartlett and a teenager called Tomlinson lay prone on the deck, protected by improvised steel upstand plates only a foot high. It was too dangerous to stand upright, so Sam had to crawl across the deck on his stomach. Bartlett was spotting with binoculars, directing Tomlinson who was operating *Lupin's* only real defence weapon, an old and battered Bren gun.

"Top window line, third from the left," Bartlett called out, followed a second later by the harsh chatter of Tomlinson's gun.

Bartlett turned as Sam approached, greeting him with a grin.

"Glad you found time to come and join us," he shouted, mockingly, above the clamour, as several bullets zipped by just above their heads. "Girl okay?"

Sam nodded as Bartlett handed him the binoculars and pointed towards the shore. "A big guy keeps appearing, directing the others. He acts as if he's the boss and they now seem to be trying to load something that looks suspiciously like a bazooka. Want me to take care of them?"

Sam focused the glasses through the smoke to where the quay jutted into the river. He could just make out a large tall man, with long tangled hair that streamed in the wind. He was well over six foot tall, with a girth to match. He was pointing defiantly towards the speeding *Lupin* whilst two of his men loaded a long grey tube, resting on the shoulder of a squatting man. For a moment Sam stared, mesmerised by the angry face of the big man and wondered if he had just seen their nemesis?

"Sam?"

"Just a moment."

He fumbled through his pockets. He still had the flare pistol Bartlett had given him hours earlier. Releasing the safety catch, he aimed it high enough to hit the wall above their heads on the shore.

"This won't hurt anyone, but," Sam mused, "let's just see what fun the effect causes."

He pulled the trigger and the flare carved a shallow arc across the river and exploded with a cascade of red stars and streamers against the wall. The effect was dramatic. The tall man threw himself sideways in surprise, inadvertently kicking the other two men who were so startled that they fired the weapon without aiming and sent the shell plunging into the water only yards from the shore. It was a small victory but Sam couldn't resist a defiant gesture and stood up, in full view, arm pointing at the hilarious scene on the shore. He stood there for long enough to be sure they had seen him before turning away. He had made his point.

"Very funny, but you should have let me deal with the thug," Bartlett grumbled.

"Best not to," Sam replied. "I have a feeling that sooner or later we'll have to negotiate with someone. It might well have to be him."

Claire appeared to be asleep when Sam returned to the mess deck. She was where he had left her in the chair; blind, lost and alone, still wearing only the torn wet dress, right hand pressing the dressing against her wound. Beside her, Teri was attending to Ryan who had a nasty burn on his leg received whilst helping Aiden with the fire, while Karen was occupied behind screens with the girl in labour.

Sam collected mugs of hot sweet tea for them both, contemplating how he might go about removing Claire's splinter. He placed a hand gently on her shoulder to wake her, and felt a repeat of the surge of static electricity he had experienced when lifting her from the skiff, wondering if it was true that some people held a counter static charge to others. Or was it something else? As she woke, her face at first creased with disorientated alarm, eyes blinking with panic as she tried to absorb the sounds around her.

"It's Sam. I'm back. Sorry I was gone a while. Things were hectic."

With the sound of his voice, Claire relaxed, anxiety replaced by the glimmer of a smile. He had a feeling no one had spoken to her since he had left.

"I'm going to remove that splinter. We'll soon have it out."

"I guess it will hurt."

"I'll be so quick you won't have time to notice. And actually, surgery is one of my specialities," he announced, making an attempt to be light-hearted.

"I'm in safe hands then."

He should have said that his surgical experience was limited to cows and sheep, a subtle point he thought it better not to mention. On a second examination, the splinter looked larger than he remembered and the flesh around the wound now looked red and swollen. He felt woefully unqualified for what he knew he had to do, but there was no one else free to help Claire, and so, with false bravado, he set about removing the spike that projected from her side.

"Where was the farm you came from?" Sam chatted as he began, trying to distract her.

"On the east side of Dartmoor, near a place called Widecombe." She drew breath, riding the pain as Sam opened the wound with the tip of a scalpel. "Not that I saw much of the place after I had been blinded," she added wistfully.

"How was your journey?" he asked, changing tact.

He had to cut her skin around the splinter in an attempt to avoid it breaking off when he tried to remove it; in a world without antibiotics nothing could be left behind; they all lived in fear of infection. Against her pale skin, the blood seeping from the wound looked a deep arterial red.

"Long, tiring, scary," she answered, cutting through his thoughts, her words short and tight. "At first, we had a tractor and trailer to ride for a while, but when we were ambushed they had to be abandoned near Totnes." Claire paused for a sharp intake of breath. "After that, all we could do was walk, taking only what we could carry and leaving everything else on the trailer." She paused before adding, "at least that's what I was told."

Claire jumped slightly as Sam began to draw out the splinter with tweezers.

"When did you eat last?" Her ribs were distinctly prominent.

"Nothing much since Totnes."

Sam was trying to keep a steady hand and not rush; he knew he was hurting Claire but there was no alternative if he was to get the splinter out cleanly. And it was resisting his efforts. He paused for a moment, wiping sweat from his eyes, before probing again at the base with the scalpel. As he worked, the thought occurred to him that others in her group certainly didn't look especially under-nourished, which increased his suspicions that they had written off Claire when trouble arose. If they were going to use her as bait, well, why waste food on the bait. A surge of anger coursed through him. Angrily, he tugged harder. The splinter suddenly released, unbroken. With a gasp and in half faint, Claire fell against him as the door swung open and John appeared with a pile of supplies for Karen.

"John, quick, hold her up while I close the wound."

Sam applied antiseptic and improvised with some plastic clips to close the wound as there was little flesh on Claire for an amateur to apply conventional stitching. That would have to wait until Karen was free.

"She looks as though she hasn't eaten in some time," John commented as he scooped up towels and disappeared, soon returning a minute later with a bowl of steaming porridge. "They kept a pan warming, figuring no one would have time to cook today, so it's help yourself. I've added extra honey."

Claire now sat upright, bleary-eyed but awake and John put the bowl in her hands before he disappeared to collect more supplies. Karen, wiping her hands on a towel, appeared beside them and paused to look at the splinter, now lying maliciously in a steel dish.

"You did well to get that out in one piece," Karen said to Sam, bending to check Claire's pulse. "Hopefully, you've helped prevent infection, but we need to get her out of those wet clothes."

A shout echoed around the room as someone called for Karen and she sped off quickly again. It was going to be a long day.

"We need to find you some dry clothes. Is there anything in your bag?"

Claire shook her head. "Everything was lost on the run from Totnes."

Momentarily immobilised, he had no idea where to start looking for replacement clothes until the answer arrived with the appearance of Ruth, her face blackened with a waxy sheen from smoke and sweat.

"Helen is asking for you in the wheelhouse," she called to Sam. "Straight away, as soon as you can."

Sam nodded. "This is Claire, she's just joined us. She needs somewhere to rest and some dry clothes. Do you think you can help her?"

Despite her tiredness, Ruth looked Claire up and down with a concerned eye. "You're about my size; I've got some spare things you can have if you don't mind odd colours, and there's a warm shower in the girls' room," she said encouragingly.

"I've just dealt with a nasty wound in her left side," Sam added. "You'll need to find protection for that."

Claire smiled. "At the moment, just the thought of a bed sounds like heaven. As for a shower, I haven't been able to wash for a week."

"Take my arm; we've a flight of stairs to manage and a corridor but I can promise a shower, fresh clothes and a bed are at the end of it," Ruth said lightly.

Both girls disappeared, leaving Sam with a growing list of demands. As he was leaving the casualty room, Karen shouted urgently for oxygen and anaesthetics from their meagre reserves. Sam didn't wait to question her, instead he interrupted Teri, still mooning over the injured Ryan, and sent her scurrying to the chiller which in normal times held the ship's fish catch. As he watched her depart, his conversation with Ruth that morning about the pair of them felt it had taken place in another world.

In the wheelhouse, Sam found Helen, Bartlett and John already waiting for him. Through the shattered front screen Sam was surprised to see they were making a south-westerly course.

"I know the compass is damaged, but isn't home in that direction?" Sam pointed over his shoulder.

"It's more than possible they're watching the route we take as we leave the estuary. Just in case they come after us, I thought it best to set a different course, until we're well out of sight of land," Helen paused. "We'll change course for home in about an hour."

Sam nodded. "Do we think they have the resources to follow us?" he asked. Until now that thought hadn't occurred to him.

"There are still some large motor cruisers afloat in the marina. One of them might have a workable engine," Bartlett replied. "At the moment it's safer to assume they'll come after us."

From the vibration through the deck, Helen had *Lupin* at full speed. She anticipated Sam's next question.

"We'll have to slow down soon; we're low on fuel and we're shipping water through damaged hull plates from the battering we received. You can probably hear the pumps hard at work now."

Sam raised an eyebrow. "Is it serious?"

"Nothing the pumps can't handle, but slower would be safer."

Sam nodded. They could always increase speed again if they had to.

"And there's one other thing," Helen continued. "John thinks they know our radio frequency; they're most likely listening to our messages."

They all turned to John. "When the men on motorbikes captured the other family at Totnes, it included Peter Fry. He was the first to make radio contact with us from the Dartmoor farms. We have to assume he told them everything."

Sam shrugged. "I think we suspected that already."

"So everything we say to the island could be listened to, unless I change the frequency," John said.

"Not the best of situations, but is it a problem even if they are listening to what we're saying?"

"It could be. It would confirm where we're heading and where home is. We must suspect that they already know that of course, but listening to our radio signals would confirm that."

"So what are you recommending?" Sam asked.

"Radio silence; at least until we get back to the island."

"But won't that worry those at home?"

"Not for a day or so. They'll think our radio set has packed up, though they might keep trying to call us, so we'll need to forewarn them we have a problem."

"Okay."

Sam turned to look at the other two for agreement. Helen nodded, Bartlett shrugged, unable to resist saying, "Though it sounds as if we're getting a bit paranoid, frightened of our own shadows. They're only a band of thugs after all."

To Sam's mind, there were things about the day which didn't quite fit that general description.

"Until we know more about who and what we're up against, we'll be cautious. Radio silence it is then. Meanwhile, let's debrief the group we've rescued. There are a number of questions I'd like answers to."

He left the wheelhouse. Sam felt his clothes clinging to his body, wet and stiff with salt and reeking of smoke. Things had been hectic and he needed time to collect his thoughts, especially about the callous way that Claire had been used for the rest of the group's survival. That didn't sit well with him. Even in their darkest days during the creation of their community on the Isle of Wight, survival was often precarious but they had never considered the sacrifice of the weakest for the benefit of the others. It was not the way of things if they wanted to retain at least some vestige of humanity.

*Lupin* turned for home about an hour later. The wind and swell were running from her stern and yet it was sometime later when Sam realised the seasickness, that had so plagued him just a few days earlier, had disappeared amidst the drama of their day. Most of their casualties were minor and they found spare cabins for the elderly woman and the expectant mother, so the mess deck could revert to its original function in time for an evening meal. Sam even found space to shower and bring his journey log up to date before joining the others. Ruth had found fresh clothes for Claire, who now sat at the table with her and the other women. She seemed relaxed, listening to the roll of conversation of the others, learning their voices and names to distract her from the veil of pain emanating from her side. They had little to offer for pain relief, but colour had returned to her face and she was now eating.

"I sorted out our new friend," Ruth said as she passed Sam's table.

"Thanks. Did she tell you anything about the journey here?"

Ruth shook her head. "Not much. She's very polite, probably still shocked to find herself alive. It must have been frightening, trapped in a world of perpetual darkness."

Sam chose to eat alone, listening to the conversations that at times erupted excitedly around him. The sense of relief was palpable after the drama of their escape from Dartmouth. For some the aftermath of danger translated into humour, the excitement of a near miss or close shave now recalled in light-hearted recollections. Sam was pleased for them; it could have so easily been very different.

Bartlett interrupted his thoughts when he stopped beside him on his way across the room.

"When you've finished eating, can I have a word?"

Sam nodded as Bartlett left.

Dusk was gathering by the time Sam joined Bartlett. The wind had dropped, leaving the promise of a mild spring evening. Bartlett drew on his roll-up, the tip glowing bright red in the twilight.

"I still think you were wrong not to let me deal with that big bastard."

Sam laughed. "It was worth letting him live just to see the pantomime the flare caused."

"So, we'll have to deal with him again further down the line instead," Bartlett said, not sharing his viewpoint.

"If we do, it will be with the memory that we made him look a fool, so more important that we spared his life. If our paths ever cross again, I'll remind him of that."

"As if that would make any difference. Bastards like him only understand one thing. He'll only view what you did as weakness."

Sam remained silent for a few moments. "If we resort to killing one another, we're doing the boars' work for them. If we react with violence every time we're frightened, a blood lust will consume us all."

Bartlett flicked his spent cigarette away. "Very laudable; but it's like telling a rabid dog to go and sit quietly in the corner. Optimistic; but you always end up getting bitten."

Agreeing to disagree, they moved on. Despite his air of bravado, Bartlett looked strained and tired, so Sam volunteered to do the midnight watch. Bartlett accepted without question, adding, "Keep everyone on their toes; they'll all be exhausted tonight. Call me the moment anything arises. Anything."

He thanked Sam and departed to find a bed.

*Lupin* ploughed her way on an easterly heading through an indigo sea lit by the dying light of the sunset. Sam had the upper deck completely to himself. He found a life-raft and sat enjoying the warmth of the last rays of the early evening. It would be dark soon, but a few minutes still remained in which to relax. Only a few days had passed since Albert Jamieson had set Sam his task and he had said farewell to Rachel amidst a clear disagreement. It felt like weeks had passed. Had he been successful? In part; they had rescued some, but only half the group had made it to Dartmouth. All the crew of *Lupin* had survived, yet almost half had received injuries of one form or another. The ship was still afloat, even if her starboard side had the resemblance of a colander. Perhaps that was the best they could have hoped for and they had certainly learnt enough lessons to add to earlier failures in countering the menace from the boar. Tired, he closed his eyes. For a moment, in his mind's eye, he saw the image of the feral boy he had almost saved, left behind. Sam had done his best but fate had decided otherwise and time hadn't played him a fair hand. In a recess of his conscience, Sam took comfort from the crude map, linking Dartmouth to the island, he had placed inside the rucksack that the boy now had. He had no idea if the boy could read or would understand it, but it gave at least an outside chance that he might one day find them.

Across the deck, a steel bulkhead door swung open and the outline of a slender figure, thrown into profile against the yellow light in the gangway behind, stumbled through the opening and on to the deck.

"Claire?" Sam knew who it was almost before he asked. "What are you doing up here?"

In her arms were a bedroll and pillows. Ruth had found her a mismatched collection of clothes, including a thick man-size jumper that seemed to completely swamp her. At least she would be warm and dry.

"I wanted to smell freedom; I still can't believe I'm here, safe, alive." There was a sense of wonder to her voice, as if she feared that at any moment it might be snatched away from her like a child's toy. "And it's still busy below deck; Ruth was kind and said I could share the cabin with them, but it's small and there are already three of them in a space for two." She paused before adding, "And I'm not welcome with the others I travelled with, so I thought it best to find my own spot. Up here will do me just fine."

It seemed pointless to say anything in reply; as was so often the case, those who wronged someone come to hate their victim to allay their feelings of guilt. He wondered if Claire already knew that.

"I was watching the sunset. Come here, there is just time for you to still feel it."

Sam guided her to the side rail, turning Claire to face the fading rays of sunlight. For a moment she was still, turning her face to the dying sun, a smile on her lips, eyes unblinking, imagining.

"Describe the colours," she asked.

Sam thought for a moment; it had been a long time since he had needed to think of anything in artistic tones.

"The sun is half an orange ball sitting on the horizon, the sea now a purplish indigo. There are fine veins of horizontal cloud, grey and pink lower down, rising to a darker blue-grey higher in the sky. As for the sky itself, it looks as though it's on fire; scarlet lower down, rising through shades of gold and salmon pink until it pales overhead."

For a while he was silent, letting Claire paint the picture in her imagination. He found it hard to comprehend what it would be like to never again see something as beautiful as this, something that he had always taken for granted. After a minute of perfect silence, the sun dropped below the horizon, eclipsing the last of its light, leaving just a fan of rays to dissect the approaching darkness.

"Thank you." Claire touched his arm in gratitude and once more Sam felt the curious tingling sensation. For a while they stood fixed beside the rail, as if reluctant to let go of the moment.

"Do you want to tell me what happened, how you came to be abandoned by your own people?"

Claire sighed. "Do you really want to hear yet another tragic story? Don't we all live with that, day in day out?"

"If you're joining our community, I'd like to know the truth of what happened," Sam hesitated. "If it's not too painful to talk about."

For a while, she continued to face towards the departed sun, gathering her thoughts.

"I don't blame them for what they did. They're not my real family; my parents are in the diplomatic service." Sam noticed she spoke of them in the present tense. "They had sent me to boarding school when my father was posted to India. He had a temporary assignment and they weren't planning to be away for very long."

Claire faced the disappeared sunset, hoping, as they all did, that if you wished hard enough, the world might revert to the way it had been.

"When the pandemic burst upon us I was almost fifteen. My parents were delayed in leaving India; something to do with the monsoon, I recall, so my Christmas holidays were with a school friend at their family farm on Dartmoor. My parents were due back in England in the New Year; I hadn't seen them for six months."

She stopped, painful memories flooding back.

"Ironic when you think of it; nature's Christmas gift for the world was the arrival of the pandemic. We only had the radio for news, so it was sometime before we heard how quickly it had spread. The farm was remote, so we were naturally isolated. It was the holidays, so we decided to sit tight and wait for the worst to abate. But it didn't, as you well know. The government covered up the appalling death rate, frightened that it would cause mass panic. I think that's what made things get out of control so quickly. All we could do was stay on the farm and wait. It was sometime later when a neighbour came to the farm, begging for help for his sick family. But there was nothing we could do; they all died before our very eyes and all our help manged to achieve was to spread the infection to our farm."

"How did you escape the virus?" Sam asked. He had heard a similar tragic story a thousand times, never with a happy ending.

Claire shook her head. "I didn't. My friend and I went down with the flu on the same day; I must have become delirious very quickly with the fever and unaware of anything for several days. My friend's parents must have nursed us until they too contracted the virus. I was lucky, if you can call it that, my body broke the fever before it killed me, but when I had recovered sufficiently to get out of bed, everyone in the farm was already dead. Including my best friend," she said with a grim finality.

'The same awful story, with the same tragic ending. Most died from the virus, an unlucky few survived to find a world full of ghosts,' thought Sam.

"So how did you come to join up with the people you've arrived in Dartmouth with?" he asked.

"I was frantic with despair; I hadn't realised at first that my sight had been affected by the virus; that's its kick-back for the body winning the battle."

For a moment, Claire seemed on edge, her emotions jousting with hysteria. She shook her head as if to clear her thoughts.

"The Carters were more distant neighbours related to the farm. They sent their son, Colin, over to the farm to investigate. He found me, digging graves, the only survivor."

They were both silent for several minutes; there was little else to say.

"To be fair, the Carters gave me a home. I'd been one of the rare lucky ones, if you can call it that. They isolated me for a while, to be certain I wasn't contagious. While I waited, my eyesight began to deteriorate, slowly at first, as the optic nerve was progressively destroyed. But the final result is always the same and you become just another blind girl."

Her final words were gaining a slightly hysterical edge from the telling of the tale. Then Claire added, "Strange though, that so few men survived the flu to go blind. Nearly all of us are women."

Sam nodded. "I guess it's the way of natural selection. If a species like ours is to have any chance of surviving, you need far more females than males. Nearly all men who caught the flu never lived to experience the blinding."

"I can't blame the Carters for not making me welcome. They were struggling to make sense of the situation themselves, without another mouth to feed."

"How did they survive unscathed?"

"Their farm was also very isolated, tucked in a tiny combe. The Carters had sense to realise very early on how virulent the virus was going to be. Jenny Carter, the mother, had lived through the epidemic of 1919 and knew how contagious it could be and so they shut themselves off completely until it had burnt itself out. They were almost totally self-sufficient, so it wasn't too difficult. But five years is a long time to live in isolation. It got easier in some respects when they found several neighbouring farms had survived in similar circumstances. When the virus burnt itself out, they pooled resources."

"So what caused the problem in the end? It can't have just been the arrival of the group of men," Sam asked curiously.

"A combination of things. Boar breed easily on Dartmoor and their attacks grew in intensity. Cows and sheep became ill, with no drugs to treat them, and pests and diseases infected the crops, and no chemicals to treat them. Things finally came to a head with the failure of the harvest last summer. We feared we were heading for some terrible disaster when, by chance, one of the other surviving farms made contact with you by radio. Knowing there was someone else out there raised our morale beyond words. For a few days we floated on clouds, only to have the bubble burst by the sudden arrival of these men on motorbikes. We first saw smoke plumes in the distance, where they were hunting for whatever they could plunder and rob."

Claire paused, re-living the experience in the darkness of her memories.

"It seems brutally unfair that fate can snatch away your hope, just at the moment it comes into your grasp. Waiting to hear if you would come and help us became almost unbearable as news of the atrocities around us filtered through."

She paused again and Sam remembered the heated debate at the forum over that particular subject.

"We were euphoric when you said you would come, but it was almost too late. We had to flee in haste, using the last remains of our fuel, and we gained a head start when the men on motorbikes found the farm after we had left. It mercifully gave us a day or so while they stripped the place of all they wanted and burnt the house and outbuildings."

She cocked her head to one side, in puzzled thought.

"I guess they do that to spread fear, as some pathetic show of strength, but at least the smoke from the burning of the farmhouse warned us that they were finished and would soon be after us."

Sam could hear the fear in her voice and thought she might not want to continue any further, but Claire seemed to need to do so.

"Totnes was important. If we could have got beyond there before they caught up with us, the other family might have survived.

Instead, the men on motorbikes got in front of us and set an ambush. The others were a mile or so ahead of us. By then, we had been delayed by the collapse of Mrs Carter."

Claire hesitated, shuddered and shook her head.

"That's when we abandoned everything. You can't outrun motorbikes with a tractor, so we left the roads and took to the woods to follow the river to Dartmouth. That's when I began to hear the Carters whispering about me. I never guessed they were planning to leave me behind. I don't think Colin agreed, but he's afraid of his father, so he does as he's told. As I said, I don't blame them for what they did. Survival of the fittest, I think you call it. They regarded me as their 'canary in the cage'; my screams would have warned them the men were closing behind them and dealing with me would buy them time, perhaps enough to make it to Dartmouth. I was simply expedient, to be left to a horrible fate, to disappear without trace. Just another unwanted blind girl, if it hadn't been for you."

It was dark, with only the full moon to light the tears that were now streaming from her sightless eyes, washing freckled cheeks as they flowed, driven by the inescapable fears of her imagination re-enacting her fate. Awkwardly, Claire turned towards Sam, gasping in surprise from the pain of the injury to her side.

"You saved my life."

"On the island, we leave no one behind," Sam said. He tried to make it sound matter of fact.

"But you chose to help me. You knew the risk, yet you still came back for me."

"If I hadn't, one of the others would," though he doubted Bartlett would have agreed to release a squad member for such a risk. Only Sam had the independent authority to make that life or death choice.

Her reply was spontaneous and caught him by surprise. Claire kissed her hand and gently stroked the soft mat of beard on his cheek.

"I have nothing on earth but the gift of my life. And that's something you've returned to me."

# TEN

Despite the trials of the day, there was a high spot during the early hours of the morning. Maureen Carter gave birth to a healthy boy. They called him Salvador to celebrate their rescue, and for the remainder of the night his gusty cries echoed through the steel passageways of *Lupin*.

Claire had chosen a sheltered space beneath the open stairway that climbed to the wheelhouse, having mapped out the layout of the deck with her cane before laying out her bedroll. Exhausted, she had fallen asleep in seconds.

Sam took the night watch until two in the morning. It left his eyes sore from staring into the passing darkness, with only starlight for company and the occasional appearance of fellow watch-keepers circling the lower deck. The hours passed uneventfully; only towards the end did tiredness begin to play tricks as a rolling swell broke with a foaming crest that resembled an approaching boat.

His watch completed, Sam searched inside *Lupin* for a place to sleep. He was out of luck; with almost thirty people on board, some of whom were injured, every space was taken and he drew a blank. So, the outer decks beckoned and he decided to follow Claire's example and sleep on deck. It was open to the sky, but offered at least peace and quiet. Until it began to rain. Drowsy, he scurried to the deck below for protection; the only dry spot he could find was that occupied by Claire beneath the staircase. Too tired to care, he slept toe to toe with her and hoped he wouldn't wake her with his snoring.

When Sam awoke it was already daylight and he was alone; Claire had gone. For a while, he allowed himself the rare luxury of regarding the day through a sleepy haze from the warmth of his sleeping bag. It was hard to make sense of their world. At least sea travel offered tranquillity that was becoming difficult to find on land and he lay fantasizing of a time when humans would roam and rule the seas while boar held dominium of the land. With a rueful smile he wondered how that scenario would eventually pan out.

Eventually, the smell of frying bacon roused his lethargy. He stowed his gear, washed in a bucket of sea water and set off to find breakfast. The mess deck was full. Ruth and her squad had organised breakfast for everyone. Karen and Teri, their usual chefs, were nowhere to be seen, having been up all night supervising the birth of the new arrival. There was just sufficient time for them all to eat before they sailed into Newport. Helen arrived to share a table with Sam, a plate of food precariously balanced on her one useable hand. With a wry grin, he offered to cut it up for her.

"Can't have you hungry as well as grumpy," he teased.

"I just wonder how we're going to explain the state that *Lupin* is in to Chairman Jamieson and the forum," Helen said morosely.

"That's no one's fault but our assailants," Sam said between mouthfuls. "Our task was to lose neither crew nor the ship and we've succeeded on both those counts."

"All the same, I didn't expect to bring my ship home with a five degree list and enough holes to use her as a colander," she said gloomily. "And a blackened and burnt aft deck."

"Let's say it's the price of our mission. We've saved eleven people, including a new arrival, five of whom are sighted. I call that success."

Sam felt better for his sleep and was determined not to let Helen burst his bubble. There was more than enough time to be concerned when all the facts had been analysed. He caught Ruth's eye as she passed.

"Can I ask a favour?" he said and smiled to her frown. "As we arrive in harbour, can you run out flags on the bow and main mast and line the decks with as many of the crew as can be spared; get them all waving and cheering with as much enthusiasm as they can."

He turned back to Helen. "Any chance we can enter Newport with our port side to the dock?"

She replied with a wry smile. "And conceal the truth of the beating we've been given?"

"Just until we've had time to tell everyone the whole story. Run the pumps at full speed too; it might ease the list."

Helen shook her head. "You'll make a good politician one day, Sam." She stood up to leave. "I can't hide the wrecked wheelhouse, but the rest shouldn't be a problem."

Gloom lifted, she limped off. Even shaking her head didn't remove the smile.

The sun came out as they approached home. As they passed Hurst Castle, the swell and breeze picked up, combing white foam in streamers from the crests of rolling waves. Sam found himself a quiet spot on the main deck rail from which to gather his thoughts. Bathed in sunshine, the island was illuminated in a patchwork of green, the canvas for their lives for the past five years.

He had been out of contact from Rachel and Lorna for the first time in five years and he felt the relief of homecoming but squeezed by a pang of anxiety. From a seemingly unknown cause things had changed during the difficult days before his departure. Sam was worried that Rachel's mood would continue to wash against him in his absence. His reverie was disturbed by a metronomic tapping noise as Claire approached along the deck, her white cane profiling the passageway in front of her. She paused a few feet from him.

"Sam." More a statement than a question, she asked with her head cocked slightly to one side.

"You guessed right. Do I smell that badly?" he teased.

"Ha. I knew it was you. I could hear your breathing and anyway, you give me space. Most people crowd my space and assume I need help."

Beneath them, the deck of the ship began to heel as Helen turned towards the distant harbour of east Cowes.

"How long before we dock?"

"About half an hour. Your new home approaches."

Sam made way as she joined him at the rail. A flock of squabbling seagulls arrived overhead to welcome them home. Since he had last seen her, Claire had showered and washed her hair which now glowed in shades of red and gold in the early sunshine, offering nature's counterbalance to the mismatch of clothing she had been given.

"The smell of freedom," she said after a while. "I guess it's a bit late to start asking, but what's life like here?"

Sam thought for a moment. The passage of time had led to so much being taken for granted but he picked up on her word freedom.

"There are about a thousand of us living here now, mostly all incomers, survivors like you. The island is largely secure and you can travel freely almost anywhere, or at least you could until we recently began to have problems with a few visiting boar. The community is divided into farming hamlets, each comprising three family units, each containing one sighted adult male and female and usually three or four blind women and children. There are few blind men I'm afraid; it's one of nature's consequences that so few men survived the flu virus. If you include children, each hamlet supports about thirty people. Every sighted male is responsible for fathering children with all the women of the family group. Because we are such a small population, every fertile female needs to bear four children, more if possible. It gives us numbers we can support and feed and allows us to grow a sighted population for the future. It's tough on the women, but until our population increases in numbers the alternative would be a steady path to extinction."

"Do women get to choose the father of their children?" Claire asked with a hint of mischief in her voice.

"To a limited extent, yes. If she really dislikes a man, a woman can reject him and is allowed two refusals; after that she starts to lose privilege."

"Privilege? Now that's a word I haven't heard in a long time."

"Well, incentive might be a better word. If she bears four children, a woman earns the right to choose her own home and live independently if she wishes. In the case of blind women, she would need support, presumably from her sighted children as the forum can't provide that. Overall, we think it's a fair system; not perfect, but then the circumstances are nothing like any of us have ever experienced."

"How do you manage for food?"

"I guess you would say we're holding our own. Every farm has to achieve a quota which it has to pass on to the central reserve for distribution. Excess beyond the quotas can be kept and either consumed by the families or used for barter. There doesn't seem to be much cheating or black market, so I think you could say it's working, though our reserves are not as strong as we would hope. But at least no one goes hungry."

Claire was thoughtful for a while. Eventually she asked the question that was troubling her most.

"What will happen to me?"

Sam took a moment before answering.

"We thought the family groups we rescued would prefer to be kept together and allocated a place in one of the hamlets. There are new ones being created as none of the existing hamlets can accommodate another family."

"But I'm not in a family member, at least, not one that wants me."

"I understand that. I need to speak to the Carters about that."

Claire gave a snort of derision. "It won't make any difference; besides I refuse to be made to stay with them." There was a grim determination in her words.

Sam hesitated before he spoke further. He felt he needed to reassure her.

"Claire, I saw what had happened to you, though you must be aware that the others are trying to spin a different tale. They say you simply got lost and they couldn't find you. Either way, we try to be compassionate as a community, whatever the circumstances. No one will make you stay in a group you don't wish to live with."

"Can you promise that?" Her face looked as tight as her words.

Sam took her arm to reassure her. "Hey, don't fret about it. You've been through enough already. I'll speak to Rose when we arrive. She allocates homes and resources and I'm sure she can find another family group who will welcome you, especially if you have any skills you can offer to the farm."

Ahead, the raised arms of the unloading cranes saluted their arrival home. The engines slowed and the bow began to turn, bringing the least damaged side to face the quay as Helen played her part of the arrival plan.

"Don't leave the ship without me," said Sam, realising he was still holding Claire's arm. The strange tingling sensation seemed to repeat itself. "Once we're tied up I'll introduce you to Rose and explain the circumstances. I'm sure she can find somewhere to live where you'll be happy."

Claire's expression began to soften and her face relaxed. At that moment, she had not a friend in the world beyond Sam but he had reassured her that everything would be okay. As he walked away, he hoped it would turn out the way he had described things.

A crowd of about sixty had gathered at the dockside. Ruth had made sure that all available crew members were assembled on deck to wave and shout with enthusiasm, which, given the battered appearance of *Lupin*, probably delighted and confused in equal measure all those who had assembled to welcome them home. Most on the quay were family of the crew and it was with a pang of sadness that Sam observed that no one from Sky Farm was amongst them.

Once moored, they ran the gangway into place and Chairman Jamieson and Connor Rigby, accompanied by Doctor Morgan and several nurses, came on board. He felt a weight lifted from his shoulders as everyone gathered around the chairman, each with an excited story to tell, and it reminded Sam how completely the responsibility for the mission had weighed upon him. Albert Jamieson worked his way slowly through the group gathered around him, smiling and nodding to all as he passed until he arrived beside Sam.

"It seems you've had your hands full," Albert said with a raised eyebrow. "You've done well to bring them all home safely, if somewhat battered."

He cast a glance at *Lupin*'s scarred exterior. "It sounds as if the men you ran into aren't particularly friendly."

"Downright hostile might be a better description," Sam replied with a wry smile. "Probably no more than we thought. We were lucky no one was seriously hurt."

Both men regarded one another in silence for a moment.

"I'm sorry none of your family could be here to greet you. We had three more boar attacks the night before last. I'm afraid one of them was at Sky Farm." He paused, palm raised. "Don't worry, no one has been hurt, mainly thanks to your preparations and the cool head of young Lorna. But sadly, another farm attacked weren't so lucky; they've had two people killed." Albert sighed. "And so the attrition starts." There was a grim undertone to his words.

Sam bit his lip, a kaleidoscope of images flashing through his mind. He felt reassured that their preparations at the farm had worked and everyone was safe, but guilty by his absence.

Albert Jamieson interrupted his thoughts. "It's best you get off home. There's a wagon with supplies waiting for you, so take that as your transport." He paused, watching a group of laughing squad members as they left the ship. "I'm calling a forum meeting for tomorrow night. Can you have your report on the Dartmouth rescue ready to present by then? I'm sorry that's short notice, but all of the crew will be telling family and friends their own versions of events and it's important the forum hears what you have to say before everyone creates an opinion of their own."

Sam nodded. He had already prepared enough notes to start the framework of a report.

"Is Mary free to type up my notes? It will help me to complete the report in the next twenty-four hours." Sam felt tired. His body ached with countless bruises and cuts acquired during their escape. "It would help if Helen and Dave Bartlett could have their reports complete before the meeting as well, so we avoid any contradictions."

'I'll ask Mary to organise that for you," Albert Jamieson said encouragingly. "Now get off home to your family and get some rest. You've pulled off something close to a miracle to complete the rescue and bring everyone home safely."

The ship slowly fell silent as all the crew hurried ashore, eager to get to their homes and families. It felt a huge contrast to the action and drama of the previous day that now so vividly marked the sides of *Lupin*. Tired though he was, Sam felt he would miss the demands and excitement of Dartmouth, despite the absurd perversity of that feeling. As he made to leave the damaged ship, Sam saw Albert walking away. Abruptly, the older man stopped and called over his shoulder, "You never seriously believed this would be a walkover, did you?" Mischief coloured his words. "That's why I sent you."

*Lupin* rested in silence, only punctuated from somewhere deep inside by the voices of Helen and the engineers who had to repair the damage. As he was leaving the ship, Sam found Claire sitting alone at the head of the gangway like a piece of discarded flotsam. Her face brightened as she heard Sam approach.

"You told me not to leave without you."

The innocence of her tone made him smile. He had almost forgotten his last instruction, but Claire obviously hadn't. Sam gathered up her few possessions, a careworn canvas satchel and a bedroll, and Claire took his arm, leaving her other arm free to scan with her white cane. They crossed the gangway to the quayside, already empty now that the crew had hurried to their homes, and they were in time to see a van depart carrying the Carter family complete with the newborn baby.

In the harbour office Sam found Rose in conversation with Karen. Rose looked up as they entered and greeted Sam with a warm smile.

"I hear you rescued a blind girl who was lost, though not without taking a terrible personal risk by the sound of it."

Rose was a cheery soul but, like so many others, had the habit of talking about the blind as though they weren't present. Sam drew Claire forward and she extended her hand in greeting.

"Claire, this is Rose, she'll sort out your personal details and help find somewhere for you to stay. But first, I want Karen to check your wound. I don't think anyone has looked at it since I got the splinter out yesterday."

Despite her fatigue, Karen took Claire away into the privacy of a small room, leaving Sam with Rose.

"I'm not sure what story you might have been told, but it's important that Claire isn't placed with the Carters."

Rose frowned. "I assumed there were two family groups and they've been allocated together to a newly established hamlet. It's going to be a bit of a problem to find somewhere for a blind girl on her own if, as you're saying, she can't join them. Most of the existing hamlets already have their full allocation of blind as it is."

She pursed her lips and flipped a clipboard of papers listing the distribution of the population of the island.

As she read the lists Rose added, "The Carters said Claire had a habit of wandering off alone and she had got lost and they hadn't been able to find her. They claim she's spreading rumours blaming them unfairly."

Sam had suspected something like this would happen, but there wasn't time to argue the details now.

"Well, let's just say the situation I found doesn't support that version of events." He paused to let his comment sink in. "We need to find Claire somewhere to live that doesn't involve the Carters. She's not a relative to them and I'm sure there are any number of farms who could use a girl, blind or sighted, and she has dairy and cheese-making skills."

He smiled at Rose. "I'm sure you can rustle something up while I go and find Mary. I'll be back in about an hour, so I'll leave it to your usual skills to organise things."

Sam didn't wait for a reply.

As luck would have it, Sam found Mary in her office in the Jubilee store building. She shared an office with two trainee clerks who were busy processing the aftermath of the Dartmouth expedition. In addition to the reports from the crew members, *Lupin*'s hold contained a cargo of precious stores, all of which had to be accounted for. It took all of Sam's persuasive skills for Mary to interrupt the process in order to type out the handwritten notes he had returned with. In silent protest, Mary passed his notes to the most junior clerk, a young boy barely old enough to shave, with instructions to type them while Sam set out to find the supply wagon he needed to return to the farm.

It took some time to find the wagon. Fortunately, some thoughtful person had already loaded it with supplies, including a precious allocation of fertilizer, milled flour, and a large jar of thick white honey. He was disappointed to find only a few jerry cans of fuel. Their stock on the farm was getting low and the cans in the wagon wouldn't go far in a busy season. Sam counted the cans; at this rate, even more horses would be needed when it came to the harvest, which in turn put ever increasing demands on their fodder stocks. With a shortage of petrol, Sam could only hope the coming year would provide a good crop for them all, including their livestock. The wagon looked well used, as did the grey-whiskered mare waiting patiently between the traces, regarding Sam with large doleful eyes. At least the driving bench had springs, and with luck he would be able enjoy a slow horse-led amble through the lanes in the sunshine on his way to the farm. Sam found a bag of oats and left the mare to enjoy a mid-morning feed while he checked the cargo and loaded his equipment into the back and returned to collect the draft of his report.

The young clerk had completed typing his report by the time Sam found his way back to the offices and collected the pages. He thanked the boy, noting there were more corrections on the pages than clean typing. As he left, Karen appeared and hastily approached Sam.

"I'm glad I found you; I think you have a problem with Claire."

"Is it her wound?"

"What? No, I've checked that. You made a decent job of removing the splinter, though it will need keeping an eye on. She looks very under-nourished, so I suspect her resistance to infection is low. No, it's more a problem with Rose; she couldn't find anyone with a vacancy for Claire. 'Not another blind girl' seems to be the common reply, and it's not helped by Rose having taken against her for some reason. In the end Rose insisted that she join the rest of the Carter family as planned and stop causing problems."

Sam looked aghast, remembering the reassurance he had given to Claire only a short time before.

"How did Claire react?"

"I only caught the tail end of the conversation. Claire thanked her for her trouble, took her satchel and cane and walked out. In the time it took me to wash my hands she had disappeared." Karen looked genuinely concerned. "I'm sorry Sam, we seem to have lost her."

"Okay," said Sam. "She can't have gone far. I'll go and look for her straightaway."

"I'd take her in if I could, but we already look after four blind girls; we really couldn't manage another," Karen said.

Sam nodded his thanks to Karen. He knew the last thing Claire would accept would be the forced return to the Carters. She couldn't have gone far, though his search would be hindered by having to take the wagon. There were three possible routes; one led farther into the harbour area, a second wound into the streets of the largely deserted town, whilst the third headed northwards, where the path more closely followed the river towards the sea. He made his best guess and opted for the last route beside the river, deciding she would try to keep close to the river as it offered the strongest point of reference.

Sam gave the mare a 'hurry-up' and was rewarded with a disdainful glare; in reply, the horse set off at her usual slow pace. He checked his watch; if he was right about her route, Claire couldn't be more than thirty minutes ahead of him. Just how far could a blind person cover in that time? He felt a pang of anxiety; if he hadn't caught up with her in a couple of miles he would have to think of another plan.

For some time the path was silent and deserted until three young children appeared with a fishing line and buckets. Sam stopped, surprised. The two boys looked sheepishly at their feet when he asked if they had seen anyone pass this way, merely answering his question with a shake of the head. He guessed they had been catching crabs when they should have been at lessons, but he struck lucky with a younger girl who told him that a blind woman with a white cane and golden-coloured hair had passed only a short time before. Encouraged, Sam moved on, only to find the path split into two directions. There was no clue which route Claire might have taken. He wondered how she would react when her emotions calmed down and she found herself in a strange place and utterly lost. One path stayed close to the river; it was only a narrow track and badly overgrown but Sam applied the same logic as earlier and led the mare to follow it. Broken tarmac continued; it had taken a mere five years for potholes to grow like sink holes, clawing giant handfuls of tarmac, leaving water-filled craters in their wake. After a short distance, the mare made her objections clear and refused to haul the wagon another step. Impatiently, Sam tried to encourage her to move on, only to be rewarded with another disdainful glare. It was an impasse as horse and man regarded one another with mutual contempt and the horse snorted through her nostrils while Sam tried bribes and threats.

"There's a boar behind you."

The voice was unmistakeable.

"Claire? What the ..."

"It's been following me since I left a group of children a short way back. I think it was stalking them."

Sam turned slowly. He couldn't hear or see anything except the wind rustling dried grass and the flicker of early spring leaves. He asked an unnecessary question.

"Are you sure?"

"If you sit there long enough you'll find out. I can hear it growling, so it's close."

Sam turned around to look for his Sten gun, remembering with alarm that the magazine was empty since Dartmouth. He hadn't brought a spare. He couldn't see Claire and knew that as soon as the horse smelt the boar it was bound to be spooked with every chance it would panic and disappear with the wagon, supplies and all.

"Are you any good with horses? This mare is rather flighty."

Claire appeared from behind a crumbling concrete wall searching her way towards his voice. He slid from his seat, took her hand and led her to the horse's head. The mare nodded vigorously when Claire arrived, which he took as a good sign, as he placed the bridle in her hands.

"Hold on tight; try talking in her ear; she might just cooperate with you."

Sam slipped away, moving to the back of the wagon. The route ahead stopped at a dead-end and he daren't try to turn the wagon around if a boar was lurking close nearby. His only option was to confront it. Without his gun, one of the jerry cans offered a solution. It had been stored upright and had a tap at the base. He still couldn't hear the boar but if Claire said it was there he wasn't going to argue about it. In his rucksack, he rummaged for a glass water bottle, emptied the contents and refilled it with petrol. He tore several pages from the back of his journal, rolled them into a tight tube and forced them into the neck of the bottle. Thus armed, and with his cigarette lighter ready, Sam set off on a boar hunt.

"Keep to the river side of the horse, just in case anything goes wrong," he called to Claire as he moved across the track.

Sam decided his best chance was to try and gain the initiative by circling behind the boar. With any luck its attention would be fixed on Claire and the horse and provide the opportunity he needed. He didn't particularly relish the idea of hand verses tusk combat with a boar when armed only with a petrol bomb.

On the opposite side of the track, waste ground rose slightly. Several buildings had once occupied the area, and broken crumbling walls and dense clumps of weed now provided ideal cover for boar. Moving carefully, he tracked left to avoid a wire fence and climbed a small wall. For a few yards, the ground in front opened out. The breeze swirled around him and his ears caught the faint sound of a deep growl. He realised that there was more than one boar. He still couldn't see anything, but his nose caught their unmistakeable odour. They had to be close. Very close. He stood still; then took a step forward, stiff with tension. This was starting to look far more difficult than he had hoped.

Unseen, a strand of rusty wire caught his trailing foot, pitching him onto his hands and knees. He narrowly avoided dropping the bottle, and cursed loudly.

To his right, he heard Claire shout and the mare neigh. The horse had smelt the boar, which suggested they had moved between Sam and Claire. Sam altered direction as fast as he could, hoping that the boar stayed close together; if they had fanned out he had a problem with only a single bottle of petrol.

He suddenly saw them, halfway across the pitted tarmac; a large fully grown male with two smaller boar on either side slightly behind it. Without hesitating Sam flicked the flame on his lighter and lit the paper spill in the neck of the bottle. At close range he threw it hard; the bottle hit the boar on the shoulder with a dull thud and fell onto the track. It smashed, showering petrol in all directions. Immediately he realised his mistake; he had been too quick and the spill hadn't completely caught alight and had extinguished as it flew through the air. Now just liquid petrol puddled, unlit, on the tarmac at the feet of the boar. As if aware of Sam's mistake, the boar at first hesitated, undecided between the horse and the man who had suddenly attacked it. By some unspoken command, the three boar fanned out. Sam had no more paper in his pockets, but scanning about him he noticed dry clumps of reed grass growing on the verge. He backed away, mimicking Ruth's tactic of swaying slowly from side to side in an attempt to confuse the boar. He squatted down and snatched a handful of reeds. Dry and brittle, it easily snapped in his hand. He held them to the lighter and snapped its flint; once, twice, three times; it refused to give a flame. The air filled with the angry growl of the large boar, head lowered to lunge and gore. Instinctively, Sam threw himself to one side but in misjudging the speed of the boar he received a numbing blow to his hip, knocking him sideways, narrowly avoiding the razor sharp tusks. The boar had made the first strike and would need several seconds before attacking again.

Hurling abuse at the errant lighter, Sam thrust flint and grass together in a final desperate attempt to ignite it. A tiny white flame grew in the grass as all three boar gathered to attack and finish him off. Working together, Sam knew they wouldn't miss a second time. He blew with as much control as he could on the tiny white flame; it flickered, almost extinguished, only to suddenly flare as the grass caught light. It shone brightly, perhaps distracting the boar for a mere heartbeat, long enough for Sam to hurl the burning torch into the petrol puddled around the boars' feet. The last thing Sam remembered was the world exploding in an enormous ball of flame.

# ELEVEN

Claire was struggling to calm the terrified mare when the heat from the fireball washed over them. Terrified, the horse shied vigorously, dragging Claire and the wagon sideways, away from the flames. For a moment, she thought the wagon would tip over as the horse strained against the traces. Before being blinded she had learnt to be a competent horserider, yet despite her past skills, Claire feared falling and being trampled under the mare. Holding on to the bridle, she had to use every ounce of her strength and weight to calm the frightened horse. It was taking a long time and she hoped Sam would return to help her. She must have called his name a dozen times as she was dragged about, her anxiety increasing as her shouts went unanswered. She knew Sam had attacked the boar; she had heard him cursing, but since the petrol had exploded she'd heard nothing except the hiss and crackle of flames. At least she was reassured by the obvious fact that the boar wasn't trying to attack her and the horse, but what had happened to Sam? Just before he had ignited the petrol, she had heard more than one deep guttural growl followed by Sam calling out in pain, and she was beginning to fear the worse.

She finally managed to draw the horse away from the heat of the flames which had now increased with the acrid smell of burning tar; the track must have caught fire. Struggling in a world of darkness, she walked into a stout oak mooring post beside the river, painfully grazing her shins. Despite the pain, at least the post offered somewhere she could tie the horse. On the side of the wagon she found a feed bag still half full of oats. It took only a few seconds to fit the bag and calm the horse enough to leave her, releasing Claire to try to find Sam. In the confusion, Claire had lost her white cane. Even without it, she reasoned Sam had to be somewhere close by. Her feet could feel the edge of the track where stone and tarmac gave way to coarse weeds. It wasn't much help but it would do as a reference line. Counting steps along the verge, she traced her way back towards the flames. There was still no sound from Sam and the closer she moved towards the fire, smoke began to fill her lungs, bringing on a bout of choking and coughing. Still following the verge, she moved through the smoke into cleaner air beyond, her sightless eyes now streaming with tears. Pausing only to clear her lungs, Claire began the process of searching the track with her feet, moving slowly across its width, from one side to the other, stepping six paces farther along for each crossing. She must have covered twenty metres or so in this fashion, but found nothing. After a while she concluded that Sam must have been closer to the wagon than she had thought when he had thrown the petrol bomb. Returning back along the verge, she crossed closer to the fire, straining her ears at every step. Her nose twitched. There was something else mingling with the pungent odour of boar. She moved closer to the sound of the fire. The barely perceptible smell became stronger; burning cloth.

"Sam?"

It was hard to manage more than a whisper with a smoke parched throat. She repeated the call several times, without any response. Frustrated, Claire dropped onto her knees, turned away from the verge and began to crawl towards the heat, groping desperately ahead with an extended hand as she moved forward, aware that his clothes might well be alight. She stopped; another wave of heat struck her, forcing her back. Groping for support, her hand brushed something soft and hot. She snatched at the material and found a woollen sleeve, and in it, a leg. She yelped; the fabric was burning.

"Sam," she shouted and tugged his arm.

Her reward was a gasping moan. Quickly, she moved to his side, hands frisking in search of more burning material. The trouser leg had burnt her hand. Hastily, she fumbled in her canvas bag and found a bottle of water and poured most of it over his legs.

"Can you move? We've got to get away from the flames."

The roar of fire suddenly increased. He muttered something unintelligible but seemed to be trying to move. Claire traced his body, found his head and emptied the rest of her water over his face. She leant close to his ear.

"I can't lift you but I can drag you. You'll have to help me; push with your feet and hands as best you can."

She grasped him under the arms and pulled. He didn't move. She hauled again. Slowly the message must have got through and he began to push with his feet. It felt like a snail's pace, but bit by bit they drew away and the heat began to ease a little. At the edge of the track, she collapsed, gasping for air, with his body lying across her legs. They both lay silent for several minutes, gasping to recover.

"Are you okay?" The words came out in a croak. "Have you been gored?"

"No, it must have missed anything major, though it caught me a hell of a whack in the side with its head. It knocked me over and stunned me just after I had lit the petrol. After that, everywhere just seemed to explode."

Sam was silent for a moment, trying to gather his thoughts. "The boar must be the survivors from the farm attacks last night. That might explain how they ended up here."

Still groggy, he prised himself off Claire's legs. The left side of his head felt numb and the blow had torn a cut in his right leg, aggravated by the pain caused by his burning trousers. Struck by a bout of retching, he struggled to his knees. The spasm passed and slowly Sam managed to stand, pausing to help Claire to her feet. Immediately, the world started to spin around him from smoke and effort, and Claire only just caught him as his legs sagged and he pitched against her. With difficulty, she managed to prop him up and together they stumble to the protection of the wagon. For several minutes, Sam rested against the tailboard with Claire leaning against him. He tore the cap from another water bottle, dowsing both their heads before drinking the remains.

"I think you've got concussion. We need to find somewhere safer to stop for a while and allow you to recover."

Sam shook his head.

"I must get back to the farm. After the attack last night I need to check everything is okay and see the situation for myself."

It had been preying on him ever since Albert Jamieson had told him of the events of the previous night. This new fight with rogue boar only intensified this feeling.

"You shouldn't move too much until you feel better."

"I can't hang around and wait. Could you handle the wagon? The horse seems pretty docile, even if she is a bit stubborn. I can just sit and give directions though she probably knows her way to the farm anyway, with or without us," he added.

Without either of them being aware, the simple decision had been taken for homeless Claire to live at Sky Farm. Claire never asked and Sam never suggested. Both were oblivious to the spin of fate and the mysterious web it wove. The future would take care of itself.

It took some time to turn the wagon and horse around and trace their way along the crumbling lanes to the farm. The horse wouldn't be hurried and twice she stopped to graze on fresh clover and grass at the roadside. Claire held the reins while Sam occasionally gave directions. They saw no one at all on the way and the day offered the peace and calm of early spring, holding out the tantalising promise of summer to come. It was as close as their lives came to normal, a day that could have seemed normal fifty or five years before, until their new world was turned upside down, as their days in Dartmouth had so painfully proven.

Sam yawned and rocked drowsily in his seat for much of their journey, still washing through the muzzy effects of concussion, barely kept awake by Claire, who persistently questioned him in her keenness to know how things worked on the island.

As they joined the track that led to the farm, Sam saw the carcasses of at least a dozen dead boar littering the land around the house. Judging by the number of kills, everyone would have had their hands full the previous evening at the farm, probably at the very moment he was enjoying a peaceful sunset on *Lupin*. By the time Sam and Claire drew to a halt in the farmyard, most of the families had gathered outside to welcome him home. Earlier, a carrier pigeon had arrived with the news that *Lupin* had returned safely and everyone began asking excited questions as Lorna gathered the horse's bridle.

Leaving Claire on the wagon, Sam climbed stiffly down. He still felt groggy, though the worst of the effects seemed to have passed. He saw Rachel standing towards the back of the group, staring anxiously at his burnt and torn clothing, with a bandage around his lower leg where his trouser leg had been cut off and a livid red weal and swelling on the side of his head. Sam moved purposely through the gathering towards her.

"You look as if you've been in the wars," Rachel tried to make it sound light, but her eyes betrayed her concern.

"No thanks to some rogue boar that ambushed us just outside of Newport."

He gazed slowly at the dead boar that surrounded them.

"It seems you've had your hands full too."

Spontaneously he reached out and drew her to him, squeezing her with a hug that tried to bridge the time since their parting. Unfortunately, there were too many questions demanding answers to give them time to linger, not least of which was Claire who needed introducing to everyone. Sam reached up for her hand and helped her down.

"This is Claire. She needs a home and as there are no other vacancies, she has come to join us here at the farm."

Despite looking equally battered, Claire had brushed her hair behind her ears, creating a golden halo against her pale skin in the afternoon sunlight, reminding him of the same natural radiance he had noticed the first time he had set eyes on her.

"Claire was part of the group that we rescued. It's a long story, but I'll tell you more later. But for now, Claire needs a home and we have spare capacity here, so I hope you will all make her welcome. She is also an expert cheese-maker, so at last we have someone living with us who will have a use for our surplus milk."

His last comment brought a cheer followed by shouts of greeting and light-hearted banter. Still holding Claire's hand, Sam turned to Rachel to introduce them.

"Claire, this is Rachel who I've told you so much about."

Normally a warm and welcoming personality to everyone she met, Rachel stared, unsmiling, at the new arrival. Sam waited for Rachel to take Claire's outstretched hand in greeting and although the hesitation lasted only a fraction of a second, Sam had noticed. Over the years they had been through so much together and instantly he felt a pang of unease, less by the hesitation, than the set of Rachel's eyes. He had seldom seen that hard glint in her eyes, and only when she had taken an immediate dislike to another person. Things were going to be harder than he had thought.

Reading the unspoken body language with perfect intuitive timing, Lorna stepped in enthusiastically. Although younger than Claire, she placed an arm on her elbow and guided her towards a barn next to the farmhouse. Lorna used the roof space above the animals as her own private space to escape from the constant noise and clamour of the younger children now in increasing numbers on the farm.

"I'm Lorna," she announced. "Let's find somewhere for you to stay. There's an area in my loft that I'm not using. It needs a bit of a clean and a coat of paint, but it will be somewhere you can call your own. And while we're at it, let's see if we can find you something to wear."

As she left, Lorna gave Sam a hasty glance which said, 'Fix things with Rachel.'

After they had disappeared into the barn, the stream of anxious questions could only be given short tired answers and soon everyone began to disperse. As they did, Jake caught Sam's attention.

"When you have a minute, there's something I need to show you." Sam was about to protest when Jake added, "I wouldn't trouble you so soon, but it's important."

Sam nodded his agreement, adding the request to his list as he walked off towards the farmhouse. He urgently needed fresh clothes and a few hours' rest.

Alone together at last, Sam ate at the farmhouse kitchen table; it was good to enjoy home food again. When he had finished eating, Rachel cleaned and dressed the wound and burns to his leg, and made a compress to tape to the side of his head to ease the bruising. She stood to one side, making a quizzical appraisal.

"If this is the state in which you return home, Albert Jamieson needs to find someone younger to run his errands."

From the tone in her voice, it was apparent her feelings for his role to Dartmouth had not abated since his departure.

"And that blow to your head is nasty, though perhaps it will knock some sense into you," Rachel added with mock cynicism. "Or not, depending on how you look at it."

She continued, "I know you'll object but I want Doctor Morgan to check you over, particularly with all the cuts and bruises you've come home with."

"Well at least I'm still in one piece. It might have been a different story if Claire hadn't dragged me from the flames of the fire after the boar attack."

Sam glanced at Rachel as he spoke and noticed with concern how she stiffened at the very mention of Claire's name. Without saying as much they moved on. Rachel told him of what had happened on the farm while he had been away, mostly daily events for a working farm; two cows were showing signs of mastitis, a young lamb had been killed, they thought by a fox, and of course the main event, the boar attack.

"Marcus counted eighteen, perhaps a few more. Without our defences we would have been overwhelmed for sure. Lorna had left several pairs of geese inside the ditch line after dark and they kicked up an enormous ruckus as the boar got close to the houses. We all retreated to the upper floors and used the roof searchlights. But what seems to have saved the day were Lorna's specials she made with her boyfriend."

Sam looked at her with a frown. "Specials? Boyfriend?"

Rachel smiled, knowingly. "She's seeing a boy from the Howe farm, Gary I think is his name. You would have noticed if you'd been home more." She paused for effect.

"Anyway, it seems they've been adapting bullets to include a small explosive charge. They've also increased the bullet velocity, and bingo, virtually every shot that hits a boar now kills outright. Much better than tracer, though handling the bullets is a risky game. Connor Rigby is impressed, enough to want to start large scale production if the test holds up and we can find a means to manufacture them."

Swapping roles, Sam made coffee while Rachel listened as he gave her a summary of his trip, choosing to deliberately underplay the confrontation with the men on the motorbikes. He also overlooked any mention of his role in rescuing Claire. As Sam relaxed, tiredness stiffened his aching limbs. Eventually too tired to continue their conversation, he grasped her by the hand and before she could object, led her to their bedroom. The house was empty; their children were at early learning lessons in one of the other farmhouses so for once they had the house to themselves. If she was still angry with him, it evaporated once they slid beneath the bed covers, their love-making arousing a degree of passion energised by the anxiety of separation. Later, exhausted, Sam fell deeply asleep within seconds, leaving Rachel to stare at the ceiling in a state of uneasy wakefulness that she couldn't explain.

Sam awoke to the clink of a cup and saucer. Light was casting dusty rays through a gap in the curtains, softening the shadows.

"Wake up sleepy head. Here's tea for you. Jake's downstairs and he's eager to show us something before it gets dark. You've got five minutes."

Rachel kissed his forehead and left him to drink his tea. Sam rolled over in the bed and stretched into a star shape, feet and hands pointing to the corners of the bed. He felt sore and stiff muscles where he didn't even know muscles existed. At that moment, the temptation to stay beneath the covers was almost irresistible until, with an explosion of noise, the door flew open, announcing the excited arrival of his two young children, Gemma and Tom. Amidst the clamour of shouts and squeals, the bed was turned into a trampoline, dispelling any thought of sleep. It took the bribes of multiple treats to calm them down, a pointed reminder of just how much they had missed him too.

Sam was still dressing as he entered the kitchen and found Jake and Rachel ready to leave, three horses already tethered in the yard. Jake apologised again as Sam swung into the saddle.

"I wouldn't normally be so pushy, but the forecast is for rain sometime tonight and I wanted you to both see something before it's washed away."

Jake nudged his horse and led away along the path used by the boar on their route to the farm. A distinct swathe had been cut through a field sown to spring barley; the young green shoots churned up by hooves in a line some three metres wide. Sam was surprised by the direction in which Jake was leading them; they had only a single field close to the seashore and he had expected them to head in that direction. Instead, their path cut inland across the fields to the east, almost the opposite direction. They rode in silence until they came to a broken gate at the edge of a field. Beyond lay a muddy track that dissected the fields and led directly to the nearest road. Jake stopped his horse and slid from the saddle.

"The boar must have busted open that gate; it was fine a few days ago," he said as he tethered his horse. "Climb down, there's something you ought to see."

Rachel and Sam followed.

"The boar started from this gate; there's a lot of commotion, dung and hoofprints up here in the lane, nothing in any of the fields on the opposite side of the track."

Jake moved through the broken gate, taking care to keep to the long grass of the verges.

"Come and look. Don't tread there, you'll spoil it."

"All I can see is mud," Rachel said.

"Look closer. What can you see pressed into the mud there where it's thickest?" Jake pointed to the wheel track lines scoring the lane.

They both looked blank for a moment until Sam said, "Tyre tracks? Not unusual, it's a track."

"True. But this lane only goes to a dead-end in a few hundred metres. And if you look, you can see these tracks have been made by a double wheel axle. We don't have one."

Jake paused, squatting down onto his haunches.

"Also, we don't have anything with a tyre pattern like that."

He pointed to the prints scored into the mud.

"It seems the vehicle didn't turn around either and the tyre tracks don't go beyond this point. I've checked; it must have reversed from the road to here."

Jake paused, allowing them to consider what he had just said.

"It rained heavily the day before, so most probably all previous tracks would have been washed away."

He looked at them both with a troubled expression.

"So, it's fair to assume these were made recently; no earlier than last night."

The implications suspended time for a moment as Rachel and Sam considered his words. They could almost second guess what Jake would say next.

"If I'm right, it means the boar that attacked us didn't walk here. They arrived in the back of a lorry."

Sam and Rachel rode back to the farmhouse alone, leaving Jake to make an impression of the tyre tracks with some plaster he had taken from their supplies.

"There could be a simple explanation," Sam mused as they rode side by side in the gathering dusk, though he felt a hollow pit in the bottom of his stomach at the thought that someone in their midst could be responsible for this. "Though at the moment, I can't think of one. A group of boar cut a pretty conspicuous path through the landscape. There's nothing the other side of the lane, so if Jake's wrong where did the boar that attacked us come from?"

Sam stopped, resting his hands on the pommel of his saddle, and looked around them in the departing light. He hadn't grown up in the countryside, being born and bred a town boy, but over the years the soft colours and security of the land had insinuated itself into his very being. He had slowly grown to love the island, and now the thought that someone amongst them might try to bring this to an end filled him with dread.

"It makes no sense. We're hanging onto this world by our fingertips. Why seek to destroy it?" he said, seriously.

Rachel laughed cynically.

"Come on, Sam. Remember some of the power crazy characters we met on the mainland before we found refuge here. People like that prey on a catastrophe like the one we live in every day. It sounds as if the gang you met in Dartmouth aren't any better than some of the psychopaths we were lucky to escape from. Just because we are trying to build an enlightened system here doesn't mean everyone else sees things that way."

She paused, looking north towards the invisible mainland.

"It seems to me that storm clouds are brewing and the threat could be far worse than a few malicious boar."

For the first time in quite a while, all the families gathered for dinner that evening. The main farmhouse, where Sam and Rachel lived, had by far the largest kitchen and by setting separate tables for adults and children, they managed to seat everyone. Marcus released a generous number of bottles from his home-made beer cellar, and as the kitchen filled with the smells of roasting lamb, the evening soon became animated, with the exchange of stories of their shared dramas the previous evening.

Lorna made space for Claire to sit with her and introduced her in the conversation with the others. Focused on the boar attack on the farm, no one raised the subject of the mission to Dartmouth, so Sam was able to relax without being swamped by dozens of questions. Earlier, Sam had asked Jake not to mention the discovery of tyre tracks in the lane; he wanted to bring it to the attention of the forum before open discussion created a firestorm of speculation and fear. It was just still possible there was a simple answer.

Over dinner, Sam listened to the coming and going of conversation as it flowed around him. It was apparent that Lorna and her hand-made bullets had played a major role in quelling the attack well before the boar gained an advantage. Some were concerned about handling bullets containing even a small amount of explosives, but the results more than justified the risk. Lorna's marksmanship and courage had also been influential; not bad for a girl who had never lived outside a town until Sam and Rachel stumbled upon her amidst the chaos of the pandemic. The dozens of conversation fragments washed around Sam as the group laughed and teased one another. One snagged in Sam's subconscious; he heard Alice, Marcus's wife, saying "... and I found this disgusting sack laying against my front door."

After dinner, as Sam excused himself to complete his report for the forum the following day, Alice's words came back to him. Intrigued, he sought her out as they cleared and washed the dishes, drawing her to one side.

"Excuse my curiosity, but I overheard you saying something about an unpleasant sack on your front step," Sam frowned in bemused concentration.

"Oh, it was nothing really. This morning, once the all-clear from the boar attack could be given, there was a horrible stench around the house. Marcus said it was probably boar; they smell something awful when they're dead. It was the dog who found the cause, behind the water trough for the horses at our front door. A sack full of putrid offal, with a terrible smell. I soon got rid of it, I can tell you. I suspected one of the kids was up to mischief and thought it would be a funny prank to stink out the house. I've yet to find the culprit but I will, you mark my words. I'm not having any more tricks like that played on me," Alice said with her arms folded, her face set to find the perpetrator.

Sam excused himself, lost in thought. He found Rachel outside, enjoying the spring evening.

"Penny for your thoughts?"

Sam shook his head slightly. "I'll tell you later. I need to complete my report before bed but I shouldn't be more than an hour or so."

"Don't be too long. You look exhausted, despite your nap this afternoon."

Sam saw Rachel's eyes dart over his shoulder as she leaned forward to kiss him and he squeezed her arm as he turned to head for the office. A few feet behind him stood Claire.

Sam sat in the darkness, troubled by worries. He had hoped to convince himself that there could be an alternative reason for the tyre tracks, but Alice's discovery of the sack dispelled any illusions. It was commonly known that boar had an attraction to rotting flesh, but no one could have guessed they would develop such a palate for the human variety. The surest way to lead boar in a particular direction was to use a lure of putrid animal protein; it had been the way they managed them on the farms Sam had worked on before the pandemic overwhelmed them. The sack Alice had found must be such a lure, with the deliberate intention of guiding the boar to their farm. The purpose made his stomach churn; the intention could only be to kill as many on the farm as possible. So someone in their midst was a murderer, and he had no idea who it was.

Around him, the house fell silent as everyone made for their beds. Sam turned his focus to the report which he had to finish for the morning. 'Keep to the facts and avoid speculating,' he kept reminding himself. The unadorned story of all that had happened to them had to be presented objectively to prevent the forum losing objectivity. Discussion of the consequences could arise when they had debated his report and then it would be down to Albert, as chairman, to keep a steer on things.

Sam spent an hour adding information to his earlier draft. He would take it to Mary in the morning for typing so that copies could be distributed to forum members before the evening meeting. His concentration wandered while writing; there was much to include but what to leave out? In a distracted moment, he balanced the relationship between Teri and her cousin Ryan, which, for the moment, he had parked to one side. If he mentioned what he knew about them in his report it would have devastating consequences for both of them, and his conscience. Yet as a forum member, he had sworn to uphold the rules of the forum. Likewise, there were the circumstances that had led to Claire's abandonment by the Carter family. Include or forget? But foremost in his concerns were the intentions of the vigilante group they had encountered. It had resulted in unprovoked violence with a purpose and intent that remained unclear, though it wasn't hard to speculate. Now, evidence had been brought to him implying that the boar attacks contained a home-grown element. But why? It seemed to Sam a perfect storm of problems were building against them in which the true purpose remained obscure.

Abruptly, the quiet night was punctured by the bark of a dog. After a few seconds it stopped, abruptly. Sam left his desk, fearing a repeat of the boar attack the previous night. It wasn't impossible that whoever was behind this might try to hit the same farm on consecutive nights. At the front door he picked up a rifle, checked the breech and peered through a gap in the window blind. An almost full moon cast a pale light, but he could see nothing outside. Sam slipped the lock and carefully opened the door, half expecting a boar to appear at any moment. Moving through, Sam closed the door behind him and moved quickly into a pool of moon shadows, listening. Even if you couldn't see boar you could often hear them growling or grumbling if they were close enough and preparing to attack. He held his breath and forced his ears to detect the faintest sounds. Something floated just within range of his hearing. Someone was playing music. Keeping close to the barn to use the shadows, Sam moved towards the source. At first it faded, drifting with the breeze, until he turned the gable corner where it became more distinct; the song of a flute played softly in the darkness. Just beyond was an open sided Dutch barn where they stacked straw and hay bales. As he approached, the sound of the flute increased, the player hidden in the dark recesses amongst the bales. Sam halted. Sitting cross-legged on a bale was Claire. He stood still, half expecting a boar to make an appearance, attracted by a modern day Pied Piper, hypnotised by the lullaby she was playing. Claire stopped mid-bar, sensing she was not alone, leaving the final notes to slowly decay.

"It's a long time since I've heard that tune. You play well."

"Not really," Claire said. He suspected she had known he was there all along.

"It's my mother's flute; it's all I have of her. I wish I had paid more attention when she tried to teach me," she added wistfully.

"Amen to that. I guess we all stand guilty of missed opportunities. May I?" Sam slid on to the bale beside her. "Still, there is a small group of musicians around Newport; I'm sure someone would be able to help you to learn more. They'll welcome you with open arms if you want to join them."

Claire sighed deeply, though Sam was uncertain whether it was of sadness or having found peace at last.

"Aren't you sleepy? It's not completely safe out here; there's always a chance that a boar who survived last night's attack might return."

She shook her head.

"I'm fine. Lorna has been kind; it's been a long time since anyone made me feel welcome. There's almost too much to take in and I can't tell the difference between night and day. It's only the sounds that change and sometimes I need the feeling of safety that night-time brings. In a sense it equalises the world around me and gives me chance to gather my thoughts. Besides, I'd hear a boar long before it crept up on me."

Sam wasn't too sure about that but let it pass.

"Well, I'm glad you like Lorna. She has a sound head on her shoulders for one so young. If an emergency arises and Lorna asks you to do something, take my advice, don't hesitate."

They sat in silence for a minute listening to the night.

"How long before I have to start producing babies?"

Claire's question was asked almost casually, with an abrupt edge to her words that caught Sam completely off balance. He wondered if that was what she had intended.

"Whoa, don't start getting ahead of yourself. You've only just arrived and you need to settle in before such things need to be discussed."

He knew that was a male perspective on a subject that featured foremost in the lives of most women on the island.

"You need to make friends first. Besides, we want your cheese-making skills before anything else," he said with a light note, trying to reassure her.

Sam stretched and yawned, tiredness was making its presence felt. "I need to get to bed even if you don't," he said playfully. "There's a busy day ahead."

As he made to leave the bale, Claire's hand stopped him.

"Before you go, can I trace your face? I need to know what you look like?"

Despite living with a community of blind women, the request caught Sam by surprise.

"Of course, though you may not like what you find," he added with a laugh.

He turned and stood in front of Claire so that she could more easily reach his face. Using both hands she started to trace his hairline and measured the texture of his hair.

"What colour? Dark, I think, by the texture," she asked.

"It was black, now it's flecked with grey; lots of grey."

Her hands moved to his ears, the left one still swollen from the boar strike, and then moved to the beard on his cheeks, chasing the profile to his chin. He could feel her breath, like a soft whisper, on his face as she frowned in concentration.

"Your beard is softer than I expected." She sounded surprised.

Claire's hands moved to his mouth, tracing the profile of his lips and Sam held his breath, feeling her fingers shape the depression directly beneath his nose, before working slowly up the sides and down the bridge. It was a form of passive sculpture, imprinting his appearance in her mind, an experience of unexpected intimacy. Or was that just his imagination? Her fingers moved on, shaping the orbit of his eye sockets with gentle fingertips, before crossing his brows to the centre of his forehead. She lingered a moment, his skin tingling beneath her fingers, a moment frozen in suspension.

"There, all done." Softly spoken, the spell was broken.

"So now you know; Beauty and the Beast," he quipped.

"Quite so, though the Beast saved me."

"And in return Beauty saved me too."

The burn on his leg reminded him how lucky he had been to have been pulled clear of the boar.

"So we're even then?"

"Yes," he said, nodding and stepped back.

Claire slid her flute into a thin velvet bag and eased herself from the bale. Sam just noticed a silent wince of pain from her lips, a reminder that the wound in her side needed checking again soon.

"Let's call it a night," he yawned expansively again. "It's unlikely there is anything about, but it's best not to take too many risks until you know your way around."

He took Claire by the arm and led her back to the door to the barn. Once inside, she moved unaided to the ladder which led to the rooms above.

"I'm sure I know my way from here."

She thanked him with a warm smile and, having already memorised the route to her new bedroom, climbed the ladder and disappeared into the darkness, leaving Sam to return to the farmhouse.

He replaced the rifle, secured the doors and switched off the office light before silently padding his way shoeless through familiar darkened rooms. Home, peaceful, secure. Or was that really only an illusion? In mid-stride a thought stopped him. If his suspicions were correct, somewhere on the island at this very moment schemed and plotted against them, someone quite prepared to commit murder to achieve their ends.

# TWELVE

Sam awoke to the sound of rain dancing on the roof. Pale light glimmered at the windows as dawn made a late appearance. He lit a candle, letting its warm yellow flame cheer the bedroom. Beside him, the bed was empty. Rachel had risen early to supervise the cull of sheep as part of their contribution to the island's food stocks. The slaughter-man was due first thing and rain always conspired to slow down everything on the farm.

Sam dressed and made his way to the kitchen, still full of the aromas of dinner the previous evening. He filled a kettle and placed it on the range to boil. Outside, the plaintive calls of sheep, not long for this world, echoed from a makeshift pen in the yard. The cull took place in a mobile abattoir and was always the event in the calendar to which he least enjoyed. Sam made tea and took a mug to the office, well away from the commotion in the yard. A folder was propped on his desk with 'urgent attention' stamped across it in red. It contained many forms and lists of their crop expectations with anticipated yields entered against those achieved the previous season. It would not make happy reading. Try as they might, the trend was a constant decline, mainly caused by a lack of fertilizer, bad weather and bad luck. The best that could be said was that they were holding their own, but to increase their population numbers, as they must, more food had to be grown or hunger would haunt their lives in the very near future.

The stamp of boots and smell of wet oilskins wafted from the kitchen. A few minutes later Rachel appeared in the office.

"I thought I might find you skulking in here."

Sam smiled. "You know me, I can't stand seeing or hearing the sheep being killed."

"It's that or go hungry."

Rachel saw the report he had written the previous night laying on the desk.

"Is that finished? Do you want me to read and check it? Your spelling is notoriously bad," she said, only half joking.

Sam left the chair and made way for Rachel. Her discerning eye would help, and allowing her a pre-meeting read through would make her feel more inclusive.

"I'll make breakfast while you read," he said as he returned to the kitchen.

Sam lit the gas under a pan of porridge, stirring in a spoonful of their own honey and a handful of wild berries left over from the previous autumn. "What do you think?" he said as Rachel entered the kitchen.

"Factual, understated, but missing the point in your attempt to avoid causing alarm," Rachel said bluntly.

"Okay?"

"You make the men on motorbikes sound like a sideshow, almost an afterthought. I would have thought three hundred odd bullet holes in *Lupin* represents a very serious matter indeed. It can only be something of a miracle that many of you weren't killed. It's obviously what they intended."

"Albert Jamieson doesn't want the forum to be given a speculated or dramatized report of what happened. It influences the facts before they can be thoroughly debated."

"I understand that, but we may not be so lucky the next time we come up against these people and, if we don't take their threat seriously, the outcome could be very different. I think it's essential you don't underestimate the potential threat they represent," Rachel said with a serious frown lining her forehead.

"We have no evidence they intend a serious challenge on us. This might just have been a small group of thugs, caught up in some drug-fuelled blood lust, using gratuitous violence to plunder isolated survivor communities."

"Or they might not be. We have little idea of the real situation on the mainland, beyond what we're told by the few survivors who have recently made it to the island. And much of what they know has been only anecdotal. The truth is, we thought we had abandoned the mainland to the boar, but while we live here in supposed security, who knows what has been happening over there."

Her words were striking a raw nerve in Sam. If he tried to inspect his inner feelings about their lives, part of him knew there was much he chose to overlook for fear of becoming overwhelmed by the possible reality of their situation.

"To be honest, I think your efforts to avoid being alarmist could mislead everyone. I think these boar attacks are a sideshow and perhaps running into this group of men in Dartmouth was the wake-up call, and not a moment too soon. If you downplay the situation, even for laudable reasons, you may leave us wide open to a far greater danger than the boar. When you present your report the entire island will be listening, one way or another. If you leave it as written, you'll miss an opportunity and may well be doing all of us a grave disservice."

The fire in her eyes underscored the conviction in her words. Rachel knew she had said more than enough, so she left Sam to make his decisions as they ate in silence.

Sam left later that morning for Newport with Giselle, one of Jake's blind wives, and her young son for company. Giselle was their fastest braille writer at the farm and had agreed to attend the forum and make notes to share with the others. She had a sunny personality, seemingly unaffected by her blindness, and their journey passed quickly as they both entertained her inquisitive four-year-old. Mary was already working in the forum building when they arrived, and immediately typed Sam's report. By early afternoon it had been copied on her ancient roneo machine and distributed to all the other members of the forum. Before the meeting was scheduled to begin, Sam found himself with the unusual experience of a few hours to himself and so decided to pay a visit to the family of Naomi Taylor, who had been killed by boar a few days before he had left for Dartmouth. Naomi's funeral was scheduled for later in the week and Sam hoped to attend. He still felt a pang of guilt over her death; had he gone with her as she had requested, Naomi might still be alive. But, then again, he might have been killed alongside her.

His plan to visit Naomi's home was triggered by the discovery of the lure used in the attack on his own farm. In the aftermath of the first attack, when Naomi had so earnestly asked him to accompany her to the next whenever it arose, he had been aware that she had found evidence she had wanted him to witness. Sam guessed Naomi had a close relationship with Linda Hue, in both a working and personal sense, and at the farm where she had lived she had no husband or partner. However, her friends were happy to allow him access to her study.

He had no idea what he was searching for. Her desk seemed to have been left untouched since the night of her death. Her journal, with daily entries of farm visits to inspect crops and animal problems, lay open, incomplete on the day she had been tragically killed. He wondered where she might have recorded any suspicions she had harboured that led her to ask Sam to join her immediately after any subsequent attacks. Working back through her journal, he carefully read her spidery handwriting for the detailed entries of the previous week, the period prior to the first boar attack. Nothing appeared to arouse his attention; only early signs of rust in a wheat crop, lameness in sheep, mild fever in a group of pigs; all meticulously listed and recorded, along with remedies and recommendations. It was all a sad reminder of the loss her untimely death represented to all of them.

Sam turned his attention to a notepad on Naomi's desk. She was an idle scribbler; its pages filled with ideas for remedies created from their limited resources; association diagrams for medical causes and effects; nothing that seemed exceptional to Sam. Examination of several manila files, scattered on the desk revealed nothing of interest. He leant back in her chair, staring at the ceiling in search of inspiration, an aimless glance coming to rest on a partially hidden wastebin, half full of discarded paper. Slowly, he removed the contents, unfurling and flattening the screwed up pieces of paper. Fortunately, Naomi hadn't torn up the things she discarded. Most were lists and notes to remind her of the never ending list of work commitments. But one stood out; it contained a series of random sketches. One depicted what Sam thought resembled a flat-bottomed punt he had seen on a visit to Cambridge in what now felt like another world. The boat was linked by an arrow to what was most probably the depiction of a boar. This was followed by many crossings out, things either badly drawn or irrelevant but beneath them was a crudely drawn house, sprouting long vertical lines. Sam couldn't see the connection, but the illustration was marked by something embossed from the page that had covered it. Sam switched on the desk light, holding up the paper to cast the imprint into shadow. Two words appeared written in bold capitals.

'Aerials. Why?'

Puzzled and intrigued, he searched the bin for the imprint page. Were the two pages connected? He had no idea and the missing cover page wasn't to be found. He sat staring at the impression, trying to see a relevance. Nothing would come to mind, yet instinct said it meant something. Or was that just wishful thinking? Almost without thinking Sam folded the paper, tucking it carefully into his inside jacket pocket. He felt a pang of guilt, as if removing evidence from a crime scene, though he had no idea why it should feel that way.

Sam paused at the lectern and gathered his notes. The forum and the public gathered in the hall had listened to his report in sombre mood and he prepared himself to face their questions. As he had planned, Sam had presented his report without elaboration or speculation, including the attack by boar at the petrol station and his brief contact with the feral boy. As Rachel had insisted, he had changed the tenor of his words to imply a direct connection between the boar attacks and the violent gang they had encountered in Dartmouth, though the truth was that if he was questioned there was no clear evidence to support his statement. As he waited for questions to begin, his knowledge of the relationship between Teri and Ryan pricked his conscience. If he kept his silence, he could only hope Ruth had spoken with them and made them see the serious risks they were taking.

Albert Jamieson restricted the number of questions he would allow, suspecting correctly that most of Sam's answers could only be guesswork. Instead he proposed that the forum security sub-committee should meet the following day to examine all the reports from Dartmouth in more detail. Sam wound up with a commendation of bravery for Ruth, and a note for the minutes of the high professional conduct displayed by Helen, and Dave Bartlett. There was little to be offered in recognition beyond entering their names in the official records, hoping that at some time in a better future, their successors would honour their lives and sacrifices.

It was a night for reports; Helen and Dave followed with their individual presentations, which dealt more with a review of tactics and equipment than recommendations on improvements if similar ventures were to be repeated. Standing with her arm in a sling and her head displaying a large square plaster, Helen's request for an armoured wheelhouse needed little further endorsement. Dave criticised squad training, adding a strong endorsement for the testing and manufacture of Lorna's explosive bullets that he had seen since returning. He also commended Ruth, recommending her for training as a squad leader with immediate effect.

That seemed to wind things up. Much needed to be discussed and a course of action agreed, but that would follow in subsequent days. Stiff from sitting, people began to stand up and, as chairs scraped on the floor, Dave Bartlett raised a hand, calling for silence. Sam noticed how yellow his fingers were, stained by the endless flow of unfiltered cigarettes.

"One final thing I want to add before we close. Some of you will already have heard that a young woman was rescued, at the very last minute, from the clutches of the thugs who were chasing her. I have to say, this action was undertaken by Sam Morten with complete disregard for his own safety. It doesn't bear thinking about what would have happened if the girl, or Sam for that matter, had been captured. I therefore request the forum make a specific commendation to Sam Morten for his personal bravery."

To Sam's embarrassment, an expanding ripple of applause filled the hall. Faces smiled in his direction, heads nodded; it was a good news story that made everyone feel uplifted. Towards the back of the hall, Sam could see Giselle making her braille notes, as stunned as he was by his public endorsement. He tried hard to smile in gratitude, but he felt his stomach drop like a stone; there was one person who would definitely not appreciate what he had done. Rachel.

"Care for a nightcap before you leave?"

Albert Jamieson caught Sam's attention as he moved towards the exit. Giselle had already left with a group of friends who would drop her off as they passed the farm and, already delayed, Sam was anxious to get home to explain Bartlett's announcement before Giselle told them. But he felt he couldn't ignore Albert's request and Sam entered his office to find him pouring a measure of Scotch into two crystal glasses.

"There are a few perks for being chairman and a bottle of Scotch every now and then happens to be one of them. Water?"

Sam nodded his head. He wasn't a Scotch drinker but sensed Albert wanted company. Albert walked towards a leather chair and raised his glass.

"To a successfully accomplished mission."

"More a close run thing than a success."

The Scotch burned Sam's throat, bringing tears to his eyes. Both men regarded one another in silence, savouring the warm glow of the Scotch and a log fire in the open fireplace.

"Bartlett's commendation for your actions is well deserved, though next time, let someone else take the risk. We can ill afford to lose you."

Sam grinned. "Anyone would have done it. You can't sit idly by and watch an innocent woman be brutally assaulted."

"Bartlett told Rigby that you also spared the life of one of the ringleaders of this gang." Albert had a spark of mischief in his eyes.

"I didn't see any purpose in wilful killing. To do so makes us just as bad them and anyway, I doubt we've seen the last of them, so it might help to have someone at a disadvantage to negotiate with when the time comes."

"So you think we'll come across them again? I thought their fiefdom operated only towards the north of England."

Sam shrugged. "I think this group are a raiding party, off marauding some way from home. John Evans said he picked up their radio messages with some sort of headquarters, which must have been in the south of England for John to be able to hear their signals."

Albert looked thoughtful, reached for the Scotch bottle and topped up their glasses.

"Do you have any thoughts you want to share? Off the record, that is."

"Only gut instinct. I don't like coincidences."

Albert raised his eyebrows. "Go on."

"These boar attacks; they're too regular. Boar seldom organise themselves into large groups, and each attack has almost the same number. I don't buy that. My logic suggests someone is behind them; manipulating them to attack us."

"Any evidence for your suspicions; gut instinct apart?"

Sam paused for a sip of Scotch.

"The boar tracks that led to our farm followed a straight line to a lane that crosses our land. It runs to a dead-end and down to the main road at the other end. There seemed to have been lots of activity in the lane where tyre tracks stopped and the tyre treads are very different from anything we have on our lorries or trailers."

Albert sat in thought for a moment.

"There is a link between other attacks and their proximity to nearby beaches. Naomi Taylor found evidence of furrows in the sand or shingle where flat-bottomed boats, such as military landing craft, could have come ashore, but so far, in every case the next high tide washes away the evidence before we can investigate it."

Sam went to a large bay window with a broad panoramic view to the south of the island. There was a time when necklaces of white and yellow lights would have sparkled in the darkness. Now, all was blackness, illuminated only by moonlight, as mankind's stamp on the landscape was progressively erased. He turned to face Albert, well aware his next words would bring to life their worst fears.

"There's more, Albert. We've made a plaster imprint of the tyre treads before the rain washed them away."

Albert nodded, watching Sam carefully over the rim of his glass.

"That's only part of the picture. The boar made a direct line from the lane to the farm without deviation. They specifically attacked the only house where our ditches hadn't been completed. Boar are cunning, but not that clever, and I don't like coincidences, as I said, especially when a sack of putrid meat was found hidden against the main door of the house they attacked. Someone must have lured them there, someone who knows the island well and I'm afraid it amounts to clear evidence that what we hoped would never arise, is actually happening. These attacks are organised, or at least coordinated, by someone here."

Albert sat with his eyes closed as the enormity of Sam's words made his burden ever heavier to bear.

"You realise that if this comes out it will rip apart the fragile fabric we've worked so hard to build. Neighbour will turn against neighbour in suspicion and it won't be boar that we fear, it will be one another, which means we end up doing the job for them. Does anyone else know about this?"

"Not at the moment, though it's only a question of time before everyone at Sky Farm pieces the evidence together. I suspect Naomi Taylor came across something just before she died, though I don't think she had chance to tell anyone or leave a record of her suspicions."

Albert pursed his lips and shook his head.

"You know we're bound by our constitution not to keep this secret?"

Sam nodded. "That's what worries me. We could argue that the evidence is largely speculative and we didn't release it until we had something concrete."

"No, we must tell the forum as soon as possible. I can't tolerate the creation of an inner clique which excludes information from others. That will bring down the entire structure of trust."

Sam was thoughtful for a moment.

"Look, perhaps the evidence needs filtering. I'm the only source of the information at the moment and I could ask for an in-camera session of the security sub-committee. That way, I've shared my suspicions with the forum in a way that could keep things confidential until we know more or have tracked down the traitor."

Albert flinched at his final phrase; the very thought of 'the enemy within' undermined everything he had worked for during the past five years.

"I've called for a meeting of the security sub-committee for tomorrow evening to discuss the implications from Dartmouth. As you were the forum representative on the operation, it seems logical for you to chair the meeting. Then you can bring up this matter under any other business. That gives us twenty-eight days before we must share it with the rest of the forum, unless the committee members vote otherwise."

Sam thought about Albert's words. There were six sub-committee members and a rotating chairman, who held the casting vote in the event of a tie. It was risky but the only legitimate way they could hold things together. He downed the last of the Scotch in his glass.

"So be it. It's the best we can do. Meanwhile, I have an idea we could follow in the hunt for our attacker, but I'll need clearance for more resources for John Evans."

Albert smiled for the first time in a while and opened the leather folder on his desk. He found a typed sheet and placed his signature on the bottom before handing it to Sam. It was the warrant for the additional resources John had requested to advance his pet project for the installation of the island-wide radio service.

"It's not a lot, but it should enable John to help you while he gets his broadcast system up and running. Keep things under wraps, I dread to think what could happen if this comes out before we've caught whoever is involved. And you've got four weeks to find them, Sam."

There was a glint in his eye as he spoke.

"Just don't bend the law too far in the process."

# THIRTEEN

Sam was tired when he arrived at the farm in the early hours, only to find that his horse refused to enter the stable. He had borrowed a young colt from the stables in Newport. Despite the darkness, the journey home had been quicker than usual, the horse nervously excited by shadows in the darkness. All had been well until they entered the farmyard. Whether it was the smell of other unknown horses or an unfamiliar barn, Sam was at a loss. The colt dug his hooves in, obstinately refusing to move. With his patience tried, Sam lost any sympathy he might have had for the young horse, which only made matters worse as the commotion disturbed the other horses in the stable.

"You can't stay outside all night you silly mutt," he half shouted in exasperation, using his shoulder to try and force the colt towards a vacant stall.

"Shouting won't get him to cooperate."

Claire appeared out of the darkness, brushed passed him and took the reins from his hands.

"You sound tired and grumpy with him; where's the stall?" She had taken Sam by surprise, appearing seemingly out of nowhere.

"To the left ten paces, then left again," Sam muttered, now adding surprise to his tired and grumpy feelings.

Claire paused for a moment, whispering to the horse, her head pressed against the colt's cheek just below his ear. The horse shook his head and whinnied, conspiring to agree that his rider was an idiot, before allowing her to lead him into the empty stall. Despite her blindness, Claire removed the saddle with a heave and dropped it at Sam's feet.

"Would you put that in the tackroom while I get him something to eat. How far have you come?"

"From Newport; about eight miles. The hay baskets are over here."

Sam took her hand and noticed, momentarily, a repeat of the tingling sensation.

"Can you find a blanket; he needs a rub down and cover up; it's a chilly night," Claire said, feeling sweat on the flanks of the colt.

They worked together and it took barely ten minutes to settle the horse in his new home.

"At least he's comfortable for the night, which is more than you'll be; the house is locked as Rachel didn't expect you home. Have you got your keys?"

Sam could detect a note of amusement in Claire's voice.

"The forum ran late. Did Giselle get home safely?" he asked apprehensively. He hadn't expected to be so late and had left his keys at the farm.

"She came straight to the farmhouse, full of excited tales of how you had rescued me. It seems she had spent the evening sitting with Ruth who had seen most of what happened. Giselle sounded very proud of you."

'But Rachel won't be,' the thought ran anxiously in his head.

"Are you okay?" Claire continued. "You sound tired and there's a dark tone in your voice."

"I'm fine. There's been no time to rest since Dartmouth. But what are you doing up in the early hours? Can't you sleep?"

"I woke when the horse entered the yard and guessed it must be you. If you can't get into the house where are you going to sleep for the rest of the night?"

"There are hay bales stored on the floor over the stables. I'll get my bedroll from the saddle and spend the night there."

It would be a poor substitute, but better than nothing, and while Sam collected a few things from the saddle bags, Claire disappeared, returning a few minutes later with a jug of milk and some stale bread and cheese.

"It's a poor supper but it's all I can find without waking Lorna and it's better than going to bed on an empty stomach."

Sam realised that he hadn't eaten for most of the day and Albert Jamieson's whisky sat heavily in his stomach. Despite the meagre fare, he was touched by the kindness of her gesture. He drank straight from the jug and in a repeat of their previous evening, sat beside Claire on a straw bale. The bread and cheese were dry and stale but at least he wouldn't be hungry.

"Is there anything in particular that's worrying you?" she asked him, probing with concern.

Sam rubbed the back of his neck; the constant barrage of problems had made him stiff with tension.

"Too many unanswered questions. Just before you arrived in Dartmouth, I discovered a young boy, living rough in the ruins. I think he was alone, I never saw any evidence of anyone else. He lived barely more than a feral existence, hardly recognisable as a human being. I made progress towards the end and managed to gain some measure of his confidence, but he slipped away, virtually into thin air. After that, with everything working out the way it did, I wasn't able to go back for him. It leaves me with the ghastly feeling that I was seeing an image of the future for our children if we're not careful."

Claire was thoughtful for a moment.

"So you feel you abandoned him and it hurts your conscience."

"Something like that," Sam replied morosely.

"Has it occurred to you he might not have wanted to be saved?"

"How could anyone not want saving from life in a hell hole like that?"

Claire shrugged. "Everything is changing, not least the psyche of the few human survivors. For some people, our idea of civilisation no longer applies. Take those men on motorbikes for example; I doubt they are the least bit interested in a life governed by rules and regulations, where they have to share with their fellow men. What they want they take, and they'll kill to get it. You might think that in the end it leads to extinction, but I doubt they even care about that. All most survivors care about is living for today. Most think they'll probably die tomorrow anyway."

Behind them, the horse snorted, seemingly in agreement.

"For many," she continued, "the struggle to remain civilised is just too hard. I heard it beginning to happen with the Carters on the farm. Becoming no more than feral, half animal, half human, may well be the only way our species can avoid extinction."

"That's a depressing thought. It's not a world I would want to live in."

"It may well be the way things work out on vast areas of the planet. Pockets of civilisation will survive as long as men like you live and breathe. It could be how our species mutates; one human, the other merely related to us only by distant history and DNA."

For a moment, in the glimmering light, Sam felt defeated by that vision of a future that Claire painted. It was all too overwhelmingly hopeless.

"Surely you don't believe we will surrender to such a dark alternative?"

Claire laughed grimly. "If I did I might as well have done away with myself a while back when everyone I knew had died. Locked in my blindness, unwanted by the Carters, I was in a pretty dark place."

She paused, sliding her arm through his.

"But, like you, I can't give up. I don't know how long my life will be, most probably much shorter than I had once expected, but if I can make some difference, no matter how small, my life will have been worth something. When you rescued me, it made me more certain of that than ever."

For a while as they sat, shoulder to shoulder in silence, Claire was worried she might have been too outspoken and honest. Eventually, Sam moved stiffly and yawned, yet reluctant to release her arm.

"Time we slept. I'll find some bales in the loft for a bed. Thanks for spending some time with me and providing supper."

"You can't save everyone, Sam," Claire said as she collected her guide stick. "And not everyone wants you to, so don't try to carry the weight of the world on your shoulders."

With that, she disappeared into the darkness leaving him with only silence as a companion.


Lorna found Sam asleep the next morning when she came to milk the cows. She made a mug of tea and perched on a bale beside him.

"Late back?"

Sam nodded.

"How are things? I seem to be spending most of my time away from the farm these days."

"It may surprise you, but we're managing pretty well without you," she said with a slight mocking tone. Lorna watched him drink his tea for a moment. "So, we have a hero in our midst. You kept very quiet about that."

Sam put down his cup as he felt a pang of concern spike through him when he remembered the story had already preceded him home with Giselle.

"The entire time in Dartmouth felt tense and ominous; no one event stands out any more than another."

Lorna stood, hearing the bellows of approaching cattle. It was milking time and she was needed to receive the cows.

"Look, it's none of my business, but you may have difficulty convincing Rachel that you didn't take one hell of a risk when you rescued Claire. Those thugs weren't playing at being tough; you wouldn't have had a chance in hell if they had caught you. Don't get me wrong, I like Claire, but I'm not sure Rachel will understand why you haven't told her about all this before she found out."

Having forewarned him, she turned to find her cows, and then hesitated.

"I know you're desperately busy, but you must try to fix things with Rachel. None of us enjoy being around her when she's unhappy with you."

Forewarned indeed, Lorna's honesty didn't tell Sam anything he didn't already know. He spent some time searching the house for Rachel, but everyone was already busy with farm work and the children were at nursery in one of the other houses. Sam felt the growing burden of his forum duties pulling him away from the farm and his family. As he made a cold breakfast from leftovers and ate alone he made a promise to himself to avoid the endless stream of tasks that Albert Jamieson was passing on to him. Only the decision to put Rachel and his family first would heal the growing rift between the two of them. But thereby was the problem. However he tried to look at the situation, threats loomed in every direction. If he turned his back on these dangers to spend more time with his family, it would only endanger them further. In the study he checked the diary for the tasks of the day, noting the red line slashed through his name as his work load had to be shared amongst the others. From the schedule he saw that Rachel was hauling felled logs in the woods, beyond their northern pasture. He felt a spike of alarm; the trees provided ideal cover for any marauding boar that might have escaped the attack on the farm. If Rachel was still mad with him, it might affect her vigilance, leaving her exposed to an ambush.

Sam donned a jacket and saddled *Rowan*, the mare on the farm he preferred to ride. He made sure to put the Sten gun and a fully loaded magazine into the saddle holster. After his experience in Newport, you could never be too careful, even within the farm. The morning air was laced with the tang of salt; nowhere on the island was far from the sea and the suggestion of a warm sunny day lifted his spirits. He resolved to remain contrite when he found Rachel. Sam found her working alone, hauling long felled logs out of the woods with *Samson*, one of their larger work horses. *Samson* wore a heavy leather yoke and harness with lengths of thick chains attached. His large feathery hooves caused little damage to the soft ground beneath the trees, and despite his size the horse could squeeze into places beyond the reach of a tractor. Back at the field edge Rachel had rigged an A-frame hoist and she and *Samson* had already loaded half a dozen cut trunks onto a waiting trailer; an impressive tally so early in the day.

"You're certainly not hanging about," Sam called out as he approached.

Rachel didn't reply, preoccupied with lifting a particularly heavy log to slide chains underneath. Sam dropped from his saddle and grasped the free end of the log, braced himself and raised it clear off the ground. With chains tensioned, Rachel then drove several spikes through links on opposite sides of the log and prepared *Samson* to haul it clear.

"So when did you get back?" she called in a diffident tone as she encouraged the horse forward.

"In the early hours. I slept in the hayloft; I hadn't taken my keys as I expected to come back with Giselle. Albert Jamieson asked me to stay behind," he added before she asked.

"We gave up waiting for you. Giselle must have been home several hours earlier." Conspicuously, she made no mention of the issue foremost in her mind but her words were tight and clipped.

Together they stopped by the A-frame, connected the chains to the lifting block and re-positioned *Samson*. Five minutes later the log lay with the others on the trailer.

"I brought coffee in a flask," Sam said. "How about having a break for a minute? The trailer is at the limit for *Samson* to haul back to the farm and anyway, I need to apologise."

"For what? Oh, the part where you omitted to tell me of your reckless exploits when it seems the rest of the entire island already knew."

Rachel had her arms folded, her face a blank mask.

"If that's what's upsetting you, yes. Look, don't turn away, at least hear my side of it."

Rachel snatched the flask from his saddle bag; in her haste to leave the house she had forgotten to bring anything to drink with her. She sat on a stump and poured herself a cup. She didn't offer one to Sam.

"I know you're angry and I'm sorry."

"Which part are you sorry for? Deliberately not telling me or almost getting yourself killed?"

Sam shook his head. "Look, what I did was no big deal. With everything else that happened in Dartmouth, I didn't see it as significant. There were countless occasions when things became difficult; this is just one amongst many. I'm not trying to conceal anything, Rachel, I just haven't had time to tell you the complete story. The way this has come out has blown things completely out of all proportion."

"Then just set it in context will you."

Sam felt uncomfortable. Fate had dealt him a lousy hand and the person who had needed to know the complete picture was Rachel. Now she had found out from someone else and any explanation he made would sound feeble.

"I've already told you that Dartmouth was a desolate place; we were ambushed by a group of boar and completely blind-sided. It was only the courage of Ruth that prevented a disaster. But there were signs of life amongst the ruins; we only saw one lone person, a young boy I think, but it felt as if eyes were everywhere and we could have been attacked at any moment. For sure, the mainland is not a safe place, and I don't mean just from boar."

After a moment's thought Rachel asked, "And you knew the men on motorbikes were a threat before they arrived?"

Sam missed the trap in the question and nodded.

"John Evans was picking up radio signals. We knew they had caught up with the group we were waiting for and what they had done to the others they had captured."

"So you knew what to expect when they caught up with you in Dartmouth?" Rachel had a grim smile on her lips, which confused Sam.

"Well, yes. It was pretty clear they would come looking for a fight, though we had no idea why."

"And you knew you were outnumbered?"

"Possibly. Most probably. Why?"

"And despite the likely consequences, you still took the risk to save a group of survivors to whom you have no allegiance and who had got themselves in this mess in the first place by their own stubborn stupidity."

There was an angry impatience in Rachel's words that Sam couldn't understand.

"That's a bit harsh. They had no idea these thugs would turn up when they did," he answered defensively.

"Really? So you don't think there is any connection between their radio pleas for us to rescue them and the men on motorbikes suddenly arriving in Devon? You said yourself they were a raiding party; why didn't they just stick to theft and plunder, with a bit of rape and murder thrown in?"

Sam felt disorientated by the cynical tone to her words. Their conversation was taking him in a direction he hadn't expected and he felt uncertain where it was leading.

"Remember, we knew these men were around before we agreed to a rescue mission. My brief was to sail to Dartmouth and rescue these people with the least risk to our crew as possible. I would say we achieved that. It was a close run thing I'll grant you, but we pulled it off with no one seriously hurt. Rachel, we can't just run away the moment a few risks need to be taken."

"And the next time?"

"What?"

"How will you handle the next time this need arises?"

"There won't be a next time, not that I can see anyway."

"So your brief was to undertake a rescue with the minimum amount of risk to the crew?"

"Yes."

Something in her tone made him feel wary.

"So where was the instruction that you, more than anyone else, were to place yourself in a situation of grave danger, without regard to the consequences?"

"I never acted without considering the consequences. Can you imagine what they would have done with Claire if they had caught her?"

"What if they had caught you both? You're saying you thought about Claire when you made your decision, but obviously not us, your family. Did you spare a moment to think what would have happened to me and the children if you had been killed? No, of course you didn't, you were too busy playing the role of knight in shining armour to worry about us."

Her final words had risen to a shout of anger, which spooked *Samson* standing beside them, and Sam only just caught his reins as the horse backed into the A-frame and brought it crashing down. Rachel's words had stung Sam in a way he hadn't experienced in all the time he had known her and as he struggled to steady the horse he felt a surge of emotion, as though he was losing his grip on a precipitous slope, the ground sliding away beneath his feet. Was it simply the injustice of her accusations, or his own guilt? He couldn't be certain which was correct. Silence stood between them. Rachel snatched the reins from Sam and led the horse to the front of the trailer, clearly angry with herself for upsetting the horse whilst blaming Sam at the same time for causing it all.

"I'll take this load back to the farm," she said with a note of resignation. "I suggest you set up the A-frame again while I'm gone."

Sam could only stand aside, knowing if he tried to stop Rachel in her current mood he would only make things worse.

"What can I do to put things right?" he asked; his words felt heavy.

"Make the right decisions."

"Rachel, I couldn't just stand by and watch an innocent woman be raped and murdered. I'm not made that way."

For a moment she didn't answer, distracting herself with harnessing *Samson*.

"That's just my point. You didn't know they would have harmed Claire; they would have more likely raped her I'll grant you, but kept her for their own fun, but I doubt they would have murdered her, whereas you … they would have killed you without a second's hesitation."

Rachel turned away to lead the trailer back to the farm.

"You can't base your life on the values that existed five years ago, Sam; the world is not like that anymore, it's dog eat dog; brutal and callous but ultimately only the toughest will survive. If you and Albert Jamieson don't realise that, well, there's not much hope for any us."

She turned and led *Samson* away without waiting for a reply.

Sam had re-erected the A-frame before Rachel returned. He scribbled a brief note to her and pinned it to one of the posts where she would be sure to see it. He was behind with his projections for their forthcoming crop harvest and needed to complete them before the next forum meeting. Anyway, trying to reason with Rachel in her current mood would only risk pouring petrol onto the flames of their misunderstanding.

A shower of cold rain swept across the farm as he rode around the fields. His boots slid in brown mud when he dismounted to count the plant density, measure heights, and compare leaf shades against a colour swatch. Despite a mild winter, all were less than the previous year, emphasising that the crops were in urgent need of fertilizer that was in such short supply. At the north boundary of their top field the land rose to its highest point. From here, with the rain clearing, Sam could see across the Solent, towards the mainland, now a dark line in the distance. He eased himself in the saddle, gently stroking the neck of the horse as he contemplated the potential for challenges that lay hidden beyond the wave-whipped waters that separated them. For five years that water had provided their protection. They had become complacent with its security. No boar could ever cross the fast currents surging between them even at Hurst Castle, where the Solent was tantalisingly narrow. They had anticipated that a few might one day come their way, but nothing prepared them for the numbers that were now pitted against them. The rain was soon replaced by brilliant shafts of sunlight, lancing through gaps in the bulbous grey clouds that illuminated the land below him in a palette of vivid greens. He could see the slash of the River Yar winding its path to the coast, the abandoned towns of Yarmouth and Freshwater in the distance gaining a brief moment of their lost past in the pale sunshine.

Rachel had shocked him. She seemed to have somehow lost her natural light-hearted optimism, and cynicism had begun to replace it. He had seen it in others before, exhausted by the relentless struggle to survive, gradually surrendering the will to go on. He felt terribly responsible; his forum duties and the recent challenges occupied increasing amounts of his time, leaving Rachel to cope alone. Things would have to change; others would have to be asked to step up and shoulder the load to free up more time for him. He had ten months remaining until the biannual forum elections took place so he made the decision, there and then, not to stand for re-election. Perhaps, when he told Rachel, it would restore her usual sparkle and repair the horrible rift that had come between them ever since he had been sent to Dartmouth.

Just then, the sun eclipsed behind the clouds and the breeze cooled to a chill that made him shiver. Whether that came from the breeze or a feeling of ominous foreboding, he couldn't be certain.

# FOURTEEN

The security sub-committee meeting took barely an hour to agree that a reconnaissance of the mainland must take place at the first opportunity. Sam chaired the meeting as Albert Jamieson had requested, Mary took the minutes, with Connor Rigby, Dave Bartlett, and John Evans included for specialist advice.

"Okay." Sam checked his notes.

"We all agree that some method of reconnaissance must be made of the mainland coast to see if we can locate where the boar attacks are originating from. That's all well and good, but how do we set about the operation and when can it be carried out?"

Chris Jones, one of the three women on the committee, raised a hand.

"It seems our only option is to use one of the planes. We've only two serviceable helicopters and we've got more pilots for planes. This isn't without risk; John has already told us he's heard fragments of radio messages from the other side of the Solent, so if someone is working against us over there they won't be too happy about us spying on them. We can't afford to lose a helicopter on a mission that a plane could carry out just as well. As a pilot myself and a committee member, I volunteer to fly the mission, though I'd need an assistant with a camera just in case we find anything."

A murmur of support seemed to come from the others.

"There is the option of *Lupin*," Sam ventured. "She should be repaired in a few days and we can arm and protect her well."

Rigby interrupted him. "That only works if we could build a flat deck on the stern to fly the helicopter and we don't have time or resources to do that quickly. An aerial reconnaissance is the only way to have any hope of seeing what might be going on."

"One other thing," said Craig, the only trained meteorologist they had. "The air pressure has been high for almost a week now, but there are signs it's beginning to weaken. If we miss the next few days, it might be several weeks before we get another clear period to fly."

Sam nodded thoughtfully. "Can we set something up in say, forty-eight hours?"

"We need a serviceable plane, fuel, and a volunteer with a camera," Rigby stated. "For safety, no flying below three thousand feet and *Lupin* must put to sea in case there's an emergency. Let's do this while the weather holds. How accurately can you make a prediction, Craig?"

"Two, maybe three days ahead at best."

For a few minutes Sam allowed the points to be debated before calling them to order for a vote. Six hands were raised in support of a reconnaissance using one of their Cessnas. Sam dictated a note for Albert Jamieson and asked Mary to deliver it while he closed the first part of the meeting, releasing Rigby and Bartlett to make a start on the arrangements. He asked John Evans to remain behind.

"I know you're not a committee member, John, but I need you to participate in the next part of the meeting which will be held 'in-camera'. That binds you to complete secrecy for twenty-eight days. Are you okay with that?"

John nodded, unable to mask a quizzical expression.

Sam waited for Mary to return. "Good. Doors locked?"

Craig left his seat and turned the key.

"Right. Apologies for the classified nature of what we're about to discuss. You'll see why in just a few minutes."

Sam paused and withdrew the plaster cast from his rucksack. It took only a few minutes to describe the evidence they had discovered following the attack on Sky Farm. Everyone sat in stunned silence, uncomfortable with the thought that someone might be working against them. Chris Jones spoke for what they all thought.

"If this is true, that person could be a member of the forum. However you look at it, whoever is involved is complicit in murder and directly responsible for the deaths of more than twenty of our people. Isn't that what we're all thinking? If this gets out, it will tear our community apart."

"That's why I've called this part of the meeting in private," Sam added in a serious voice. "It's hard enough for us to live with the possible facts. If it becomes common knowledge before we root out the culprit there's a serious risk that people and hamlets will turn on one another in fear and suspicion. So, the question is, what are we going to do about it before things get out of hand?"

"Should we not consider the details you've presented as circumstantial. It's just possible that your evidence is arriving at the wrong conclusions." Angela, an eternal optimist, tried to put the case for an alternative interpretation.

Simon Grey, more of a hawk than Angela, interrupted, "There were rumours a few nights ago, prior to the attack on the Moore's Farm, that someone said they saw lights and heard the sound of a large motor running less than a mile from the farmhouse. The claim got overlooked amid the drama of the attack but I think we should go back and look for more evidence."

"Well, we have nothing concrete but it's more than just suspicions." Sam said looking pointedly at the plaster cast of the tyre print. "And there is still the issue of the lure for boar that we found against one of our farm buildings. I suggest we set a timescale, say a week, and make our own discreet enquiries. We need an excuse to check on all the lorries operating on the island and see if anything comes up. Meanwhile, can any of our small planes be flown at night?" Sam's question was directed to Chris.

"Planes yes, but we've only got one pilot qualified and safe to land and take off on instruments. Why?"

"The boar attacks come in darkness. A plane, even flying at height, should see moving headlights and help us check on anyone driving around at night. We could then direct a Landrover to stop and check what's going on." Sam laughed drily. "You never know, we just might turn up a lorry full of boar."

Sam asked John to wait as the meeting dispersed.

"You've said before that you can pick up fragments of messages between the groups we encountered on the mainland?"

At first John looked surprised by the question. "Only weak signals, seldom anything that makes a lot of sense."

"Far off?"

"Not necessarily. Their equipment doesn't seem to be any more powerful than ours. Most of the signals would be within a fifty-mile radius."

"So not far from the coast on the other side of the Solent."

"Yes, possibly, though I've never heard any mention of their location. It's usually about problems with motorbikes or a night of drinking if they've found a store of alcohol or found some poor community they've come across." John shuddered.

"Nothing about us? Or boar?"

John shook his head, anticipating Sam's direction of thought.

"Sorry I can't be any help there. I do keep a log of what I hear; it might be useful if you looked through it."

Sam sat in thought for a few moments.

"How close are you to covering the entire island by radio?"

He knew it was John's pet project, held back by limited resources and the recent trip to Dartmouth.

"Closer than I was; the extra fuel allowance the forum gave me helped to survey locations for masts and hunt for equipment."

John was one of the few island members excused from farming duties, his time was taken up with repairing and installing electrical equipment from their meagre resources.

"You travel most of the island. Have you ever seen any large aerials, apart from your own? I'm thinking of the northern part of the island in particular."

John shook his head. "No one would have need for one; it's been years since anything from long range has been heard. Most of my listening hours are just a monotone of static. It's like hunting for a needle in a haystack. I'm afraid the world is a silent place," he added.

Sam nodded. The day of radio for communication and entertainment had been left behind long ago. "Just the same, I'd be grateful if you'd keep your eyes open. Keep it to yourself if you see anything, but let me or Chairman Jamieson know as soon as you find anything unusual."

John weighed his words for a moment.

"Do you think someone on the island is hiding the use of a radio from the rest of us? I've never heard anything from close by, or any island based signals."

Sam drummed his fingers on the table top. "You can't cover all the frequencies every hour of the day. But if these boar attacks are coming from beyond the island and are coordinated with the help of someone here, a radio link would be essential. If you do see something, keep your distance. If anyone here is involved, they're covering the tracks very carefully and they've already conspired in the deaths of more than twenty innocent people so far."

Rigby caught Sam as he left.

"We're on for tomorrow. Take-off shortly after sunrise to get the benefit of shadows for photographs. Craig predicts the weather will hold until late morning at least, though the air pressure is beginning to drop already."

Sam nodded; the sooner it took place the better.

"Is that all okay with Chris?"

"Cromford is flying, not Chris. He's ex-RAF and more experienced. Jean Haynes will accompany him to take photographs if they see anything."

Sam felt a pang of unease. He had no doubt of George Cromford's flying ability but he had a reputation for being hot-headed, which probably appealed to Rigby.

"Take-off at six in the morning. We'll fuel the plane tonight and check radio links with John Evans. The flight plan has been agreed; the aim is to fly the mainland coastline from east to west, from Selsey to Milford via Southampton Water. Cromford doesn't think it will take more than a couple of hours, so he should be done well before the weather starts to break up."

Rigby was gone before Sam could comment. For some reason, he wished Chris Woods could have flown the mission, but without Rigby's support it wouldn't be possible to change things.

The meetings had continued later than Sam had hoped, so he borrowed one of the cars the forum kept spare for essential use. He found keys for an ageing Vauxhall Velox and felt a tinge of nostalgia as he opened the driver's door. His father had owned a similar model when Sam was a boy, and the smell of the interior brought back a flood of long forgotten memories.

Dusk was settling on the landscape as he set out for home. The Velox boasted a radio, quite a luxury in its day. Out of curiosity Sam switched it on. As the set lit up, he noticed it was tuned to the home service. In another time and place, the evening news or music would have kept him company; now the channels were silent except for the constant hiss of static.

As he drove he played with the tuning dial, vainly hoping for a surprise. The unfilled potholes in the road surface now limited his speed, but it was still quicker than horseback. Sam flicked his headlights to full beam and on impulse he took a sudden right turn onto a single track lane. It would save him several miles and he might make it home in time to join everyone for dinner and spend some time with Rachel.

Without the lights on full beam, Sam would never have seen her, set back as she was a short distance from the road amongst the trees. In an instant he had passed, not wishing to believe what his fleeting glance had told him. He braked hard and the Velox shuddered to a halt, sliding on the broken road surface. Sam reversed a short distance and skewed the car to shine the lights into a small copse. He hadn't been mistaken. A forlorn shape of a woman was hanging from a tree branch. Death shadowed them every day, but confronting it unexpectedly was always a shock. He sat stunned for a moment, watching the pathetic form swing like a pendulum on a rope as the evening breeze swirled through the trees. Reaching for rifle and knife, all thoughts of home and dinner evaporated. His days were long and hard and, for a second, he was tempted to find someone else to deal with this sad tragedy. He could report what he had seen in the morning; a few hours wouldn't make any difference. Then it crossed his mind that this poor woman might still be alive. Running hard, he quickly covered the short distance in hope if not expectation. In the light of his torch, the body of a young woman was hanging tantalisingly short of the ground, her long hair had matted around her face, her tongue swollen and protruding, vacant eyes stared accusingly into the night. Sam guessed she hadn't been dead for very long; hungry crows were yet to find her. Although he knew most of the neighbouring hamlets hereabouts, he didn't recognise the woman.

Finding a suicide hit even a stranger with the pain of grief and waste, and Sam set about cutting her down to care for her remains. Drawing his knife, he looked around for something to stand on. There must have been something that she had used to stand on before she jumped with the noose around her neck but to his surprise, there was nothing; he would have to climb the gallows tree and cut the rope from above. Sam was desperate to get her down and stop the obscenity of the back and forth pendulum swing, yet he hesitated. His torch followed the line of the rope above. He expected to find it knotted around a higher branch but instead it passed over in a continuous loop, descending at an acute angle to ground level behind a nearby tree. A black cloud of doubt seemed to settle in around him.

Something was very wrong here. The rope was cross-twisted around the stout trunk of a tree and secured to a large stake driven into the ground a short distance beyond. As he shone his torch at the body, the hairs on the back of his neck prickled with fear. What he had stumbled upon wasn't suicide at all. The woman had been hanged deliberately.

Sam cut the rope at ground level and lowered the woman to the ground as gently as possible. He left the rope and its anchor in place as evidence. He checked for a pulse but her cold body was long past any chance of revival. It was a struggle to carry her body to the Velox, but fortunately the rear doors were wide which helped him to lay the stiffening body across the rear seats.

As he started the engine Sam recalled that Linda Hue lived on a farm fairly close to Newport. The fuel gauge on the car wasn't working, which added to the tension of the situation, so he headed back towards Newport by the way he had come and hoped he wouldn't have to spend hours trying to locate Linda.

It took many miles and several wrong turns before he found her. Linda was already dressed for bed but changed immediately when he explained what he had found.

"We must take the body straight to my lab. We can collect Doctor Morgan on the way; I need him to validate the cause of death."

The small clinic on the island was closed at night and it suited Sam's purpose to keep his discovery to themselves until they knew more about the cause of death. It was essential as few people as possible knew what he had found until the forum had been told.

They carried the body on a stretcher into Linda's lab. Working with a combination of speed and dignity, Linda undressed the body on an examination table and covered her with a white sheet while they waited for Doctor Morgan to arrive.

"Somehow suicide seems the saddest form of death," Linda mused, staring at the lifeless form in front of them. "Perhaps futility and waste exaggerate the act."

"We all fight our demons; some just get overwhelmed by them," Sam said. "Before Doctor Morgan arrives," he continued, "could you check under her nails, just to see if there is any blood."

Linda looked at him questioningly but found two small dishes and a scalpel. The woman appeared to have dirt under her nails. Most people had to undertake manual work and their nails often were forgotten, even amongst women. Linda worked quickly, taking a sample from the fingers of both hands before adding distilled water to the tiny powdered scrapings.

"Care to share with me what's on your mind?"

Sam was silent, watching the samples dissolve as Linda gently agitated the dishes. It didn't take long for the solution to stain into a deep burgundy colour. Blood?

"Check her body carefully for scratches and bruises, Linda. I didn't see any as you undressed her." For a moment their eyes met. Sam nodded. "I think you might find this wasn't suicide."

When Doctor Morgan arrived, Sam requested that he and Linda examine the body and prepare a report on the cause of death as soon as possible, with the added request that they kept it confidential until the next of kin could be found.

"There doesn't seem to be any ID, but someone usually comes forward as soon as a person goes missing. The forum will organise a search. Perhaps you could share your conclusions as soon as possible with the chairman, even if they're only provisional."

With that, Sam left hastily to find Connor Rigby.

The length of cut rope hung limply from the bough over which Sam had left it. Sam and Rigby stared at the frayed rope strands where he had cut it several hours earlier. The noose lay on a mat of dead leaves below.

"In my haste to cut her free I didn't think to protect any footprints. Mind you, everywhere is covered in leaf litter, so any evidence will be hard to find."

Rigby listened in silence. Their only light was an oil lamp that cast ghostly shadows outside the immediate radius of its yellow glow. Sam had briefed Rigby on what he had found and he now tried to evaluate the scene for himself. In the five years since the island community had been established there had been a few suicides, most commonly amongst those unable to cope with all their loved ones lost or dead. In all that time there had not been a single murder.

"How old is she?" Rigby asked.

"Not sure yet; we've made no identification. Early twenties I would guess. Linda will know soon enough."

Rigby pulled a pad and measuring tape from his bag and made a rough sketch.

"Hold the cut ends of the rope together."

Rigby measured the distance from the base of the noose to the ground.

"Roughly how far was she suspended?"

Sam imagined her toes, writhing frantically for purchase, anything to remove the choking clasp of the noose.

"About a foot of clearance, not much more. If it's not suicide, whoever was responsible for this intended her to suffer," he added with a shudder.

Rigby didn't answer, instead he busied himself with measuring distances and rope angles to complete his sketch of the evidence.

"And there's nothing around from which she could have jumped? Ropes don't shorten or tie themselves back on their own accord."

Rigby turned towards him, features sharply defined in the light of the lantern.

"It's a big ask to believe someone has done this. It's nearly always suicide in the end when you bring the evidence together, despite the emotions that lead you to think otherwise. Don't distort the facts to suit your opinion, Sam."

"There was blood under her nails."

"Doesn't prove she was murdered, even if you find the scratches to match."

"Most suicides we've had have been blind people and this girl was sighted," Sam said.

"How do you know?"

"There was a pair of glasses in her pocket."

Rigby still didn't appear convinced.

"Well, there must be something here we're missing, something that will prove what happened one way or another. We'll have to come back in daylight."

Rigby was tired and they both had an early start ahead of them.

"At the moment, I've more to worry about than an unfortunate suicide. It's hard enough trying to protect and keep everyone else alive to worry over much about the dead," he said with an air of finality intended to wrap things up. He moved slowly away, leaving Sam to collect the lamp.

Sam paused, making one last pass with the lamp in a circle immediately beneath the hanging rope. On the far side, something shone amidst the leaves. He stooped, carefully brushing the brown leaves aside.

"Rigby, wait," he called after him.

With ill-concealed impatience, Rigby returned. "What?"

Sam had cleared a small area of dried leaves with his hand, in the middle of which shone a small brass button, its cap impressed with the swirls of a seashell. On the back of the button was a thin piece of white cotton fabric, its edges torn and frayed. What stood out most strikingly were three brown lines across it. Dried blood.

"What was the girl wearing?" Rigby asked, though he could guess the answer.

"Jumper and trousers. Nothing white and certainly no brass buttons."

Rigby nodded. From his bag he produced tweezers and a small brown envelope. With the tweezers, he raised the fabric to his nose and sniffed it several times before holding it out to Sam. He caught the faint fragrance of perfume, a luxury in their survivalist world. Rigby looked hard at Sam as he dropped it into the envelope.

"Well, if it doesn't belong to the dead girl, we'd better start looking for someone with a torn white blouse with a missing button and scratches around the throat. It seems we have a killer loose on the island."

"And it's a woman."

Sam switched off the engine and lights and left the Velox to coast quietly to a stop. The farmhouse was in darkness, but a quarter-moon shone from a cloudless sky. He parked the car and walked the remaining distance; if there were any boar about he should see them in the moonlight. The house was locked and secured; with five young children and two blind women to protect, Rachel was strict when it came to night security, even if it meant another hungry night on hay bales for Sam. The horses stirred and stomped in their stalls as he passed them and he spent a minute re-positioning bales and laying out his bedroll before taking a bucket to the tap in the yard for a cold wash before a few hours on a lumpy hay mattress.

"Meeting like this is becoming a habit." Claire's voice called softly from the darkness.

"Forum business went on late. I was in two minds to sleep in Newport, but I need to check on things at home and grab a change of clothes." Sam was aware he'd stripped off to wash, not that it would make any difference to Claire.

"Lorna and I thought you might be late back and saved you some dinner; I'm afraid it's cold but it's better than stale bread and cheese. Come up to our rooms; I'll light a candle for you." She left before Sam could reply.

Claire had already memorised the layout of the barn and seemed to move around with almost the agility of the sighted. She heard the creak of the ladder as he climbed, a match flared and lit the kitchen space she shared with Lorna.

"I lit a candle beneath the plate when I heard you return; it will be warm enough if you give it a minute."

"Thank you."

It had been a while since Rachel had the time to consider his personal needs. But then, he had left her to run the farm and raise their children without him. He cast a look towards the curtain screening Lorna's bed space.

"Won't we wake Lorna?" Sam said in a whisper, noticing that Claire had brushed her hair and tied it back with a dark blue ribbon. Her hair reflected gold in the light of the candle.

"She's staying with Gary, the boy she's become very friendly with. They're working on improvements to the bullets to destroy boar. Too many seem to pass straight through their bodies without exploding. Lorna says range is not an issue, so no doubt they'll come up with something better. She said that if the main house is locked you're to use her bed rather than the hay bales."

Sam ate hungrily as they sat side by side in mutual silence.

"Would that be okay with you … I might snore."

"You did the last time we shared a bedroom," Claire teased, reminding him of their night on the deck of *Lupin* while returning from Dartmouth.

"I think you'll find it more comfortable than a hay mattress, though you're welcome to sleep in the stable if you prefer."

Sam yawned in response. In truth he was bone-achingly tired, but, for the moment, he was happy to enjoy a few minutes of company. He cleared the plate and stretched.

"How are things for you? Have you started to settle in?"

"This is paradise after what went before. I sometimes have to pinch myself to be sure it's real and Lorna is endlessly kind and generous. She's already found some equipment for me to start making cheese, but I need more before production can begin. If Rachel will allow me to stay here, that is."

Her final sentence gave Sam a jolt.

"Why shouldn't you stay; we've more than enough space and we need someone with experience to make cheese."

Claire shrugged. "I don't think Rachel likes me very much. I sense she thinks I get in the way of the farm routine."

Sam sighed. "I don't think it's your presence that's the problem. There are huge and unfair demands on Rachel at the moment and I'm not helping things. Once this current situation with boar dies down I'll be able to spend more time here and things will settle. Just be patient and stick close to Lorna; things will come right in the end."

Claire nodded.

"Yes, of course they will. Thank you."

She tried to smile at Sam but her words lacked conviction as she disappeared behind a curtain to find her bed.

# FIFTEEN

For a few brief moments, the Cessna hung motionless in a pale sky, like a searching hawk, black against the golden ball of the rising sun. The wings waggled mischievously as the plane banked steeply towards the north-east. After the clamour of take-off, only the melodic song of a disturbed skylark filled the silence left by the departing plane.

Together, Rigby and Bartlett strode off towards the low building where John Evans had set up his radio room amidst a small forest of aerials, leaving Sam watching the plane disappear towards the eastern horizon, in company with Chris Jones and Albert Jamieson.

"I'll be glad to see them back." Chris spoke for them all. "Why do I feel so anxious?" she asked in self-reflection.

"Cromford is a good pilot, perhaps our best. I'm sure they'll be alright," Albert offered in reassurance, but it didn't lift Sam's feelings of lingering doubt. "There's nothing more to do here until they return and there's tea in the radio room so I suggest we go and join the others."

They filed into a room already jammed with equipment and the other waiting members of the forum. The air was already blue with cigarette smoke, dry voices accompanied by the throb of the generator rumbling noisily just outside. Conversation buzzed around; it was all surprisingly upbeat, encouraged by the feeling of at last doing something positive to counteract the boar attacks.

Sam took a large mug of tea from a tray as he entered. At the far end of the room, John Evans sat at his desk, radio receiver and transmitter arranged in front of him, their luminous dials glimmering through the smoky air. Beside him sat his assistant Jaki with a large wax-coated map covering the entire sweep of the Solent spread out in front of her. A series of red crosses marked the coast of the mainland at regular intervals, each cross numbered for the radio call points for Cromford as he flew over the landmarks. By this method they could plot his position without disclosing it to anyone who might be tuned to their frequency. Sam noticed a large spool-to-spool tape recorder and microphone, set up to record Cromford's radio signals at the flick of a switch. As Sam drank his tea the speaker abruptly interrupted their thoughts.

"Hello Ant Hill, this is Grasshopper, turning two hundred and seventy degrees at stage two." Cromford's distorted voice gave notice that he had crossed the Solent safely and was turning westwards above Selsey Bill.

"Roger, Grasshopper. Fly safe."

John was worried; suspicious that the men they had confronted at Dartmouth had worked out their frequency and could listen to their radio messages. A measure of basic security seemed only common sense, though even that would be pointless if someone close to the forum was passing information across the Solent.

Following Cromford's message, conversation continued in subdued tones. The mainland had become largely unknown territory in recent years and who knew what dangers might lay in their path. Sam stood to one side, his focus of attention straining to catch any periodic reports from the Cessna. They all paused to listen when Cromford circled the plane for a while around Portsmouth harbour. This was the first possible location for a sign of activity, but all he found were rusting warships and a few wrecked ferry hulks, driven ashore from broken moorings.

They flew on, the clock hands slowly counting the minutes of their flight. Fuel wouldn't be a problem for several hours yet, but large cloud banks were already massing towards the south-west horizon as Craig had predicted. For the moment they were in the clear, with the wind direction held firm to the south, but it wasn't expected to last. They would have little time to spare if problems arose.

Slowly, Jaki drew a blue line on the map, extending between the red crosses as the flight unfolded. Cromford turned the Cessna and flew the length of Southampton Water, circling several times to consider anything that aroused his interest. The inlet at Hamble provided interest for a few minutes and in the radio room they could hear the click of the camera shutter as Jean took photos. On their second circuit, Cromford reported it was only a false alarm.

The returning shoreline proved equally fruitless, a graveyard of empty jetties and sinking ships, leaking oil slicks casting rainbows on the surface of the water, the clear evidence of mankind's evaporating presence. Within a few more years even these would be gone. The blue line extended to the southern tip of Southampton Water and Cromford reported turning westwards. The main areas where they had hoped to find evidence of activity seemed to have passed, leaving a silence of disappointment to settle into the room.

"The damn things must be coming from somewhere." The muttered comment summed up everyone's thoughts.

Interest seemed to be wavering when a few minutes later, Cromford reported turning north towards Buckler's Hard. Chris frowned.

"That wasn't on the flight schedule."

The plane had deviated from the prescribed route to follow the estuary of the Beaulieu River. Sam shrugged; Rigby had obviously agreed with Cromford that he could adjust his flight plan as he saw fit. A few extra miles were well within the range of the Cessna. After a few minutes, the radio crackled again as Cromford circled above Buckler's Hard.

"Turning south a hundred and eighty degrees."

As Jaki added an extra red cross to the map, no one in the room appeared particularly interested.

"Hold on. What's that?"

Chris shot a glance at the loudspeaker as John switched on the tape recorder.

"Where?" They just caught the sound of Jean's voice in the cockpit.

"Look, over there, by that ramp area."

Suddenly interested, everyone in the room held their breath, crowding towards the speaker. The click of the camera shutter was just audible.

"I'm circling; turning back. Take more photos when I overfly that ramp." Cromford said something else to Jean that they couldn't hear as the engine note was throttled back. "Damn, we're too high. I'm going down for a better look."

"No, that's against the plan," Chris spoke with sudden alarm in her voice. "Jean's got a powerful telephoto lens; there's no need to lose altitude, it's too risky."

Rigby held up his hand, calling for silence as they strained to listen intently.

A few seconds later they heard Jean's voice, tight with anxiety.

"Not below three thousand feet, I can see enough … What's that?"

"Where?"

"In the trees; I saw a flash. Look, there again." Fear suddenly tightened her words. "Cromford, please climb before …"

A noise, like someone striking the outside of a steel dustbin, cut her short.

"Oh no … Oh no, oh god …"

Jean's words echoed through the speaker as they all stared, aghast. The engine note roared with acceleration.

"We're on fire," Jean managed to scream before her words were abruptly cut short, leaving only the hiss of static.

Amidst the stunned silence of the room, only John Evans voice spoke, "Grasshopper, do you read me, this is Ant Hill."

Dry mouthed, John struggled to repeat the call several times. Only the hiss of static answered.

"Grasshopper, this is Ant Hill. Please respond."

Ashen-faced, John turned towards the others. "Nothing. What do I do?"

"Keep calling," Rigby shouted angrily. "There could be a simple reason for this."

John turned to his microphone, repeating the call continuously in the vain hope that whatever had happened had passed.

"Jean said there was fire," Chris directed the words towards Rigby. "We clearly said they weren't to descend below three thousand feet." Her anger seethed beneath the surface. "Who allowed Cromford to ignore that instruction?"

Rigby paused, walking with Bartlett towards the door.

"The pilot had to have discretion; he's the one trying to get the job done. We couldn't tie his hands; he's the man on the scene," he shouted angrily. "We don't know what's happened. They could as like as not turn up here in the next half-hour, so let's stop being alarmist. We're not nursemaids; Cromford has more service experience than all of us put together, so let's just wait and see." Rigby glared at Chris and Sam and strode out of the room without another word.

Chris turned to Sam, shock clearly lining her face. He held her gaze for a brief moment as he called to John Evans.

"How many fishing boats have put to sea?"

"Three, but only one has a radio."

"Call that boat and instruct them to move as fast as possible towards Buckler's Hard. Tell them to stand off the coast by at least a mile and look for red smoke flares. Only if they see the smoke should they move any closer. It's a long shot, but we have to try."

Sam turned towards Albert Jamieson who was standing at the back of the room, eyes closed, his face grey and lined.

"Chairman?"

Albert nodded. "How long will their fuel last?"

"An hour and a half; two at the most," Chris replied, her voice tight and hoarse.

"John, call them every ten minutes for the next two hours. Tell the fishing boats to search until dusk; earlier if the sea gets up. They're not to go close to the shore; if they see smoke they must just report the position. We'll send another plane to check it out." Albert paused and turned to Chris Woods. "Chris, can you prepare a plane and be ready for that?"

She nodded, grateful for something to do and left to prepare the other Cessna for take-off.

"Sam, when you're done here, can I see you in my office?" Albert said softly.

He nodded in reply. "I'll stay here until we hear something or they run out of fuel."

As Albert left, Sam's instinct told him there wouldn't be a happy outcome.

As Craig had predicted, the weather began to deteriorate. The orange windsock spiralled angrily in the gusts, streaming in a north-easterly direction. Sam watched its dance, semi-mesmerised; at least it was something else to think about. Dave Bartlett appeared beside him, an eternal roll-up smoking between nicotine stained fingers.

"Weather's folding up."

Sam nodded. The blue sky had disappeared and the cloud base was becoming lower as the wind increased while they searched an empty sky for any sign of the returning Cessna.

"Fuel ran out ten minutes ago," Sam uttered with a note of finality.

Bartlett drew heavily on the cigarette and blew smoke as an epitaph to their failed operation.

Sam shrugged. "We knew the risks."

He watched Chris walking towards them from the direction of some parked planes. He had let her run through all the warm-up checks, principally to keep her occupied.

"Did John tape all of their radio transmissions?" Bartlett's question seemed casual.

Sam frowned. "I think so, though we heard enough to know what they said."

"Wasn't there part of the exchange between them that we couldn't hear, just before Cromford decided to descend? Perhaps the tape picked it up. We might hear what they said if we turn up the volume and played around with treble and base levels."

Sam looked surprised. "It might, but I doubt it will tell us anything; things seemed to happen so fast."

Chris arrived, glaring angrily and interrupted them.

"So you're just going to write them off then?"

Sam turned patiently towards her. "No, the fishing boats are still searching. They'll continue until nightfall, even with the wind rising. But it's no longer safe for you to fly in the forlorn hope we might find something."

"We don't know what happened to them. For all we know they might still be alive, waiting desperately for us to rescue them." She spoke the words with a sharp tongue that searched for someone to blame.

"I'm sorry Chris; that's the final decision. If we had heard something, or had the fishing boats seen a flare, the risk might be worth taking. The danger is too great; no one is setting off in just vain hope. We simply can't afford to lose anyone else."

She looked deflated, her leather flying helmet dangling in her hand, her face a conflict of emotions. Sam took her arm to guide her towards the radio room. The first spots of rain had arrived as the wind strength increased; it was no time to stand outside hoping for the impossible.

It took only a few minutes to re-wind the tape spools and run through the recordings. The microphone had been positioned directly in front of the speaker and had picked up a broader range of sounds; smaller events, like the click of switches and the whistle of slipstream could now be heard. John re-wound the tape to the moment Cromford reported turning at the exit from Southampton Water.

"What are we looking for that we haven't already heard?"

Bartlett exhaled blue smoke. "There was something said between them just after Cromford told Jean to take more photos as they flew over Buckler's Hard. If we turn up the volume we might catch what was said."

John re-started the tape. It ran for a few seconds before Jean's voice broke the silence.

*"Where?"*

*"Look, over there by that landing ramp."*

*The click of a camera shutter.*

*"I'm circling; turning back. Take more shots when I overfly that ramp."*

Their voices murmured: their heads must have turned away from the headset microphone. The engine note eased as Cromford throttled back.

*"Damn, we're too high. I'm going down for a better look."*

Bartlett interrupted.

"Hold it there. Re-wind, increase the treble and turn up the volume."

The murmur became a more distinct rumble.

"There's definitely something there. Add the base tones and slightly less volume."

John re-wound the spools and adjusted dials. Bartlett leaned forward, ear hard against the speaker. John pressed play. Within the room the sound was indistinct, but Bartlett soon pulled away, a wry look on his face.

"Got it." He nodded towards Sam. "Your turn."

Sam took his place, positioning his ear by the front of the speaker. He heard Cromford say *"going down for a better look"*. There was a pause. The engine note softened as it was throttled back. Sam could imagine Cromford banking the plane to give a better field of view. *"Look, those rectangles; make sure you get them, they're landing craft unless I'm very ..."* A loud crack cut off his words. But it was enough.

Sam stood away and met Bartlett's quizzical gaze.

"No question?"

He shook his head.

"No. Cromford had seen what we were looking for: landing craft."

Albert Jamieson sat with steepled fingers, eyes closed as if asleep. Linda Hue and John Evans had just left, leaving Albert and Sam to assess the events of the previous twenty-four hours. Sam gazed out of the rain streaked window, now arriving in horizontal squalls under the gusting hand of the wind. Events were moving quickly, leaving both men with the breathless feeling of running to catch up. Sam broke the silence, looking pointedly at Linda's report on Albert's desk.

"So we now know for certain that the girl I found was murdered."

Albert nodded slowly, his eyes still closed. Linda had carefully examined the nameless girl's body and found signs of bruised banding around both wrists, inflicted by fighting to release her hands from ropes that had bound her. Linda presumed the missing ropes were removed after she was dead.

"Why hang her; they could simply have shot or stabbed her?" Albert asked.

"To make it look like suicide. We weren't supposed to find her for some while, by which time any evidence would have been largely destroyed by animals and decomposition. It was only by luck I took that track as a short-cut and saw her in my headlights. Otherwise, it might have taken weeks for anyone to find her, even if someone had reported her missing." Sam paused before adding. "And with no identification on the body, we still don't know who she is."

Albert opened his eyes. "Someone will know she's missing. She can't have hidden away completely for these past five years." Albert stretched, staring at the ceiling. "With our resources so stretched, it's going to be hard to start a missing person hunt as well." He paused in thought for a moment. "Can we find someone to sketch her likeness? We could copy it and send it to every hamlet on the island and wait for someone to come forward."

Sam looked uncertain. "That supposes she came from the island in the first place." He let the thought hang in the air before adding, "It seems the best hope we've got in the circumstances, though I wouldn't hold my breath on the chance of success."

Albert stood and joined him at the window. "So, landing craft."

"That's definitely what Cromford said. Photos would have made it conclusive, though even if he was right, we don't know they are being used; they could be just abandoned military hardware that Cromford stumbled on by accident."

"Coincidence?" Albert ventured.

"Too much so; boar don't get here by swimming the Solent. And then there's the radio chatter John has just picked up. I know it's a bit garbled but someone knows we've lost a plane already. And most of what John heard was on the same frequency used by Cromford." Sam hesitated, a worried frown on his forehead. "What disturbs me most of all is that John didn't decide on the exact frequency to use until yesterday. Someone must have told them."

Albert Jamieson sighed; they were going backwards fast with each turn of events. "Two more deaths in the past twenty-four hours. We can't sustain this attrition rate, Sam."

In his words, Sam heard the full weight of responsibility that Albert had on his shoulders.

"Still, four new births in the same period."

He tried to sound optimistic, though you couldn't run their community with only a population of ten-year-olds. Albert knew that only too well. With so few survivors, time was always running against them and every death brought the collapse of their island community a step closer.

"So, their motive for attacking us?"

Sam pondered the question. In the dark hours it was starting to keep him awake. The answer had to be simple demographics; someone wanted the island for themselves and they didn't want their system for running it. If they could kill enough islanders, they could simply walk in and take over. Using the boar was a simple and efficient means of achieving this and they had access to an unlimited number if they could catch them. Sam had done the numbers. At their current rate of sighted deaths the island would be unsustainable in less than two months. And he didn't need to remind Albert Jamieson of that grim fact.

# SIXTEEN

Sam woke, surfacing through sleep with a feeling of disorientation. He had slept in his own bed for the first time in many days. When he returned to the farm he found word of the loss of the Cessna had preceded him. Everyone had given Sam space to come to terms with the consequence.

Later that night, he and Rachel made love for the first time in weeks. It had arisen quite naturally and went some way to restoring the natural chemistry between them. Afterwards, in the flickering light of a candle, he re-told the disastrous events of the previous days.

"So no one has come forward to report a girl missing?" Rachel asked, puzzlement in her voice. "Isn't that odd, when there are so few sighted women on the island?"

"We're making a sketch of her likeness to issue to every hamlet. Someone must know her." Sam avoided any reference to his suspicion that she had been murdered. "We wouldn't have found her when we did if I hadn't taken a short-cut; no one uses that track very much any longer."

"It must have been tough for you to have to cut her down and carry her body to the car." Rachel was leaning on one elbow, regarding Sam with genuine concern.

"I've had more pleasant jobs. At first I wasn't certain she was dead, that there might still be a chance she was alive, but her neck was broken. Her face looked somehow ... serene. There was nothing that could be done."

After a few minutes thinking, Rachel asked, "And Cromford?"

Sam sighed. "Like Icarus he flew too close to danger. We warned him not to go below three thousand feet. But you know Cromford; he thought differently."

"Is there any chance they could have survived?"

"It's an outside chance at best. Cromford is an experienced pilot but something happened to the plane. We can't be certain, but we think someone shot at them."

He didn't mention the final, garbled message about landing craft or the fact that the Cessna had been deliberately destroyed might clearly point to the fact that someone had something to hide.

"So the men that attacked you in Dartmouth? You made them sound no more than a gang of thugs. What were you expecting to find by inspecting the mainland coastal areas? Surely we would have heard if anything larger and more organised had spread this far south?"

"The gang we ran into were just a scavenging party, probably let loose to rampage out of control. Word of mouth spreads fear and creates a myth. There must be someone with brains and a plan behind all of this; it's not happening by chance. We'll just have to wait and see what turns up."

"So we just sit back and wait for them to attack us?" Rachel's voice bristled as she spoke.

"They'll contact us soon enough," Sam said, trying to placate her. "If we can find where they're operating from, we can work out a plan to frustrate them. In the meantime, we have Lorna's special bullets to help deal with the boar that arrive here, so at least we've made some progress to defend ourselves."

Rachel didn't look convinced but she decided to let matters rest. After a moment she changed tact, asking the question that had been on the tip of her tongue since Sam had returned.

"This new girl, Claire; when are you going to find her a permanent home?" Her question, so casually asked, caught Sam off balance.

"New home? I thought we had space here. And we need a cheese-maker," Sam yawned, trying to feign tiredness to avoid the question.

"Most of the hamlets need a cheese-maker. And anyway, she doesn't fit in here."

"You surprise me," Sam said casually.

"With such a high ratio of women to men it's hard enough to keep things on an even keel. Add the wrong woman into that mix and you have problems. Claire's personality doesn't suit the set up here with the other women and we've no clear role for yet another blind girl so you have to find her a new home as soon as possible."

With that, Rachel let the matter drop, though Sam, pretending to have fallen asleep, suspected it was only temporary. She blew out the candle and, within moments, tiredness overwhelmed her too, leaving Sam awake, disturbed and troubled by what she had just said.

Making an assessment of their crop and animal yields occupied most of the following morning. Sam urgently needed to hand in their yield predictions, which were already overdue. The day was one of sunshine and showers as Sam and Rachel rode off to inspect their fields of milling wheat and spring barley. A recently planted field of potatoes was too early to evaluate, though it showed promise provided the blight kept away. The mild winter had advanced the cereals, though a lack of nitrogen left the fields looking pale and thin. A count of plant numbers in a given square showed a decline on the previous year. Their report wouldn't make encouraging reading.

"Cow pregnancies are down too," Rachel added as they remounted their horses. "The bull doesn't seem to be making a success of his job. I think he'll have to go for steaks and we'll need to find a younger replacement."

Sam felt a tinge of sadness. He was fond of their Hereford bull, but a decline in calves would bring a drop in their milk yield, already under threat from a thin grass crop. He stared silently into the middle distance, trying to push away the feeling of overwhelming depression as problems bore in on them from every side, providing ever more questions than answers.

They arrived back in the yard to find the farm in a high state of excitement. Jake ran over.

"Thank goodness you're back. Lorna and her boyfriend have caught a male boar alive on the edge of the woods. No one knows how to handle it safely, but you worked with them before the pandemic, so you'd better come quickly and help."

Sam quickly gathered ropes, netting, and sacks and followed Jake across the fields to the edge of a large area of deciduous woodland that bordered the farm. Scenting, and hearing, the angry boar, even from a distance, made the horses flighty and nervous.

They found that Lorna and Gary had cornered and netted a large fully grown boar that had killed one of their sheep in a nearby field. The boar was entangled in the thick mesh of a net, which had been tied and anchored to a number of stout trees as the boar raged and charged back and forth to release itself. Around it, several excited dogs danced and barked, further goading the ensnared animal. From a quick glance, Sam could see the net wouldn't hold the boar for long. Lorna was buzzing with excitement; the capture of a live boar was a rare achievement, but Rachel had quickly arrived at the same conclusion as Sam and set off back to the farm to collect her blowpipe and tranquillising darts that they used on other unpredictable animals on the farm.

"When we found the dead sheep we had a feeling a boar was around and so took a net and ropes with us just in case." Lorna's face was flushed, her voice excited.

Sam circled the snared boar. Close up, he could see its enlarged bottom tusks, stained by the recent kill, the edges and points honed sharp by the long top incisors. It had already worked out that its bottom tusks could be used to saw the rope mesh, and several holes had already appeared. Sam hoped Rachel would return quickly or all they would be able to give Linda would be a dead boar, shot before it could escape. Linda would be delighted with a live specimen; how she would undertake her evaluation was a mystery, given the aggression of the animal.

It took four darts from Rachel's blowpipe to finally subdue the boar. Alice, who Lorna had once described as the farm shaman, had concocted one of her recipes for a tranquilliser, normally used as an alternative to anaesthetics, though its strength could be unpredictable and only used on humans in small doses in an an emergency. The boar keeled over, and they hastily tied its feet together and secured a thick sack hood over its head, before re-netting the animal. 'Hog-tied', Sam could only hope the lorry they had summoned from Newport would arrive before the boar woke up. Sweating from exertion, the four of them stopped to admire their handiwork.

"That was a first," Jake spoke for all of them. "I had never appreciated the bastards were as physically strong as that."

Up close, they could appreciate the boar was twice the weight of a man and in recent years, the tusks had developed in length, the angle of the lower pair now flatter, sharpened to a razor edge by the downward curving top incisors

Sam laughed grimly. "Their hatred for us never diminishes. They no longer fear us and our scent excites a blood lust they have acquired in recent years. Now that the virus they carried has virtually wiped us out as a species, their instinct seems to tell them it's a fight to the finish; either them or us, and at the moment they seem to be on the winning side." Perhaps not surprisingly, no one disagreed with him.

When the lorry arrived, the boar had begun to stir. Hooded and groggy, it took a worrying period of minutes to manhandle the heavy beast onto the flat bed of the lorry and lash its net basket down securely to the floor. As the lorry departed they all felt a sense of relief; at least now it was someone else's problem.

Later on, Sam, Marcus, Jake, and Rachel gathered in the office to complete their crop projections for the forum. Taken all together, they weren't as bad as they had feared, but it still made unhappy reading.

"So our conclusions are," Marcus summarised their bottom line, "we've increased the area of our crops which uses more fuel, but the overall harvest will still have declined by at least ten percent. Fewer cows are pregnant and it's the same with the ewes. The chickens seem okay, but eggs laid are also declining. The only encouraging point is the pigs; they seem impervious. They'll even eat the dead boar carcasses given a chance," he said with a note of black humour.

"Any improvements we can make?" Sam asked in the silence that followed, looking at the last empty section on the form.

It was Jake who answered for them all.

"Yeah. Turn the clock back five years. We might stand a chance then."

It was becoming the norm for the forum to continue late into the night. As always, Chairman Jamieson tried hard to keep a tight control on the scope of their discussions, but the range of urgent topics seemed endless. With almost thirty people killed in the past few weeks, it had been decided to hold a combined church service for everyone rather than individual funerals. Arrangements for their communal burial were in full swing when a young woman burst into the room with a message. The room fell silent for a few seconds as Albert Jamieson absorbed the contents before passing it to Connor Rigby, who was moving before he had even completed reading the message.

"All squads immediately to the Hollins' farm," he shouted, still looking at the slip. "At least sixty boar counted so far. Bring all the special ammunition you can lay hands on."

Sam slammed his files shut and moved quickly to accompany the dozen or so forum members hastening to leave. Albert caught his arm.

"Sixty?" he said in a hoarse voice. "Is that possible? It's double the number they've previously attacked us with."

Sam hesitated for a moment and turned to look directly into the older man's eyes. "If that's correct, we can take it as a response to the reconnaissance Cromford was trying to undertake. Whoever is behind this wants to make a point, so god help the Hollins; sixty boar will overwhelm them if we don't get there immediately."

It promised to be another long, sleepless night.

It was bad, though it could have been worse. The boar had broken into the farm stables but despite that, the Hollins had closed their ears to the screams of the horses and remained secure inside the farmhouses. By the time the first squads arrived their entire stock of ammunition had been almost used up in the darkness. The farmyard was full of rampaging boar, where a dozen or more worked in unison, trying to batter their way through a vulnerable door into one of the farmhouses, aware their prey hid within its walls. Ruth, in her first role as a squad leader, used a grenade to blow a hole in the gable wall to let the terrified cows escape.

It was a pale smoky dawn before the fight was over. Exhausted squad members sat slumped wearily around the smoking ruins of barns and a silage store. There had been no serious injuries but three squad members had received burns. Everywhere Sam looked he saw blackened faces, everyone silently processing the shock from the number of boar they had confronted. Rigby strode past, fuming in anger despite the eventual success of the night. He paused and turned to Sam.

"I'm needed here to mop things up but I need you to go straight back to Newport and call an emergency meeting of the security committee. We need a strategy to get a grip of this. We can't just keep waiting for them to attack us before we respond to a situation. We've got to stop them before they land or at least be closer to the beaches if that's where they're being landed." Rigby gazed around them; the milking parlour was a smoking ruin, the barn a morgue full of dead horses. "It stops now, tonight, before we lose all our farms." He paused, failing to bite back his anger. "Call the committee meeting, Sam, and get this sorted. Fast." He stormed off, not bothering to wait for a reply.

It was mid-morning by the time Sam had returned to Newport and contacted all the committee members he needed. As he climbed from the Landrover, distracted by Rigby's terse and alarming conclusions, he almost walked in front of a passing wagon guided by Lorna, with Claire seated beside her.

"You're a sight for sore eyes. What are you doing here this time of the morning?"

Lorna climbed down with a puzzled expression. "It's our usual day for delivery and collection." She looked amused, which only served to remind Sam how out of touch with the farm routine he was becoming. "When you didn't come home last night we guessed there was a problem and we came to see if you were okay."

Sam shook his head wearily. "Sixty boar attacked the Hollins' farm. We've had our hands full."

Lorna looked shocked. "Sixty? Surely that's not possible? Is everyone alright?"

"More or less. The defence system worked, mainly thanks to your specials, though it was touch and go for a bit. No fatalities but three squad members have serious burns, and the farm is in a pretty bad state."

Lorna was pensive. She was obviously shocked by the news of the attack, but Sam sensed there was something else on her mind. Curious, as he waited, he turned to Claire now holding the reigns in the wagon.

"Hi, Claire," Sam called up to her. "What brings you into town so early?"

"I need to see Karen for a check on my wound, so I tagged a lift with Lorna." Claire took Sam's grubby hand, extended to help her down from the wooden seat. "Can you point me in the right direction for Karen's room?"

Lorna took the horse and wagon to offload their produce at the distribution centre next to the Jubilee store building, and Sam took Claire's arm. Together they walked the short distance to the medical centre.

"How is the wound?"

"Still sore but healing, thanks mainly to your prompt intervention and Alice's herbal remedies. Lorna teases Alice, calling her a shaman and a witch. I'm not sure what that makes you; your prompt attention probably spared me a nasty infection."

There was a lightness in her voice which Sam found uplifting after the grim night he had just spent. For a short distance the path they followed narrowed, forcing them closer together. Sam noticed she didn't hurry to withdraw as it widened. Arriving at Karen's clinic, he held open the door for Claire to enter.

"Karen's door is the second on the left. I could be here a while yet, but Lorna could collect you and take you back to the farm."

He let go of her arm with reluctance, immediately missing the warmth of their touch. Claire beamed her smile in thanks as she turned to explore her way independently down the corridor with her guide cane.

Later, Sam found Lorna loading five-gallon jerry cans of fuel onto the back of the wagon.

"Claire should be finished with Karen by the time you've completed loading. Let me give you a hand with those."

Lorna had their farm's monthly fuel allocation in jerry cans to position around the wagon to evenly distribute the weight. Hauling sacks of flour and dried beans, along with a few large bags of fertilizer, was heavy work, and after a while they both had to pause for breath.

"There's a problem at the farm," Lorna managed to say between gasps for air. It was obviously what had been on her mind from the start. "It's between Rachel and Claire. Somehow a tap on the milk storage tank got left slightly open and many gallons of milk spilt out before anyone noticed. Rachel blamed Claire. Claire and I had been filling the batch tank to start some cheese-making using some of the surplus milk. Things didn't go well."

"Go on." Sam could feel her words had a yet more ominous undertone to them.

"Rachel lost the plot and began shouting at Claire, and when she tried to defend herself, well, Rachel lost her temper and said some unpleasant things."

"Accidents happen," Sam tried hard to be balanced. "Things get said in the heat of the moment which aren't really meant. I'm sure when Rachel ..."

Lorna shook her head. "Afterwards, last night, Rachel told me to bring Claire into town to get her wound checked. She also said I must take her to Rose and tell her to find Claire somewhere else to live. She said that Claire is making mistakes all the time and continually tells lies to cover up. She says Claire doesn't fit in on the farm and insists she's returned to the Carters who she arrived here with. Immediately."

Sam stared in silence, digesting the implications of Lorna's words.

"Look, it's nothing to do with me," Lorna continued defensively. "I get on well with Claire and this is a rotten job I've been given to do. But Rachel is the boss when you're not around and I'm in no position to argue with her. Hell, not even Marcus or Jake will stand against Rachel when she's in a wild temper, so what can I do? Even if I think she is being unfair."

Sam had the disturbing thought that the social fabric at the farm was starting to be strained by his continual absence and beginning to unravel, as if invisibly a loose single thread had been pulled, only to lead to the entire garment to come undone.

"I'm sorry, Sam. I warned you there was friction between Rachel and Claire arising. I know you're desperately busy and this is a lousy time for a problem like this, but things won't repair unless you find the time to sort this out with Rachel."

Sam felt exasperation well up inside him. It wasn't Lorna's fault; she was only the messenger but he couldn't suppress his feeling of anger.

"For goodness sake, I've been through this with Rachel only the other day. When Claire first arrived here Rose couldn't find her anywhere to stay. If anything, the situation is much worse now. We have five farms wrecked by these attacks and half the communities on the island are grieving for loved ones. We have space at our farm and it's our job to make things work for the newcomers."

The words exploded from him, sweeping over Lorna with the force of a physical blow. Shocked, she took a step back.

"Look," Sam softened his tone. "I'm sorry. The thing is that Rose isn't here at the moment. I passed her at the Hollins' farm and she won't be back for some while, if at all today, with that mess to sort out and people to re-house. When you and Claire are done here, you go straight back to the farm; don't linger; there are any number of rogue boar about the island. Tell Rachel you've seen me and I'll be back just as soon as I can."

He turned away, exhausted as much by his own emotions as the never ending stream of demands being imposed upon him. "And remind Rachel that not so long ago the three of us were strangers here too," he said, perhaps unfairly not bothering to looking back at Lorna.

# SEVENTEEN

Sam stretched back in the bath letting the warm water soak the aching fibres of his body. It had been days since he had managed anything more than the briefest of showers or a quick body wash. He lay back in the tub, feeling the room swim around him in a mist of warm steam as the door swung open and Rachel entered, a glass of home-made beer in her hand.

"A well-earned treat, though I suspect it will send you to sleep, so don't drink it too quickly until you've told me everything."

Without invitation she quickly stripped off and slid into the bath with Sam, turning her back to stretch against him, squirming to fit her body into his grooves and niches with the familiarity of the last five years.

She spoke with a lazy tone that hid the seriousness of her words. "You may have convinced everyone around the dinner table tonight that things are okay, but why am I left with the feeling you're not giving us the complete story?"

Sam shuffled and wrapped his arms around her body.

"You know me too well," he said, trying to sound light and mischievous at the same time. "The truth is, we really don't know a lot more than I told the others. But given that everything happens for a reason, it's not hard to guess where these attacks are taking us. But, there seems no point in causing anxiety by guessing until more pieces of the puzzle fall into place."

"So you're happy to just rely on evening flights along the coast and sending *Lupin* to sea on patrol every night?"

Sam sighed wearily. "That's what we agreed at today's meeting. With Lorna's special bullets we're containing the boar attacks, and there's a chance the flights and *Lupin* will intercept some of the boats carrying boar to the island before they are landed. If we manage to capture someone red-handed it could tell us a whole lot more. Until then it's the best we can do and it avoids putting too many of our people at risk."

With a spare hand, he took the glass Rachel had brought him and sipped the beer, enjoying the distinct hoppy taste.

"How many pilots can fly in darkness?" Rachel asked.

Sam hesitated. "Only Chris Woods at the moment. There are two men who are capable pilots and they can help with navigation while they learn instrument flying for night-time. We just hope that they get up to speed before Chris becomes exhausted," Sam paused. "We really couldn't afford to lose Cromford," he said with a sigh.

Despite their recent differences, the act of laying wrapped together in the bath made them feel like their old selves again, at least for the moment.

Rachel broke the silence. "Shouldn't we do something to fight back? You said Cromford had found the source of the attacks. Why don't we sail across the Solent in *Lupin* and sort the problem out?"

Sam yawned. "That's what Rigby thinks we should do; load all the squads onto *Lupin* and sail over and start a war."

"Well, why not? It's better than just being a sitting duck."

Sam eased his back in the bath. "Because it's the trap they want us to fall into. Whoever is behind all of this obviously doesn't feel confident enough to attack the island wholesale; it could be why they're starting with groups of aggressive boar. If we just sit tight and deal with what they send against us, eventually they'll have to show their hand and we'll have an idea of exactly what we're dealing with."

"What does Albert Jamieson think?"

"He disagrees with Rigby. He wants to sail over under a white flag and try and negotiate with them."

"What's wrong with that?"

"When the right time comes, nothing. But first, we have to force them to a stalemate at least, or better still, make them feel they're losing. Talking will only work if we're in a position of equality or strength. We've got to try to fool them into thinking we're stronger than we really are." Sam paused, measuring his next words. "Though that won't be easy with a spy in our midst."

For a moment Rachel was silent, evaluating what he had just said. She turned to face Sam, sending a wave of soapy water over the bath rim. "Someone here, on the island?"

"Looks that way."

Rachel sat back, knees drawn together beneath her chin. She looked at Sam thoughtfully. "That girl you found, the one who hanged herself. Anyone come forward to identify her?"

"No. But its early days; her likeness was only distributed a couple of days ago."

"What if no one does?"

Slowly, Rachel was peeling away with her questions, like stripping the layers of an onion. Sam wondered where she was taking this.

"It might suggest she was killed for something she had discovered, something someone wanted kept secret."

Rachel frowned. "I thought you said she killed herself? It was suicide, wasn't it?"

"Linda Hue has found evidence that she couldn't have killed herself. We think someone murdered her, but wants us to believe it was suicide."

"So the spy and the girl could be connected. And it is murder," Rachel said, eyes staring wide at the thought. In five years there had been suicides on the island but never a murder.

"If we can find out anything about her it could lead us to her killer. Until then, we must say nothing; not even to Lorna, or anyone else on the farm for that matter. Sooner or later someone will make a mistake. But until they do it's essential to sit tight and keep them guessing."

Rachel stood up, found her towel and stepped from the bath.

"Since when did you become Sherlock Holmes?" she said with a wry smile on her face. "Not sure I ever noticed this dark side of your character before."

Sam stretched. "It's one of my hidden assets. With any luck I'll surprise you with my deviousness. Perhaps it will be enough to keep us all alive."

Rachel dried herself and threw the towel at him in the bath as she grabbed a gown from the back of the door. Despite having borne two children, the hard farm work and a simple diet kept her body lean and taut, accentuating the size of her breasts.

"I'm not certain your measured approach to our situation is the right one, but who knows," she said wistfully. "I'll back you if you need support, but there's one condition. As soon as all of this is over, Claire leaves this farm. That's my terms and they're not negotiable."

She had left and closed the door before Sam could think of a reply.

Three moonlit cloudless nights followed. No one ventured forth from the mainland. After the pace of recent events, the island had a chance to draw breath. No more boar attacks took place and it gave the opportunity for Chris to rest and concentrate on training the others with their night flying skills. Worryingly, it became apparent that the two pilots thought most able to assist her would take longer to train than they had hoped, especially as one of them almost crashed the Cessna trying to land with instruments only.

On the fourth night the wind rose to gale force but they all spent an untroubled night, safe in the knowledge that the sea conditions would prevent any attempt to cross the Solent. They used the time to good effect, replacing ammunition stocks and experimenting with a simple tripwire system to be fitted to the approach paths to the farms. It worked on the principle that a marauding boar would break a taut line and immediately set off an alarm bell, powered by a battery, in the nearest farmhouse. It wasn't a hundred percent reliable and was prone to false alarms, usually caused by foxes or deer, but at least it was something of a first line of defence.

Sam used this quiet time to source replacement parts for their worn out tractors and farm machinery. It meant a lot of scavenging in unused farms and workshops. In the process, he discovered a disused factory in Newport where a local cheese-maker had once operated. Large hand presses, thermometers, and moulds lay gathering dust on wooden benches. Delighted with his find he returned to the farm to collect Claire, and with the Landrover returned to the factory so she could pick the items that were of most use.

The factory had been vandalised, probably by desperate people in search of food in the aftermath of the pandemic. The building was littered with debris and wreckage, so when they entered the building, Sam held Claire's hand to guide her through the wreckage. Together, they wandered the disused rooms, Sam describing the equipment they encountered, much of which was a total mystery to him. One item in particular aroused Claire's attention; she could feel a large circular stainless steel vat sprouting an assortment of dials, tubes, and pipes.

"Can you find a manufacturer's nameplate somewhere?" Claire asked as she ran her hands around the cold metal of the rim.

"It could be on the outside of this tank," said Sam, on hands and knees searching the outer casing. "Wait a minute, there's an embossed plate on the back. If we can pull it away from the wall I might be able to read it."

Claire gripped the front edge as Sam squeezed himself into the narrow space behind it. Together they lifted and slid the legs gently forward.

"Hang on, I think I can read it now. I can't see the manufacturer's name but it says *50 gallon pasteurising cheese vat with swing arm, curd blade and motors*. Is that any use to you?"

Claire was motionless, her brow furrowed in concentration. With her hair tied back in a ponytail, Sam could see her pale blue eyes more clearly. They appeared surprisingly animated, as if trying to absorb the invisible Aladdin's cave of treasures around her. The frown vanished, replaced by a smile that lit up her face. Not unblemished, but beautiful despite life's trials. With surprising agility, Claire followed around the edge of the vat to where Sam was and kissed his cheek in a spontaneous gesture.

"You've no idea how much this will help. It will so change things for me on the farm; it might even help prove that I have some value to Rachel," she added wistfully, head cocked to one side.

"Why do you try so hard to help me?" Her question wasn't an afterthought.

"Why?" Sam asked. Her unexpected display of affection had caught him off balance.

"Most people only see my disability; I'm more a millstone than a person." She held up her hand, knowing Sam would try to protest. "It's true. I hear it in their voices and, in part, I understand. But you're different. You make me feel normal, equal to the others and that gives my life a value and purpose."

Sam tried to laugh dismissively but when he spoke, his words came without thinking.

"The world is filled with the disabled. Most are blinded, I'll grant you, but the rest of us are scarred by trauma and loss. How do you measure one against the other, apart from one being visible, the other hidden inside us. The blind are no more a millstone than the rest of us. There are so few of us left that if we don't care for one another, blind or sighted, there won't be a future as we would want to recognise it."

"So you don't believe that only the strongest will survive? Isn't that what the natural world is based upon."

Sam shook his head. He could see from Clare's expression and by the tone in her voice that she had been wounded by being cast off and left as bait in Dartmouth, a feeling aggravated by Rachel's blunt rejection.

"I've thought a lot about that afternoon in Dartmouth," he paused, perhaps conscious of the dangerous ground his emotions were leading him towards. "Fate wasn't aware that you were blind or sighted, or of me for that matter. Yet it spared us. I can't believe that wasn't for a purpose."

His own words caught him by surprise. Since that afternoon, the injustice of Clare's situation kept coming back to him, now aggravated by Rachel's earlier ultimatum. He knew he had already said too much but he wanted to say more. Beside him, he felt Claire's presence like an electrical charge, enticing him to say things he hadn't consciously thought. Perhaps they lay in his subconscious all along and he had tried to ignore their presence. He couldn't retract his words; in truth, he didn't want to. Time held them both in suspension, neither able to move forward or back. Claire gazed sightlessly beyond him, waiting, listening, while Sam snared in a tangle of confusion and shock as he realised his protective instincts towards her had grown without him being aware. She was younger than him by a margin of years. He had interpreted his feelings for her as paternal, so denying what he had actually felt from the first moment they had met.

Anticipating his turmoil, Claire turned away towards the direction of the door. "We need to get back to the farm, just in case some rogue boar finds us here."

Sam felt that was unlikely, but it served as an excuse and gave him refuge from the emotions he was struggling to control. Claire lit up his world, and try as he might to deny it, her radiant spirit both confused and overwhelmed him.

After the forum that evening, Sam took his turn to supervise the night flight. The forum meeting had been inconclusive as too many unresolved matters stacked an ever increasing number of problems against them.

In the radio room, Sam listened with half an ear as radio signals passed to and fro between John and Chris now somewhere above their coastline in the darkness. The flight had been uneventful so far with only the occasional bank of sea mist and veil of thin cloud to trouble the flight. Sam could detect the tiredness in Chris's voice as flying night after night, in the absence of a relief pilot, took its toll. He played with the idea of aborting the evening mission; it looked as though it would be a repeat of the previous flights, and terminating the operation would bring some much needed rest for Chris. Around him, everyone was busy with their roles in the operation; John in regular voice contact, while Jaki, sitting beside him, carefully plotted the course of the plane in wax coloured pencil on a plastic coated map.

Craig joined Sam, his brow furrowed with concern for a developing weather pattern he couldn't make sense of as he showed Sam a chart of his barometer readings, taken during the previous thirty-six hours. It left Craig mystified and concerned.

"It looks like a series of pressure waves, plunging from high to low in a matter of a few hours, as if some giant storm is pushing from behind, compressing everything in front of it."

Sam only understood the basic elements of the weather with its effect upon the farm. So far it had been a soft benign spring and for once even the weather hadn't worked against them, leaving one less thing they had to worry about. At least until now, it seemed. But then, Craig wasn't the anxious type.

"Is there anything we need to be concerned about? It's April, winter should be behind us by now."

Craig's face creased in concentration. "I don't know; it's just a gut feeling, but I don't like what I'm seeing."

Sam placed an arm on his shoulder in encouragement. "Keep an eye on things and the moment anything changes to cause you concern, let Albert Jamieson or me know immediately. It will be best to be careful."

Craig nodded and went away to compile the latest readings that had arrived earlier by carrier pigeons from weather stations in hamlets dotted around the island.

In the radio room, alone with his thoughts, Sam rocked gently in a swivel chair. Trust the weather to add yet another potential problem to their list. It was late, and Sam was tired and as he listened, half-distracted, to the routine radio messages between John and Chris Woods his thoughts wandered to the murdered girl he had found. They had circulated an artist's impression to every hamlet on the island, but so far no one had come forward to identify her. Did that go further to support the suspicion that she had been murdered? It was hard to stay objective when so many problems demanded attention. In a similar vein, their search for the matching tyre treads, discovered in the mud of the lane had also revealed nothing. They had found similar patterns, but the widths were wrong and it had drawn a blank.

Likewise, John had visited most of the hamlets on the island in his search for aerials and found nothing that resembled a transmitter mast. Admittedly, signals could be made from anywhere, but to transmit to the mainland required a mast of a fair height. His conclusion was that whoever was conspiring against them was covering their tracks with great care.

'Luck had better break in our favour soon,' Sam mused to no one in particular, and, lost in his thoughts he almost missed the abrupt interruption of the radio signal.

High above the island, with only moonlight illuminating the coastline below, the sensation of loneliness was intense. It was a stark reminder of their plight; no ribbons of streetlights shaped towns or villages and most hamlets could ill afford to run their generators for external lighting. Chris had completed the westward leg of her flight, turning above the Needles, standing out like white teeth in the moonlight. She headed south, circled over Freshwater and flew over the sleeping island to re-join the north coast just east of Yarmouth. On the outward journey, banks of sea fog had gathered in wandering clumps and she had flown much of the time using only her compass and stopwatch. Now, a freshening onshore breeze bumped her wings, mixing up the cold turbulent air. Newtown Bay, invisible in its misty cloak only a few minutes ahead gleamed like beaten silver. She nudged the trainee pilot in the seat beside her, reminding him to check his course and bearings against the profile of the coastline now clearly visible below them.

For the countless time, Chris checked her instruments as they approached the entrance to the bay. To her right, five or six miles ahead, a few solitary lights were just visible, marking the runway north of Newport. On course and on schedule, they would cross the Medina River in a few minutes and begin the easterly leg of their course to Ryde and then on to Bembridge. Most of their population lived on the rural farms, reminding Chris that as she flew over what had once been thriving towns and villages, the only things she disturbed were rats and mice, hiding from the boar, in their domain amongst the ruins.

Chris blinked. With tired eyes, the instrument lights cast ghosted images, playing tricks of illusion. As the westerly shore of the bay ahead came clearly into view, a light flashed on the water.

It shouldn't have been there.

Without hesitating, Chris swung the Cessna into a tight banking turn, throttling back to soften the note of the engine as she did so.

"Anthill, this is Searchlight. We may have a contact."

"Searchlight, please repeat." In the radio room John jumped up in his seat, unsure what he had just heard, Chris's words distorted by static.

"Anthill, this is Searchlight, there's a light, no, three lights, at the head of the bay; must be close to the entrance at Newtown. Have we got anyone there because if not …?" Chris's words drifted away as she concentrated on maintaining a fix on the lights.

Suddenly alerted, Sam leapt to John's side. "What can she see?" he asked.

Chris answered without waiting for John to repeat the message.

"I'm banking now. There are lights on land, could be vehicle headlights, they're moving, I think. The other … wait, the lights have gone out … I can see a dark rectangular shape in the water, hard against the shore … it could be fifty feet long, maybe more."

"Where's *Lupin*?" Sam snapped the question to John.

"Returning to Newport as it happens. She ran into thick fog east of Ryde so there seemed no point in going any farther," Jaki answered, pointing to her track lines on the map.

Sam couldn't resist a smile; perhaps luck might be on their side for once after all.

"Ask Helen to get *Lupin* to Newtown Bay as quickly as possible. And switch to your frequency just in case anyone is listening," Sam said to John.

"Chris?" Sam called directly into the microphone. "Can you circle over the bay and keep us posted on what you see? And whatever you do don't lose height," he added as an urgent afterthought.

"Roger that."

At that moment, the door flew open and Rigby entered. They headed straight to the large scale map of the island pinned to the wall.

"I think we may have hooked a prize," Sam pointed to Newtown Bay. "The fog has cleared on the return leg of the flight. Chris has seen lights here," he said, pointing to the end of the bay. "Onshore, they could belong to a lorry and there's a large rectangular shape just offshore."

"Landing craft?"

"It could be. Do you have anyone in this area?"

Rigby shook his head, his finger tracing the network of lanes and tracks that fed into the island from the marshy shores of Newtown Bay.

"We've a squad on *Lupin*, another on standby here, but one squad won't be enough to block all the options."

The door opened and Ruth appeared, newly appointed as a squad leader.

"How many members do you have here tonight?" Sam directed his question to Ruth.

Rigby answered first. "Six, including Ruth."

"Okay, if we split the squad in half, Connor you could take two, and leave the other three with Ruth. If you're quick, you should be able to block both ends of this road here," Sam pointed to the road that ran east to west along the bottom of the bay and into which all exits fed. "There's no cloud tonight and the moon is still high so Chris might be able to give us a direction for the lorry, even if it travels without lights. They must head south, there's no other route out of the bay area. If you leave now you might just be in time to cut them off from both directions."

A brief glimpse at the map confirmed the logic of Sam's suggestion. Within seconds Rigby and Ruth were both running for the door.

"And we need the driver alive; he's no use to us dead," Sam shouted to their disappearing backs.

A few minutes later their headlights briefly lit the control room as their accelerators raced the engines. After they had departed, Sam had a sudden feeling of alarm; he had forgotten to warn them of the likely contents of the lorry. Thirty very unhappy boar. And the driver of the lorry might not be male.

Helen had never been given a direct instruction to take *Lupin* to full speed, plus whatever else she could force out of her ageing engines. She had been caught by surprise when John switched to a new frequency; more so when he gave her an interception position in the Solent due north of Newtown Bay.

"You must make all speed. Push *Lupin* as hard as you dare and try not to let them escape," Sam instructed.

Now, with the regulator sat at *Full Ahead* and a fluorescent wake streaming from her bow, the deck of *Lupin* vibrated under the torque from her racing screws. John had passed on the last known position for what they assumed was the landing ship, estimating it was travelling northwards at a maximum of ten knots. Pushed to full speed, *Lupin* might make eighteen knots. When they had plotted the courses it was obvious it would be a close run thing to stop the fleeing vessel from reaching the protection of the mainland shore. Aware of the sudden commotion, Aiden, squad commander on *Lupin*, joined Helen in the wheelhouse.

"Looks like they've discovered an intruder. We should catch up with them about here," Helen pointed to a spot on her chart of the Solent, approximately two-thirds of the way between the island and the mainland. "My guess is they're not going to be too happy when we arrive. Our main instruction is to prevent them escaping, the second is to take them alive. So I'll leave their capture to you then," she said with a wry smile.

Aiden nodded. He and his team had rehearsed this scenario many times. After Dartmouth, *Lupin* had hastily been given better protection with a powerful searchlight and a heavier calibre gun. Despite the improvements, he knew that practising on dry land and repeating that drill in the middle of the Solent in darkness were two very different things.

*Lupin* surged onwards as Helen searched the darkness ahead with a precious pair of night-sight binoculars. The shallow low-profile vessel would be difficult to spot, even in the gentle swell of the Solent. In fact, without radar, if it was a landing craft it would be next to impossible to see until they were right on top of it.

Despite Sam's wishful thinking, Chris had soon lost track of the lorry driving without lights in the narrow hedge-lined lanes. Immediately, she switched her attention to the vessel leaving Newtown Bay. From her altitude, the wake of the fleeing ship gleamed green on the silver waters of the bay. Far off, in the distance to the east, she could just make out *Lupin*'s wake, cutting a course astern of the craft below. If they passed too far behind the vessel, it would be next to impossible to see, so she had to try something to help them. Switching on all the plane's navigation lights, she banked steeply, aligning her flight path with the wake below. Helen couldn't hear the plane above the rumble of *Lupin*'s engines, but the sudden appearance of lights in the sky in front of them were unmistakeable amidst the backcloth of stars. Curious, Helen watched the lights turn sharply, retracing the flight path back towards the island, only to suddenly turn again and repeat the original track. It was obvious Chris was trying to send them a message.

"The ship is somewhere on the line of her flight," Helen shouted to Aiden. "It's somewhere between the plane's turning points."

Aiden disappeared up to the wheelhouse roof. A powerful beam of white light lanced through the night as he powered up their new searchlight. Slowly, the beam traced the track ahead, but revealed only rolling wave tops. Helen heard Aiden curse with frustration. The Solent wasn't especially wide and at their current speed, the mainland coast, with all its hidden dangers, was rapidly approaching.

In the plane, Chris changed her tactics. She could see the searchlight hadn't picked up the landing craft, so at the end of her run towards the mainland she made a steep turn which changed her path to a right angle to the craft's direction of travel.

"Pay attention; I hope you're watching," Chris muttered.

Aiden saw the Cessna's lights diminish, before shining brightly as the plane changed direction and flew directly towards them. He swung the searchlight across the sea towards the plane's line of flight, guessing that Chris was using her lights as a direction finder for his searchlight. For a moment there was only open sea until, hidden amongst the waves, a low dark shape appeared, white foam creaming along its sides. In the wheelhouse, Helen saw the craft at the same moment.

"Gotcha," she shouted triumphantly. "Aiden, hold it in the beam; don't lose it." Pausing to grab the loudhailer, she called to the coxswain as she moved to the port wing. "When we're within fifty yards, turn to a parallel course and match his speed. We're going to have a chat."

*Lupin* rolled uncomfortably as they changed course. For long seconds the craft disappeared. When Aiden picked it up again, the distance separating them had closed dramatically and Helen could now hear the roar of its diesel engines, straining at maximum speed to escape. She braced herself against the rail as the coxswain changed course again, *Lupin*'s engines easing back as he set a course to shadow the fleeing vessel. Helen switched on the loudhailer, pressing the mouthpiece to her lips.

"Hove-to and prepare for us to board."

Her metallic words echoed across the waves. She waited for a response. Beyond her right shoulder, a deeper shade of black outlined the approaching mainland coast. They were closing at a mile every six minutes and the skipper of the landing craft must have fancied his chances of reaching safety. Abruptly, he turned sharply towards *Lupin*, aiming to pass behind her stern. Helen repeated her instruction twice more on the loudhailer, her last call answered by a series of loud cracks and the whine of several gun shots. They had given their answer.

"Keep the light on him," Helen shouted to Aiden as she re-entered the wheelhouse and grabbed the wheel from the coxswain.

Helen knew what had to be done and couldn't ask anyone else to do it. As the landing craft passed astern, *Lupin* surged to full speed again and, with the rudder hard to starboard, she heeled alarmingly as Helen spun the wheel and turned, her screws threshing the dark sea. The other skipper had gambled and played his hand, but misjudged how quickly Helen could turn to counter his move. Within seconds, he was broadside on to the path of the racing *Lupin*, her engines at full speed, her high razor bow carving a straight path towards the midships of the fleeing craft now immediately in front of her.

# EIGHTEEN

Just as the dawn coloured the western sky, Ruth returned. Until that moment, Sam thought he had her measure. It took a lot to make her angry, but to say Ruth was fuming when she entered their control room was an understatement.

"They must have heard us miles away, racing around the countryside without a second thought for stealth. We knew where they were and could have used the back lanes to work around them and catch them by surprise."

Ruth hurled her rucksack against the wall in frustration and stood with hands on hips, struggling to regain her composure.

"Having heard us approaching some miles distant, they would have known they couldn't outrun us with a fully laden lorry. As it was, we saw the fire before we caught up with them and by then it was too late. Whoever was involved had disappeared into the darkness, leaving the back of the truck open for the boar to escape and the entire rig ablaze. So now we haven't a clue about their identity, the lorry's totally burnt out and we have thirty hungry boar roaming the countryside. The best opportunity we've had to catch them so far has just gone up in smoke."

Ruth was careful not to name Rigby, but it was obvious that she held him responsible. His impulsive tactics had already contributed to the probable deaths of Cromford and Jean, and now a golden opportunity to break into the gang attacking them had slipped between their fingers like dry sand. Sam avoided asking her to calm down; he guessed that would only make things worse. He picked up her rucksack and handed it back to her.

"Get some rest. We'll get the helicopter flying as soon as it's light. I'm afraid we'll need you again to track down the missing boar."

The radio room overlooked the harbour quay used for *Lupin*. They could see smoke coiling from her funnel long before she came into view, so by the time she was tied to her mooring points everyone had assembled to swing the gangway into position. It was a relief that *Lupin* appeared to have escaped serious damage, with the exception of a line of gouges which now veined her flanks emanating from the dent in the front of her bow.

Albert Jamieson, Sam, and John Evans were the first to board *Lupin* and were met by Helen, ashen-faced with her arm still bandaged from Dartmouth. Behind her, between two squad members, stood a downcast bedraggled figure with his wrists tightly bound in front of him. Helen nodded to the men as they stepped onto the deck.

"In the end we had to ram the landing craft. I tried to avoid it and head them off, but I had no choice. We were only a mile or so from the mainland coast and the helmsman," she gestured towards the figure behind her, "was very quick and agile. Another few minutes and I would have been putting *Lupin* in danger and he would have slipped the net. We called on them to stop several times, but their only answer was to fire shots at us. I had to stop them, so I rammed the landing craft. There was no other way."

Helen paused, gulping for breath, anguish written on her face.

"There was a crew of three; we only found him in the water." Normally stoic, Helen looked both shocked and stunned. "I think I've drowned the other two," she said, her eyes glancing from one to the other, appealing for reassurance.

Albert stepped forward and hugged Helen. "It was unfortunate but necessary. In the end, you were only carrying out your instructions to protect the rest of us." He nodded towards the handcuffed man. "He made his choice when he wouldn't stop, so he must take his share of the responsibility for what's happened."

The moment was interrupted by Rigby's arrival on deck, a gaggle of tired squad members trailing behind him. Until that moment, their captive had appeared disconnected from what was happening around him. Suddenly, his eyes were alert; without appearing to move, he shrank away, out of sight of the advancing Rigby.

"You started without me." The words came as a shout. "This is the prisoner? Well, no matter, we'll take this over from here and soon have some answers."

Rigby grabbed the man and propelled him towards the gangway. Before anyone could react, Rigby and his cohort were crossing the gangway with the captive.

Finally, Sam moved. "Aiden, come with me. Ruth, accompany Chairman Jamieson back to the forum building."

Sam and Aiden pursued Rigby but he must have taken a short-cut and by the time Sam and Aiden entered Rigby's office the terrified captive was already tied to a chair, eyes wide with fear at the prospect of whatever awaited him. Sam didn't hesitate.

"Connor, a word outside, please. Now." He didn't want to have the inevitable argument in front of the others.

"Aiden, don't let anyone touch this man while I'm out of the room."

The man's eyes glanced nervously from Sam to Rigby, trying to assess who had the most authority. Once outside, Rigby raised his chin to speak.

"If it's a cosy chat you're wanting, Sam, it will have to wait until I've had a few words with the prisoner."

Sam wasn't certain exactly what he wanted to say or by what authority he could stop Rigby. He had glanced at the bedraggled figure in the chair before they had left the office. Close up, he looked hardly more than a teenager and was shaking violently. Sam's only hope was to delay Rigby for long enough to allow Albert Jamieson to work out what to do.

"You can't interrogate him like this. To get answers from him you'd do better to find him some dry clothes and something to drink. While that's happening, we can talk about what to do with him."

Rigby smiled cynically. "You know, I like you Sam, but there are times I think that if things were left to you, we might as well run up the white flag here and now and not bother to resist. Some of us have got to be prepared to get our hands dirty. So, stand aside and let's find out what this little runt knows; no frills, no cosy get-to-know-you chat, just the straight truth before another farm is attacked. Straight talking, with a few broken teeth and some bruises if necessary. Or, is our safety no longer a priority for you?"

Sam took a step back, trying to avoid confrontation. "That's unfair Connor, you know me better than to insinuate that. But strong arm tactics aren't the way to get to the truth. That kid in there is so scared he'll tell you whatever you want to hear to stop you hurting him, and it's unlikely to be the truth. At least let us find out what he's doing here before putting any pressure on him. That way we may get a few honest answers."

Rigby laughed. "And just how long are you prepared to invest in such softly, softly tactics? I'm only asking, because it's a neap tide in two days and it would be helpful to know if these guys intend to dump boat loads of boar on our doorstep in an attempt to really hurt us."

Sam felt Rigby was losing what little patience he had as they argued over the fate of the boy, when Albert Jamieson's voice suddenly intervened.

"That will be all, councillors." Sam suspected he had been standing out of view, close enough to hear what had been said. "I'll deal with this."

For an instant, Rigby's expression jumped from surprise to defiance, as though for a moment, he contemplated challenging the chairman. He hesitated, perhaps uncertain of the strength of his support if he openly defied Albert. Sam felt an uncomfortable shiver run down his spine, aware that one day soon this might finally happen if their luck didn't change.

Rigby apparently thought better of it. "That's your call, chairman. Do you want me to guard the prisoner while you interrogate him?"

Albert produced a smile. "That won't be necessary for the moment, Connor. I suggest you get some rest; you've had a long tiring night and we're bound to need your expertise when it comes to rounding up the escaped boar that now roam the island."

He made no accusation, but his words made it clear that he knew Rigby had thrown away the opportunity to capture the lorry a few hours earlier. Behind them, Ruth stared impassively ahead, her eyes focused on some distant point. Sam didn't need two guesses to know it was her frustration that had influenced Albert.

"As you wish," Rigby snapped. "I won't be far away if you have any problems."

He threw a suspicious glance in Sam's direction and set off to collect his squad.

They re-entered the office where Aiden stood beside their captive. Albert Jamieson closed the door gently, making it obvious he wasn't going to lock it.

"Please untie this man."

Aiden checked, making certain he had heard the instruction correctly before releasing the ropes from the chair.

"And his wrists, please."

For a moment Aiden again looked doubtful, thought better of it and did as he was instructed. Their captive rubbed his raw and chafed wrists.

"What's your name, son?" Albert asked in a neutral tone.

"Longmarsh, David Longmarsh." He glanced nervously at them. "I don't mean no harm. I didn't want to come here; they made me do it."

His words came out in haste, tumbling over one another in a desperate attempt to try and plead his case before anything unpleasant happened to him.

"One thing at a time." Albert Jamieson held up his hand. "Ruth, could you find David some dry clothes and something to drink. When did you last eat?"

For a moment the boy looked disorientated, as though he hadn't expected to be treated fairly. "Not since yesterday." He looked nervously from one to the other. "Look, you've got to release me. They'll do terrible things to my Cynthia if I don't return soon." His final sentence resembled more a cry from the heart than a plea to be released.

Albert looked at Sam. "We'll get to that in good time, David."

Behind him, the door closed as Ruth left. Albert slightly shook his head in Aiden's direction as he made to release the holster cover to his gun. Aiden clipped it shut again.

"Very shortly, David, I'm going to leave you and Sam here to talk." Albert nodded in Sam's direction. "He has my complete authority to make decisions on your fate, so you can make your requests then. We have a community here based on rules and fairness, but you must realise that your attacks on us make it difficult to be generous towards you. How things work out for you will hinge on how much you can help us. Do you understand?"

Sam noted how Albert's voice remained calm and measured, but not without heavy inference on his words. Longmarsh nodded his head, wide-eyed and open-mouthed.

The door opened and Ruth re-entered with clothes and a blanket over one arm and a tray of food and a steaming mug in the other.

Albert beckoned Sam and Aiden outside while Ruth stood guard and allowed Longmarsh to change from his wet clothes.

Albert frowned. "Judging from Connor's mood, the entire island will know soon enough that we're holding him here. Aiden, I need you to set a reliable guard on this door and allow no one, not even Connor, to enter at any time. We must avoid emotions being whipped up into the frenzy of a kangaroo court, which means we need to find out as much as possible from him quickly, in a humane manner." He paused. "Sam, you've not got long I'm afraid, so be firm and direct with your questions. You can appear to be on his side but make it clear that many people here won't be anywhere near so accommodating unless he is helpful. Ask Ruth to take notes and hand the only copy she takes to me when you're done."

Albert Jamieson left, bound for the unenvious task of dealing with Rigby. The sinking of the landing craft and rescue of a solitary survivor were all they had to show for their night's work, but even that could slip through their fingers unless they moved quickly.

Longmarsh was ravenous. Once dressed in the assortment of dry clothes, Sam gave him a few minutes to drink and eat while he collected his thoughts.

"Okay, let's get down to things," Sam kept a neutral expression as the boy ate, fixing direct unblinking eye contact with him.

"My name is Sam, Mr Albert Jamieson is our chairman. I'm an elected forum member and in that capacity I need answers to my questions. The quicker you can provide them, the more help I can give to you. Do you understand, David?" he said, deliberately using the boy's first name.

Longmarsh nodded his head. Sam glanced at Ruth who was sitting beside him, legs crossed and poised with pencil and paper to make notes. She had tied back her long dark hair in a ponytail and whether through tiredness or for effect, she looked bored by all that was happening. Sam returned his attention back to the boy.

"How do you come to be here? You must have known the boar you ship over in the landing craft are intended to attack us. Hardly an act of friendship, wouldn't you say?"

For a moment, the boy's mouth tried to shape words but nothing came out. Sam pushed a glass of water towards him.

"Drink and try again."

If it was an act, he was making a convincing job of it. Longmarsh drained the glass and wiped his mouth on the back of his hand.

"Okay, let's begin again and you can start by explaining how you came to be involved in what is obviously an attack upon our island."

"It's not how it seems," he began. "Before the pandemic I'd been living near Lulworth Cove. I'd been a fisherman all my life with my dad who ran a small inshore fishing boat, mostly crabs and lobsters. Living near the sea is all I've ever known. When the pandemic arrived, all my family caught it; they were dead inside a week." He shook his head, still bewildered at the enormity of the event despite the passage of the years. "A few of us survived, many blinded, but as we weren't far from Dorchester and we had the sea to fish from, we could get by from looting warehouses and shops in the town. But gradually the boar increased in numbers and it became too dangerous. You can live well from the sea and one of the women in our group was good with seaweed and wild plants and we could grow things like potatoes and vegetables. We were surviving okay until these thugs on motorbikes suddenly turned up a few months ago."

Sam let him take a pause, frowned and leaned back in his chair.

"So how did you avoid the pandemic?"

"In a police station in Southampton. I had too much to drink with some mates on a night out in town. I was stupid enough to take a swing at a policeman when he tried to stop us being rowdy. When they arrested me, the desk sergeant took a dim view of me and kept me locked in a cell for a couple of nights to cool off; two nights that ended up lasting several weeks. As it turned out, he saved my life, though it took days of shouting and hammering to get someone to come and unlock my cell. I almost died in there."

Sam looked at him sceptically.

"Let's go back to the arrival of the men on motorbikes as we call them? From my experience, they're not well disposed to friendly conversation. How does it happen that you're still alive and working for them?"

"At first the group who found us were only interested in taking the women away. Then it occurred to them that as we were fisherman we would be of more use if they left us to carry on. So they came back twice a week to take most of the fish we caught. One week we were short on catch; the weather had been bad so we hadn't been able to go to sea. They weren't prepared to listen and decided to teach us a lesson. They took one of the women away and badly beat up her partner. We never saw her again." His face creased with distress at the memory.

"Okay, that bit I can understand, but how do you get from being a simple fisherman to sailing a landing craft full of boar across the Solent? You must be aware you're hardly taking them out for a pleasure trip around the island," Sam said sceptically.

"Things changed about a month ago. When the men arrived for the fish as usual, they brought a lorry. They said we were wanted in Portsmouth. We had no choice, we either had to agree to go with them or they would take our women away. Have no doubt; they're mean enough to do that without a second thought."

Sam paused in his questions, watching Ruth catch up with her note taking.

"And Cynthia. How does she fit into this story?"

"She's not a story," Longmarsh said sharply, suddenly angry at Sam's sceptical tone. "I found Cynthia a couple of days after I escaped from the police cell. She had survived contracting the flu virus, but it had left her blind. I was searching houses for something to eat and heard shouting. There was a boar in the garden of the house Cynthia was in with a few other survivors. It had killed anyone venturing out of the house to search for food. The wretched thing was waiting there and Cynthia became more terrified each time someone failed to return. If I hadn't found her, I don't think she would have survived very much longer." For a moment he seemed suspended, lost in thought.

"She's brave and resourceful, blind and pretty, which only makes her vulnerable for one thing only in the eyes of these men." His words brought Claire's situation abruptly to the fore in Sam's mind. "By doing their bidding, I manage to protect her. There aren't many of us who can navigate the Solent in the dark. The deal is always the same; if I don't go back, her protection is over and they'll take her to the brothel they run in Portsmouth. It's how they control us and make us do what we're told. Cynthia would never be able to cope with that; she would rather kill herself than endure it. I'm no good here to you," Longmarsh appealed. "I'd just be another mouth to feed, so you might as well let me go." His voice rose progressively as he spoke, choked with emotion.

Sam leant back in his chair, placing his fingers together. He still felt the need to challenge Longmarsh.

"Actually, I don't have to do anything. You seem to forget that you're still the one attacking us. I'm only here to protect my family and our community." He left space for Longmarsh to consider his words before continuing.

"So, if you want me to help you, you've got to come up with something to offer me in return." Sam weighted his last words to give him a way out. "Something that will really make a difference for us." He stood up abruptly, his chair scraping noisily on the concrete floor.

"Where are you going? Why are you leaving?" Alarmed, Longmarsh shot a nervous glance in Ruth's direction, appealing or imploring for her help, Sam couldn't be sure.

"I've more important things to check on; I suggest you think about my offer while I'm gone."

He nodded to Ruth. She followed him outside the room.

"Watch him. See how he behaves while I'm gone and listen to what he says. When I return, if you think he's lying or he tries anything that makes you suspicious, change position and sit on the opposite side of me."

Sam heard Ruth turn the key in the lock behind him. He felt confident Ruth could handle being alone in the room with Longmarsh, but felt reassured when he found that Aiden had appointed two large men to guard the access to the room.

"If Ruth calls for help, only one of you must enter. While I'm away, no one is to have access. No one," he said with emphasis.

Both men nodded in agreement and Sam hurried away to find John Evans. While questioning Longmarsh, an idea had slowly begun to crystallise and he urgently needed John's help to make it work. He found John in the radio room, in his usual position, headphones clamped over his ears, his fingers delicately adjusting the frequency dials.

"Much happening?"

John shrugged. "A little. They already know we've sunk one of their landing craft."

Sam frowned. "How would they know that so quickly?"

The question was rhetorical, but John spoke for what they had both already guessed. "Because someone told them?"

"That was quick. Hear anything from our side of the Solent?"

John shook his head. "But then, they've started changing frequencies, so they must have guessed that we're listening for them. But, I only catch fragments of what's being said." John's words posed yet more questions at a moment when it was answers that were needed more than anything.

"Do you have a small radio set? I'm thinking of something that could send a message in morse code, with a range of ten or twenty miles," Sam asked.

John looked puzzled. "I've got an old army set that would fit the description. The batteries would need charging before I could test it, but it should still work. Why?"

"I'll tell you later. Get them charged and make sure it will work. Can you have it ready to go in a few hours?"

John nodded. "If I can run the generator for longer, it could be ready in say, three or four hours, but I'm using a lot of fuel for the generator," he said with a worried look on his face.

"My instructions. Go ahead as a priority and I'll be back shortly."

Sam left the radio room and as he crossed the courtyard a breathless Craig intercepted him, waving another series of coloured graphs in front of him. Another lesson in meteorology was the last thing Sam needed at that moment.

"I've been trying to find you. This strange ripple effect on the pressure cycle I told you about earlier is still happening." Craig looked anxious, wrestling with something he plainly didn't understand. "In fact, the cycle is getting faster and the range of highs and lows are increasing."

Sam cast a fleeting glance at the graphs. "Meaning?"

"I don't know, but my instinct tells me something nasty is coming our way and I don't think it's going to be very pleasant. I want to raise a storm warning for the entire island as soon as possible. I don't think it will be very long before we find out what's in store for us and people need time to prepare."

Issuing an extreme weather warning was a rare event; at that moment it was the last thing they needed, especially if it turned out to be a false alarm. The problem was, if Craig's suspicions were founded and they did nothing, the consequences could be disastrous, especially as they were in their main growing season.

"Okay. I agree. Go and see Albert Jamieson immediately. Tell him what you've just told me and that I agree with you. We need to raise an alert just in case. Everyone will then have the chance to prepare and move livestock and equipment into cover. I'll be free in a few hours, but don't wait for me; ask Albert to authorise this now and let's get it done immediately."

Sam hurried away without waiting for an answer.

Ruth unlocked the door at the sound of Sam's voice. Standing to one side with her back to the wall, arms crossed and her face impassive, she said nothing as he entered, showing no hint of what had happened in his absence.

"So, David, what do you have to offer me?" Sam said, his voice feigning disinterest.

Longmarsh stared ahead, his expression a picture of total loss. He shook his head. "I'm sorry. I've racked my brain while you were gone, but I can't come up with anything other than what I've already told you. There's nothing I can add that might be of help to you. I'm a mere pawn in their hands, and yours for that matter; no more than a puppet dancing on the strings for whoever pulls them."

He looked morose and deflated. Sam sat down and drew up his chair without responding. Ruth sat beside him, in the same position she had occupied before he had left. 'So', thought Sam, 'she believes his story'. At least that was some progress.

"That's a shame, David, a real shame." He paused for effect. "But let me try and help you."

Longmarsh blinked and he looked up, a tremor of hope ghosting his face as he waited for Sam to continue.

"Do you know morse code?"

"Morse?" he said with surprise.

"Yes, electric signals made with dots and dashes," Sam answered impatiently.

"I'm a fisherman, I've worked on boats on the sea since I was a kid. Of course I know morse. I'm not fast, but I learnt to be accurate. In recent years, ship to shore radio became more common." Longmarsh looked puzzled. "Why?"

Sam ignored the question. "I've an offer. If, and it's a big if, we let you go, you will have to give me your promise that you'll work for us." He paused, fixing his stare on Longmarsh's face. "But I can only release you back to the mainland if you supply the information I need."

Longmarsh looked bewildered, his head nodding vigorously to agree to anything, even if it had yet to be explained. Sam kept his face impassive.

"I'm deadly serious about this. Our people are dying, partly because of your actions. If we give you a boat and send you back, you'll break your word at your peril and someone, not necessarily me, will let a message slip on the radio waves that makes it clear you're working for us. From what I know of the men you work for, they're unlikely to wait to ask you for an explanation. So do you understand?"

The nodding continued with even greater rapidity. "Yes, of course, I promise I won't let you down." His voice was hoarse in urgent desperation.

Sam couldn't avoid a brief smile. "You don't know what it is yet."

"Anything. Just tell me."

Sam explained his plan.

"So, when they give you the landing location for your next trip to the island, you must code it and send it by morse to us. The transmitter we'll give you has the range, and the code will be simple to remember. It's just in case anyone on the mainland is listening in."

For a moment, David looked thoughtful. "But how do I smuggle the transmitter ashore? They're bound to search and question me."

"We'll seal the equipment into a waterproof barrel. Can you find one of your crab or lobster pots in the dark in the sea near Buckler's Hard?"

"I think so. They have reflectors attached to them so they glint in the moonlight."

"Good. You can secure the barrel to the marker buoy and go back to collect it the next time you go out. I presume they still let you fish when you're not dumping boar on us?"

"Yes, but will the radio work? The sea is still cold in early spring?"

"We'll line the barrel with insulation. The most you might need to do is charge the batteries. Someone will be here shortly to explain how to use the transmitter and help you memorise the instructions, along with a simple code you'll be given. Nothing in writing."

Sam was in a hurry now, anxious to move on with Craig's warning of bad weather and storms preying on his mind.

"One more thing; how are you going to explain things when you get back to the mainland? After all, you're the only one to survive from the landing craft."

Sam didn't mention the spy in their midst on the island. He was certain that word had already been sent to the mainland, confirming that someone from the landing craft had been rescued and questioned. Whoever was behind the boar attacks would not be pleased if they found out that Longmarsh had spent many hours answering their questions, only to miraculously turn up on the mainland a day later.

Without answering, Longmarsh's eyes darted uncertainly from side to side, his fear of the men on motorbikes and what they were capable of, clearly written in his expression.

"Listen, what were the names of the men who drowned?" Sam asked.

David looked puzzled. "Jim Dere and Kevin Weston."

"Was either of them a committed bike man? Someone who might try to fight his way out to get back to the mainland?"

"Kevin was a nasty piece of work. He was put on board to make sure we did exactly as we were told. He'd stick a knife in your back at the first opportunity. I won't miss him."

Sam sat in thought for a minute. He needed a plan. If they devised a story that would make its way to the mainland he knew it had to be plausible enough to protect both Longmarsh and their own plans.

Albert Jamieson arched an eyebrow when Sam told him the plan.

"Will Ruth be able to keep to this story?" Helen asked from a chair in the corner, an element of doubt in her voice.

"Only the five of us know Longmarsh's real name. Even Rigby never got that far," Sam said with a wry grin.

In the interim, Albert had done a good job of calming things down, especially Rigby who had been roaring around like a loose cannon.

"So let me get this straight," Albert continued. "Our story is that when you left the room to find John Evans, leaving Ruth to guard 'Kevin Weston' he drew out a concealed knife, held it against her throat and forced his way out when you returned, locking both you and Ruth into the room as he escaped."

"And Aiden." Sam shot a glance at him standing near the fireplace, warming his back. "It was Aiden who dismissed the men guarding the door. Our story will be that we captured and questioned 'Weston' not Longmarsh and it was 'Weston' who escaped. I guess his body will eventually wash up on the mainland. No one must ever mention David Longmarsh's name. When questioned he will tell them that with the sinking of the landing craft, he swam to the island, hid for a day, and then stole a boat which he then used to return over the Solent."

Albert looked uncertain. "And where exactly is Longmarsh/Weston now?"

"We smuggled him into a disused cottage in Newtown Bay for a few hours until we send him back to the mainland."

Albert didn't look convinced. "It all seems very underhand to me," he said.

"Our situation doesn't give us any option. We have to assume that whoever is our traitor is giving the men on the mainland real-time information, even what's discussed in secret within the forum. If anyone gets even a hint that we've questioned Longmarsh, his cover story won't last five minutes. This will only work if they can be made to believe we interrogated 'Kevin Weston' and he drowned using a stolen boat to cross the Solent. It's our only chance to make real progress; if Longmarsh can send us a message with the location of the next landing, we can scoop up the entire operation," Sam said, concluding his argument for the deception.

"Assuming he man doesn't double-cross us," Helen said sceptically.

Sam ignored her doubts. "I don't think he will," he said with conviction. "If it does go wrong, we'll have to persist with our night flights until we strike lucky again. How many more of our people will be killed while we wait for that to happen?"

As dusk began to fall several hours later, Aiden, Helen, and Sam stood overlooking Newtown Bay, watching a battered whaler cut a wake towards the Solent.

"How do you rate his chances?" Helen shivered in the unseasonably cold wind, as the boat dug its bow into the rolling south-westerly surf, now surging into the bay.

Sam exhaled between his teeth. "Odds-on. If he makes it across safely. Anyone getting back to the mainland in this sea will look committed to their cause. Hopefully, the story we've spun will protect him. If it doesn't …" Sam left the sentence hanging in the air.

"Will the radio work? It looked pretty battered," Aiden asked.

"The radio's tough enough. Not too sure about the batteries though," Sam added.

Even if Longmarsh made it to Buckler's Hard before the weather broke, as Craig had predicted, he still had to hide the radio, make it ashore safely and tell a convincing story to a very unpredictable group of men. Perhaps the odds Sam had given were too optimistic. They would know soon enough.

Ruth arrived from the lakeside, plastered with thick mud almost to her waist. She had helped launch Longmarsh in the whaler from the reed beds that fringed the bay. Sam noticed that she never complained or shunned the most unpleasant tasks and he smiled at her with gratitude; he hadn't fancied the job himself.

As Aiden and Helen turned away towards the shelter of the Landrover, Sam said to Ruth, "I never got a chance to ask what convinced you he was telling the truth."

Ruth shrugged. "Female intuition. He only asked if we still recognised marriage here on the island and if I could find him something he could use as a wedding ring for Cynthia. Apparently their captors had stolen the previous one he had given her. It didn't occur to him to plead with me for help for his own sake, so I figured his story was genuine."

For a few minutes they watched in silence as the whaler disappeared into an approaching squall.

"I did learn one thing you might find useful."

Surprised, Sam turned towards her.

"I showed him the picture of the girl you found hanged," Ruth said, still staring out to sea after the disappearing boat.

"And?"

"He said he recognised her. She was caught a few weeks ago, trying to steal a boat to escape across the Solent to the island. He said normally they would have killed her for that, but instead she just disappeared."

Ruth shuddered.

"Maybe it explains why no one has come forward to identify her. Only one person here knows who she is. And they are complicit in her murder."

## NINETEEN

Sam awoke to the impression that the world around him was roaring like all the demons in Hades. He lay in a narrow bed, struggling to collect his thoughts and remember where he was. He knew he had ridden back to the farm into the teeth of a rising gale, which had been head-on most of the way. Luckily, the horse he had chosen appeared indifferent to the conditions and, apart from a few squalls, the rain held off for most of the journey. Now, as he lay in his bed, the rain hammered deafeningly on the roof above him and the barn shuddered under the concussive force of the gale.

Groggy with sleep, he levered himself onto an elbow. It was still dark as he looked at the luminous watch hands on his wrist and was shocked to find it was already eight in the morning. It had been well past midnight when he had finally ridden into the farmyard. The weather had deteriorated as Craig had predicted and Sam offered up a silent prayer that David Longmarsh had reached the mainland before the worst of the storm arrived. It would have been a close call at best.

Sam eased his tired legs over the edge of the bed. The room held a faint lingering scent which reminded him that he had spent the night in Lorna's bed. The farm had been in darkness when he arrived in the early hours and the house had been locked and shuttered in anticipation of the storm. Only Claire remained to keep her nightly vigil when he was away, intuitively aware when he would return. Despite the weather, she had appeared out of the darkness as he led the horse to the stables which were now full of horses brought in for safety. Claire took the reins from his hands.

"I'll bed her down; go and wash, there's a plate of food warming for you upstairs."

Sam was too tired to argue and besides, Claire could settle the horse in a fraction of the time he would take. He hadn't eaten a hot meal in two days and felt suddenly gripped with hunger as he wearily climbed the ladder to the attic room. Lorna's space was empty but a shiny metal plate of food sat next to the stove, in which the dying embers still glowed. He eased himself into a chair, feeling the ache of tiredness in every muscle in his body.

Perhaps one day life would be easier though Sam wasn't sure it would be anytime soon.

After a few moments he got up, stripped off his day old clothes and was washing in cold water in a ceramic bowl on a stand when Claire appeared at the top of the ladder. The thought amused Sam that being undressed in front of a sightless woman made no difference as Claire handed him a towel. Sam wondered if it belonged to her and a thin smile played on her lips as if she had just read his thoughts.

"Everyone was exhausted after the scramble to bring in the livestock and bring the cows to shelter on the low ground. Also, all the windows needed storm shutters," Claire continued, "and that took longer as the weather got worse. I heard we were amongst the last to receive the weather warning." She paused, gingerly testing the temperature of the plate. "Seems our faithful messenger pigeon got lost," she said with an amused smile. "Your dinner's ready now."

She handed Sam a knife and fork as he sat at the table.

"After you've eaten, you can fill me in with everything that's been happening."

"Thanks." He looked ravenously at the plate in front of him.

Sam watched her while he ate and Claire collected his discarded boots and moved his oilskin to a better place to dry. As she moved, the candlelight shone through her hair, creating a golden halo around her head. The candle must have been lit as a gesture for Sam; it made no difference to Claire, his eyes taking in the details of her face. The dark rings around her eyes from when she had first arrived were slowly disappearing and her face was filling out after long weeks of starvation. He also noted that colour was returning to her skin, subduing the freckles on the curve of her cheeks below her eyes. Claire smiled, perhaps she sensed his gaze.

She sat on the chair opposite and recounted the events of the past days. The animation of her words underscored how much the security and company of the farm had come to mean and, despite her handicap, how hard she worked to be included. It was almost possible to believe that the strained relationship with Rachel would eventually become a thing of the past. But, despite his wishful thinking, there lurked a pang; somewhere beyond his ability to understand, that there was something in Rachel's animosity that warned him that he might one day have to burst Claire's bubble of happiness and find her somewhere else to live. For now though, the music of her voice and a full stomach must have tipped Sam over the threshold of exhaustion. Claire's hand gently shook his arm.

"Bed. Now."

He gazed around, confused with sleepiness.

"Lorna's gone to stay at her boyfriend's farm," Claire said. "She said you were to use her bed if you came home late."

On drowsy legs, Sam just made it to the bed behind the curtain and Claire covered him with a patchwork quilt as he fell into the arms of sleep.

During the night, a thunderstorm of enormous force swept over them. Sam was largely oblivious, uncertain whether the ear-splitting noise of the storm was real or a dream. At one point, he felt the bed move, a small voice said, "I'm frightened," and Claire slipped into bed with him.

He realised that blindness exaggerated the experience of a storm; without sight, lightning offered no forewarning of the ear-piercing cracks of thunder when they arrived. Lost in sleep, he was only vaguely aware of her shaking hands gripping his back and arm. How long they remained so he couldn't tell, but the space in his bed was empty when he woke in the morning. The day would prove to have plenty of drama of its own and Claire made no mention of what happened in the night. Perhaps, he thought, it had been no more than a dream.

In a rare interlude in the storm, Sam scurried across the yard to the farmhouse. In the lobby he found Jake morosely staring at the barometer.

"Welcome back," Jake said over his shoulder. "Can't make head nor tail of this instrument; one moment the dial is spiralling into low pressure, the next it's spinning back to high pressure off the top the scale. Do you think the damn thing could be broken?" He gave it a sharp tap with his knuckle. The needle didn't budge.

Sam found Rachel in the kitchen; she looked relieved to see him.

"I was worried you hadn't made it home before the storm broke." She glanced at the shuttered windows as they shook violently. "Is this really happening? The weather seems to have forgotten it's May."

Sam smiled weakly. "Pressure's rising, so perhaps the storm has blown itself out."

Rachel hugged him. "We were stretched yesterday without you. Any chance you can stay home, at least for a few days. The children miss you."

Sam nodded. "I won't be going far while this storm lasts and at least we can't receive any more surprises from the mainland. No one will attempt to cross the Solent in this."

Their hug was interrupted when the door burst open. Lorna, clad in oilskins and riding boots, entered, dripping rivers of rain water onto the kitchen floor, her hand guiding Claire inwards as she kicked the door closed against the wind.

"I'd swear the temperature has dropped five degrees in the past half-hour," her excited voice echoed around the room as she hauled off her dripping clothes. "I made a dash for home as soon as the wind dropped a bit. It's backed around to the north-east; if I didn't know better, I'd say it was about to snow."

Everyone in the room looked incredulous; with conditions as they were anything seemed possible. Lorna continued.

"At least we don't have to go out and feed the livestock in the barns." She paused to nod in Claire's direction. "I found Claire finishing the horses as I stopped at the stable. And she's fed and milked the cows as well, so we're spared that job this morning."

A murmur of grateful thanks went round the room; Sam noticed Rachel remained tight-lipped.

As the main farmhouse was by far the largest building, it made sense for everyone to spend the night there, sharing the generous sized rooms in anxious anticipation of what the storm might bring. The kitchen was now full of people preparing breakfast and they gathered all together around the huge table to consider their situation. Only Marcus and his son, Peter, were missing.

"Marcus told me he had spent the night worrying about the sheep, especially the younger lambs," Claire told everyone as they sat down to eat. "Marcus and Peter came into the stables first thing while I was filling the hay nets. They hitched *Samson* to the small trailer so they could take hay bales up to the top pasture," she added by way of explanation. "I expect they will be back very soon."

Those around the table smiled in Claire's direction, adding a few words of agreement as the conversation flowed onto when the storm might blow itself out. They divided equally between those who thought it was over and those who predicted that worse was still to come. Distracted by the storm, no one thought to question Sam on the events of the previous day. He was happier with things that way, preferring that the story he and Ruth had concocted to protect Longmarsh was best avoided until it had been fully tested.

With breakfast over, Lorna volunteered to climb to the crows-nest to see if there was any sign of Marcus and Peter. Despite their earlier optimism, the storm showed no sign of ending. Within minutes, Lorna was driven back inside. The sleet she had encountered earlier had turned to snow, driven horizontally into a howling blizzard. But her efforts weren't unrewarded; she had been able to make out the broad figure of *Samson* entering the farmyard with Marcus and Peter astride his back. It still took quite a time before the door opened and Marcus and Peter stumbled into the shelter of the house, both dripping water and snow.

"This brutal weather will kill half my lambs at this rate." Marcus looked at Jake urgently. "If we could take your dogs and open the large Dutch barn, we could get most of them down here into shelter before this gets worse."

Jake shrugged. "It would take a bit of clearance; I hadn't expected to accommodate livestock this late in the spring and I've got the combine harvester in there, stripped down for servicing." He looked thoughtful for a moment. "Perhaps if we close off the yard at both ends we could bring them down. They'd get some shelter closer to the house. This storm can't last much longer, surely," he added, more in hope than expectation.

Lorna listened thoughtfully. "Rather than risk bringing them down here, it might be better to breach the top stone wall and let them into the woods. That way, the sheep could find shelter amongst the trees or at least behind the wall."

They started to weigh up the options. The sheep were hardy, but the lambs had been born late and were ill-prepared for the sudden appearance of a bitter chill. To further exacerbate the situation, Peter looked out of the window.

"It's snowing hard," he added in wonderment. Their normal temperate climate on the island meant none of the younger children had ever seen real snow before. As the wind whipped flakes streamed past the window everyone stared at one another in bewildered amazement and shook their heads.

"Bang goes my potato crop," Marcus added morosely. "And some of the roof glazing has broken on the glasshouses."

"Most of the cereals are going to suffer too," Rachel added. "Did anyone turn the heating boiler on to protect the early salad crop?" Their silence confirmed her answer.

It fell to Sam to find something optimistic to brighten their gloom. "Well, at least one thing is in our favour; boar don't like the cold any more than we do. And I can't see anyone venturing across the Solent, so at least we don't have to worry about their attacks for now." He received a few half-smiles in response.

It snowed with almost white-out conditions for the next few hours. Soon it was drifting into graceful curving snow banks against walls, blanketing the rutted landscape of a working farm. It brought a peaceful beauty to their otherwise troubled world, only to be transformed into a nightmare by the unseasonal timing. Their food production was already precarious; now the growing white landscape spelt devastation to their already limited expectations.

Around mid-afternoon the snow stopped as abruptly as it had started and the younger children didn't hesitate to leave the warmth of the farmhouse to play in the pristine gleaming world outside. Within minutes all the children were outside and building snowmen to resemble the images they had only previously seen on Christmas cards found in derelict shops.

Marcus and Peter immediately set off to check their sheep, again harnessing *Samson* to an improvised sled to tow more bales of hay to the higher pasture. Unnoticed, Lorna and Claire slipped away to the barns to feed and milk the cows just in case the break in the storm became short-lived, and Sam and Jake organised a human chain to pass logs from the barn to the house. Even in the sunshine, the air bit arctic cold on a light north-easterly breeze which left the promise of an even colder night ahead. They passed logs from hand to hand, fogging the air with the breath of their exertions. Most laughed and thought the worst was over. Sam wasn't so sure.

After a while of wild play the children lost interest in the snow as gloved hands became wet and cold and snowball fights soon lost their attraction. With a mountain of logs stacked indoors, everyone went inside, leaving Sam and Jake clearing pathways and lagging exposed water pipes. They worked in distracted silence, each so lost in his own thoughts that they almost missed the first spirals of snow preceding the imminent return of the storm. Before either could comment, the largest flock of seagulls they had ever seen raced low overhead from the south-west, not pausing to settle on the farm or its buildings. Jake gazed after them.

"First time I've seen that many in a flock. Do you think they know something we don't?"

It took less than five minutes for the weather to provide an answer. The sun was eclipsed behind a roiling black cloud front, which caught them by surprise as the wind abruptly veered to the north. The first gust arrived with enormous force, sweeping up anything still loose in front of it and almost knocked over both men. Somewhere, a door slammed hard, adding the sound of breaking glass to the melee. As Jake ran for the house, Sam called urgently for Lorna and Claire who were still milking in the barn. They were safe enough at that moment, but if this wasn't an isolated gust, they could soon become trapped. And there was no sign of Marcus and Peter. An hour had passed since they had left. The high pasture and the shelter of the wood was a good mile from the farmhouse and Sam hoped they had seen the storm well before it hit them but, so far, there was no sign of *Samson*'s imposing figure. Sam ran back to the farmhouse and found Rachel frantically screwing a ply panel over the shattered glass in a kitchen door. She smiled at him as she worked.

"So much for optimism."

"With luck it won't be as bad as the first storm," Sam said, though he was alarmed by just how quickly the storm had spiralled in on them once again.

A white blizzard was streaming past the windows within minutes, obliterating their efforts to clear the pathways in a fraction of the time it had taken to clear them. Almost half an hour passed before two figures appeared in the blizzard as grey outlines, locked arm in arm and approaching the farmhouse. The door Rachel had just fixed swung violently open, and Lorna and Claire tumbled into the kitchen.

"Where did that come from?" Lorna gasped out, without expectation of an answer, and a wide grin on her face despite the situation.

Sam shook his head. "Any sign of Marcus and Peter?" he asked in a hushed voice.

Lorna shook her head.

"They'll be fine with *Samson*," Claire said in encouragement. "They'll cast off the sled and ride him back as they did last time. A storm like this won't daunt a brave horse like *Samson*."

Sam shot a look in Claire's direction, hoping she was right and he was about to thank her for again for milking the cows when an enormous crash shook the entire house, leaving the rooms full of frightened wailing children. Jake gathered the children into the central living room, now protected in the lee of the gale. He had to shout above the screaming voice of the wind.

"It's the roof platform, the crows-nest we erected around the chimney to fight the boar. The weight of snow and force of the wind must have got too much for it." He looked into the yard from a side window. "Most of it's in a heap outside in the yard now."

It was Rachel who reacted first. "I'll check the roof from the attic. With any luck, with so much snow covering the roof the tiles will have been protected from damage."

"Luck seems something we have precious little of at the moment," Sam muttered as she disappeared up the stairs towards the attic.

She returned as the first kettles had begun to boil on the kitchen range; in extreme situations they always resorted to the comfort of tea.

"All seems okay. There's some snow blowing in at the eaves but the roof doesn't seem to be damaged, at least from what I can see from the inside. We'll just have to hope that the boar don't try and creep up on us now we've lost our roof platform from which to deal with them," she added, attempting a joke to make everyone laugh.

The storm continued; a conveyor belt of gale force wind, often gusting to hurricane strength, drove blizzards of snow interspersed with brief periods of arctic bright sunshine. It was during one of these clear periods that Marcus and Peter finally rode into the farmyard astride *Samson*. The huge horse was frosted with snow and at first glance resembled some prehistoric beast from another long distant Ice Age. Both men had to be helped to dismount, their thin winter clothing making them on the cusp of exposure. Monica threw blankets around them and boiled hot water bottles and they were hurried towards the warmth of the stove, while Lorna and Claire coaxed the tired horse into his stall in the stables.

Despite the reflection of the snow, dusk arrived early, drawn in by the dense cloud mass that raced above. For a while, the snow stopped falling, though the wind showed no promise of easing. Their only encouragement was that the barometer had stabilised and was slowly beginning to rise, albeit at a snail's pace. Perhaps the following morning would bring respite, though not in time to save anything of their year's crop. But that was a problem for another day. For the moment they were warm and secure, with the comforting smell of a hot meal cooking on the range spreading through the house. Without the endless demands of the farm it felt in some ways a bit like Christmas, enabling the adults free to play continuous games with the children.

After dinner, Sam, unused to inactivity, sat dozing in front of a huge log fire. They had switched off the generator to save fuel and the children had been bathed and chased to bed when, unexpectedly, a blaze of headlights intruded into the soft light of candles and oil lamps. Sam roused himself with a start, a sudden premonition that his peaceful evening was about to be rudely interrupted. The sound of voices and stamping feet soon reached him from the front hall; a door slammed, a cold draught haunted through the house. Someone shouted his name. Reluctantly, he dragged himself away from the warmth of the fire to find Bartlett and two other men standing in the hall, their boots and coats crusted with snow.

"I didn't expect to see anyone here on a night like this," Sam ventured.

Bartlett grinned wearily, drawing deeply on an eternal roll-up.

"It's taken us an hour just to get here in the Landrover. Nothing else would get through. As ever, there's an emergency." He paused exhaling a cloud of blue smoke. He looked at Sam with red, rheumy eyes. "John's received an emergency distress call."

Sam groaned silently and looked at him with genuine surprise. "Where from? Not the mainland again?"

"No. It's from a yacht in the Channel. There are eleven people on board and they've lost their mast in this storm. It seems they have managed to rig some sort of a sail, but they don't have much steerage, and they're coming this way fast, driven on by the gales. They're signalling for help from anyone who can hear them. We can't get through to Albert Jamieson; too many big drifts, so John suggested to call you. Helen's already with John, so we're not without a plan, but we need authority to use forum resources. We need you to come and authorise that. Now. The yacht will be here in a matter of a few hours in this storm and there's nothing to warn them of where to arrive on the island, especially in the dark."

He paused briefly to allow Sam to absorb the implication of his words.

"Grab your coat, Sam, it's time go." Bartlett turned to head to the door. "And there's one thing more you need to know."

He stopped and turned to make sure Sam was following.

"This yacht has come all the way from New Zealand."

## TWENTY

Their drive to the farm near Newport, was faster, using the wheel tracks in the snow made from the outward journey. John had some of his radio sets at home where he spent hours vainly searching the frequencies in the hope that, like a desperate man panning for gold, he would occasionally find 'pay dirt'.

They entered the attic radio room where the gale force wind moaned amongst the roof tiles, a mocking accompaniment to the static hush of radio frequencies. John nodded when he saw Sam.

"Has Dave put you in the picture?" His words had a Welsh lilt which became more accentuated with excitement and anxiety.

"He's explained the situation as of a couple of hours ago. Has anything changed since then?"

John shook his head. "There is a yacht called *The Shepherd* captained by a chap called Kit Napier who seems to be in charge. Earlier today the storm almost capsized them and broke their mast. I can't imagine how they're coping; nothing should be at sea in these conditions. It's a miracle, if you ask me, that they haven't already sunk, and with four kiddies on board as well. Must be terrible for them."

Helen stepped out of the shadows of the room. "Napier is proving to be one hell of a seaman. Somehow he's rigged a storm jib on what remained of the mast. It's providing him enough to run with the wind, which swung from north to south-west again a few hours ago, but he hasn't much room to manoeuvre or change his direction."

"What's their position?" Sam asked.

John pushed a map of the Channel across the desk. A red line, marked in pencil, snaked across the map, ending with a cross.

"As best we can estimate, they're here," John pointed to the south-west of the island. "It makes them about thirty miles from us."

"And coming this way fast," Helen added.

"And the plan?" Sam asked, though in these conditions any workable plan seemed unlikely.

"With his limitations to manoeuvre, if he adjusts his course now he might just be able to pass to the south of the island and try to get into a port in the protection of the eastern shoreline. If he gets it wrong by just a few degrees, he'll miss us and run aground on the French coast. Not surprisingly, he doesn't favour that prospect, especially as we're the only voice he's been able to raise in days."

"And the Solent?" Sam wondered if it would offer better protection.

"And get through the narrow channel at Hurst Castle in this gale? Not a chance," Helen said.

Sam shrugged. Helen knew best.

"We need to move quickly and fix some lights for him to see. If we position them close to derelict lighthouses it will give Napier reference points to aim for." Helen pulled the chart closer. "We've got some old military searchlights that could be operated by mobile generators. If we position them here, here, and here," she pointed to the old westward facing lighthouses clearly shown on the map, "and shine their beams in an arc, there's a good chance Napier will see them." Helen paused. "Provided it doesn't snow again."

"How long do we have?" Sam asked, the memory of the snow filled roads from the farm prominent in his thoughts.

"We have to have the lights switched on in a couple of hours. Any more than that and Napier won't have time to adjust his course."

Sam frowned. "Sounds impossible, given the weather conditions."

"Some of the searchlights are stored in the old lighthouse in case they ever needed to be used." Sam hadn't seen Bartlett enter the room and his voice surprised him from the darkness. "We could use JCBs with wide buckets to plough the way and dig through any drifts. The Landrovers just need to tow the generators and carry fuel and tools. If we start out now we should make it in time, though the essential light at St Catherine's Point might be the last to be switched on."

Within fifteen minutes, the Landrovers had been fuelled and hitched to their equipment trailers. Bartlett had roused several squads earlier in the afternoon and most had made it to Newport despite the conditions. As soon as each JCB was ready, the convoys set out, those heading for St Catherine's Point and Bembridge being the first to leave. John had worked miracles since the Dartmouth rescue and found enough working radio sets to make sure that he could stay in contact for as long as their ageing batteries could hold their charge. Anxious to help, Sam joined the last Landrover to leave, heading for Bembridge on the east coast if by some miracle the yacht made it to that protected side of the island.

It was one in the morning when Sam's small convoy pulled into Bembridge. They had to stop frequently to allow the JCB to dig a path through the drifts on exposed sections of the road and twice had to use the chainsaws to remove fallen trees. While they waited, Aiden, leading the Bembridge team, used the time to run through the instructions for operating the searchlight. Meanwhile, Helen sent continuous updates estimating *The Shepherd*'s position; the yacht was unlikely to arrive much before three in the morning. The wind had dropped from the earlier hurricane strength but even in the shelter of the eastern shoreline, the sea was driven into mountainous waves with white combing crests.

Bembridge was dark and deserted, but the route down to the sheltered harbour had been cleared by the handful of men who fished from the small disused port. In the boatyard they found the locked shed containing the light, but in their haste to leave Newport no one had picked up the shed keys and they spent a frustrating twenty minutes breaking open padlocks. Moving on fast, they followed the road around the harbour to the sandy track that rose on the promontory of land enclosing the south side of the bay. At its mouth, the harbour entrance was surprisingly narrow, which only added to Sam's doubts about their plan. Even if Napier could get the yacht this far, the sea in the bay churned in a confusion of colliding waves, creating a turmoil of currents in the narrow entrance. Foaming breakers could strike the yacht from all sides as it tried to ride the wind, any one of which looked capable of capsizing any boat that broached across them. Sam wondered anxiously if the yacht had any fuel left for its engines. They would certainly need it.

They positioned the light on the highest point and Aiden tied everyone to safety lines as they hooked up the light and the generator in the teeth of the howling gale. From the protection of the Landrover, John reported on the radio that the two lights on the exposed west-facing coast were already in operation, including the one marking the landward side of the Needles. But to the south, Bartlett and his team were struggling to get through to St Catherine's Point, their route continually blocked by fallen trees now buried in deep snow.

Once the electrical connections were made they started a test run, only to find that the generator wouldn't start. The dark cold air filled with curses as the men fumbled with hand-held torches to find the cause of the problem, their frozen fingers eventually tracing the fault to moisture condensing in the ignition system. More precious minutes were lost as they battled the elements to dry it out. Then an urgent message was heard from Dave Bartlett, advising he had given up trying to get through to St Catherine's Point; instead he planned to use a position on the high cliffs a few miles to the north-west. With the furthest to travel, he had taken one of their few spare lights. Now battling against time and the elements, it had proven to be a wise decision.

Somewhere amidst all the noise, Sam caught a broken radio message, confirming that Napier could see the light now operating at the Needles and he had changed course towards the south-east. With St Catherine's Point still lost in the darkness it was ever more essential that Bartlett and his squad got their light into operation as soon as possible.

To add to their difficulties, it began to snow again. They managed to start the generator just in time to allow the heat of the engine to keep things dry and the generator running. It left them free to operate the light now at the mercy of the wind and snow, which cut like a knife through their clothing.

"How long can the light run for?" Sam shouted, cupping his hands against Aiden's ear.

"These generators are thirsty beasts. A couple of hours; perhaps a little more. Let's hope the survivors aren't late." Aiden paused, staring at the frothing turmoil in the harbour entrance, visible despite the darkness and driving snow. "It will be a hard enough job to navigate that, even with the searchlight. Without it, they won't have a chance of making it."

Attached to safety lines, the men were still being blown from their feet by the strength of the gale. Radio messages came through intermittently, sometimes only in fragments, and reluctantly they decided to risk turning off the generator to save fuel. With the light off they could shelter in the Landrover, feeling it shudder continuously against the force of the wind. Huddled together, time seemed to pass slowly as they waited, checking their watches every five minutes. For a while the radio fell silent and the air of anxiety increased palpably every time it squawked with static. Without the light the world around them descended into a claustrophobic coal black void, lit only by the dials of the radio set and accompanied by the thunderous roar of the raging sea.

When it came, the clarity of the message surprised them; Napier's voice so clear that he could have been in the Landrover with them.

"Newport, this is *The Shepherd*; we've rounded St Catherine's Point." There was a brief euphoric moment, quickly dispelled when he added. "We're taking in water; don't know if the pumps will hold it." He paused before adding with a note of irony, "Don't suppose there's a chance of a rescue?"

As if to underline the seriousness of the situation, the hurricane gusted with such violence it almost overturned the Landrover.

The radio waves fell silent after Napier's message. Huddled together for warmth, they waited an hour before starting the generator. To their surprise the wind swung to the south-east and Sam felt certain that it would be easier for the yacht to enter the harbour. If it was still afloat.

Intermittently, Aiden tried to contact the yacht. He was answered only by the hiss of static, making little progress until, abruptly, the radio died. Cursing their luck and struggling in wet oilskins, Sam wedged a torch between his teeth as he fumbled to change the battery in the shelter of the Landrover, only to find that the spare was lifeless too. Most of their equipment was now decades old and they were paying the price now at this time of crisis. As if they hadn't got enough challenges, the generator suddenly coughed and shuddered to a stop, refusing to be re-started. The engine had seized.

"Give us a break," Aiden shouted to the wind, taking a swipe with a wrench at the dormant machine in frustration. "They haven't got a chance of finding us without this damn useless thing."

Even if they had some spares, repairing the seized engine would take too long. They were helpless, knowing that the foundering yacht would sink, desperately searching for a light to safety that no longer existed. Unable to face the shelter of the Landrover, they all scanned the dark ocean and sky with a handful of flares as a final hope. Straining their eyes into the spray and darkness, none of them saw the white lights crawling up the track from behind them.

It wasn't until the approaching engine began to labour that its deep throated roar made them turn in surprise. Coming towards them, lights blazing, was a battered tractor, hauling a laden trailer through the snow. Astonished, they watched as the machine drew alongside the dormant searchlight. In the glow of instrument lights, Sam could just make out Javed in the driver's cab, Ruth perilously clinging to grab-handles beside him. Dressed in oilskins many sizes too large she climbed down, her face wet and gleaming with excitement in the headlights.

"Made it; we followed your tracks," she blurted out, her words a mixture of relief and excitement. "John thought you might have problems with that generator so we added another one to the supplies we had already loaded. We've also brought extra bedding and food. He guessed you might also have problems with the radio, so we've got spare batteries."

Grinning from ear to ear, Sam searched for the replacements, while the others manhandled the heavy generator off the tail of the trailer. With batteries loaded he switched on the radio. The dials slowly lit up and within moments he made contact with John. But before they could speak, the voice of Napier cut across them, his words terse and strained.

"What's the problem, guys? I can't see any lights."

"It's good to hear from you Napier. We're just fixing a few small problems. I'm about to fire a red flare; tell me if you can see it."

He waited, tense with anticipation. Over the howl of the wind he could hear the sound of voices shouting in the background over the radio.

"Got it. We've just seen something, low down, some way off on our port side. But we're going to need more than that, and quick." Napier's words were sharp and to the point. "We're taking on water faster than we can pump out. I'm changing course now towards the flare, but you're going to have to use the searchlight beam if we're going to stand any chance of getting into harbour."

Sam glanced towards the group working feverishly to prepare the new generator. Ruth and Javed were battling to fill its fuel tank from a jerry can, while Aiden and the others connected power cables to the searchlight. Sam fired another red flare into the sky on the premise that anything was better than nothing. Beside him, the generator coughed into life and stalled, then he heard Napier's angry voice on the radio.

"For god's sake, stop firing flares and give me a cone of light."

Again the generator coughed, spluttered, and coughed again, then clouds of white smoke belched from the exhaust; the starter motor gave a dry metallic whine and the engine gulped and roared into life. Someone switched on the light, the powerful filament glowing pale orange. For long seconds it seemed that it was all they were going to get until suddenly, a beam of dazzling white light shot into the maelstrom of the night sky.

Over the thunder of the sea, Sam just managed to catch Napier's words. "Okay, we can see you. Lower the beam to just above horizon and give it twenty degrees more south-south-east. Hold it there until I tell you, then swing the beam to light the harbour entrance."

The generator was now roaring at full power, four men bracing themselves to hold the direction wheels of the light steady while being soaked in freezing spray. Everyone had done their best; one way or another it would all soon be over.

Minutes ticked slowly by, the radio silent. Below, the sea raged into the harbour entrance, throwing up fountains of spray as the wind driven waves collided. Even if Napier managed to slip through the narrow entrance, the boat would still face a hostile sea. The radio squawked.

"Move the light to the entrance." Napier shouted the words, terse and abrupt.

At first all Sam could see was a red light that appeared to be floating in the sea. It disappeared, only to rocket skywards as a huge wave thrust a white hull high into the air where it seemed to hang motionless before the bow crashed forward, the stern rearing up at a precarious angle as a monster wave carried the boat forwards, before dropping it stern first into the approaching trough. The scene looked terrifying.

The light beam now fell onto the opposite side of the harbour entrance; it looked impossibly narrow. As the yacht rose again Sam could just make out a tattered jib sail lashed to the mast. Below the howl of the wind Sam could hear the forlorn growl of diesel engines, the screw thrashing air as the stern was once again tilted at a crazy angle as the next wave arrived. But instead of sliding down the back of the wave the yacht seemed to settle on the top, surging forward as it surfed the combing crest. As it finally crashed backwards into the trough the bow was struck by a wave racing towards the entrance, only this time from the harbourside. By some miracle the yacht was through.

Leaving Aiden to manage the searchlight, Sam leapt into the Landrover, determined to get to the jetty to help Napier moor the boat. The coast road was free of snow and it was only a matter of minutes before he was driving onto the quay, headlights on full beam to guide Napier to the shore. The profile of the yacht appeared again, still fighting a violent sea, as Sam slammed the Landrover door shut behind him. He could just make out three figures on deck, frantically throwing over side fenders and mooring lines to protect the sides of the battered hull as the yacht raced forwards at speed, threatening to smash into the jetty in the final act of her battle with the storm.

A wave crashed into the jetty, soaking them with its spray. In the trough that followed, the yacht suddenly jibed, diesel engines screaming at full speed in a frantic race against the next wave. Napier held the rudder hard over, forcing the yacht to turn violently through a half circle, heeling sideways at a crazy angle, pointing her bow to take the next wave head on and stalling her forwards motion in the process. With her head into the wind and sea, Napier raced the engines into reverse and the yacht was hauled backwards against the side of the jetty where waiting hands grasped mooring lines and bound her hard against the bollards. The engine note died away like a fading sigh in the turbulent night. *The Shepherd* had arrived. Their mysterious visitors were safe.

## TWENTY-ONE

"You saved our lives."

Napier's Kiwi accent gave Sam a start as he joined him at the window, watching the churning waters of the small harbour in the grey light of early morning. Sam had been staring at *The Shepherd* as she rolled and pitched against her mooring lines. Her wet sails lay in unfolded heaps on her deck; the fractured stub of her main mast pointed skywards like a broken finger and her sheets and lines were knotted and tangled in a spaghetti of rope and wire.

They had all spent what remained of the dark hours on mattresses and air beds that Ruth and her team had set out in the canteen of an abandoned holiday camp in Bembridge. Ruth had provided food and hot drinks for everyone, but many had been so badly seasick, a combination of the dreadful sea conditions and unremitting fear, that few had wanted to eat. Now, most slept soundly on in the morning, while Sam and Napier watched the continued rage of the storm. Napier handed Sam a steaming mug.

"Fresh coffee, courtesy of the farmers of New Zealand."

"Getting your yacht through that narrow entrance was no mean feat," Sam nodded at the salt stained hull of *The Shepherd* moored just outside.

Napier yawned and languidly stretched his six-foot frame. At a glance he looked about thirty, with a tanned weather-beaten complexion and salt-bleached blond hair.

"We couldn't have made it without your help. We owe you a great debt," Napier said, his tone matter of fact. "The gale would have blown us straight on to the French coast. In these conditions I don't think that would have been a pleasant prospect." Napier laughed at the thought. "Not least because I can't speak French."

"So," Sam started on the subject that had his curiosity aroused, "you're a long way from home. What brings you half way around the world to yet another troubled land?" The question had been on the tip of his tongue ever since they had welcomed ashore Napier and his crew of three New Zealanders and two rescued Spanish speaking families with three young children.

Napier sipped his coffee and delved in the leather satchel he wore across his chest. "I suppose you could call me a glorified postman." He produced a cream envelope and handed it to Sam. Stencilled on the front of the envelope were the words *For the Boss*.

Sam regarded it with raised eyebrows while Napier added, "It's to whoever is in charge here. It's from our Prime Minister."

The look on Sam's face changed from surprise to incredulity. "Prime Minister? I thought ...?"

"Of South Island, New Zealand. By some miracle of foresight, we avoided the pandemic and had no boar farms to add to the problems." He stood for a moment, watching the storm try to tear *The Shepherd* from her moorings. "When the pandemic took hold in China and the Far East, our government acted fast and closed our ports and Auckland airport. It wasn't popular at the time; many thought we were being inhumane and selfish." Napier shook his head, lost in reflective thought. "But by the time we started arguing about the policy, half the world was already dead. Turns out that our early decision saved us. Very quickly we realised something terrible had happened and managed to organise some sort of rescue operation, but it was already too late; North Island had been devastated by the virus and became a happy hunting ground for the large numbers of boar that had broken out of their farms. It swamped our resources; we rescued a few survivors ... but now North Island is just boar land, no different to your mainland here."

Sam twisted the envelope in his hands and felt a strong temptation to open it, but that was the prerogative for Albert Jamieson, so he tucked it into his pocket and asked the question repeated so many countless times in the past five years.

"How many of you have survived?" The largest group Sam had seen in one place since the pandemic was here on the Isle of Wight.

"At the last count, about four hundred thousand, of which about ten percent are blind." Napier watched Sam over the rim of his cup as the shock sunk in. "We think we're the largest single surviving population on earth. In all our travels, we've never found any evidence of anything close to our numbers."

Sam frowned, struggling with the maths. "But surely, America must hold large populations too? I know we haven't heard

anything from them, but it can only be a matter of time before …"
He halted. Napier was looking at him stony-faced.
"So you don't know?"
"Know what?"
Napier drew a breath. "The pandemic entered America from the East and the medical authorities misjudged its virulence from the start. They knew it could be bad from what they had heard from the Far East, but nothing prepared them for what arrived and they lost control of it in a matter of days. It raged like a forest fire from coast to coast. There was one unexpected consequence; very soon no one turned up to work at any of the nuclear power stations the Americans have for generating electricity. Seems the clever designers thought of every possible eventuality that might befall their wonderful invention, except one; the day when no one would turn up for work ever again." Napier paused to allow the enormity of the thought to sink in. "Seems it didn't take long for things to go wrong, and with no one to fix the problems, or flip the off switch, things very soon got out of hand. We've no idea exactly what did happen, but we can guess. Now, vast areas of America and Canada are little more than a radiated waste land. All that survives are boar and cockroaches; those bastards actually seem to thrive on the radiation," he said with a grim note of irony, before adding, "Have you checked your radiation levels here?"
Sam could only shake his head. It had never occurred to them to do so and anyway, they had no Geiger counters. He was dumbfounded, lost for words. If Napier was telling the truth, their hope for a resurgent America, who would one day arrive with a rescue plan, had in a single moment become no more than a mirage.
Napier continued. "Well, you need to check the radiation. We stopped in a small harbour in the Channel Islands before the storm began; the radiation levels were high, far beyond normal background levels. The wind blows the fallout across the Atlantic, with nothing in its path. Radioactive particles will be falling in the rain, especially when the wind comes from the south-west and will affect all of you here too, in low doses if you're lucky."

Sam looked stunned. If Napier was correct, the harvests they were struggling to grow were being washed in a poisonous radioactive soup.

"What about Asia, or Africa?" There had to be at least some good news somewhere.

Napier shook his head. "We found that about a year after the pandemic, plague festered its ugly head in the Far East, probably from survivors in the slums of India, who knows. It spread even faster than the pandemic, with more or less a hundred percent mortality amongst the starving survivors in Asia. Boar did the rest, opportunist bastards that they are."

"Africa?"

"From the few survivors we've found, a lethal virus called ebola is rampant throughout the continent. There are fewer boar about, but a deviant form of cockroach has developed with a paralysing sting. And like boar, the roaches thrive on rotting human flesh."

Sam shuddered. He exhaled, long and slow, as though frightened that the very air around them might be filled with radiation and viruses.

"So, mother earth has finally decided to have done with us. First she maims us and then sets out to erase what few vulnerable survivors remain."

The finality in his words needed no answer. Distractedly, he pulled out the envelope Napier had given him.

"Anything positive in this?" he asked grimly.

Napier gazed seaward, a thin smile on his lips.

"I think you'll find it's an invitation."

"An invitation?"

Sam said the word, laced with irony. "What to, the party to celebrate the end of the human race?" He found himself laughing at the tragedy of such an idea, though for the life of him, he couldn't think why.

"An invitation," Napier repeated evenly, "to come and join us."

Sam was silent, distracted with the enormity of Napier's words. Napier gave him a moment, and then continued.

"For a while we thought that enough of the world's population had survived to regenerate across the globe. Sadly, the discoveries of our travels tell us that it won't, not in a thousand years, if ever. Global numbers are far smaller than we ever dared to fear. South Island has been blessed, or cursed, depending on your viewpoint. No pandemic, no boar, and we're missing the worst of the radioactive fallout coming from America, and Russia too, most probably. It would explain why the fallout is detectable in so many parts of the world. And you may be right; maybe mother earth does intend to wipe us out completely, have done with mankind once and for all, as if we're a failed experiment. But it might still be possible to convince her to give us one last chance. Few of us there might be, but it's not over yet, and we're not going down without a fight. A copy of the letter you're holding has been given to every group of survivors we find. It lays out our principles, values, and desires for a new society, a new *homo et fidem spem* that will live in faith and hope with the planet that bears us. The letter asks you all, sighted and blind, to come and join us."

He paused, his expression now showing his emotions.

"Before it's too late."


Albert Jamieson arrived as Sam and Napier were finishing breakfast. He was accompanied by Rigby, John, and a four-man squad, towing a trailer filled with extra supplies. Albert's face had taken on a grey drawn pallor and he was sweating, despite the bitter cold. He still had a broad smile to everyone he met.

"Even in daylight, that was a tough journey. Goodness knows how you got here in the dark," he said to Napier.

"It was an amazing feat of seamanship for our friends here to get into the harbour without capsizing." Sam paused to introduce Napier to Albert Jamieson and the others. They all shook hands, aware of the huge number of questions waiting to be asked from both sides. Sam gave Albert the envelope that Napier had handed to him.

"This is for you. It seems that Napier is an emissary, from the government of New Zealand."

Everyone looked astonished; even Rigby gasped, while John just smiled, and Albert repeated, "New Zealand?"

On the far side of the room Sam saw their boat engineer Joe Cramer arrive. "Look, before we bombard Napier with a thousand questions, why don't we let him make an evaluation of his damaged yacht with Cramer? Then we can start sorting out what repairs are needed to get his boat seaworthy again. While that's happening, you can all read this letter and I'll bring you up to speed with everything I've been told so far."

Napier departed with Cramer. Sam found a side room that looked as though it had once been an office, complete with scuffed wooden desk and a swivel chair with split seams and protruding filling. He suggested that Albert had the room to himself to read the letter while he organised the treat of Napier's fresh coffee for them all.

"Are you okay, Albert?" he asked with concern as he settled him at the desk.

Albert winced and had a smile that was slightly mischievous. "Nothing that a whisky wouldn't fix."

Unconvinced, Sam left him and went to join Rigby and the others who were busy laughing with Ruth and some of the other squad members.

"Is this man for real?" Rigby asked sceptically as Sam arrived. "Are we really expected to buy his story? Why would anyone sail all the way from New Zealand just to deliver a letter making some crazy offer? For my money, they're no more than a Trojan horse for the mob attacking us." He paused to look at the yacht, still rolling against the quayside in the heavy swell. "I think a few blunt questions need to be asked of our new friend Napier; then we'll soon find out the real story."

Sam laughed. "Connor, not every visitor we receive deserves the third degree. Before you try electric shock and fingernail extraction, just consider the facts. For a start, there are two families on board who are Spanish," Sam nodded in the direction of a small group now eating breakfast at one of the tables. "Napier picked them up from Galicia in northern Spain on the way here. The crew and their yacht are simply the advance party for a much larger operation. Napier says their mother ship, *The Aotearoa* is currently anchored in Gibraltar and will come north if he finds a large group who want to be rescued."

"Very generous of them, but personally, I don't buy philanthropy; it doesn't fit my view of the world as it now exists," Rigby replied caustically.

At that, they all smiled.

"Connor, you're just becoming a suspicious old man. Give the world a break for a moment, it might just not be as bad a place as you think."

Sam sounded light, conveniently not mentioning the stories of plague and radioactive fallout Napier had described; in the midst of their current crisis, anything positive had to be good news.

After about ten minutes, the door to the office opened and Albert Jamieson beckoned them in. He returned wearily to his chair; on the desk in front of him were three typed sheets of cream paper. Albert waited for them all to enter.

"I recommend you take turns to read this letter before anyone starts to ask questions. Then we'll discuss what to do about the contents."

Sam waited until last for his turn to read the letter. He knew much of it already from his conversation with Napier, though the letter laid out more clearly how New Zealand had fortunately avoided the pandemic that had engulfed the world, and included a summary of the constitution by which the survivors in New Zealand now lived. The final paragraph listed the terms of their invitation to any peace loving people who would join them on South Island. Sam returned the letter to Albert with an anxious look; the man looked ill despite his assurances to the contrary.

"Okay," Albert began. "To start, can I have an initial comment from you all in turn. Please keep it short."

Sam was surprised to see Albert had included Ruth in their gathering. She wasn't a forum member, but then neither was John or Aiden for that matter. The speed of events was blurring the boundary lines very quickly and maybe that was a good thing.

"Connor?"

"An elaborate hoax," Rigby said, arms folded.

"John?"

John cast an uncomfortable glance in Rigby's direction. "In the circumstances it's impossible to think it's fake. Somewhere in the world had to be spared. We all hoped it would be America, but I'll take New Zealand as an alternative any day."

Albert nodded. "Ruth?"

She was leaning against the wall; Sam guessed it was to take the pressure off her maimed leg. "I think it sounds plausible, but like Connor, I think we should be careful and make sure we don't drop our defences until we're certain of the truth of the facts." Her answer carefully avoided isolating Rigby; she probably could anticipate what Sam's answer would be.

"Sam?"

"Having watched them fight to survive the storm last night, I believe what we're being told. There is a way to validate what Napier has said and that's for us to speak directly with *The Aotearoa* in Gibraltar. Napier must have the equipment on the yacht with the range to do that and we could ask if John can use it and make a connection for you, Mr Chairman, to speak to them directly."

"And that would prove what, exactly?" Rigby cut in. "We could be talking to some thug in Portsmouth for all we know."

"Simple," Sam retorted. "Craig spent many years in the Royal Navy. He once told me he had been based in Gibraltar. All you have to do is ask the captain of *The Aotearoa* to look out of his window and describe the dockyard. Then Craig can confirm if he's telling the truth."

Napier returned with a long list of replacement equipment and repairs needed, and a grey box containing a Geiger counter.

"It's not as bad as it looks," Joe Cramer said in his laconic Scottish brogue. "A week and we'll have her fixed to rights again."

Cramer had known little about boats before he came to the island, but as an engineer he learned fast; it was all machinery to him.

"We'll have to find a new mast in Newport; there's nothing the size of *The Shepherd* in Bembridge and the weather will need to improve a lot before towing her around the coast."

Sam called Rigby over to join them. Napier was about to explain how to use the Geiger counter and take the readings, something in which he wanted to include Rigby. If they both verified the readings across the island it would help avoid future disputes. Rigby tapped the instrument's dials sceptically.

"How come you Kiwis seem to be such experts in nuclear radiation? I thought all you knew about were sheep and grass," he said provocatively.

Napier grinned at his words. "Courtesy of a group of Californian survivors who managed to sail across the Pacific Ocean in the boat that is now *The Shepherd*. The truth of what had happened in America in the days immediately following the pandemic came to New Zealand with them. One of the survivors had been working in a new atomic power station on the west coast near Los Angeles."

Rigby was impassive. The proof would be in the readings they took across the island. "We'll see, though I've yet to see any of our sheep glowing in the dark."

Albert Jamieson interrupted them, asking Napier to join them in his temporary office. The table had been moved to the middle of the room with chairs set around it. Albert sat at one end and invited Napier to sit beside him. Sam noted that Rigby took a chair at the opposite end as a ploy to distance himself from the proceedings. A long tray, set with thermos and mugs, was placed in the middle of the table along with a freshly cut rose, the colour and emblem of their island. A partly opened rosebud was also pinned to Albert's lapel to signify his status and welcome an important guest. Albert started by introducing Napier.

"I think you've been introduced to everyone here, Mr Napier."

"Just call me Kit or Napier, please."

Albert nodded and paused, looking at the letter in front of him. "No doubt we have a lot of questions to ask one another. Time is short and serious discussions should only take place when a full forum of all members can assemble. However, these extraordinary weather conditions prevent that at the moment."

Napier nodded. "We find the climate is changing everywhere on the planet. Some blame it on the radioactive fallout … Others blame the boar," he added with mild amusement.

"And you would know, of course." Rigby fired a caustic shot.

Napier smiled at the barb. Relieved, Sam thought, 'He's a seasoned performer; he's used to handling this.'

Napier continued. "It seems logical. Boar emit a lot of methane from their digestive process and this could be combining with the radioactive dust in the atmosphere; it will take the planet decades to absorb that, just as it did with the dust when the dinosaurs became extinct."

"So, an expert in history as well." Rigby's words verged on contempt as he sat staring with a bored expression at the weather beyond the window.

Albert smiled, ignoring the comments. "In the short time we have, could you explain in more detail the surprising invitation we have received from your government? It's an extremely long way from New Zealand. There are about a thousand of us living on this island and I can't see us all fitting onto your yacht."

A ripple of laughter circled the table, lifting the mood. Rigby pointedly refused to laugh.

Napier continued. "We set out on this mission in the hope of finding groups of survivors prepared to come and join us. Presently, our mother ship, an ageing passenger liner, *The Aotearoa*, is docked in Gibraltar. She has space for a couple of thousand people at a squeeze, but there's no point in using up precious fuel if no one is there to be rescued. Which is where my job comes in."

"Rescued?" Rigby cut in. "I don't recall anyone here sending out a distress message saying 'please come and rescue us'." He fired an accusing glance at John before continuing. "Why don't you all come and join us here instead; our island is big enough to absorb tens of thousands more and, after all, we are your mother country, so it would be merely reversing emigration back to the homeland."

Napier nodded. "A fair comment, except as I've already said, everywhere we travel we find the climate is changing, often quite dramatically. Are you having harvest problems?" He paused and raised an eyebrow, looking out of the window at the stark white light reflecting from the drifted snow. "Perhaps more importantly, I think you need to check the island for radioactive fallout from the American power stations. It might not be too high, but there could well be enough to be absorbed into your food chain. The animals will react first; have you found a drop in fertility, with poor general health and early deaths from unknown causes?" He watched as his question was answered by the intuitive glances between them.

"We're told the plumes of radioactivity will continue for years, perhaps decades, as these power plants burn through their broken reactors. You might not get the worst of the fallout; that's already swamping continental America, but the prevailing wind is from the south-west." Napier paused with a shrug of the shoulders. "How's your human birth rate standing up and what's the incidence of cancer?"

"None of your damned business," Rigby barked at him.

Napier shrugged. "As you wish; but if you want to invite us to stay here, don't expect too many volunteers to come and join you. On balance I'd say the prospects aren't particularly attractive, as you'll soon discover with the loss of your harvest and the radioactivity check."

Albert Jamieson interjected, stalling Rigby's next repost. "Kit, you have to understand, this island is our home, our refuge *in extremis*. Most of us have grown very attached to the community we've had to fight to establish. We know nothing of New Zealand and, as generous as your offer is, you may find the fighting spirit still holds amongst us and many may wish to stay and see things through, whatever unknown difficulties await us. To abandon our homes to boar for a second time will be a step too far for many, no matter what the odds against us might become."

To Sam's ears they were elegant words, though he doubted their grip on reality. "Mr Chairman, may I make a point. We pride ourselves as a surviving beacon of democracy. The forum must debate this offer from our friends ..."

"If they really are our friends," Rigby's blunt words cut across him, aimed at annoying Sam in the process.

"... but at the end of our discussions, should it not be down to each individual on the island to decide to stay or leave, irrespective of what the forum prefers or recommends?"

Albert leaned back in his chair. Sam's suggestion cut new ground; beyond elections, voting had only been used once before when they had set up the constitution for the island.

"It would seem fair, I'll grant you, but a vote might well split the island. If a substantial number choose to leave, where does that leave those who wish to stay? It's hard enough to maintain a viable community with our current population. If we halve the numbers, those remaining would struggle to survive. And what of the future for those who are blind?"

Ruth, seemingly distracted, was writing notes on a pad on her knee. "Mr Chairman, forgive me for interrupting. I'm not a forum member but I would like to endorse your point about preserving our community. I've always thought of it like a beehive, in which we all stand, or fall, together. It can't be just for the forum to decide unilaterally, on its own. In this instance that could be too divisive. We've never done things that way and we mustn't start now. But, even if less than half choose to leave ... well, you're right, it would most likely spell the end for those who remain."

Ruth looked directly at Sam. "So I propose that after the forum have discussed and debated this offer from New Zealand, the options are put to the island population in the form of a referendum; everyone, men, women, children, blind and sighted, all vote. A straight majority decides for us all." Ruth placed emphasis on her final words. "If only one more person votes to leave than stay, then we all leave together."

"Or we all stay if a majority of one votes to stay," Rigby interjected.

Everyone nodded in agreement, and, for a while, they all sat in silence.

John was the first to raise an arm. "I second that."

Rigby sat silent, withdrawn behind a mask of his own thoughts. Albert Jamieson made a careful note at the bottom of the letter of invitation in front of him. Looking up, he announced, "I propose that, on the matter of a referendum, it will be put to the forum as soon as we can possibly call an emergency meeting. Any referendum can only come as a result of that meeting and after we've checked the radiation levels across the island."

As they all gathered to leave, it began to snow hard once more and Sam noted with curiosity that the merest of smiles, barely concealed, seemed to play across Albert's lips.

# TWENTY-TWO

In daylight, the return journey to Newport was easier. A few miles inland, Sam, travelling in company with Rigby and Aiden, came upon a farm with an array of glasshouses. The devastated scene confirmed their worst fears. Snow had drifted high against the side walls, and glass roof panels lay in broken shards under the weight of snow, leaving the plants and salad crops blackened and shrivelled amongst a blanket of white. A short distance beyond the wrecked glasshouses, an orchard appeared ravaged by the storm as fading spring blossom stained the snow around the base of every tree. There was no sign of anyone; the nearest farm buildings were a mile or so farther along the road. Sam looked at Rigby and Aiden, both lost in thought; if this scene repeated at every farm on the island, the implications for their crop loss would be catastrophic.

Sam had asked Aiden to join him with the excuse of driving the Landrover. More importantly, his presence would help prevent arguments erupting between Sam and Rigby. He would have preferred to have made the journey alone, but excluding Rigby would have left his reports of the storm damage open to dispute, especially given Rigby's antagonistic attitude towards Napier.

Around midday, the gales finally blew themselves out, leaving a breeze from the south to clear the sky and offer a slight rise in temperature. Slowly, snow turned to slush and the Landrover made better progress, except where drifts had swept across the open road. Every few miles or so they stopped, often wading knee deep through softening snow, to get some idea of the extent of damage. Bypassing Newport to the south, they aimed for the coast. As expected, the snowfall reduced as they drew closer to the sea but here the wind damage was greater, with orchards and woodland littered with uprooted trees, roofless barns and hay and silage stacks flattened. Arriving in Freshwater they found the main road blocked by a collapsed gable wall which had taken most of the adjacent roof with it. There was no point in going any farther. As they sat drinking coffee from a flask, it was Aiden who summarised their thoughts.

"Well, if what we've seen so far is representative of the entire island, we're in big trouble."

"I've seen worse," replied Rigby. "If the storm hadn't washed up those jokers on our shores with their fancy tales we'd just mend and make do, pick ourselves up and just get on with life as before."

"But it's not," Sam said more sharply than he intended. "Life is not as before. Any ordered stable world came to an abrupt end five years ago. We've soldiered on, yes, fighting boar, absorbing everything that's been thrown at us. But this storm will be a game changer." He was unable to hide a growing feeling of sadness.

"So what, we throw in the towel?" Rigby replied. "None of us expect a long and easy life. Nothing's changed from where I'm sitting."

"Perhaps not for us, but think of the children and the coming generations. This storm has destroyed most, if not all, of this year's harvest and we're left with little, if any, way of replacing it quickly." Sam hesitated, staring at the white landscape surrounding them. "At best, our reserves are down to six months and then only if we issue strict rationing. You know as well as anyone that it'll take more than a year for the next harvest. And who's to say that won't fail as well."

Rigby regarded Sam sceptically. "You don't know that for sure, no one does. But I'd rather go down fighting than run away from my home to a place I know nothing about; if such a place exists."

Despite Aiden's presence, Sam felt his anger surge. "What you can see out of these very windows is clear enough evidence of our future. Turning your back on that is way beyond just wishful thinking."

Rigby shrugged. "So says our new agricultural expert. Weather is a balancing act, you take the good with the bad. I'm for sticking things out and I'll wager most people on the island will agree with me. Okay, so Albert Jamieson might get his democratic referendum agreed by the forum, but remember, you only need a majority of one."

"Either way," Sam called out to Rigby's departing back as he strode off through the snow.

It was nearly dark by the time Sam approached the farm on the grey mare he had used a few days before. Having seen enough, they drove back from Freshwater to Newport to find that John and Albert Jamieson had returned, leaving Joe Cramer to organise the yacht repairs with Napier and his crew. On arriving, they made a brief report of their findings to Albert who listened with a grim expression, the details confirming his worst fears.

"There's little we can do for now," he said. "We'll organise a thorough survey of the entire island as soon as conditions permit. I'll call a forum meeting in the next day or so, but until then, I suggest you all head home to your families and get some rest."

As Sam made to leave, John fell in step beside him. "I've heard from David Longmarsh," he said, his face wreathed in the first smile Sam had seen in a while.

"When?" Sam asked, surprised.

"Last night, during the height of the storm. He probably used it as a cover, hoping no one might be around to listen. It was only the code word we gave him, but it proves our link is working."

Sam nodded. The news was encouraging; if nothing else, it confirmed that Longmarsh had won the race back to the mainland. During the previous twenty-four hours, boar attacks had been relegated to something of a sideshow, but this was a stark reminder that their problems were only in temporary abeyance.

It was a good thing that the mare knew her way to the farm. Exhausted, Sam fell asleep in the saddle and only woke on hearing Lorna's voice as the mare ambled through the slush that covered the cobbled farmyard. He dismounted, stiff and cold, passed the horse to Lorna and entered the warm glow of the kitchen where Rachel greeted him with a hug.

"Welcome home, stranger," she teased.

"We've been busy."

"Aren't you always." She turned to a huge pot on the stove. "You must be starving; come and sit down and tell all while you eat."

In their small world, news that Sam was back quickly circled the farm and very soon the kitchen was full, everyone keen to hear the latest. Despite their limited communications, gossip still found a means to spread quickly around the island and they had already heard a version of the appearance of a strange yacht in the height of the storm. As he ate, Sam gave an outline of the events of the previous night. Too tired to deal with the fallout of bad news, he didn't tell them about a disease ravaged world almost void of humans. People could only cope with so much bad news at one time and they had yet to discover just how seriously their farm had been damaged by the storm.

"An invitation to go and live in New Zealand? Are you serious?" Jake couldn't keep a note of incredulity from his voice.

"It seems they could be the only large population group remaining, with most of their communities and infrastructure intact. And they have the added advantage of never trusting the experiment in mass boar farming, so they're free of the menace. So far, no boar have crossed the Cook Straight to South Island. Their major problem is oil, just like us, and if we don't join them, there is little, if anything, they'll be able to do to help us on a regular basis beyond the possible occasional delivery of supplies."

Sam hesitated and decided to avoid the subject of the radioactive fallout. It was yet to be established how big a problem they had. Again, he avoided too much bad news.

"There's talk of a vote for everyone on the island, a referendum, to be held when all the details and facts are known. A straight majority must decide for us all, one way or another. No one can be left behind." He paused, allowing the idea to gain some traction.

Lorna shouted with excitement. "Imagine, New Zealand. What an adventure."

Marcus didn't sound too sure. "Why would we go to the other side of the world? This island is our home, we belong here. We've given blood, sweat, tears, even our lives, to build what we have now. I wouldn't be happy to let a handful of boar and one bad harvest chase me away."

Brave talk, and in the nature of these things, Sam could see his point of view. At that moment, he could only nod in acknowledgement, too tired to take forward a debate on the full implications of their situation. He sat back, listening, as the bubble of excited conversation washed around him and with eyes half-closed, he realised that Claire was missing.

Later, as he washed dishes at the sink, Lorna nudged his elbow, his saddle bags looped over her arm. "I've fed and watered your mare."

"Thanks. Where's Claire?" Sam tried to sound casual.

"She says she's not feeling well," Lorna said with a sigh, adding, "there's been more cross words with Rachel over her share of the farm tasks. It was bound to happen, with all of us under lockdown in the house while the storm lasted." She hesitated, giving Sam a knowing look. "The problem isn't going away, Sam, in fact, it's getting worse."

Sam awoke to the sound of bird song; the early morning chorus. He was confused to find himself alone in bed, and then remembered a troubled night. Their daughter, Gemma, had developed a temperature and after being roused several times, Rachel had decided to sleep with the children to be on hand if they woke again. Sam glanced at the clock, surprised to find it light so early, only to remember the covering of snow outside. It might be fast turning into wet slush, but not before it had destroyed most of their crops.

The house was silent as he dressed and quietly descended the stairs in his socks. He decided he would tour the farm to evaluate the scale of the damage before anyone else appeared. Questions lay ahead to be answered and it was important to make an assessment before they began making plans. In the kitchen he paused to fill a thermos before setting off to wade through the wet snow that covered the yard to the stables.

The mare Sam had ridden the previous evening gave him a discouraging look and gently shook her head. He smiled as he passed by. "You can sleep in," he muttered to her softly and continued to the stall occupied by *Rowan*, the horse he usually preferred to ride on the farm. Returning from the tackroom with his saddle, Sam caught sight of a figure moving in the shadows near the bottom of the ladder to the loft.

"Sam? Is that you?" Claire asked with a note of uncertainty.

"Claire. How are you? When I got back last night, Lorna told me you were unwell." He had been meaning to check on her before bed, but his intentions had been interrupted when Gemma woke.

"I'm fine," Claire replied.

She didn't sound particularly convincing but Sam thought it wiser not to probe any deeper, though her issues with Rachel were becoming plain to everyone on the farm. When she stepped forward into the light, he could see dark circles around her eyes, accentuated by a pale drawn face.

"Now that the snow is starting to melt, are you up to an early morning hack? I want to inspect the farm before I'm called away again," he added with a note of humour. "And it'll give me a chance to update you on what has happened in the past few days, which involves you as well."

Although Claire had clearly been upset, she rewarded Sam with a smile, weaker than normal, but a smile just the same.

Claire saddled her own horse while Sam was still tightening his girth strap. She had been given a boisterous young piebald called *Frisco*, who no one else had patience with. At first he had seemed an inappropriate horse for a blind girl. Whether *Frisco* was aware of her handicap or not, Sam suspected Claire had a natural empathy with the unwanted horse and their relationship developed immediately into a meeting of minds with the result that *Frisco* responded to Claire's every word or gesture, much to the bemusement of all his previous riders.

Softened by the rising temperature, the snow masked the sound of the horses' hooves as they walked through the yard, their steps marked only by a cushioned slush rather than the hard impact of steel shoes on cobbles. Sam strapped a map of the farm to his right knee so he could record an accurate picture of the damage wrought by the storm, and once clear of the yard they mounted the horses.

"You're behaving mysteriously." Claire's sense of humour seemed to have returned now they were riding clear of the farmhouse.

"Just checking. I'm away so much I'm beginning to lose touch."

Sam rode on, not wishing to expand further. There was much he wanted to tell her, but felt the need to get farther from the farmhouse before he said more.

He had three coloured wax pencils, each on a cord tied to the map, so he could code the condition of their crops in various fields; blue for fields that might recover after the storm, orange would be marginal, and red signified total wipe out.

They crossed the first paddock closest to the farm. It was used for the horses throughout the year and Sam felt a sense of relief when he saw grass shoots sprouting vividly through the covering of snow.

"Tell me what you can see," Claire asked, curious to hear a picture of the state of the farm. She rode beside Sam, partly as a consideration to his horse, *Rowan*, who became nervous whenever *Frisco* walked behind.

"I'll try to, but it's only part of a bigger story; when we stop in the shelter of the woods I'll tell you more."

That appeared to satisfy Claire and for the next half-hour she seemed happy to ride in mutual silence, alone with her thoughts in a world of her imagination. In some hamlets, blind members also rode, but usually needed a lead rein attached to a sighted rider. Claire seemed to have complete confidence in *Frisco*, using him as her eyes, sensing his moods and his ability to keep them both safe. As they rode, the devastation wrought by the storm was plain to see. To Sam's left, a potato crop reared black and stunted, the entire harvest destroyed, while to his right, fields of winter wheat were blown flat, hidden by a thick carpet of snow that bent and flattened the early shoots. On his map, an alarming number of fields were now marked with red crosses and it was most likely that this would be repeated on other farms throughout the island.

As they crossed the top pasture leading up to the shelter of the copse, dozens of white mounds marked the icy tombs of those ewes and lambs who had perished before Marcus had breached the stone wall. They reigned in the horses against the dry stone wall through which Marcus and Peter had hastily broken out an opening to allow the surviving sheep to gain shelter from the storm amidst the trees. Looking south from the woods, Sam could see a thin column of white smoke rising from the farm chimney. Around them, the mounds of their dead flock cast purple shadows on the snow as a weak sun ascended slowly in the eastern sky. Sam thought it was a grim bonus that Claire's blindness spared her from the sad sights around them. He exhaled a long slow breath, leaving a white cloud of crystal vapour hanging in the arctic air.

"That doesn't sound too good," Claire said from beside him. "Long heavy sighs are seldom the prelude to good news."

Sam didn't respond immediately, instead he distracted himself pouring coffee from his flask. He handed a cup to Claire.

"Here you are, made from fresh coffee beans, all the way from New Zealand."

Puzzled, she sipped in silence, processing what he had just said. "That's a long way to go for a decent cup of coffee."
Sam waited for Claire to finish drinking before he replied. "A lot has happened since the storm began." He refilled the cup and took a sip. "Let's start from when I left during the storm."

He chose not to rush the story. During his telling, *Frisco*, in search for warmth, moved closer to *Rowan*. Sam felt a shared moment of intimacy as he began describing the night of the storm after he had left the farm. As the story unfolded he noticed that Claire sat with eyes closed as she imagined the dramatic arrival of the yacht. When he told her the boat and crew had travelled half way around the world from New Zealand, he heard a sharp intake of breath. Without pausing, Sam moved on to explain how the South Island had been spared the catastrophic effects of the pandemic, its population remaining more or less intact, without any boar to prey on them.
"They're short of the usual things; oil, medical supplies and imported goods, but food doesn't seem to be a problem. They were largely an agricultural economy before the pandemic, so after the shock of what had happened to the North Island and the world at large, things continued much as before. It took a while for them to get organised, waiting very much like us for a radio message, contact from America or Europe. When they heard nothing, they became suspicious and embarked to investigate for themselves."
Sam was interrupted by the sound of snow sliding from the branches of a pine tree behind them, landing with a dull thud on the ground that caused both horses to shy, spooked by the sudden noise behind them. After a minute, Sam continued, describing the pandemics of disease that Napier had found to have ravaged Africa and Asia. A greater shock was the environmental disaster that had laid to waste vast areas of North America where nuclear power stations had released huge quantities of radioactive fallout with no one alive to control them.
"The New Zealanders have discovered very few groups of people that remain to be found. Napier claims we're the first group of any size they've come across for some years."
He paused to allow Claire to assimilate the implications of what he had said.

"That sounds far worse than I ever imagined. It's a lot to take on board," Claire said eventually, her voice distant, trying to imagine a world now largely devoid of the human race.

He nodded, forgetting she couldn't see his gesture. "There is one thing though that brightens the gloom. They've brought a letter from their government suggesting that we join them and start new lives in New Zealand."

"All of us? How big is their yacht?" she asked incredulously.

Sam laughed. "Not the yacht. There's an old passenger liner they've brought with them. It's currently waiting in Gibraltar until Napier completes his search, as far north as the Hebrides and Norway. Though now he knows what the men on the mainland are capable of, I think he'll be cautious if he makes it to there."

Sam noticed Claire shudder as he reminded her of their narrow escape. She was thoughtful as he drank his now cold coffee.

"I think you'll find a lot of people won't want to leave the island though," she said eventually. "For most it's a haven, a secure home, and there are many still hoping that one day they might yet hear from their lost loved ones; even though the inevitability of loss becomes ever more real. If we leave, it will be the final act of abandoning any hope of ever finding them again."

Was she thinking of herself perhaps? An only child of parents whose love had been boundless, how could Claire discard her dream that they might one day be reunited. Hope, no matter how futile, burns eternal and Sam thought better than to add anything more on the subject; they all carried personal trauma in one guise or another.

"Yet the future only looks a comfortable place if you are considering one problem at a time." He felt her sightless gaze rest upon him.

"To do otherwise would be unbearably pessimistic."

"Even if our challenges take choice away from us?"

She hesitated. "This sounds like bad news."

"It's shaping up that way."

Sam paused to rub *Rowan*'s neck while *Frisco* stamped his feet, looking hopefully for something green to eat beneath the snow.

"Go on."

Sam continued. "Just think about it; the men who attacked us in Dartmouth were scavenging, stealing food and taking whatever else they could lay hands upon. That was before this storm arrived, which means they're primarily driven by hunger. They will have heard stories about our island, that there's ample food here, and my guess is that their ultimate intentions are aimed at us, helping themselves to whatever we have created. Their ravaging through the south of England clearly states they're not remotely interested in law and order or any form of society, it just gets in their way. Far simpler to apply the theory that 'might is right'. At the moment, I think they're using boar to soften us up and weaken our resolve. Eventually, I think an offer will come, but it is intended to arrive in the form of a threat."

"They hardly seem prepared to listen or negotiate."

"Quite. But they can't all be thugs. That's just a tool; there will be a brain somewhere behind this, someone quite prepared to use violence to achieve his, or her, ends. To counter that, we need to hold together and defeat their softening-up tactics. An offer must eventually come, or they'll starve. I have a suspicion they're not strong enough to make an outright attack against us. But there lies the problem."

"You think that will change?"

"Eventually; probably sooner than later. Our population numbers don't grow quickly enough to let us farm a bigger area and grow more food. Plus the storm, with the damage it has wrought, will set us back years. Which leads us to the problem."

"How so?"

"My guess is they were facing hunger long before the storm struck. Here, it looks as though it has destroyed most of this year's harvest. Even if next year is good, we're going to have to live on our meagre reserves and we'll all experience hunger before things improve. And that's an optimistic scenario. Had things stayed as they were, we might have had a sufficient food surplus to buy them off, for a while at least. But now? It leaves us with nothing to offer in negotiation. If they threaten us, and I suspect they very soon will to avoid starvation, we have two options; surrender to their demands or fight it out. Either scenario ends in disaster."

The picture Sam painted left Claire in stunned silence.

"So that leaves the invitation from New Zealand. Do you think it's a serious option? Most of what you've outlined is speculation, and even if you are correct, I can't see people surrendering the island without a fight."

"By which time any chance of escaping will be gone. If we delay, just to prove my point one way or another, it'll be too late. We have about a month, during which time Napier will complete his search and turn for home. And that will be with or without us."

"But how do we resolve this? People will have strong views and feelings. You make it sound so simple, so black and white."

"By means of a vote; a referendum in which everyone has a vote."

"And what, you think we'll agree to leave here, for an uncertain home and future on the other side of the world?"

"Yes, well, at least after the options are clearly presented."

*Frisco* jostled impatiently, bored with listening to human conversation, stamping his hooves in the snow.

"You may find more opposition to your plans than you think," Claire said, making more of a statement than a question. Sam felt a sudden chill, this time not only from the wind.

"Go on."

"It's not my place, I'm merely a blind incomer."

"Meaning?"

Claire looked awkward, her expression suggested the need to say something that her memory was trying to avoid.

"You can't start saying something and then stop," Sam said, with more irritation than he intended.

"It's just that there has been talk here, on the farm, suggesting that since Dartmouth you've become too consumed by forum affairs and as a result your judgement is now... questionable ..." she trailed off, shaking her head in discomfort.

"Don't stop."

Claire gazed at the snow below her; she couldn't see it, but that didn't prevent her knowing it was there.

"The others think the turning point was when you rescued me from these men in Dartmouth. No one says it to my face, but there's talk that the praise you've received has gone to your head."

Claire winced visibly as she said her words. *Rowan* bucked impatiently, uncomfortable with the sudden change in mood of her rider. Sam was shocked into silence, less by the words than the thought that it might be Rachel who held such an opinion of him.

Claire broke the silence. "If you do win your vote, the referendum, what happens to those of us who are left behind?"

The question stunned Sam, perhaps because her tone contained a sharp note of anguish, mollifying his anger at the judgement of the others.

"Stay behind? No one will be left behind. We will either all stay, or all go."

Claire laughed. "I doubt that your recent New Zealand friends will extend their invitation to the blind from here when they've already more than enough of their own to care for. Besides, there are some on the island who won't want to take newcomers like me."

For a second, Sam seriously thought that Claire was only joking. He knew she had ample reason to feel unwanted and discarded, but it was only when he looked at her face that he saw tears casting wet trails down her freckled cheeks. It pulled him up short; the blind still cry tears, even in their darkness.

Sam tried his best to reassure Claire, but his efforts sounded hollow even to his own ears. Later, as they rode back into the farmyard, they were greeted by the sight of John's green van parked in the slush of the melting snow. John got out as Sam eased himself stiffly from the saddle.

"Can I have a private word, Sam?" John looked white with cold as he cast a worried glance at farmhouse. "For your ears only, at the moment." A strong Welsh inflection coloured his words, the usual signal he was anxious.

Claire had heard John's request and she took *Rowan*'s bridle from Sam. For a moment, her hand, surprisingly warm, lingered deliberately on his in a token of thanks. Perhaps his words hadn't been totally wasted after all.

Sam led John to the far side of the stable barn where the sun felt warmer in the shadow of the wind. John stamped his feet.

"Bloody snow; never could stand the stuff, even back in the valleys," he grumbled.

"You haven't come out here just to moan about the weather," Sam said with a grin. "And I'll be seeing you shortly at the forum."

"Ah, I needed to speak to you before then," he hesitated, uncertain, rubbing hands together for warmth. "See, there's been another message, on the distress frequency," John paused. "Family groups, adults and children, about twenty in all. Desperate they are, too."

Sam knew what was to come before John spoke.

"They're pleading for us to rescue them."

# TWENTY-THREE

It is a sad truism that the bearer of bad tidings often takes the blame. After John had left, Sam called everyone on the farm together to discuss the urgency of their situation in more detail. With the storm damage he had previously seen across the island and his early morning inspection of the farm, it was essential that they considered the future before he left for the evening's emergency forum meeting. Despite Claire's warning, he hadn't anticipated their reactions or the consequence of a constant stream of bad news which was beginning to unpick the security of the home they had striven to build.

Pinned up on the wall behind him was the colour-coded map he had prepared earlier from his inspection of the farm with Claire. He tried to ignore the shocked intakes of breath as he described the crop damage in fields, where so much time and sweat had been spent trying to create a harvest. Without thinking, Sam overlooked the feeling of futility his description of the hard facts might bring. Unaware of his effect on the mood in the room, Sam pressed on regardless, keen to illuminate their plight before Rigby's counter arguments could influence them. In so doing he had made one fatal flaw in the process; his words evaporated everyone's hope.

"In addition to the storm, there is one more fact we need to consider."

Everyone listened in silence as he painted a picture of the state of the world the New Zealanders had discovered on their journeys. He continued, without pause for comments, and went on to described the disaster caused by the unmanned atomic power plants in America, explaining the effect of the conveyor belt of radioactive fallout that streamed eastwards across the Atlantic on the prevailing winds with their island lying directly in its path. As he stopped talking there was a momentary silence followed by a slow metronomic hand clap; from Rachel of all people. Sam hesitated, suddenly unnerved by a warning shiver, a foreboding, that spiralled like an electric shock down his spine. It was Rachel who spoke for the room.

"Quite a depressing picture of our future wouldn't you say, presented so eloquently by our able leader."

Sam couldn't tell if it was a question or a statement, her final words laced with cynicism, eyes flaring angrily in his direction. Shocked, he was lost for words, suddenly fearing a public disagreement with Rachel. Had she seen him return with Claire from their early morning tour of the farm? He hadn't set out to hide it and would have invited Rachel to join him if Gemma hadn't kept her up most of the night. He became uncomfortably aware that he had submerged them all in a gloom of bad news; too much detail in one go to compensate for the guilt of his prolonged absences. Too late, Claire's earlier warning rang hollow in his ears. With more than a hint of panic, he fumbled with an effort to lift their spirits, trying to turn to an optimistic perspective of their future.

"There is reason to have hope for the future." He paused to clear his throat. "When the forum meets later today we'll be asked to consider the proposal from the New Zealand government. It will involve a referendum to transfer the island's population; every one of us, to New Zealand. All of you will get a vote, including children and those who are new to our community, and in the case of the very young, their parents or guardians will have the powers to make a proxy vote on their behalf. There is a lot still to consider; the crew of *The Shepherd* have brought a copy of their constitution and the detailed terms of their invitation. Chairman Jamieson is studying the detail before tonight's meeting as we speak, so I'll have more to tell you afterwards. Meanwhile, given our current circumstances, I think it's fair to say that this offer could be our salvation."

His final words were greeted by a cold silence, which Sam at first translated as a deep and thoughtful consideration of what he had told them. He had just begun to collect his notes when the room exploded in a barrage of angry questions hurled in his direction.

"How long have you known about this radiation issue, leaving us here in some sort of poisonous soup …"

"What makes this story true? Only the word of strangers we've never met …"

Questions flew at Sam from all sides. His eyes desperately sought out Rachel for support, but she stayed silently to one side, her face expressionless, unable to hide the look of cold anger in her eyes.

"... as for being chased away by a few thugs on motorbikes and a mob of boar, I think your words are defeatism, they're a disgrace ..."

"Any radiation here could be natural background levels, here since the beginning of time ..."

"Have you seen these smoking nuclear reactors for yourself? How can you make these wild claims and terrify us when you don't have the first idea what you're talking about ..."

Fear leads people to behave out of character, and in the face of their onslaught, Sam could only stand aghast and friendless, stumbling to find answers to their anguish. The meeting was fast dissolving into chaos in which he had few answers. Only Claire, standing alone at the back of the room, had an expression of horrified compassion on her face. She had forewarned him of their mood and he had badly misjudged the depth of their concerns. The best he could do was let their anger burn its course. Eventually he held up his hands in a gesture of surrender.

"Okay, I get the message." Sam had to shout to make himself heard. "To be honest, I'm as worried as all of you. We're being buffeted by ever changing events, on an almost daily basis. The forum is trying its best to keep everyone included, but you have to appreciate that things are happening so quickly it's difficult to keep you all informed."

Sam paused, feeling almost overwhelmed by tiredness, though perhaps it was disappointment, of having so plainly failed to communicate adequately, even with those closest to him.

"You must understand that the forum is working night and day in the island's interest," he could barely make himself heard, "with decisions that often require immediate action." He paused again, looking slowly at everyone gathered in the room. "Sometimes there just isn't time to consult everyone before action is required. That's why we elect a forum; to make decisions, even if some of us disagree with them."

For a moment, Sam's appeal seemed to have earned him space. "As you know, elections to the forum take place every two years. I've already decided to stand down before then, just as soon as this current crisis has passed. It's impossible for me to do so now; half the forum are either sick, giving birth, or have injuries from the boar attacks; we only just have enough councillors as it is and there is no time for elections at the moment. We need to get to a period of calm for that to take place, so you'll just have to trust us until then. When it's over, I'll resign my post on the forum and devote my time to be here with the rest of you, where I belong."

At last Sam's emotional words brought the room to silence. Before anyone could say anything more, he collected his things and left the room.

Sam made a quick departure for the forum meeting in Newport. He felt personally stung by the criticism and although he acknowledged that he was reacting with a degree of self-pity, he needed time to let it wash through. He had deliberately avoided Rachel after the explosive meeting in the farmhouse, fearing a confrontation and uncertain how he might respond if they tried to talk. For the moment, time would have to heal things between them. Sam was tightening his saddle girth strap when a shadow fell across the horse's flank.

"How you've just been treated was unfair," Lorna said, "but I did warn you things were coming to a head. Most of us are shocked, worried, and upset, particularly Rachel. I don't think they intended to attack you personally. Your news lit a fuse and things got out of hand. But you're not doing enough to resolve the most important issue. It's between Rachel and Claire."

Lorna paused, giving space for Sam to respond. Silently, he continued adjusting the saddle.

"I'm sorry everything is so difficult, but please don't resign from the forum. Despite the anger and emotions, we all desperately need you to stay on board and help guide these worrying events."

Lorna's distress was written clearly on her face. It was always hard for him to be mad with her so he relented and gave her a smile.

"I know. It's not your fault, but in my present mood, I'd resign tonight if I had the chance." He held up his hand. "But I can't. Since the boar first appeared here on the island, it's felt that the sand in the hour-glass is running ever faster against us.'" He sighed deeply. "The truth is, we've became complacent in recent years and now things are catching up with us at an alarming rate. What we need is unity more than anything; the time for arguing can come when we've achieved what's most important. Survival."

Sam swung into the saddle. "And for the record, it's not Claire that's the problem; it's our spirit of unity, or more importantly, what's fast becoming the lack of it."

He gave the mare a sharper dig with his heals than he intended and was gone before Lorna could reply.

For some time after leaving the farm he rode with only the horse for his compass. For a while he was happy to avoid all decisions, least of all the route to Newport. Fortunately, the mare knew the way; they would get there when she was good and ready. Oblivious to the passing landscape, with only the soft steps of the horse for company, Sam was surprised to find himself in the lane which passed the woods in which he had found the mystery dead girl. Without the white blanket of snow, Sam might not have noticed the flowers that marked the spot of her passing. Subconsciously, the scene sparked his curiosity. A bunch of brightly coloured freesias stood proud against a backdrop of white. Sam tethered the mare, slid from the saddle and looked carefully around him. From the verge of the lane, a line of footprints led into the trees. Puzzled, he withdrew his rifle from its scabbard. He doubted there would be any rogue boar about in these conditions, yet the prints were fresh, only wind-blown snow filling the impressions. They had obviously been made since the storm had passed. No tracks appeared along the lane, but he found footprints crossing from the fields on the opposite side. Whoever had made them had left by a different route; or was still there.

"Hello."

His shout was answered by a pair of rooks, cawing angrily as they rose into the air. He waited, called again, looking for movement in the woods, aware there were ample places to hide amidst the camouflage of drifted snow and fallen leaf cover. Behind Sam, the mare blew clouds of white vapour into the cold air, her ears pricked in nervous anticipation. Had she heard something, or just tuned in to the unease of his voice? He shouldered his rifle; if anyone intended harm, he had been exposed in full view for several minutes. He turned and paused to stroke the neck of the mare to steady her, then followed the footprints. They led to the flowers in the centre of the clearing directly beneath the bough that had supported the noose. In an ordinary glass jar pressed into the snow was a delicate cluster of bright flowers, their petals vibrating gently in the breeze. 'No hedgerow flowers, these,' Sam thought, 'but something grown for beauty by someone with a love of flowers.'

In a circle around the clearing, the snow held the imprint of a single trail of footprints. Whoever had made this gesture appeared to have acted alone. In the far corner, the footprints moved away in the opposite direction to their entry, deeper into the cover of the woods. He followed for a short distance. There were no obvious trails, the prints swerving to avoid denser pockets of vegetation or drifts of snow. He resisted the temptation to follow any further. It seemed quite possible that he had disturbed whoever had placed the flowers when he approached on horseback. The spot was isolated, so his arrival would have come as a surprise, and someone could have circled around behind him. Hastily, he backtracked, stopping briefly to ponder the flowers once again, a silent epitaph to a murdered girl. He had gained little, but as he rode away a thought occurred to him; the footprints were small and must have been made by a woman or perhaps a child. Coupled with the shell patterned button Rigby had found earlier in the clearing, it could be that the footprints and button belonged to the same person.

Distracted by the day's events, Sam couldn't remember the rest of the journey to Newport. When he arrived, he was surprised to find *The Shepherd* moored at the quayside, having sailed under tow from Bembidge by *Lupin* as soon as the wind had died down earlier that morning. The yacht was already a hive of activity, her broken mast dismantled, hatch covers opened to dry out her flooded interior.

"She'll look better when we give her a new mast."

Napier had seen Sam ride into the harbour area and came to stand beside him, cleaning his hands on a piece of cotton waste, a broad grin lighting his tanned face.

"I hadn't expected to see you here. How long do you think the repairs will take?" Sam asked as he dismounted.

"It will be quicker now we're here; more equipment and yachts to cannibalise for replacement parts. Several of our hatch covers were smashed or ripped away; that's how we shipped so much water. Plus a few leaks in the hull, but they can be easily repaired." He cocked a raised eyebrow in Sam's direction. "I can't thank all of you enough; fair to say you saved our lives," Napier added with sincerity. "Picking the sheltered harbour of Bembridge was inspired. In those conditions, I don't think I could have got her into safety anywhere else."

Sam waved a hand of dismissal. "We'd do the same for anyone in the circumstances; well, almost anyone," he added with a rueful smile, looking north towards the Solent.

Napier nodded. "Ah yes, I hear you've been having problems with a band of troublemakers. How extensive do you think they are on the mainland?"

Sam was thoughtful for a moment.

"Hard to know, exactly. They appear to be fast and mobile, living off the land, taking everything they want by threat and force. They don't seem to take kindly to anyone who stands in their way. After you leave here, be careful if you go to the mainland." He looked at Napier with genuine concern. "When are you planning to sail?"

Napier cast an eye over the yacht.

"We need to be on our way from here in no more than a week. *The Aotearoa*, our mother ship, is waiting in Gibraltar for the fuel tanker that accompanied us from New Zealand. We found that the naval fuel depot there still has reasonably full tanks, so we'll fill up while we can. So I have to finish my search here by the end of June and head back to Gibraltar for the start of the long haul home." Napier stretched with a loud sigh. "'We've all been away from home for a long time." He was interrupted by someone shouting his name from inside the yacht.

"I'd better go; we keep finding problems. We need to talk more; maybe I'll see you before the party?"

"Party?"

"Yes. It seems we're not to be allowed to leave here before we've danced with every eligible female on the island," Napier said with a broad grin. "Saturday night in some disused sports hall on the edge of town, I believe. I understand everybody on the island is invited." He turned and hastened away to another shout of his name. "I'll see you there."

He was gone in a moment, leaving Sam pleased, if surprised, and he turned to lead the mare to the stables with a perceptibly lighter step. Although he had only known Napier a short time, there was something about conversation with the tall blond Kiwi that lightened the problems that surrounded around him. Sam already felt they would all miss his optimistic charisma if he sailed back to New Zealand without them.

The agenda for the forum meeting was the longest they had ever considered. Despite Chairman Jamieson imposing a strict timescale on members' opinions, it was the early hours of the morning before their business had concluded. Predictably, the most controversial points had been the invitation from New Zealand and the appeal to rescue the small group of survivors John had made contact with as they struggled towards Weymouth.

Albert Jamieson tabled the consequences of the recent storm as their first item of discussion. On this point at least, there was almost universal agreement; further rationing had to be introduced immediately while a detailed assessment of the damage and loss to their harvest was prepared. Every councillor brought tales of gloom and devastation from their fields and orchards and even the most sanguine amongst them found it hard to be optimistic about their prospects. There was no lack of ideas for recovery, but when the farms damaged by boar attacks were added to the mix, it was hard to avoid the prospect of a hungry future.

It was in the midst of the discussions of pending hardship that Albert introduced the offer from their New Zealand visitors. News had travelled like wildfire and, knowing it must be a prominent point of debate, all hamlets had sent their representatives to be present. It was with an air of attentive silence that everyone listened to Albert's impartial resume of the situation. He temporarily suspended questions, and instead, invited Napier to join them to make a personal report to the forum before embarking on open debate.

Napier was impressive, which, along with his seamanship, was probably why his government had selected him as their ambassador. He kept to a tight storyline, describing how, by good fortune, the South Island had avoided the pandemic and quarantined the island at the outset. As catastrophe had raged around them, engulfing all in its path, the pandemic had mercifully passed them by, leaving their population and its fabric virtually untouched. Mother earth, so intent on destroying mankind wherever he, or she, held on, appeared prepared to cast a benign eye on this tiny outpost of civilisation. Their constitution, which he read out, was not dissimilar to their own, though Sam was surprised to hear they had banned the death penalty, even for proven capital crimes.

"But don't be deceived," Napier said. "Our grip on this world is fragile at best. One slip or mistake and we too could easily go the same way as the rest of the planet. To our north, the boar reign supreme, for at least the immediate future. Beyond that, plague and disease still rampage, wherever it can find human existence. We survive by our wits at best. Our population, and the spirit that it supports, is just enough to give us an edge to hold back the tide that will overwhelm us if given the chance. We think strength in numbers is our main asset to future survival; our mutual survival. We hope, when you have given due consideration to our invitation," he paused, holding the word in suspension, "you will all vote to come and join us and embrace the fight for the future of mankind."

He paused, sweeping the room with a purposeful stare.

"Together."

After Napier had left them, Albert Jamieson adjourned the forum for a break, and the room quickly filled with voices, all expressing a kaleidoscope of opinions. Sam helped himself to coffee, courtesy of the New Zealanders, and stood to one side. He could only admire Albert's deft hand at work, utilising decades of hard learnt committee skills. He sensed there was a wide and emotional divergence of opinion amongst forum members from whom Albert would need a decision of unity in the coming hours. Debate on the offer from New Zealand was next on the agenda and, with emotions running high, it would be far from straightforward. In one corner he could see Rigby in animated conversation with a group of supporters. Rigby had moved fast, gathering forum members of a like mind against the very motion of a referendum. Whilst Rigby plotted, Albert moved quietly from group to group, applying a hand on the shoulder at one moment, a discrete word in the ear of the next.

It was late by the time the meeting reconvened. After he had started procedures, Albert looked tired and distracted. Sam feared something had arisen during the recess which was preying on Albert's mind. Even so, he didn't miss anything, using his experience to weigh and assess the arguments and outspoken opinions washing around him. When they resumed, Sam was surprised by the absence of the secretary, Mary, who had been replaced by a younger woman he hadn't seen before. Recognising that the next part of the forum would be long and detailed, Sam guessed she had left to begin processing the minutes for early morning distribution, leaving her replacement to take the next set of minutes.

It had been agreed that every member should be given the opportunity to speak on behalf of their hamlet on the offer from the New Zealanders. Each speaker would have to summarise their opinions in two minutes during which there could be no interruptions or questions. Three minutes of debate on each point would be allowed after each speaker had said their piece. Even running the discussions on a strictly timed schedule, it still took three hours for every forum member to speak. At the end of the session, Albert Jamieson made a resume and began the process of calling for a vote on allowing a referendum in which every island inhabitant would vote. He was at pains to point out that this should include both children and newcomers, with those below the age of ten represented by the proxy vote of their parents or guardians. As Albert concluded his statement, a low murmur of voices rolled around the chamber. Sam was uncertain whether the mood would be for or against acceptance. After his mauling earlier in the day, he felt a worrying premonition that the issue wouldn't even get as far as a vote. As the vote approached, Mary returned to take over from the young secretary, who now looked exhausted, her shorthand notebook filled from cover to cover. Despite the lateness of the hour Mary looked impeccable and as impassive as ever; Sam wondered what thoughts lay hidden behind her inscrutable facade.

Everyone took their turn to express the opinions of their hamlets, and when the large wall clock showed two in the morning they were still far from done. Sam guessed it would take until sunrise. Albert sat with eyes closed for long periods, though Sam doubted he slept. Eventually, the last presentation was concluded and Albert struck his gavel to bring the forum to order.

"For the moment we have heard enough opinion to bring us to a vote on the matter in hand. The detail, for and against, can be continued and debated in the period of time preceding the referendum. This must take place as soon as possible and I therefore call for a show of hands from all councillors, firstly, to allow the referendum to proceed. The second vote will be on not holding a referendum but to resolve the matter only at the forum on behalf of the island."

The room went deathly quiet. Albert Jamieson looked up, surprised. Rigby sat with his arm raised.

"Councillor Rigby?"

"Mr Chairman, I dispute your call for a referendum. I consider the principle of your proposal would be unconstitutional and shouldn't even be considered for a vote by the forum. We have no provision in our constitution to do this, which we consider," he looked at his supporters gathered around him, "to be merely an expression of your own personal agenda."

Rigby placed extra emphasis on the last two words. Sam felt his chest tighten at Rigby's words; so this was how his attempt to unseat Albert Jamieson would manifest itself, by creating a vote of no confidence in their ageing chairman. There was silence, all eyes riveted on Albert who sat motionless in his chair, eyes hooded, fingers steepled. For a moment Sam feared that Albert hadn't properly heard Rigby, until his hand stretched out for the leather bound copy of their constitution on the secretary's table beside him.

"You're quite correct, councillor Rigby. And, if that was the terms by which this motion were to be tabled, I would indeed be exceeding my powers. However," Albert opened the constitution at a tagged page, "amendment 13E allows the following. *'Where one third of the members, or more, present a motion and request the forum to give said motion attention and discussion, resulting in a vote, the chairman shall be bound to grant permission'*."

Albert closed the book and stared unblinkingly at Rigby.

"I call for a show of hands from those councillors present who propose and second the motion that a referendum shall be discussed and voted upon by the forum."

For a moment the room seemed shocked by the sudden authority with which he spoke, so completely at odds with his manner only a few minutes before.

"Those calling this motion, please show your hands."

His gaze didn't waiver from Rigby as he waited, realising that the issue was less about the motion than a vote of confidence in him as chairman. Chris Woods raised her arm, trying hard to avoid smiling as she was joined by others, including Sam.

Albert Jamieson was still staring at Rigby when he asked sternly, "Secretary, are there more than ten proposers?"

The normally implacable Mary looked shocked as she counted.

"Twenty-one, Mr Chairman," she said in an uncertain voice.

Albert looked thoughtful. Rigby had shown his hand and eight others had joined the attempt to unseat him. Albert nodded. For the moment at least, his position was secure. Slowly, a smile creased his tired face.

"I think you have your answer, Connor."

# TWENTY-FOUR

Sam left the blissful fog of sleep and felt the world shaking around him.

"Sam, wake up."

He opened his eyes at the sound of John Evans' voice. Sam blinked at the hard light of day, stiff and drowsy from only a few hours' sleep, stretched out on the floor on chair cushions.

"Give me a moment." Even yawning felt stiff and painful.

John disappeared in the hopeful search for coffee, leaving Sam to process the events of the previous night. The vote to allow the referendum had been passed, despite Rigby's intervention, initially giving Sam an overwhelming feeling of relief, only to be tempered by his disquiet over their final topic. It was almost daylight when they had finally wound up their arguments over mounting another rescue bid for the twenty or so survivors struggling to get through to Weymouth. With their meagre resources already stretched to the limit, and the experiences in Dartmouth still raw in their minds, it felt a step too far. Time and again, Albert Jamieson had reminded them of the values that held them together. To turn away from a plea was an affront to what they stood for, irrespective of the cost. The forum had been exhausted and red-eyed when the proposal to go ahead had finally been passed at four in the morning. This time it hadn't been unanimous as had previously been the case for the Dartmouth rescue mission. Sam felt uneasy; they had only a few days to prepare, which felt all too soon, especially with the avalanche of problems that were still engulfing over them.

With protesting muscles, Sam dragged himself from the cushions he had laid out on the floor in a corner of the main hall. He had been too tired to attempt the journey back to the farm and anyway, the list of things requiring attention in the morning grew ever longer. When John returned with mugs of coffee and fresh doughnuts, Sam read from his expression that he was about to add yet more to his list headed 'urgent'.

"I've heard from our friend across the Solent," John said, excitedly between gulps of coffee.

Sam paused, mid-bite. John handed him a slip of paper on which were written a chain of numbers, followed by the date and time.

"My god, it's tonight."

Sam looked and sounded genuinely shocked. Another boar attack was about to happen and they had a chance to intercept it.

John nodded. "I left a tape recorder running while I was attending the meeting. The morse signal must have arrived in the early hours while I was at the forum." He looked pale and drawn like the rest of them, with red circles around tired sunken eyes.

"Where have they chosen?" The coordinates left Sam none the wiser.

"Newtown Bay again. They obviously fancy their chances among the creeks and marshes, especially with the shallow draught of a landing craft. But there aren't many roads out of the area and, as we know in advance, it should be straightforward to set a trap and snare them. The snow has mostly melted on the roads, so with a bit of luck we'll catch them red-handed."

"Boar-handed," Sam added with a grin.

Perhaps their luck looked brighter for once.


Napier caught up with Sam as he walked to Albert Jamieson's office.

"I see you're busy, but can I have a minute?"

Sam nodded. John's news had further pressurised his already tight schedule, but he enjoyed talking with the New Zealander. They walked along the riverside beside a varied assortment of battered and careworn boats, the early sun steadily warming the storm battered landscape. *The Shepherd* rolled gently at her moorings, proudly displaying her new mast with all the debris of her fraught arrival cleared away and her hatches and side rails replaced.

"Things seem to be going well," Sam gestured in the direction of the yacht.

"We'll be ready to leave in three or four days; certainly by the end of the week. Not before the party though," Napier said with a broad grin. "No mariner will pass up the opportunity to dance with a pretty girl."

Sam laughed. There was something about Napier that would lighten even the darkest situation.

"Somehow I don't think you just want to talk of dancing with pretty girls."

"No." It was Napier's turn to grin. "I hear you managed to get agreement to hold your referendum."

Sam let out a long breath. "Just; not without a few battles on the way."

"When will it be held?"

"We've allowed three weeks to hear all the opinions and arguments, for printing the ballot papers and making arrangements for casting the vote. It's a first for the island; we've never had to do something like this before, so we're going to have to make it up as we go along."

"How do you see the outcome?"

Sam had a tight lipped expression. "Logic would suggest we should accept your invitation, but ..."

"This is home for you all, why leave at the first sign of trouble," Napier said with a note of irony in his voice.

"Something like that, though it's far from the first sign. Our position on the island has been precarious from the moment we all washed up here. We've made a lot of progress in the five years but it's not enough. The truth is, we're going slowly backwards and things are in decline. Our population isn't increasing fast enough and neither is our food production. We're increasingly living off our reserves, with fuel and machinery being used up at an unsustainable rate. Add to that this storm, which has just wiped out this year's harvest and made things a whole lot harder. To be honest, it's beyond an uphill struggle."

As if to emphasise Sam's point, a gang of squabbling seagulls screamed above them, endorsing his sentiments. He knew he sounded grim, but couldn't stop himself from adding, "Apart from that, things are just fine and dandy, but only if you forget about a band of vigilantes just across the Solent, who want to take over the island for themselves with the help of a seemingly endless supply of boar." He couldn't avoid a sardonic smile.

Napier was staring down the estuary as he listened. "So no problems then; provided you make the decision to join us in New Zealand."

Sam shook his head wearily. "There are some amongst us who would rather go down fighting than give up and leave. But what solution is that for our children, who won't have any future worth speaking of if it's the wrong decision and we lose the fight after you've left without us?"

Napier struck a match and lit a small cigar, blowing perfect smoke rings gracefully into the air. Sam smiled; it was a deliberate gesture, reminding him he hadn't seen or smelt a cigar, small or large, in years.

"Fight on regardless of the cost. It was an admirable virtue twenty years ago when the threat was clear and tangible and you could count the odds. But today?" He let the question hang, eyes focused on a distant horizon.

"We have put democracy as a keystone of what we're trying to create. We can't suddenly become dictators just because we fear where the storyline will end," Sam added with a wistful note.

"Laudable, but …"

"But what?"

Napier sighed. "It's not for me to try to influence things, but …"

Sam laughed. "You're going to anyway."

Napier sat on an old timber spar and regarded Sam thoughtfully.

"We'll sail for the north the day after the party. In the meantime, I've heard from *The Aotearoa.* She'll be sailing in six weeks from Gibraltar for home, so I'll have to cut short my search. I must be back here in roughly four weeks from now."

Sam was tempted to ask how he was able to contact *The Aotearoa* so far south at the entrance to the Mediterranean, but thought better of it; that was John's speciality, not his.

"So soon. I had hoped we might have a little longer."

"*The Aotearoa* has done her work and the oil tanker has arrived from home and they're filling her tanks from storage in Gibraltar. We've gathered our survivors and the crews want to go home. It's been a long voyage and we can't sit around indefinitely waiting for others to make up their minds."

Napier spoke in matter of fact terms; perhaps that was the way of New Zealanders. He stretched his legs and crossed his feet, regarding Sam as he created another smoke ring.

"Once we leave, I doubt we'll return for many years. I would try and get a supply ship to you at some point, but there are so many priorities and I can't give any guarantees, much as I might like to."

Both men stared into the other's eyes. Napier was making his point clear and simple.

"Make sure your people know this when they vote. If they choose to stay, well, it's their right to do so, but they'll need to understand that you'll all be on your own and its more than likely we won't be back for a long time; if ever."

It was later that afternoon that Sam stood in the doorway at the top of a flight of steps at the entrance to the forum building. The sun had warmed the stone walls around him and made a dazzling reflection from the heaps of shovelled snow, now melting at the roadside. He had to remind himself it was late May, not the depths of winter. For the first time in a long while, Sam had just become a man without a list of demands. Albert Jamieson had appointed Connor Rigby to oversee the approaching night operation to intercept the boar and their handlers from the mainland. They would use four squads; Chris Woods would fly the Cessna, coordinating with *Lupin* to cover the Solent. It had all been carefully scheduled; what could possibly go wrong?

Excluded, or rested, as Albert had tactfully put it to Sam, he felt uncomfortable with Rigby's heavy hand at the helm. There was always a risk that something could go awry; if they made things too obvious, it would signal that they had been warned in advance and jeopardise their attempt to break the cycle of attacks and also endanger the safety of David Longmarsh, thereby destroying the chance for any future tip-offs. And so Sam fretted.

In addition, Craig had been appointed by the forum as their coordinator for the rescue mission to Weymouth. Craig was a safe pair of hands; a cautious thoughtful man, who sometimes worried about things to an extent that slowed his decision making. But Dave Bartlett had again been placed in charge of the five squads to be sent for protection, with Aiden and Ruth as lead squad commanders. They had learnt a lot from the Dartmouth expedition, and though the right people were in place to improve safety, Sam still felt anxious. Tired to his very core, he ought to have felt elated to be stood down; after all, it had the added bonus that he could show to Rachel he was putting his family before his commitments to the island. For some reason he couldn't identify, now that he was free, it didn't feel that way.

In an attempt to dispel his fears, Sam started walking alongside the river, trying to recover what normal life felt like. At the quayside, *The Shepherd* had now been lifted clear of the river, suspended on rope slings hung from a tall crane. A man stood on a scaffold frame beneath her stained hull, blue and white sparks describing cascading arcs from his welding torch.

Soon, Napier's expedition would be over. Would he depart without them, never to return? Most probably, if the numbers so loudly speaking against leaving were anything to go by. And how could he convince anyone that continuing their life here on the island was a lost cause, when even his own family group seemed so firmly opposed to it?

Distracted, he left the riverside and wandered down empty side streets. It had been months since he had last been this way. Most of the streets were still covered in snow, the adjacent buildings stripped of anything of value. It was a sad sight; at least the previous owners weren't alive to witness the desolation of the scene. The street led into what had once been a popular commercial high street. The shops, forced open and looted, were derelict and bare. With barely a casual glance, Sam passed a shop front that had been a clothes store. From the outside, the place appeared to have been picked clean, as hungry vultures will lay bare a carcass to the bone. In a corner of the shop window someone had arranged a group of naked mannequins around a small table, set with cups and a teapot. Two figures sat on wooden chairs while behind, three more stood, heads turned, in the appearance of animated conversation. One even held a cup and saucer. The scene was a grotesque parody for a world long departed.

On impulse, Sam stepped through the shattered front entrance. Faded clothing, discarded in the act of looting, littered the floor amongst shards of glass. Napier's leaving party must have lingered somewhere in the back of Sam's mind. It had been years since Rachel or Lorna had worn a new dress and whilst he doubted there could be anything left in the shop, it was at least worth a quick search. After the gloom of recent weeks he could imagine the smiles of delight on their faces if he, of all people, returned with new dresses. As he suspected, the store looked empty, but at the back a door hung to one side on broken hinges, opening into a storeroom. The room was lit by a cracked overhead skylight, with three walls lined from floor to ceiling with shelves and hanging rails. The lower shelves and rails had been stripped bare, but at a higher level, some stock remained untouched. A wooden ladder rested in the far corner and Sam climbed it to investigate. He had struck lucky and found a storeroom that contained women's clothing, only to realise that he had no idea of female sizes. The first items that came to hand were labelled small or large, and what little remained had received the attentions of mice or moths. In a corner was a neat stack of garments in ageing cellophane wrappers. Sam felt a wave of nostalgia as he found fashions from the past; a bright orange dress with the hem a mile above the knee, polka dots and abstract patterns that Picasso would have been proud of. They had been such innocent days, when the future promised only peace and love, when all the while their annihilation approached in a cocktail of viruses that no one could have ever imagined.

Sam shook his head; a trip into melancholia no longer served any purpose. Hindsight could never alter their present, or their future predicament. He put the orange dress to one side and continued searching. Nothing useable came to hand until he found an untouched box in which were a dozen or so neatly folded dresses, all in a dark blue material that resembled silk, still wrapped in cellophane. The top few had faded and spoiled, but lower down he found several that had survived remarkably unmarked. He opened one to examine it. The yoked neck had a trim of white lace but the size looked too small for Rachel or Lorna. He found a size number on the label and checked the others in the box but they were all the same. The thought came to him that if not for Rachel or Lorna, perhaps the dress would fit Claire. In the weeks following Dartmouth she had slowly lost her stick thin emaciated figure as her female shape began to return. The only clothes he had ever seen her wearing were hand-me-downs, often shapeless and mismatched cast-offs, given on the assumption that a blind girl had no care for how she might look. Sam felt a pang at the thought; in his limited experience any woman, blind or sighted, worried about her appearance. He couldn't resist grinning to himself; it wasn't hard to imagine the delight the dress would bring Claire, especially when the party was only a few days hence. Had the idea been in his subconscious from the start? It was best to dismiss such a notion without further thought, deciding it was simply an opportunity of fate that he hadn't sought, that chance had lain in his path.

It was a short time later, when he left the dilapidated store with the dress wrapped in brown paper, that the world seemed a brighter place than when he had entered. As he stepped outside, the sun shone, the sky was blue, his steps felt lighter.

Alas, life is seldom as simple as that for very long.

# TWENTY-FIVE

The following day, a glorious sunrise mocked them with a blaze of pink and gold. Sam awoke, haunted by worries. Attempts to foil the next boar attack and catch the traitor would have been taking place overnight, and in the absence of any news, Sam felt excluded. He knew that was irrational; Albert Jamieson's words had been very clear when he had said, 'Go home to your family; spending time with them is long overdue.' Astute as ever, Sam knew Albert was right, but the fact didn't stop him fretting on the outcome, especially when he had left things in Rigby's hands.

The farm was silent as Sam collected *Rowan* from her stall. She nudged him firmly, a reminder that she felt as much ignored as the rest of the family. Above the stables, the loft was empty; Lorna was away helping Gary again, and Claire was surprisingly absent, having spent the night in Newport. Sam felt a pang of disappointment when he had discovered her room was empty. He had arrived home with the dress and instead of enjoying the delight of her reaction, he had left the brown paper parcel on her bed. Claire's absence had brought about a noticeable improvement in Rachel's mood; the atmosphere around the evening dinner table lighter than it had been for some while, and it led Sam to suspect that Rachel had played some part in whatever had kept Claire away from the farm.

As he led *Rowan* across the yard, the sun rose over the woods to the east, changing the dawn's grey light from white into gold. Sam climbed into the saddle, feeling the warm strength of the horse beneath him as she moved with effortless ease and ambled forward. This was always his favourite time of the day; today felt no exception, despite the disaster that awaited him in the blackened fields around them. Sam had expected to be the earliest riser and was surprised to find Jake already busy with the plough in one of their best fields for cereals. The snow had melted to reveal a crop of spring barley, flattened and broken against the ground. Seeing Sam approach, Jake switched off the engine and swung open the cab door.

"Can't you sleep either, or has Rachel kicked you out of bed early?"

Sam laughed. "I wanted to see how bad the damage is without the camouflage of snow. You started early."

It was a large field and almost a third was already scored with parallel furrows from the plough blades.

Jake shrugged. "Well, the crop can't be saved, so there's no point in waiting. We've enough seed to re-plant with a bean crop, so the sooner it's in the ground the better. This field drains quickly so I thought I'd get a head start; if the weather gives us half a chance we could still get a crop from it."

"How's the fuel situation?"

Jake shrugged. "Awful. When it's gone we'll have to team up the horses."

Sam sensed *Rowan* giving him a nervous glance. "We'll have to release more from reserve. The forum knows that; we're just waiting for all the calls to come in from across the island. There won't be enough to give everyone all they want, so we'll have to use our allocation carefully."

For a while they discussed the options for some of the other fields. The winter wheat might have survived in some locations, but the potatoes and most of the green vegetables were a total loss, and the entire greenhouse crop had been destroyed, as had the orchards and soft fruit.

"How are the sheep?" Sam asked, anticipating the worst.

"We've lost three-quarters of all the spring lambs and a substantial number of ewes. The cows are fine, but we've lost the first grass cut, so silage making will be late. Our biggest silage clamp had its covering shredded by the gales. It's still buried under deep snow so most of it will rot. The future looks like hungry cows I'm afraid."

"Which in turn will wipe out our milk yield," Sam said morosely.

Jake, usually the optimist, nodded in reply. "Any bright ideas? We've virtually no concentrates left to feed them with."

"Go to New Zealand?" Sam said as he rode off with a departing wave of his hand.

Later in the morning, Sam came across Claire seated in the old bus shelter, about half a mile from the farm, beside the road where buses no longer ran. Having toured the farm he had followed a circuit that brought him again to the clearing in the woods, as though drawn by magnetism to the spot where he had found the murdered girl. He entered the woods from the north side, still looking for clues, as he carefully picked his way through the trees. The flowers in the glass jar had been replaced with another bunch of freesias. He skirted carefully around the clearing, but found nothing; whoever was placing the flowers there was taking great care to cover their tracks.

None the wiser he took the lane back to the farm, allowing *Rowan* to amble at a gentle walk, and used the time to reflect on the consequences if the referendum failed and they decided to turn down the invitation from the New Zealanders. Lost in his thoughts, Sam would have ridden past the dilapidated bus shelter without a sideways glance if *Rowan* hadn't stopped abruptly; she had recognised Claire immediately.

"Good morning, *Rowan*."

The horse blew her a greeting through her nostrils.

"Good grief, Claire? What on earth are you doing sitting here? There aren't any buses due today, or any other day for that matter," Sam added with mock irony.

"Hi Sam, I guessed you were back."

Stiffly, he swung himself from the saddle where he'd spent the past three hours and walked over to join Claire, leaving *Rowan* to forage the verge for her late breakfast amongst the weeds.

"I called at your room when I got back last night. No one seemed to know for sure where you were."

She seemed to ignore his implied question.

"You know, when I want to be on my own I like to come here to think; no one travels this way any longer, and facing south it makes a warm suntrap." Claire wore a broad brimmed straw hat and a sleeveless shirt with a long skirt hitched up to tan her legs.

"As for last night, I got a lift with Lorna into Newport. Karen, the nurse who treated my wound, has been asking for more girls to volunteer for training as nursing assistants. So I applied." She paused to move her guide stick to make room for Sam to sit beside her.

He had a look of astonishment as he sat down, only narrowly avoiding saying the clichéd words, 'Nursing assistant? But you're blind'.

Perhaps Claire read his mind; she smiled at him as she covered her bare legs with her skirt.

"Karen wanted me to complete an assessment immediately. She's desperately short staffed, so I took her tests last night. And much to everyone's surprise," she paused, still smiling, "I passed."

Sam laughed, as much at himself as his delight for Claire, belatedly remembering that blind members of their community were everyday fulfilling roles previously only considered for the sighted. It was a simple matter of numbers; there just weren't enough sighted men and women to undertake all the tasks to hold their community together.

"Have you been to the farm since you got back?" Sam asked the question, aware he had a subconscious motive.

Claire yawned and stretched in the warming sunshine. "I have."

He noted a hint of mischief in her voice. "And I guess you've heard about the party to be held for the New Zealanders before they leave at the end of the week. I don't know who will be going from the farm, but everyone is invited, so you must go too. I've no doubt they'll be hoping for lots of pretty girls to dance with."

"Is that what you think I am?" For a moment Claire's question caught him off balance. "One of the pretty girls?"

"Yes, you are. Very pretty, actually."

Sam surprised himself with his words, spoken softly with disarming frankness. Claire had a faraway wistful smile. Her eyes blinked, perhaps fighting back tears.

"That's nice to know. No one has said that to me for years." She turned, gazing sightlessly in Sam's direction. "I've not seen an image of myself since I was sixteen, and I never will again. Can you imagine what that's like?" Her voice caught at the end of her words.

He remembered how she had traced the profile of his own face. Without sight, it was the only method the blind possessed to create a picture of an image. Sam took her left hand in his and led her fingers to her face. He started on her forehead, gently touching her fringe with her fingertips.

"Your hair is naturally straight and fine and its red tones glow gold in the sunlight," he said softly. "Your fringe could do with a trim, but even wonky, it complements your face," he said lightly. Sam led Claire's fingers across her forehead. "Your skin has developed a warm glow from the sun, which makes the freckles almost disappear. Your eyes are almond-shaped," he traced their orbit, "the palest blue-grey." Sam paused to let her absorb the description she would never see again. "Your face has lost the hungry look you had when we first met, so your eyes are back in proportion."

He moved on, tracing her cheekbone, running around to her ears, describing the path to her chin. He stopped and swallowed, gazing at Claire's mouth. Not perfect, with a recently healed scar in the left corner, but beautiful, nevertheless. Gently, he traced the small depression beneath her nose and followed the profile of her top lip. He moved silently, stopping at the scar. He wondered if she knew it was there, before shadowing the shape of her bottom lip, finally coming to rest on the curve of her chin bone. Suddenly unsure of himself, he drew his hand away.

"There, all done. Guided tour complete."

Sam tried to speak with light humour in an attempt to avoid the sensation he felt from physical contact with Claire; this time even more intense.

She spoke into the space he left. "You're silent. What's wrong? Am I disfigured by the scar? I know it's there."

"No. The scar is small and complements your face. Your mouth is," he hesitated, "perfect." Sam swallowed, desperately seeking words to protect him from his own emotions. With a laugh, he added, "I'm sure those handsome New Zealanders at the party will all fall in love with you."

He just about pulled it off, ending on a carefree note as he shook his head, aware of how narrowly he had avoided the temptation to kiss her lips and abandon himself to a journey of mystery.

"I ought to get back." Sam shook his head; the spell was broken, part of him wishing it could last forever, but instinct warned of how dangerous that might be.

Claire stood up, brushing paint flakes from the wooden seat from her skirt. "Lorna told me there is a path near here that leads through the woods back to the farm; a short-cut I believe. It would be nice to explore it if you have time to guide the way."

Sam realised her suggestion was the path that approached the farmhouse concealed by the barns. Walking together into the farm in the current atmosphere, an innocent act in itself, might be misconstrued by anyone who saw them. Perhaps that had already occurred to Claire, he thought.

"Come on, we'll let *Rowan* lead the way. The path will be wide enough so we can hold the halter and still walk either side."

By means of a plank bridge, they crossed the roadside ditch which ran full of meltwater. A track meandered to a gate that led through a pasture meadow towards a small coppice, beyond which was another field that bounded the farm.

"You'll need to hitch your skirt again; the long grass is still wet." With a flourish, Claire gathered the hem of her skirt and bound it with a knot at mid-thigh height.

"There; wet feet but a dry skirt," she said with a laugh.

They walked in silence as they crossed the field, *Rowan* now eager, sensing the path led to a dry stable and a bag of oats.

As they approached the trees Claire asked, "Why did you do it?"

"Do what?"

"I found the parcel on my bed when I got back first thing this morning."

"Ah, yes. Well, a girl must have a dress for a party. I found it in a derelict shop in Newport. It's a small size but I guessed it would fit you. Only one colour though, dark blue silk. I hoped you wouldn't mind," Sam added cautiously.

Claire laughed. "For a girl who doesn't own a dress, the colour's a minor detail. But you haven't answered my question; why did you give it to me?"

Sam fumbled for an answer; how could he give a truthful reply when he didn't want to admit the answer to himself. Possibly Claire already knew his anguish. How easy it was for women to be open about their feelings.

"Because I care." Sam swallowed, impelled to say more, intuitively afraid of going further, afraid of the consequences.

"Well, that's alright then," she answered, as if she knew what was left was best unsaid.

With *Rowan* between them, they walked the shaded path through the woods with only birdsong as their accompaniment. If anyone saw them, they would appear as two individuals leading a tired horse, and as they emerged from the trees, Claire paused to lower the hem of her skirt.

"I'll take *Rowan* from here. It will save you a detour to the stables and I'm sure you have a busy day ahead."

Sam smiled to himself; her words told him that she was aware of their situation without it needing discussion. As he released his grip on the halter, their hands met; an innocent gesture, but with power beyond words.

It was always going to be a difficult farm meeting, but it was Jake's son, Thomas, who surprised everyone with an inspired idea. Everyone involved with the farm had gathered around their large table in the kitchen with the purpose of deciding what could be salvaged from their ravaged crops and what would be needed to get some sort of harvest before the winter. They had all inspected the damage, and after an hour or more, a provisional list had been agreed to pass on to the forum. When the totals were added up it gave Sam a furrowed brow; their requirements amounted to almost a complete year's re-allocation, which, if multiplied by every farm on the island, was beyond their reserves to meet. It was Jake who highlighted their biggest problem.

"It's all very well to list our needs for seed, fertilizer, and chemicals, but if we don't have the fuel for the machinery ..."

A major re-plant would require almost an entire year's fuel allowance and they had little reserve left from their current allocation.

"So what, we just sit back and starve," Rachel cut in with an acid tone to her words.

"There's always the horses." Monica tried to sound optimistic.

"Which, if we work night and day, would allow us to plant less than a quarter of what we need." Rachel punched her words across the table, aimed at Sam, who had made notes in silence for most of the meeting. He knew about their reserves. Fuel, or a lack of it, was the eternal albatross that hung around their necks.

"If we draw this quantity of fuel from our stocks," he tapped the sheet in front of him, "multiplied across the island by every farm, our reserves will be too low to cover next year's harvest."

"So, we starve this year, in hope of salvation next?" Sam winced at Rachel's scorn.

Everyone looked at him for an answer, but he had nothing to offer. Rachel's words were basically true; it crystallized their situation; they were losing the battle to hold on, even on this last outpost of their homeland. Without fuel they would soon lose electricity, the loss of drugs and chemicals would diminish medical care and the ability to grow their own food. When you factored in the attacks from across the Solent and the conveyor belt of radioactive fallout carried on the wind ...

Sam had learned his lesson. He wasn't about to spell out the truth for them, for he knew many would choose to fight on whatever the odds, even if it risked their children being subjected to enslavement to the men orchestrating the attacks, or dying from starvation and radiation sickness. Some would never admit defeat.

To his own astonishment, Sam began to laugh, at first as though at some private joke, until, without control, it accelerated away from him, echoing around the room. Faces that normally looked to him for reassurance now stared wide-eyed, almost frightened. Even Rachel looked stunned. He wiped his eyes as he collected himself.

"I'm sorry for that. It's just that the genie is well and truly out of the bottle, but none of you can see it."

His judgement was harsher than he intended, unfair perhaps. He should have said more, but lost the will to, surrendering instead to an embarrassed silence. The moment was saved, or interrupted, by Marcus's son. Thomas was, by most opinions, alternative. Still a teenager, he was old enough to remember their world before it abruptly came to an end with the arrival of the pandemic. The effect on his mind from the trauma of the early years was incalculable and everyone accepted Thomas as simply different. Recently, he had taken to wearing the hat of a Chinese coolie, with a cord tied beneath his chin. He had spent the entire meeting doodling distractedly; he often spent hours filling a sheet of paper with a random maze of lines. To those around him the result was often unfathomable, until he began to shade the gaps in between the lines and eventually revealed an image of often stunning intricacy. As he spoke, he continued his shading.

"I've heard it said that there's fuel in Gibraltar, where these New Zealanders have their base. Why don't we go and get some from there."

He spoke without looking up, without pause or hesitation. For a moment, everyone in the room ignored him.

"It's a hell of a long way to go for a few gallons of petrol," Jake quipped, and everyone laughed.

"Gavin says that Craig, his dad, was stationed in Gibraltar many years ago and there are huge tanks of fuel still there. That's why these New Zealanders have made a base there. We could send

*Lupin* back with them, loaded with empty tanks, and they could show us how to fill them up."

There was a further ripple of laughter at Thomas' words, as no one ever listened seriously to what he said, until Marcus interrupted them.

"Just a minute, he might be onto something. We know there are storage tanks here and on the mainland with fuel in them, but we've never been able to open the valves and use the pumping system. If the New Zealanders know how to do that, by sending *Lupin* with them and filling up our tanks we will have learnt how to do it in the future ourselves. We may even be able to tap into the storage tanks across the Solent."

"How much could *Lupin* carry, do you think?" Sam asked.

No one seemed certain, but a quick multiplication of their own needs pointed to fifty tons being sufficient for their replacement harvest.

"It would provide every farm with at least five hundred gallons," Jake dared a note of optimism.

Everyone began talking at once, while Thomas continued his shading, oblivious that he had come up with an idea that would ward off hunger for the entire island for at least another year. If it worked, they would perhaps be able to return to Gibraltar with an empty ocean tanker and alleviate their constant fear of fuel shortage.

When the meeting had dispersed, Sam came across the sketch Thomas had been working on. It depicted an intricate image of a petrol pump for cars, and filled the page in sharp edged black and grey tones with the face of the dial depicted by the macabre image of a human skull. Sam wondered who he had based it upon.

It was two of their eldest children, playing outside after lunch, who saw the columns of smoke coiling skywards in the distance. Hearing their shouts, Sam ran outside with the others. The day was still, allowing the smoke, thick and black, to rise vertically in spiralling tubes before flattening into mushroom heads as they reached for the clouds. Sam guessed they were about five miles distant, each separated by several miles.

"Only one thing I know that burns like that," Marcus said grimly.

The statement didn't need an answer; they all knew he meant farms.

"There must have been more attacks last night," Rachel added, casting a questioning glance at Sam for his reaction.

He felt his stomach tighten and knot, unable to express his fears in case he let slip anything that might expose David Longmarsh on the mainland. He had heard nothing about the previous evening, so it was best not to jump to conclusions. It hadn't been his operation to oversee, so it was essential he did nothing to intervene until someone made contact. Still, however you looked at it, burning farms had to be bad news. In silence they watched the distant pyres, lunch forgotten.

Almost unseen, a van pulled into the yard containing two men who Sam vaguely recognised. They climbed from the vehicle carrying an orange metal box, and the taller of the two walked directly towards Sam, recognising him from the forum.

"Sam Morten? I'm Geoff Edwards and this is Larry White." They shook hands. "We're here to conduct a survey of any radioactive material that might have fallen onto this farm. It's part of the island wide survey as instructed by the forum. If we could borrow a couple of horses, it shouldn't take more than a few hours to complete. I'll give you a copy of the results afterwards and warn you of any dangerous hot spots you need to avoid."

Sam frowned. "Avoid? I didn't think the problem was going to be that serious."

Edwards shrugged. "It's a steep learning curve for us all. We've completed ten surveys so far and each one seems to have a few high radioactivity areas. In some cases the readings are almost off the scale, particularly where run-off streams feed ponds for livestock."

They were speaking as they donned rubber suits, gloves and masks. Edwards saw the look of alarm on everyone's faces.

"I know; it makes us look like something from an old horror movie. If it's any comfort, it feels even worse to wear than it looks." He tried a joke to lighten the mood; "like working in a sauna in a plastic bag. Still, the job's got to be done."

Lorna and Claire appeared with two horses, and within minutes the inspectors were preparing to depart with a map of the farm fields.

As they were leaving, Sam asked, "Know anything about those smoke plumes?"

"Nothing more than there's been a general call for a boar alert." Larry White added, "I heard there have been major attacks on the Hazelwood and Carpenter farms, just before first light," he said through his mask. "Last I heard there had been casualties, but that's only hearsay."

Anxious at the news, Sam asked Jake to accompany the two men on their inspection. He felt he should have gone himself, but the ominous sight of the smoke plumes worried him. Once they had left, he climbed to the farmhouse attic, taking binoculars and a map. They had modified a dormer window to give access to a small balcony from where a ladder climbed to their roof platform, yet to be repaired after it had collapsed in the storm.

The extra height gave Sam a better view over the northern half of the island, but he couldn't get a clear sight even with the binoculars. Fuming with frustration, he could only speculate on what had happened and felt even more isolated as he battled with his feelings of exasperation. So much of the day felt a contradiction; bathed in warm sunshine, amidst piles of drifted snow, groups of children were taking full advantage to release their pent-up energies in a world where invisible poisonous radioactivity might lurk at any corner. If you shut your eyes, and mind, if only for a brief moment, their lives had the appearance of normality.

A few short minutes later, that illusion came to an end. An iridescent carrier pigeon, arrived with a red message tube secured to its leg and tripped the alert bell when it entered their loft. In a few short minutes, everything had changed.

# TWENTY-SIX

Albert Jamieson was dead-heading roses in the courtyard garden when Sam finally arrived.

"The first blush of flowers have all been destroyed by the cold wind and snow," Albert said over his shoulder as Sam dropped his rucksack onto a garden chair. "If I remove these now," he paused to snip with his secateurs, "we should get another chance a few months from now." He straightened up, easing stiff muscles in his back. "Thank you for coming at short notice."

The message had asked Sam to meet Albert as soon as possible. Although the message contained few words, he could guess what they needed to discuss.

"Take one of the chairs, I'll find Mary and organise some tea for us."

Albert picked up a bucket of dead rose flowers and disappeared into the office building adjacent to the garden. Sam eased himself onto a canvas deckchair. Against the east wall of the courtyard, he could still catch the final warmth of the day as dusk approached in the lengthening shadows and falling temperatures. He had been anxious to leave the farm as soon as he had received Albert's message, but had to wait until Edwards and White had returned with their evaluation of the radioactivity concentrations on their land. No one seemed to clearly understand what the 'Rem' numbers meant, but Napier had shown them the level on the dials of the Geiger counter at which things became dangerous. The readings showed that their best fields were reasonably clear, with just a few hot spots to avoid. The problems arose in the water courses; streams, ponds and brooks, where their animals drank, were all extensively affected. The only advice Edwards and White could offer was that these dangerous areas should be fenced off immediately until a possible solution could be found. The problem was that no one seemed to know exactly what that would mean.

Albert returned and took the chair beside Sam. He was still wearing a broad-brimmed sun hat, and the soft evening light warmed the grey pallor of his face, lending an almost healthy glow that Sam hadn't seen on him in months. For some while they remained in mutual silence, broken only when Mary arrived with a tray of white porcelain cups with an elegant teapot. Albert swirled the pot gently before he poured and as he passed a cup to Sam he said, "I sometimes think things go wrong because they are meant to, not just because of human error or frailty."

Sam concentrated on stirring his tea, giving space for the older man to share what was troubling him.

"Success last night wasn't intended for us. Everything that could go wrong did so." Albert paused to sip his tea. "We sent four squads to the landing point in Newtown Bay as young Longmarsh had told us. On the narrow lanes one leading squad collided with a deer and a second squad ran into the back of the first, seriously injuring the two men in the front and blocking the road for several hours. The remaining two Landrovers had to reverse for the best part of a mile only for one of them to back straight into a ditch. While all this was happening, Chris Woods taxied into a soft section of the landing strip, one wheel on the Cessna became stuck, and we bent the undercarriage strut when we tried to tow her free."

He sipped his tea for some time. If it all wasn't bad enough, Sam sensed there was more to come.

"On top of that, Helen ran *Lupin* aground on a mud bank near the entrance to Newtown Bay that must have formed in the run-off from the storm. They had to wait for the high tide to re-float her, by which time our visitors from across the Solent had offloaded their cargo and disappeared."

To Sam, it sounded like a total fiasco and he only just avoided saying so.

"There's more," Albert continued with tired words. "The boar that had been landed attacked two farms just before sunrise. Sadly, at the Carpenter's farm there were fatalities. We had just sent word to alert all farmers in the north of the island when, for the first time, the attacks happened in the south. A mother and daughter were doing early morning milking when the boar entered their farm without warning. They became cornered and alerted the rest of the farm with their screams. Everything went haywire after that and, as a result, four of the family were killed by the boar."

Albert sounded devastated. It was a total disaster, but saying that would only tell Albert what he already knew.

Sam drew a deep breath. "So we're back to square one. We'll just have to hope David Longmarsh can tip us off again before the next attack."

He paused, his attention caught by a figure that moved in the shadows of the cloistered courtyard behind Albert. Following Sam's eyes, Albert turned in his chair just as Mary appeared, moving with her usual silent grace.

"If you've finished with me, Mr Chairman?" she said with her usual impeccable manners.

"Of course Mary; I've kept you far too late as always. Please be off home and don't rush in the morning; I'm sure we can manage without you for just a few hours," Albert said with a smile.

Mary nodded in wordless reply, slipping back into the shadows as effortlessly as she had appeared. For a while, both men sat in silent communion over their tea; Albert contemplating his next words, while Sam sat in troubled anticipation.

"I don't know if you have heard, but one of the injured in last night's accident is Craig's eldest son, Gavin."

Sam shook his head.

"Yes, and it's serious, I'm afraid. We expect Doctor Morgan to perform the impossible but, sadly, he can't achieve miracles. It doesn't look too good, though I suppose there is always hope."

"It must be hard for Craig. I know they're a close family, one of the few complete families to survive the pandemic."

Albert nodded. "Which brings me to my main point. In the circumstances, I can't ask Craig to continue to lead our rescue mission to Weymouth; it simply wouldn't be fair to ask him. I'm afraid I have to ask you to go in his place."

Sam's immediate thought was, 'No, not again.' From the moment John had told him of the distress message he had received, he had felt unease about another plea for rescue so soon after Dartmouth. To Sam, it was a puzzling coincidence that after years of silence, a second desperate group could appear so quickly. Obviously, Craig couldn't be expected to continue, but there had to be others on the forum who could take his place? Plus, there would be Rachel's reaction to take into account when she found out.

"We'll be sending Aiden and Ruth as principal squad leaders. Helen has agreed to skipper *Lupin* again, but Dave Bartlett has had to stand down. He's very ill at the moment. Doctor Morgan has diagnosed lung cancer, and the prognosis isn't very optimistic."

It took a moment to absorb the news; jokes that Bartlett was literally smoking himself to death were nothing new, but confirmation of the consequences still came as a shock.

"He's a very private man. He lost his wife and children in the aftermath of the pandemic. He'll be a sad loss to us until he recovers, but Aiden knows the ropes and is a competent leader." Albert hesitated. "And he, Helen and Ruth have all asked for you as the replacement for Craig."

Sam winced at his words, aware it made it even more difficult to decline. "What are Bartlett's chances?" he asked.

Albert shook his head. "Not good. All Doctor Morgan can offer is palliative care. He's thought of removing the cancerous lung but we've barely enough anaesthetic."

He watched Sam with concern. Had he heard of the difficulties in his personal life? Albert never spoke of gossip, but little happened on the island without him knowing. For several minutes he was silent while Sam was thinking of someone to replace him. The problem was that the constant boar attacks had already side-lined many suitable alternatives; others amongst the women were ruled out with pregnancy and childbirth, and advancing age and ill health eliminating more of the men. It left a mere handful fit and active to call upon for ventures such as Weymouth.

Albert sat patiently, watching the sun disappear behind the tiled roof to the east. Sam was desperate to decline, to resign from the forum with immediate effect for that matter, but how would he be able to face anyone on the island, or himself, when things were so worryingly stacked against them. Leadership was a mysterious art, he decided. He had no training and little awareness of his own role, and while some had begun to bitterly oppose him, others relied heavily on him for guidance and direction. Either way, he knew he didn't have it in his conscience to turn away, whatever the personal cost.

"I'll go to Weymouth," he eventually said with a heavy heart.

With just a few words he feared he had embarked upon a defining act in the rift in his relationship with Rachel.

Exhausted by the previous day, Albert left for home. Sam now had to plan an operation that he thought was dangerously ill-advised. He had less than seventy-two hours to pull the threads together and began immediately by despatching messages to attend a meeting early the following morning to everyone involved in the forthcoming operation.

The party organised for Napier and his crew was to be held the following evening, attended by everyone on the island who could be spared. The repaired yacht would set out on the final leg of her mission the morning after, hangovers allowing. Sam had heard that several teenagers had already volunteered to go with them as deckhands and though he wondered what use they might be, there was the bonus of experience and the almost certainty that Napier would have to return them before setting course for Gibraltar and home. That gave them possibly four weeks to organise and complete their referendum. It was going to be tight.

As darkness fell, Sam stared out alone at the river Medina which lay slick black in the fading light. It was low tide, with only the masts of moored boats visible above the harbour wall, pointing like accusing fingers at the indigo sky above as pinprick stars slowly appeared. Was one of them responsible for their dire luck? 'Catch a falling star and put it in your pocket' Sam hummed the well-known tune in thoughtful irony. In truth, there were as many theories for their plight as opinions, but no one knew, nor would they ever know, how the planet's foremost life form could come to be laid as low as they were.

The door opened behind Sam. He hadn't heard anyone enter the building but Chris Woods came into the room carrying two glasses and a half empty bottle of home brewed red wine.

"Don't you have a home to go to?" she teased, placing the bottle and glasses on the desk. "I saw you still working as I passed and wondered if you needed company."

Sam guessed that Chris would have already heard that he was to take over the leading role from Craig in the Weymouth operation. He noticed her face had a look of concern as she poured two glasses and passed one to him.

"It's no secret that I have reservations about Weymouth," Sam said abruptly. They touched glasses and drank. "But someone has to do it. How's Craig's son?"

Chris pulled a face. "Paralysed by a broken neck." She emptied the glass. "Another consequence of Rigby's bull-in-a-china-shop tactics."

Involuntarily, Sam let out a deep sigh; it put his own problems into perspective. "Aren't you flying tonight?" he asked, trying to change the subject.

"No. It's Geoff Foster's first solo mission. He's passed the tests and seems competent to fly by instruments. It's simple enough, so long as you don't get lost. And on that point, what are you doing tomorrow evening?"

Sam looked surprised. "I guess I'll show my face at the party for our New Zealand friends and then try and get an early night. Why?"

"I'm rostered to fly. I said I would so the younger ones could have a night off. Parties are rare enough and I didn't want to deprive them of their fun, but I could do with some company; preferably someone who can read a map. Our usual plane is still being repaired, Foster will use the spare and so I'm flying the bigger twin engine model and I could use a navigator."

Sam thought for a few moments. It had been years since he had last flown in a plane and that had been whilst doing his National Service. The opportunity brightened his mood and it would also give him an insight into how that crucial part of their security was performing.

"What time do you need me?"

"High tide is around one o'clock, so take-off is eleven-thirty and I'd need you half an hour before then. You'd need to be at the airstrip by eleven, so you can party until then. No drinking I'm afraid." She filled their glasses again. "I'm taking advantage tonight as I only need to be at the airstrip to watch Foster take off and land and offer advice if he needs it." She paused, thoughtfully. "How do you think Albert Jamieson looks?"

"Tired; he needs a break like the rest of us."

"He has a heart condition and I think he's deteriorating. Doctor Morgan does his best, but with too much work and limited drugs …" Chris left the sentence to answer itself.

"Once the current crisis is over we must make sure he gets a decent break. He'll have earned it." Sam tried to sound positive.

He noticed Chris was biting the inside of her cheek nervously.

"But what if the worst is yet to come?" she said in a worried voice. "Albert Jamieson is not young and he's not a well man."

Sam drew breath. "I know, but we'll have to cross that bridge when we come to it. Albert provides the glue that holds us all together; he won't stand aside while there's still breath in his body. In the meantime, the rest of us must do our bit and take as much of the load from him as possible."

As he spoke, he realised that he had answered his own dilemma. He didn't want to go to Weymouth, but to refuse would have contradicted what he had just said, and he realised he had accepted it to share the strain on the man he highly respected.

Chris nodded and emptied her glass.

"Well, time to go. I'll see you tomorrow evening then. Don't work too late."

She turned to leave, picking up her bag and flying jacket, throwing her final comment over her shoulder as she did so. "And don't forget to ask Rachel to dance at the party tomorrow night."

She was gone before Sam could find an answer, and amazed by how much they all knew about the private lives of each other.

## TWENTY-SEVEN

"I presume it's pointless asking you not to go to Weymouth?" Rachel's voice was flat, resigned.

"I told you, Craig's son has been very seriously injured. There's no way we can expect Craig to continue." Sam had again returned late and needed to leave early. At least they weren't arguing; the house was still silent and abed and raised voices would have been heard by everyone.

"You could cancel the entire operation; it's not impossible for people to make their own way here. I recall that we had to."

Sam heaved a heavy sigh. "Rachel, we've been over this. It's the same story as before; we're bound by the words of our own constitution to go to the aid of those in need."

Rachel laughed sharply. "And who will come to our assistance in our hour of need?"

"I thought that's what the New Zealanders are doing?"

"On their terms, maybe. You said yourself they've issued an ultimatum that they won't return if we don't leave with them."

Sam frowned; he felt that was an unfair interpretation of what Napier had said. Rachel's recent moods led her to interpret things through a distorted lens and it pained him to think that his actions could have so evaporated her usual sunny optimism. He reached out for her hand, only to find hers withdraw from his touch.

She pursed her lips and said, "And I suppose you're going to tell me this has nothing to do with Claire volunteering for this trip?"

"What?"

"Oh come on, don't try to pretend you don't know. She volunteered to help Karen, to do her bit to help the island." Her final words were pure cynicism.

"Claire going to Weymouth? That's ridiculous. What could she achieve, she's blind, for goodness sake." Suddenly exasperated, Sam raised his voice, his words sounding hollow as they echoed back at him.

"So it's fine for sighted men and women, with families, to take unnecessary risks, but not the blind; after all, they need to be protected at all costs. Especially the pretty ones."

Sam was reeling, the bite in Rachel's final words leaving him momentarily speechless. "I don't have time for this nonsense," he abruptly replied, gathering his rucksack.

"You never have time," she blurted. "So you won't deny it then?"

"Deny what?" he shouted with anger, as he made for the door.

"What everyone else can so clearly see but you," she retorted at his back.

Sam hesitated, slowly turning to face Rachel. He feared he knew what her next words would be.

"Don't say it, don't you dare say it. That will cross a line between us, one that could be difficult to forget."

"Is that a threat?"

Sam shook his head. "I simply don't understand. Why are we doing this to one another, when our grip on all we have and hold dear is so precarious? Everywhere I look I see grief and bereavement, yet all we can do is snarl at each other like angry dogs."

Standing facing one another, the distance between them was a mere arms' length, but at that moment it felt like light years. He was desperate to bridge the gap but didn't know how to.

"There is only one thing that can heal the rift. And if you're too blind to see it," she paused for breath, "then I'm not going to spell it out for you. Until you face up to the situation, we're trapped in this impasse."

Her face looked twisted with pain, but as Sam made a step forward she shook her head, leaving Sam, his arms spread in exasperation, lost for an answer. He felt wretched, but what could he do? Slowly he turned and walked back to the door. As he opened it, he heard Rachel's voice, now stilled, quiet, behind him.

"Just ask her to leave, Sam. That's all you have to do."

He closed the door and left without a reply.

Sam stopped on his way to Newport to again check the clearing where he had found the nameless girl. The flowers still remained, slightly faded, less perfumed. Something in their fragrance struck a chord he couldn't place. Cultivated flowers were rare; no one had time to grow them when there were more pressing things to do every hour of their daily lives. Had he encountered the fragrance before, possibly recently? Nothing came to mind, but Sam was puzzled, like an itch that couldn't be scratched. He lifted the flowers from their sunken jar. The stems were loosely tied with a pale green ribbon. As he turned the bunch in his hand, he noticed a black character, '&', stencilled near the end of the ribbon; an 'ampersand'. It seemed meaningless; the only purpose he knew for the symbol was the abbreviation of the word 'and'. It didn't make any sense, least of all the murder of a young woman, yet the clues in the lonely clearing intrigued him. Along with the fragrance of the freesias, he felt sure he had seen the symbol recently, somewhere other than the keys of a typewriter. Distracted in thought, Sam released the ribbon and tucked it into his pocketbook, replacing the flowers into their humble vase. Were the flowers a conscience gesture or the symbol of grief for a life that couldn't be acknowledged?

As he rode away, Sam was only too aware that mystery excited the imagination. It could mislead, though the early morning sunshine, with its dappled sunlight, held no feelings of ghostly haunting. The leaves on the hangman's bough above him shimmered, as if calling out the dead girl's parting warning, yet there was not even a breath of air. Somewhere, this spot hid the keys to their future. But finding those keys was another matter.

John looked at Sam thoughtfully.

"It just occurred to me that you might have heard names mentioned at some point when you listened in on the thugs on the mainland."

"Occasionally. There seems a wide choice that crop up."

"I hadn't thought much about a particular name for years and I've been trying to join the dots together recently and I wondered if any names had regularly crossed your path on the airways."

John frowned. "Nothing specific immediately came to mind. When names are mentioned, they seem to be less specific; 'the big man' comes up a lot and there is someone called 'the inquisitor'. A lot of blasphemy flies around, crude names, but there doesn't seem to be any consistency. Someone called 'the hangman' is there a lot." John shuddered. "I'll look back through my notes. Is it important? Do you recognise any of these names?"

Sam shrugged. "Nothing comes to mind. I'm trying to make sense of something associated with the death of the mystery girl in the woods. What little evidence we have could conceal a message or clue. Those names are a long shot and I'm not certain why they could be relevant, but see what you can find."

Sam left their Newport offices in search of Napier, who he found loading stores and supplies onto *The Shepherd* in the harbour. Patched and sporting a new mast, the yacht looked almost ready for sea.

"Just the engine strip-down to complete; we took on a lot of sea water in the engine room in the storm. Best to check everything out before we set off. We should be done today, possibly tomorrow."

Sam noticed a flag displaying a silver fern on a black background that now snapped taut in the wind at the stern.

"I thought your national flag included the Union Jack and the Southern Cross?"

Napier grinned. "There didn't seem much point in continuing with it, especially as we weren't sure if the home country even existed any longer. We felt a new page had to be turned, as though we were giving birth to a new country, so we've adopted our Maori name, *Aotearoa*; *Land of the White Cloud*; it seems especially poignant in the circumstances." He pointed towards the stern. "That's our new flag, the living vibrant symbol of our precious homeland," Napier said with pride in his voice.

Sam laughed. "I think our new flag, if we were to have one, would show 'Boar Rampant'; not much else seems to prosper at the moment, least of all humankind," he said with a grim note of humour.

"I've been using our old name, New Zealand, while I'm here to avoid confusion. I had hoped it would appeal more." Napier nodded to a poster stapled to a telephone pole. In bold print, the banner line read,

*'Say NO to running away; NO thanks, New Zealand'*

"Looks as if your people opposing the idea have been quick off the mark. On reflection, if our new name had been used from the start it might appeal more," Napier added thoughtfully.

"Rigby certainly hasn't wasted much time. The thing is, how many will support him?"

Napier looked at Sam with a raised eyebrow, but neither had an answer; time alone would tell and Napier returned to continue loading their supplies.

"Don't forget the party tonight," he shouted over his shoulder. "I heard the band rehearsing yesterday; they sound good, so be sure to bring your dancing shoes." He waved casually as he disappeared down the hatchway.

Sam grinned, shouting after him, "You obviously haven't seen my dancing."

Somewhere deep within the bowels of the yacht, Sam could just hear Napier's deep, booming laughter.

Sam was finishing his lunch when Linda Hue approached his table with a tray. The forum building had a café of sorts which offered a daily menu, but dishes were improvised and sometimes re-heated from the previous day. She chose a seat opposite Sam and studied the plate of food in front of her.

"I'm sure I ate this yesterday," she muttered with an amused frown. "Boiled, with butter; fried today."

"You know the adage; waste not, want not."

Linda poked her lunch with a fork. "I think they call it wholesome, it's certainly not haute cuisine. Cooked at least six hours ago, I would guess," she said with an exaggerated sigh, tearing at a baguette; at least the bread was fresh baked. "I was hoping to catch you. Albert Jamieson wants to hold Melissa's funeral the day after tomorrow."

"Melissa?"

"It's the name we've given to our mystery dead girl from the woods. No one has come to identify her and I'm afraid we can't support the refrigeration of her body any longer. If anyone turns up to claim her, identification will have to be done from photographs."

"I can't see anyone coming forward," Sam muttered, adding, "I should be able to attend the funeral though; the Weymouth operation is scheduled to begin the following day."

A thought suddenly struck him. "Is there a chance I could read your autopsy report before we bury her, assuming there's no cremation?"

Linda looked at Sam, weighing up his request. "It would have to be in my office. There are several specific points I've tried to answer which Albert Jamieson wouldn't want in the public domain, but I see no reason why you shouldn't read the report," she said, fixing his eyes with hers, aware of listening ears at the tables around them.

"Would this afternoon be a good time? I wouldn't need long, so I'd be clear in good time for you to get ready for the party tonight."

"Ah, the celebratory send-off for our handsome New Zealanders."

Sam laughed. "I'm sure that's a female perspective unlikely to be appreciated by any of the male population."

"But so good for our gene pool," Linda said mischievously. "I hear several of our young women have volunteered to accompany them as support crew; to gain ocean sailing experience of course, but I wouldn't mind speculating they all return with far more experience than just sailing."

The afternoon was taken up planning the strategy for the Weymouth rescue mission. With the lessons learnt from Dartmouth still sharp in their memories, Helen, Aiden and Ruth worked hard with Sam to create a plan that avoided the mistakes and surprises they had made only a few weeks previously. Extra steel protection had been welded to *Lupin*, now displaying a rust stained hull and moored at the quayside. For the next trip, additional weapons had been added along with a more powerful radio and aerials. As a consequence, Helen had taken to referring to the trawler as her 'flagship'. Sam nicknamed her the Admiral; minus a fleet.

Aiden and Ruth asked for an extra squad and more ammunition and supplies. Karen would once again provide medical services with three assistants, reminding Sam of his shock at the inclusion of Claire in what he considered a risky operation at best. On the positive side, the sea route to Weymouth was only half the distance and they would be better prepared and equipped. So far, John's radio contact with the survivors hadn't shown any evidence that any men on motorbikes might be shadowing them. They could only hope things stayed that way.

Everyone parted early to prepare for the evening festivities, the first time in many long months for the chance to be carefree, if only for a few hours. Sam had a change of clothes with him and decided not to return to the farm; he would meet everyone who could come from the farm at the party instead. Showered and changed, he closed the door to the room he used as an office and set off to pay a visit to Linda Hue's lab before she left for the evening.

"The report is on my desk. Could you return it to the bottom drawer when you've read it. I hope you find the clues you might be looking for," she said with a questioning glance in Sam's direction.

"And the body?"

Linda looked surprised. "In the fridge on the trolley, if you need to inspect it."

"I'll let you know," he replied casually, opening the manila file on her desk.

The file contained a dozen pages, bound together by a tag. The first page was a summary of where and how the body had been discovered and her gender, colouring, ethnicity and an estimate of age. Interestingly, the 'name' box was now entered as 'Melissa'. Sam noticed that in the 'weight' box Linda had entered 'under-nourished', an ever increasing prospect for them all in the months to come.

The second page contained a line drawing of a female body, with notes and arrows identifying all the significant marks and injuries Linda had discovered. The luxury of photo film had become a precious commodity as their stocks degraded with time and none could be spared for autopsies, but each note on the diagram was clearly linked to a numbered description on the evidence pages. A large section of the report was concerned with the likely causes of death. Sam skimmed through this, already aware that Linda had been unable to decide if death had been caused by strangulation or a broken neck. Whatever had been the cause, the poor girl had met an unpleasant end. All bruises and abrasions were listed, but without any speculation as to how they had been caused. He read quickly through the rest of the autopsy notes, but failed to find anything to trigger the question that nagged somewhere at the back of his mind, something he had seen during the frantic seconds after he had cut the girl from her gibbet and searched in vain for a glimmer of life.

He left the report on the desk and stood at the window and watched the sun sink slowly in the west. In the absence of help from the report, the evidence he sought must be somewhere on the body, so he was left with only one option. He turned and stared unenthusiastically at the grey, full-height door to the fridge. Death was no stranger and it held an all too regular presence in their lives. Yet the manner in which this girl had met her end still disturbed him; if he hesitated or turned away, the opportunity would disappear, buried in the ground with her body in the next few days.

Sam opened the door. The fridge was lit by a stark white fluorescent light and the body lay on a grey steel trolley, covered by a single white sheet. He felt pity, aware of the hard cold emptiness of the room and had to resist the ridiculous urge to find a blanket to keep her warm. If it was redemption he wanted for her, he would have to inspect her body. Anything he might have seen, no matter how fleetingly, could only have been on the parts of her body exposed when he found her. He folded back the sheet to expose her face and arms and was struck by the pale grey waxy texture to her skin, the hollows of her body collapsed and sucked in around the bones. Her face looked strangely aged, yet serene in the sleep of death. Sam checked her face and neck. The bruises were black and yellow, the skin peeled back to reveal the mortifying flesh beneath. He moved quickly to her hands and checked both wrists; the sooner he got through this the better. Nothing. This was a fool's errand, he thought. He covered the exposed body; dignity restored. Should he leave? He was never going to find anything after the extended period since her death. He half turned away. The only other part of her body exposed when he had found her were her legs and feet. At the time he had thought it sadly pathetic that she hadn't been wearing any shoes; as if that would have made any difference.

He lifted the sheet at the bottom of the trolley. The right foot, bruised and torn from her death throes, revealed nothing; the left appeared the same. Instinct made him lift her foot, the joint now locked and rigid. Just above the tendon was a small black mark, a tattoo,that still stained the parchment texture of her skin. He knelt down. There was no mistake. The tattoo was the same mark as that on the ribbon he had seen earlier; '&'

'Ampersand,' he muttered.

The missing twenty-seventh letter of the alphabet.

# TWENTY-EIGHT

With most of the island in attendance, the party for the New Zealanders was a great success. For one evening, all thought of their difficult lives could be put to one side. For once, the older generation could allow the young, who had suffered most from the loss of an innocent childhood, to let their hair down. The hall was packed; no tickets needed. Every hamlet supplied food and drink, with dance music provided by a varied assortment of musicians and an ageing record player assisted by a catalogue of vinyl records during the intervals.

Committed to fly with Chris Woods on her late night patrol, Sam avoided the bar. Despite, or perhaps because of that he found it difficult to enjoy himself. He had been prepared for Rachel's cold shoulder approach. After she had arrived, she joined a larger group from adjacent farms and kept herself busy for most of the evening amongst people he barely knew. When he caught up with her she was polite, but for the most part kept herself detached, lost somewhere in the crowd. As guests of honour, Napier and his crewmen entered into the spirit of the evening with an exuberance that came from long weeks at sea, adding an invigorated excitement to the occasion.

Sam noticed heads turn when Claire arrived with Lorna and several other young women. She was wearing the dress he had found, her hair was cut and styled to just off the shoulder, where it shone with flashes of gold as she moved in the lights. In Sam's eyes, recalling the first time they had met, it was an amazing transformation and he had a feeling of pride in how she stood out in the crowd. Not surprisingly, she spent the evening partnered by a succession of young men, who guided her as they moved around the dance floor. No dancer himself, Sam was pleased to see Claire enjoy herself, such a contrast to her recent past. Things were as they should be; the night was about feeling carefree, a release valve in their sea of problems.

Conscious of the glare of gossiping eyes, he deliberately avoided talking to Claire or even passing too close to her. Perhaps it was the enforced distance that caused the unexpected pain he felt when he saw her in the arms of one of the New Zealanders for a slow dance, with the hall lights dimmed for added effect. Though she gazed at her partner with sightless eyes, the look of innocent happiness in her face caused a pang that caught Sam by surprise. Aware he was watching her, certain he was staring too much and surprised by his own feelings, he left the hall for the quiet outside. As it was, there was less than an hour until he was scheduled to leave to meet Chris Woods and he needed a cool head for the challenges of the night ahead.

The night was clear, spangled with bright stars and a half moon which was climbing lazily above the horizon. Sam felt for his tobacco pouch and pipe; the pouch was almost empty and there would be little chance of more when it was all gone. The cool of the night had cleared his mind as he packed the bowl, struck a match and filled the darkness with aromatic smoke. A felled log lay nearby and offered a good seat. He sat alone, listening to the music that drifted from the hall and tried not to worry about the coming days, reminding himself that life had a habit of working things out, no matter how much you tried to direct things. The pipe bowl glowed and smoke burnt in his throat. For a few brief minutes it was the limit to Sam's world. There were other feelings too, emotions he couldn't identify that gripped his chest in a vice, sometimes making breathing difficult and his head spin.

"You need to give that up or it will be the death of you."

A voice surprised him from out of the darkness. Claire had followed him from the hall; day or night made no difference to her when he thought about it.

Sam laughed. "I'm surprised you think I'll last that long? I'd figured the boar would get me long before this ever became a problem," he replied, holding his pipe at arms' length. "How did you know I was out here?"

"Lorna saw you leave; she said you had a sad look in your eyes when she spoke to you." She paused, feeling for the edge of the log on which he was sitting. "Like any good Red Indian, I just followed the smell of White Man's smoke," she said light-heartedly, adding with a serious tone, "I was disappointed you didn't ask me to dance." She perched beside him and smoothed down her dress with her hands.

"Oh, I'm not much of a dancer and anyway, I don't think I could compete with the string of eligible young men vying for your attention." He tried to make it sound a joke but somehow knew he had failed. "Besides, I have to leave shortly; I'm flying tonight with Chris Woods as her stand-in navigator."

The sounds of music and fun filtered towards them from the hall. Intuitively, seeming to read an unspoken note of sadness, Claire stood and moved directly in front of him.

"We could always have our dance out here, in the moonlight. Then no one will see how awful you are."

As so often, she laughed with her words, and grasping his arm, pulled him towards her. He just had time to discard his pipe before sliding his arm naturally around her, his left hand outstretched to hold hers. For a few short minutes they moved together to the strains of a slow song from a bygone age sung by a young man with a wonderful voice. Sam felt the warmth of her back and he was slightly intoxicated by the smell of her perfume with her head close on his shoulder. He just caught her words close to his ear, "Liar, you're better than you pretend."

As the song concluded, neither seemed keen to let the moment go, until a door opened, casting out a bar of yellow light and approaching voices forced them apart. Like a spirit, Claire slipped away into the darkness as a laughing couple ran past, eclipsing the private secret of their moment.

It was some time later when, out of the blue, Sam suddenly gave a sharp ironic laugh when he realised that they had been dancing to the strains of the popular ballad he had once known, *'Where fools rush in'*.

It somehow seemed prophetic.


John turned on the grass runway lights and Chris eased the throttles forward, the propeller disappearing into an invisible disc in front of them. The Cessna bounced energetically down the grass strip into the darkness towards a jagged jet black line that marked the divide between earth and sky. Thin veils of mist kissed the front screen, their speed increased, and the bouncing ceased abruptly as gravity released its grip on the little plane. They were airborne. Chris trimmed the Cessna and for a few minutes they flew eastwards, slowly gaining height. Sam checked the compass and turned to the clipboard on his knee, which he could just see in the light of the instruments.

"Come round a hundred and eighty."

"One hundred and eighty," Chris answered, adjusting the settings and easing the control stick and rudder, bringing the plane into a gentle turn.

Through the side screen Sam could see only the blackness of night. Without artificial lights he could clearly make out a myriad of stars and galaxies that filled the night above them. He gazed in wonder at the thought that it was exactly as their forebears would have seen at the dawn of creation; everything in its place, unchanged and unchanging. Millions of years hence, the scene would probably still be much the same, though he doubted humankind would be around to witness it.

The turn complete, Chris brought the Cessna to level flight, their nose now pointing in a westerly direction and she adjusted their flight path to trace the coastline, following a route just a short distance landward from the sea. Sam noticed the altimeter held at three and a half thousand feet; Chris would fly precisely to their agreed flight plan.

"From here we can see anyone approaching across the Solent or making a landing, though we'll have to change course to make a circuit around Newtown Bay where they still favour the creeks and channels for offloading boar. Keep your eyes on the port side as well, just in case you can see any headlights, though I guess they'll switch off their lights if they hear our engine, but you never know."

Chris paused, calling in their position to John, now far behind in the control tower, a rather grandiose title for what was little more than a wooden cabin on a scaffold tower.

"Light one should appear in thirty seconds," Chris prompted Sam, gesturing to the stopwatch on his clipboard and the map on his knee, on which a cross and number were written in red ink.

Within seconds, a bright light beamed at them from the ground. Sam noted the time lapse and adjusted their course, advising Chris and John simultaneously. Seconds later, the light disappeared. He felt the Cessna buck in the cold air and watched Chris re-trim the plane as they settled onto his new course. His headphones crackled.

"Newtown Bay dead ahead. We'll do a complete three-sixty around the bay to the landward, so keep an eye on my position as I complete the circuit. And watch out for lights on the ground or the wake of a boat; *Lupin* is in port tonight so there'll be nothing of ours at sea," Chris instructed.

It was far from a pleasure flight. Even without the potential excitement of activity below, the workload was considerable to just keep alert and on course. As they circled Newtown Bay, Sam used binoculars to focus to the north in the direction of Buckler's Hard, where they suspected the boar attacks originated. For a few minutes the marshes below were obscured by mist, but the view across the Solent was clear, with pale moonlight reflecting like beaten silver on the surface of a calm sea.

"Can you make out anything," Chris asked as she trimmed the banking Cessna again.

Sam adjusted the focus, searching for a significant dark landmark in the distant blackness. As they swung back onto their westerly course, tiny jewels, pinpricks of light, swam into the eyepiece. Sam checked his compass; it must have been Buckler's Hard.

"Well, they're the only lights to be seen on the mainland coast, bang on the correct bearing. I can't see any detail, but you can bet they're up to something."

"Another attack tonight?"

"Who knows; I think they'll miss the tide, but landing could be taking place right now."

He mentioned nothing of David Longmarsh. They had received no prior warning from him, but that didn't necessarily mean a landing wasn't planned. On balance, Sam decided to keep faith with David, and radioed the presence of the lights to John without suggesting they call an alert.

They flew on westwards and fixed their position from light two near Freshwater before turning out over the sea just west of the Needles. Even on a calm night, the white rock pinnacles were clear in the moonlight ringed in a phosphorescence of surf. Chris flew the return leg back towards Cowes, now choosing a course about a mile to seaward, so that Sam could maintain clear sight of the shoreline and any lights approaching the coast. With most people involved at the party, anything near to the shoreline would warrant investigation.

Apart from the dance hall, which shone like a beacon, the entire island was in darkness and their flight became more of a training routine. They flew as far as Bembridge, giving Sam a view of the coast from the air, bringing back memories of the wild stormy night and the impossibly narrow harbour entrance. As they turned above the deserted town, Chris called time for home.

"Would you like to take the controls?"

"Me? I can't fly."

"Well, there's no excitement tonight and the conditions are calm, so no better time to begin to learn."

It took less than ten minutes to fly the return leg to Cowes, in which time Sam's main achievement, apart from not crashing the plane, was to progress from being terrified, with hands locked rigid on the control stick, to sensing the movements of the Cessna as he relaxed and began to adjust their flight with rudder and ailerons. He even managed a turn above Cowes for the landing approach towards Newport before Chris took control, leaving him to watch with new respect as she flew on instruments for the final approach towards a terrifyingly short chain of landing lights. Feeling the dropping sensation of their rapid descent, Sam held his breath while fleeting shrouds of mist accelerated past them, until the wheels touched down with a gentle nudge. They bounced and bucked on the grass surface, brakes squealing, and slowed at the end of the lights before turning to taxi back to the control tower. John appeared in the darkness, guiding them with hand flashlights to the wide doors of an open hangar. Once inside, Chris shut down the engine and a stilled silence returned.

"Another successful mission," she announced with an audible sigh of relief, the first indication she had given of the strain that continuous night flights made on her. It would be not a moment too soon for the other trainees to reach a level of competence and share the burden.

"Well done," Sam said in encouragement. "What you're doing is no mean feat, night after night."

He gave Chris a hug, acknowledging that another competent pilot was needed urgently. John walked over to close the hangar doors, a sheepish grin on his face.

"Well done. A quiet night."

Sam handed him the flight log, removed his flight helmet, and ran his hands through his hair.

"Time for bed, I think."

He felt exhilarated but exhausted, even though their flight had lasted barely an hour; any thoughts of returning to the party had evaporated from his mind. As he made to walk back to their control room, John held Sam back, waiting for Chris to move beyond hearing range. He looked awkward.

"Actually, there's someone waiting to see you. I've given her a blanket, shivering with cold she was. She asked for you. I think you had better come and see."

Sam found Claire, seated on a threadbare sofa in what served as a staff rest room.

Astonished, he asked, "What on earth are you doing here?"

Claire smiled at him, a thin blanket draped around her shoulders. "I think there was a mix up. Lorna wanted to leave the party to join Gary and some friends for an all-night session. She said she had arranged for Rachel and the others to give me a lift back to the farm." Claire shrugged. "I guess there was some misunderstanding and I got left behind."

"You're here?" he said with a puzzled frown. "What about the party?"

"Everything wound up about midnight."

Sam glanced at the clock on the wall which now read one-thirty, as Claire continued. "The New Zealanders love to party but they're making an early start. Kit Napier said some words of thanks to everyone and ushered his crew off to bed. Lorna left and I found the rest of the farm group had gone. I remembered you said you were flying tonight and the road from the hall led directly to the airstrip. I couldn't think of anything else to do. Sorry."

Sam shook his head. Accident, or deliberately left behind, he wondered.

"You walked all the way here in the dark?"

Claire smiled. "Night or day; makes no difference to me. And I had my guide cane, so I just followed the kerb or the verge. I took a tumble on the way though." She lifted the hem of her dress; drying blood had seeped from a cut on her knee.

Sam had to bite back a spasm of anger. "Stay there. I'll clean that."

He found boiled water from a kettle and a first aid kit from his rucksack. Infection haunted their lives, so even the simplest of cuts needed careful cleaning. He knelt in front of Claire, her foot braced on his knee, washing away the blood and dirt and soaked a cotton swab in antiseptic. The wound, quite deep, seeped blood.

"This will hurt," he warned her.

"I've heard you say that before," she smiled to camouflage a wince.

He dressed the wound with care, suddenly conscious of the paleness of her skin.

"You'll have a painful bruise but the cut should heal without stitching. Are these the only shoes you have with you?"

They were thin-soled, already badly scored from the walk to the airstrip.

"I came in the Landrover. I didn't think I'd have to walk home," she added with a wry note of humour, stifling a tired yawn.

Sam thought for a moment. The excitement of the evening had left them both exhausted. Chris Woods had given him a lift to the airstrip and the prospect of finding a car with any petrol to take them home was slender. There was the mare at the forum stables he often used, but she would have to carry both of them and the journey would be interminably slow. He knew John had left already, but Chris's battered car was still parked outside and there remained the option of a re-used hostel in Newport, sometimes used by forum members when meetings ended late. If he could find beds there, he could organise a car for the morning.

Chris dropped them off on her way home. The hostel was in darkness except for a dim nightlight in what had once been the reception area where keys to the rooms were hung on hooks on a board. The hostel rooms were popular, it was party night after all, and only one key remained on its hook for an attic room on the top floor. Sam led Claire to a chair.

"Wait here for a moment. I'll go up and check no one is using the room. I'll only be gone a few minutes."

There was no power for the lift, so Sam had to climb the long staircase to the attic. Using the flame of his lighter for guidance, he found the door, its number hanging upside down on a solitary screw. The key turned a dry stiff lock. In a glass jar on a bare dresser he discovered a candle stub and lit it. The room was empty and contained only a narrow single bed. In a tall cupboard, he found clean bed linen and blankets and threw them onto the mattress, too tired to make the bed properly. At least there was a spare pillow; without a second bed, he would have to make do with the floor.

When he returned to the ground floor, Claire had fallen asleep in the chair where Sam had left her. For a moment he contemplated waking her, but even if he did, her knee, its white bandage showing a stain from seeping blood, would make it difficult for her to manage the long climb upstairs. There was nothing else for it; at least she was light. Sliding his left arm under her knees, he hooked his right arm around her back and gently lifted. Her face was only inches from his. Asleep, lost from the cares of the world, Claire's face looked at peace, a thin sleepy smile on her lips. Despite the scar and the odd blemish, with strands of loose golden hair plaited in a tangled thread across her cheek, the effect left him transfixed, oblivious to the seemingly endless rise of the stairs.

He pushed the slightly open door with his foot. Inside the room he kicked the door shut and gently laid Claire on the bed. In the dim glow of the candle he removed her shoes, tempted by the thought of undressing her. Maybe she wouldn't mind but he felt slightly embarrassed at the thought of seeing Claire with no clothes so instead he laid thin blankets over her sleeping form, flattening the creases in her dress. He kept one blanket and a pillow for himself and turned to blow out the candle.

At some point in what remained of the night, a hand reached out and grasped his arm.

"Don't be silly."

Words, intoxicated by sleep, floated through the darkness.

When Sam finally woke to the morning light, he found himself in the bed; slightly cramped and still fully clothed, but with Claire curled up asleep on his chest.

## TWENTY-NINE

Sam guided Claire to the bathroom door and went to find breakfast for them both. They had woken, still clothed, entwined together in the small cramped bed. Her hair, now a pale red in the morning light, had lain like cobwebs across his face, her shoulder tucked beneath his arm where she had squirmed into his body in her sleep. Neither spoke, each sensing the presence of the other, Sam could feel her breath against his neck and smelt that delicious body perfume a woman brings to a man's bed. Tiredness had spared the obvious temptation and Sam tried hard to convince himself that he'd had no thoughts of stepping over that line, but he doubted that anyone seeing them leaving the bedroom together would have believed that.

Some while later, he returned to the attic room with mugs of tea and fresh pastries that someone had thoughtfully left on a tray in the hostel lobby. Even on the morning after the party, Newport's bakery had been busy from first light. Hungrily, they ate and drank in companionable silence, as though it was an everyday event.

"We need to get to the quayside. Napier will sail with the morning tide," Sam said while re-dressing Claire's injured knee. When she didn't respond, he glanced up. She had her eyes closed, a smile on her lips.

"What?" he asked, frowning.

"Nothing."

The word, shaped like a sigh of contentment, left him mystified.

Despite the previous late night at the party, the quayside was a hive of activity as *The Shepherd* made final preparations to sail. At first, Napier was nowhere to be seen, but a helium balloon tethered to the stern was in the progress of being wound down from high above. Some minutes later Napier appeared at Sam's side.

"I've just been talking to Ross Clark, skipper of *The Aotearoa*," he said, giving Sam a very deliberate look. "He can be here in five days sailing time if you need him in an emergency. I've given John Evans the means to contact him. For the avoidance of doubt, your call sign is 'White Cloud'. He'll only respond if you signal with that, so don't forget to use it or you'll be talking to yourself; we don't want *The Aotearoa* wandering into any unexpected traps," he said with a speculative glance to the north.

Someone called his name and Napier made a brief wave to the yacht; time was pressing. At the end of the quay a small group of young women looked on as the yacht prepared to depart, wiping red eyes with handkerchiefs. Sam looked puzzled. "I thought you were taking extra crew with you?"

Napier laughed and shook his head. "So the boys would hope, but I need a crew of men for the task; it's not a game out there in the ocean. And you breed pretty girls on this island of yours." Napier paused and couldn't resist a mischievous glance at Claire, who was standing beside Sam. "I need to run a tight ship and there's no place for mooning love-struck Romeos. Besides, you know what they say about absence."

He stopped to help haul ashore a fuel line that had been topping up the yacht's tanks. Napier bit the side of his mouth, a sign he was fretting about something.

"We'll be back in about four weeks; I'll look forward to hearing the results of your referendum then," he said in a voice loud enough to be heard by everyone gathered around them. He bent his head between Sam and Claire. "Do your best to get the right outcome. But if the worst were to happen," he casually pushed a tightly folded square of paper into Sam's pocket, "that's how to connect to the fuel rig at Gibraltar. I'll just hope you won't need it."

Without another word, Napier kissed Claire on the cheek, gave Sam a breath-squeezing hug, and was gone. The engines of *The Shepherd* rumbled into life and their flag, with its black ground and silver fern, stretched taut in the breeze at the stern. Slowly, the yacht cast off from the quayside, turning towards mid-channel with the tide. Napier waved once from the stern wheel platform and after a few minutes all they could see were her mast tops as *The Shepherd* slid downriver with the ebbing tide.

It was Claire who spoke first. "I think he's worried about us," she said wistfully.

Sam looked around, a vacant feeling inside him.

"He's not the only one."

"Do you think we'll see them again?" Claire asked.

Sam was thoughtful for a moment. "I hope so. I really do hope so."

In silence, they waited until the last sight of the mast tops had disappeared. Without looking at Claire, he reached for her hand, not particularly caring if anyone saw them.

"It's time we made a move," he said, lightening his tone. "We've got our own boat to catch."

Sam left Claire at Karen's surgery for the final briefing for nursing staff prior to leaving for Weymouth. He had received a note from Linda, reminding him that Melissa's funeral had been arranged for that morning. After Napier had left, cloud banks rolled in and turned the weather grey and wet. Not ideal for a funeral, not that the dead would care very much, he mused.

The island had several clergy and they had agreed to a general unified service for most weddings, baptisms and funerals. Titus Toms, florid faced and hard drinking, was chosen to oversee Melissa's internment. Despite his reputation, Toms was a surprisingly compassionate man; when it came to funerals, he had plenty of practice. A fresh grave had been dug in a corner of the Newport churchyard. Toms had arranged for turf to cover the mound of newly dug soil, and a basic wooden cross had been erected with the name 'Melissa' already etched on it.

There were few mourners; Albert Jamieson, Linda, John, Ruth and Sam. Doctor Morgan arrived last, just as the graveside service began. The internment lasted a mere ten minutes, but Toms made an effort to mark the poor girl's passing, referring to her as 'our sister Melissa, lost in tragic circumstances, but loved nonetheless.' As the coffin was prepared to be lowered into the ground, Sam wondered for whose benefit the words were for; Melissa couldn't hear them. His mind wondered to the scene of her death and the presence of the flowers. Would the person responsible make an appearance at the funeral? No one gathered around the grave seemed to be remotely possible candidates. Were the flowers an act of grief, or simply respect for a girl who had died alone simply because of what she knew?

"Ashes to ashes, dust to dust," Toms intoned, as the ropes slowly lowered the coffin.

Beyond those gathered around the grave, in the porch entrance to the church, a shadow moved amongst shadows, indistinct, but someone there nonetheless. Sam withdrew, moving in a circle around existing gravestones, keen to get to the church before the 'someone' vanished. The grass to the churchyard was long and uncut and he stumbled on a fallen gravestone. By the time he picked himself up, whoever he had seen had gone; the church porch was empty. He checked inside the church; nothing but shadows thrown by guttering candles. He slumped into a pew, rubbing a grazed shin from his fall. Had he imagined things? Simply trying to fit evidence to suit his conviction that Melissa had been murdered? There seemed to be no end to the riddle. As Sam left the church, he hesitated in the porch. There were no flowers but a fragrance lingered, a fragrance he had smelt before in the clearing where he had found Melissa. Freesias, definitely, but there the flowers had been placed as a token. No, that wasn't the connection. He had encountered the fragrance again recently, here in Newport. Freesias were out of season, unless grown especially, that much he knew, so could it be a woman's perfume, extracted from the flowers. He knew many women made their own perfume using flower extracts, and roses were a particular favourite. This wasn't roses, but he couldn't remember where he had come across the smell of freesias in recent days.

With a wave, their lift dropped Sam and Claire at the old bus shelter. There were no pool cars available, but luckily they had found a neighbouring family returning home after the party who could offer them a lift. Dropped at the shelter, they chose the route across the meadows and woods they had used a few days before as a short-cut to the farm. After the gloom of the morning, the clouds had broken and the afternoon turned bright and dry, with a warming breeze. Sam knew that Claire had enjoyed the path the first time he had shown her the way. However, this time he had an ulterior motive; he intended to persuade her to back out of the trip to Weymouth. He took Claire's hand to guide her.
"A few more times and you'll know the path with your eyes closed," he said in jest.
Claire stopped and withdrew her hand. "Get behind me."
"Pardon?"
"Do as you're told and get behind me." She waved her guide cane firmly in his direction. "Don't forget what I was like the first time you met me. Another performance could easily be

arranged," she said in a tone of mock anger, a barely concealed smile on her face.

With Sam behind her, she took his hand in her left, guide cane in her right.

"Now, I'll lead and you follow. Okay?"

"Whatever madam commands," he mocked, playfully feigning submission, curious to see how Claire would manage; she had only walked this way once before. He imagined the scene from a childhood cartoon, depicting the march of elephants in a line, tail to trunk, and laughed out loud at the thought of how they must appear; a blind girl leading a sighted man.

The path crossing the meadows was clear, with bare earth bounded by stands of tall grass struggling to regenerate after the storm. Open fields would be one thing, Sam thought the woods would pose a far greater challenge. For a while he tried closing his eyes too, walking into a black void, experiencing the world from Claire's perspective of eternal darkness. They must have made a curious sight if you thought about it, the very embodiment of the blind leading the blind. Unnerved, Sam sprung his eyes open, aware it was something Claire could never do, to find they had reached the beginning of the path through the woods. She paused, hesitating, realising the way forward had changed. Sam resisted the instinct to intervene, waiting to see how she would resolve the change in terrain. Her cane searched tentatively, measuring the way forward, reasoning that footfall must have worn a depression into the path. Finally satisfied, Claire nodded to herself, moving off with a tug of his hand. Halfway through the woods, the path split. Claire raised her head, sensing the air like a spaniel, waiting for some mental compass to resolve her dilemma. Purposefully, she chose the right fork. It was the wrong way.

"Could we stop for a moment, I've a lace that's come undone." Sam resisted telling Claire that she had made a mistake; he had an alternative agenda and pretended to tie his lace.

"Actually, there's something I want to ask you."

He had seen a fallen tree close to the path. Side by side they sat on its moss covered trunk. Taking a deep breath, he said, "I need you to do something for me."

"If I can." Claire had a curious smile.

"You've injured your knee and I think that's enough of a reason for you to withdraw from the trip to Weymouth."

Her smile faded. "But that wouldn't be true and everyone would know that."

"I don't think Weymouth is a place for someone who can't see," he said bluntly.

Claire nodded. "So those with disability should never put themselves at risk? More to the point, it's fine for those with sight to put their lives on the line, but not those of us who are blind." The blunt directness of her words made him wince. It wasn't what Sam had meant.

"Without vision, the place could be a death trap. Remember Dartmouth?"

"Indeed I do," Claire sounded a cross note. "I remember my sighted partner happily leading me, oblivious to the two men just around the corner, who, I would point out, I could clearly hear talking."

"Well, yes, that's true, but it's not as simple as that."

"How is it more complicated? Those of us without our sight can hear, smell, sense things that those with sight don't. I would point out that you would have led us into the arms of those two men if I hadn't stopped you." She turned towards Sam, chin raised in that defiant gesture he had seen before. "Bullets kill; eyes don't provide immunity to that fact."

Sam sighed with exasperation; he was losing his argument fast.

"Look, put bluntly, I don't want you to come. No other blind person has volunteered; why should you be the first to experiment with something so potentially dangerous?"

Claire reached for his hand and turned her head in Sam's direction.

"I know you only want to protect me. But you can't always do that, not in this instance. If I want to be seen as equal in this community, I have to do this, whatever the risks it may involve." She smiled patiently. "And I'll have a big advantage over the rest of you; I can't see what there is too be scared of."

Sam had to admit he was beaten. When they started walking again, he took the lead. He didn't mention Claire's mistaken path; it would serve no purpose. And so Claire would go to Weymouth. Had he allowed what were only premonitions to rule his head? They had learned lessons from Dartmouth and there was every reason to believe this would be a simple humanitarian rescue mission. But then again, that's what they had thought the last time.

With unspoken agreement, they parted company just beyond the woods, taking separate paths to the farmhouse and barns. Claire was still wearing the dress for the party. As she walked away he noticed how well the dress outlined her profile; totally out of context in a hay meadow, where barefoot, her shoes in her spare hand, she looked for the world like some guilty girl stealing home after a late night party. In part, the image was correct, with the exception that she had been deliberately abandoned and wasn't stealing home in guilt. Merely a blind girl left to find her way alone.

Sam found the farmhouse empty. After the late night party, the morning tasks had started later. He showered and packed his things for Weymouth, and moving between rooms, his premonitions continued to haunt him. Would this be the last time he would see this place and the security and comfort it had given him for the past five years? As he strapped the Sten gun to his rucksack he felt his spine give an involuntary shiver. Looking up, he stared at his reflection in the mirror. He looked scared, he decided; no matter how he tried to avoid this mission fate had decreed otherwise and led him back to it. He gave himself a grim smile; grey now flecked his beard and the crows-feet around his eyes seemed more pronounced. He straightened his back; his shoulders had become more rounded, weighed down by the problems they faced. He thought briefly of Albert Jamieson who was probably only in his early fifties, sometimes looking twenty years older, paying the price of leadership ten times over.

'Stop moaning, Morten,' he muttered to himself. He thought of the wild boy he had met so briefly, living like an animal in Dartmouth, and David Longmarsh just across the Solent, in fear amongst the men of violence. He gave his image a mocking glance and turned away saying, 'Never mind, things could be worse.'

As he turned away from the mirror, Sam thought he heard the voice of his reflection whisper in his ear, 'Things most probably will. Very soon.'

Later that afternoon Sam and Claire left the farm together. Only Lorna had returned in time to see them off, full of apologies for abandoning Claire the previous evening. As usual, her open-hearted sincerity made it easy to forgive her. She hadn't been responsible for what had happened and seemed more embarrassed that no one else was there to say goodbye to them. The excuse that everyone was too busy had a hollow ring to it.

*Lupin* was scheduled to sail on the evening tide with the aim that they would enter Weymouth harbour at first light the next morning. They were collected from the farm by an ageing van, already almost full with fellow crew members. Sam had suggested this as part of a new initiative to create team spirit amongst them all from the very outset. They arrived in time to help loading the final stores and equipment. On the outside, *Lupin* looked much changed from the trawler in which they had travelled to Dartmouth. Now, she was adorned with rust-stained steel plating, welded to her wheelhouse and hull flanks to offer better protection. Helen had wanted to re-paint her ship in battleship grey, but a lack of time and manpower had made that impossible. Meanwhile, Sam quite liked the shabby red-rust exterior, it served to understate *Lupin* and cloak the improvements they had made.

Shortly before casting off, Albert Jamieson arrived and came aboard. He spoke and thanked every crew member personally as a departing gesture. It was a small token, but its significance outweighed a lack of fanfare, giving everyone on board a spring in their step that Sam hoped would last until they returned. Albert left Sam to last, regarding him with a level gaze; his mouth smiled but his eyes were troubled.

"God speed Sam. Bring everyone home safely." He produced an envelope from his pocket with Sam's name written by hand on the front. "This may help you when you get to Weymouth; just in case."

The two men shook hands; Albert's grip seemed firmer than before. His grip continued, even as the notes of the departure siren were dying away. The older man seemed reluctant to let go.

At slow ahead *Lupin* moved with the tide downriver. It was a very different send off from the Dartmouth trip. This time only a few family members were at the quayside, waving, silent and thoughtful. Sam looked at the envelope that Albert had given him, puzzled that he had written his name by hand instead of the usual procedure of having forum business typed. The letter could wait until Weymouth, he decided. Whatever it contained, he would open it when they arrived.

# THIRTY

On board *Lupin,* Sam started to feel a release from the problems that crowded upon him on the island. Once clear of the Medina river, Helen swung westwards into the Solent, running at full speed along the north coastline of the island towards Hurst Castle and the open seas beyond. There was barely any swell, the evening was calm and the sky now a riot of colour from the setting sun. For once, Sam could actually look forward to the coming hours, unlike his previous nauseating journey to Dartmouth. They all ate together in the canteen, which would then become a dormitory and casualty station when they had moored in Weymouth the following day. Over dinner, Sam moved from table to table, chatting and trying to remember names of the newcomers to their team. He saw Claire at a table with Karen and two other nursing auxiliaries, all wearing purple lanyards for identification. He was conscious of watching eyes, so he greeted her with no more than a passing hand on the shoulder, focusing his attention on conversation to the group as a whole.

Once clear of the narrows at Hurst Point, *Lupin* turned to the open sea and Sam felt the engine vibrations slow to a gentle throb. Helen wouldn't try to enter Weymouth until daylight, so there was no need to hurry once they were clear of the dangers that lurked in the Solent. On deck, the watch circled *Lupin* as before, each squad member enjoying the last of the light before darkness settled upon them. Sam climbed to the upper deck behind the wheelhouse, secretly hoping Claire might join him before the ship closed up for the night. He circled the upper deck, a half-bowl of tobacco glowing in his pipe, and saw a small figure at the rail, watching the efflorescent wake churning behind them. Expectantly, he moved towards the figure, but it was Ruth who turned to greet him. He nodded in surprise but then turned to watch the last of the light fade into indigo.

"I find it clears the mind, don't you?" he said.

She turned towards him, a pensive frown lining her forehead. "You've heard the news, I expect."

"News? Well, nothing in particular." Uneasy, he waited for her to tell him.

Ruth sighed. "Last night after the party, Teri and Ryan were caught together; in the act so to speak. There can be no doubt about their relationship."

Sam hesitated as the implications of Ruth's words sank in. "I thought you said she had seen sense; that they had stopped that part of their relationship."

"That's what she told me," she said with exasperation. "She actually promised me, as a condition for our remaining silent about the truth." Ruth paused. "And there's more; Teri is pregnant."

Sam groaned. "I guess there's no chance that someone else is the father?"

"Not a snowball in hell."

"Who knows?"

"By now, the entire island. Two of the older forum members were on watch last night. They heard something they thought was suspicious, went to investigate and, as I said, caught them in the act. Before anyone could intervene, they had reported them. Teri is three-months pregnant and is determined to brazen it out. She's openly admitted that Ryan is the father."

Sam looked aghast, shocked that things could fly out of control so quickly. "Will she incriminate you in this?"

With a tight smile, Ruth said, "That's a certainty. She'll fight like a tigress to avoid an abortion and Ryan being sterilized."

Sam gently touched her shoulder. "Remember when you're questioned, you were only carrying out my instructions. I told you to discuss an arrangement with Teri. Knowing what you did, your obligation was to take the matter to a forum member, a task you fulfilled by discussing it with me."

"Won't that cause problems for you?"

"Probably. I'll be censured for bending the rules, an indictment put on record against my name." He let out a long breath. "Rules are rules; we all get into trouble when we break them, no matter how well meaning the intention may have been."

He watched her shoulders slump. They had tried to deal with a difficult problem sympathetically, and would now suffer the consequences.

"Now the chairman will have to deal with this and we'll have to trust in his judgement. Meanwhile, tomorrow is a busy day; put the matter out of your mind and get some rest. Nothing else can be done until we get back to Newport," Sam said with a heavy heart.

The problems he thought they had left behind had just caught up with them.

Sam spent the night on deck, once more beneath the stairway to the wheelhouse. The race of chainlinks as Helen dropped anchor roused him from sleep. He packed his bedroll and joined her, the smell of coffee wafting over him as he opened the door. One of Helen's improvements had been the provision of her own hotplate actually in the wheelhouse. In the gloom of early morning the space was lit by the dim red light of the hotplate. Combined with the smell of coffee, it created a surprisingly homely feeling in *Lupin*'s working heart. Helen poured him a mug.

"Courtesy of our departed friends. They're a bit like missionaries, travelling the world with the gift of coffee. If our plans to grow coffee on the island fail, I'll be off to New Zealand in an instant," she said with a rueful smile.

Sam took the offered mug, warming his hands on the outside. "If that need ever arises, you may need this," he paused to search for his pocketbook and withdrew the slip Napier had given him. "It lists how to access the fuel store at the old naval base in Gibraltar, and any other port on the way, for that matter. Best keep the instructions here; you never know when you might need it," he added with a sanguine tone.

Helen, ever meticulous, reached a manila folder and carefully filed Napier's instructions. They both stared into the darkness, each with their own dreams or fears for the days ahead.

"Weymouth?" Sam gestured towards a deeper black line on the horizon ahead. Not a single light shone out.

Helen nodded. He noticed she still carried her injured arm awkwardly; a legacy from Dartmouth, and silently hoped Weymouth wouldn't be a repeat.

"High tide in four hours. If you can take the watch, I'll grab a few hours' sleep," Helen yawned as she spoke.

Around them *Lupin* moved gently with the swell, the ship slept and the other squad members of the watch changed point every fifteen minutes. They were well prepared this time, but in the darkness the unknown awaited them.

The next morning life on *Lupin* held a distinct déjà vu feeling. Their approach at Dartmouth had served them well and Helen saw no need to change anything this time, moving *Lupin* with meticulous care through the bay. If anything, the wider expanse of water made life easier than the narrow confines of the river, though a small forest of half sunken masts marked a minefield of underwater obstructions. Unattended boats had been torn from their moorings; some had capsized and sunk in the main channel but most were in the eastern arm of the bay where they appeared to have been thrown by some giant's hand, forming a spectral fleet of shattered masts and upturned hulls with only ghosts for crew.

They came to a halt a short distance from the mouth of the River Wey, at the entrance to the harbour and marina. Helen dropped anchor and allowed *Lupin* to swing with the incoming tide until her bow pointed seawards, her entry marked by a ribbon of red marker buoys she had sown in the clear channel as they entered. Her escape route to sea secured, Helen could leave the landward side of things to Sam.

Fat, moisture bloated clouds rolled in from the south-west, driving occasional squalls of horizontal rain before them and casting a sombre mood over the derelict town. Using binoculars from the top deck, Sam and Aiden scoured the surrounding buildings for any sign of life, human or boar. At first glance the town looked in better shape than Dartmouth, with less evidence of fire damage or collapsed buildings. Even cars and lorries, parked around the harbour in ordered ranks, looked as if they were waiting for their owners to return. Only a crust of seagull droppings stood testament to the length of time they had sat disowned.

"It's strange," Aiden said. "I always find a new place spooky. Until I get to know it," he added with morbid humour.

"Hard to believe I used to have summer holidays here with my parents," Sam answered wistfully. "Seeing everything like this makes me think it must be a distant memory from another life."

A rain squall cut them short, obscuring even the short distance between boat and harbour, and forcing both men to retreat inside where Claire and another nursing trainee were serving breakfast.

Sam waited, touched with impatience, for everyone to be served before approaching Claire.

"Tea with one spoonful of honey, please."

Claire nodded and handed him a steaming mug from a tray. "I tried to catch up with you last night, but I found you on deck already talking with another woman," she teased.

"Alas, business," he quipped in response.

"Always so popular."

"Perhaps tonight, between nine and ten?" he asked hopefully.

She smiled. "If I'm free. I'll have to check my diary."

Fleetingly, he touched her hand. "Please do," he whispered, and moved on.

By mid-morning, the winch and raft were connected to the slipway that led to the old ferry terminal and Aiden already had two squads landed ashore. Before leaving to join them, Sam visited John in his radio room.

"Any news from the survivors?" he asked.

"Not since yesterday."

"How far away?"

"Hard to tell exactly, they spent the night in a village north-west of Dorchester. They're on foot, travelling with children and towing carts, sticking to tracks and lanes for safety, but they couldn't have been more than twelve miles away, so their target for arriving today sounds plausible. The signal has been a bit intermittent though," he said in his Welsh lilt.

"Do your best. I'm going ashore but send a message to me if you hear anything."

John nodded in response, donned headphones, and disappeared into his world of dials and frequencies.

Sam re-joined Aiden and his squad, leaving Ruth and her all-female unit to set up their harbourside base and prepare the small tractor and trailer they had brought for the operation. Aiden chose to investigate the immediate area around their harbour base, primarily to check for boar and also for any survivors. Sam joined them, taking up his usual role behind the rear point of their star formation.

Weymouth was eerie in almost the opposite sense to Dartmouth. Absent were the wrecked and derelict buildings; instead the reverse applied, with shops, obviously looted of their stock, closed and shuttered, waiting patiently for their owners who would never return. Even the streets were mainly clear, with vans and cars parked neatly at the kerbside. Only flat perished tyres and a thick layer of dust and grime gave lie to any sense of what had once been a normal world.

Aiden led them along the quayside north of the river toward the town bridge, detaching two men to check the side streets as they passed. All were dressed with full equipment, another lesson learnt from Dartmouth. As they walked, watchful for anywhere that might conceal a boar, Aiden used a loudhailer to call out a message for any survivors. The only answer he received was the screeching call of seagulls, which added to the tension they were starting to feel. As they approached the bridge, Aiden paused, hand raised, and dropped slowly to a crouched position. They all followed suit and he beckoned Sam forward. The star expanded as Sam passed through; nervous fingers primed safety catches on their weapons as eyes searched the buildings around them. He arrived next to Aiden and crouched down beside him.

"What do you make of that?"

Aiden pointed to the right of the road junction ahead where the quayside road met the main road and crossed the bridge. At first Sam couldn't see what he meant, until his eyes found a raised flower bed. Though ravaged by the recent storm the bed was bare of weeds and instead was planted with early season flowers in a layout announcing the previous year, '1963'.

Puzzled, Sam shook his head. "Someone likes flowers?" he ventured.

"Not only that, look another fifty yards to the right, at the road crossing."

He pointed farther along the main road. Sam followed his arm. A pair of yellow globes on striped poles stood guard on an empty black and white pedestrian crossing. Nothing unusual about belisha beacons; except these flashed their warning lights in a synchronized dance.

Aiden glanced at Sam. "Now, in a world without electricity don't you think that's more than a bit weird?"

They remained in position for some time, transfixed by the scene ahead at the junction. Nothing happened or changed, so after a while, Aiden moved the squad, tracking left over the bridge, in the direction the surviving group were likely to arrive, away from the bizarre flashing lights. For a while, Aiden and Sam walked in step.

"How can this be happening?" Aiden posed the question, more to himself than Sam.

"The world has become a strange and unpredictable place," Sam offered, remembering some of the events in Dartmouth for which no logical explanation could be found. "There will be a reason, but we don't have time to find it. If it doesn't threaten us, we move on and get the job done and get out as quickly as possible." Wise words were all well and good, so long as you could keep a curb on your imagination.

Beyond the bridge they followed a road where the marina on their right was filled with smashed and sunken yachts and motorboats. Here, the storm had obviously wreaked its havoc. Aiden halted at the next junction, where the main highway crossed their path heading due north. Aiden had instructions only to protect their landing position and to forgo a search of the town. He decided they had gone far enough and now needed to pull back. Before they left, he hammered a post into the soft verge and fixed a board, signed with a large red arrow pointing towards the old ferry port, hoping it would help any exhausted group of survivors when they finally arrived.

As they turned to retrace their steps, one of the squad called out, pointing towards a terraced row of shops on the other side of the main road. All the properties looked empty with the exception of a pharmacy shop in the centre of the row. Its doors were closed and locked, the shutters raised and the display in the main window as complete and untouched as the moment before catastrophe and collapse had engulfed them. Aiden frowned and glanced in Sam's direction, another question in his eyes.

"How is this possible?"

Leaving the squad to guard the road outside, they prised the shop doors open with a crow bar and went inside the pharmacy. Their footprints, in a crust of five years' dust, marked a path across the floor. It was plainly obvious that the only recent visitors had been mice who had made nests with some of the bandages. Aiden turned through a circle, noting shelves and cabinets stocked with all sorts of products, awaiting a normal busy day of trading. He stopped and stared at Sam.

"And now you're going to tell me there's a perfectly plausible reason for this? When every other shop in town has been looted and stripped to the bones?"

Sam looked as bemused as Aiden. "There will be a reason. Whether it's plausible or not is another matter," he said distractedly. "Either way, we need to take everything we can and get back to the harbour as quickly as possible. Call Ruth on the radio and ask her to send forward the trailer. I'll walk back to meet and guide them here." He took a final look around. "Just one thing, Aiden. Turn off your imagination." He grinned in encouragement, though it was more to hide his own unease.

Walking back alone through deserted streets was never a pleasant experience. Weymouth could have been an exception; the shops were empty but not vandalised, the streets full of leaves and the debris of nature, not burnt out cars and the flotsam of looting, but Sam thought the ordered feel to the place only made the situation more disconcerting.

He met the tractor and trailer crossing the bridge, driven by Gloria, a West Indian member of Ruth's squad. She pulled him aboard with a surprising strong grip that matched her wide beaming smile, and accelerated away in a cloud of blue smoke before he had even managed to sit down. Swinging the wheel enthusiastically towards the main crossroads on the other side of the bridge, Gloria was obviously enjoying the spirit of adventure to the full, only to stop abruptly, spilling Sam into her lap. In another time and place, this would have been funny, spoilt on this occasion by her reason for coming to such an abrupt halt. In front of them, the previously dormant set of traffic lights at the crossroads now flashed red, amber and green.

Gloria stared ahead, wide eyed. "Sam?" she gasped, astonished.

"I know." He drew a deep breath to regain his composure, before muttering, "Someone is playing with us."

Helen moved *Lupin* clear of the harbour area on the evening tide. There had been no sign of the group they had been sent to meet. John offered any number of reasons for their delay, but his words only made Sam increasingly nervous. The story of the lights in a town without people or electricity had spread through the ship like wildfire, embellished by tales of shadowy figures appearing and vanishing at will. It was all innocent fun, so Sam had no problems with morale; it was with practical considerations that they had problems. John had encountered strong interference throughout the day across all radio frequencies, including those he used to keep in contact with their base on the island.

"It must be atmospheric conditions," he said, scratching his ear, distracted by his thoughts. "Otherwise, I'd have to say someone was jamming my signals, and to do that they'd have to know in advance the frequencies I'm using, which isn't possible; unless someone is telling them." He cast a worried glance in Sam's direction.

Dinner in their mess deck was a light-hearted affair, not least because Gloria had discovered a huge stock of cosmetics and perfumes on the shelves of the pharmacy. Such luxuries were now in very short supply on the island and Ruth was under considerable pressure from her female squad members to make a return trip the following day to liberate the rest of the stock. But Sam was worried; Helen had reported an overheating problem with one of *Lupin*'s overworked diesel engines, informing him that in an emergency they wouldn't be able to run at full speed. They felt tense at their evening meeting in the wheelhouse, and the final decision to continue with the operation had to be made by Sam. Even John, normally so passionate in support of the operation, was undecided, and Helen was unhappy to continue with engine problems. Given half a chance Sam would have followed his intuition and aborted their plans, but the image of a group of exhausted survivors watching *Lupin* disappear over the horizon, haunted his imagination. 'Abandoned to their fate,' would be hung like an albatross around his neck.

"Okay. This is how I see it. The problems with the radio signal and *Lupin*'s engine aren't serious enough to abandon our mission, provided things don't get any worse. Odd things are happening ashore I'll grant you, but nothing that threatens the safety of *Lupin* or our crew. We must avoid our imaginations getting carried away," he added, more in self-reproach.

"So," he paused for breath, "I vote we stay, for another twenty-four hours, no more. We'll gather again tomorrow evening and review the situation. Hopefully before then we'll be well on our way home, with an extra twenty mouths to feed and care for. Helen, keep *Lupin* ready to sail at a moment's notice. Aiden, only two squads ashore at any one time." Sam was thoughtful for several seconds. "And in the morning, clear the canteen for casualties, just in case."

With a crew mainly made up from younger members of their community, the light-hearted atmosphere continued long into the evening. When Sam passed through the ship after the meeting had broken up, he found Claire at the centre of a circle of conversation with several younger male squad members who all seemed keen for her attention. He felt a spasm of irritation; the weight of decision he had made sat heavily on his shoulders, and at the very moment he needed to share his burden with Claire, he found her distracted by the attentions of the younger men. Nodding briefly to groups as he passed, he quickly left the canteen, seeking the fresh air and solitude of the upper deck.

The moon had risen, a segment cut away as though from the bite of some malevolent giant. In the moonlight the sea shimmered, mercifully calm, accompanied by the sound of laughter that spiralled up from below. Sam found a life-raft and sat down against it to rest his tired and aching limbs. Staring into the darkness for answers, he found only loneliness. Finally, he realised he was guilty of indulging in self-pity, so decided to try to get some sleep. He positioned his bedroll in his preferred spot behind the wheelhouse steps, and despite everything, he was asleep in minutes.

At some point in the night, a pressure came against his back as someone else squeezed into the narrow space under the stairs. He stirred to find that Claire had arrived to share the space with him. Though neither spoke of the evening, Sam wondered if she understood how he felt. It was not the time for explanations, they just shared being together without words.

When he awoke early the next morning she was still asleep, on her side and curled tightly against his back, the soft shadow of a smile on her lips, as though she found something in her dreams amusing.

# THIRTY-ONE

The following day started with promise. The early threads of daylight veined the morning sky when Helen nosed *Lupin* carefully back to her mooring point, a stone's throw from the entrance to the river and harbour marina. Ashore, deserted buildings were profiled against shades of grey as the sky slowly lightened from the east. No mysterious lights winked to tantalise the imagination, the only sign of life was the flock of hungry gulls wheeling and cawing in their wake. Sam watched as mooring lines were re-connected, and Helen slowly spun *Lupin* around so that her bow pointed towards the open sea. While this was happening the raft was made ready to winch their first squad the short distance to the shore. By now it was a well-practised routine. As Ruth lowered the last of the equipment to accompany her all-female squad, John appeared beside Sam, his face alive with an excited smile.

"The signal improved overnight; the atmospheric problems seem to have cleared so I've been able to speak to home and, more importantly, the survivors. They're only five or six miles away and though their progress is slow, they should be here early this afternoon, so we should get ready to receive them. I've told Helen we could be on our way home on the evening tide."

Sam nodded in agreement, relieved to know they could soon be on their way back to the island with the possibility of arriving home before midnight. Below, Javed, now a squad leader, joined Ruth on the raft to help with the loading. In a few minutes the winch began to haul in the cables, and the laden raft grounded onto the concrete access ramp where the tractor and trailer had been stored overnight.

The sun rose above the dark line of the horizon and they swiftly unloaded the raft while Javed prepared to return to *Lupin* for more equipment. Sam planned to go ashore on the next raft and so he returned quickly to his locker to collect his things. While donning his jacket, the crisp rustle of paper reminded him of the letter Albert Jamieson had slid into his pocket at their moment of departure. His name was written on the front in Albert's distinctive copperplate style. Sam frowned as he slit it open. Even a handwritten note, no matter how brief, theoretically contravened the rules. A single piece of white notepaper was inside and contained a single paragraph.

*If you run into anyone from across the Solent again, irrespective of the circumstances, use your best efforts to open up a dialogue. Don't get caught up on lengthy details but arrange for me to meet them, under a flag of truce if necessary. I would suggest Hurst Castle as a neutral spot. It serves no purpose to just carry on attacking each other; only the boar benefit in the end. I request you keep this to yourself until arrangements are finalised.*

*Albert Jamieson*

Sam stared at the note, surprised by several things but perhaps most of all that Albert had written privately to him. Did he suspect the spy in their midst was a forum member or was he anxious to avoid Rigby stepping in to prevent any form of negotiation before they had even begun?

When Sam returned to the deck, he found that Javed had already re-loaded the raft and embarked on another trip ashore, leaving Sam behind. Boxes were piled high on the raft including some marked with a red cross, as precious medical supplies were ferried ashore to create a dressing station. He had expected another squad to be sent, but it looked as though two trainee nurses were on the raft instead. The women scrambled ashore at the landing ramp, one guiding the hand of the other. It was Claire.

Sam experienced a sudden spike of anxiety. There were eight people now on the shore and only Ruth had any real experience in an emergency. As he watched them unload the raft, the radio crackled into life. John had refurbished more mobile sets and batteries, so at least over short distances they could communicate. Javed's voice called from the earpiece.

"The pulley block this end has sheared. Can someone bring over a spare? We can't send the raft back until we've replaced it."

Sam set off hastily in search of spares. *Lupin's* engineers were already occupied with the overheating engine and had no time to hunt for a spare pulley block, and Aiden, in company with another squad, had gun parts laid out and stripped down for cleaning. Frustrated, Sam could only bide his time, searching storerooms and cupboards for what he needed.

A message arrived from Javed, requesting that his squad be sent over in the inflatable as soon as possible; he didn't give a reason.

At the same moment, Sam tried to contact Ruth and failed. He thought the most likely reason being a faulty battery in her radio. It was the last straw. Moving at a run, he found John and took another radio and a newly charged battery for Ruth.

"Tell Aiden I can't find a replacement pulley set. He needs to mobilise Javed's squad immediately and get them across in the large rib; there's no raft until we replace the broken pulley. I'm going ashore now in the smaller inflatable before things come totally off the rails." Sam paused to throw the radio into his rucksack and grabbed a spare magazine for his Sten gun.

"There's another problem, Sam," replied John. The larger rib got punctured yesterday and I'm not totally sure it's been repaired."

Sam looked at John with utter disbelief; unfairly, his Welsh accent suddenly irritated him. "Then get it fixed," he shouted. "Or use a life-raft or rowing boat if you have to, but get another squad ashore immediately before we have a disaster on our hands." Sam knew he was behaving unfairly but the ordered start to the day was rapidly sliding away from them unless someone quickly got a grip of things.

The outboard on the inflatable started reluctantly and Sam accelerated to full speed too hastily, almost tipping over in the process. He tried to think calmly, he would only make matters worse by charging around like a bull in a china shop. The truth was that the strange business with the lights the previous day had disturbed him more than he was prepared to admit. And he had eight people stranded ashore, and one of them was Claire. He aimed the inflatable to the seaward side of the pier, not trusting himself with the swirling currents in the river mouth, and chose a rusting ladder to climb instead. He hitched the inflatable to a ladder rung and found Javed and Gloria waiting for him at the top of the ladder.

"Where's Ruth?" Sam asked tersely.

"She's taken three of her squad and has gone forward to check the main road on the other side of the river. It was part of her plan for today, though I think her girls were keen to indulge in a bit of liberation from that pharmacy you found yesterday," replied Javed. "They left before we had a problem with the pulley system," he added as an afterthought, noticing the angry expression forming on Sam's face.

Sam bit back his words. There was no point in losing his temper but more importantly, there was still no sign of the back-up squad preparing to leave *Lupin.*

"Get back to the ship now and get your squad here as soon as possible; even if they have to swim across," Sam barked at Javed, as though the whole mess was his fault. "I'll take over here until you get back." He turned without waiting for a reply, shouting, "Gloria, come with me," before adding, "and where the hell are your guns; do you remotely suppose they're going to fire themselves if we have a problem?" Sam stormed off, leaving Gloria trailing in his wake. With Javed returning to *Lupin* and Ruth absent, it left only the two of them to protect their shore base, and Gloria wasn't even carrying her gun.

Sam's mood hadn't improved by the time he caught up with Karen and Claire. Except it wasn't Karen but Jenny, a girl of the same colouring and stature and easily mistaken from a distance.

"Make way for Mr Grumpy," Gloria called ahead breezily, warning them both of his mood.

"Where's Karen?" Sam snapped, ignoring Gloria.

Without waiting for an answer he turned to bite back at Gloria, only to find her hoisting a Bren gun over her shoulder, its size out of proportion to her shortness. What Gloria lacked in height she made up for in width and someone must have decided it made her ideal for the larger weapon. Her disarming smile, enhanced by a set of brilliant white teeth in contrast to her chocolate skin, stretched the entire width of her face when she saw Sam's incredulous expression.

"I've got my marksman's badge too," she said, reading his thoughts. "Just don't see no point in humping around a big heavy gun like this everywhere I go."

Reprimanded, Sam turned back to Claire and Jenny. He felt the pressure of Claire's hand on his arm before he could open his mouth to speak. The usual sensation between them returned, finally diffusing his anger and restoring calm. It had been a while since they had been able to make physical contact and he suddenly realised how much he had missed her.

"One of the new men slipped on the gangway stair as we were preparing to leave; Karen had to stay behind as she thought he had broken his wrist," Claire said with a smile to match Gloria's, reminding Sam not to jump to hasty conclusions. He nodded as the tension slipped away, though the feeling that things were coming unravelled still lingered.

"Show me how you've set things up here," he asked, keen to move them from the exposed position on the quayside to the shelter amongst the old warehouse buildings.

There were just the four of them; blind Claire, and Jenny, who seemed a pleasant but quiet girl, somewhat ill-suited to unexpected surprises, which left only Sam and Gloria until Ruth or Javed returned with their squads. Without any clear reason, the numbers made him feel increasing uncomfortable.

Sam turned abruptly to Gloria. "Find yourself a wall and keep an eye on the old fort across the river," he grumbled.

She gave him a questioning look but he shrugged in reply. Perhaps the fort's dark brooding bulk intimidated him, but it had occurred to him that no one had crossed the river to check out the old building. Resigned to his mood, Gloria nodded and wandered off to find somewhere suitable to conceal her considerable presence.

Before leaving, Ruth and her squad had erected an old bell tent just back from the quay, in the shadow of an old brick warehouse building. From here they had a clear view of the access road rising towards the bridge and on towards the centre of town. *Lupin* was nearby, moored a short distance beyond in the estuary. From where they stood, they were overlooked from the top of the old fort, even though a crumbling stone wall ran along the quayside. Sam shook his head; he was becoming fixated on detail, equal in measure to his worries from the delayed return of Ruth, Javed and their squads; he wouldn't rest easy until they were back.

Half an hour later there was still no sign of them. The bridge road was silent and although there was activity on *Lupin*, the inflatable was yet to appear in the sea. Sam was trying to distract himself with Claire and Jenny. Lessons had been learnt from Dartmouth, and the tent, with its front segment propped open, had a trestle table set out with medical supplies and food and drink. The number of survivors they anticipated was twice the size of the Dartmouth group and they had been told there were children and pregnant women. They had set up several camp beds, erected drip stands in readiness and several canvas camp sinks just inside the front opening.

"You've done well." Sam tried not to sound patronising; he was genuinely impressed.

"It's what nurses do," Jenny said, pleased with his compliment. "Claire and I set things up; Karen's the triage expert." Sam didn't miss her anxious glance towards *Lupin*.

Gloria also reassured him. She had positioned her gun in a gap in the quayside wall, a spare magazine at its side, and was now smoking behind a higher section of wall from which she could still see the top of the old fort across the river. There was no doubt that Ruth had trained her well; Sam could only hope that training wouldn't be needed.

Perhaps to distract him, Claire casually asked Sam to help her lift some heavy boxes containing medical equipment, all still carefully sealed in cellophane. There was little to do, but at least it gave them the chance to be together for a few minutes.

"Your voice sounds tight, are you worried?" Claire asked him as together they lifted a box containing large bottles of antiseptic onto a table.

Sam laughed. "No hiding anything from you is there? The truth is, we're not trained soldiers and we're not particularly suited for this sort of operation either. These places are dangerous and I don't like plans that change without a plan; especially when you're involved."

"So it's okay to put girls like Jenny and Gloria in harm's way, but not me?"

"I'd rather no one was in danger, but I'm just worried I might not be able to protect you if something goes wrong."

"Do I need protecting?" she queried.

"Claire," he grumbled. "This is no time for fencing over equality. If things go badly, people could end up getting seriously hurt." His voice showed the pain he felt and his words were clumsy. "I couldn't bear to lose you," he suddenly blurted out. "I'm sorry, it's just the way it is. If anything happens, well, just promise you'll stick close to me."

She frowned. "What could go wrong?"

Sam had to leave her question unanswered as they were cut short by Jenny approaching with mugs of tea. He felt frustrated; he had only been able to say half of what he wanted and any chance to talk further had ended. He moved away but was relieved when Claire caught his arm and squeezed it for reassurance.

Gloria was doing an excellent job of looking bored. Sam handed her a mug of tea into which she tipped three spoonfuls of honey.

"Not much happening. Just a plain ugly old building with hosts of squabbling seagulls."

"That's the way I prefer things. Any sign of Ruth and the others yet?"

Gloria shook her head. "Guess they've been busy clearing out that shop we found yesterday; it's got the things we girls are in short supply of on the island."

Sam nodded, reminded that Ruth had probably agreed to go back to the shop in the interests of morale for her squad and the women back home. Still, she could have chosen a better moment. With no sign of Javed either, Sam radioed John.

"Got the rib fixed. Now we can't get the damn outboard started," John grumbled. "Dirt in the fuel system, I'm hearing. Shouldn't be too long now though."

"Any news from the survivors?"

"Nope. But I guess they're busy trying to get here." Then John added with a note of unease, "There's one other thing though."

"Go on."

"Well, it's the radio transmissions from across the Solent. They've gone quiet."

"So?"

"Well," he said in a measured tone. "Last time they did that so abruptly was just before they attacked us in Dartmouth."

It was Sam's turn to be quiet, with a growing hollow feeling in the pit of his stomach.

"Just get Javed and the others here as soon as possible. Make them row across if they have to." He cut the link before John could reply.

Gloria glanced at him, one eyebrow raised in question.

"Have you got a steel helmet?" he asked her gruffly.

Gloria nodded.

"Wear it then," he barked, and walked away.

Alone, Sam drank his cold tea, trying to fill the hard void in the pit of his stomach. Across the bay, a stiff breeze whipped short wavelets into a sharp chop with white foamy crests, the cloud breaking and clearing from the north-east showing large gaps of blue sky. Opposite, the sun lit the face of the old fort, softening some of its ominous appearance. Beside *Lupin* the large inflatable had been lowered into the water, wreathed in clouds of grey smoke as they tried to start the obstinate outboard motor.

Gloria now sat with her back against the low wall, ignoring Sam, slowly and methodically loading another magazine with polished brass rounds, plainly considering the entire process to be a complete waste of time. Jenny and Claire, with their immediate work completed, had found a couple of discarded plastic chairs and now sat together in quiet conversation. And so they all waited. Even the sun came out to make an appearance and join them. Sam bit on the unlit stem of his pipe to ease his anxiety, and wondered, more in hope than expectation, if Ruth might have found a tobacconist on her scavenging foray. If she had, it would ease some of his annoyance about her absence. With the warming of the sun, time seemed to tick by at a lethargic pace. He checked his watch; it was only five minutes later than his previous check and still only mid-morning. On the positive side, if the survivors arrived on schedule they could all be safely back on *Lupin* in a few hours.

Abruptly, Claire stood from her chair, brushing her hair away from her ears, her head cocked to one side.

"I can hear an engine," she said frowning, concentrating to locate the direction it was coming from. All Sam could hear was the rhythmic hush of the sea, but went to join her, as if it would make a difference.

"Where?"

"Over there." She pointed across the river, beyond the bridge.

Almost simultaneously, to their seaward side, an engine barked and coughed into life, chased immediately by the sound of cheering. Javed and his team had finally started the obstinate outboard. The tension that hung over them began to ease. Hopefully, in just a few minutes, their long tense wait would be over.

Gloria yawned and walked over to join them, releasing the chin strap from her steel helmet with a gesture of contempt. She looked at Sam and rolled her eyes.

"Drama over," she said, her tone implying he had over-reacted.

At the same moment, Ruth appeared, driving the tractor and towing a trailer piled high with boxes under a cargo net. Two girls from her squad sat on top, waving enthusiastically, the third stood on the back of the tractor behind Ruth. They were in high spirits, which underscored Gloria's sceptical opinions. With a roar of acceleration the inflatable left the side of *Lupin* at the same moment the girls on the tractor crossed the bridge. With perfect timing both squads would arrive together, confirming in Gloria's mind that Sam had been behaving in a way that warranted an apology.

Suddenly Claire flinched, turning her head towards the river beside them, her eyes blinking rapidly, as she tried to identify something new, out of place, floating at the edge of the range of her hearing. Shadowing her gesture, Gloria swung slowly around, staring across towards the old fort. Opposite, a huge flock of gulls rose as one, screaming into the air. From this new direction intruded a sound they knew only too well, slowly increasing in volume; the raucous chainsaw rip of approaching motorbikes.

Sam hesitated, confused, uncertain. He frowned. Gloria opened her mouth to speak, "What the ..."

And in the next second, all hell broke loose.

# THIRTY-TWO

It is a basic law of physics that light travels many times faster than sound. Looking up the road towards the bridge, a surreal scene seemed to evolve in slow motion as the tractor and trailer carrying Ruth and her girls disappeared in a cloud of dust and splintered masonry. Fractions of a second suddenly extended to minutes. Sam turned his head towards *Lupin* in time to see the inflatable disappear in a fountain of a hundred small geysers, as if caught in a hail shower of huge stones. Hypnotised by the surreal images, his eye caught sight of Gloria, seemingly moving in slow motion, eyes white and huge in her brown face, head bent forward, arms outstretched like the embracing horns of a charging bull. Headlong, airborne, almost frozen in time, her body collided with Sam and Claire, lifting them from their feet, knocking them to the ground like bowled skittles, as everything around them flew apart. Then sound arrived; the song of a hundred jack-hammers and the unmistakeable hard metallic rattle of machine guns, followed by the impact of bullets on stone and concrete. Shattered masonry filled the air around them, accompanied by the zip-buzz of ricocheting bullets. One word screamed in Sam's mind. Ambush.

It lasted for eternity; in real time, mere seconds. Gloria moved first, rolling off them and crawling towards Jenny who was laying a few feet away, her right arm bent unnaturally behind her back. Open-mouthed, Claire lay beside Sam, blood already staining her golden hair.

"Are you alright?" he managed to gasp, tasting blood and dust in his mouth.

"Only bruises and cuts, I think. What happened?" she asked in a frightened voice. "Where are the others?"

Sam moved, wincing from pain in his ribs. "Go to Jenny. She's a few feet in front of you," he instructed. "Gloria's already with her. Keep close to the ground and help drag her back behind the wall to your right. Don't stand or even try to kneel up. I'll check on everyone else."

Sliding painfully on his stomach, he dragged himself to the low wall that ran along the riverside. From the direction of the bridge there only came silence. A line of empty steel drums lay at the roadside a short distance away and Sam crawled to their protection before daring to raise himself for a better look. He could see that the tractor and trailer now lay on their sides, skewed at an angle against the side of the road. Scattered around, like dolls cast aside by an impatient child, lay bodies. He knelt, transfixed. No one moved.

"Oh no, please, no."

The urge to help was irresistible, but beyond the steel drums the wall quickly tapered out, leaving a wide gap of open ground to be covered before he could get to them. Sam slumped down as the first waves of overwhelming shock and grief swept over him.

"Oh what have I done," he cried out as the realisation that they had walked into a trap suddenly burst upon him.

Painfully, he crawled back and leaned against the wall just as the air was again filled with the ear-splitting rattle of sustained gunfire. Nothing seemed to come their way so Sam assumed it was aimed at *Lupin*. Apprehensive, he strained his ears for the sound of someone returning fire. Nothing. What the hell was Aiden playing at? He could surely see what had happened to them; they needed *Lupin* to react to protect them in the same way as she had in Dartmouth. But this wasn't Dartmouth. There, they had been lucky and mercifully escaped without loss. He already knew this was going to be very different. He tried to slow his breathing. He needed to think, but the feeling of panic was overwhelming, freezing his mind. His first priority must be to protect the small group around him. The rescue of Ruth and the girls would be next, but to achieve that he urgently needed Javed and his squad and support from Aiden on *Lupin*. Whoever had ambushed them was shooting from the old fort. If he could get Javed and his squad in position, they could provide cover fire while he and Gloria tried to get up the road to Ruth and the girls.

"So where the hell are you, Javed?" he burst out angrily.

Forcing back panic he began to crawl back to Gloria and Claire. With Gloria's help, Claire had moved Jenny behind a high concrete wall. A blood stained dressing was already taped around Jenny's forehead and her arm was in a sling. She looked pale and groggy.

"Jenny fell awkwardly and dislocated her shoulder. Gloria put it back in," explained Claire with a wince as she cleaned several nasty cuts on her hands. "The head wound is deep, it needs stitching, but we'll have to deal with it later." She paused, words drowned out by another sustained burst of firing.

"Are you hurt?" her hand grasped Sam's arm in concern.

"Cuts, bruises and a few cracked ribs by the feel of it." He took her hand in his and squeezed it.

"Anyone seen Javed and the others?" he called out hopefully.

Hearing his question, Gloria crawled over to join them. "You'd better check out the bay," she said. "Be prepared, it's not a pretty sight," she warned.

With a final squeeze of Claire's hand, Sam swallowed a feeling of dread and, crawling on his stomach, moved towards the opposite side of the quay. Once behind the old warehouse he eased himself to a standing position, wincing from the dagger sharp pain of his injured ribs. Leaning against the wall, he took deeper breaths, trying to clear his head.

As Gloria had said, he didn't have far to look. A short distance away the orange inflatable wallowed empty, half sunk, its outboard motor reared up at an acute angle clear of the water. A body lay half in and half out of the punctured boat, two more rose and fell with the swell as if in some macabre dance. Even worse was the black smoke pouring from *Lupin*'s funnel. Helen's priority was her ship and she had already raised anchor and was preparing to leave. In desperation, Sam waved frantically, hoping that someone would see him, the awful dread of abandonment adding to his swirling cocktail of emotions. Released from her anchor *Lupin* swung her stern to the landward, her newly welded, rust-streaked plating offering a smaller target and better protection to the gunfire now streaming from the old fort. It was undoubtedly a wise move, but Sam couldn't understand why no one on board was shooting back. He waved again. With his hand above his head, he felt a warm wet line of blood run up his sleeve from a bad gash across his hand. He found a handkerchief in his pocket, and knotted it around the palm. Looking up from tying the knot, Sam noticed a head, then another, bobbing in the sea, slowly moving towards the quayside as another burst of gunfire rang out and showered sparks against *Lupin*'s hull. For the moment, Sam was absorbed by the two figures in the sea. He had to get their attention and direct them to a steel ladder fixed vertically to the quayside in front of him. The beach farther round was another option and better protected, but was a greater distance to swim. Taking a risk, he stuck his head around the corner of the building and shouted for Gloria to join him. It would mean leaving Claire and Jenny, but her help would be the only way to get the two survivors out of the sea. Gloria arrived beside him surprisingly fast.

"If we can find a length of rope and make a lasso, we can throw it to them when they get closer to the quayside and haul them in," Sam shouted.

Gloria nodded and disappeared into the warehouse building behind them, leaving Sam to try and signal to the swimmers. He could clearly make out Javed's head and they were both wearing lifevests. Javed was supporting the second person, who lay with her head against his chest as he struggled to swim with the other arm; he was beginning to tire. Gloria returned with a length of frayed, oily rope in which she had already tied a noose at one end.

"Down the ladder," Sam shouted to Gloria. "Throw the noose end of the rope to him."

Sam's ribs hurt badly every time he took a breath, so hauling the pair out of the sea was going to have to be a task for Gloria.

It took four attempts to get the rope to Javed and he had considerable difficulty trying to slide the lasso under the arms of the girl he was supporting. At last Gloria began hauling the rope and re-climbed the ladder. Once the rope was in place, Gloria threaded it through a mooring hitch and, looping the end diagonally around her body, she began to haul the injured girl clear of the sea. Eyes bulging and body taut with strain, Gloria raised her inch by inch to the safety of the quayside. The girl was breathing but barely conscious, two conspicuous bullet wounds staining her saturated clothing. They found a discarded door to use as a stretcher. They would need to drag it over the rough surface like a sled as they rounded the corner of the warehouse and came into the view of the old fort again. Sam led the way on all fours, with Gloria hauling the door with the girl tied to it with the rope. Gasping from the strain, she only just remembered to shout a warning to Sam.

"When I left to help you, I gave your Sten gun to Claire for their protection. Be sure to shout to her as we approach; we don't want any accidents."

'Oh wonderful,' thought Sam, 'a nervous blind girl let loose with a loaded sub-machine gun is all I need.'

They crossed the open stretch without being spotted while the attention of their attackers was drawn to *Lupin*. In the brief lull, Jenny and Claire had dragged their undamaged medical equipment into a safer location. Jenny looked pale but had the use of one arm, while Claire looked more like a pirate with a dressing taped around her own forehead and iodine stains to the cuts on her face and arms. When she heard Sam's voice she handed the Sten gun back with a look of relief.

Gloria carried the wounded girl to an old bench they had dragged from the warehouse. With Karen stranded on *Lupin*, they would have to improvise and make things up as they went along, and Sam went in search of dry clothes for Javed who sat shivering and exhausted, propped with his back against a wall. As he left, Javed grasped his arm.

"Where's Ruth?"

Sam nodded in the direction of the bridge. "I'm afraid they were caught on the open road just after crossing the bridge. Things don't look too good; I can't see any movement."

When he returned he found Javed had moved forward to gain a better view. Sam joined him and passed him his binoculars. "As things stand, we're trapped, completely stuck. We can't go forward, or back and we need help from Aiden and *Lupin*, which to add to our problems ..." He held up his rucksack, punctured and shredded by several ragged holes. He pushed his hand inside and pulled out their only radio, now a tangled spaghetti of wires and twisted metal.

"So we can't contact *Lupin* either," Javed said, grimly.

"On the plus side, someone on board must have seen us pull you from the sea. But ..."

"... Helen has instructions to save *Lupin* at all costs, with or without us," Javed completed the sentence for him.

For several minutes they sat side by side against the protection of the low stone. Even raising their heads an inch too far could be fatal.

"They must have been watching us from the moment we arrived," Javed said grimly.

Sam nodded. "I think the entire operation has been a hoax they set us up for from the very start and we've blindly walked right into their trap," he said with a note of recrimination.

"Why? What's their purpose?"

"Same as Dartmouth. It's the Trojan horse theory. If they capture *Lupin* intact they can sail straight into the heart of the island unopposed. We're hardly likely to sink our own ship on the off chance, just because there's been no radio contact for a while. If they get their hands on her, it could be game over for all of us."

Gloria was sitting beside the injured girl, giving her own blood directly into the girl's arm. Sam looked at her anxiously.

"Has to be done. We're the same group," she quipped with a wide-toothed grin.

Claire arrived with a tray of steaming tea mugs.

"Extra honey for Gloria," she said, pointing to the largest mug. She nodded to a spare mug for Sam.

"Can I have a word?" she asked.

Space to stand up was limited, but they found a place to talk near the back of the building.

"Are you okay," Sam asked in concern.

"I'm fine." Claire paused and took a deep breath. "I think Ruth is still alive."

"Alive?"

"I can hear her. If I crawl as far as the end of the protecting wall, I can hear Ruth calling out in pain," she hesitated, before adding firmly, "I want to go out and get her."

"What?" Sam looked aghast. "You can't do that. No one, sighted or blind, can cross the open gap beyond the steel drums. There's no wall and it's completely open to the fort. It would be total suicide to try."

"But we've got to try. We can't just leave Ruth and the girls lying there." She set her mouth in the resolute line he had seen before when she became determined. "Ruth has always been kind to me; I can't just leave her out there. I owe it to her at least to try and save her."

"Look." Sam was holding both her hands, as if she would run off at any second on her wild rescue attempt. "I know how you feel about Ruth, we all like her a lot, but there's nothing that can be done at the moment. Promise me you won't try and do anything rash," he said, rubbing the blood-caked skin on her hands.

"How's the other injured girl we've just brought in?" he said, trying to change the subject.

Claire smiled thinly, guessing he was trying to distract her.

"Jenny has more advanced training than me so we've been able to staunch the bleeding and given her blood from Gloria plus some morphine. She's comfortable, but we need Karen urgently. This," she gestured around her, "is only a dressing station at best. She needs proper medical help quickly."

Impulsively, he held Claire close in a tight grip. "You're needed here. There may be more wounded, including Ruth, that we can rescue, but working out how to do that is my problem, not yours. We'll need you here for when we bring them in, not off trying to do something heroic."

Gloria stood in the protective shadow of the higher end of the stone wall, a length of torn white sheet tied to the end of a broom handle. Sam was beside her, Albert Jamieson's letter still in his breast pocket, reminding him of his duty to the island. It wasn't the kind of negotiations he had intended, but the need to get to the dead and wounded was paramount, overruling any other options. Javed, restored and dressed in a rag bag of dry clothes, stood back out of harm's way with the girls.

"Not quite what we anticipated," Gloria said in a doubtful voice.

Sam shook his head. "We've got to give it a try. Our people are going to die if we don't get to them soon." He nodded to Gloria. "Okay, give it a try; long slow arcs so that the white flag can be clearly seen."

She looked badly disgruntled by the job she had been given and reluctantly extended the broom handle beyond the end of the wall. The sheet made a loud crack when swept upwards and reversed in direction.

"I don't see this doing any good with this bunch of scumbags," Gloria grumbled.

"Try it more slowly. We want to make sure they can clearly see …"

His words were cut short by a burst of gunfire, accompanied by the shock of bullets hammering into the walls around them. As the dust settled, the white sheeting hung in shreds from the end of Gloria's pole.

"I think you just got your answer," she said tersely.

"So we're agreed," Javed said with a note of finality.

Sam nodded reluctantly. Time was running out, leaving no alternative but for one of them to try and swim back to *Lupin* and organise their rescue. Though tired, Javed was by far the strongest swimmer amongst them and the amount of time exposed in the sea would be critical.

"How long do you think you'll be able to protect me for?" Javed asked, trying hard to sound unconcerned.

"I've enough ammunition for five magazines. Say, five minutes maximum; if I'm careful. After that, you're on your own," Gloria said with genuine concern.

"We'll just have to hope that Aiden can help us. Remember to fire a green flare when you get to *Lupin* so we know you've arrived okay." Both men shook hands briefly. "I'll help you down the quayside steps where you landed." Sam took a deep breath. "Five minutes after that … we'll pick a fight."

With a wave, Javed left Gloria filling the last of her magazines. He was about to embark on the race of his life.

When Sam returned, he found Jenny and Claire already lying on the floor, covering the wounded girl who now lay between them. Breathless, Sam slid into place beside Gloria, spare magazines at his side. She handed him a pair of gloves and a bucket. He knew the gloves were for removing hot empty magazines, but the bucket?

"Piss into it. The barrel is going to get red hot so we'll need to cool it down," she said in an amused voice.

Together they watched the second hand swing around to the five minutes mark on Sam's stopwatch. When the hand reached twelve, with her eye pressed tight against the telescopic sight, Gloria started a war. Their plan was to make the five magazines last for the time Javed would need to swim to *Lupin*, but things seldom go to plan, and halfway through their allotted time, Sam was forcing their last full magazine into the gun. Fear and excitement had left him unable to pee, and despite the gloves he had already received several nasty burns to his hands.

"It's the last one," he shouted.

"What do we do when this runs out? Throw rocks?" Gloria adjusted her sights and fired a short burst for the countless time.

"Pray for Aiden to come to the rescue," Sam muttered to himself, ears ringing from the deafening cacophony.

Silence; a dull metallic click announced the magazine was empty. Javed was on his own now. With more than a minute left of the time they had allotted for him to swim back to *Lupin* the firing from the fort began again within seconds of their final burst. Gloria gave Sam a hefty shove.

"Time to get the hell out of here," she shouted, dragging him with her as they both rolled sideways away from their position in the wall. Seconds later an explosion blew the wall and their gun apart.

"Well, now we know one thing; this mob have brought their bazooka with them again," Sam shouted.

Following the explosion, the firing fell away to single measured shots. As they shook off debris, Sam imagined Javed valiantly swimming towards *Lupin*, surrounded by violent geysers and the whine of bullets. They had done their best in an unequal struggle and he could only hope it would be enough. As the painful vibration from the explosion died away in his ears, a new sound entered the arena; a deep percussive throb, followed by loud explosive cracks from the direction of the fort. Sam and Gloria both ventured a hasty glance around the corner of their refuge. A chain of explosions were dancing slowly along the parapet of the old fort, spurting clouds of debris into the air as it advanced from one end to the other. They watched, mesmerised. Having reached the far end of the parapet, the chain of explosions reversed, working their way back towards the starting point, an occasional vein of tracer marking a path from *Lupin*.

"It's an automatic cannon," Sam whooped. "Someone on *Lupin* is actually using a cannon."

He recognised the sound from his National Service training several years before. As the explosions continued, the entire length of the parapet was turned into a smoking ruin. Lying at their feet were the remains of their white flag attempt at mediation. Now at last, Sam felt they had a chance.

Sam glanced anxiously at his watch. Ten minutes had passed since Javed had started swimming. The distance was not much more than a few hundred yards; he should be back on *Lupin* by now. The waiting was almost unbearable and Sam found himself clutching Gloria's hand, the burns an agonising reminder of what they had just been through. Seconds ticked by on his watch; neither of them could breathe.

The firework whoosh of a rocket came as a surprise, followed by a loud crack, high above their heads. Open-mouthed, they watched the green flare, slowly swinging in the breeze as it descended to earth. Javed had made it.

Any celebrations were short-lived. Sam went to check on Claire and Jenny to make sure neither had been hurt by ricocheting bullets and to share the news of Javed's arrival. He found Jenny struggling alone with one arm to lift the wounded girl back to her improvised bed.

"Where's Claire?" Sam asked as he bent down to help Jenny.

"Just after you left us, before the shooting started, Claire said she needed the toilet," Jenny gasped from the effort of lifting. "I thought it was just nerves, but she hasn't returned."

"Where?" He shouted, suddenly anxious.

"Round the back. There's a bucket behind a curtain."

The space was empty. The realisation of what Claire must have done suddenly kicked in.

"Oh no," he gasped out loud. "You silly, stupid girl."

Rage and fear surged through him in equal measure. He needed no second guess where Claire had gone. After all, she hadn't actually said she wouldn't try to do what he had strictly forbidden.

# THIRTY-THREE

Driven by adrenalin and fear, Sam crawled almost as fast as he could run. Panting so hard that he was starting to hyperventilate, he paused where the protection of the quayside wall came to an abrupt end. Anxiety had ridden on his back the entire way, half expecting at every turn to come upon Claire's body. She must have come this way and without her sight it was impossible to believe she could cover the distance without being shot. From where he knelt, gasping for breath, there was little over a hundred yards to the wreckage around the tractor; he could see the overturned wheels above the camber of the road. There was no sign of Claire, or Ruth and the girls for that matter. For about half the distance ahead the wall was completely missing, leaving the road completely exposed. Only an overturned car offered any protection. Despite the pounding *Lupin* had given the walls of the old fort, anyone still there would have a clear view of him, regardless of whether he walked or crawled. With grim resignation Sam knew there was no point in weighing the options; he only had one choice.

"No point in crawling, I'll die on my feet if I have to," he shouted angrily, hauling himself upright.

Sam had never been an athlete, but he ran as he had never done before, not pausing to think of consequences, driven only by his need to find Claire. It took only seven or eight seconds to cover the fifty yard gap, but it felt a lifetime. Whether he dived or stumbled into the protection of the next section of wall he couldn't tell, but the pain of yet more cuts and grazes was enough to tell Sam he was still alive.

For a moment he lay unable to move, his painful chest heaving, shouting in pain and exaltation at having survived. By some miracle he had got this far, but even if he found Claire, how were they going to return down the same road again in one piece? Right now though he had to go on, crawling towards the heartbreak he feared was ahead of him.

He came first upon two of the girls, who only minutes before had been riding, carefree, on the rear of the trailer, their bodies now spread-eagled where they had fallen in the road beside the upturned trailer. Carefully, he checked them for signs of life. Both were dead. He groaned out loud. Until that moment, a part of him had hoped he might find them wounded, but alive. The towing tractor lay on its side, some way beyond the trailer, its nose rammed into the gable wall of a small building. Sam crawled hastily over, apprehensive of what he was about to find. Behind the protection of the tractor body, another girl, Alice, lay on her back in the road. Beside her, Ruth sat propped against the wall, eyes closed, with one hand pressing a dressing against a large blood stain on her chest. Between the two girls, with her back to him, knelt Claire, her medical pack open, blood soaked hands working feverishly on another wound to Ruth's thigh.

"Claire!" Sam shouted her name as he approached and crawled beside her. "What are you doing?" He hadn't intended to speak so sharply, but his emotion and relief mixed into anger in his words.

"What does it look like," she said evenly. "Here, press your hand against her leg and hold this."

She grabbed his hand, applying it to a dressing pad, already warm with fresh blood, while she tore open powdered antiseptic and another fresh dressing, before pushing his hand away as she searched with her fingers in the oozing blood from the wound. She swabbed it, poured on the powder and pressed the dressing into place.

"This is the exit wound," she said, biting off adhesive tape with her teeth. "The entry is on the back of the leg. All I can do at the moment is try to stop the bleeding. Now, press down hard while I strap it," she shouted, raising Ruth's leg, using her remaining hand to bind the bandage.

He was amazed by Claire's composure; within moments, a dozen turns of bandage and tape had been spun around the leg. He sat with his back against the tractor as he watched her work to care for Ruth and the other injured girl. Both had a capital 'M' written on their foreheads in drying blood, indicating that Claire had given morphine to both of them, broken phials littering the road. Occasionally, Ruth's eyes fluttered open, sliding in and out of consciousness, sometimes offering a brief smile of recognition. He thought she looked comfortable, but was having difficulty breathing.

'Two out of four,' Sam thought grimly, and sadly shook his head. Claire closed her medical bag and crawled over to sit beside him.

"That's the best I can do for now; it's not much, but at least it's slowed the bleeding and eased their pain. Alice is in a more serious condition and we need to get them both back to *Lupin* quickly."

"First things first. Getting back down that road is the first challenge." Around them, echoes of single sniper's shots replaced the all-out attack. "How on earth did you get here?" Sam asked, his voice rising.

"I walked. When you and Gloria started your war, I reasoned that no one would spare concern for a stumbling blind girl."

She tried to smile but her face, pale and afraid, betrayed the courage it would have taken to achieve what she had done. There was no point in staying angry with her; it wouldn't help their situation and if he thought about it, she had never said she wouldn't go to help Ruth. When he warned her against it, she had only smiled in reply. He should have guessed what she intended.

"So, the problem is how we get back down that road carrying two badly wounded girls. Is there any chance Ruth could walk if you help her?"

"Not a chance. And it's not two, it's four girls."

"Four?" His mind took a second to connect. "We can't possibly manage to carry the dead bodies as well," he said, an incredulous note in his voice.

"Well, we can't leave them here," Claire said. "There are boar hunting around; you know what they'll do if we leave the bodies behind. These girls belong to us, we can't just abandon them because they've been killed."

"Boar? I wondered when they would show up. Are you sure?"

Claire nodded. "I could smell them, lurking around somewhere close, shortly before you turned up. They're bound to smell our presence with all this blood around."

"Well, for sure we can't stay here."

Sam turned to cautiously peer around the side of the tractor. Smoke drifted from the parapet of the old fort and there was no sign of movement, but that didn't mean there was no one there waiting for them to make a move.

"There's something else I heard when I got here." She paused, waiting for Sam's attention. "Motorbikes."

"Well, what a surprise. Any idea of the direction the sound was coming from?"

Claire was thoughtful for a moment. "The sound started from over there," she pointed in the direction of the old fort, "and seemed to circle around behind me," she said, pointing over her shoulder.

Sam was silent while he took in what she described. If Claire was right, it meant their attackers were trying to surround them on all sides except the sea, and he guessed they would soon try to close off that escape route too.

With a crash, the trailer fell back onto its wheels. They held their breath, waiting for the shots to come. Sam threw everything out of the trailer, sparing only what appeared to be medical supplies. Having decided not to wait any longer, they had to make a fast dash for their quayside refuge. The only way to carry the dead and wounded was in the trailer. Their first idea had been to upright the tractor and use it to tow their dead and wounded girls, but the ambush had smashed the tractor, puncturing its sump and radiator and splintering the distributor. It wasn't going anywhere.

"Could we push the trailer by hand, together?" Claire suggested.

It was possible, but slower. At least the road had a slightly downhill gradient in their favour. They would have to hope that their attackers were lousy shots or that *Lupin* would use her gun to distract them. How Sam wished for a functioning radio.

On hands and knees, they pulled the bodies of the dead girls closer to the trailer. Unpleasant though it was, their plan was to lay the dead bodies on top of Ruth and Alice for protection.

"We'll have to move quickly; no stopping if one of us falls over, so hang on, whatever happens."

It took agonising minutes to carefully lift Ruth and Alice into the trailer. Ruth was conscious, but weak. She beckoned to Sam as she lay propped against the rear flap.

"Give me your revolver," she croaked in a hoarse voice. "You can't push and shoot at the same time and besides, I'm a better shot than you are," she said giving him a half-hearted smile.

Sam had left his Sten gun with Gloria, so his pistol was all they had. Provided Ruth stayed conscious, it was a good idea; he only hoped they wouldn't need it. Laying the dead bodies on top of their two live friends was tough, but soon they were ready.

"Okay, no point in waiting. Once we start, there's no stopping," he repeated, shouting in an attempt at bravado.

As he started to move away, Claire suddenly placed a hand around the back of his neck, pulling his face to hers. Without hesitating she kissed him, deliberately, full on the mouth, a searching kiss that spoke more than words could ever do. He gasped in surprise as they parted.

"Just in case," she whispered and turned to push the rear of the trailer.

It took half a minute to cover the first few yards; thirty seconds of exposure. Momentum was hard to generate, but a combination of a clear road surface and favourable gradient soon began to work in their favour. Sam could hear Claire gasping with effort, and he felt the towing hasp bite into his hands.

They had covered about thirty yards before the first shots rang out. Sam flinched but nothing seemed to be aimed towards them. Seconds later there came several more and he heard something resembling supersonic bees, making zipping sounds around them.

"Push harder," he shouted, as if it needed to be said.

Another shot rang out, followed instantaneously by the excited chatter of a Sten gun. Sam had left his Sten with Gloria to protect Jenny and the other wounded girl. Now he could only hope she had seen him and Claire with the trailer and was using the gun to try and protect them. With any luck *Lupin* might join in as well. Until then, they were exposed and on their own.

They had covered about half the distance when Sam thought he saw a shadow move beside a building to his left. It could have been nothing, perhaps a wild dog, or a boar. For a moment the shooting stopped.

"Sam," Claire said in alarm.

He looked up. Twenty yards ahead, two men were in the road about six feet apart, blocking their path; both were wearing black leathers. With a sinking feeling Sam could see they carried sub-machine guns on slings; both were pointing directly towards them. He stopped, feeling the un-braked trailer push hard against his back. For several seconds they stared at one another in silence, each evaluating the other.

"What do you want? You're blocking our way and we have injured women in the trailer. We need to pass." The words left Sam breathless from the effort.

The taller of the two men gestured skywards with the barrel of his gun. "Up. Hands above your head."

Sam dropped the hasp and reluctantly raised his hands. If he ran now, would that distract them long enough for Claire to get away? He doubted it; the other man looked alert and would be after her in a second. And anyway, they would be abandoning Ruth and Alice in the trailer.

"Kneel down," the taller man shouted.

So this is how it is going to end, Sam thought grimly. He heard the click of a safety catch. Slowly he knelt. Their assailants held all the options. But there was one thing everyone had overlooked. The ear-splitting crack reminded him of ice shattering on a cold winter's day. The tall man in front of him took a staggering step back, and then another, dropped his gun and keeled over backwards, falling prone, flat on the ground. The second man responded instantly, dropping to one knee, eyes wild and alert. Anger flared in his face as he turned the gun towards Sam, still kneeling with hands on his head. He forgot to look at the trailer. Two more sharp cracks followed. The man sprung to his feet in surprise, made to run and fell forward into the road, his gun skittering away.

Shocked, Sam slowly raised himself to a standing position. Behind him in the trailer, the vacant eyes of a dead girl stared at him from an almost sitting posture, a bloody hand around her chest, another holding Sam's pistol on her left side. Beneath the dead body, he could just make out Ruth's face, gasping with the pain and effort of her wounds. She had just shot both men.

"More morphine," Ruth demanded. "You owe me," she added with a painful grin, bloodless lips stretched over bared teeth.

Claire shook her head. "Too soon, sorry." She fumbled for her water bottle, spilling much of it across Ruth's face as she pressed it to her lips and re-positioned an improvised pillow beneath her head and eased her back down.

"Rest. We'll have you safe soon," she said with more certainty than Sam felt.

Ruth grunted through her pain, "Bastards." Somehow she still managed to smile.

Sam dragged the two men's dead bodies clear of the road and came across a clasped leather satchel. Inside were maps and papers. In haste he threw the satchel over his shoulder; whatever value they might have would have to wait until later.

Taking the strain on the tow end of the trailer again and with Claire pushing once more, two things seemed to happen simultaneously. First, a single shot rang out from the direction of the old fort. Sam heard the whine of a ricochet and instantaneously felt the sensation of a hot sharp knife stabbing him in the foot. He made an involuntary grunt and tried to ignore the pain. As his head cleared he could hear a deep throbbing noise from the direction of *Lupin*. As she inched her way, coming slowly astern towards the shore, the parapet of the old fort disappeared again in a cloud of dust and flying debris. An umbrella of protection would last for as long as *Lupin* kept firing. Running, hobbling, shambling along, they had made half the remaining distance to safety before Sam's ankle finally gave way, pitching him sideways into the gutter at the edge of the road. The trailer wheels narrowly missed running him over as it passed by, now driven forward only by Claire, obliviously pushing, with every ounce of her strength. 'There can be no stopping,' he had pronounced at the start. Now, as she couldn't see him, she couldn't know he had fallen; she had just one mission; to get the trailer and the wounded cargo to safety.

Sam was left lying in the debris at the side of the road, chest heaving, gasping for air like a landed fish. His boot was full of blood and he couldn't move his ankle. Even crawling was going to be slow and difficult and he had nothing to protect himself with if anyone else caught up with him. Despite that, the irony of the situation made him laugh as he watched Claire and the trailer fade away from him; four dead and badly wounded girls being hauled to safety by a diminutive blind girl; it was absurd and heroic in equal measure.

Gloria found Sam dragging himself along the road. He saw her crawling towards him, large smiling eyes in a brown face, a long bladed knife clamped tightly between her teeth. Exhausted, he thought she looked both the most beautiful and scary woman he had ever seen. He climbed onto her broad back, his arms crossed around her neck, and together, Gloria dragged them both back to safety. It felt an age since he had left the safety of their dressing station and to his delight, Javed, half-dressed in a wetsuit, stepped forward to help Gloria in the final yards.

"I got shot in the foot," Sam exclaimed as he slid off Gloria's back and dragged himself to a wooden bench.

Their small protected space suddenly seemed full. Javed hadn't returned alone. Two new squad members were unpacking sealed bags and, most important of all, Karen was there, busily organising care for Ruth and Alice. On the floor in the corner sat Claire, a blanket covering her shoulders, exhausted, but already connected to a drip stand where a bag filled with her blood. They would all have to donate quickly if the wounded were to be kept alive.

Sam shuffled over to sit beside her. Words weren't necessary, just being together was all that mattered. Javed joined them, ripping open a sealed bag as he did so.

"You'll need this." He placed a radio set in Sam's hand. "And it's got a spare battery."

Sam checked his watch, the glass in its face now badly cracked from one of his many falls. It was early afternoon, only hours since he had set out that morning from *Lupin*. It felt like days.

Sam winced as Karen dug deep into his foot for the bullet while he called Helen on the radio.

"Are you okay?" Helen asked.

"I have been better," he grunted in reply.

"Look," she continued, "the risks are too great until high tide. We've no idea of the depth or obstructions at the quayside. High tide is safest."

Sam glanced at his watch. "That's still five hours away," he said, passing a meaningful look at Karen who had moved to Alice's makeshift bed. She shook her head with a pensive expression.

"We can't wait that long, Helen. Alice is very weak and Karen needs to get her to *Lupin*."

Helen sighed heavily. "You could try stopping this stupid war and ask these idiots for a truce to help the wounded."

Sam laughed. "I've already tried that; what's left of the white flag is proof of their answer. Besides, it's most probably *Lupin* they're after; the longer we wait, the greater the chance they'll alter their plans and come up with something better to catch us all. There's no alternative, you either come and get us now," Sam paused, "or sail immediately. Without us."

Helen cut the link without an answer. There was a metallic noise and spurt of blood from Sam's foot as Jenny, who had taken over from Karen, prised the bullet free.

"Gotcha," she said with satisfaction, offering the dish containing a bright metal slug for his inspection.

"For something so small, it hurts like hell," he grumbled.

"Think yourself lucky it was only a ricochet. A complete bullet would have probably taken your foot off," Jenny said.

She was dressing the wound as Javed arrived, having climbing onto the roof above them to get a better view of things.

"Can you get ready to donate more blood?" she asked Javed.

For the present, their situation was better than they had been for some time, but that could change in an instant, thought Sam. Their future rested in Helen's hands. And the incoming tide.

Some while later, Javed slumped onto the bench beside Sam, weary from his exertions and his donation of another pint of blood.

"See anything from the roof?" asked Sam.

He nodded. "Activity on the groyne." Javed looked worried. "And they've already moved a couple of motorboats to the far end. It suggests they're thinking of cutting off our escape route."

They both sat in thought, hoping Helen would have also seen the boats.

"How long do you think we have?" Sam asked.

"Not long. They've probably worked out that the gun we've fitted to *Lupin* can only fire from the stern. If they try to rush us from all sides it's going to be impossible to hold them off."

It had felt like the day would never end, but to their surprise, the final attack came quickly. With the currents of the rising tide, Helen cast off and slowly drifted towards the quayside. Javed was the first to notice *Lupin* drawing nearer, so they abandoned the protection of the dressing station and set out for the quayside, desperate to avoid being seen until the last possible moment. When *Lupin* was already halfway to the quay, the attack began again. This time they were using something bigger to fire at *Lupin* from a position in the main town. Helen engaged the engines and pulled alongside, lowered the gangway and stretchers were run aboard. Impatient to leave, Helen ordered 'full ahead' almost before loading was completed. A hail of crossfire struck *Lupin* from their attackers, enraged that their prize might slip between their fingers. Despite the damage she was receiving, nothing was going to stop *Lupin*. Clear of the quay, Helen raced for the clear channel. Until the inevitable happened.

Despite repairs, the overheated engine suddenly seized. With only one screw working and racing at full speed, *Lupin* slewed violently to port before Helen could make a correction. Thrown off course from the narrow channel she had so carefully plotted, *Lupin* came shuddering to a violent halt. They had run aground.

For a moment everything stopped, including the gunfire attack. In the eerie silence, everyone paused to take stock of the situation, even their attackers. With Claire's support, Sam hobbled to the wheelhouse, accompanied by a deep shuddering vibration beneath his feet as *Lupin* strained her remaining engine to full power to pull herself clear from the grasping mud bank. After less than a minute, Helen shut down the engine just as they entered the wheelhouse.

"We're stuck fast," she shouted in angry exasperation. "I'll just burn out the engine if I keep trying. We'll have to wait for the tide to lift us clear."

"High tide is still three hours away," Sam said calmly. "We can't wait that long."

Helen shook her head. "There's nothing else we can do. There's been no dredging for more than five years; there must be mud banks everywhere around the mouth of the river."

In the silence, they could hear the sound of feet running fast up the stairway. The door opened and Aiden burst in, rapidly followed by a breathless John and Gloria.

"Quickly, can you move *Lupin* astern?" Aiden asked. "I can hear outboard motors being started. I think they intend to come aboard." Fear tinged his words as he looked at everyone in the wheelhouse.

Helen shook her head. "I'm sorry. We're not going anywhere anytime soon." She turned to look at Sam. "There's no choice; we'll have to show a flag of truce or face the consequences."

They silently digested the implications of her words. Neither option had much appeal, but what choice did they have?

"How strong is the bow?" Aiden asked suddenly.

"Strong? Helen said. "*Lupin* is a deep sea trawler; she's designed to operate in arctic waters, so her bow is especially reinforced. Why do you ask?"

Without waiting to give an answer, Aiden ran towards the door.

"I think I can try to clear the mud we're stuck on by blasting it clear with explosives. Get the engine ready to go full astern," he shouted as he disappeared down the ladder.

"If he doesn't blow the bow clean off in the process," Helen muttered with a sigh of weary resignation.

They could now see motorboats being prepared on the open beach behind them and on the groyne in front of them. The attack would come from all sides; it was only a matter of time. Aiden had deployed all the squads on board into what little protection they could find on deck, while he packed explosives into waterproof boxes. Working carefully, he taped them to the longest poles he could find, before connecting detonators and yards of charge cable. Crawling across the foredeck, Aiden and Gloria dragged the explosives on their poles to the bow and dropped them into the sea as far as possible on either side of the bow. It was their final gamble. Aiden signalled to Helen in the wheelhouse. *Lupin*'s remaining engine trembled into life, her decks drumming as the revolutions increased. Aiden held his breath and pressed the red button. For a moment, nothing seemed to happen until, simultaneously, two huge geysers of water fountained skywards, followed by a deeper rumble that shook every one of *Lupin*'s rivets. Aiden felt the hard jolt as the bow leapt violently upward. The protesting engine screamed, and then by some miracle *Lupin* slid backwards, clear of the grip of the sucking mud. Helen, now at the wheel while her coxswain hurried below deck to check for damage, set about running her ship to safety and raced for the larger swells of the open sea.

Weymouth fell slowly behind. They had escaped. Although Sam knew they must remain vigilant for the entire journey home, a sense of immense relief swept over everyone on board. Their trial was over.

Taking stock, the mission had been a disaster. Even if their escape was triumph enough, it was a bitter victory, scarred by the five dead bodies they sadly carried homewards. Sam felt traumatised by that fact. He made himself tour the ship, comforting and encouraging everyone in the manner that Albert Jamieson would have done. Seeing him limping on his injured foot, everyone greeted him warmly, but there was only one thing they all wanted to talk about; the inspiration of a blind girl who, acting alone and against the odds, had saved the lives of those badly injured and retrieved the bodies of two more, hauling them in a trailer, under gunfire, to safety. Sam noticed with a wry smile that there was no mention of him in their picture of the events. But then, that was the way it should be.

# THIRTY-FOUR

With only a painful foot for company, Sam spent the night alone. His mind spun like a kaleidoscope with the events of the previous days, making sleep an intermittent friend. His bed in the hostel, shared with Claire after the party for Napier and his crew, now felt cold and friendless. His body craved the warmth of her presence; in reply the bed offered only cold loneliness.

Although they had slipped the clutches of the mud bank and their attackers, the cost was the damage to the bow plates of *Lupin*. Even at reduced speed, the challenge to keep her afloat taxed their limited resources throughout the return journey, needing every pump they had on board to keep her from sinking. On arriving back at the harbour in Newport everyone with medical training was mobilised to help with the casualties. Alice's condition had been a desperate battle for Karen and her assistants to deal with during their slow journey home, and the exhausted nurses found no rest; many of *Lupin*'s crew were wounded, any one of which could turn septic if not given prompt attention.

In the early hours, Sam found his way to the hostel for a few hours rest, only to be woken suddenly by someone hammering on his door. Chris Woods entered, bearing coffee and breakfast.

"Thought you might appreciate a friendly face," she said. "How's the foot?"

"Sore, actually. It hurts like hell."

"Bullets usually do. Think yourself lucky you haven't lost your foot."

"Such a comfort," Sam grumbled. He looked at the tray Chris had brought. "Have you just come to gloat or is that for me?"

Chris smiled and perched on the edge of his bed.

"We'll share, and then I need to get you on your feet. I've heard what you've been through, but we need to get you up and moving around. I'm sorry, but the grieving families will be coming to Newport this morning to collect the bodies of their loved ones. Some words from you will bring comfort so I'm afraid you need to make it clear that their sacrifice hasn't been in vain."

Sam slumped back onto the bed. It was too soon to re-live the trials of the previous day but he knew he couldn't avoid it. He lay there, staring at the ceiling.

"You know, it was a set-up all along. They were waiting for us to fall into their trap," he muttered. For a moment, he struggled to keep his composure. Now the adrenalin had gone, the enormity of what had befallen them fell with a heavy hand upon him. "Sacrifice not in vain? It was an absolute shambles; it's a miracle any of us survived."

"I know," Chris said, her words softening. "But you can't say anything about that. Leadership is about maintaining faith; smoke and mirrors if you like. Albert Jamieson is absolutely broken up by this. He insists on carrying all the blame for the deaths." Chris paused, holding up an open palm to stop Sam interrupting. "You went on his instruction; we all know you disagreed with the operation from the very start and that lifts most, if not all of the responsibility from your shoulders."

"Yes, but …"

"No buts," Chris cut in. "The feel-good stories of the heroic efforts of Claire, Javed, Aiden, and even you leading them still with a bullet in your foot, are already circling the island. When things go badly, it's what people want to believe that's important. No matter how you see the true picture, you've got to spin the story to find the positive. You have no choice. Without it … well, I don't have to spell out the consequence."

The families of the dead arrived throughout the morning but no one came from the farm to support Sam or Claire. It was a heartbreaking process; time and again Sam had to repeat the story of their ambush without portraying it as a disaster. Chris stayed at his side, joined in with hugs of comfort and helped to wipe away the tears. Despite the tough world in which they lived, day in, day out, violent death always had the power to shock.

At one point, Rigby made an appearance. He passed no comment and offered his qualified support, though Sam could detect a concealed agenda written in his eyes. Albert Jamieson stayed throughout. He looked drawn, hollowed out by what had happened, yet he still managed to provide meaningful words whenever the opportunity allowed. As they left, he caught Sam's attention.

"Are you feeling okay?" He looked with concern at Sam's shoe-less foot. "Could you come to my office tomorrow sometime? Sorry to ask, but I do need to talk to you." It wasn't a question; the sadness in his voice made it more like a plea.

After the last of the casualties had been collected for burial by their families, Chris found a quiet room for Sam.

"You need to get home to get some rest. I'll find a car and drive you back to the farm."

Exhausted, Sam nodded his thanks. "Can you find Claire? She's been working all night. I need to take her back with me."

"Ah, our young blind heroine," Chris said wistfully. "I'll see what I can do. Meanwhile, John's waiting outside to have a word with you before you leave if you're up to it."

John entered the room as Chris left. Like everyone else, he looked tired and red-eyed.

"How's the foot?"

"Hurts." Sam managed a smile.

John was silent for a moment. "So it was a set-up all along."

Sam nodded. "Heard any more from the supposed 'survivors' we went to rescue?" he said, an ironic note to his voice.

John stared at the floor for a moment. "Well, sort of." He looked uncomfortable. "Actually, there's been a message. For you. Personally."

Sam looked bemused. "Me?"

"Yes." John looked at the paper slip in his hand.

"Shortly after we managed to escape from Weymouth, I picked up a signal on the same frequency the survivors had been using." He looked directly at Sam. "The messenger said simply, 'Say hi to Sam Morten for me,' then cut the signal, laughing hysterically."

When they found Claire, she was asleep in a chair, her arms and clothing streaked with blood stains. Her duties complete, she now hadn't slept for twenty-four hours or more. Sam and Chris carried her to the car and laid her on the rear seats. A scarf had been tied around her head to keep her hair back, revealing a wide cut on her forehead which had leaked blood into her hair.

"Let her carry on sleeping when you get home. Cleaning up can happen afterwards," Chris suggested.

As they travelled to the farm in silence, Sam measured the word 'home'. It might be true for him, but for Claire he wasn't so sure the term applied any more, or had ever, for that matter. They had always thought of the island as secure, a place of refuge and safety in a wild and dangerous world, but recent events left a huge question mark against that description.

News of Weymouth had reached the farm before they arrived. Only Jake and Lorna were on hand to greet them. Shocked by Claire's appearance, they helped carry her to one of the spare rooms in the farmhouse without waking her. Leaving Lorna to stay with Claire for a while, Jake and Sam retreated to the kitchen. Jake set a kettle to boil.

"Rachel's not here. She's been spending time helping out at the Robinson's place at Rainbow's End. They've got a farm just off the road to East Cowes and were hit hard by a boar attack a few weeks back," Jake explained, leaving Sam uncertain of the inference in his words. "You caught us by surprise, returning last night," he continued uncomfortably. "But I'm sure Rachel would have gone over to Newport to collect you this afternoon when she finished at Rainbow's End."

Sam gripped Jake's shoulder to reassure his discomfort.

"Do you want to talk about it?" Jake asked.

"We lost five people, all young sighted women. We could have lost more. Quite a number seriously injured to cap it all. That tells you all you need to know."

Sam filled a bath, fell asleep and woke some time later, ravenously hungry. When he returned to the kitchen he found Marcus and his wife busy preparing supper. They hugged him in greeting but nervously avoided making eye contact and anything other than superficial conversation. Sam made a sandwich and retreated to the office. If Albert needed to see him he was bound to need his report on their ambush in Weymouth. It would be best to get it written while things were still clear in his mind.

Sam completed his report at the first attempt. He normally struggled for words, but this time the entire sequence of events just flowed, the narrative more or less wrote itself, defining a watershed in the history of their island. When he had written it, Sam stretched and sat back, abstractedly pressing his lips together at the memory of the kiss shared with Claire. 'Just in case', a statement made in the face of possible death, when passion overcame fear and made her courage all the greater. It would always remain a privately shared memory that would never need to be explained, just a moment of intimacy that would always exist, no matter how fate wove their future.

At some point, Sam must have fallen asleep in the chair. He awoke, feeling stiff and thirsty and wandered into the kitchen for a drink.

"If you're looking for Rachel, she got back half an hour ago. She saw you were asleep and left you in peace. She's gone to gather silage bails in the top pasture," Monica explained. "Not that there's much to store, but we have to try. She said to tell you she'd be back for dinner."

Sam had limped into the kitchen on his injured foot and Monica probably guessed that walking or riding the mile or so to their top pastures in his current condition was beyond him. He wandered through the house to check the room in which they had left Claire asleep. If Rachel returned and found her sleeping in the main farmhouse he was uncertain how she might react. There was only an impression of her body on the bed; the room was empty, so Sam hobbled across the farmyard to the barn. From the stables he could hear movement above and hauled himself up the ladder on his one good foot. It was Claire.

"You were asleep when I looked around the office door. I thought I'd come back here and take a shower." Her hair was wet and she had wound it in a towel. Despite her rest, tired lines spread out like rays of sunlight from the corners of her eyes. "Has anyone checked your foot today?" she asked.

"Too busy. It hurts enough to remind me it's still there though."

"Sit on the chair. I'll open the dressing and change it."

Claire unwound the bandages, now stuck together with crusted blood. When she got to the final twists, she began soaking the fabric with warm water to separate the layers.

"Sometimes, people can be unexpectedly kind. Despite her own worries, Alice's mother, who is also blind, has offered me a retriever puppy to train as my guide dog. She insists it's a small token for saving her daughter's life. I keep trying to explain that I wasn't alone, but she didn't want to listen," she added in a bemused voice.

"You can thank Ruth for that," Sam winced as the dressing pulled away from his wound. "She's well aware that you were the only one prepared to go and help them. Both Javed and I dismissed the idea as far too dangerous."

"So I get the praise and you take the pain," she replied, delicately feeling the wound with soft fingertips. She could feel the wetness still oozing from the hole, though it was less than it had been.

"How does the wound look," she asked, swabbing away the blood.

Sam peered at the ragged hole torn in the side of his foot.

"Red around the edges. Quite angry looking."

Claire soaked it in antiseptic. "Your body is fighting back. You really ought to keep off the foot for some time though; you'll need a crutch to help you move around until it has healed."

"No antibiotics I suppose?"

"Not as such, but our herbal specialist, Allison, has a store of biotic potions. They certainly helped heal the gash in my side."

Sam pulled a face. "Her witch's brews; I seem to remember they taste vile."

"A small price if they work," she teased. "I'll get you some." Claire re-dressed his foot in thoughtful silence. "When do you think you might next go to Newport? I'm keen to meet the puppy and start the bonding process."

Sam thought of Albert Jamieson's request to meet with him. "Tomorrow or the next day at the latest; I could give you a lift if it helps."

Her face lit up with delight at the suggestion. "Don't go without me."

She was fizzing with excitement. Though showered, Claire had yet to dress and was wearing an old faded kimono-style wrap, a size too large for her, but it was tied tightly and clung to her body, expressing the curves of her breasts and hips. Mesmerised by her appearance, the image lingered long after Sam had left Claire to dress.

Sam had almost overlooked the leather satchel he had taken from the man Ruth had shot in Weymouth. He found it at the bottom of his rucksack where he had pushed it for safekeeping, shortly before the bullet hit his foot. The leather was good quality with a deeply aged patina, and there were brass buckles and clips.

Inside he found mainly scraps of paper, though whoever had been carrying it must have had a certain degree of authority, as amongst the rubbish he found an assortment of warrants and directive notes. Nothing stood out as particularly useful until, in an inner side pocket, he found a selection of maps, numbered and neatly folded. Most had been torn from a road atlas and were marked to indicate where food and fuel might still be located. A faded map of Dartmouth caught Sam's eye, indicating in red the route on which he had first encountered the men on motorbikes chasing Claire. The map implied that the dead man could have been amongst the group who went on to mount the attack on *Lupin* in the harbour. At the back of the folder he also found a map of Weymouth. The old fort was ringed in red, along with the groyne and various buildings and road junctions in the main town. It seemed to confirm that the ambush had been planned well in advance, creating the spider's web into which they had been snared. Most of what he found was of interest but told him little they didn't already know. He carefully re-folded the maps, replacing them as found, in preparation for handing over the satchel to the forum to see what the other councillors could make of the contents.

Deep in thought Sam almost missed a slim outer pocket, concealed by a hidden zip. He opened it. Inside was a thin plastic wallet containing another folded map. Attached to it was a piece of paper on which were the tide tables for various points in the Solent and the Isle of Wight for the month ahead. He unfolded the map. It was of their island; their home. He spread the map out. Along the north facing coast a dozen red arrows marked beaches and disused ports and harbours, each arrow linked to a letter and number.

"Well, well, what have we here," Sam mused to himself.

There was nothing to indicate the purpose of the map and its markings, but it wasn't too much to think that it was probably a landing plan for the Isle of Wight. He looked thoughtfully at the map. Did this represent the men's plan to take over the island by force? If his suspicions were correct, luck might finally have smiled in their favour and given them advanced information they needed to protect themselves. Trying not to let his imagination get ahead of him, Sam refolded the map and was about to return it to the satchel when he saw something written on the back. He unfolded it again, this time laying it face down. Just a single line was written. It gave him a chilling sensation down his spine as he read it.

*'Find Morten alive.'*

Under the words was a symbol he recognised immediately: '**&**'

# THIRTY-FIVE

Rachel didn't come home to the farm that night. Concern arose after dinner when she hadn't returned from baling in the upper pasture. As they were about to mount a search, a carrier pigeon arrived with a message telling them she had been called to Rainbow's End to help with a problem calving. Over dinner, Marcus explained the situation in more detail.

"Robinson lost his wife and daughter, killed in a boar attack a few weeks ago. With that and recent injuries, they're running Rainbow's End on a knife edge. Despite your absence," he looked in Sam's direction with a mischievous grin, "the rest of us are coping well enough here, so it seemed only fair to help them out."

The reasoning appeared quite logical, though Rachel's timing seemed more than coincidental. Before bedtime, Sam sent a return message to her, asking if she could be home the following morning. His meeting with Albert Jamieson was approaching and he needed to catch up with their life together before Albert made further demands on his time.

Bearing a glass of Allison's 'evil brew', Claire found Sam as he made his way to bed. Without asking, she pushed a thermometer into his mouth. When she removed it, he read his temperature back to her.

"It's on the high side. Drink this." She thrust the glass into his hand.

Sam pulled a face of disgust as he drank, but Claire's gesture made a pleasant change; the feeling that someone actually cared for him was an odd experience; the first in some time.

"Ask Doctor Morgan to check you out when we go to Newport tomorrow. We don't want your foot to get an infection," she said, which he suspected was also a reminder for her visit to meet her new puppy as had been promised.

Whatever had been in the drink, Sam slept without dreams until daybreak. His foot still hurt, but now just a dull throb, more like toothache. Even his ribs only gave a stabbing pain if he twisted awkwardly. The house was quiet, with no sign of Rachel. Anxious to see her, Sam dressed and collected *Rowan* from her stall. If Rachel was unable to return to the farm, he would have to ride over to Rainbow's End and speak with her there. She had her horse to get there, so if he followed the path through the fields he might come upon her returning.

He rode in something of a daze, his head re-living the nightmare scenes from Weymouth on a constantly rotating carousel of images, each scene viewed from the critical perspective of hindsight. He would be called upon to give his report at the next forum meeting, where his decisions in Weymouth would be analysed by the rest of the committee. Sam would have to explain the tragic consequence of so many deaths and he anticipated criticism for his actions. It was an uncomfortable prospect. Sam was roused from his reverie at the sign for Rainbow's End. He felt a pang of disappointment that he hadn't encountered Rachel on the way.

Leaving the track, he directed *Rowan* onto an overgrown path that led towards a collection of rusting buildings grouped around a farmhouse with a red tiled roof. Meeting Rachel here, rather than in the home where she belonged, was far from what he had hoped for. A small wood screened the farm buildings as he approached. A tall man suddenly stepped from the trees to stand in the drive in front of him. Broader than Sam, with a greying beard and a shotgun tucked beneath his arm, Jeff Robinson blocked his path. *Rowan* halted, sensing uncertainty. At first, Sam assumed that Robinson hadn't recognised him. They each studied the other in silence. Sam spoke first.

"Jeff," he nodded in greeting. "Sam Morten. I was sorry to hear of your recent loss. I've come to see Rachel; I think she's here."

Robinson showed no sign of having heard what he had said. "I heard you walked into an ambush in Weymouth?" His words held an edge of criticism.

'Word travelled quickly,' Sam thought.

"That's true enough. We had our work cut out to get back to the island," Sam replied, waiting. "Rachel?"

"In the main barn. Been up calving most of the night. My wife used to do everything with the cows, before ..." His words trailed away.

Sam nodded, aware that his wife and daughter had been killed during the recent boar attack when they had been trapped in the milking parlour. It explained a lot about the man's demeanour.

Sam nudged *Rowan* to move on. Reluctantly, the horse stepped around Robinson and left him standing in the lane, staring back along the path in the direction Sam had just travelled from, momentarily lost to all human contact.

Sam found Rachel in a pen made of woven chestnut, bottle feeding a young calf.

"No mother?" he called out.

Rachel turned, startled; she obviously hadn't heard him approach.

Sam continued. "I guessed you were busy, so I thought I'd come and find you instead. How are things?"

He wanted to step forward and kiss her in greeting, but something in her eyes warned him not to.

"We lost the mother last night. That's the second in as many days and we can't find another to adopt this little one," Rachel said. "How's your injured foot?"

Obviously she had also heard the news about Weymouth.

"Sore, but I'll live." He tried to sound light-hearted but was impatient to draw her into a more personal conversation about them. Instead, Rachel remained disengaged, engrossed with feeding the orphaned calf.

"Can we talk when you're done?" he asked.

"Say what you have to say now. I'll be busy for some while yet." The chill in Rachel's words didn't encourage him.

Sam drew a breath. "I can see you're busy here, but when are you coming home?" He hesitated. "I need some time with you." At least his words were said with warmth.

For a moment she didn't answer. When the bottle was empty, she moved away to refill it from a steel jug.

"It's not the birth mother's milk, but it's better than nothing," she muttered, almost as if she hadn't heard his question.

"Rachel?"

She completed refilling the bottle and snapped the teat back on top.

"When am I coming home?" Rachel pondered, and shot an accusing glance at Sam. He couldn't read what the look meant. "That's not a question for me to answer."

"Sorry?"

"Only you can answer that quesiton."

Confused, he said, "I don't follow you."

"It's simple. I can't return to my home," she paused to emphasise the last word, "until you find your little heroine somewhere else to live." Her words, laced with ice, bit hard. "I would have thought with her new-found popularity, any hamlet on the island would welcome her with open arms. Wouldn't you agree?"

She stared hard at Sam, a cynical smile on her lips, awaiting his response. A wave of enormous weariness swept over him.

"Why start things this way, with an ultimatum?" he said, exasperated. "We've had people come and join us ever since we arrived and set up the farm. Why pick a fight over Claire, who needs a home as much as we all did when we first escaped from the mainland to start a new life here? Do you remember how it was for us?"

She ignored his question. "The difference is that we didn't choose that she should join us. You did. You chose. You never asked me if I agreed."

Rachel raised her voice, frightening the calf that was trying to reach the bottle she held in her hand.

"When are you next going to Newport?" she suddenly said, moderating her tone as she turned to encourage the calf to suckle once more.

Her question confused Sam.

"This afternoon; I've got to see Albert Jamieson. I expect it will be to arrange the funerals for the five dead girls I brought back from Weymouth," he added bitterly, as though the fact had slipped Rachel's mind.

"Don't you dare use that sort of remark against me," she hissed at him. "I'm truly sorry that they have been killed, but it's grossly unfair to bring a tragedy, for which you are at least partly responsible, ..." she paused for breath, "into an argument between us."

"Why can't you understand that this won't get sorted out until you get Claire out of my house," she shouted, gulping in emotion. "Just find her somewhere else to live. Today. Not tomorrow, or whenever you think this imagined crisis of yours will be over." She stared at Sam, anger burning in her eyes. "If you want me back on the farm, do it today, this afternoon. If not … I'll hold you responsible for the consequences."

Sam stood back in shock, feeling wretched. This was all going so badly wrong. After all they had been through, it came down to a shouting match, hurling threats at one another at a time when he most needed someone to share his worries and fears. Despite his own feelings of anger, he knew that from Rachel's perspective she wasn't asking for something she wasn't entitled to; the right to control matters in her own home. Yet granting her that wish would mean the total betrayal of all he had promised Claire, casting her off into the shadows of the storm clouds he could clearly see bearing down upon them, to become just another blind girl in a world where the sighted, so often, cannot see. It felt like cutting off a part of him, destroying the values he prized so dearly.

Rachel turned her back on him with a wave of the hand. He felt dismissed, cut off until further notice. He rode away with a heavy heart, carelessly nudging *Rowan* harder than he intended in an attempt to put as much distance from the truth as possible.

It was a sunny afternoon as Sam and Claire took the wagon and headed for Newport. She could barely contain her excitement, chatting brightly, any trauma of the previous day temporarily suspended. In contrast, Sam had to pretend, forcing himself to conceal the turmoil within. Whatever happiness the prospect of a guide dog represented, he faced breaking the most important promises he had made to Claire. He could try to hide behind that it was the only decent thing to do for Rachel, that the situation had been forced on him by her ultimatum. Did that change the responsibility for his actions? Whatever happened to Claire in the days that would follow, would it result with him blaming Rachel for forcing his hand, and poison what remained of their relationship? He felt miserable. He just wanted the whole thing to be over. If Claire noticed that he seemed withdrawn, she didn't show it and he realised he was about to destroy one of the few things that brought light into his troubled world. And for what purpose? The situation was impossible. By the time he had gathered the courage to speak, they were already in Newport and it was too late. No, it would be better to tell Claire after she had met her dog; at least then there would be something precious left for her to hold on to.

Sam dropped her at the house in which Alice's mother was staying to be close to her daughter in hospital. "I'll be back in a couple of hours," he said softly as he left her, knowing it was the last time they would part in trust and happiness.

He left the wagon at the warehouse. They had requested extra seed and whatever fertilizer could be spared, and he asked for it to be loaded while he met with Albert Jamieson.

The sad fallout since his quarrel with Rachel was that it had consumed all his emotional energy, leaving neither time nor space to consider what Albert might want to discuss. In the leather satchel he had found, Sam carried the report he had prepared, detailing the events in Weymouth. He intended to ask Mary to type and distribute it to the forum before their next meeting. For some inexplicable reason he hesitated to approach her, remembering the handwritten letter which Albert had given him to take Weymouth. The call to meet him made it more likely that Albert wanted to read and discuss the implications before it was circulated to the committee members, especially Rigby, whose silence since Weymouth spoke more than words. Perhaps it was best that even Mary did not have sight of his report until Albert had decided what action to be taken.

Mary led him into Albert Jamieson's office. The chairman was sitting with his back to the room, staring out of an imposing set of French doors that fronted a large windowed bay looking out over a panorama of the island. Mary bent and gently spoke in his ear.

"Councillor Morten is here, Mr Chairman."

With a momentary look of confused surprise, Albert slowly turned in his chair. Quickly gathering himself, he thanked Mary, requested a tray of tea and waited until she had left before speaking.

"Thank you for coming at this difficult time, Sam. Please come and sit with me in the window."

Two winged chairs had been positioned either side of the bay window, a small table between them.

"How is your foot?" Albert asked with genuine concern, making small talk until Mary returned.

"It's only a flesh wound; it will heal." Sam tried to sound dismissive.

Albert nodded and sat thoughtfully for almost a minute before speaking again.

"I called a full meeting of the forum this morning. I'm sorry not to include you but …" He gestured towards Sam's foot. "I knew you would agree anyway. We've placed the island in a state of emergency."

The door opened and Mary interrupted them as she entered with a tray. "Shall I pour?" she hovered.

"No, thank you, Mary."

"Do you need me to stay and take notes?" Her eyes looked in Sam's direction without appearing to see him, focusing somewhere far beyond.

"That won't be necessary, Mary."

Albert's tone was quiet but firm, and Mary left quickly, leaving Sam puzzled by a sensation, almost like a passing breeze, though he couldn't put his finger on what it was.

"A state of emergency?" Sam looked deliberately at the satchel on his lap. "With what I have discovered in here, that sounds not a moment too soon."

Normally perceptive, Albert didn't respond to his words. Sam was accustomed to his mentor looking strained and unwell, but today was different. The pallor of his skin seemed to have gone and there was light again in his eyes, and the shaking of his hands seemed to have eased as he poured amber coloured liquid from a pot into the cups. Albert handed a cup to Sam.

"There is something else we must discuss," he said.

'Ah,' thought Sam, 'this is the business concerning Teri and Ryan'. Out loud he said, "I'm sorry, I didn't hear that Teri and Ryan had been arrested until after I left for …"

"It's not that," Albert cut across Sam, uncharacteristically swatting the words away like an annoying fly. "There's something else I need to tell you."

Sam sat back in his chair, waiting, apprehensively. Albert drank his tea, moistened his lips and gathered his words.

"I've called another full forum meeting for tomorrow evening. It is imperative that you attend." He paused.

Sam sat and waited, puzzled that two forum meetings should be needed in such quick succession.

"At tomorrow's forum," Albert paused, "I will resign as chairman, with immediate effect." He sat back, allowing Sam to absorb the implications of his statement. Then he continued.

"It is my intention to nominate you as my replacement, for the immediate duration of the state of emergency or until such times as an election can be held. In a time of crisis, the chairman is required to nominate his replacement in case something happens to him. The responsibilities of this office must continue, seamlessly, for reasons of island security."

He held a plain white envelope in his hand, addressed to the forum, in his distinctive handwriting. With what was written on a sheet of paper inside the envelope lay the future of their island. His eyes looked directly into Sam's, his words without emotion, spoken with firm authority.

"In accordance with the rules laid down by the forum, this letter will appoint you as chairman. Only you know of my decision at this time and I must ask for your decision to my proposal no later than tomorrow morning."

Sam spent the next hour using every argument he could think of to try to persuade Albert Jamieson to change his mind. Albert countered every impassioned point Sam put forward until eventually, as they both tired of talking, Sam played his final card.

"Why not appoint someone who actually wants the job, because, be certain of one thing, I don't."

"It's partly for that very reason that I want you to take it. We both know that Rigby is desperate to step into my shoes. He has many excellent qualities, but leader of our community isn't one of them. I guarantee he would bring disaster upon us all, and you must think the same if you're absolutely honest. I know you don't want the job; that's part of what makes you most suitable and why the majority of forum members would want you as their leader. They would be fearful of what Rigby would try to do if he became chairman."

Albert paused. He seemed to be struggling for breath and Sam noted the strained tiredness had returned to his face.

"There are enormous problems facing us, Sam. Things might have been difficult up to now, but it's nothing compared with what I fear lies ahead."

For a moment, he seemed to be swamped by his emotions. He gathered himself.

"Sam, I'm no longer able to face the mounting challenges, my judgement is being called into question, by me as much as anyone, and rightly so. I must stand aside for someone younger and more able. I need you, we all need you, to take the chairman's role in my place. It's what the majority of the forum would vote for when they are asked." He hesitated for a moment before continuing his impassioned plea.

"Make the right decision, Sam. Save something from this situation before it overwhelms us."

Shocked, Sam still tried a final counter argument.

"But the referendum? Surely that's our solution; a positive vote offers the answer. If we leave with the New Zealanders, it's the best way to resolve the most pressing of our problems," he said, suddenly energised.

Albert regarded him with sad tired eyes.

"Do you really think our nemesis across the Solent will allow us that much time? The spy here will have already told them of our plans and intentions. They will know Napier and his crew have left and when they're most likely to return. Do you think they're just going to sit back and allow us to play our little democratic games? They want the island and its resources, that is beyond doubt, but they also want to enslave our people to run the island for them. I've seen it all before and it's what they've done everywhere on the mainland. They're not planning to let us run away and spoil their plans. The end game is approaching rapidly, Sam. We must have the right person to lead us when it arrives."

It was over. After five years of unstinting service, nothing would alter Albert Jamieson's intentions. He ushered Sam out of his office through the French doors, suggesting that he might enjoy the gardens in the evening sunlight as he left. As Sam stepped through the open door, Albert took his hand and held it for a long time, looking him directly in the eye as he did so.

"Make your decision, councillor Morten." Sam was surprised by the use of his formal title. "Whatever you choose, it will be the right one."

With that, Albert turned and closed and locked the doors.

## THIRTY-SIX

Sam found Claire, sitting cross-legged on a stone wall, plaiting a coloured ribbon around a leather collar. He had taken longer than he had expected. A call on Doctor Morgan to have has foot examined had delayed him.

"Have you seen Albert Jamieson recently?" the doctor had asked, prising the dressing dried with blood from the wound. Sam yelped. "I take it that's sore," the doctor muttered. "That's a good sign."

"So everyone keeps telling me," grumbled Sam. "I met with Albert before I came here."

"How did you find him?"

"I thought he looked better than he has been for a while," he answered tentatively.

Doctor Morgan examined his wound, carefully cleaning away the blood before soaking it in iodine.

"What I wouldn't give for antibiotics," he mused. "I hear our friends in New Zealand have got a lab making a basic range of them," he said, throwing the comment casually into the tableau of reasons for a positive outcome of the referendum. "Albert Jamieson worries me. I thought his problems were because of work and strain, but I suspect there's more to it than that." The doctor seemed to be talking to himself, re-dressing Sam's wound as he spoke. "I can't seem to put my finger on what's wrong." He tied the bandage tightly around Sam's foot and pinned it in place. "There, that should be okay; keep an eye on it and try to keep off it as much as possible. The bullet probably broke the bone, but I can't be certain without an x-ray." He tapped Sam's shoulder. "And you're not hurt badly enough to use up one of our precious x-ray plates."

"So I guess your dog's female," Sam said, noting the pink ribbon between Claire's fingers.

She beamed a smile in answer.

"Yes, a retriever. She's three weeks old and so gorgeous. Grace, Alice's mother, says she can come and live with me in a few weeks or so. Her guide dog training can't start for some time, but it will be wonderful to have her with me so soon."

Sam twitched the reigns, setting the loaded wagon on the road back to the farm. For a moment, the lightness of their conversation lifted the feeling of dread in the pit of his stomach, allowing him to imagine a time in which all he and Claire ever spoke of were bright ordinary things of everyday life, a place that was difficult to imagine for any of them any longer. As the wagon creaked through the lanes, Sam tried to shape the words that he feared would shatter the bond of their friendship forever. Claire chatted on, seemingly without a care in the world. For the first time, Sam found it impossible to focus on the sound of her voice. His mind spiralled, rudderless, between Claire, his duty to Rachel, and the answer he must give to Albert Jamieson before next morning. Anguish was squeezing the very life out of him from demands that wouldn't wait for answers.

For a while the sun shone as they wound through the streets of Newport; the island had the appearance of a normal spring day. Once clear of the town, the horse ambled slowly along quiet lanes where nature was striving to repair itself from the storm damage. Claire stopped her light chatter; Sam almost hadn't noticed. Perhaps she had become aware that he was distracted and was listening to the silence.

"I think I can smell rain," she said. When he didn't respond, she added, "a penny for your thoughts?"

Sam sighed. "Albert Jamieson isn't well. I guess I'm worried about him, that's all," he said, covering up the truth.

Claire nodded, but he was aware that she probably sensed it was far from the only reason.

The rain clouds crept upon them unnoticed and all too soon, large fat drops arrived as she had predicted. They hadn't brought coats, expecting the balmy spring weather to last through the week. The rain fell like rods, vertical, wet and soaking. Searching in the wagon, Sam found a plastic sheet but it was not quite large enough to cover them both and as they passed a side track, Sam saw a broad ash tree with a leaf cover that had miraculously survived the gales and snow. He led the horse down the track, drawing to a halt beneath the tree.

"The rain looks set for some time. We'd better stop and shelter," he said, easing his aching foot carefully from his seat and tethering the horse.

He held out a hand to help Claire climb down. "We could shelter beneath the wagon with the tarpaulin over us and the supplies."

The wagon had large spoked wheels intended for the rough ground of the farm, so there was enough height beneath the main trailer to sit on the plastic sheet and be protected from the downpour above. With a light-hearted laugh, Claire fumbled her way beneath the wagon, searching with her hands for a spot to sit down.

"This feels like fun," she said over the drumming of the rain above them.

Her dress was already soaked through, so Sam removed his jacket and draped it over her shoulders.

"Thank you, kind sir," she said, a gentle reminder to a bygone age.

He felt the bottom fall out of his stomach. This was going to be far worse than he had ever imagined. He sat silent for some while, just listening to the rain, lost for words.

"Claire."

Eventually he found the courage, his voice tight with sorrow and emotion. "There's something I've got to tell you."

"Yes."

For the first time, her voice sounded hesitant. Did she suspect something? He knew she would react stoically to what he was about to tell her, which made the whole wretched situation even worse. His mouth was dry, the words he had planned so carefully lost somewhere in the deluge around them. Despite her soaked clothing he could feel her warmth, a glow that radiated from her body whenever he was close to her. He tried to move away but it was as if some force of magnetism kept him rooted to the spot.

"It's just … I can't …"

Claire waited patiently, then asked softly, "Can't? Can't what?"

"I can't go on like this. It's impossible … to continue like this."

His words came in a flood and seemed to suck the very energy from the air around them. Her face was turned towards him, only inches from his; her expression, just visible in the shadows, questioned and searched in the darkness.

"It's hopeless," he said forlornly, now finding anger at their situation, suddenly shocked as heart and head fought one another.

"I just … I love you; more than life itself." The truth burst from him, unexpected, without control.

"I've loved you from the first time I saw you and held you in Dartmouth."

He paused, shocked by his outburst. This wasn't what he had planned to say, what he had rehearsed, what he must tell her. Something beyond his control had taken over and he felt powerless in its grasp.

"Part of me refused to believe it. I convinced myself that once the drama of our escape was over, sense would prevail," he laughed weakly. "But instead, it just gets worse, every hour, every day, like a fire that won't be extinguished," he said feeling wretched.

"I'm sorry, you must think I'm stupid, that I'm behaving ridiculously. I'm years older than you and should know better. I'm probably embarrassing both of us, making an impossible situation even worse." The words cascaded from his lips in a torrent that wouldn't be stemmed.

"I feel utterly wretched. For you, for Rachel, the children, even myself. But it's hopeless. I love you beyond anything I've ever known. That's all there is to it."

He finally fell silent, conscious that tears were streaming down his face, that emotional truth had finally taken over and said what had lain hidden all along and wouldn't be denied.

Claire leaned over and stroked his face, her thumb gently rubbing away his tears, while her fingers sought his mouth, exploring his lips. She said nothing; what was there to say; she just leaned gently towards him, her lips searching for his, and kissed him. Around them the world disappeared, cocooning them in a veil of rain and soft sound. Slowly, as she kissed him, Claire unbuttoned the front of her wet dress. He was vaguely aware of her body beneath, her skin pale and freckled, soaked almost translucent.

"I know," she whispered. "I've known all along."

It was everything. All that could, or needed to be, had been said. In its space, love took control, and changed their lives forever.

Sam woke, surprised he had slept, thinking what had gone before had been no more than a dream. Lying naked in Claire's arms dispelled that temporary illusion. He moved his shoulder and woke her in the process. They were entwined together on his jacket with only their wet clothes around them. It had stopped raining, the fresh silence broken by the sound of dripping water onto the tarpaulin from the leaves above them.

"Hello," she said playfully, yawning, sensing he was exploring her body with his eyes. "And what do we do now?" The question seemed to be asked without much expectation of an answer.

Sam leant on an elbow, hesitating while he enjoyed her nakedness. They had crossed a line, as lovers will. Now there was no going back.

"I've no idea. I've never been in this situation before," he said with a mere hint of mischief. He kissed her, gently, as if to remind them both that this really was happening, and fell onto his back beside Claire.

"It will be impossible to conceal this. We'll have to tell the truth and let the others decide. We'll almost certainly have to find somewhere else to live, it's Rachel's home and for that reason I'd prefer to do the right thing."

"Where shall we go?"

"Well, Newport, to begin with. It will be more convenient for the forum; that takes up a lot of my time anyway. Newport would be good for you too so that you can be with your guide dog and start training."

Sam looked at his watch. It was already late afternoon; they had stopped beneath the ash tree for longer than he had thought. Their relationship, and its impact on Rachel and the rest of the farm, had to be resolved before he could even begin to word his reply which he knew would disappoint Albert Jamieson.

He found a nearby stream to wash in and helped Claire to dress, aware that these ordinary things were now about to become a part of his everyday life. The horse was hungry and seemed impatient to move on. Sam gave Claire his jacket and flicked the reigns, guiding the wagon back to the farm which had been his home before love intervened.

"No regrets?" she asked after a short while. "I'd quite understand if you have second thoughts."

Sam reached across and took her hand, squeezing it gently.

"Part of me is sad. We're going to affect so many lives, but I can't bear to be apart from you. Things will work out as they must, it's no longer in our control. But that's not the only reason I was silent."

Claire turned her face towards him in question.

"This afternoon, Chairman Jamieson asked me to consider something important that I don't want. I've got to decline and I hate disappointing him. Albert isn't a well man and I feel I'm going to let him down at a time of crisis, but there's no avoiding it."

"Would it help to talk about it?" Claire offered.

"Unfortunately, I can't. Not even with you. But, it's a decision for tomorrow, so let's get to the farm and face the music there first."

Dusk had begun to gather as they approached the farm, riding on the wagon hand in hand. The smoke from the farmhouse chimneys rose above the trees; a melancholic reminder that this was once their home. As Sam steered the horse into the track leading into the farmyard he noticed a vehicle parked directly in front of the house. At first he thought it was from the Robinson's farm; perhaps Rachel had borrowed it to return before dark. But as they got nearer, he could see that it was an unusually smart green Landrover, similar to the one kept for the official use of the forum chairman. Sam frowned, puzzled. He had only seen Albert Jamieson a few hours earlier and wasn't expected to give him an answer until the next morning. So what on earth could have arisen to bring Albert to the farm so soon?

Everything in the house seemed normal when they entered. Marcus was laughing about something one of the children had said and turned when he saw Sam and Claire enter.

"You have visitors," he said. "I've asked them to wait in the lounge. Two men and a woman; they said it was forum business. It's the quietest place in the house at the moment," he said, and as if to underscore the point a line of excited children raced past, chasing one another.

Puzzled, Sam turned and headed towards the lounge, brushing Claire with his hand for reassurance as he went. "Just give me a few minutes to get this sorted out." He left her, feeling a pang of misgiving that something had so soon intruded between them.

Sam found a log fire burning in the hearth as he entered, dancing shadows around the room. Two conspicuously armed men who he didn't recognise stood with their backs to the flames, warming themselves. Chris Woods rose up out of a chair, and turning towards Sam revealed a serious face, her eyes red and wet with tears.

"Chris?"

Sam shot a glance at the two men, neither of whom introduced themselves.

Chris cleared her throat. She didn't smile.

"What's the matter?" he asked, unnerved.

"Sam," she paused and took a breath, glancing at the taller of the two men who nodded. Chris continued.

"It is my sad duty to have to tell you that our chairman, Albert Jamieson, was found dead in his office three hours ago." Chris checked her watch, "at approximately four o'clock this afternoon. It's thought that it's from heart failure. Doctor Morgan will need to conduct a post mortem to be sure."

Chris opened the leather bag she carried across her shoulder and withdrew a white envelope, identical to the one Sam had seen only a few hours earlier, now with the seal broken, signatures and times written across the opened flap.

"This has been authenticated as the constitutional will of Chairman Albert Jamieson, written as required when a state of emergency exists on the island. In his will, he has named, in the event of his untimely death, his immediate successor, until such times as a leadership election can be organised."

Chris paused and handed the envelope to Sam. He withdrew the single sheet of paper and scanned the distinctive copperplate handwriting in shocked silence. Albert was dead. It wasn't possible. They had only been together a few hours earlier and Sam had thought how well he had looked, much better than in recent times.

"I can't believe it," he finally said. "I can't ..."

Chris cut across him. "As of four-thirty this afternoon, it was agreed by an emergency quorum of the committee that in accordance with Chairman Jamieson's instructions, you, Sam Morten, are to be formally sworn in as chairman this evening. These two men are now your bodyguards and you are requested to accompany them as soon as possible. Please collect your personal things as quickly as you can. I'm afraid a lack of time and pressing events won't even allow us to grieve. Something urgent has arisen. Your presence is needed in Newport immediately."

Rachel entered the bedroom as Sam threw a change of clothes and a few personal things hastily into a bag.

"What's happening?" she asked in a flat tone of voice.

"Albert Jamieson has died. It was sudden, unexpected, shortly after I left him this afternoon."

"Actually, I meant about us."

Sam had his back to her as he zipped the bag closed.

"My friend, Albert Jamieson, has just died," he repeated, slowly turning to face her. "Against my wishes, the role of chairman is to be passed on to me." He felt angered by her seeming lack of compassion and only just managed to suppress it. "Something has arisen and I'm needed immediately."

Rachel had a hard look on her face. There was a time when they could have shared this moment, halving the burdens to come. But no longer.

"And Claire? When is she leaving?"

"Tomorrow," Sam said abruptly and reached for his rucksack. "I'll arrange for Lorna to bring her to Newport. For the foreseeable future I'll have to stay there to run the forum." He paused to gather himself. "Claire will come and live with me."

"So you're leaving me and the children, abandoning the farm and everyone here for that slip of a girl."

"The farm's yours. It's your home; you've pretty much been running it these past few months without me and you've still got Jake and Marcus to assist you. I'll help whenever I can, but until the state of emergency is over, you won't see very much of me."

"I don't believe what I'm hearing. What about me, the children, the farm and the rest of us?"

For a moment, a hostile silence descended between them, each feeling angry with the other. Pressed from so many sides, all Sam could do was turn away, needing urgently to leave, but desperate to reach an understanding with Rachel that the sands of time seemed determined to prevent.

"So, you still don't have the courage to admit the truth." Rachel threw the barb at his back. "Cowardice won't sit well on the shoulders of our newly appointed leader," she added provocatively.

Sam paused, staring at the wall. "Don't make me say something that will only hurt us both."

"The truth wouldn't be as bad as your pathetic denials all the time."

He turned, frowning. "I've fathered children with other women; it's part of my civic duty as a man to try to keep our community alive. You never complained before," he shouted back, exasperated.

"That was different. You were never in love with any of those women. What you did was pure biological necessity."

"That sounds strange. I thought we all agreed to call it free love, a re-structure of society in order to survive."

"Free sex," Rachel corrected. "Love is different. I thought you always loved me; just me. Now I know you love her more. You just won't admit it."

They were interrupted by a knock on the door. Lorna's uncertain voice interrupting them, "Sam, they're waiting. They say you have to leave now, immediately."

Sam looked at Rachel with sadness, a look filled with the history of years, and shrugged his shoulders.

"Honestly, what more can I say. I'll take Claire to live with me in Newport, out of your sight. Please stay here in your home on the farm, with the children, where you belong. I'll try to do my best for you all."

He grabbed his bags and moved past her.

"Don't expect me to wait for you to come back."

The pain in her words struck him like a knife. He hesitated, his hand on the door latch.

"Maybe you're right about one thing, Rachel. I am a coward. But I love Claire, and I need her beside me to get through a task that I've never sought and may yet end in failure. For all of us."

He left with Rachel's eyes burning in anger at his back.

It was the fastest journey Sam had ever made to Newport. Chris drove, handling the Landrover with the same accomplished ease with which she flew the Cessna. One of the bodyguards sat in the front beside her, the other shared the back seat with Sam. From now on, these two would be a constant shadow in his life.

The lights burned in the forum building as they arrived, accompanied by a subdued hum of activity. Sam was escorted to the chairman's office where only a few hours earlier he had taken tea with Albert Jamieson. A dozen forum members had assembled. The chairman's ring, with its embossed gold seal, lay on a piece of purple velvet on Albert Jamieson's desk. Sam paused to collect himself; it was now his desk.

The formalities were over quickly and passed in a blur, Sam reciting the chairman's oath of office as the ring was placed on his finger. Lost for words, he gazed at it, aware that only a few hours earlier, his friend's hand had warmed this very same gold band. Those present took turns to grip his hand in congratulation. Only Rigby stood apart, distant and silent. After only a few minutes, Chris and Aiden interrupted the proceedings.

"We need you to come straight away, Mr Chairman." The words sounded odd; it would take a while to get used to his new title. "There's someone you need to meet."

As everyone made way for Sam to leave he paused.

"Can you give me five minutes?" he asked.

Aiden looked at his watch and nodded reluctantly and ushered everyone out of the room.

"Connor, would you stay behind please," Sam asked.

With everyone gone, Sam closed the door and moved round to stand in front of the French doors where he had bid goodbye to his friend, not knowing it was for the last time. He turned and made eye contact with Rigby.

"I didn't seek this position, Connor."'

Rigby shrugged. "Why accept it then?"

"To stop you from doing so," Sam said bluntly, without smiling.

His abrupt words surprised Rigby, the shock clear upon his face.

Sam opened the leather satchel, withdrew the maps and slid them across the desk towards Rigby.

"Ever seen these before?" The tone of accusation in his voice was unmistakeable. "I found it in this," he lifted the satchel for Rigby to see, "hanging around the neck of a man who tried to kill me in Weymouth. He would have done so if Ruth hadn't shot him. I'm beginning to wonder if you might know who he is?"

"If you're implying what I think, then you're mad, as well as a fool."

Sam withdrew the map.

"Mad I might be, a fool I'm not. Someone in this building is leaking all our plans to these people across the Solent, before we can even implement them." He stared at Rigby. "You won't be surprised to know that I'm deeply troubled who that person might be."

"If you're pointing a finger at me, well, that's preposterous, an outrageous slur and accusation. If I was the traitor, you," he pointed an index finger in contempt, "wouldn't be standing here now, I can tell you. Look somewhere else before you make your ludicrous accusations."

"Time will judge what's ludicrous," Sam said grimly. "Meanwhile, I want you to plan to mobilise every man and woman capable of firing a gun, and work out a strategy to repel an attack from across the Solent. You can use that map to plan your strategy. Do it immediately, with Aiden, and tell no one what you're doing. We don't have very much time. I'll need your answer by the morning at the latest."

Rigby stared at Sam with smouldering hostility.

"And if it's you who is betraying us, don't bother telling your friends across the Solent. They know already," Sam said, leaving the room without waiting for a reply.

Sam was led to the secure room in which David Longmarsh had been held and questioned. It had no windows or doors to access the outside, and he noticed a new security lock and spyhole had been fitted. Now, one of Aiden's squad sat guarding the door. Sam raised an eyebrow. Flipping the cover to the spyhole, Aiden peered inside and seemed for a moment to have difficulty finding whoever was inside.

"Ah, there, I see you." Aiden leaned away. "The only thing he has said since we found him washed up this afternoon is your name, the same name written on the crude map pinned to his chest. His behaviour is erratically aggressive and we suspect there could be a knife hidden somewhere. I can't see how it's possible he could know of you, but can you take a look yourself; he's in the far left corner, squatting on the floor."

It took a moment to focus through the tiny spyhole. Sam blinked several times; the first to clear his vision, the second in complete astonishment. In the corner was a figure that looked more spider-like than human, clad in filthy rags. Sam watched as a leg, bare-footed, stretched out, toes flexing like grasping fingers, a wasted dirty face, small, even for a child, rotated from side to side, the gaze fixed on the door.

"It can't be possible." Sam stepped back from the door, astonished. "Get me a plate of biscuits, bread, anything we have." Aiden and Chris exchanged a look of alarm. "Immediately, please. And get ready to unlock the door and let me in."

It seemed unbelievable. Sam was looking at the same feral boy he had left behind in Dartmouth several weeks before.

# THIRTY-SEVEN

It felt like entering the cage of a wild animal; one armed with a knife. The door closed behind Sam, the metallic click of its lock echoed around the room. When he had first met the boy in Dartmouth, there had been space around them, space to run if things had turned nasty. Now he was enclosed by the claustrophobic presence of four walls which concentrated the smell of his emaciated unwashed body.

Sam walked slowly to the middle of the room and stooped to place the plate of food on the floor where the boy could see it. He back-stepped to the door and squatted down, not daring to take his eyes from the boy for an instant, clearly remembering how fast he could move when he chose to.

"So, we meet again," Sam said, more to himself, adding, "how on earth did you get here?"

The boy seemed not to have heard him, twisting his head at unnatural angles as he scrutinised Sam and the food simultaneously. His eyes stared, unblinking, their whiteness dazzling in a weather-beaten face blackened by the grime of unwashed years.

"I'm Sam, do you remember," he said pointing to himself. "Sam." He reversed his finger. "You are?"

The boy didn't reply, but instead extended his folded limbs languidly towards the bait laid out to tempt him. The contents disappeared in a flash, almost before Sam had seen any movement. He could see the crude map he had left for the boy now pinned to the rags on his chest. Somehow, he doubted the boy could have done that himself, which implied someone must have done it for him? Through the creased and weather worn paper, Sam thought he could see something written on the back. Seeing was one thing, persuading the boy to let him remove it was another matter entirely.

Behind Sam, the door slowly opened and another plate of food slid into the room. He heard Chris's voice in subdued tones.

"John needs to talk to you. He says it's urgent."

Sam pushed the door shut. Everything was becoming urgent, but things would have to wait their turn. The boy was still watching him intently, finishing the food on the first plate; at the same time his eyes jumped between Sam and the second plate beside him. Sam realised he had his attention, something the boy wanted. Could they negotiate for the map on his chest? Sam began the process once more.

"I'm Sam." He said it twice, before pointing again at the boy. "You are? What's your name?"

The boy kept staring at the plate of food, but his mouth had begun to shape silent words. Pointing, he said, "Sam." He repeated the word, as though weighing it, measuring a long-used sound. Slowly, his finger reversed to point to himself. He hesitated for a moment.

"Stupid arsehole."

"What?"

The boy jabbed himself with his finger. "Stupid arsehole."

Encouraged when Sam burst out laughing, the boy repeated the obscenity many times over, his voice rising excitedly, until Sam interrupted him with raised palms.

"Stop, stop." He wiped the tears of laughter from his eyes.

"We're going to have to find something better for you than that. For the moment let's call you Tom."

He studied the boy's face more clearly. The bruises and split lip explained that he might have received such a derogatory name from someone who had given him a beating in the process. Sam pointed at him once again.

"Tom, your name will be Tom."

The boy looked thoughtful, though most of his attention was fixed on the new plate of food beside Sam.

"Tom. Are you hungry?" he held up the plate in his direction.

The boy looked at the plate with covetous eyes.

"Okay, it's yours, it's for you. But I need something from you." Sam unsheathed his knife. "This is my knife."

He held it out for the boy to see, while with his other hand he knocked on the door behind him. It opened and, with great deliberation, Sam handed the knife to Chris's outstretched hand.

"Now, can we do the same with your knife?"

He held out the plate with one hand, the other an outstretched palm for the knife. The boy looked uncertain while Sam remained squatting, patiently waiting, offering the plate and then slowly drawing it back, leaving his extended palm slightly forward.

"You're perfectly safe here; I need your knife."

Slowly, a hand reached inside the rags and produced a slim knife. With his eyes fixed on Sam, the boy held it out to him, his spare hand reaching for the plate. And so an exchange was made. The boy ate with the same animalistic intensity while Sam passed the lethal knife out to Chris.

"John really needs to see you, Sam."

"Two minutes; just one more thing I need."

He searched his pockets. When the boy had eaten the food, Sam held out his palm again. On it lay his compass, with its silver spinning needle. He handed it to Tom.

"You can have it," he said, laying the compass into the boy's hand and closing his fingers around it. "But I need this." He pointed towards the map pinned to his chest.

For a moment the boy appeared confused, looking instead at the second empty plate. Sam nodded and grinned.

"More food, Chris. Quick as you can."

Slowly, he moved closer to the boy. The smell was overpowering; they were going to have to do something about that. As another plate of food arrived at the door, Sam slowly released the pins that held the map to the boy's rags. While Tom consumed the third plate of food, he pressed out the folds and creases of the now much faded paper. Had this boy really found his way to them with just his crude hand-drawn map? He saw his name, scrawled on the front of the paper, and turned it over.

*Morten. Hurst Castle. 9.00am Thursday morning. Be there; alone.*

For a moment Sam thought he recognised the handwriting.

"You're just imagining things," he muttered to himself.

Still sitting on his haunches, staring at the map, Sam looked for clues. The future that Albert Jamieson had predicted was fast becoming reality. Inescapably, fate had rolled her dice once again and it had fallen to him to be the one to pick up the consequences.


John fell in step with Sam as they walked back to his office.

"So, there's less warning than last time; the attack is scheduled for tonight."

Sam nodded. "They seem to be fond of Newtown Bay."

"Marshes are ideal with a flat bottomed craft. The actual landing point could be anywhere, they can pick any number of places and change them at the last moment."

Despite the lateness of the day, Mary was still at her desk. Conscientious to a fault, she wouldn't go home until she had prepared the paperwork and briefing notes for the new chairman. Sam politely interrupted her.

"Could you send messages to Aiden, Dave Bartlett and Craig, and ask them to meet at my office within the next half-hour."

Mary made notes and disappeared.

"I know Bartlett's unwell, but I want his opinion to support Aiden," Sam said to John, his lips pursed in thought. "Meanwhile, have a look at this."

He handed John the folded map he had taken from Tom. John exhaled through the gap in his front teeth.

"Only gives you two days to prepare. You can't go alone, it could be another trap. What do you think they want to meet about?"

"I couldn't begin to guess, but I doubt it's to say sorry for attacking us. I need to ask Tom some questions and we need to find out how he got here, who he has seen, and who wrote the message he carried to us."

Sam was silent for a few moments, thinking.

"How long would it take to set things up to make contact with *The Aotearoa*?" he asked.

John sounded surprised. "It needs the equipment Napier left us. I'd need to fill and launch the helium balloon to tow the aerial to the correct height and some time to start the generator and warm up the VHF radio; say, two, three hours. It's the first time I'd be doing it but I'd probably get quicker if I do it often enough."

"Could you do it in the dark? Alone."

"Alone?" John scratched his head. "Well, it should be possible. When are you thinking of?"

Sam looked out of the windows at the darkness.

"Before daylight tomorrow morning. Do you think you can set it up? You must tell absolutely no one what you're doing, even forum members. If anyone asks, just say it's a weather balloon or something like that."

Perplexed, John departed in a hurry. He had barely six hours until dawn.

Sam smelt cigarette smoke and heard a hard hacking cough as Dave Bartlett entered the room. He was the first to arrive, smoking a roll-up despite, or perhaps because, of his prognosis.

Dave looked much thinner, his skin jaundice yellow. Sam was pleased to see him, though saddened by his appearance.

"Take a seat," he offered.

Bartlett shook his head and joined Sam at the French doors.

"I hear condolences and congratulations are due in equal measure," he paused, a racking cough again shaking his body. "We're going to miss Albert Jamieson. He'll be a tough act to follow."

Sam wasn't sure if that meant Dave thought he wasn't up to the job, but let it pass and decided to take advantage of a few minutes they had alone together.

"I've asked Rigby for a plan to mobilise the island," he said. "How many squads do you think we can put together?"

Dave drew on his cigarette, silently calculating.

"Assuming you can call on about two hundred sighted men and women, that's fifty squads maximum. Leadership would be your problem, so that reduces to, say, forty, more than likely thirty to be effective. Why?"

"I think we must expect a visit from across the Solent," Sam said wistfully.

A few pinpricks of light appeared in the distance, otherwise all was in darkness.

"Given what you know of the quality of training for our people, what are the odds if we're outnumbered?"

Dave shrugged. "Hard to say. It depends on many factors," he said, breathlessly. "If you're defending you have the advantage, but anything more than two to one and you're going to be in trouble."

"Beyond that?"

"Try bluffing and negotiating," Bartlett said, cigarette in mouth.

"And if that doesn't work?"

Dave shook his head. "Surrender. You might at least be left with something."

Sam was silent, searching beyond the windows for a better answer. They might indeed be left with something, but he doubted it would be anything that any of them could live with. He thanked Dave as the door opened and the others began to arrive. As he turned to greet them, he realised he had forgotten to ask Dave how he was feeling, though given his appearance he probably didn't need to ask.

Clearing away the maps and paperwork after everyone had left Sam was shocked to realise how quickly his role had changed. Instead of his usual hands-on involvement, all he could now do was stand back and watch things develop in the hands of others. In the short space of thirty minutes, Sam had been able to insist on a stealthy approach to the approaching night, sealing off the only roads out of Newtown Bay and awaiting those transporting the boar to become entrapped in one of their many road blocks. There were only a few routes out of the marshy creeks and channels, so with luck their plan should work this time. They definitely needed a success after the near disaster of Weymouth.

Chris left to get her Cessna airborne, leaving Jaki, John's assistant radio operator, in charge of communications. Craig agreed to direct the land operation, with Bartlett and Aiden in charge of the six squads they had selected to use. *Lupin* couldn't be used; her bow was still under repair, which left her unseaworthy. But with the Cessna flying, Chris and her co-pilot could provide the best opportunity to sight any vessels crossing the Solent.

Sam felt more confident; he had placed a brake on the operation and all he had to do was wait for things to develop. He treated himself to a small whisky, deciding he would wait half an hour and then visit the radio room to check on progress.

It took less than thirty minutes for things to start going wrong. Sam was climbing into the Landrover when lights raced into the car park, tyres scattering gravel as a car skidded to a halt. Chris jumped out, leaving the engine running.

"Someone has sabotaged our planes," she shouted. "There's sugar in the fuel tanks. Neither Cessna is going anywhere anytime soon," she added furiously.

"Is there anything else at the airfield you can fly?" Sam asked, checking his watch. High tide was still an hour away.

Chris shook her head. "Nothing we can use in the dark. We've put all our resources into keeping those two airworthy," her voice rising. "Bastards. It'll take days to strip down the engines and sort this mess out."

Sam placed a steadying hand on her arm. "We'll just have to manage without you. We still have surprise on our side, and Aiden and Dave Bartlett are on the ground in the area with their squads."

They were both silent for a moment, then Chris spoke for them both.

"I'm really worried. This is too much of a coincidence. What if someone has guessed, or knows, that we've been pre-warned? It wouldn't take much to change their plans, and without 'eyes in the sky' they could move their landing to anywhere on the coast and we'd be none the wiser."

Sam felt a feeling of emptiness form in the pit of his stomach that went beyond a misplaced operation. If their plans went awry it would be yet another setback. He tried to remember all that had been said at their briefing meeting just a short time before. A misplaced plan was problem enough but David Longmarsh's fate was something he really didn't want to think about.

"When did you last run the planes' engines?" he asked.

"What? This afternoon, a normal routine in preparation for a flight; we do it every day. There's nothing out of the ordinary in doing that. They were both fine then," she said in exasperation.

The reality of the situation suddenly dawned on him.

"Get back to the airfield. I'll meet you in the radio room shortly." He jumped into the Landrover.

"Get me John Evans in the radio room, quickly," he growled to both of his bodyguards.

If his fears were correct, he had to find John immediately and tell him to send a warning message to David Longmarsh in the hope that it wasn't already too late.

Filled with anxieties about the ongoing operation, Sam sat in the radio room while John tapped out a coded morse message of warning.

"Do you think it will be in time?" John said, his Welsh accent accentuated again.

Sam sighed. "If whoever tipped them off is close enough to our decision making to warn them that we know of tonight's operation, it's a logical guess that we must have someone working for us on their side of the Solent. Hauling in Longmarsh in for questioning will be their next step and something tells me that won't be just for a friendly chat."

He gazed at the wall of illuminated dials and switches. They had done the best they could. They just had to hope that Longmarsh received their warning in time.

Almost a mile above them, a helium balloon danced in the cold air, its anchor cable attached to the winch on the front of the Landrover. If anyone asked, they would say it was a weather experiment, part of the aftermath of the great storm. In the back of the Landrover, Sam and John sat hunched around a radio set, their faces ghostly in the green light from the dials. John had found a way to power the VHF set from the Landrover's electrical system, and with the engine running to power the radio they gained some warmth against the chill of the spring night. Occasionally, the Landrover rocked like a cradle from the cable straining to hold the balloon, towing their ariel skywards. Patiently, John worked the dials, chasing the frequency he had been given by Napier for contact with *The Aotearoa*, far to their south in Gibraltar. So far, John had been calling for almost an hour without reply.

"Perhaps they're all asleep, though you'd think they'd keep a radio watch," he mused. "Napier said we could call at any time."

"Could they have changed the frequency?" Sam asked.

This was beginning to look like another disappointment on a night that had started so encouragingly.

"I could try the emergency frequency, but other, less friendly, ears might be listening," John replied.

Sam looked at his watch. He'd told Chris and Jaki where he would be and he had already been with John far longer than he had expected. It was again beginning to look as if every turn they made ran into an obstacle. He wasn't impetuous by nature, but time wasn't exactly an asset they had in abundance.

"Keep trying," he said. "Just make sure you allow enough time to bring the balloon down before daylight. This must be kept a secret, at least for the time being."

He didn't add, 'until we find the spy in our midst.' After all, there even remained the outside possibility that John was the person they sought. He dismissed the thought, aware he was becoming suspicious of everyone around him. Sam could only hope his coming meeting at Hurst Castle might give a clue to who the informant was.

For another half an hour they persevered, John calling the code name Napier had given them every five minutes. He received only the hiss of static in reply. Beyond the windscreen the eastern sky was growing noticeably paler by the minute. Dawn was approaching.

"Five minutes more," Sam said, resigned to failure.

John nodded, checked his frequency dial once more and called for the penultimate time.

"White Cloud calling Aotearoa." He repeated it several times, leaving the channel clear between calls, in hope of a reply. Silence was the only reward.

Sam sighed. "Better call it a night," he said in a flat voice. "Let's start to wind the balloon …"

"White Cloud? This is Shepherd. Are you receiving me?" A metallic voice suddenly blurted from the speaker above them.

Sam grabbed the microphone, a wave of relief sweeping over him as Napier's voice echoed in the confines of the Landrover.

"Hello Shepherd? It's a surprise to hear from you. Are you all okay? We've been trying to raise *The Aotearoa* on this frequency, but it sounds as if we've found you instead. How are things?"

"We have been better." Contradictorily, Napier's voice projected its usual bright optimism despite his words. "We're by Ramsgate and ran into problems. As far as we can see, the Channel is choked with huge quantities of debris; big stuff that would punch a hole in our hull if we ran into this size of wreckage. It seems to be washing down the Thames, probably as a result of the storm inland. We've seen huge fires to the west in that general direction towards the London dock areas, and a smoke column visible fifty miles away. I thought we could get through it, but it just seems to go on forever. We've been stuck here for several days already, so we're falling badly behind on our schedule. How are things with you?"

"Like you, things have been better. We've also run into a problem," Sam added, trying to sound matter of fact.

For a moment, static interference drowned out Napier's words. All they caught was "… turn back. We could get back to you in a couple days; if you'll have us, that is." He even managed a laugh.

"I'm not sure about that. I don't think the girls here have recovered from your last visit yet," Sam added jokingly, his spirits lifted by talking to Napier again. "More seriously, Kit, we've got a problem. I think we're going to need your help very soon."

As it turned out the conversation with Napier was the high spot of the night. Everyone returned in the daylight, the squad members complaining of the waste of a sleepless night. Their leaders just looked fed up and thoughtful. No one said very much in Sam's presence; even Bartlett kept his thoughts to himself. The news of the sabotage of their planes was evidence enough that things were deteriorating rapidly. Sam, John, Chris, Bartlett and Aiden convened in his office for a tired breakfast meeting.

"Well, there wasn't a sign of any lights. If anyone was in Newtown Bay last night they either slipped away across country or they're still hiding somewhere in the marshes," Aiden said through a tired yawn.

"Or it was a deception, deliberately fed to give us false information," Bartlett looked at Sam questioningly. "We've only got the word of your informant to go on."

Mary entered the room, carrying breakfast on a tray for them. She said little. Even she looked tired and drawn, having stayed late to provide the administrative back-up Sam needed in his new role as the chairman. She left them in silence as they helped themselves to the contents of her tray.

"Someone tipped them off," Chris said, reading everyone's thoughts. "It would explain the disabling of the planes, which must have happened only shortly before I went to the airfield to prepare for take-off."

"Or just coincidence," Bartlett said, as he walked over to the large wall map of the island which Sam was already studying.

"If they changed their plans at the last minute, where would they have chosen to dump their cargo of boar?" Sam was tracing the northern shoreline with an index finger. "I can't imagine they would haul the boar all the way back to the mainland even if there had to be a change of plan."

They all gathered around the map to consider the question, while eating and drinking.

"It would make sense to land them close to Newport; risky, but it's where they could do most damage," Craig suggested, jabbing a finger in the direction of Cowes at the river entrance. "They would have the tide in their favour for a few hours, so there was plenty of time to choose their ..."

Unannounced, the door burst open, interrupting him. Without waiting, Gloria strode into the room, making a direct path towards the French doors which she struck with the sole of her boot, and emptied the entire magazine from her Bren gun. As the deafening noise died away, Gloria's smiling face shone through the cordite smoke.

"Boar," she shouted exuberantly. "Right outside your windows if you thought to look," she chided. "The grounds are full of the bastards."

As they all rushed to find their own weapons, Sam heard Aiden's voice, with more than a note of irony.

"I guess that answers our question then."

# THIRTY-EIGHT

It became a drama that unfolded for most of the morning. Aiden had been spot on when he guessed that the alternative to Newtown Bay might be on their very doorstep. The fact that no one had thought of it sooner was almost a cause of disaster. By the time they realised what was happening, Newport was over-run with boar. Two had actually forced their way into the corridors of the clinic and they had to be destroyed in the corridors, filling rooms with the echo of gunfire and cordite smoke. It was a miracle that no one was killed, though two people received injuries that would take weeks to heal, prolonging the constant drain on their numbers.

By early afternoon they felt confident that most of the boar had been rounded up and destroyed. The timing of the attack wasn't lost on Sam and the others as they gathered wearily in his office again where, red-eyed and blackened by smoke, they slumped in an assortment of chairs that Mary had hastily provided.

"I can't see much point in a meeting at Hurst Castle," Craig announced angrily. "They attack us with boar one minute and then summon us for a cosy chat the next. People like that only understand one thing; and it comes in the form of a mailed fist, not a white flag."

Sam was standing with his back to them. He had called a forum meeting for later that afternoon in the hope of obtaining their agreement to his meeting at Hurst Castle. Despite the latest attack, they more than ever needed a clearer picture of what they were up against. That could only be achieved by going to the meeting and listening to what they had to say, even if it came in the form of a threat.

"If you go alone to this meeting I'll wager it's the last we'll ever see of you," Bartlett warned, a faint smile confirming his earlier offer to go in Sam's place.

"Time will tell on that count," Sam replied. "But I don't intend to go alone." He pretended not to notice the surprised look on their faces. "Meanwhile, as things have died down sufficiently, I suggest we all try to get some rest. It will no doubt hot up in the days ahead."

As they filed out, Sam asked Aiden and Chris to stay behind.

"Can you send our two helicopter pilots to see me as soon as possible?" he asked Chris.

She nodded, a furrowed brow posing a question.

Sam smiled. "Best not to ask."

As she left, he turned to Aiden.

"And can you ask Gloria to come and see me. I've got a job that requires her skills if you can spare her."

Gloria had just returned from her favourite sport, boar hunting, and arrived smelling strongly of cordite. As she entered, she gave the shattered lock on the French doors a sideways glance.

Sam grinned. "Just one point for the future, Gloria. Next time you want to open a door, would you mind unlocking it first, even if there is a boar on the other side," he said jokingly as he offered her a seat. "Whisky?"

Surprised, Gloria nodded, and Sam filled glasses for them.

"I never had chance to properly thank you for saving my life in Weymouth. Without you there would most probably be a different chairman sitting here right now." Sam sipped his drink; Gloria downed hers in one. "I've asked you here because I have another task for you, one you can refuse if you want to, though I would be more than grateful if you can accept it." He paused, watching her carefully. "I need someone to accompany me, as my bodyguard, to a meeting on the mainland. It will be with the men who ambushed us in Weymouth and who have now attacked us again in the heart of Newport."

If Gloria was surprised she hid it well. "Do I get to kill some of the bastards?" she asked, enthusiastically.

"I hope that won't be necessary. I was thinking more that your presence would scare the hell out of them," he said with sincerity. As Gloria was almost twice his size any man would think carefully before upsetting her.

"We need to attend the meeting tomorrow. Have you ever flown in a helicopter?" Sam had a moment of doubt, wondering if Gloria would actually fit inside the small cockpit. "It's not a long trip but we need to be impressive. Whatever tactics they try to play, we mustn't look phased; just give your trademark scowl with that man-eater smile and clean your nails with a hunting knife; you know the sort of thing. And if I say anything of a conciliatory nature, give me a smouldering angry look, as though I'm committing treason."

"And will you be committing treason?"

Sam smiled. "That, Gloria, is for everyone to guess."

He drained his whisky. "Do I take it that you agree to come with me?"

Gloria rolled her eyes dramatically. "Why do I end up feeling that without me you'd only get yourself into deep trouble and need rescuing again?" With that, Gloria reached across his desk and gave him a bone crunching handshake of acceptance.

Claire passed a pair of excited, if puzzled, helicopter pilots as she made her way to Sam's office.

"Am I pleased to see you," he whispered into her hair as they hugged. "I had hoped Lorna would have brought you here sooner, though we've had a busy night of things as it turned out. Is she still here?"

Claire hesitated and shook her head.

"She didn't. Bring me here, that is. Things became difficult at the farm after you had gone. I'm afraid Rachel left with the children during the night, and by this morning, well, let's just say I wasn't exactly Miss Popular. In her absence, Lorna had to do most of Rachel's work and no one else was available to bring me to Newport either. So *Frisco* and I managed it on our own," Claire said, with a note of personal satisfaction.

"I'm sorry I left things in such a mess."

Sam held Claire's hands, fingers entwined, gazing into her face. There was a livid red mark high on her left cheek, but such was her delight at accomplishing the journey on her own that he avoided asking how she had acquired it.

"You managed the journey on your own, without help?" he asked in astonishment.

Claire smiled. "I've travelled the road by wagon often enough and I had memorised most of the sequence of twists and turns, so it was straightforward enough to just follow my intuition. Despite his moods, *Frisco* is a clever horse. We got lost a couple of times, but fortunately our combined instincts served us well."

"Well, don't do that too often. There were boar roaming loose again during the night," he gently chided, secretly admiring her determined independence.

She gently pushed against his chest and took a partial step back. "And there you go again. You forget, I can hear and smell a boar long before you would ever set eyes on one."

He leaned forward and kissed her forehead, silencing her words. "Come on, I need to rest before the forum meeting. We must get something to eat and find a room for the next few nights, until things get sorted out."

As they left the forum building, Sam carried her bag over his shoulder. Almost light as a feather, it contained everything in the world that Claire possessed. He held her hand through the corridors of the building, oblivious to what anyone may have thought and gossiped about.

It felt almost like home; the same attic room in the hostel they had used after the party for the departing New Zealanders. This time they made love warmed by the afternoon sun. Afterwards, Claire lay awake, while Sam snored gently beside her. She guessed he had seen the painful bruised swelling on her cheek. He hadn't asked about it and she had no intention of telling him how she had got it.

The row with Rachel had erupted almost as soon as Sam had left the farm; pent up emotions, fuelled by weeks of frustration, had suddenly flared into an incandescent flash of rage. Cornered and confronted, Claire could only silently take the accusations thrown at her. To say anything in response would only add petrol to the flames, yet staying quiet only served to accelerate Rachel's anger out of control. Tormented by Claire's silence Rachel had struck her, hard, knocking her head sideways against the wall.

What followed was lost to Claire in a misty daze of sound; Rachel crying, Monica and Lorna intervening to separate them. Lorna found an ice pack for Claire's head and by the time she recovered, Rachel was gone, taking her children with her. She didn't say where she was going.

Claire didn't need to be told to leave. Everyone in the house fell silent in her presence; conversation stopped when she entered a room, and even Lorna moved silently around her. Claire spent a sleepless night, packed her bag early the next morning, and left the farm before anyone else had stirred and set off for Newport with only *Frisco* to guide her path.

Later that afternoon, Sam presided over his first official forum meeting. Before the meeting began, Sam at last found a few private minutes to spend with his dead friend. As he sat beside the open coffin, looking at Albert's lifeless face, the speed of transition between life and death never ceased to amaze him. Was it because Albert was aware of the voice of mortality calling him that he had expressed his wish that Sam should lead the forum? Their final words had been shared in the doorway to the garden. Still shocked by the proposal to appoint him as chairman, Sam hadn't paid enough attention to that last handshake or their final seconds of eye contact. He longed to re-live those last moments and to be able to ask the questions that could no longer be answered.

They started the meeting by holding a minute's silence for their departed friend and chairman. In the hushed quiet of the meeting chamber, Sam tried to gauge the atmosphere in the room around him in an attempt to decide where support might be found. He knew his proposed visit to Hurst Castle would be controversial. In the next hour or so his position would be put to the test. It was probable that were it not for the tragic nature of Albert Jamieson's death, Rigby and his supporters would have already made a determined effort to unseat Sam from the role of chairman. As it was, the majority of the forum, led by Chris Woods and Craig, rallied around him from the very outset and helped to secure his position, if only until the crisis was behind them and a proper leadership election could be held.

As he suspected, his proposal to go to the meeting at Hurst Castle proved controversial. Most were against the idea of Sam attending, with the exception, ironically, of Rigby. That was probably because if Sam failed to return, his position would be wide open for Rigby to replace him as chairman. Sam listened to the lively debate without interruption or reply. Beside him, Mary filled pages in her notebook with shorthand symbols that he found surprisingly calming in their unreadable rhythm, almost as unfathomable as Mary herself. When everyone had the opportunity to give their opinion, Sam went through the protocols for a vote. He had made a straw poll as the discussion progressed and suspected with alarm that the result would go against his participation, by some considerable margin. They were interrupted when John Evans entered the room and approached the platform with his arm raised.

"Mr Chairman, I need a private word. As ever, it's urgent." The Welsh lilt to his words was once again pronounced; John was anxious.

"Can it wait a few minutes?" Sam asked.

John shook his head. "I think you'll find it extremely relevant to your debate."

Uncertain, Sam adjourned the meeting for ten minutes. Albert Jamieson would never have allowed a halt at such a crucial stage but Sam felt a need for anything that might help change the likely course of the vote.

John led Sam to the canteen, in which a solitary woman was preparing tea and coffee for the forum. In the low light Sam saw the room wasn't completely empty; two figures sat at a table in the corner, wrapped in blankets, cradling hot water bottles. One was a pretty blonde girl, blind eyes darting around as she strained to absorb the strange sounds around her. Sitting beside her was the wet and bedraggled figure of David Longmarsh.

"So if I hadn't overheard the message on the radio of the landing craft, I don't want to imagine what would have happened to us when we returned."

David cupped Cynthia's hands as he spoke, trying to reassure her. "She's lived in fear for so long, Cynthia can't really believe we're here at last."

"Well, you're certainly safe now," Sam said calmly, pushing his own worries to one side, "safe and free." He omitted to say 'for the moment.'

He was rewarded with the first suggestion of a smile on Cynthia's face. Behind them, Gloria was listening, having followed with his bodyguards.

"Gloria, can you find a hot shower for Cynthia and some dry clothes, please?" Sam checked his watch; he needed to return to the forum as quickly as possible before Rigby created too much mischief in his absence.

"David, we'll sort you out in a few minutes, but if you're up to it, I need some information from you straight away."

Sam resumed the chair and looked around the table, giving every member a measured stare.

"I'm sorry for the delay."

Someone muttered, "disgraceful," but he let it pass.

"I was delayed," he continued, "because of the actions of someone in this room, someone who deliberately sabotaged our attempts to prevent another boar attack last night." Sam paused, turning to stare at the boar carcasses still lying in the gardens beyond the windows.

"Instead of capturing the ringleaders and their lethal cargo, we've ended up with boar right here in the centre of town. It's little short of a miracle that no one was killed, though several more of our people have been seriously hurt."

Molly Reid, one of Rigby's supporters, interrupted Sam.

"What evidence do you have to make such accusations against forum councillors? Are you claiming that one of us in this room is a traitor? If such a person exists and is sending messages to the mainland, it could be anyone on the island and possibly one of the newcomers that you welcome with such open arms. It's disgraceful."

The point of her barb was obvious but Sam bit his tongue and remained silent, listening to the rumble of support for Molly Reid's comments from around the table. He held up his hand for silence.

"My evidence comes from an informer we have had in place on the mainland. Last night, as the boar operation was beginning, he heard a message on the radio that clearly stated we knew where and when they were to be landed. The message was timed during the hour following our forum meeting when we had agreed our plan to intercept them. It also coincides with the period when our planes, the only eyes we have for protective surveillance, were sabotaged."

"And how did your supposedly reliable informer miraculously manage to escape his captors?" Rigby asked, his words pronounced with deliberate cynicism.

Sam looked stony-faced. "He's the boatman who is forced to ferry the boar here while his girlfriend is held hostage to ensure his cooperation. Last night, fearing his time as our agent was running out," Sam paused, "he hid his girlfriend on board the boat in the hope of giving their captors the slip while they were unloading the boar here on the island. Fortunately for them, he overheard the radio message. It came from someone here on the island, warning the mainland that we knew about the operation in advance. It seems whoever sent the message must have been in a hurry and broadcast in plain language, which was lucky for us."

"Was the voice recognisable?"

"The radio signal was too distorted. But the message was clear enough to tell our protagonists across the Solent that they had a spy in their midst. If our informer had returned to the mainland, he knew he would be taken for questioning. We can all imagine what that would entail."

"That doesn't explain how the informer conveniently managed to escape," Rigby continued.

"With the boar unloaded in a new location, the supervising crewmen started drinking to celebrate their successful drop-off. They hadn't received any instructions from the mainland beyond moving the drop to a different location. Realising what was to come, our informer took the life-raft and rowed with the girl back to the island. They were found this morning, soaked and exhausted, on the beach west of Cowes."

Sam paused and took a drink of water, listening to the murmurs around the room, and then continued.

"All this is very interesting, but that's not my main point. When the boar transport set out from the mainland last night, our informer saw a considerable number of landing craft tied up at the quayside in Buckler's Hard. They were in the process of being loaded with men, and you don't have to be a crystal ball gazer to guess their destination." Sam paused to let his words sink in. "It will be here, our island, our home."

Sam left the room to give the members a chance to evaluate what he had just told them, holding back the vote on his proposals.

In the cloakroom, he met Dave Bartlett, sluicing his face with cold water.

"Are you okay?" he asked.

Bartlett nodded, his face hollow and drawn. There was no point in asking more.

Sam hesitated. "You've heard the news of our informer?"

Bartlett nodded again. "John Evans told me." His voice was dust dry and tired.

"How many men do you think they might be assembling?" Sam asked.

Bartlett shrugged. "Can't be certain, but if the number of landing craft is half correct, it's more than you'll be able to manage."

Sam watched as Bartlett walked slowly away, hands cupped as he lit an eternal cigarette. As he left, Sam realised he knew nothing at all of Dave's past. He could only hope that one day soon there would be time to ask him.

He returned to the meeting room, now full of voices of opinion. The gavel felt strange in his hand as he called them to order, a job Albert Jamieson had done for so many years. It took him longer to achieve silence.

"Thank you. We still have to vote on my invitation …"

"Summons, you mean," someone shouted.

" … to meet at Hurst Castle. Okay, I don't like it any more than the rest of you, and we can speculate for hours about what they're planning. In the end, the only way to find out is to go and talk to them. It won't be pleasant, but at least we'll find out what we're up against. If we don't, we're flying blind, and we'll have no way of knowing how all of this will end."

Despite his efforts to obtain their agreement, part of him had secretly wished they would vote down his proposal. The thought of the meeting filled Sam with dread, even with the presence of Gloria at his side. But if it worked, and they returned alive, they would at least have some sort of picture of the future. It was a big 'if'.

Counter arguments kept disrupting the vote and it required several attempts and break periods to allow tempers to cool before enough discipline could be imposed to allow a vote to be counted. In the event the ratio was two to one. Sam had won his first vote at the forum.

When Sam and Claire entered the room, the boy, Tom, greeted them with a smile.

"Hello, Tom."

Sam pronounced his words with deliberate care. The more language the boy heard, the faster his language would recover. Sam had questions for him to which he needed answers. He had asked Claire to join him in the hope that she would be able to interpret more of his rusty, odd sounding language. They had changed his room for one with a small window, a table, chair and a bed. It felt less like a prison but Tom still preferred his usual position, squatting in the corner. The rags he wore had been replaced by clean clothes, though judging by the smell, no one had yet been able to persuade him to wash.

"This is my friend, Claire," Sam introduced her, repeating her name several times as Tom tried to shape it. "She'll be your friend too."

Tom stared at Claire with a puzzled smile, his gaze seemed transfixed by her hair. While he sat distracted, Sam produced the map that had previously been attached to the rags on his chest.

"Who pinned this on you?" He held the map against his chest in a similar position. "Did a man do it?" he asked.

Tom seemed to ignore him, still fascinated by Claire, his gaze unwavering. He muttered something Sam couldn't catch.

"Touch hair. I think that's what he said," Claire said.

"Do you mind?" Sam asked her, taking her hand and leading her closer to Tom, still crouching in the corner. He left a short distance between them.

"Come," Sam beckoned to him. "Come and touch her hair." He repeated it several times, running a strand of Claire's golden hair between his own fingers.

Slowly, Tom unravelled himself, curiosity overcoming his doubts. He stepped forward, head turned almost horizontally, his gaze fixed on Claire. Sam felt a tremble of apprehension; if this went wrong, all he had was a set of handcuffs.

"Touch hair?" Tom said again.

This time Sam heard it clearly. Tom took another step forward and Sam held out his hand to him. For the first time, Tom placed his hand in his without looking at him and stretched towards the curve of hair at Claire's shoulder. He rubbed it between his fingers and seemed mesmerised, while with his spare hand he rubbed his own filthy, string-like locks.

"Do you like Claire's hair?" Sam asked. "We could wash your hair and make it feel the same," he offered. He had no idea if Tom understood, but a brief smile played on his lips.

A few minutes passed, the door opened and Gloria arrived with a plate of food for Tom. She placed it on the table. For a moment, Tom seemed undecided, torn between the food and Claire's hair. Unsurprisingly, the food won.

"Tell me the questions you want answering," Claire said while Tom wolfed the food. "Why don't you leave me to talk to him. I'll meet you back at our room later."

Sam felt uncertain; he couldn't trust Tom completely and it felt as if he was leaving Claire alone with a wild animal, one who could see, while she was blind.

"Only if Gloria can stay with you," he finally said.

He looked at Tom who had taken the last of the food off the plate and had returned once again to the corner of the room. This was progress, but still a long way to go to bring him back to civilisation.

Sam nodded to Gloria as he moved to the door. "If he so much as makes a move against Claire, stop him."

Gloria looked at Sam with derision while he slid the handcuffs into her hand and left.


Sam found Ruth sitting up in bed without an oxygen mask. She smiled weakly as he approached.

"No bowl of fruit or flowers? Poor visitor you are," she said in a dry husky voice.

He leant forward and kissed her forehead.

"Good to see you looking better," he said. "You had us worried for a while."

Ruth nodded. "Fortunately, it didn't spoil my aim."

There were dark shadows of pain around her eyes but some colour had returned to her face.

"I've just been told about Albert Jamieson. That's so sad; he was a good man."

"The best. He'll be a tough act to follow," Sam added wistfully.

"So, we've got you to lead us now. Am I supposed to salute you?" Her humour was irrepressible.

"Only when you're better," he answered, jokingly.

"Look, I'm sorry to disturb you, but I need to run some things past you."

Sam described the proposed meeting at Hurst Castle and the intervention of the betrayal by someone in their midst the previous evening. He trusted Ruth's clear-sighted pragmatism, her opinions unobstructed from the combative instincts of men.

"They always know our plans before we can even begin to carry them out. Our spy seems to pass information on as soon as we have agreed what to do," he said. "Do you think I am walking into a trap, as most people seem to think, or is there a genuine chance of negotiation?"

Ruth lay silent, eyes closed, for several minutes. Sam began to think she had fallen asleep.

"Weymouth, followed by Albert Jamieson's death, are the game changers. These men across the Solent are strong and desperate at the same time. They want the island for themselves, that's been obvious from the very start, but why fight for it if we can be forced to surrender? Weymouth was another attempt to weaken us. Had they been more successful, and killed us and captured *Lupin* they would have reckoned that Albert would sue for peace; surrender, in all but name." She paused, gasping for breath. Sam handed her the oxygen mask.

"The boar attacks are taking too long and they haven't weakened us enough," Ruth continued, hooking the oxygen mask back on its clip. "And now, after the death of Albert, they've got you to deal with. In my opinion, they think this is their chance to negotiate. If they remove you from the picture," she said enigmatically, "they're left with Rigby, and he'll fight until we're all dead, which is not what they want."

Ruth lay back against the pillows, the colour drained from her face from the effort of talking.

"If you want my honest opinion, the main trap that now exists is in the words they use. And you won't discover that without talking to them."

Exhausted by talking, Ruth started to fall asleep. Sam squeezed her hand, eager to leave her in peace.

"Get better soon, Ruth, we need you on the forum."

Heartfelt words, but she hadn't heard them.

"So, that's all Tom could tell me; two men, one large and hairy, the other smaller, bald, and with a beaky nose."

Claire yawned. She was tired and didn't ask why Sam needed to know so urgently. The bruise on her cheek had turned to a purple-yellow and as they slid into bed, he saw a cut line of dried blood, camouflaged by the fringe of her hair. He was about to ask how she had come by them when she added, "Oh, and he said 'there are lots of men, no girls'."

With that, Claire wriggled back against him, and fell asleep. Somewhere in the early hours, she stirred, aware that Sam was talking in his sleep beside her. He kept repeating a name she couldn't clearly make out, as though its owner tormented his dreams. She didn't need to be told he was worried and guessed that asking him would only increase his anxieties. It was far safer to follow her instincts. With silent kisses she aroused him, using love to wash away his demons until the morning light arrived.

## THIRTY-NINE

The air was as clear as crystal, the sun hovering somewhere below the horizon. Sam and Gloria stood together, hands in pockets, hunched against the early morning chill. Beside them, two black sleeping locusts squatted on the grass, the island's last remaining working helicopters. The pilots checked their clipboards and set their watches to match Sam's. One of the helicopters was fitted with a tubular framework that looked more appropriate for crop spraying. Gloria had given a questioning eye at Sam when she saw it. To her mind, it didn't offer much as a means of protection. "Wait and see," Sam said with an amused smile, reading her thoughts.

He turned to brief the two pilots for the last time. "Split second timing will be imperative." He turned to the pilot flying the helicopter with the tubular rig. "Take off thirty minutes behind us. Keep as low as you can all the way and don't start your approach until Casper," Sam pointed to the other pilot, "gives you the 'Go' signal. Stealth is essential, only a single pass, don't be tempted to try a second pass whatever you see happening on the ground."

Sam paused to look at his watch apprehensively. The moment was approaching. "Okay. Everyone clear on what we need to do?" They nodded their agreement. "Good luck. In an hour or so it should all be over and we'll be back here safely."

Gloria rolled her eyes at that suggestion. Chairman he might be, but she still clearly doubted his talent as a strategist.

Sam had never flown in a helicopter before. In normal circumstances he would have enjoyed their brief flight to Hurst Castle. Lit by the early sun, the Solent below was aqua blue, flecked with white caps in the stiff westerly breeze. Today though, he tried to close his mind; fear rode as the invisible passenger in the helicopter. He had said nothing about his meeting to Claire, she hadn't asked about it and she would only worry if she knew where Sam was going. He decided the best thing was to just focus on his plan and find out at the meeting what they wanted. Getting out of Hurst Castle might be problematic and be dependent on precise timing. Lingering for a sociable chat wouldn't be an option.

They followed the north coast of the island as far as Fort Victoria, its angular walls dark in the morning shadows, and crossed the narrow strip of water to Hurst Castle. In the lee of the walls on the north side was a large bell tent. No one was visible, but two flat bottomed motorboats lay beached in the protected lagoon beyond. Sam tapped the pilot on the shoulder, shouting to make himself heard above the noise of the rotors above.

"Drop us about a hundred yards north of the tent, then climb back to three thousand feet. Keep that tent in sight at all times. Remember, the moment we reappear, signal the other helicopter to start his run in. If we haven't reappeared by the time you get to reserve on your fuel gauge, you must leave."

Sam repeated his instructions again to emphasise the point that the helicopters must be saved at all costs. In the event of the plan misfiring, the second helicopter pilot knew what he had to do.

Their helicopter descended to hover a few feet above the ground. As Sam prepared to jump out he paused and turned to Gloria.

"Perhaps it's best you stay on board and leave me to go alone," he said, feeling a pang of concern for her safety.

She leant forward to shout in his ear.

"It's easier if I come with you now. It saves me having to rescue you later when you've made a mess of things." Her sarcastic message reassured him.

Within seconds they had scrambled clear and the helicopter lifted quickly away, rapidly climbing to a height to resemble a noisy black insect high against a backdrop of white blousy clouds. Their ears re-adjusted as the clatter of rotor blades subsided, to be replaced by the serenade of a skylark that had risen from the fields beyond. In the lee of the castle walls, shielded from the westerly breeze and bathed in warm sunshine, for a brief moment it was possible to enjoy the delusion that all was well in the world.

Sam stopped some yards from the bell tent. He didn't like the idea of entering until he had seen who they were supposed to meet.

"If you're waiting for an invitation, we could be here all day," Gloria said, marching forward and wrenching open the entrance flap without bothering to unfasten it.

Inside was a folding table with a tray bearing a whisky decanter and glasses. There were no chairs. Gloria stood aside to allow him to enter. It was hot, the smell of warm canvas reminding Sam of boyhood camping trips held in the balmy days of childhood just after the war. He turned through a complete circle, checked his watch and said in a loud voice, "Twelve minutes and we leave."

A shadow entered the tent from behind them, followed by two men wearing worn black leathers; both carried sub-machine guns. Gloria's nostrils twitched at the smell of their unwashed bodies.

"No guns allowed. Hand them over butt first," a man with a full beard confronted them.

Sam made no comment, holding out his pistol by the barrel. The man snatched it away, removed the magazine and threw it into the corner. Turning to Gloria, he snapped his fingers impatiently. She smiled as he tried to take her gun from her. Misreading her expression, he missed her empty hand, arriving out of nowhere and enclosed his outstretched hand in a vice-like grip. The man jumped and gave an involuntary shout of pain, Gloria only releasing the pressure when the gun fell from his grip to the ground. He was swearing and cursing, his face creased in anger, and he balled his other fist to swing a punch.

"I wouldn't do that if I were you," Sam said. "Gun or no gun, she'll snap your head off before you've even thought of pulling the trigger."

The man massaged his crushed fingers while Gloria, still smiling, kicked the fallen gun disdainfully to one side.

"If you want something, you only have to ask," she said, imitating the high pitched voice of a young girl. "And ask nicely."

"What an amusing tableau." The voice came from the entrance behind them.

Sam was motionless. He didn't need to turn. It was a voice he hadn't heard for five years.

"Hello, Whistler," he said to the man who had just entered the tent, a voice that had followed them in his dreams in the years since they had last crossed paths. "I had often wondered when you would show your face again."

Sam kept his gaze fixed on the two men still standing in front of him. The second he recognised as the tall broad man he had last seen on the quayside in Dartmouth, Sven. He was wearing a loose leather jacket, his mane of long hair tied back in a knot, his trousers a size too large with the waist gathered in with orange twine. He looked thinner than Sam remembered. The third figure was to his left, wearing a threadbare cord coat with a velvet collar, despite the warmth of the day. Whistler.

Whistler made a rough dry laugh in greeting.

"Well, well, if it isn't my dear friend Sam Morten. I knew all along, in fact I was certain, that all this unnecessary intransigence must be the work of my old friend. And now you've aspired to high office too I hear, chairman of the island forum, in fact."

The two men eyed one another, like a mongoose and cobra locked in a deadly dance.

"We were never friends, Whistler," Sam said. "Get to the point; what do you want?"

Whistler stepped forward, opened the decanter and poured three glasses of whisky.

"I said to come alone." He pushed a glass in Sam's direction. "But," he sighed elaborately, "I guess a pet gorilla doesn't count."

Sam ignored the insult, raising a slight smile, though not for the reasons Whistler might think. Gloria cleaned her nails, appearing not to have heard; a bad sign.

"You've nine minutes, Whistler. I suggest you don't waste them on pointless slander."

"Always the moralist, you never change, Samuel." He sipped his whisky. "I always liked that about you; uselessly impractical in our new world, but praiseworthy nevertheless."

"Nine minutes," Sam reminded. "I asked you what you wanted?"

Whistler ignored him. "Nine minutes, nine hours, nine days. Why such a rush, Samuel?"

Sam sighed, already bored by the unnecessary charade. "Because in nine minutes, no, eight and a half actually, if I don't reappear outside, free to walk away, one of my helicopters will drop something very unpleasant on this very spot."

He glanced sideways at Gloria. Her face had taken a decidedly puzzled expression.

"Threats, Samuel, just idle threats; so unnecessary."

"Not a threat, Whistler, just a statement of fact. I repeat, what do you want?"

Whistler laughed, though it was edged with an uncertain note. Perhaps he had been perturbed by the look Gloria had just given. Impatiently, Sven suddenly slammed his fist on the table.

"Let's stop this bollocks right now. Just cut their throats and be done with it. We're going to take the Isle of Wight by force anyway."

Whistler placed a steadying hand on the big man's arm, a blank expression replacing his sickly smile.

"Easy, Sven," he said in soothing tones. He smiled at Sam. "Sven gets ... upset from time to time. But the truth is, Samuel, my dear chap, we need your island and we intend you to give it to us, willingly, and with gratitude for our kindness."

Sam fixed his expression. "Well, you'll find we have a very generous immigration policy. You're welcome to put in applications to come and join us. We can only take small numbers at any particular time, but you might be lucky, if you meet our standards."

Whistler's smile hardened. "Games, games. We both know that's not how it's going to happen. We just need you to hand things over to us. There will be changes yes, but benefits for you all nevertheless."

"And what might they be?"

Whistler appeared to look for the answer in the conical roof of the tent. "You'll be allowed to live on your farms, perhaps not in the style you're used to. There will, of course, be ... accommodations."

"Such as?"

"Sharing. Your food stocks, your homes and, almost as important, your women."

Sam chose to ignore the implications of his words.

"I can understand the attraction of our island. For a start, there are no boar, apart from the ones you bring to us. But surely you have enough food and women already, why uproot yourselves when we could trade peacefully, in coexistence."

Whistler shot a sideways glance at Sven.

"Alas, the boys have big appetites, and supplies are ... limited. As for women, well, they tend to be ... a little careless with them. As a result there are nowhere near enough to go around." He paused with a sick grin on his face. "Too many men; it tends to cause friction and knowing how you so believe in a sharing society …" He left the words hanging.

Sam looked thoughtful. "But as you already well know, there's at least one major problem with this idea. Unless we can double the farm food production, there isn't remotely enough to feed us both."

"Then someone will have to work twice as hard or go hungry." Sven thought he was being clever and smiled at his own words.

"Or, if you're proposing a shared proposition, you stay on the mainland and we'll send you as much food as we can spare on the basis of fair barter and exchange," Sam offered.

"Would you include a regular allocation of women in your sharing proposition?" Whistler asked.

"Only if they volunteered."

"Which is highly unlikely. In my experience, if left to their own devices, women seem strangely reluctant to share their lives with real men. A little … masculine guidance is usual needed in the matter." Whistler laughed at his own wit.

Abruptly, Sven turned to Whistler. "Why are we wasting time talking? We outnumber them; they'll be crushed in a day." He swung back to Sam. "For the avoidance of doubt, the deal on the table is the only one on offer," he poked a finger in Sam's direction. "Hand over the island to us. Period. We run things now and in return for our generosity in allowing you to live, you will work for us. Simple as that."

"Our island is a democracy. We need to meet and discuss such an offer," Sam replied.

"Twenty-four hours is what you can have. Answer by tomorrow." Sven hit the table again to emphasise his point.

"I'd need at least two weeks," Sam said, folding his arms, ignoring Sven as he stared at Whistler.

"Boys, boys, let's not be too hasty. What's a little time between friends? We could give you three days," Whistler proposed, "if you make concessions, that is."

Sam shook his head. "Ten days minimum."

Whistler sighed, spreading his hands. "Five days is the best I can offer you. And for that I will need at least a dozen of your youngest women to prevent the boys becoming, shall we say, impatient and fractious." An unpleasant smile creased his face.

"Pick them pretty, but robust. They're going to have to work hard to keep everyone amused for five days."

Sven turned his head and spat demonstratively. "You can include a dozen wine barrels as well. And, five days, not an hour more." He glared menacingly across the table.

Sam felt his stomach make a cramping twist. He looked deliberately at his watch. Six minutes remained.

"It will be hard to find twelve women to volunteer for such a task," Sam offered. "What about enough wine and food to fill a boat and no women?"

"Both," barked Sven, pounding the table again with his fist.

Sam stared into Sven's eyes. He had spared his life in Dartmouth, he knew the man remembered that, but if eyes are windows to the soul, all Sam could see was a psychotic killer. He was playing for time; five days would be tight, but his plan might just work if they could be persuaded to keep to their word.

"Okay. Give me twenty-four hours to sort out the boats, though it will take at least five days to bring the forum to the right decision on what I have to tell them."

Sam felt Gloria stiffen and glare at him. He hoped Whistler had seen her look, though whether it was fake or not was another matter.

Whistler smiled triumphantly. "Always the pragmatist, Samuel. I think a toast to our new mood of cooperation is called for."

He pushed a glass across the table towards Sam. As they raised their glasses, he saw the tent flap behind Whistler begin to open. He drained his glass, wiping his mouth on his cuff.

"As a token of our new relationship we thought we'd send you home with a parting gift," he said and snapped his fingers.

Two men entered the tent, half-carrying a ravaged figure between them. Barely recognisable, it was Jean, the girl who had flown with Cromford, hands tied in front by a rope that dropped to a shackle joining both ankles, her hair matted and face swollen purple with bruises. Her eyes stared vacantly, her mind lost somewhere in a mist of violence.

"I'll grant you the boys have had some fun with her, but at least she's still alive. I think that clearly displays our humanity," Whistler couldn't resist laughing. "And she's yours to take back with you. It dispels the malicious rumour I hear you bandy about that we actually eat our prisoners."

Sven stared at Jean as she was dragged past him. Gloria moved to catch Jean before she fell, producing a knife concealed in her sleeve and cut the rope ties. Impulsively, Sven lunged for Gloria's knife hand, failing to notice the lightening movement of her left hand, which locked onto his wrist in mid-air. For a brief moment, Sam almost felt sorry for him. Sven's leering smile transformed to one of pure agony as his wrist was dislocated. He jumped back, groaning like a wounded animal. Gloria had no need for words, her actions usual spoke clearly for her. In one movement, she scooped Jean into her arms, nodding her head towards the tent flap as she did so.

"We're done," Sam said. "Five days, Whistler, you'll have your answer."

"Indeed," said Whistler, watching with a self-satisfied smile as two additional men appeared through the flap and painfully snapped back Sven's wrist joint.

"Samuel. Just one point to consider as you leave. In case the thought of double-crossing us should possibly occur to you in the coming days, remember, we've generously accommodated Jean these past weeks. I would hate to think you might choose a course of action that could jeopardise the well-being of the pilot that was with her. If we hold him, that is? But then, that's for you to guess."

Sam looked nervously at his watch as they walked away from the tent. If the plans were running to schedule, they had barely a minute to spare. In front of them the helicopter was rapidly descending, while in the tent behind them he could hear raised voices. Whistler and Sven were arguing and he didn't need to guess what about. Gloria now carried Jean over her shoulder; it was quicker than trying to help her to walk. Sam risked a glance over his shoulder. A dozen armed men had suddenly materialised from a door in the castle and were following them at a brisk pace. As he had anticipated, it appeared that Sven intended to over-rule Whistler all along and was trying to take things into his own hands.

"If I tell you to run, don't ask why," Sam said to Gloria.

The helicopter was now hovering just a few feet from the ground and less than a hundred yards ahead of them, the downbeat pulse of its rotors drowning out all other sound. Behind them, the line of men had spread out and had begun to move faster. Amidst the noise no one heard the second helicopter, still invisible but approaching fast from a westerly direction at little more than head height. Sam called out to Gloria to start running.

"Faster," he shouted as she started to get breathless with carrying Jean.

The second helicopter suddenly burst over the castle wall, flying straight and low directly above the heads of the men, spraying a dense brown cloud over them. Alarmed, many threw themselves flat to the ground, unstrapping guns in a last minute attempt to shoot at the low flying machine, but it was too fast and too low. For Sam and Gloria, slightly ahead of the men, the stench of ammonia was immediately suffocating, their eyes streaming tears and throats burning. Behind them everyone was enveloped and soaked in the brown vapour cloud; the men were retching, coughing and choking.

Running fast, Sam and Gloria arrived at the hovering helicopter in front of them. Gloria more or less threw Jean into the rear seat before diving in behind her. Sam was barely half way through the side door when the pilot pushed the throttle hard forward, moving the stick and pedals to climb and bank away from the chaos below.

"What the hell was in that stuff?" Gloria shouted, coughing and wiping her eyes at the same time.

With the violent departure of the helicopter, Sam was trying to close the side door and haul himself into his seat. "Prime Isle of Wight liquid pig manure, undiluted of course," he shouted euphorically. "If they haven't taken a bath in a while, they'll certainly need one now."

His plan had worked to perfection. Even if they had appeared to leave running with their tails between their legs, his final statement had at least partially corrected things. As they flew homewards in the company of the second helicopter, Sam enjoyed a rare moment of triumph. He knew the feeling wouldn't last, but it reassured him that Whistler and his band could be beaten.

A small group had assembled at the airstrip to greet their return. Doctor Morgan and Karen, both delighted and shocked in equal measure, briefly examined Jean before whisking her off to hospital. Meanwhile, Sam and Gloria shared the relief of having survived.

"I thought the big hairy guy, Sven, was going to kill us on the spot," Gloria said with a laugh.

Sam shrugged. "That certainly wasn't Whistler's plan, at least for the moment. He's about as reliable as a cobra, but keeping us alive suits his purposes. Despite that thug Sven's intervention, it might just give us the one thing we most desperately need. Time."

Gloria shook her head. "Only if you supply them with a dozen women. Where the hell are you going to find anyone willing to submit herself to those monsters, even if it's for the good of the island?"

"I have a plan," Sam grinned. "But there's a queue of people waiting for me, so while I see to them can you do something for me?"

Gloria looked at him warily. "So long as it doesn't involve being shot at."

"I need you to find as many female shop mannequins as you can lay hands on, plus wigs and clothing. Don't bring them to the forum building. Find an empty lock-up somewhere and come and find me when you've got it all together. Oh, and tell no one what you're doing," he added as an afterthought.

Gloria left with a bemused expression and Sam turned to talk with Chris who had been waiting patiently for him.

"Glad to see you made it back okay," she said, wrinkling her nose at the smell that lingered on his clothes.

"That was another close call," he said with an audible sigh of relief. "But that's not what you want to see me about," he added, reading her troubled expression.

Chris nodded. "It's best that John tells you what he's found," she said as she led the way from the airstrip towards the radio room.

John looked genuinely pleased to see him.

"It's glad I am that you're home safe," he said as Sam entered. "As per usual, we have a problem."

Sam groaned inwardly. "Go on."

"I've found a radio aerial."

It took a second or two to sink in.

"Where?" Sam asked cautiously.

"Concealed in a small copse close by some farm buildings. I'd been doing some calculations, trying to identify the most likely places to position a radio for a reliable signal across the Solent. I was trying to save time and avoid driving around trying to find a needle in a haystack, so to speak. I made a list and have tried to visit all the possible locations whenever I travel around the island. By pure luck I seem to have struck lucky. The aerial I found is hidden by trees, extending just above their canopy. Not by a lot; in normal circumstances I wouldn't have seen it. But the storm has stripped a lot of leaf cover and there's a relay box up quite high on the branches, close to the crown. It must have been glinting in the sun and that caught my eye. Made me suspicious, so it did, and I went to investigate. At the base is a stack of cut logs with a small space inside enough for one person and a radio set. It's so well camouflaged you'd never notice it unless you were really looking for something, and judging by the footprints, it's been used recently."

"Where is it?" Sam asked cautiously.

Chris and John glanced at one another.

Chris spoke for them both. "Connor Rigby's farm."

John led Sam, Aiden, and Chris through the woods to where he had discovered the radio aerial. Fortunately it was possible to approach the spot without entering Rigby's farm. Sam had travelled there in the back of the Landrover, thinking that everything Rigby did could be interpreted to incriminate him, but a radio mast didn't prove that he was the person using it.

Sam followed John and saw that the aerial had been hidden with deliberate care.

"Someone has been very careful," Sam muttered, deep in thought. "But this location doesn't necessarily make Rigby our spy."

"A radio would," John suggested.

Sam nodded, though not totally convinced.

"Do we arrest Rigby and the rest of the farm and bring them in for questioning?"

Sam shook his head. "No, that feels too heavy handed at the moment."

"We can't wait," said John in an exasperated voice. "This is the break through we've been hoping for. We can't hold back now."

Sam stared at the log pile and its enclosed space. The evidence was compelling, but in reality they had nothing that couldn't be easily denied. It was true they had the good fortune of a break through, but what they needed was the final piece of the puzzle and for that they needed to catch the perpetrator in the act of sending a message.

Sam nodded to Aiden. "We need what the Americans call a stake-out, someone with the patience to stay concealed and watch for who turns up. A job for Javed?"

Aiden thought for a moment, staring at a fallen tree now partially covered by thorny briars.

"We could position Javed over there. It's fifty yards away, but if we connect a line to the entrance of the radio hide, it would alert him the moment someone tries to use it."

It had the shape of a workable plan until Chris reminded them it could take days before anything happened.

"Nice idea, but Javed could be here for a long time waiting for an appearance. How would he sleep, or take a piss for that matter, without missing someone? Surely, if Rigby is only a couple of hundred yards away it's pretty compelling evidence?"

Sam suddenly smiled.

"I think I've got an answer. I've called a forum meeting for tonight to report on my meeting this morning at Hurst Castle. If we hold out a big enough carrot, our traitor will be tempted to send a message as quickly as possible. The story doesn't have to be true, just so long as it is plausible and urgent. That way, we can leave temptation do the job for us and catch them in the act of transmitting the message. Simple!"

## FORTY

Claire found Sam still fully dressed, coiled up asleep on the bed in their attic room. She waited, sitting silently in a chair, listening to him breathe, enjoying the warmth of the late afternoon sun through the open window. Newport was alive with speculation about Sam's meeting with Whistler and his gang across the Solent, leaving Claire slightly piqued that he had said nothing before leaving that morning. He would have had his reasons, but the dangers in the meeting alarmed her; it was probably why he had kept it so secret. She kicked off her shoes and slid onto the bed beside him, squirming into the warm space between his arms as he lay on his side. For a moment he feigned sleep, then yawned and opened one eye to peer at her.

"Evil woman," Sam said, yawning a second time. "You've woken me up. Am I to be granted no peace?" He jabbed her playfully in the ribs.

"Not if you go off on foolhardy adventures without telling me." She kissed his neck.

"You would only have worried."

"So, that's a woman's lot. We have to endure far more than men, don't forget, so please don't keep things from me just to protect me," she started to search with her fingers in the area at the front of his trousers.

Sam kissed her on the forehead, checking his watch over her head.

"Nice idea, but I've got an emergency forum this evening and we need to make a visit first."

He had overlooked how quickly Claire had learned a woman's tricks; in seconds she had opened his fly zip and was teasingly searching inside.

"We could be very quick," she whispered in a small voice, adding seductively, "just in case your meeting goes on into the early hours."

Sam pretended protest. "It's a time of crisis and all the woman can think of is sex."

"There are far worse things," Claire said in a provocative voice as she pushed him with surprising strength onto his back and sat astride him, releasing the buttons on the front of her dress. She could be a demanding lover at times.

In the early evening sunlight, Sam led Claire into the clearing in the woods where he had discovered the dead woman, 'Melissa'. His bodyguards remained with the Landrover, giving them a few minutes of privacy. Arriving at the spot, Sam halted. On the brief journey from Newport, he had explained to Claire the outline of what had happened, making no mention that the evidence pointed to murder. It was important for Claire not to be prejudiced by his conclusions; after all, the purpose of the visit was to see if it triggered something he had missed.

He stepped away, allowing Claire time to absorb the space around her. A short distance beyond, a meadow pipit sang joyfully, accompanied by the soft evening breeze of late spring, ruffling the regenerating leaf cover around them. In another time and place it would have been a romantic setting. He knew it was a long shot; what could a blind girl discover that the sighted world had missed. He made no mention of the fresh flowers at the spot 'Melissa' had died; he assumed Claire would note their presence from their strong perfume. Watching her carefully, he leaned against a tree and just resisted the urge to light his pipe.

Claire slowly turned full circle. "There are flowers, fresh, with a strong perfume. Nearby, a fox has cast his scent." For a while she was still, listening, absorbing natural sounds and smells around her.

"There's hawthorn, spring flowers and a pair of birds serenading one another over there," Claire paused to point towards a field hedgerow. "And I can smell freshly dug earth somewhere near." Her final point aroused Sam's interest.

"Where? Can you point to a direction?"

Claire held out her hand. "That way I think, though the breeze could be playing tricks around us."

Slowly, she led Sam away from the clearing, tracing the route of the smell farther through the trees. For almost ten minutes they wandered, hand in hand. Sometimes the smell was stronger, at others it disappeared altogether. They found nothing.

When they returned to the clearing, the flowers had gone. Someone had been watching them. It sent a shiver down Sam's spine but he decided not to tell Claire.

The visit was made to try to find a new lead in a mystery that confounded him. Instead, they discovered nothing new except that someone thought their presence a threat and removed the flowers. Hastily, they returned to the Landrover where his bodyguards waited impatiently. Neither of them had the flowers, nor had seen anyone.

Abruptly, Claire stopped.

"What?"

"The first smell I noted, the flowers, not the hawthorn." She paused, turning towards the clearing. "I've noticed it before recently, several times." She cocked her head to one side, searching her memory. "Yes, that's it. In the forum building; perhaps someone has fresh flowers on their desk. In one part of the building it's quite strong."

Sam was about to ask her more when one of the bodyguards called to him, pointing to his watch urgently. The forum meeting couldn't wait. As the Landrover drew away with Sam and Claire sitting in the back, Sam leaned close to Claire's ear.

"Tomorrow, can you do something for me? Search all the rooms of the building. If you trace that smell you've just mentioned, come and tell me immediately. It might be best if you tell no one what you're doing," he said, squeezing her hand to emphasise his point.

"Well, that just about sums it up," Sam said at the conclusion of his report to the forum. "We either hand the island over to them, or they will come and take it and make us suffer the consequences."

For once a stilled hush prevailed in the forum chamber. Sam hadn't anything new to report; most had feared the intentions of the vigilante group on the mainland from the moment the boar attacks had begun. But now, hearing it first-hand, brought an unpleasant reality to the situation.

"So what are our options, if we have any?" Craig asked.

"Perhaps our chairman will recommend running up the white flag," Molly Reid interjected sarcastically, no doubt speaking for Connor Rigby who sat stony-faced in his usual seat. A murmur of discontent circled the room, tinged with notes of anxiety and anger. Sam allowed it to pass for a few seconds before responding.

He smiled and said abruptly, "Actually, I recommend we strike first." His outburst shocked the room into silence. "They won't be expecting us and if we act quickly and decisively, we may yet force them to make some acceptable form of accommodation."

His words echoed back at him and he stared grim-faced around the forum. He was certain that one of them was an informer; his words were aimed at that person. Sam was a good actor; he had no intention of allowing what he was proposing to actually happen. In a brief conversation before the forum with Bartlett and Aiden, both had insisted that such a course of action would tempt complete disaster.

"When?" Rigby asked sarcastically. "How soon do you remotely suppose we should organise such an attack? You've already told us that we've only got five days to agree to their demands."

Sam glared stonily back at Rigby, remembering the radio aerial they had discovered near his farm. "A day to plan and evaluate, a day to organise. We attack on Thursday, before dawn. Bartlett is already preparing a plan of action and we'll need you Rigby, to coordinate our resources. Use every available squad you can get."

To Sam's ears, the plan sounded like a prescription for suicide; Bartlett had already told him as much. But as a hoax, all he needed was the informer to take the bait and expose himself. Or her, for that matter; Sam had his doubts about the loyalty of Molly Reid as well. Aiden had confirmed that Javed would soon be in hiding in the woods. What they needed now was the informer to make a hasty visit to their radio hide on Rigby's farm to send an incriminating radio signal to forewarn Whistler and his henchmen.

"That was uncharacteristic," Rigby said as the forum broke up.

Sam was surprised; he hadn't anticipated such a comment. Rigby would have expected him to recommend some sort of pointless negotiation, a form of veiled surrender, resulting in a life of oppression along the lines of 'making the best of a difficult situation'.

"Always do what our opponents don't expect. It helps to keep them off-balance," Sam said.

He shook his head with a false smile on his face, not for the reasons Rigby supposed, but with the image of his words being transmitted on radio waves very soon by the man standing right in front him.

"Speak to Bartlett, he's experienced in military things. We need an all-out effort and we've only got forty-eight hours to organise it." He cut the conversation short, aware that if he went too far, the flaws in the plan might become glaringly obvious.

John looked perplexed when Sam asked him to contact Napier again.

"As well as listening for a signal to the mainland? I'll need Jaki to help me," John said, rubbing his hands together in a sign of anxiety.

"Whatever you need. Just make sure she understands the need for absolute secrecy," Sam replied.

With the forum over, there was little for him to do but wait. Aiden arrived to confirm that Javed had been concealed to overlook the radio hide and Gloria was positioned with a squad close by as back-up. John had chosen a small clearing in the trees at the end of the airfield. Screened by dense scrub and trees, it was ideal to conceal the Landrover while he listened for a transmission from their informer. It was now all about timing. To be absolutely certain, they had to wait for the radio transmission before springing the trap.

Sam stood down his usual bodyguards. Even they had to rest sometime, so he walked back through the empty streets alone to the hostel. For a few short hours his plans could develop in the hands of others. Aiden knew where to find him if he needed him and John was unlikely to be ready to contact Napier for a few hours. Sam found their room empty with no sign of Claire. He kicked off his shoes and eased himself onto the bed, the sheets still holding her lingering scent. He hadn't intended to sleep; he was more anxious to frame a workable plan for the coming days, but needed to speak to Napier first to tie the threads together. Instead, sleep had other ideas.

In his dreams a sound of hammering echoed in his ears. He blinked, suddenly awake. The hammering returned, shaking the bedroom door. He lit a candle and, still dressed, fumbled for the door lock. Aiden entered without waiting to be invited. The luminous hands on Sam's watch showed it to be three in the morning and Aiden's face looked ghostly tired and strained in the candlelight.

"We've been outwitted again," he said, exasperated. "Javed is in hospital with a lump on his head the size of a tennis ball. We found him, badly concussed, close to the entrance to the hide. When the trip line was triggered, someone must have waited for Javed to appear and used a club on him from behind. The doctor says he should be okay, though it will be a while before he can tell us anything." Aiden paused. "Sorry, Sam. They've slipped through our fingers again. And to make things worse, John picked up a signal an hour or so later warning the mainland of our plans, so they must have a second aerial in another location to use as a back-up."

Sam cursed loudly. "What the hell do we have to do to catch this slippery eel at the very heart of our operations? Something goes wrong every time. We do our best, but we're being outsmarted every time," he groaned, ominously aware that time was running away from them with ever increasing speed.

Aiden left and Sam set off to locate John Evans. It was approaching dawn when he found the Landrover in the clearing that John had described. Inside, Sam found him and Jaki, side by side, listening intently across the frequencies. John twisted around, easing the tension in his aching back, stiff from hours bent in concentration over the dials. Sam raised a questioning eyebrow. John shook his head.

"Someone is jamming our VHF frequency. Seems they know what we're up to." He threw his headphones aside in frustration.

"So no word from Napier then?"

"Nope." John shook his head. "Across the Solent, they keep one step ahead of us all the time."

Sam nodded. Another night that had started with such promise had ended in disappointment. He beckoned John to join him outside and was surprised to see him light a cigarette. He didn't know he smoked.

"I can't remember the last time I slept in a bed. These damn things are all that keeps me going at the moment," John said with a morose expression. "Has it occurred to you that we might need to be looking for more than one traitor amongst us?"

"The thought had crossed my mind," Sam said.

He cast his mind back to the sight of 'Melissa' hanging on a noose beneath the bough of a tree. Was that the work of only one person? He had always harboured a doubt, but no evidence had presented itself either way. After the past night, he was no longer sure.

"It seems that Javed walked into an ambush."

John nodded. "And it never occurred to us that one person would be using the radio while another stood watch outside. As soon as Javed crept forward to investigate, bingo. Whoever was keeping watch smacked him over the head."

"When did you hear their message to the mainland?"

"About forty-five minutes after the incident with Javed. Enough time to move to a back-up location," John added ominously. "And we don't know where that is."

After a moment Sam said, stating the obvious, "Well, I guess that's one plan of ours that we won't be implementing, not that we had ever intended to anyway."

"And if we can't contact Napier? I realise talking to him is important; you can't just be asking him about the weather," John said.

Sam looked away. The eastern sky was paling from indigo to grey; it would soon be light, the start of another day. Only he and Napier knew what plans they had considered; plans that he couldn't share with anyone for fear of tipping off Whistler, which only emphasized the importance of catching the spy ring, as it now obviously was, amongst them. In the absence of contact with Napier, Sam would just have to continue in the desperate hope that his far away friend could pull off miracles.

And so the night left them empty handed. On the brighter side, Gloria arrived at the forum offices with a van laden with the ransom items Sam had agreed to send to Whistler and Sven, though with certain things there were a few, not so subtle, changes.

"You're not exactly Mr Popular with some people we visited," Gloria said. "There was a distinct reluctance to give up such a substantial quantity of alcohol."

"Did you get the mannequins?"

Gloria nodded. "Yes, though several of them are men, not women," she said with a frown. "Even if these guys are desperate I can't see them being fooled for the real thing."

"They only have to see the mannequins from a distance. As for the alcohol, it's more value to us if they drink themselves into a stupor for a few days. We need anything that can buy us more time."

Gloria laughed. "Well, there's gallons of the stuff in the van. Where do you want it taken?"

"Yarmouth. You should find Helen and her engineer in the harbour with a couple of serviceable motorboats. Did you get enough wigs?"

Gloria rolled her eyes. "I got everything, including dozens of house bricks you asked for, though I can't imagine what you want with those."

It was Sam's turn to laugh. "You'll find out soon enough when we get there."

Later that morning, Sam called a meeting with Rigby, Aiden and Dave Bartlett. He sent Gloria ahead to Yarmouth with other female squad members with specific instructions to dress and prepare the mannequins in a sitting posture.

"Have you found what I asked for?" Sam asked as he greeted Bartlett.

Bartlett nodded and looked quizzical. "The time switches took some finding; no problems with the plastic explosives and detonators. Why so many?" he said and convulsed into a fierce bout of coughing.

Sam grimaced at his barking cough. "Just a firework display I need you to arrange for me. We'll discuss my idea after the meeting."

Rigby arrived, plainly disgruntled. "If you want an update on your hair-brained scheme for a pre-emptive attack, you'll have to wait until tomorrow. I only started looking into it last night," he said crossly.

Sam shook his head. "Not today. I want us to discuss this." He laid out the folded map from the leather satchel on the desk in front of them. He gave space to consider the obvious implications.

"The threat we are faced with gives us two options; we either surrender the island and everyone who lives here, or we try to repel them when they try to land here. Neither option has a happy outcome." Sam pointed to the arrows on the map. "We must assume they are the locations shown on this map."

"So no more touchy-feely attempts at negotiation then," Rigby said sardonically.

Sam ignored the barely disguised insult. "We still have our pre-emptive strike to consider," he continued. "But if that fails we will be left with only unpleasant options. So, in the absence of anything better, I want you to devise a plan for opposing them with all the resources we will be left with."

"Which is about two hundred partially trained squad members, with about a hundred amateurs in reserve who can just about fire a gun," Bartlett added in a matter of fact voice.

Sam shrugged and stared at the map. "Well, whatever happens, we need a workable plan to give us at least some sort of a chance. On the evidence David Longmarsh has brought us, we'll almost certainly be outnumbered. We need a plan that, in the worst event, will hold them back for two or three days. Beyond that," Sam said with a heavy sigh, "I doubt if any of us will still be alive to worry about the consequences."

"Why two or three days? Are you still planning to hold this fancy referendum of yours? Democracy lives on," Rigby taunted, provocatively.

"Something like that," Sam answered dismissively. There seemed little point in rising to the bait.

He left them discussing a possible plan. It was pointless wasting precious time batting away insults. Based on the options he had just outlined, the outlook was grim. It was a shame that Rigby's ego would still prevent him working with a team, even at such a perilous time. Despite everything, Sam knew in the end they would sink or swim on the success of the secret plan only he had agreed with Napier. They just had to gain the time to pull it off.

Sam caught up with Claire, absorbed and excited by her morning visit to meet her puppy, now interestingly called *Pilot*. Somehow it seemed an appropriate name for a guide dog and together they paid a visit on Ruth, now out of bed and seeming to be on the mend. Claire tactfully excused herself and went off in search of Alice, sensing that Sam needed space to talk to Ruth.

He quickly brought Ruth up to speed on everything, trusting her confidentiality without having to ask for it, and gave her the facts without embellishment. Ruth eased herself into a chair beside the bed. She was no longer on a drip but Sam noticed the oxygen mask was still in regular use. For a moment she stared at the ceiling.

"So, today's Tuesday. How long do we have?"

It was easy to talk with Ruth, she always managed to keep one step ahead of his thinking.

"They will come at us no later than Friday."

"Is that enough time?"

Sam pursed his lips. He didn't have an answer to that question. Ruth nodded at his silence.

"Well that's it then; I'd better get dressed," she said with grim humour.

"Don't you think you should rest more?" Sam said with genuine concern. "A few more days?"

Ruth laughed. "I've got a portable oxygen bottle and a crutch, what more does a girl need." Unsteadily, she pulled herself to her feet. "I'll see you at the next forum meeting then." She drew the curtains around her bed, ushering Sam out while she dressed but then called to him as he made to leave.

"By the way Mr Chairman," she gently mocked. "Don't forget about Teri and Ryan. I hear some inspired genius has locked them up as the best idea for keeping them apart."

Sam and Gloria watched the rib towing a pair of rowing boats, linked by a rope, through the harbour entrance.

"Well, they look more convincing from a distance," Gloria suggested as the boats rolled gently with the swell.

"That's all they have to do," Sam mumbled in reply.

He raised his binoculars and looked westwards towards Hurst Castle. John had broadcast the message that delivery was underway on Whistler's radio frequency.

"Personally, I can't see them being impressed by what we're sending them. I know they're desperate and not that fussy, but a boat full of tailors' dummies isn't going to cut it."

"Hopefully, the second boat full of alcohol will, at least for a few days," Sam replied, binoculars still trained on the mainland coast. A few yards away, John sat in the Landrover, eternal headphones clamped over his ears. Dave Bartlett sat beside him.

Sam handed the binoculars to Gloria. "Call me the moment you see something appear from behind the castle," he said, walking towards the Landrover.

"Anything?" he called to John.

"Just excited chatter," John answered without looking up.

Beside him, Bartlett sat slumped on a seat, eyes closed, a smouldering cigarette between his fingers. It seemed that he could sleep and smoke at the same time.

"That's a lot of effort for just a hoax," Bartlett said, eyes still closed, aware Sam was looking at him.

"All we need is to buy a few extra days."

"I can't see you're going to gain very much from trying to pull the wool over their eyes. I figure these men are pretty desperate for many things, especially women and food. Somehow I can't imagine them seeing the funny side of our little charade."

Sam didn't answer. The mannequins in the boat had been dressed and made up to appear genuine, if only from a distance. Each one was secured to two house bricks; Sam's intention was to leave no evidence from the tableau that was about to unfold. After that, they would have to wait and see how things worked out; what else could they do.

Gloria called for Sam's attention. "We've got company."

Even without binoculars Sam could see the wake of a high speed motorboat carving a course towards their convoy of rowing boats. He turned to John, already calling the towing rib on the radio. All they needed now was a substantial slice of good luck.

He looked pensively at Bartlett. "Are you confident your men know what they've got to do?" he asked. "Timing is everything."

"And waterproof cabling," Bartlett quipped as Gloria handed Sam the binoculars. Only half a mile separated the high speed motorboat from their two little boats. He drew a deep breath and crossed his fingers.

"Okay," Bartlett shouted. "Tell them to begin."

Within seconds of his instruction, the crew of the rib cast off the line from the boats and their cargoes. With its engine accelerating, the rib wove an arc around the boats, hastily turning away from the rapidly closing high speed motorboat. Seeing the rowing boats now set adrift, the motorboat accelerated, bow wave high as the outboard motors raced to full throttle, sending a deep-throated rumble across the sea. For once things seemed to be going to plan. The rib slowed and hove-to a short distance to the south. They were under strict instructions to linger only a few seconds to avoid putting themselves at risk.

"Go now," Bartlett shouted, binoculars fixed on the closing distance of the motorboat.

For several seconds nothing seemed to happen. Sam felt his stomach twist. On the foredeck of the motorboat several men had their binoculars trained on the rowing boats, examining the cargo. Sam focused back to the boat of mannequins, just in time to see it lurch in the water, as though pushed upwards by a large passing wave, before settling once more into the sea. Drowned out by the roar of the approaching motorboat, a dozen small explosive charges had just detonated. And blown the bottom out of the boat. Or so Sam hoped. His plan had included replacing all the buoyancy bags with large rocks. In addition, Bartlett had placed his charges to detonate simultaneously, the small blasts removing all the underside of the boat in one piece with the aim of sinking it in seconds. None of its fake human passengers were to escape. The boat founded in seconds, not tipping, but settling vertically into the sea. Within seconds only a few hands and arms, left loose when the mannequins were strapped in, rose to grasp forlornly for rescue, as the boat and its cargo slid gracefully beneath the waves of the Solent. To the eyes of the approaching motorboat it should appear that the boat had been hit by a large wave and tragically sunk, taking the 'women' to the bottom of the sea. He doubted Whistler would fall for his ruse, but if he couldn't prove Sam had double crossed him it might make him stay his hand for just a few days.

Bartlett grinned with satisfaction. "That bit worked," he said.

"We just have to hope that the channel is deep enough so the boat would go straight to the bottom," Sam added.

Gloria had a squint-eyed look. "You don't really think they're going to fall for that, do you?" she said.

Sam shrugged. They would find out soon enough. The other boat laden with supplies had been deliberately left afloat and he was betting that with drink inside them, Whistler's men wouldn't be asking too many questions. The price of success was time. The thing Sam needed more than anything was a few extra days.

# FORTY-ONE

By the time they had returned to Newport, the area beside the river around the forum building was filled with men and women from the hamlets, chatting in the late afternoon sunshine. The decision to mobilise the island's sighted population meant, in practice, that each community released six of its sighted members, leaving most farms to be run by sighted teenagers and the blind. Sam moved through the groups as he arrived and thought how enthusiastic they looked. Such impressive progress had been made since the catastrophe of the pandemic five years previously and he had a heavy heart to think it was all about to be destroyed because survivors still found it impossible to co-exist together, despite the odds stacked against them. Even if they could withstand the onslaught soon to be released upon them, how many would be left alive to pick up the pieces and still deal with their nemesis, the boar?

"Any chance of trying to contact Napier tonight?" Sam asked John as he entered the forum building amidst the bustle of people.

"I'll try; usual time, usual place," John replied. "Do you think your plan with the boats worked?"

"We'll find out soon enough."

Sam looked at John with concern; he looked almost asleep on his feet. "When did you last get some rest?" he asked.

"I can't remember," he smiled weakly. "But you know what they say about sleep; there's plenty of time for that when you're dead."

In black humour, Sam walked off to deal with the endless stream of demands.

"Lorna and Jake came to see me while you were out," Claire said as they shared a hastily improvised meal.

"How are things at the farm?" Sam felt a pang of guilt as he asked. He had planned to pay a visit to Rachel and the children. Where did the time go?

"They both seemed a bit down. Lorna said she was missing us, Jake said Marcus and his wife keep arguing with everyone. It seems that you and Rachel were the glue that bound them all together; now you've both gone, that equilibrium has broken down," Claire said with a sad expression, aware of her unintended responsibility in disrupting the lives of everyone at the farm.

Sam reached across the small table they were sharing and squeezed her hand.

"You mustn't blame yourself. If anyone is to blame, it's me, though it's not helped with Whistler and his gang continually attacking us. The constant threat hanging over us has turned our lives upside down. I know I'm neglecting things, not least you," he squeezed her hand again. "But what can I do differently? I don't want the role that's been thrust on me. Apparently, fate thought otherwise."

Claire had a worried look as she asked, "Do I need to be scared about the future? You can give an honest answer."

Sam gazed into her face; her eyes were still, listening for his answer. Fear was no stranger to Claire and he knew he couldn't avoid the truth.

"We all need to be scared of what lies ahead. Our strength as a community is unity of purpose. We're outnumbered by Whistler and his men, but working together counteracts that. What we need more than anything is time, and to gain that we have to find the informer here before it's all too late. If only we could stop the leak of all our plans, we'd stand a better chance. Until we do, quite frankly our prospects are starting to look bleak."

About an hour later, Bartlett and Aiden knocked on the door to their room. Claire made them tea as they briefed him.

"We've been chatting to David Longmarsh," Aiden said. "At first we still weren't totally confident he was telling the truth. To be more certain Dave asked questions to see if he contradicted himself. Longmarsh tells a convincing tale and stuck to his story, so we have to accept that his information is reliable. We think he must be telling the truth. His girlfriend Cynthia proved to be particularly useful and we think she's too frightened to be lying."

Aiden paused. "She seemed certain that a lot of new faces have recently arrived in their area; Scots, Irish, northern accents, ex-soldiers and a lot out of the prisons."

Bartlett took over the narrative. "Add to that, about a dozen landing craft have been brought around the coast, presumably from Poole Harbour, including some large enough to carry vehicles. Longmarsh said they heard large vehicles moving around at night, so that makes sense." He paused, staring through his eternal veil of cigarette smoke. "And that's the game changer. If they have found some tanks, even old ones, that work and can be driven, we're in big trouble."

Shocked, Sam stared at them both for a moment. "Any ideas on numbers?"

"Of men, probably not as many as we first feared. Given the number of landing craft, perhaps three or four hundred. But that makes no difference if they can bring tanks with them," he said with a shake of his head.

Sam went to look out of the dormer window; his back to the two men. It had begun to rain, streaking the glass with beads of raindrops. Behind him, Claire poured tea into mugs, filling time while they waited for his response. Sam shook his head, as though silently arguing with himself.

Eventually he asked, "Can you work out a plan for me, tonight? Assume we don't oppose them when they land, avoiding contact or conflict unless it's absolutely necessary, but use every resource we have to take the entire population on a progressive retreat down the island. Blow up every bridge, block every road junction. Assume we fall back continuously, without fighting. Delay and obstruct to be the mantra. Avoid casualties, keep everyone organised and together. Use the squads to screen everyone while they retreat behind them, like a form of rear guard."

"Rigby won't like this," Aiden said in an uncertain voice.

"Then don't tell him," Sam turned to stare hard into his eyes.

He walked over to the table and supported himself on the back of a chair.

"I need a plan that gets us to Friday at least, preferably Saturday. A scorched earth policy. Leave nothing they can use, except alcohol. Dump every drop of the stuff on the island and leave it wherever you can block their path and make it obvious where it's been left. Anything to slow them down."

Bartlett lit another cigarette from the dying stub of the previous. "Just one point on this magical plan of yours? Where exactly are you planning to take us? The island is not particularly large and eventually we'll end up in the sea."

Sam grinned. "Southwards. I'll tell you where when I know for sure. Just tell absolutely no one what you're planning, especially Rigby. That's absolutely imperative." He smiled in encouragement. "And can I have the plan for first thing in the morning. Just in case they pay us an early visit."

Sam awoke to the sound of rain drumming on the slate roof directly above his head. He fumbled for his watch on the bedside table; the luminous hands showed three o'clock. Sometime in the next half-hour, John would try to contact Napier, and Sam needed to be there. He twisted uneasily in bed. So much of his plan rested with Napier and his silence over the past few days was eating into him.

Reluctantly, he slid out of the warmth of the bed. Claire stirred, making a light snuffling noise as she balanced between sleep and wakefulness. He lit the gas ring beneath an enamelled kettle, made tea before it began to whistle, and dressed by candlelight.

Since his ruse in the waters off Hurst Castle, there had been no response from Whistler. Sam had no idea if that was positive or not. Sven and his henchmen hadn't received the women they were hoping for and he could only hope the generous quantity of alcohol they had sent had overcome their disappointment, at least for a few days. He had sworn Gloria and her girls to silence but one of them would eventually let something slip, so he could only hope that it wouldn't happen too soon.

Sam found one of his bodyguards asleep on the sofa at the foot of the stairs. He tapped his foot to wake him. The forum had become increasingly anxious about his personal safety in the aftermath of the meeting at Hurst Castle and insisted on extra security.

"We need to make a visit," he said, handing the sleepy man a mug of tea, leaving to gather oilskins for them both.

He could hear the rain, driven against the windows by the wind. Good news for while it lasted; Sam couldn't see Whistler or anyone else making a move in bad weather and a turbulent sea. He made a note to ask Craig to prepare a forecast for the rest of the week. Two or three days of unseasonably windy weather would be worth their weight in gold right now.

They drove without lights and on low revs to find John, passing through the early morning streets of Newport. John's Landrover was in the same clearing near the airstrip, a metal cable attached to the front winch, disappearing into the dark sky above them, making the Landrover rock and dance energetically in the wind.

"Keep a watch for anyone who might have followed us," Sam told his bodyguard. "It's not impossible that someone might come snooping around. I'll send a flask out to you shortly."

When Sam climbed into the back of the Landrover little appeared to have changed since his last visit. John and Jaki sat hunched over their radio sets, headphones clamped over their ears. John turned when he entered; Sam raised his eyebrows in silent question but John shook his head.

"Nothing yet," he said. "Perhaps it's too early."

"Keep trying," Sam said and found a spare seat in the corner uncluttered by equipment.

After a few minutes John switched on the microphone and issued his call sign. "This is White Cloud calling Shepherd. Do you read me?"

He repeated it, switched to loudspeaker and sat back. The hiss of static rolled around the cabin, whispering through a cloud of white noise. John had once described how, in the early years after the pandemic, he had sometimes encountered voices, plaintively calling a plea for help, in an endless repeating rota. He had tried countless attempts to contact them, only to realise that he was probably just talking to a tape recorder. In desperation, the callers had recorded their cries for help as a final act, leaving the tape to spool until the batteries ran flat long after their deaths. No one ever replied to John's calls. Only the dead were listening.

And so he tried to raise Napier, repeating the message every five minutes for the best part of an hour, without success, the silence imposing a feeling of gloom on the three of them.

The rear door opened and it was the bodyguard who broke the spell. "Anyone got some coffee?" Rainwater cascaded from his glistening oilskins.

John passed a half-empty flask. "Sorry, we got distracted."

The man nodded his thanks and disappeared. Two seconds later the morse receiver kicked into life with the 'get ready' signal. John leaned across and checked the tape spool and the frequency, just in time for the machine to spring into life. Punched tape coiled out onto the desk in a frenetic chatter. The silence was deafening when it stopped. Judging by the timing and the frequency adjustments John had made, Sam expected the message had come from Napier, though using morse was a surprise. Slowly, John ran the tape through his fingers, writing down the letters as he did so. It took only seconds to de-code. Anxiously, he glanced up, staring at Sam, his face ghost green in the light of the radio dials. He handed Sam the pad on which he had written the message. The sentence, written in black pencil, left little doubt. Whistler had found Longmarsh's morse transmitter.

'Well, Morten. You asked for it.'

A single line of words, ending with '&'

Just before it became light they wound down the balloon and aerial. There had been no word from Napier. Sam left John and Jaki to close things down and he set off with his bodyguard to the farm to find Rachel and the others. When he arrived, he met Marcus crossing the farmyard. He seemed genuinely pleased to see him.

"I had hoped you would bring a trailer of supplies with you," Marcus said, half joking, as they gripped hands in greeting.

Sam tried to smile. "Sorry. This isn't a courtesy call. Can you gather everyone together? I need to talk to you all." He paused for a moment. "Are Rachel and the children here?"

Marcus looked worried. "Rachel is still at Rainbow's End. We've no idea when, or if, she intends to return." He pursed his lips. "What with Jake, Monica, and Lorna summoned to Newport to mobilise their squads, your arrival sounds serious."

"So who's left to help with running the farm at the moment?" Sam asked with concern.

"Just me and three of the eldest boys. Peter's good, Michael can be helpful if he tries, and several of the blind girls have skills with the livestock, but we can't achieve much more than milking and feeding. As you know, we desperately need to do more re-seeding. We've got less than a third completed and we're stuck until we receive more fuel and supplies. Any idea when we can expect something, when this crisis might be over?" Marcus asked anxiously. "We were only just coping before the storm and now with this business with the boar, we're going backwards fast."

They had reached the kitchen door before Sam could give an answer. What he had to tell everyone wasn't going to make pleasant listening. While Sam waited for everyone at the farm to assemble he sent a carrier pigeon to Newport with a message explaining where he was and asking Mary to arrange a forum meeting for later that day. It had become a sign of the times that people became anxious if they didn't know where to find him. Someone had lit a fire in the main lounge. Though it was spring, grey bulbous rain clouds gave a gloomy feel to the day and the warm flicker of orange flames added a helpful lift.

"It's good to see everyone," Sam began. "I would have liked to have got back sooner but things have been hectic. I'm glad to see you're all doing so well in difficult circumstances," he said in encouragement. "Things are not easy at the moment," Sam paused, glancing around the room at their expectant faces.

"I wanted to speak to you personally before you receive a directive from the forum, which could come as early as tonight," he hesitated, choosing his words with care. "It might cause you concern."

No one spoke; all waited, their expressions asking the questions.

"Very soon and without provocation, we could be invaded by an armed group from the mainland. We have feared it might come to this for some time and tried our best to avoid such an outcome. I have to warn you it looks as if our attempts are about to fail. Even with as many islanders mobilised as possible, this gang from the mainland could be much stronger than us. Many of them have previous military training and they have access to military equipment on the mainland. When guidance arrives, you must all move immediately to a village a few miles south of Newport; further instructions will be given to you there. You will only be able to take what you can carry. Everything else must be left behind. Everything. So pack carefully."

He paused, looking at the ring of shocked faces staring at him. Very soon, all the other forum members would have to repeat this same conversation in every hamlet on the island. It wasn't going to be pleasant or easy.

"What about the animals? The cows will need to be milked and they'll need to be fed at least twice a day," Monica said, her voice a mixture of fear and concern.

Sam fixed his face and took a breath, knowing he would have to limit the truth for all their sakes.

"Feed and milk them as you come to leave and turn them into the fields so they can fend for themselves until you can get back. If you leave extra hay bales, they should be okay for some while. By then, one way or another, this crisis should be all over."

Sam drew breath; there it was; the truth, at least in part, had left his lips. The price? That they would obey the instructions when it arrived, and save their lives. He had expected a tirade of angry questions but instead everyone fell silent as they processed what he had just told them. Only Peter spoke up with an obstinate glare in Sam's direction.

"This is our farm, these are our animals, our friends. We can't just abandon them to bureaucratic instructions that order us to leave. What are you threatening to do if we refuse to obey you?" he said.

Sam looked at the floor. The challenge didn't surprise him; in Peter's position he would probably have felt the same. He took a deep breath.

"You're right. We can't order anyone to leave their farms. Instead, I'm begging you all to do as we ask. If you don't, and things go badly for us, you will be left to the mercy of men who care nothing for our values. I can't sugarcoat the situation; I've met the leaders of this gang and they leave no room for compromise. They want our island and our people to work for them, and only on their terms. It's as blunt as that; there are no options, no shades of grey."

This time a gasp passed around the room; several of the women cried out and burst into tears, followed by some of the children. For several minutes Sam was ignored as family members comforted one another, until Monica came in his direction, anger now burning in her eyes.

"I think you had better leave; you've caused enough trouble for one day," she nodded towards the door.

Sam shrugged, hesitated, and said, "You may well have contempt for how I've behaved in the past few months and what I've just told you," he told her, only inches separating them. "But if only for the sake of the children, do precisely as you're instructed when the moment comes, as painful as that may be."

Monica glared back at Sam for a second, her face now blank and expressionless. She glanced at the door.

"Go, before this gets out of hand," she said, almost spitting the words in his face, leaving him with the feeling of utter rejection, thrown out of his own home.

Sam had to make a circuitous route to Rainbow's End. His bodyguard drove the Landrover, leaving him to brood over his lack of success at the farm. Albert Jamieson would have made a better job than he just had, but then Albert had always held the respect of the community, even with those who disagreed with him. That was something he was a long way from acquiring.

They approached Rainbow's End along the farm track and found a large fallen tree trunk barring their path, supported on oil drums at either end. Sam climbed from the Landrover.

"I'll be no more than half an hour. Turn the Landrover around in case we need to make a quick return to Newport."

He ducked beneath the barrier and set off in the direction of the farmhouse. He had barely covered fifty yards when a figure came walking down the drive towards him.

He resembled his father; the young man was the image of Jeff Robinson. He barred Sam's path, a rifle cradled across his chest.

Sam stopped. "I've come to speak to Rachel," he said. "I have reason to believe she's still here."

"Who's asking?" Though he must have recognised Sam, the younger Robinson had his father's surly manners.

"Sam Morten. But you already know that. Rachel lives with me at my farm."

Robinson waited, his face impassive.

"Can you tell me where she is?" Sam asked, trying hard to keep impatience out of his voice.

"Somewhere in the fields. Don't exactly know where. We're rounding up sheep, so they could be anywhere. I'll tell her you came."

"Where are my children?"

"With Rachel, chasing the sheep I would guess."

He made no effort to move out of the way or allow Sam any farther. The farm covered hundreds of acres and Sam had no idea where to start searching for her. For a moment, both men silently eyed one another with barely concealed dislike. Sam wagered that Robinson wouldn't physically restrain him if he tried to push past him, but what would that achieve? It would still be like looking for a needle in a haystack.

"If I write a message, you must make sure Rachel knows I've been here looking for her and reads what I've written. It's very important."

Robinson nodded but didn't answer. Sam sighed inwardly; without causing an argument, it was probably the best he was going to get in the circumstances. He hastily wrote a message on a page of his notebook, tore it out and folded it, writing Rachel's name on the outer face. He handed it to Robinson.

"Please be sure she gets this; it is important."

"I said I would," he said as he took it and waited for Sam to leave.

"Just one thing before I go." The man in front of him certainly wouldn't win any prizes in the personality stakes, but at least Sam had his attention. "This evening or tomorrow morning at the latest, you're going to receive instructions from the forum. For the sake of all of you, be sure to take them seriously and act on them immediately."

Robinson gave an upwards jerk of his head, as if he had just smelt something bad. "Ah yes, the forum." It was all he had to say; his tone spoke more than his words.

As Sam turned and walked away, he realised that trying to persuade people to do the right thing and save themselves was going to be far harder than he had feared, and yet they were in a situation that wouldn't grant them the luxury of time to argue the point.

Chris Woods met Sam with a beaming smile as they met in the car park on the quayside.

"We've got one of the spare planes operating," she said in a bright voice. "It's a twin engine machine and I can fly it, at least in daylight. The rain should pass through by lunchtime, so I thought I'd make a visit across the Solent and see what's going on."

"That's the best news I've had so far today," Sam said with a grin. "Just make sure you keep safe and come back in one piece. And take someone with you."

"Well, you're not coming, that's for sure. You're needed here."

Rigby approached, carrying a file and folded map.

"I've got your plan for this ludicrous pre-emptive strike you misled the forum to consider." He handed the documents to Sam, casting a dismissive glance at Chris's direction.

"Don't worry," she said, reading his expression. "I've found another plane to fly. I'm off to cross the Solent."

With a happy wave she walked away, leaving Rigby to have words with Sam. Rigby watched her figure disappear with a thoughtful expression.

"We'll talk in my office." Sam announced, leaving Rigby to follow him.

Rigby laid out his maps on Sam's desk.

"We only have boats for about thirty squads, which limits what we can do." Rigby pointed to the various areas that landing craft might assemble. "Southampton is blocked by too many sunken wrecks; Portsmouth is a possibility, Buckler's Hard is the favourite. The critical factor is we can't do the strike until Saturday. There aren't enough boats in the right place until then and we need fuel and squad training for landing from boats."

"Saturday's too late," Sam said.

"It can't be done before then. We've trained for fighting boar, not jumping out of boats," Rigby snapped. "By the way, where's Chris off to?" he asked with questioning interest.

"She's going to fly over most of the port areas they could be using to gather their landing craft. It will be critical to know how advanced their preparations are."

Rigby nodded. "Well, no amount of wishful thinking can speed up my plan. You'll see on the last page I've prepared an estimate of our casualties. It doesn't make pleasant reading," he warned.

With a deep intake of breath, Sam nodded and turned to the final page. Written in black and white only confirmed what he had already feared, but it didn't lessen the shock. Seeing the look of surprise on Sam's face, Rigby smiled.

"I suppose those figures explain why you've cut me out of the loop and are exploring a separate proposal for retreating without a fight as part of your capitulation plan."

So he had guessed. Sam ought not to have been surprised.

"Just a contingency plan. If they attack us, the odds aren't exactly in our favour," he said without looking up from the map.

"Makes me wonder what other schemes you're dreaming up without telling me."

Sam gave the appearance of being distracted. "The forum makes the plans, Connor, you know that. It's my job to take the overview and put the options before them." He studied the map intensely without seeing it, listening to Rigby's body language.

"Well don't think too hard, Morten. If your personal life is anything to go by, strategy is not one of your strong points."

Sam looked up from the map. The barb was intended to provoke an argument. He smiled. "Thank you, Connor, I'll bear in mind what you've said."

With that, he opened the door and waited for Rigby to leave.

Unrequested, Mary brought in a tea tray.

"Your young lady is waiting in my office," she said without expression.

"Thank you, Mary. I'll come and collect her," he said politely. His tone implied that if Mary had wanted to help, she would have just brought Claire to his office with the tray.

"Ah, found you at last," Claire said as Sam greeted her with a kiss and led her by the hand through the labyrinth of corridors. "I had begun to wonder where you had disappeared to."

She had spent the morning with *Pilot* and for a few minutes she distracted Sam with her stories of playful training while he poured tea and laughed at their hilarious antics. It brought an idea to mind.

"Claire, I know your puppy is very young, but could you manage to look after it by yourself? Say, immediately, tomorrow at the latest?"

"I think so. She certainly responds to me already. I'm not sure Alice's mother would agree though."

"She won't have a choice I'm afraid. I think you should get together everything you need to care for a dog immediately, today."

"Okay. Why? Your voice has gone all serious again. You're scaring me."

Her mouth held a serious expression as she paused to sip her tea. Claire pulled a face.

"Sorry. I didn't mean to frighten you," Sam added. "Just thinking ahead."

"It wasn't that." She returned her cup with a thoughtful expression. "That tea tastes funny."

"Perhaps the milk has gone off," Sam sniffed the jug. "I'll get some fresh."

"No, don't bother. I'm not thirsty anyway," she said with a puzzled frown. "I'll gather together everything I can find for *Pilot* this afternoon. If I'm to take her now, I think you'll need to speak to Alice's mother and explain the necessity. That would carry more weight and might better convince her."

"Good idea. I'm just going to the airstrip. I'll call on her when I come back."

Sam and Claire hugged quickly as he handed her the guide stick and led her to the door. As he did so, he felt Claire hesitate and pause.

"Just one thing," she said. "That smell of fresh flowers in the woods the other day. I knew I had come across it before." She paused. "I noticed it again today in this building."

"Where?"

Claire shrugged. "I'm not sure. In one of the corridors, I think. Is it important?"

Sam hesitated, still holding both her hands in his. When he spoke, his voice carried an edge of urgency. "If I led you through the building do you think you could identify it again?"

"I think so. It was quite pronounced, but only in one area."

"Look, it's important I go out now. I need to see Chris Woods when she returns, but immediately I'm back we need to scour the building. Organise your things for *Pilot*; I'll be back here in an hour at the most," he kissed her on the forehead. "And be sure you don't tell a soul about what we've just discussed, even if anyone asks what you're doing here."

Sam left with his mind reeling. He needed to move quickly but had to see Chris first. If the landing craft were still where David Longmarsh had seen them they would be safe for a while longer. If they weren't, it meant the 'end game' had commenced, a thought that he dreaded and feared in equal measure.

The Landrover came to a halt in a shower of loose gravel. John, Craig and Angela were grouped together with binoculars outside the radio hut, staring anxiously northwards. Sam slammed the cab door and moved quickly to join them.

"We've lost contact with Chris over Buckler's Hard amidst a storm of shooting," John shouted, his words pinched by the binoculars. He put them down, turned and added, "It's almost as if they knew she was coming and were lying in wait for her."

"Any sign?" Sam looked up, following their direction.

"Nothing yet, though we can't see much from this distance," Angela said.

They were silent for a few minutes, straining eyes and ears for some sign of Chris's return. John turned to Sam with a sudden flare of anger.

"It's a repeat of what happened to Cromford. Again, they knew Chris was coming before she even arrived." He looked at Sam morosely. "They know what we're doing before we can even make a start. At this rate we've no chance if we can't keep anything secret for more than five minutes," he added in exasperation, his words suddenly whipped away as a twin engine plane roared only feet above their heads, skimming from the sea at wave top height.

Chris was back. She made a long turn beyond the airfield before returning to touch down in a pin-point landing and taxied over to where they were standing. Aside from a few dents and holes, the plane looked little worse for wear. She opened the cockpit door and climbed onto the wing. Sam stood aside from the others; he needed to control his emotions to keep his thoughts clear. Once again, they had been betrayed and he struggled to contain his anger as he waited to speak to Chris. He watched, waiting, while Chris removed her helmet and headphones.

"Are you okay?" he asked as she came over. Behind her, he noticed her assistant being helped shakily to the ground.

"We got the full treatment; a laid on reception. More bullets than you ever want to see close up. Fortunately, that beauty," she indicated the plane over her shoulder with her hand, "has a real turn of speed, so we were probably going much faster than they expected. Virtually everything missed us," she said with an exultant smile.

"The landing craft?"

"Loads of the buggers. But at least they're still there, in Buckler's Hard. For how long is another matter. From what I saw, most of them seemed well-loaded," she added with a worried frown.

Sam felt the tension suddenly slip out of him. They had won that round by the skin of their teeth, which was little enough to be satisfied with. Suffice to say, it meant respite, at least for a day or two more.

Chris was on an adrenalin high; he almost felt sorry to deflate her. "Who did you tell where you were going?" he asked with a calmness he didn't feel.

"What? Tell? No one. Just you and Rigby."

For an instant, their eyes met in a second of realisation.

"Precisely," he said, though the word brought him little comfort.

Sam was late back in Newport, only just in time for yet another emergency forum meeting. He found Ruth in an empty room in a quiet part of the building. To his astonishment, she was dressed and in a wheelchair, oxygen bottle and mask taped to the rear handles. She still looked pale and drawn but with her presence he felt both relief and concern in equal measure. Javed stood beside her, sporting a broad bandage around his head and they were joined by Aiden and Gloria with three squad members, plus Simon Grey.

Sam quickly briefed them about Chris's eventful flight and listened to their advice before leading everyone into the forum meeting. The buzz of conversation in the room was so animated that their entrance went almost unnoticed, until someone became aware that Gloria and her squad members had positioned themselves in front of every exit door. The room rapidly descended into an expectant silence as, unsmiling, Sam walked to his seat. He started without preamble.

"This afternoon, one of our members made a dangerous flight to check the situation on the mainland. It is only by good fortune and her expert flying skill that she wasn't killed. Again, our adversaries had been forewarned of the plan, tipped off in advance. Only three people knew about the flight and its destination; myself, Chris Woods ... and Connor Rigby. Only one of us could have told them that Chris was coming; the same person who does so on every occasion we plan an operation to protect ourselves. On the mainland, they know our intentions almost before we do ourselves. But then, of course they would, wouldn't they, Rigby?"

Rigby stood up, ashen-faced.

"You idiot, Morten," he retorted. "It's common knowledge that we don't like each other, but I would never have believed you could stoop to this level of utter stupidity."

"Whether I'm foolish or not is a measure of judgement. But today's act of treachery, coupled with the presence of a hidden VHF aerial we discovered on your farm," Sam paused, making an almost imperceptible nod of the head, "leaves no alternative but to take you into protective custody, at least until we've completed our plans to protect ourselves."

Given her size, it was a surprise that Rigby failed to notice Gloria until she closed the handcuffs onto his wrists. It made everyone in the room gasp in surprise. A few of Rigby's supporters started to protest, but Sam's mind had been made up before the meeting and he wasn't about to conduct an inquest here and now. Aiden arrived with several of his squad, and vigorously protesting, Rigby was led away, his shouts of abuse deaf to Sam's ears, leaving the meeting to subside into an uproar of shouts and commotion.

Sam leaned back in his chair, staring at the ceiling. In the circumstances he had no alternative but to act; Rigby's complicity was blatantly obvious. Yet it still left a shadow to cloud his thoughts. At that moment Sam had remembered he had completely forgotten to meet with Claire and search the forum building. But Rigby didn't wear perfume.

## FORTY-TWO

After the forum meeting, Sam found sleep impossible. Rigby's supporters had made a determined attempt to disqualify Sam from his role as chairman. He had never seen the council so divided, as harsh words and accusations, many of them aimed at his private life, were thrown across the chamber. If their situation hadn't been so precarious he would have resigned there and then, triggering an immediate election for a new chairman. Sam closed his eyes, unable to drown out the arguments and bickering that swirled around him. Were they really so blind to what awaited them that they were prepared to fight over petty feuds and insults? He felt deflated. The evidence so far implicating Rigby had left no other alternative than to remove him. Yet what people demanded was strong leadership, no matter how flawed; Rigby offered that.

The ear-splitting crack of a gavel striking desk shocked the room into silence.

"Enough." Ruth's voice, rough and dry with fatigue and pain, echoed around the room. She stood with difficulty, crutch beneath her good arm to support her injured leg, glaring angrily at everyone in the room.

"This is self-indulgent insanity," Ruth said in acid words of exasperation. "Doing this is beyond the realms of 'fiddling while Rome burns'. I've met these people who are attacking us, up close and personal, and I can tell you the experience isn't one to repeat. Do any of you have a remote idea of what awaits us if we fall into their hands? Are you really that blind?"

Ruth paused, gasping for breath and gave a challenging look to everyone in the room. She took a gulp of air from her mask and continued.

"Of course you're not. It's fear that makes us pretend the nightmare won't come true if we try to pretend it's only a dream." She paused again, struggling to breathe, a palm raised to stop any interruptions. "Bear with me for a moment," she paused again for a few seconds.

"My friends, if we are to have any chance of surviving we have to work together, even if, for some of us, that means accepting things we don't like. For that to succeed we need leadership. We all admired Albert Jamieson for his wisdom and judgement. And it was his decision, shortly before he was prematurely taken from us, to appoint Sam Morten as his successor. I've seen enough of Sam in a crisis to convince me that Albert's choice was the right one. What confronts us is the biggest threat we've faced since the pandemic. Once this is behind us we can decide, by a democratic vote, who we want to lead us. If Sam Morten makes mistakes and we disagree with his leadership, we can vote to dismiss him and elect someone else. But until then, this infighting must stop. To put it simply, fate, and Albert Jamieson, have decided that Sam Morten must lead us through this time of crisis and there it must rest."

Ruth slumped into her wheelchair, waving away offers of assistance as she sucked oxygen through her mask. She refused to be taken back to the clinic, sensing that only her presence would prevent attempts to unseat Sam as chairman.

The outfall of Ruth's intervention brought agreement on the plan to begin withdrawing from the north of the island, and it was passed unanimously. Bartlett and Aiden had prepared a working plan in amazingly quick time and instructions to evacuate the northern hamlets sent out immediately. Reluctantly, they had decided that people would be told it was a temporary necessity, that once the crisis had passed they would soon return to their homes. As the members dispersed, Sam was thoughtful, knowing that returning to their homes was unlikely. He took out the plan he had found in the satchel in Weymouth. It clearly showed arrows pointing towards their northern ports, from Yarmouth in the west, to Ryde in the east. Despite its logic, they couldn't be certain that this was the plan they faced, but in the absence of anything else it would have to do. Bartlett and Aiden had decided to leave the ports undefended, watched only by a few men with scramble bikes. All the squads would be held inland, blocking roads and junctions and protecting the hamlet groups as they withdrew southward through Newport. Their immediate destination was Rookley where the village hall was already being prepared to receive them until the situation became clearer. As a plan it offered a decent solution which should spare lives. But the reality was heartbreaking. Everything had to be left behind, people could only take what could be carried, and Sam knew the only way they could be persuaded to leave their homes was if they were told it was only temporary. Fortunately, as the evacuation gained momentum, no one thought to ask him about what would happen next. Perhaps they had no wish to hear it.

Claire was sitting in front of the open dormer when Sam finally awoke.

"There's more noise this morning, people are moving around," she said as he stretched and yawned.

Claire had prepared the last of their coffee on the gas ring. It smelt delicious.

"How long have you been sitting here?" Sam asked, drawing up a chair and sliding an arm around her shoulders.

She stretched lazily against him, like a preening cat. "For an hour or so. You woke me, talking in your sleep."

Sam sipped his coffee, reminding him that it would be sometime before he enjoyed such luxury again and that this was probably their last night together in the room. A lorry rumbled past in the street, shaking the building as it headed south.

"Claire," he said her name with deliberation. "I need you to be brave today. A lot of new things are about to happen and you must keep your focus and try not to get scared," he said in an encouraging tone.

She turned her face to the rising sun which streamed into the room, eyes closed, comforted by the sensory feeling of its warmth while she absorbed the implications of his words.

"To start with, we must go and collect *Pilot* as soon as you're dressed. I'll come with you to help."

He noticed she had made a sling from a canvas bag, to be carried over her left shoulder across her breast. Claire nodded, a broad smile now lighting her face at the thought of collecting the dog.

"Before we do that," she reminded him, "we must go to the forum building so I can show you the room I discovered the smell of the flowers."

Sam started in surprise, suddenly reminded. "Which room? Do you know what floor it was on?"

Claire frowned. "Not the ground floor, and I don't venture up to the very top floor, so somewhere in between," she paused. "I heard the chatter of typewriters, if that's any help."

Sam quickly drained his coffee and watched Claire while she washed and dressed, calmed by the very ordinariness of her actions. Though she couldn't see him, she knew he was enjoying the sight by the smile of on her lips.

The forum building was buzzing with activity when they arrived. Mary and her staff had worked late into the night typing out multiple copies of the forum instructions. All that remained now was to put into action what was written on paper.

Claire and Sam started their search of the building. Claire discounted the ground floor, but Sam insisted on leading her from room to room, silently pausing in every space to give time for her to use her acute sense of smell. They drew a blank; it was the same on the first floor. As they moved to the second, Sam realised he had no ready plan if Claire not only identified a room, but the person wearing the fragrance. That thought reminded him that questions to Rigby still awaited him.

Slowly they searched each room on the second floor leaving the largest, the administration room run by Mary, to last. After the previous late night, the room was now only staffed by two women. Claire moved past them without any sign of recognition. They walked slowly, moving from empty desk to empty desk, with the merest shake of the head from Claire. Mary's desk was in the centre of the room, left neat and orderly despite the late hour of the previous night. Claire hesitated, her eyes dancing to silent thoughts. Sam watched her in rapt attention; this was the strongest reaction he had seen from Claire in the entire building. Seconds ticked past, he held his breath, only released by an abrupt shake of her head.

"Nothing," Claire said.

"I know you never go up there," he said, "but we might as well check the top floor. Just to be sure."

Claire shrugged, his suggestion seemed like a waste of time. The top floor was given over to storage and archives, much relating to the days before the pandemic. To Sam, it smelt of dust and dry paper. It hardly seemed promising, but while they were there it still made sense to check every space. Predictably, their search was fruitless; the only reward was the view, which, from the extra height, showed a panorama of their derelict and disused town, through which columns of vehicles were now slowly winding their way in a southerly direction. Sam watched them with a sad eye, his mood dark with thoughts of the day to come.

The evidence implicating Rigby was very compelling, but instinct made Sam suspicious that he wasn't acting alone, that he must be part of a ring conspiring against them. Very soon, they would have to decide on their 'end game' and it was necessary to find all the informers in Rigby's ring before their final plan was leaked to Whistler.

They wandered, room to room, finding nothing.

"Okay," Sam said. "We'll have to finish here. Nothing ventured, nothing gained," he said with a note of forced optimism. He held Claire's hand as they descended the stairs, squeezing it gently for encouragement.

"I don't understand it. The smell was unmistakeable when I passed through the other day. If only we could have checked then," Claire added wistfully.

"If only I hadn't forgotten," Sam said in self-reproach.

He needed to check on the progress of the evacuation orders, so as they arrived back on the second floor he decided to see if Mary had returned to her desk. The office was still empty; the two women who had been there earlier were busy with a temperamental Roneo copier in the next door. There was no sign of Mary. As Sam led Claire farther into the room, he stopped abruptly. Mary's desk, so immaculate only minutes before, was now an utter mess. He dropped Claire's hand and ran to the desk. The blotter and filing trays were still in place, but now void of papers, and all the drawers beside the desk were open, stripped out, empty.

"Kind of you to abandon me," Claire said. "You could have told …" She stopped abruptly mid-sentence and hesitated. "It's here; I can smell freesias. Did we pass this way the first time? I must have missed it."

"No, you didn't," he said grimly. "The person wearing that perfume must have been watching us and returned while we were upstairs."

One of the two women at the copier came back into the room. Hurriedly, Sam turned to her. "Have you seen anyone here in the past ten minutes?"

The woman nodded. "Just Mary, with a large box of papers and documents."

"Where did she go?" he tried not to sound too anxious.

"Down the stairway. I assume she was heading for the forum chamber." The woman smiled, hoping that she had been helpful.

Without hesitating, Sam grabbed Claire's hand. "We must be quick; just run, I'll guide you." With a tug they were moving before she could reply.

Sam felt a pang of dread as they approached his own office. The door was open. No one was inside, but his desk, always kept in immaculate order by Mary, was now littered with papers, rifled and scattered, cast on the floor. The side drawers, to which only he was supposed to have a key, hung open and empty.

Sam shouted angrily in frustration, striking the desktop with his fist. "For god's sake, give us a chance," he bellowed, his words echoing down the corridors.

He didn't need to look any further to know all their maps and detailed planning lists were missing. Claire jumped when he shouted, then gathered and composed herself, uncertain at first who he was angry with.

"For what it's worth, the same perfume is here too," she said.

Sam exhaled a deep sigh. "Thanks, I had already guessed that. We were on the right track, just ten minutes too late. I think we now know the identity of the traitor. And she's just stolen everything, including all of our detailed plans for saving everyone."

Sam didn't have to wait long for more bad news. As if by magic, Gloria arrived at his open door. She had heard his shout. Doctor Morgan and Linda Hue accompanied her, both wearing tight pensive expressions on their faces. Gloria frowned as she entered. "You've two visitors who want to see you urgently." She paused, taking in the unexpected chaos of the room. "You had a row with someone?"

Sam didn't bother to explain. "Take two squads and go to Mary's home as quickly as you can. Keep her there until I arrive; lock her up if you have to but don't let her get away. And be careful; she might be as thin as a rail, but she could be dangerous."

Sam closed the door as Gloria left, turning to Doctor Morgan and Linda with a brief apology.

"I'm sorry about that."

They both cast fleeting eyes over the scattered papers.

"Can I offer you anything?" Sam asked.

Doctor Morgan shook his head, spreading his hands.

"I'll be brief; I can see you're busy enough. We've completed the autopsy on Albert Jamieson." He paused to swallow. "I'm afraid to tell you that Albert was being poisoned. Linda has found traces of cytisine in his body which, coupled with his heart problems, was enough to kill him."

Sam stared at them in shock. "I don't understand. How, why, who would want to kill Albert, of all people?"

"Cytisine is found in laburnum seed pods," Linda explained. "If you boil the pods and make tea with the extract, you have a subtle slow release killer. On the afternoon he died, it seems a concentrated dose was served to Albert. As to why? If you find the 'who' you'll probably discover the why."

A noisy tractor rumbled past, towing a trailer, momentarily drowning out their words. After weeks of fruitless searching, the pieces of the jigsaw puzzle were falling into place. All they needed now was enough time to process the complete picture. As the sound of the tractor died away, a fist hammered urgently on Sam's door, interrupting their thoughts.

"Come in."

Chris Woods burst in. "They've gone. I've just completed another check flight over Buckler's Hard. All the landing craft and ships must have sailed during the night. On the way back I flew along the coast from Yarmouth to Ryde, but there's nothing to be seen." Chris paused for breath, grinning with excitement. "It looks like they might have called it all off. Perhaps they were just bluffing all along."

Sam shook his head and walked over to the large map of the Isle of Wight on the wall. He measured the distance of an hour's sailing with the span of his hand and was silent in thought.

"Chris, can you find Aiden and Bartlett and ask them to come here as soon as possible. Find John and Craig too, if you can locate them."

He turned to Doctor Morgan and Linda.

"You're welcome to stay but things are about to get hectic. Thank you for your briefing. There's a certain person I urgently need to talk to, so you'll have to excuse me. I'll tell you what I find out straight away. In the meantime, could you keep this appalling news about Albert Jamieson to yourselves?"

They left with a nod of agreement, and Sam set out to have a conversation with Connor Rigby. It was more like a verbal fencing match than a conversation. For half an hour, Rigby parried every question Sam asked, answering with counter questions and belligerent accusations. Sam achieved nothing concrete and though he doubted Rigby had the skills to use a radio set with the aerial they had discovered, it became obvious that Rigby's relationship with Mary was closer than he had been aware. The one mistake Rigby made was to try to protect Mary whenever Sam tried to implicate her. They needed answers in a hurry and it was obvious that he wasn't going to get them easily from Rigby.

He was interrupted by a message from Gloria; Mary was missing from her farm. Mary's friends had told Gloria she spent a lot of time at an old boat-house in Wootton Creek. Tracking her down and cornering Mary there hadn't been difficult. It was almost as if she was waiting for them to arrive. Now they had her contained in a stand-off at the boat-house, demanding to see Sam.

Sam left Rigby, still seething anger at his detention. For the moment, it was more important to find out why Mary had betrayed everyone at the cost of so many lives. Sam bumped into Bartlett and Aiden as he left the building.

"Have you heard from Chris? This morning, when she flew over Buckler's Hard, she found the landing ships have left their berths and disappeared." Both men looked surprised. "I very much doubt they've given up and there are any number of places they could be hiding. Can you increase your readiness and ask Chris to fly again this afternoon, if only to check on anyone crossing the Solent."

The Landrover came to a halt a short distance from the disused ferry ramp near Fishbourne. Driven at high speed, it had been a quick journey from Newport. Gloria was waiting for him.

"We disturbed Mary loading the boat to the right of the house on the other side of the river. She ran into the empty boat-house and when we approached she fired a couple of warning shots and demanded to speak to you."

Sam used his binoculars to survey the scene. The incoming tide had already surrounded the boat, which was fitted with a large outboard motor. In the boat-house, tattered blinds had been lowered at the windows. They couldn't see Mary, but she could probably watch them from the darkened interior.

"We think she could be in one of the attic rooms. She would be able to see more from up there," Gloria said. "While you speak and distract her, we'll cross the river farther up and work our way around behind her. If she won't surrender we can always lob in a grenade as a last resort."

Sam shook his head; he needed Mary alive, providing answers.

"Have you got a boat handy?"

"There's a small inflatable with paddles." Gloria nodded towards a black rubber dinghy drawn up on the mud.

Sam left Gloria with specific instructions that shooting Mary would be an absolute last resort and walked down to the muddy banks of the creek.

"Mary. It's Sam. I'm unarmed and coming across," he shouted. There was no reply.

"This is not a good idea," Gloria muttered as Sam pushed the dinghy into the swirling waters. "Don't expect me to come and rescue you when she takes you hostage."

Sam pretended not to have heard. He eased into the boat and rowed his way the short distance across the creek. The boat-house was set back a short distance above high tide level and a gravel track ran in front of it. He hitched the inflatable to a mooring post and jumped ashore, trying to avoid getting his feet wet. The irony of the jump made Sam smile; in full view, Mary could shoot him dead in a moment, while he was worrying about wet socks. He walked up to the house, pulse racing, palms outstretched.

"Are you there, Mary? I've come as you requested."

He tried to hide the sadness he felt. She was a woman at the very heart of their community, trusted by all who knew her and yet she had chosen to betray them to Whistler of all people.

"Stop right there, Sam Morten, that's plenty close enough."

He was about ten yards from the boat-house, close enough to talk without their words being heard the other side of the creek. Sam lowered his hands, trying to relax his shoulders.

"Why are you doing this, Mary, why make it like this?"

She was silent for almost a minute, waiting.

"I have my reasons," she said, "as you have yours for coming here. And that's not for a cosy chat."

"And why is that? Why did you ask me to come here, Mary?"

"Because we both want something the other has."

Sam hesitated. "Why did you do it? What earthly reason turned you against us to cause such harm?"

She ignored his plea. "I have something you need, but first, I want fuel and your guarantee I'll leave here alive."

"And what do I get in return?"

"Information. I can tell you where and when Whistler and his men intend to land. It won't help you very much, they outnumber you, and you already know that, but it might help you change your plans and negotiate with Whistler."

He had a tremor of misgiving. His plans were formed on the map he had found in Weymouth and Mary already knew that. But if that was no longer Whistler's plan, they were in ever deeper trouble.

"I already have a map showing where they intend to land; why would I need to make a deal with you for information I already have?"

Mary laughed. "That's long out of date. Whistler guessed you had a copy and it served his purposes to let you think you knew more than you do." Her words carried a cutting edge, turning his misgivings to something closer to fear.

"Then why don't you try telling me?"

"Don't get ahead of yourself, Sam. I want fuel and your word on my safe passage first. And just in case you need reminding, your time is running out just as fast as mine."

Sam certainly didn't need reminding. He turned and shouted to Gloria to bring two jerry cans of petrol across the creek, quickly.

"I take it you're going to the mainland?"

Mary ignored his question. "Put the fuel in the boat when it arrives, connect the fuel line and start the engine."

"So why did you need to murder Albert Jamieson? He was never anything other than kind towards you," he asked as they waited.

"I had orders to put you in his place. I knew he intended to stand down and pass the role to you, but Whistler couldn't wait. Besides, Connor could never be persuaded to accept you as chairman by any means other than the sudden death of Albert Jamieson. Whistler thought you'd be a soft touch and that he could just threaten you and walk right in and take over," she said with contempt. "He was mostly right."

"So you murdered a good kind man just because you thought I was a soft touch?" Sam could have quite happily wrung her neck at the thought of what she had done.

There was a splash of oars from behind him as Gloria made a hopeless mess of rowing across the creek. She arrived wet and in a bad mood.

"Put the jerry cans in the boat, connect the fuel line and start the engine."

Sam waited in silence while Gloria did as he asked. He was quietly seething that Albert's murderer was about to slip away. Yet the price was the information that might yet save them. Would Albert think it was a price worth paying? The boat's engine spluttered into life in a cloud of smoke, interrupting his thoughts.

"Thanks, Gloria. Go back across the creek. I'll finish up here."

Gloria hesitated, giving a questioning look at the boat-house. "You're letting her go?"

Sam nodded. "There is a price. I think it's worth paying."

Gloria hesitated. For a moment he thought she was about to disobey him. He wouldn't have blamed her, but he badly needed her to cooperate. Undecided, she weighed the options, until, with a shrug of her substantial shoulders, she climbed reluctantly back into the dinghy. Mary waited until Gloria had reached the other side of the creek before speaking again.

"Walk to the front door and turn around to face the creek."

Her voice now came from the shadows on the ground floor. Sam walked over and turned his back. The door opened and something hard, the barrel of a gun, pressed against the centre of his spine.

"Haven't you forgotten something?" he reminded Mary.

"No. You're my insurance policy, so you're coming for a boat ride with me first. I doubt they will shoot me while I hold a gun to your back. I'll drop you beyond the harbour and complete my side of the deal once we're out of range. Tell them not to shoot if they want to keep you alive and at least have a chance to save their families."

As they walked towards the boat, Sam shouted to Gloria, his mouth dry with fear, making words difficult to form. "Don't shoot, I'll be fine; we've made a deal. I need her to stick to her side of the bargain," he said, reminding Mary as she pushed him roughly in front of her towards the boat. Gloria didn't reply.

They paused to unhitch the boat before climbing in, Mary always keeping Sam between her and the opposite side of the creek. Sam sat facing her in the stern, her index finger pressed firmly against the trigger as the barrel rested inches from his heart.

"You steer, I'll tell you where to go."

They drifted from the shore with the current before Sam lowered the spluttering engine and turned the boat towards the harbour entrance. Even here, he could smell her freesia perfume, the elusive scent that had finally given her away, now nauseatingly close. His anger at taking too long to recognise it left a bile taste in his mouth.

"Why did you do it; why betray us all?" he asked.

"Because Whistler holds my daughter. He caught her a year ago when she tried to make her way here to join me. She's all I have left in this world and he holds her hostage. He taunts me with a photograph every month. What choice have I got but to do what he says? No mother could sacrifice her daughter to someone like him."

Her words were so wretchedly sad that Sam could have almost felt sorry for her had the price of her betrayal not been so appallingly high. Yet, by the same token, wasn't he abandoning the possibility that Cromford was still alive and held hostage by Whistler?

"And Rigby? Does he know about all of this? You can't have worked on your own. Dealing with the boar when they were landed is far more than one person could ever manage."

"Rigby was my cover. I knew he was in love with me so I led him on and encouraged him. Love makes you blind, something you should know only too well." Mary let her words hang in the air for a moment.

"Did Rigby suspect; probably. But there is so little love in what's left of this world that when you find it, looking the other way is the easiest thing. Rigby might be a fool to love me, but he's not a traitor. He protected me by not asking questions. But you're right. There are others, sympathisers to a cause different from the future that you and Albert Jamieson have mapped out for us. But I'm not going to help you out with finding them," she said with finality.

Sam sat in silence, pondering what Mary had just said. As they cleared the harbour entrance she turned slightly to check the way ahead, momentarily exposing the underside of her forearm normally covered by long sleeves. Sam caught a fleeting glimpse of a small tattoo. It passed in a second; the missing letter of the alphabet he had encountered before: '&'

Beyond the arm of the western breakwater, Mary directed Sam to take the boat to the shore. Hidden from view from Gloria and her squad members, they hove-to a short wading distance from the shingle beach. Mary backed away from him, her gun still aimed at his chest.

"Time for me to be gone," she said wistfully. "I should kill you now. Just think of the chaos that would cause. For sure, it would guarantee Whistler's success. And be heartache for that pretty blind girl you're so fond of ..." Her words filtered out, distracted by her own heartache for a daughter held hostage.

"You also murdered the girl I found hanging in the woods?" Sam said, unable to stop the ring of judgement in his words. "Why? What harm had she done?"

Mary looked away, avoiding his eyes.

"She discovered the full extent of Whistler's intentions and was about to tell the forum everything. The only way she could be stopped was by disposing of her in a way that would look like suicide. And to make an example to the rest of our group."

"It didn't work though, did it?" His words were full of reproach.

Mary shrugged. "You were lucky. I never expected you to re-visit the spot where she died."

"Where you murdered her," he reminded. "Where remorse made you make your one big mistake."

"Ah yes, the freesias. But that's not going to affect the outcome. It's already too late for that."

Sam shook his head; he had just heard murder justified for expediency.

"And so I have to allow you, responsible for the deaths of countless innocent people, to just slip away?" He couldn't conceal the contempt he felt, despite the justification caused by the blackmail for her daughter's life.

"Which you'll do if you think there's a slender chance it could change the outcome for the rest of you. My life for a thousand. Sounds a good deal from where I'm sitting," she added smugly.

"Then give me my part of our deal, Mary. Tell me what I need to know."

"Climb over the side and wade to the shore."

She gestured with the gun, moving to the stern seat as Sam reluctantly eased himself over the gunwale and into the shallows. Once he was clear of the boat she continued.

"You're looking in the wrong direction, Sam. Whistler's not landing at any of the northern ports. I sent him details of the beaches south of Freshwater and Bembridge Harbour. He intends to cut the island in half from east to west and trap you all like rats in a sack." She paused to look at her watch. "And I think you'll find it's too late already. Landing time was an hour ago."

With a wave of her hand, Mary accelerated the engine, swung the bow to the north and headed out into the swell. Within seconds she was hidden by the rolling waves, quickly erased from their lives forever.

'Caught like rats in a sack.'

Sam repeated her departing words as he ran back towards the deserted port. Mary's departing taunt couldn't have been more aptly worded. The hours lost in time could mark the difference between freedom and slavery.

Fate tried one final twist as the Landrover raced through the lanes towards Newport; they got a puncture, adding yet more delays to any chance they might still have to thwart Whistler.

An hour later, Sam sprinted into the forum building and was immediately struck by the silence of the building. With the news he carried, the thought crossed his mind that it was probably the last time he might experience the feeling of calm security the building had grown to offer them. He rushed through the corridors, searching for someone to help in an eleventh hour bid to stave off disaster.

His office was empty, but a murmur of voices drifted from the adjacent forum chamber. Bursting in, he hoped to find someone to begin organising an emergency plan. He stopped dead in his tracks. Ruth sat in her wheelchair, the large wall map from his office now pinned on a board behind her. At her side was Javed, head still bandaged, making notes, radio and headphones draped around his neck. Beside him, Jaki adjusted and tuned dials on a radio set. To Ruth's other side, the two women he had last seen in Mary's office were making notes and passing instruction slips to a group of teenage messengers. Ruth looked up as Sam entered, the words bursting from him.

"I've discovered their real plan. We're looking in the wrong place. It's not the northern ports at all; they started landing at Freshwater and Bembridge two hours ago. Their plan is to cut the island in half."

"We know," Ruth said in a dry husky voice through a tight smile. "Chris discovered them entering Freshwater on her reconnaissance flight after you had left and we couldn't contact you. I suggested Chris fly on to Bembridge where she saw them landing there as well. Their intentions seemed plain enough."

"To catch us like rats in a trap," Sam said, repeating Mary's words.

Ruth nodded. "I thought it was a good move that you had already begun evacuating farms in the north of the island. The problem is that a lot of the farm families, and nearly all of our squads, were still north of the road line they're likely to use to cut the island in half," she said with concern. "So in your absence I took the liberty to pull back all the squads as quickly as possible and speed up the evacuation to the south." She pointed to the blue arrow lines she had marked on the map. "It will be a close run thing to get everyone to safety but, with a bit of luck, we should do it." Ruth paused, gasping. She applied the oxygen mask to draw air for her damaged lung while Sam examined the map.

"What are the red crosses?" he asked. They appeared on all roads running from east and west towards Newport.

"Chris reported seeing some tanks and lorries leaving their ports of entry. We had excavators on standby, so I gave instructions to dig wide trenches across all those roads. I doubt if it will hold them up for long, but anything will help."

Sitting in her wheelchair Ruth looked small and exhausted, but her presence of mind was in no way impaired by her physical injuries. Her prompt action might well have saved the situation. Now, only time would tell.

Everyone seemed to know the task in front of them. Outside, convoys of tractors, vans, and lorries carrying families from the farms streamed by, heading south. Ruth's prompt initiatives amazed Sam. She was obviously tired so Sam insisted she rest on Albert Jamieson's old camp bed set up in his office, while he took her place.

Stars were moved on the map with the reported positions of the relentless advance towards Newport. Watching the map with alarm, Sam's bodyguards began to insist that he and the forum should leave Newport immediately. Boxes were hastily packed and loaded into a lorry when John appeared with a box of ageing radios and batteries; communications during the coming hours would be critical. Sam still kept their final destination secret; Mary had admitted there were other sympathisers on the island; to declare his hand too soon could prove fatal.

"Where's Claire?"

Amidst the commotion, Sam assumed she was somewhere in the building and he needed to get her to safety. He recalled that earlier he had sent her to collect her dog but that was many hours ago.

"Has anyone seen Claire, a blind girl, pale skin and auburn hair, in her early twenties," he shouted as a sudden influx of people entered the room for instructions. At first, no one seemed to respond, so he called again. A woman he didn't recognise appeared at his side.

"I don't know anyone called Claire, but we've just come down from our farm near Northwood. Some of the farms in our area didn't receive the first evacuation order, so it's all happened in a bit of a rush. As we travelled the road past the old prison, we saw a girl that fits your description. She was riding fast on a piebald horse and heading north in the opposite direction. She said she was taking a message that hadn't been delivered to her home farm." She looked at Sam anxiously. "Unless her people are already on their way, I can't see them making it here before all the roads from the north are cut. Plucky, I'll say that for her, especially being blind and everything. I hope she makes it; there aren't many people left to help her if she gets lost."

She walked away, leaving Sam reeling. All Claire had were her wits and *Frisco*. And that was asking an awful lot from both of them.

# FORTY-THREE

It took several minutes for Sam to regain his composure. He stood in front of the island map, measuring and re-measuring the route he knew so well. A fit and rested horse might canter ten miles in an hour. Keeping to the tracks and lanes would help, but with a sightless rider who didn't know the short-cuts? How many times had *Frisco* made that journey? Over the years he had ridden the same route on countless occasions and found that some horses learned the route almost without effort, while others continually got lost if left to their own devices. Maybe if he returned to the farm now in the Landrover he could get there and back in less than an hour.

Beside Sam, Javed moved a marker an inch closer on the road from Bembridge to Newport. How long did they have before Whistler and his men arrived on their doorstep? Sam scaled the distance with outspread fingers. They had only four miles and one of Ruth's ditches still to cover. How long? The question gave a different answer every time he asked it. At least the advance from Freshwater was making slower progress, but that could change in a moment.

He zoned out from what was happening around him; questions washed over him and were left unanswered, waved away with a 'give me a moment'. It was Claire he was worrying about, not some strategic plan, and he needed to be decisive now. Sam made for the door, beckoning his bodyguards. There was still time; he could get to the farm and be back before Whistler arrived in Newport. But he didn't notice Gloria. As he reached for the door handle, her substantial figure loomed in his path.

"Where are you going?" she asked, blunt and direct.

"My home farm may not have received the evacuation order. I need to go there immediately. I won't need you this time."

He felt irritated; why did he always end up having to explain himself to this woman? She glanced over his shoulder and slightly nodded her head.

"Sorry, you're not leaving. Your place is here and anyway, I hear Claire is already dealing with that problem."

"Don't block my way, Gloria." Sam pushed against her to make his way past. She stood unmoveable. "Gloria, I instruct you to stand aside."

In response, Gloria folded her arms. Sam was about to turn to his bodyguards for help when Chris interrupted their confrontation. "Thank you, Gloria, that will be all," she said in an even voice. "Sam, I need you with me, and we need to leave. The forum must meet as soon as possible and it can't be in Newport. I must have your instructions on where to set up a temporary base." She hesitated. "Look, we'll send someone on a scramble bike to search for Claire and the others, but you can't go."

Her final words left no room for negotiation. Sam turned to confront her and was shocked to find how the room had changed in such a short time. While he had been alone with his thoughts, Ruth had returned to her desk and was again overseeing the developing situation with Javed. Beyond them, Bartlett stood in the bay window deep in thought, lost in a smoke screen, and Chris had the forum minutes book held open in her arms. She drew him to one side.

"Mr Chairman," she gave Sam his official title. "Everyone knows their job. We just need your authorisation; it's how the system works. Spare the details, let the rest of us look after that. But I need your instruction to call a forum; everyone is fleeing south and we need to meet urgently to agree the next step and tell them where and how this present crisis ends. The forum must convene this afternoon to stop everything descending into chaos; the village hall in Rookley looks the nearest safe place at the moment."

Sam nodded in agreement, aware that everyone was watching him as they went about dismantling their lives.

Chris continued. "One more point. Rookley is reaching saturation point with the influx of everyone. We need to start moving them on immediately. Where should we send them, Sam?"

She was recording his instructions in their prized record book which bore the complete history of their struggle over the past five years. Now written by hand, gone were the typed measured entries made by Mary, copies of which he now knew were treacherously forwarded to Whistler.

Sam hesitated a moment, gazing out of the east facing windows. Columns of black smoke spiralled high into the blue morning sky as Whistler's men approached, rampaging through their lives. The 'end game' approached. Like an incoming tide, it had remorselessly advanced towards them for weeks. They had tried every means to hold back the evidence that foretold this moment. Now the black stains told him it was here, on the island, and closing in fast. Decisions could no longer be postponed.

With a heavy heart, he said, "St Catherine's Point. Get everyone south to St Catherine's Point as soon as possible."

At least Mary wasn't there to hear his words. Chris nodded and made notes in the record book. She grasped Sam's arm.

"You must go, Mr Chairman," she said formally. "It's already long overdue to get you to safety. We must move you immediately."

She nodded to his bodyguards and he was led away without further protest, shadowed as ever by Gloria. In the car park, as the Landrover started, he held back for a moment, staring northwards. Because of his position, he was about to be taken to safety, but what of Claire and his children, Rachel, and friends? In the end he had failed to protect any of them, and now their fates rested in the hands of others. No one heard his words, muttered as he climbed into the back of the Landrover.

"Where are you, Napier? For god's sake, where are you?"

Their small convoy sped south; Sam's role now symbolic, maintaining the stability of leadership. There was little of a practical nature he could do; their community had begun their journey and it would now be organised by those around him. His task was to project an aura of calm confidence, an act to bring reassurance by his presence. As they abandoned the forum building, Chris had despatched two volunteers on scramble bikes to speed north in the hope of finding Claire and the others and guide them to safety; it had been the only way to get Sam to leave, and then rumours began that lorries and the rattle of caterpillar tracks could be heard in the eastern suburbs of Newport.

A few miles short of Rookley they came to a halt in a long column of stationary vehicles, held up by a tractor with a punctured tyre. It completely blocked the narrow road so there was no alternative but to wait until it could be repaired. Much to the annoyance of Gloria, Sam left his Landrover and began to wander back towards the north, anxious at any moment to catch sight of Claire and the others. He mingled with those also in the traffic jam; he was impressed by their forbearance, no one complained, all looked forward to returning home when the crisis was over. Sam could only smile reassuringly, patting shoulders for encouragement, while the reality of the situation rested like a stone near his heart. If the truth came out now, it would only cause panic and fear. There would be time enough for that later on if things didn't work out. As he moved through the stationary column of traffic, he found that rumours of his actions against Rigby had spread far wider than he had expected and he encountered an endless stream of questions about Rigby's treachery. His conversation with Rigby in the final minutes before leaving Newport had been cold and terse. Rigby had listened in silence as Sam told him of his exposure of Mary and her subsequent admissions as she escaped the justice of the island. Sam told Rigby he was a gullible fool, blinded by his own self-importance, but not a traitor, and was free to leave Newport. If Sam had expected gratitude in return, he would have been disappointed.

The puncture repair on the tractor took longer than expected, so Sam found a quiet space in an adjacent wheat field, flattened and destroyed by the storm, which already felt a distant memory. He found a rusting gate and sat with a pipe for a few reflective minutes. Nearby, in a hedgerow, a corn bunting called out its jangling song notes, unaware of the trials of those around it, while somewhere nearby he imagined he heard the growl of a hunting boar. He could have been mistaken. For the moment they were quiet, but out there somewhere, they were waiting for their chance, content for the moment to watch their human foes fight one another. For the past five years, man and boar had fought one another to a standstill.

"And now all we're doing is finishing the job for them," Sam muttered bitterly.

Gloria appeared like an apparition beside him. He should have known she would never be far away; she always performed a brilliant act of invisibility.

"Why do I waste my time trying to keep you alive when you try your hardest to kill yourself with that disgusting habit," she said, dramatically fanning away his pipe smoke with her hand. "We leave in five minutes. Be ready."

If anyone kept his feet on the ground it was Gloria.

Despite their efforts to move people onwards, Rookley was still choked as hundreds more descended on the village. Sam found an empty room in the village hall in which to hold the last forum meeting they would ever hold on the island. The thought sent a cold chill down his spine; the forum had been a constant point in all their lives from the very beginning. Outside, a shuttle of tractors and trailers were already transferring family groups down the narrow lanes to the open fields around the lighthouse at St Catherine's Point. Ruth had despatched an advance group carrying several old marquee tents and they were already erected to receive people arriving. For the children the whole thing was a huge adventure, a change from their normal routine, an excuse to miss school. But for the adults, the phrase 'it's just a precaution' was beginning to wear thin. Sam fixed a smile on his face and hid his personal heartache, and moved amongst them for reassurance.

Ruth arrived in a van carrying field kitchens, holding herself together by sheer force of will. She climbed painfully from the van and waved the driver on towards St Catherine's Point.

"Are you okay?" Sam asked the pointless question.

Ruth had a tight smile. "This will teach me to go hunting for cosmetics." She coughed, and winced, remembering their disastrous venture to liberate the chemist shop in Weymouth.

"When we left, Whistler's men were already in the streets of Newport. Luckily, they focused on our forum building and plundering the centre of the town, so we slipped away without any trouble. To all intents, the north of the island is now sealed off, though with a good map you could find a way through on tracks and lanes." She paused to catch her breath. "No sign of Claire or the others yet?"

Sam shook his head. Ruth smiled gently.

"There's time yet. A lot of people are still following; most will be using the side roads." She gave him a moment to gather his composure before asking, "When do you intend to hold the forum meeting? Many councillors have already arrived and are anxious to move on to keep their family units together."

"I'll give it another half-hour. There should be enough of us here by then to hold a full meeting. Ideally, I'd like every member here, but ..."

"And Rigby?"

"After what Mary told me, I've released him. I don't think even Rigby will have the gall to attend until things heal and people are prepared to forgive him."

Ruth nodded. "I need to sit down. Is there a quiet room where we could talk for a few minutes?"

Sam led her into the village hall just as another party of about twenty arrived. He searched their faces, but there was no sign of Claire amongst them.

"Did you remember to release Teri and Ryan?" Ruth asked.

Sam stopped in mid-stride. "Oh my god. I completely forgot?" For a moment he looked stunned until he saw the smile on Ruth's face.

"It's okay. After you had left, I forged your signature for their release. It will be the least of my crimes before this situation is through."

Sam ushered Ruth to a chair and found her a mug of tea. For a while they sat in compatible silence until Ruth raised an eyebrow and spoke.

"The end game? Assuming that you accept that I'm not working with Mary, it would help if you shared with me how all this finishes. I've supported every step you've made so far and I can understand why, in the circumstances, you've chosen to keep the final gambit to yourself. I can buy that. But St Catherine's Point leaves us nowhere else to run." Ruth paused for breath. "So, Mr Chairman, what's next? How do you plan to get us out of this predicament we're faced with?"

Sam stood and moved to the window, stretching tired limbs. In the fading light of afternoon, trailers were still loading groups of people to transfer southwards. Very soon, Rookley would be deserted. And there was still no sign of Claire.

"We have a window," he said, "probably no more than twenty-four hours. Beyond that we have to assume that Whistler will have discovered what we're up to. Once that happens, we'll be in serious trouble," he said bluntly.

"As if we weren't already. Okay, so what are you planning? We've moved a thousand people or more to a lonely spot on the southern tip of the island in the expectation that we know what we're doing. So what do we tell them? From where I'm seeing things, 'swimming for it' looks like the only option we've got left?"

Sam laughed at her final words. "Five days ago I managed to speak briefly with Kit Napier in a rare radio contact. He had more than enough problems of his own to deal with, but we managed to discuss the growing crisis here and the probable outcome. Remember the man you shot dead in Weymouth? I only saw him fleetingly, but there was something about him, the yellow bloodshot eyes I think, that told me who we were up against. That was the moment I knew that it must be Whistler and his drug culture that was involved somewhere in all of this. It told me enough to know there was unlikely to be a happy ending for us here on the island. I decided to gamble. Before I went to Hurst Castle I decided to contact Napier."

Ruth sipped her tea, looking at him over the rim of the cup. "So no chance of the referendum vote then?" she said cryptically.

Sam shook his head, stretching his arms.

"And the result of your little chat with Napier? I know he's something of a magician, but not even he can fit a thousand of us onto *The Shepherd* if that's what you're planning."

Sam turned to face Ruth. At last there was a smile on his face.

"Not *The Shepherd*, but *The Aotearoa*, with ample room for all. And with luck she'll be here tomorrow."

Ruth had many more questions to ask him, but they had to be put on hold as forum members spilled into the room, anxious to start the meeting. They made a brief headcount. Only one forum councillor was missing; Rigby. Chris stood in as secretary and they all gathered around Sam and Chris. Outside, the last stragglers funnelled past the windows.

Sam spoke uninterrupted for twenty minutes explaining in detail what he had described to Ruth just before the meeting. Everyone sat in sombre silence, digesting the implications. Simon Grey, well known for his hawkish views, eventually broke the silence.

"I still don't understand why you're so against further negotiations? You say you know this Whistler clown well, but you don't want to try some accommodation with him. But on what basis? One ten-minute meeting at Hurst Castle? You seem to forget they handed Jean back to us as a token of good will."

"A token of what?" Craig Ainscott interrupted. "Their humanity? Look at the dreadful state the poor girl is in."

Sam intervened. "Negotiating with Whistler is like leaving a cobra loose in your house as a pet. It may appear disinterested, but one day, beyond any doubt, it will strike you. Whistler employs the tactic of 'bonhomie', lulls you into believing he's your best friend in the world, and insinuates himself into your trust and confidence, gifting you an answer to all your misery and problems in the form of hallucinogenic drugs. It's what he always does, as sure as day follows night."

"Surely they can't all be as bad as Whistler. There must be some who are decent amongst them?" Angela asked.

"That's not how he works. Before the pandemic he was friendly with someone called Dressler who ran an illegal LSD lab hidden in Wales. He opened Whistler's eyes to the power of controlling people through addictive drugs. His devious schemes should have all come to an end with the catastrophe of the pandemic, but Whistler managed to survive and avoided being blinded. In the aftermath, he saw a limitless opportunity to use his knowledge of the power of drugs to exploit the grief and helplessness of survivors. When I briefly searched the man Ruth shot in Weymouth, his eyes were yellow and bloodshot, with dilated pupils. It made me suspicious, and when I met Whistler at Hurst Castle, the pet thug he brought with him displayed the same eye symptoms and an arm that showed more needle pricks than a pin cushion. Whistler controls people by drug dependency, that's how he induces them to do terrible things. He makes addicts of the worst thugs and turns them into rapists and murderers. It scares the rest, even those not using drugs, to be submissive to his bidding."

Sam paused to gather his emotions. "If there was any other possible alternative, I would be the first to support it. We can't stand against them with any chance of winning the fight without unsustainable loss of life, and submitting to Whistler is to choose a life of misery and slavery. But if we seize the opportunity to go to New Zealand we stand a chance to grow with our children and re-build in freedom. Then, at some point in the future, we can return stronger and take back our land and our homes."

There was silence in the room following Sam's impassioned plea. In their hearts, everyone must have known the reality of their situation but hearing it so graphically put into words was another matter entirely. Standing by the door, Gloria attracted his attention, pointing to her watch and making a wind-up gesture with her hands. In the few minutes available for open debate, some predictably critical accusations were thrown at Sam from people who had been Rigby's supporters. Distressed feelings made their barbs sting, the most personal accusing him of deliberately hiding the truth and misleading everyone by drawing the entire population to an isolated part of the island to cling to an exposed clifftop like lemmings. Someone even stood and shouted for a vote of no confidence in Sam. By now he was becoming inured to criticism, his mind distracted, counting the minutes of Claire's absence. He felt overwhelmed by the tiredness of weeks of remorseless strain and couldn't even summon the energy to argue in his own defence. On this occasion it was Chris who intervened, shouting above the melee of voices and calling for order.

"This might well be the last time we ever hold a forum on British soil, so let's not descend into the conduct of a bear-pit," she shouted. "Remember, as our situation has deteriorated, who amongst us hasn't looked in suspicion at our fellow councillors, speculating about the identity of the informer in our midst? Our chairman might well have concealed the truth of his final plan, but if that saves the majority of our community, it will have been worth the price."

Chris glared at them, daring anyone to contradict her.

"In the end, who amongst us could be trusted with so many lives at stake?" she added in a soft voice, paused, and looked deliberately at Sam.

"Mr Chairman, would you propose the motion, please."

Sam moved to the middle and turned to meet the eyes of everyone present. Beside him, Chris was poised, pen in hand, ready to register their final vote.

"I call for a show of hands on the proposal that the free community of the Isle of Wight, every child, woman, and man, will be taken by sea to a new home in New Zealand, where at the invitation of their government, we can live in peace and freedom, until such times as we can return to our homeland."

On the first count, there were three abstentions. Sam stood to speak.

"Our presence here, on the Isle of Wight, has been so brief as to be almost insignificant. But for as long as human civilisation remains, it will always stand as a beacon of light, of how a tiny disparate community, thrown together in adversity, can live within the principles of law and order, hope and decency. We chose not to fight and kill one another, not because we are cowards, but because it is the right thing to do," he said with both pride and sadness in his voice. "This isn't the end, it's only the beginning. Our example must be a guide for human beings wherever they survive on the planet and, if for that reason alone, I ask you to set aside personal prejudice and make it a unanimous vote."

For the last time in their brief existence as a forum, Sam finally got his way.

As the forum departed, Sam couldn't stop himself staring northwards into the darkness. The scramble bike riders that were despatched as they left Newport had now returned, having found Sky Farm abandoned and burning. There was no sign of Claire or any of the others. He ached to see her appear out of the darkness, but the road from Newport was now silent and deserted. For a moment he felt tempted; he could still distract his bodyguards with some final errand, take the Landrover and head north in search of Claire, anything to ease the pain inside him. But he knew that watching him from the darkening shadows, Gloria would anticipate his every movement. Leaving now, no matter how compelling his personal need, could plunge everything he had achieved into question. He was their leader, the choice of fate against his will. The path was no longer his to choose; he was as much a follower as those he led.

Reluctantly, he wandered towards the Landrover. As if by itself, the door opened and Gloria's large ever supporting hands pushed him inside. He had sent everyone to the cliff top refuge at St Catherine's Point. It was time to join them.

No one had ever seen the entire population in one place at the same time. Accumulated like so much flotsam during the previous five years, nearly a thousand people now huddled together, spread in the fields beside the dark lighthouse at St

Catherine's Point; a thousand people who now looked to Sam for their safety. They were gathered in hamlet groups around three large marquees which served as field kitchens, latrines, and a makeshift hospital in which two women were already in the advanced stages of labour. Farm polytunnels were being hastily erected for accommodation; rain was forecast overnight and things would be rudimentary at best. Everyone had now been told by their forum members of the final phase of the rescue plan. Sam had expected to become the focus of their anger; after all, he had concealed the truth of their departure until the very end, after they had all moved on the promise of a prompt return. Now, tall columns of smoke hung over the north of the island, staining the dusk sky, dispelling any illusions of life under the rule of Whistler and his men. Sam moved with a forced display of optimism, visiting every hamlet group in the open fields. Everywhere, people asked the same question, "When will *The Aotearoa* arrive?" rolling the unusual sounding name around their tongues as they became acquainted with a new language. He gave the same answers each time; "Soon, very soon," or "tomorrow most probably." The women seemed relieved by what Sam said, children squealed with excitement about their forthcoming adventure, whilst men just nodded, expressions dead-pan, unhappy with the thought of leaving their homes and possessions without so much as a shot being fired. But at least so far, they were safe.

The buildings surrounding the lighthouse had been taken over as a control centre and eventually Sam caught up with Bartlett and Aiden who were trying to complete a plan which would hold off Whistler and his men when they found them at St Catherine's Point. They had the usual large map of the island pinned to a wall, now tagged in coloured markers as their journey came to an end. Behind them, their homes were in the hands of their adversaries; in front of them lay just the sea and their future in the form of a rusting passenger ship somewhere over the horizon. Bartlett pointed to the map.

"We've blocked the four main routes into Niton, the last village on the road above us." He paused, coughing hard into a handkerchief visibly stained with fresh blood.

"If they break through the road blocks with their tanks and lorries, we're making bombs using socks stuffed with plastic explosives and coated in sticky tar and grease. If they're using lorries and tanks, they'll have to stick to the roads and we can drop the home-made bombs on them from the buildings that line the streets. If that doesn't stop them, it's down to the horror of street fighting. Beyond that," Bartlett paused, "it's down to you, so make sure that everyone is rescued before that happens."

Sam stared at the map. "How long can you hold them back?"

Bartlett was silent for a moment. "Once they find where we are? Five, six hours could be doing well." He looked at Sam. "How long do you need?"

"Twenty-four hours?"

Bartlett looked back at the map. "Then you'd better start praying they don't find us too soon."

Later that evening, on a pyre built close to the sea, they cremated Albert Jamieson's body. As they started the improvised ceremony, a misty drizzle that had set in an hour before lifted to reveal a sky full of brilliant stars that shone in tribute on a man they had all admired. Craig predicted more rain later in the night, but for that brief window, it seemed the gods smiled on a murdered man who had selflessly led them from the beginning. Chris Woods read the eulogy, re-counting Albert's time in London where he had been council leader throughout the height of the blitz, adding an amusing story of his disagreement with Winston Churchill when he had visited to inspect bomb damage to their local streets. Albert had won no medals; he showed heroism of a different kind, the quiet type that provides the glue that holds communities together in the face of adversity.

Unaccompanied, a thousand voices opened their lungs and sang 'Jerusalem' to the stars in memory of a good friend. He was nothing more, and nothing less. As the pyre was lit, Sam read the closing passages of the service for the passing of the dead as the flames consumed his friend's body,

"… *We will remember him.*"

Their simple service over, people dispersed to their tent refuges for the night. Sam lingered by the warming glow of the dying pyre, alone with his thoughts and fears. His job was almost complete, a task Albert, anticipating the future, had deliberately passed to his care, unable any longer to carry the final burden himself. Albert had seen what was to come and knew that he no longer possessed the strength to cope with the challenge. Now, with Claire and his children lost, Sam felt his own inadequacies, real and overwhelming, visit him like vengeful ghosts. Unable to rest, he walked back to the lighthouse. Earlier, he had found Ruth trying to settle into a cramped space in one of the polytunnels. He insisted it was no place for someone with a perforated lung and a bullet through the leg and, with difficulty, had persuaded her to take the bed provided for him in the lighthouse keeper's cottage. She looked worn out by the day, only her indomitable spirit driving her to work through the night.

"There's nothing much left to do until daylight, so I insist you rest. We'll be busy enough in the morning no matter how much you do tonight," he told her. The bed was hard and she looked cold, so he hunted for a spare blanket, wrapping it around her weakened body. "Hardly luxury, but better than a plastic tent."

He left Ruth to sleep and found a space with a bed, but no mattress, and a hard wooden chair and small table; something he needed more than the bed at that moment. From his rucksack he produced his notebook and a creased and battered envelope and sat down to write. For once, the words came easily, and he wrote in a single pass, tore out the page, signed it and closed the envelope with the seal on his ring. "Just in case," he muttered as he slipped the envelope into the pocket of his jacket.

He leaned back in the chair and closed his eyes. Where was Claire and what had become of her? He remembered their first kiss in Weymouth, just before they had set out to push Ruth and her wounded girls to safety in the trailer. The memory almost overpowered him. Wiping away tears with the back of his hand, he left the meagre comforts of the room to walk away the hours of the night.

Amongst so many worries, one in particular nagged at the back of Sam's mind. In the years before, he had visited St Catherine's Point to obtain fresh fish and crab from the few boats that operated out of nearby Reeth Bay. From those visits, knowledge of the almost hidden inlet had helped to shape his decision agreed with Napier to direct *The Aotearoa* to St Catherine's Point to rescue them. Even if Whistler had been told by Mary that they were planning to escape by sea, Sam was banking that he would assume they would need a major coastal port or level beaches at the very least. To the casual observer, St Catherine's Point only offered a coastline of rocky reefs and cliffs. He doubted Whistler would consider the Point a likely refuge; there were far more promising alternatives a short distance along the coast. Just in case Whistler's scouts discovered that they were at St Catherine's Point, Bartlett and Aiden had blocked the only available approach routes from the north, and Ventnor in the east.

Ill at ease, Sam walked the camp boundaries and surrounding fields in the dark, fretting about the lack of detail he had of Napier's rescue plan. He had been encouraged by Bartlett's idea to block the roads above, but he had a suspicion that it still left an unprotected track entering Niton from the west. Sam knew a coastal road entered the village along higher ground above Gore Cliff which was set inland from the coast. With limited resources, Bartlett and Aiden had dismissed this as a likely route into Niton. Sam remembered from the map that the road swung away from the Point as it approached from the west, leaving a sloping area of wild rugged moorland through which a network of paths and sheep tracks threaded their way towards the shore. Whistler would only need a map to see the paths would access by foot down to the flat plateau next to the lighthouse around which everyone was now huddled. Covered by dense bracken and gorse, Whistler's men could easily descend unseen until they burst into the fields amongst them. Disturbed by their vulnerability, Sam changed his walking route to check where the paths crossed their perimeter. With only the moonlight for company, he headed off alone across the fields, back-lit by flickering flames from the oil drum braziers kept burning in the gaps between the polytunnels. The wind had dropped and the world was stilled; disturbed occasionally by the cry of a child, hushed by parental voices. Though he couldn't see her, he guessed Gloria would be following him somewhere in the darkness.

Once clear of the tents, Sam followed a stone wall to the northern limit of the fields. Beyond the wall was a belt of thick gorse, bracken and scrub, dense and overgrown in long years of neglect. There seemed little chance of access through these thickets, especially where the land beyond rose steeply towards the inland cliffs, but Whistler and his men only needed to find one clear path. Sam reached the edge of the field on the westward side where the wall curved back towards the sea. He lit a paraffin lantern and shone it at anything that resembled a path. Eventually, he found what he was looking for; a clear gap in the scrub approaching from the north and a barely discernible path slashed in a zig-zag line as it wound inland towards Gore Cliffs. He decided at first light to send a squad to block and guard the route at its top extremity. With his plan to close this 'back door' in the morning, Sam turned to re-trace his steps back to the main camp. For the first time since leaving Newport, he started to relax. Mid-stride, he stopped abruptly. Some distance away, carried on the cold night air, he thought he heard something. He cocked his head and held his breath, listening intently. It came again; a cough and the soft sound of what might be muffled hooves, moving higher up, just below Gore Cliff. Had his fears been realised already and Whistler discovered the path he was so worried about? He stood stock still, straining his ears. There came more sounds, moving left to right on a parallel path. He recalled the track, with the distinctive name of 'Old Blackgang Road', that threaded itself amongst the trees. If it was someone approaching, they had already circumvented the barricades in the village to the north and east and would soon meet the steep lane that led in a final descent into the very heart of the camp. Sam quickly backtracked towards the lighthouse, calling anxiously for Gloria, and like a ghostly apparition, she and two black figures seemed to appear out of nowhere.

"I think I can hear someone on the upper road," he hissed. "If I'm right, they're soon going to meet the lane that drops to the lighthouse. We need to stop them before they get that far."

He sent one man hurrying back to the camp to bring help. It left only three of them to defend the camp until he returned.

"It could be late arrivals coming in," Gloria whispered, loud enough for the world to hear. "We had better be sure before we do anything."

Despite the moonlight, under the canopy of trees the darkness was impenetrable. Sam heard the click of a safety catch beside him as Gloria prepared herself. Seconds ticked slowly into minutes as the sound of feet and the rattle of equipment continued to approach. Sam extinguished his lantern and fumbled for his torch, his thumb on the 'on' switch in readiness. The sounds altered; hooves now striking tarmac as they turned down the hill towards them. The murmur of voices became more distinct; whoever approached, they weren't making much of an effort to conceal themselves. At Gloria's suggestion, Sam held the torch stretched out at an arm's length to his side; if anyone shot at the light, he wouldn't be standing directly behind it. After barely a minute, the sounds rounded the uphill curve, thirty or forty yards in front of them. A deep, male voice, drifted through the night.

"The burning flames we saw have to be down here somewhere; there's nowhere else it could be."

As Sam pressed the 'on' switch of the torch, he realised there was no need to shout a challenge. The words had been spoken in a New Zealand accent. A few yards ahead, in the light of the torch, was the tall blond-haired figure of Napier. He shielded his eyes with one hand, whilst holding a horse's bridle with the other. The piebald shied nervously, pulling sideways against the light, disturbing two small children who sat one behind the other across its back, leaning against the figure of a woman with hair that shone red and gold in the torchlight.

Against the odds, Claire had finally made it, and by some miracle, brought his children with her.

# FORTY-FOUR

Claire slid from the back of *Frisco* and handed the two exhausted children to Sam. For what felt like eternity, he could only stand and hug the three of them, his face buried in Claire's hair in relief, the children squashed between. Napier held the horse by the bridle and once Sam had gathered his composure, the two men hugged in greeting.

"Am I glad to see you," Sam said incredulously. "I'd all but given you up for lost."

The group was larger than he had first thought. But where was Rachel? Napier's three crewmen and a large family group, left behind during the hurried evacuation, milled around them, tired and relieved to have made it to safety. Voices sparred with excited questions, impossible to answer in a single moment and Sam led them into their improvised camp to the marquee that served as their field kitchen. In the dim light of the braziers, he found tables and chairs and went in search of something to eat and drink, taking Napier with him. Two women had remained on duty throughout the night and had been filling bowls with what had remained from the previous evening. Sam looked at Napier, his face a broad smile of relief.

"I had begun to fear that something serious had gone wrong," he said.

Napier smiled wearily. "Faced with so much wreckage and debris and sunken ships blocking in the channel, we turned back shortly after we spoke on the radio about your deteriorating situation, only to find someone had begun to shadow us. Initially, we managed to give them the slip in the fog, but every time we used the radio, they seemed to home in on us again. They must have been using some radio tracking device. It happened too many times to be a coincidence," Napier explained.

"And *The Aotearoa*?" Sam asked, unable to resist the most important question, part of him dreading the answer. "Did you manage to get my message through to them?"

Napier grinned. "I did. As it happens, they weren't in Gibraltar." Sam looked startled.

"I had discussed your situation with her captain before we left here to head north. We both agreed that as your circumstances sounded more precarious than you were letting on, we decided he would start to sail north as a precaution. When we spoke, *The Aotearoa* was already anchored off La Rochelle in France. It was just as well; since their arrival, bad storms in the Bay of Biscay have delayed further progress."

Sam sighed deeply with relief. "How long before they arrive?" he asked tentatively.

"Today, perhaps tomorrow," Napier replied.

Sam looked worried. "Tomorrow could be too late. If our opponents manage to sober up, they could be here in a matter of hours. Can you contact *The Aotearoa* and ask them to hurry."

Napier shook his head. "They'll be coming as fast as they can and anyway, we had to leave our radio on board *The Shepherd* in Newport. We could try to use John's set here, though radio silence is now essential as someone has a direction finding set-up and might be able to intercept *The Aotearoa* before they can get here."

Both men were thoughtful for a moment. The odds against them were high no matter how they played their hand.

"They were obviously tracking us with some determination," Napier continued. "I think they intended to board the boat and take over *The Shepherd*. If they hear us talking to *The Aotearoa* they may well be able to fix her position and that could completely upset your escape plan."

Chris, awakened by the sound of excited voices, arrived with Gloria carrying blankets and dry clothes for the new arrivals. As they ate, Claire and Napier began to describe the coincidence of events that had brought them together. Claire picked up the story.

"I left before you returned as soon as I heard a number of farms in the north of the island hadn't received their instructions to leave. *Frisco* did all the work. Clever horse never made a wrong turn, but we didn't make it as far as the farm. We were approaching through the woods you and I had used several times before, and from a distance I could smell burning and hear the crackle of flames and shouts. I thought I was too late, tried to backtrack and ended up getting badly lost. It must have been some while later that by sheer chance I heard children crying, and had to focus on trying to find them. I discovered Tom and Gemma sitting beside the dead body of a man; I don't think it was anyone from our farm." Claire paused frowning, concentrating her thoughts. "Tom called him Mr Robinson but couldn't explain why they were with him. We hid for a while and in the distance, I could hear more voices, shouting. I didn't recognise or like the sound of them. As the farm was burning, I decided it would be safer not to take the children back there and so set off in the direction of Newport in the hope of finding you there."

Claire ate before continuing. "The return journey was difficult; there seemed to be groups of other horsemen everywhere and I guessed they could be the men we had seen in Weymouth and Dartmouth. Anyway, none of them sounded particularly friendly, so we had to spend a lot of time hiding; not easy with a horse the size of *Frisco*." Claire made a wry smile at the thought. "As a result, I got completely lost and we would probably still be going around in circles if I hadn't come upon Kit and his crew," she said with distinct relief in her voice.

Having listened to Claire's account, Napier took up the story. "We were late getting back to the Isle of Wight, having spent two days investigating a distress signal from somewhere near the coast at Boulogne. We searched, but found nothing. It was probably a radio set left with a repeating tape message; or a trap. After that, it was a cat-and-mouse chase with a couple of big motorboats, obviously hunting for us. Only sea fog and darkness saved us in the end and we managed to avoid them."

They were suddenly interrupted by Ruth, awake and working, despite Sam's wishes that she should rest. She entered in her wheelchair, glanced at the two children now eating hungrily at the table, and nodded Sam to one side. She looked at him pensively.

"We've accounted for everyone now here in the camp, including those from Sky Farm; they were late arrivals and must have been missed on the first headcount. But, so far, no one from Rainbow's End has made it." Ruth paused. "I'm afraid Rachel isn't here yet," she said, looking towards the children with concern. "There's still time; stragglers are arriving all the time and John is trying to raise others on the radio. He left a number of spare sets at Rookley and is already in contact with one group who found them and are on their way here now."

"Keep me posted the moment you hear anything," Sam said, his forehead creased in a worried frown. "Claire said she thinks she found Jeff Robinson dead beside the children."

Sam assumed Robinson would have been with Rachel. He was becoming more and more alarmed about her; what could have happened. It was hard to imagine any circumstances in which she would have been willingly parted from the children.

Having eaten, Sam changed the exhausted children into warm clothes and Chris found them a bed to share; the same one Ruth had slept in earlier. Satisfied they were asleep and safe, Sam returned his attention to Napier.

"When did you get into Newport and how were things there?" he asked.

"We sailed into the river on the rising tide early yesterday afternoon, using just the jib, no engine. That probably saved us. We could have only missed you by an hour or so. Your forum building was already on fire, we could see the blaze from a distance."

Sam felt a pang at the thought of the building that had served them so well being destroyed.

"The blaze alerted us just in time. Things had obviously gone wrong, confirmed when we saw a group of men on the rampage. Forewarned, it gave us the chance to slip *The Shepherd* in amongst the other boats on the west side of the river. No one noticed our arrival; we were just another mast amongst dozens of others. We had just tied up to another boat when we saw a blind woman trying to lead a horse along the quayside road with two small children on its back. It was a miracle that the men wrecking the forum building hadn't spotted her." Napier glanced at Claire. "The colour of her hair was a give-away. I couldn't believe at first it was Claire. Luckily, she knew of the plan to evacuate Newport and head south, which tied in with our plan to gather at St Catherine's Point. We've spent hours walking here. We couldn't stay where we were in Newport and sailing *The Shepherd* back down the river was far too risky. We also found the family group with us now. They had a map and instructions to get to a village called Rookley. When we found the village empty I guessed you'd gone on to St Catherine's Point, so we pushed on. We had to make a diversion from the route you must have used because a group of Whistler's men have built a road block about three miles south of Rookley. Fortunately, we had two of my crew scouting ahead, so we knew about it before we walked into them." Napier unfolded a tattered map. "If any islanders are still coming south, they need to take this lane here to avoid them," he pointed to a road that led to the west, "or better still, leave the roads and head across country. It's tough going, especially with children, but far safer. Off-road you've also got the benefit of woodlands if you need to hide."

Napier shrugged wearily, all too aware that their fate now hung in the guise of an aged and battered ship, *The Aotearoa*. For a while, they all sat in silence, each alone with his thoughts. Claire had fallen asleep, leaning against Sam's shoulder, so with only a few hours remaining before daybreak, he lifted her into his arms and found them both a bed.

It felt like only a few minutes later when Chris shook Sam's shoulder and beckoned him outside. It was light; the air moving slowly to the sound of a thousand waking voices, reminding Sam of the significance of this day for all of them.

"John has made contact with the group from Rainbow's End," Chris told him. "The good news is, they've reached Rookley and found one of the radios John left behind. It sounds as though there's about twenty of them, including Rachel." Chris paused.

"And the bad news?" He could tell by the note in her voice.

"Someone is following them. Unless they can lose them, they're going to lead them straight here."

Sam was less worried about that than the thought they might be captured before they got to the Point. It was about six miles by road if they used the direct route. Making a diversion to throw off their followers might be safer, but could easily double the distance.

"Could we rush a team of Landrovers north to pick them up?"

"Ruth has thought of that already, but John thinks they've probably taken to the woods to hide and has lost signal with them, so we can't arrange where to pick them up. We can't risk using the road north, so it will have to be a track or lane somewhere to the west and for that to be possible we need to make contact again."

Chris saw the worried look on Sam's face.

"Try not to worry; there's still time. If Rachel is leading them she'll have thought of alternatives already."

Sam had left Claire asleep. There were questions to ask her, but they would have to keep. The smell of freshly baking bread and hot porridge drew him in the direction of the field kitchen. He passed several squads leaving to protect the 'open door' path that he had found during the night on their western boundary; the arrival of Claire, Napier and the others gave clear evidence of their vulnerability on that side of the Point.

The field kitchen was already full of early risers, hungry after a chilly and uncomfortable night in their tents. Amongst them, Sam discovered Napier, energetically polishing a large stainless steel tray.

"I need this as a radar reflector. I'll fix it to the weather vane at the top of the lighthouse. It might help *The Aotearoa* locate us," Napier said.

Sam avoided the question foremost in his mind. Napier probably knew no more than he had already told him, but at least the reflector was evidence that *The Aotearoa* was coming.

For a while, Sam lingered amongst people eating breakfast. Once the events of the day started, hot food would become hard to provide, so most had decided to take advantage while it was available. With surprise, Sam saw Jake enter the tent, followed by Monica and Lorna; the remainder of the Sky Farm group trailed in behind them. Initial relief gave way to hugs and tears as many unanswered questions floated to the surface.

"The children are here safely," Sam told them. "By some miracle, Claire found them and brought them with her."

For a moment, they all looked from one to the other in stunned silence.

"Claire?" Jake asked, surprised. "Jeff Robinson came to the farm to collect the children and return them to Rachel at Rainbow's End. How did Claire …"

"She heard you might not have received the warning to leave the farm, so she came back, alone with *Frisco*, to tell you. She found Sky Farm on fire and Robinson dead in the woods with the children sitting beside his body. Why in heaven's name did you let him take the children at a time like this?" Sam asked, anger suddenly flaring.

Defensively, Monica intervened. "The children miss one another since you and Rachel parted; they've all grown up together from birth and since your split up," she paused to make her point, "we have to let them get together regularly, especially as there are no children of the same age at Rainbow's End. Sometimes, Jeff Robinson comes to collect them; it's not unusual."

Hearing the strained conversation, Lorna, forever the peacemaker, intervened, asking, "Where did Claire find the children?"

"I'm not sure exactly; close enough to Sky Farm to hear and smell buildings burning. I assume it must have been in the woods close to there."

Jake looked at Lorna. "Or it could have been the Wainwright's place. The track to Rainbow's End passes quite close if you stick to the woods."

"When did you all leave the farm?" Sam asked.

Lorna continued. "Late morning. I had just fed the cows when the messenger arrived on a scramble bike. The instructions told us to prepare to be away for a few days, until things get sorted out. We milked the cows and turned out all the livestock into the fields. But now we find ..."

"It's a bloody mess and we're not being told the truth," Marcus interrupted angrily. "What happened to this precious referendum of yours? Talk about dragging us away under a false pretext. It's a dis..."

The bark and rattle of small arms fire cut his words short. Everyone strained to be certain of what they were hearing. Within seconds, the gunfire was accompanied by the sound of engines and the clatter of caterpillar tracks, punctuated by several loud cracks and deafening explosions. A few children wailed, sensing the apprehension of their parents.

"There go our barricades," Sam muttered to himself. Whistler had found them sooner than he had hoped.

After a while, the firing eased; only the echo of engines and tracks could be heard in its place, followed by two loud explosions. Abruptly, the engine noises stopped, leaving the faint sound of distant cheering. While they anxiously waited for news, Sam exchanged glances with Ruth and Chris and they immediately began circulating to calm everyone. Napier returned, having fixed his improvised radar reflector to the top of the lighthouse, and sensing the unease, he drew Sam to one side.

"Start sorting the sequence for loading *The Aotearoa*. Don't let people stand around worrying about what they've just heard," Napier suggested. "When you've done that, do a headcount, issue warm clothing, make hot drinks, anything that prepares them and keeps them occupied and distracted. A thousand panicky people is definitely something to avoid."

"How many trips will it take to take to transfer everyone to the ship?" Sam asked.

"*The Aotearoa* will probably send strings of lifeboats, each towed by a boat. Work on forty to a lifeboat; that will be roughly five or six trips but they'll double up, which will make it quicker; assuming everyone wants to leave and not hang around for your referendum," he added mischievously. He had obviously overheard part of Sam's conversation with Marcus.

"I think they just heard their answer to that question," Sam quipped, wistfully. "For the time being at least, democracy is suspended."

Their first casualties arrived; one had burns, two more had received minor gunshot wounds, but they came with good news that their squads blocking access through the village had disabled a tank. The tank had tried to force its way through their barricades, become jammed, and been blown up, completely blocking the route to the Point from the east. The respite might only be temporary, but winning the first round lifted everyone's spirits.

During all the excitement, no one had noticed banks of sea fog rolling ashore. Within seconds, visibility had dropped to less than fifty yards. Sam was uncertain if it was good news, but took it as positive that Napier was now walking around with a broad smile on his face.

"It hampers them more than us," he offered, ever optimistic.

"It may help to hide us, but how will *The Aotearoa* find us if it stays as thick as this?" Sam asked anxiously.

"Simple; the radar reflector will give them a fix on our position. They'll drop anchor a mile or so offshore to avoid the rocks, and sound their siren. In one of the outbuildings is the searchlight that was brought here to guide *The Shepherd* on the night of the storm. The generator and the light should be powerful enough to be seen some way out to sea, even in this fog. The rescue boats can take a fix on that. It's tricky, I'll grant you, but not impossible," Napier added with a broad smile, omitting to add that for any of this to work, *The Aotearoa* needed to arrive before Whistler and his men got their act together.

Awoken by the noise, Claire found Sam with the help of Lorna. For a moment, they both held hands with his two children; Claire with a wide smile on her face that he found so irresistible. The reason sat in a canvas sling, tied diagonally across her chest. From its folds, the small face of a retriever puppy peered out at a confusing world. Sam couldn't resist laughing.
"How on earth did you manage that?"
"Alice's mother kept her safe for me. She's a bit scared by everything that's going on, but great for distracting the children when the shooting started," Claire said with pride.
Lorna interrupted, tapping Sam's arm.
"I need to get back. I can take the children to be with their friends until Rachel and the boats arrive." She noticed the unhappy shadow that crossed Sam's face. "Don't be too hard on everyone. It's become very difficult since you and Rachel left. It completely upset the balance of personalities. When Jeff Robinson arrived to collect the children, well, let's say that he's very forceful and obstinate. We tried to persuade him to let them stay and evacuate with us but he insisted on taking them back to Rachel. I think that all along he had no intention of leaving Rainbow's End, which may explain why he's dead and Rachel is not here," she added in a worried voice.
Sam let his anger subside. He knew the children would be happier with their friends and reluctantly he passed them over to Lorna.
"They're in your charge until Rachel arrives. If things start to hot up, bring them back to me immediately." Stern words, but he hugged Lorna for reassurance.
A temporary lull settled over the Point. Bartlett and Aiden had formed a horseshoe perimeter using most of their squads. They were spread thinly, but there was nowhere for Whistler's men to slip through. Below, everyone waited in the fog, ears strained in the hope that *The Aotearoa* would arrive soon. The camp fell quiet and for a while, Sam and Claire discussed their departure for

when the boats arrived and evacuation began. Predictably, they disagreed; Sam wanted Claire to leave with the women and children as soon as the elderly and medical patients had been loaded into boats. Claire shook her head.

"I leave when you leave," she said determinedly, knowing Sam would want to stay until the very end. "That's how it has been for us from the very beginning and I'm not changing things now." Claire folded her arms, a thin tight-lipped smile confirming the discussion was closed. Inwardly, Sam groaned, but admired her obstinate courage nevertheless.

Somewhere in the fog beyond the shore, the drone of an approaching motorboat could be heard above the sound of the surf. Sam felt his heart leap; he left Claire and started running towards Reeth Bay. John appeared out of the fog and ran alongside him.

"So what do I tell them?" he asked urgently.

After many hours of silence, Rachel and her group had made contact. Despite leaving the roads and cutting across country to the west, they were still being followed and needed help.

"Tell them not to stop or slow down. They must be less than four or five miles away. Tell them to push on, no matter how tired and exhausted they are. If they can get to the Blackgang Road we'll be able to help them. Time is critical so they mustn't stop and try to hide any longer."

Easy said, but difficult for women with small children. John looked unhappy but ran back to his radio set in the hope of speaking to Rachel. Sam arrived at the beach, cursing Jeff Robinson's obstinacy which had delayed the departure from Rainbow's End. It meant getting to safety for Rachel was going to be touch and go. Napier was already at the beach, his head cocked to one side, straining to listen.

"*The Aotearoa?*" Sam asked.

Napier shook his head. "Not one of ours; the engine note is too deep for one of our motorboats. I think someone is searching for us, trying to find our access point to the sea." He shot an urgent glance at Sam. "Tell everyone to be as quiet as possible, especially the children. Sound travels, even in fog."

Gloria and Javed had arrived with their squads and were spreading themselves amongst the rocks around the bay. Sam chose a nervous looking teenager and sent him sprinting back to camp with instructions for complete silence. "You have my authority to insist that everyone keeps quiet." He slapped him on the back and sent him on his way.

As the approaching engine note turned to a deep rumble, Sam moved closer Javed to Gloria.

"No firing unless it's absolutely essential; and tell everyone to stay alert."

Staring into the fog created images in the imagination. The engine note was ticking over at low revs, sometimes increasing, then fading, in a varying tempo. Several times, Sam thought he saw a shadow appear in the centre of the bay. Gloria must have seen it too for he saw her finger tighten on the trigger of her gun, her eye pressed ever more tightly against the telescopic sight. Sam squeezed her shoulder and shook his head. For minutes they all held their breath; the engine note drifted from left to right, passing close to the rocky entrance shelf and then on towards the lighthouse. Napier guessed that the motorboat crew could hear the swell breaking against the rocks and, in the fog, decided to keep their distance.

A collective sigh was palpable from amongst the rocks; they were safe for a while longer, and someone in the squads passed around a hipflask. Sam left Javed's squad on watch at Reeth Bay and walked back to find Claire and the others. As he went through the gate in a stone wall, a fresh burst of firing echoed from the east in the direction of the Ventnor Road. The sound was louder, worryingly closer to their camp. Reality had reasserted itself.

The sound of gunfire became a constant backdrop, varying in tempo but always there. Chris caught up with Sam as he crossed the field.

"Our headcount is complete; about fifty are still unaccounted for, including Rachel and the group from Rainbow's End."

Sam nodded in silent acknowledgement; it was inevitable that some people would choose to take their own chances.

"With any luck, Rachel and her group will be here shortly. We know they're well passed Rookley." Chris tried to sound encouraging.

Sam was momentarily distracted by the sight of Napier and a dozen men winching a searchlight on a pulley system up the side of the lighthouse tower. The generator was already in position to power the light and signal to *The Aotearoa*, which they all hoped would soon be anchored offshore in the fog. It reminded Sam of the night *The Shepherd* had arrived; at least there was no howling gale and blinding snow blizzard to deal with this time.

Searching the camp, he discovered Claire with Karen's medical team, moving stretcher patients to the cottage positioned just above Reeth Bay.

"They'll be the first to be loaded into the boats when they arrive," Claire said. "It makes sense to get them as close to the beach to speed up the process of loading. Any sign of *The Aotearoa*?" In the sling across her chest, *Pilot* poked her head out to inspect the world. Distracted, Sam stroked the puppy's head.

"Not yet, but then, it could be anchored just a mile away and we wouldn't see it."

At the top of the lighthouse the searchlight was at last in position and cables were being slung and connected to the generator below, promising that operation of the light was imminent. Sam hugged Claire quickly and left. He needed to find Bartlett and Aiden to plan how their squads would withdraw from their posts when the time came and ensure that no one was left behind. He met Aiden with several teenagers descending with an empty trailer down the track from Niton. "We need more ammunition," Aiden said, sending the youngsters ahead while he spoke to Sam. "Sheer weight of numbers are pushing us back, but at least there are no more tanks to force their way through," he said with a tired grin. "Any sign of a rescue yet?"

Sam shook his head. At the lighthouse, the generator suddenly kicked into life and Napier switched on the searchlight for a moment.

"It looks as though the fog is thinning. It's nowhere near as dense as it was a short time ago," Aiden said encouragingly, glancing seawards.

Sam wasn't so sure. "How long can you hold back Whistler's men?" The sound of shots subsided, only to suddenly increase in volume as he asked his question.

"That depends on how hard they want to try. At the moment, no one seems to be taking any chances. They've probably decided to wait until it gets dark and then try to overwhelm us in a big rush. But that could change at any moment."

As Aiden spoke, the trailer returned, filled with ammunition boxes and he left with it, adding his shoulder as it was pushed uphill in the direction of the firing.

Sam returned to the camp and found Ruth surrounded by a group of about thirty people, each taking turns to draw a number out of a bag.

"It seems the fairest way to organise the loading sequence after the sick and elderly are in the boats. We need to prevent panic and a free-for-all. Each group leader has agreed to draw a number for their hamlet."

"How long do you think it will take to get everyone loaded and away?" Sam asked.

Ruth pulled a face. "I'm not sure, but two hours is possible."

"That could be too long; is there any way to do it faster?"

Ruth had a look of exasperation. "A thousand people? I'll do my best but I think it will be tough to complete it in two hours. Still, we're getting good at performing the impossible."

He smiled weakly. "I know, miracles take a little longer."

Sam left in search of John who had set up his radio in the lighthouse to use the aerial positioned above the lantern. As usual, John sat bent over his set, tuning the VHF frequency dial, repeating his call sign, following with their grid reference on the map.

"I keep calling *The Aotearoa* but get no response," he said, morosely. "I'm adding our position in case they can receive but not transmit; we wouldn't want them to go to the wrong place by mistake," he added in his Welsh lilt.

"Do your best. Anything from any of the missing groups?" Sam asked, feeling his own spike of anxiety.

John shook his head. "Nothing. I keep calling and listening. I hear that fifty people are still out there somewhere. Do you think they'll make it?"

"Whistler's men can't be everywhere, so there must be gaps to slip through. It's a question of finding the way before it's too late," Sam added hopefully.

Outside, someone shouted that the fog had cleared so he left John and climbed up the long spiral stair to the lantern room. Napier had positioned the searchlight on the balcony and one of his crew was patiently repeating the signal light sequence for the distress sign *S.O.S.* So far, no one had responded. Around them, the fog had almost lifted, but dense banks, like wandering clouds, continued to hide anything beyond half a mile from the shore. Sam scanned what he could see of the near horizon with binoculars, hoping some shadowy shape would appear, only to be disappointed. From the landward side, the gunfire continued sporadically. The stand-off suited their purposes, but he wasn't optimistic that it could continue for very long.

Sam descended the lighthouse and returned to find Claire. The field kitchen had baked fresh bread and Claire had acquired half a loaf for them to share. Pale in the remnant of the fog, a watery sun warmed the camp, lifting their spirits, as Sam found them a sheltered spot to eat.

"Who do you think killed Robinson?" he asked, tearing the loaf into equal pieces.

"Your boy Tom said they hid from four men on horseback. When we joined up with the other group of people just south of Newport, they said that groups of men were already roaming the countryside on stolen horses." Claire paused to share a crust with *Pilot*.

"Gemma said that Mr Robinson had heard horses approaching and made them hide under leaves beneath a dense clump of briars and they were not to come out until he said so. They heard him arguing and shouting with some men and then there was shooting. They hid for an hour or so, but when he didn't return, they sneaked out to look for him and found him lying in the lane. His horse was missing."

"How far from the farm do you think they were?" Sam looked up thoughtfully, as a fresh bank of fog rolled over them.

Claire frowned. "That's difficult to be accurate. I could smell smoke and hear the crackle of flames, but it might not have been our farm burning, I suppose. *Frisco* and I had become completely lost and disorientated and the children didn't know where they were. It was only by using their eyes and *Frisco* that we found our way back to Newport, though what we would have done if Napier hadn't seen us ..." Her words drifted away.

"You took an enormous risk going back to the farm on your own," Sam said wistfully, taking her hands in his. "One of these days you're going to have to stop doing things like that."

Claire had a winning smile. "Someone had to. I heard that the messenger sent to warn the farms in our sector of the island had failed to return to Newport. I was worried that our farm had been missed out. You weren't around, nor would you have had time when you got back, so someone had to go before it was too late for everyone to leave."

For a while, their conversation drifted into an intimate silence, each propped against the other's shoulder, happy just to be sharing a quiet moment together. Claire stroked *Pilot*, while Sam draped his arm around her neck, distractedly playing with her hair, lost in a moment of careless magic. Leaning against each other, he fell into a doze, while Claire sat motionless, barely daring to breathe in case she disturbed him.

They must have sat like that for a while, until the spell was broken when calls for Sam were urgently shouted from Reef Bay. He woke with a start and grabbed Claire's hand.

"Keep with me this time; I'm not going to lose you again."

They ran to the shore and found Javed busy with the radio summoning support from more squads. He turned to Sam as he arrived.

"That motorboat is back." A fog bank had settled in the still air, eclipsing the view of the bay. "I thought we'd seen the last of it, but just as the fog returned we heard an engine approach the entrance to the bay, probing for a way in. It's moved eastwards at the moment, but I have a suspicion it will be back."

He couldn't hide the note of anxiety in his voice. Barely had he spoken than the growl of an engine approached again, the note dying away somewhere in the middle of the bay. With the jingle of equipment, another squad arrived and scrambled in amongst the rocks.

"Don't open fire until we're certain of their intentions. In the fog, they might still think this isn't the place," Sam whispered to Javed.

The engine note picked up again. A boat was definitely entering the bay. Slowly, a shape materialised out of the fog, pale grey at first, slowly taking the form of a motorboat. As the fog cleared, a tow hitch became visible at the stern hauling a thick cable that at first disappeared into the mist, until another shape appeared. A lifeboat, slowly formed into a chain of five, each gently tugging the other with tentative apprehension. For a moment everyone on the beach crouched mesmerised, unable to believe their eyes as the boat approached the beach, before grinding to a halt on the shingle. Clearly stencilled on the bow of the boat, in freshly painted black letters, was a single word; *The Aotearoa*.

# FORTY-FIVE

By the time Sam and Javed had reached the surf line in the bay, another motorboat with its string of bobbing boats had arrived to join the first. The first boat contained three crewmen plus a helmsman in the stern of each following lifeboat. As the boat ground into the shingle, a steel grapple was thrown ashore and a man dressed in sea boots and a worn yellow oilskin leapt onto the beach. He hailed them in a deep salt-dried voice.

"Anyone in need of a lift?"

The accent was unmistakeably New Zealand. "My name is Ross Johnson, second officer of the *The Aotearoa*," he shouted with a broad smile as Sam and Javed approach. "Rumour has it that you guys need some assistance," he said in understatement. "We've anchored to the west of the lighthouse where we could get closer to the shore and the sea channel is clear of rocks."

Before he could say any more, Napier arrived breathless having run all the way from the lighthouse, his face wreathed in smiles of relief at the arrival of his friend.

"What took you so long?" Napier boomed as he bear-hugged Johnson.

"Finding this spot," Johnson responded. "Your directions were as lousy as ever and we wouldn't have found you at all had it not been for your radio operator transmitting your position coordinates."

Within minutes, Ruth and Chris appeared at the beach. With time ticking away, they came with enough support to immediately begin loading medical patients and the elderly into the boats, and the first family groups had already assembled ready to be led down to the beach. More helpers arrived and the boats were quickly prepared, spurred on by the appearance of thick smoke drifting down to envelope them from fires now burning in Niton. For a while, Sam and Claire stood together in the shallows at the water's edge, helping some of the stretcher patients into the boats until a breathless teenage girl arrived with a message for Sam.

"From Mr Bartlett," she said as she handed him the slip of paper. Sam read it hastily. It confirmed what he had feared.

*'Get a move on; we're losing ground fast.'*

Two loud explosions echoed across the fields, causing a momentary wave of panic through the assembling families. Several young children began to cry in alarm and parents looked around, anxious to find the source; two smoking craters now lay in the fields. Malevolent as ever, Whistler had guessed their intentions and stepped up his action to stop them slipping away.

Sam turned to Claire. "Stay here and help with the boats. Whatever you do, don't leave the beach. I'm going to check things farther back."

Claire looked alarmed and then nodded as he left, jogging up the track towards the fields. He took the young messenger with him. She looked barely fifteen; earnest and frightened in equal measure, determined to do what he might ask of her.

"Go and tell Mr Bartlett we're loading the boats. *The Aotearoa* has arrived but we need another hour at least. Got that?" Sam spoke to the girl slowly and deliberately, repeating it to make sure she delivered his message correctly. Still breathless, she nodded and started to run fast up the track, back towards the sound of the fighting. At the top of the lane, Simon Grey was despatching the first of the numbered family groups towards the beach, their faces a mixture of excitement and anxiety. All were led by women; their sighted men were holding back Whistler's men in the houses and woods above them.

Sam made a point of smiling encouragement at every group leader, adding the words, "Don't run, but don't hang about or stop."

Within seconds, a long crocodile of people were funnelling past him; perhaps an hour would be enough. Amidst the crowd, Sam saw John pushing through the throng towards him, radio and aerial now strapped to his back. Sam greeted him with a hug.

"You did it," he said. "Without your radio messages giving our grid coordinates they might never have found us." He paused, moving aside as another group set off for the bay. For once, John looked happy.

"Any news from Rachel and her group?" Sam asked, suddenly serious.

John shook his head. "I keep trying, but no response." He saw the anguish on his friend's face. "There's still time; they could appear any minute. None of Whistler's men seem to be on the western side, so the lanes should still be open."

Sam nodded, there was too much happening to dwell on things. From his vantage point on the fields above the bay, he could see the first string of boats already loaded, their tug drawing away in a clockwise circuit around the tiny bay as another string entered. *The Aotearoa* lay at anchor to their west and he could just see a spiralling column of grey smoke rising from her funnel. To get to her meant a slightly longer route closer to the coast, but avoided the larger waves farther out to sea. With any luck, almost a quarter of their number would soon be on their way to safety.

A few minutes later, Karen appeared, leading a line of stretchers and walking-wounded. The first casualties were being channelled down a path from the village, a stark reminder of the fighting going on there. Sam guided them into the descending queue and found boards to speed up loading into the boats. He searched the rising ground above them with his binoculars. The tree cover was dense so he couldn't see much; only smoke rising above the trees betrayed the closer proximity of the fighting. Trying to collect his thoughts, he spent a few minutes circulating, repeating the same message to every waiting group of people.

"Don't panic; there are plenty of boats; keep close to the group in front of you and be prepared to move quickly when your turn comes."

To his amazement, three women were still running the field kitchen, serving hot food to a dwindling number of passing people.

"Time to go, ladies," Sam called to them. "You've done more than enough. Shut down now and get into the queue for the boats. Don't wait. Go," he said, smiling.

As they methodically dried their hands and closed up they reminded him of the string quartet forlornly playing to the end on *The Titanic* as the ship sank. He hoped their own outcome would be happier.

With John shadowing him, Sam wove his way back to the beach. The second string of lifeboats had already loaded and he estimated that almost half those waiting had already been evacuated. It had taken a little more than half an hour, and another string of empty lifeboats was being towed back into the bay. Claire was waiting, soaked to the waist from wading to the boats. He gave her a swift hug and kissed her.

"Keep up the good work, don't get too cold," he said protectively. "I want you in a boat soon."

Claire turned her face up to him, alive with excitement. Sam wondered if blindness was partly an asset in a situation such as this.

"I leave when you leave," she repeated. He didn't have time to argue.

Ruth was too busy to feel ill, though she looked it. "You're doing a fantastic job," Sam called to her above the clamour of their evacuation. "I actually think we're winning."

He drew Ruth to one side as they waited for the next string of boats to tie up at the beach. Taking both her hands in his, Sam tried to rub some warmth into them. After a few moments, he withdrew the envelope from his inside pocket. It had Chris's name written on the front.

"I'm about to give this to Chris Woods," he said, trying hard to sound casual yet fighting his own emotions. "If anything happens to me, I'm nominating you to lead our people. The future will be difficult, even if things work out as we hope, and they will need good guidance. You're the one who must take them forward, Ruth. Everyone respects you and they'll need wise leadership."

Ruth opened her mouth to interrupt him, her face a mixture of shock and astonishment. He pressed his index finger against her lips, shaking his head.

"There's no time for discussion, but I ask you in all sincerity to carry out this duty in the event that things go wrong and I don't make it to *The Aotearoa*. For the sake of everyone we save today, you must take up the role. Your bravery and judgement have the respect of everyone, me included."

Sam paused. Ruth's face looked confused enough already. Chris Woods would have to sort out the transition with Ruth if the need arose. He kissed her on the cheek, squeezed her hand and left, making a note to himself to tell Chris to include Ruth on the next string of boats and get her to safety.

"John, I want you to stay here on the beach until I get back," he called out as he passed him. He left without an answer, searching for Chris, who he found with a clipboard as family units were loaded into boats.

"I think you'll guess what this is," he said as he pushed the envelope into her hands. She glanced briefly at the front and looked at him in open-mouthed surprise. "In the event, make sure it is enacted."

Chris was floundering to reply. Sam stopped her.

"Now, keep up the great work. I'll be back shortly."

"Where are you going?" she asked quietly.

"To find Bartlett and Aiden. Ask that nice Mr Johnson to make sure a boat with a powerful engine and space for a couple of dozen is waiting here in half an hour. We don't want our brave rear guard to have to swim for it."

Sam was gone before Chris could answer. He made the same request as he strode past Napier who seemed to be enjoying himself, using his considerable strength to hurl children and young women into waiting boats.

"And one more thing" Sam said as Napier lifted a pregnant woman into a boat. Napier suddenly looked up, aware of the serious note in Sam's voice. "If anything happens to me and I don't get back in time, get Claire away in a boat, even if you have to tie her up."

Napier looked at Sam with a concerned eye, nodded and turning away said, "You'd better not be late then," and playfully dumped a waiting child into the next boat.

Trying to get rid of Gloria was like trying to shoo away a faithful dog. Sam stopped several times as they climbed the steep lane towards the sounds of gunfire, now coming from the lower end of the village. Gloria was always ten paces behind him, a look of mild disinterest on her face, her gun supported on a strap over her shoulders.

"You don't have to do this," he called to her as they sheltered against the gable of the first house they encountered. "I'm here to speak to Bartlett, not fight a war."

Gloria ignored him and followed from doorway to doorway as they crept along the street. Bartlett had fortified the houses that overlooked the last junction of the two main approaches to the lane they had just climbed. Somewhere amongst the pock-marked ruins, the remaining squad members still crouched, protecting the safety of their loved ones in the fields below. It was time to decide how best to get this rear guard all down to the bay and evacuated before they were over-run or cut off.

Sam found Bartlett in a first floor room in a house with a view along both approach roads. A V-shape had been created in front of a tall window, built from a stack of bricks and blocks, with a slit at the centre of the 'V'. Sam slithered across the debris littered floor to join him.

"How's things?" Sam asked as he came up beside him.

"Stalemate for the moment. Until they bring up something big and nasty to knock these houses down."

He had an ancient Lewis gun propped on some bricks aimed through the slit and was busy filling a circular drum magazine with bullets during a brief lull in the fighting. He handed a spare magazine to Gloria to load for him while he lit a cigarette.

Sam nodded. "You've all done a fantastic job. Very soon, we will have all our people on board *The Aotearoa*. We now need to get the rest of you away." He gave Bartlett a questioning look.

Bartlett blew a smoke ring, one of his favourite party tricks.

"It's going to be tricky; they're pushing all the time. Must know we're up to something." To underline his words, a burst of sustained gunfire erupted from the house opposite. "Aiden's busy again," Bartlett muttered. "How long do we need?"

"Fifteen, twenty minutes, once everyone is clear of the village," Sam said and just rolled out of the way as a burst of firing smashed into their room, filling the space with a choking cloud of dust and brick fragments.

Disengaging wasn't going to be easy. Gloria loaded the magazine and handed it back to Bartlett.

"Best get going soon then," Bartlett said, peering through his gunsights and returning an ear-shattering burst of gunfire. He pushed a hand-held radio across the floor to Sam.

"Call Aiden and tell him to pull everyone back down the road. They must withdraw through the houses and avoid the streets. If you're quick, you can meet in the lower lane where you can't be seen."

There were half a dozen men and women in the other rooms around them. After speaking to Aiden, Sam gathered the group together.

"We need to go now; no delaying. We'll use the back gardens for protection. Once we get moving there'll be no stopping until the beach."

As if to make his point, in the next room Bartlett started firing again.

"Okay, wait for me downstairs. I'll get Bartlett."

They all filed down the stairs without comment, just relieved to be alive and returning to their families. It left just Sam and Bartlett alone in the house.

"Time to go, Dave." Sam tugged firmly on his arm, noticing the grenades on the floor next to the Lewis gun. They would help cause a distraction.

"You go ahead. I'll follow," Bartlett replied, not taking his eye away from the gunsights.

"Dave?"

"One of us has got to stay, and personally, I don't fancy the walk. Plus, I'm a better shot than you." He smiled at Sam. "Go. Now. Twenty minutes might be optimistic."

Sam gripped Bartlett's right hand. There were tears in his eyes, remembering the final time he had taken Albert Jamieson's hand, feeling the warmth of life force within it. He lingered for a moment before leaving, feeling shocked at his friend's insistence at staying. In so doing, he would deign cancer the final word.

On the ground floor, the others had gathered together several wounded and the bodies of their fallen friends, killed during the morning's fighting. Fatal casualties had been mercifully few and they were determined to take the bodies with them for a decent burial. Sam felt another shock of grief course through him; amongst the dead was the body of the teenage girl messenger he had despatched to Bartlett only a few hours before.

They met up with Aiden and his group just beyond the village, where the lower lane dropped steeply to St Catherine's Point. Sam counted twenty-one, including three who had been killed. Only Bartlett was missing.

"Okay, quick as you can, straight to Reeth Bay; there's a boat waiting."

Sam checked his watch. It had already taken five minutes to get this far. They left immediately, Aiden leading, Sam and Gloria at the rear. Within moments, the hard metallic rattle of a Lewis gun ended a temporary silence, continuing in short intermittent bursts. Towards the bottom of the hill they joined a worn path that broke away to their left, now littered with discarded items as people had moved hastily to the waiting boats. Within minutes, the path joined the final track. Through the trees they could already hear the noise ahead of the surf breaking on the shoreline. Above the sound of their rasping breaths, Sam had an ear for Bartlett's lonely Lewis gun, now their soul protection from the rush of Whistler's men. After a brief silence, short bursts became a long continuous hammering note; then two loud explosions ripped the air, followed by a stilled silence. Bartlett had heroically paid the price and bought them a few precious minutes.

As they sped past the last cottage to the beach and the upturned fishing boat on the slipway, Sam could see the boat ahead, rising and falling in the surf. It waited patiently, several figures already on board, engine ticking over.

Sam stopped abruptly in mid-stride and turned. From behind, on the wind, he thought he heard someone calling his name. It came again a second time, whispering as he turned. His eyes searched the empty track behind; no one was there; the track was empty. He shook his head as though trying to clear a mist that had formed around him.

"Sam. Come on man," Napier shouted, urgently calling him.

The rest of his party were already piling into the boat. He saw Claire standing in the bow, her face full of anguish, waiting, knowing he was close by. Gloria had boarded the boat and was standing behind Claire.

On the beach, John was waiting for him, radio suspended from his hand, headphones discarded around his neck, his face ashen with shock.

"What?" Sam hesitated. "What?" he demanded.

John looked at him, eyes red, staring.

"They haven't made it," he said.

"I don't under…"

"Five minutes ago, I heard from Rachel." John swallowed hard. "She said, *'We're surrounded. God help us. Tell my children I love them'.*"

Sam stood rigid, stunned. A hard pain rose in his chest, bringing with it the appalling realisation that fate had played her final hand.

"Sam, are you there?" Claire searched for him with her voice, frightened, pleading.

John gripped his arm, shaking Sam vigorously into action. "Quickly. Into the boat."

Voices were calling him, their sounds receding into the distance. In minutes Whistler would be here, yet Sam was frozen, immobile, unable to move.

"Sam, where are you?" Claire's voice begged again, desperately.

Napier jumped from the boat and ran towards him. Both men met with their eyes. Napier outstretched his hand.

"I can't," Sam said hoarsely. "I can't leave."

"You must," Napier said, reading his thoughts. "There's nothing for you here, only death. Come on, everyone's waiting; they need you, man."

Sam shook his head again. "I can't leave. I can't leave Rachel behind. I can't. This has all happened because of me."

"Sam, there's nothing you can do; Rachel may well be dead already. Sacrificing yourself will serve no purpose, it won't help anyone."

Sam pulled briskly away from his friend.

"Then I'll find her and bury her," he barked.

Sam strode into the sea, reaching for Claire's outstretched hands, white and cold, shaking violently. He drew her to him, aware she knew what he had decided to do, that what she most feared was coming true. He pushed his face into her hair, his tears plastering the golden strands to his face.

"You know I have to do this; for Rachel, for the children, for us. We have no future if I leave Rachel behind, abandon her to Whistler. I love you more than life itself, but I can't go without her, without knowing. It's not over yet; I must go back and at least try to find her."

Claire was weeping silently. There was nothing words could say when fate had already chosen their course. For a moment, she clutched frantically for him, trying to pull him into the boat, but he forced himself away; their time had run out.

"I'll catch up. A few days, I promise you. I'll catch up."

Sam turned to Napier, pushing him towards the boat.

"Go. Now. Give me the key for *The Shepherd*. I'll figure out what to do, how to sail her. I'll find others that need rescuing, someone must be able to sail. I'll catch you up; Gibraltar, Cape Town, wherever, but for god's sake go before it's too late."

With Napier's key for *The Shepherd* in his hand, Sam stumbled to the shore; even the back-tow of the surf was trying to pull him to the boat.

"Never give up hope for me," he shouted to Claire. "Hold on to that until I find you. I will come after you, I promise my life on that, but it must be this way, we both know that."

Sam steeled himself and backed away resolutely. At the edge of the surf, he paused, nodded to Gloria, who for once regarded Sam with sad solemn eyes. She nodded back, and locked her arms firmly around Claire.

"Goodbye," he shouted through his tears. "I will come after you. Don't give up hope."

He waved once more as the engine roared into life. Sam hesitated for a second, his will weakening, his eyes memorising Claire's face. If only …

Then he turned his back and walked away.


Up ahead, the sound of approaching voices drifted down the track. Whistler's men. The scrub up to his right was dense, an almost impenetrable thicket of coarse briars and bracken; it offered his only chance to avoid capture. Between a blackthorn and gorse bush, Sam decided to turn off the track.

He had saved all that he held dear, except Rachel, who now most probably hated him almost as much as she did Whistler. The irony of the moment wasn't lost on him. Sam had striven to avoid his fate ever since he had survived the pandemic, sometimes aware that death had walked only one step behind him.

He stopped, suddenly too exhausted to take another step and anyway, why bother when his fate was already decided. He thought he heard a voice, calling his name, on the wind. Perhaps death was already here to collect her dues? He gave a bitter laugh, realising he had come without a gun or his rucksack.

"I think you forgot something." A voice called from close by.

Sam turned around. On the path behind him came a lonely figure, bedraggled and soaked with salt spray; his gun dragging along the ground in one hand, rucksack in the other.

Claire.

Guided only by the fading notes of his laughter, she stumbled blindly along the track towards him, heartbroken, determinedly searching for the man she loved and wouldn't leave.

"What? Why …" he choked as his arms closed around her.

Moments later, Sam led them both away from the track into the dense thicket of brambles and bracken. Now, only seconds separated them both from the hands of the men who had pursued Claire in what seemed a lifetime ago in Dartmouth, where destiny had joined their paths together. The fog had cleared and to the north, where Rachel was now either dead or held captive, the cloud parted to reveal a piece of broken sky, so blue it took the breath away.

Sam didn't need answers; his life had been bound with Claire's long before this moment. Apart, life no longer held any purpose for either Sam or Claire, each in their way dependent on the other.

One sighted with the dream of a hopeless vision, the other blind with the vision of a hopeless dream.